EMPIRE

ALSO BY STEVEN SAYLOR

Roma: The Novel of Ancient Rome
A Twist at the End: A Novel of O. Henry
Have You Seen Dawn?

ROMA SUB ROSA®
CONSISTING OF

Roman Blood
The House of the Vestals
A Gladiator Dies Only Once
Arms of Nemesis
Catalina's Riddle
The Venus Throw
A Murder on the Appian Way
Rubicon
Last Seen in Massilia
A Mist of Prophecies
The Judgment of Caesar
The Triumph of Caesar

EMPIRE

THE NOVEL OF IMPERIAL ROME

STEVEN SAYLOR

St. Martin's Griffin
New York

TO THE SHADE
OF MICHAEL GRANT

EMPIRE. Copyright © 2010 by Steven Saylor. All rights reserved. Printed in the United States of
America. For information, address St. Martin's Press, 175 Fifth Avenue, New York, N.Y. 10010.

www.stmartins.com

The Library of Congress has cataloged the hardcover edition as follows:

Saylor, Steven, 1956–
    Empire : the novel of imperial Rome / Steven Saylor. — 1st ed.
        p. cm.
    ISBN 978-0-312-38101-1
    1. Rome—History—Fiction. I. Title.
    PS3569.A96E47 2010
    813'.54—dc22   2010021663

ISBN 978-0-312-61080-7 (trade paperback)

First St. Martin's Griffin Edition: September 2011

10 9 8 7 6 5 4 3 2 1

History is scarcely capable of preserving the memory of anything except myths.

—GUSTAVE LE BON, *THE CROWD*

CONTENTS

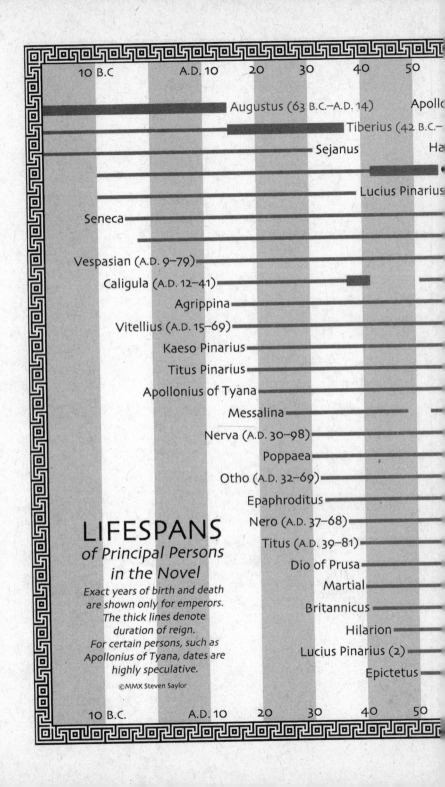

10 B.C   A.D. 10   20   30   40   50

Augustus (63 B.C.–A.D. 14)   Apollo

Tiberius (42 B.C.–

Sejanus   Ha

Lucius Pinarius

Seneca

Vespasian (A.D. 9–79)

Caligula (A.D. 12–41)

Agrippina

Vitellius (A.D. 15–69)

Kaeso Pinarius

Titus Pinarius

Apollonius of Tyana

Messalina

Nerva (A.D. 30–98)

Poppaea

Otho (A.D. 32–69)

Epaphroditus

LIFESPANS
of Principal Persons
in the Novel

*Exact years of birth and death
are shown only for emperors.
The thick lines denote
duration of reign.
For certain persons, such as
Apollonius of Tyana, dates are
highly speculative.*

©MMX Steven Saylor

Nero (A.D. 37–68)

Titus (A.D. 39–81)

Dio of Prusa

Martial

Britannicus

Hilarion

Lucius Pinarius (2)

Epictetus

10 B.C.   A.D. 10   20   30   40   50

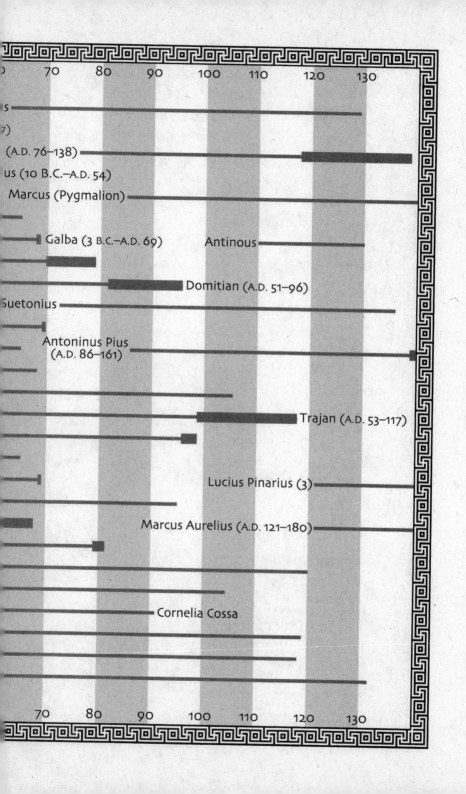

70 80 90 100 110 120 130

s

7)

(A.D. 76–138)

us (10 B.C.–A.D. 54)

Marcus (Pygmalion)

Galba (3 B.C.–A.D. 69)   Antinous

Domitian (A.D. 51–96)

Suetonius

Antoninus Pius
(A.D. 86–161)

Trajan (A.D. 53–117)

Lucius Pinarius (3)

Marcus Aurelius (A.D. 121–180)

Cornelia Cossa

70 80 90 100 110 120 130

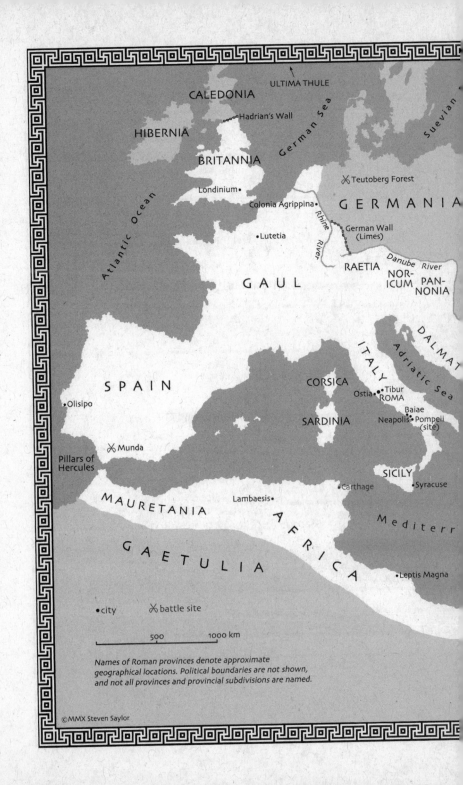

ULTIMA THULE

CALEDONIA

HIBERNIA

Hadrian's Wall

German Sea

Suevian

BRITANNIA

Teutoberg Forest

Londinium•

Colonia Agrippina•

GERMANIA

Rhine River

German Wall
(Lisipo

Atlantic Ocean

•Lutetia

Danube River

RAETIA

NOR-
ICUM

PAN-
NONIA

GAUL

DALMAT

ITALY

Adriatic Sea

SPAIN

CORSICA

Ostia•• Tibur
ROMA

•Olisipo

SARDINIA

Baiae
Neapolis• •Pompeii
(site)

Munda

Pillars of
Hercules

SICILY

•Carthage

Syracuse

MAURETANIA

Lambaesis•

AFRICA

Mediterr

GAETULIA

•Leptis Magna

•city   battle site

500   1000 km

Names of Roman provinces denote approximate
geographical locations. Political boundaries are not shown,
and not all provinces and provincial subdivisions are named.

©MMX Steven Saylor

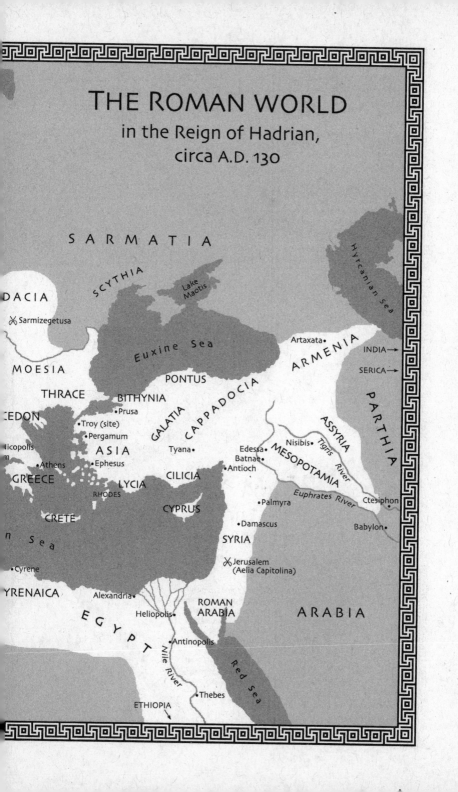

THE ROMAN WORLD
in the Reign of Hadrian,
circa A.D. 130

SARMATIA

SCYTHIA

Lake
Maotis

DACIA

✕ Sarmizegetusa

Euxine Sea

Hyrcanian Sea

Artaxata •

ARMENIA

INDIA →

MOESIA

PONTUS

SERICA →

THRACE

BITHYNIA

CAPPADOCIA

PARTHIA

CEDON

• Prusa

GALATIA

ASSYRIA

• Troy (site)

Nisibis •

Tigris River

licopolis
n

• Pergamum

Tyana •

Edessa •

MESOPOTAMIA

ASIA

Batnae •

• Athens

• Ephesus

• Antioch

GREECE

CILICIA

Euphrates River

Ctesiphon

LYCIA

RHODES

CYPRUS

• Palmyra

Babylon •

CRETE

n
Sea

• Damascus

SYRIA

• Cyrene

✕ Jerusalem
(Aelia Capitolina)

YRENAICA

Alexandria •

ROMAN
ARABIA

ARABIA

Heliopolis •

EGYPT

• Antinopolis

Nile River

Red Sea

• Thebes

ETHIOPIA →

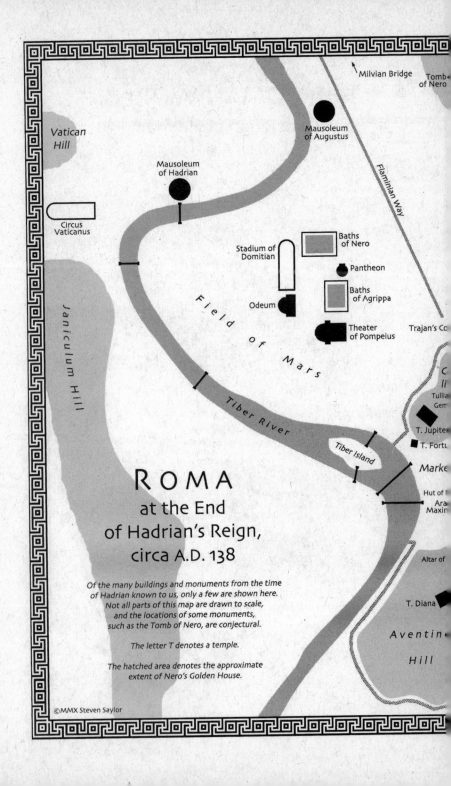

Milvian Bridge

Tomb of Nero

Vatican Hill

Flaminian Way

Mausoleum of Hadrian

Mausoleum of Augustus

Circus Vaticanus

Baths of Nero

Stadium of Domitian

Pantheon

Baths of Agrippa

Odeum

Theater of Pompeius

Trajan's Co

Janiculum Hill

F i e l d   o f   M a r s

C. li

Tullia Gem

T. Jupiter

Tiber River

T. Fort

Tiber Island

Marke

ROMA
at the End
of Hadrian's Reign,
circa A.D. 138

Hut of
Ara
Maxim

*Of the many buildings and monuments from the time
of Hadrian known to us, only a few are shown here.
Not all parts of this map are drawn to scale,
and the locations of some monuments,
such as the Tomb of Nero, are conjectural.*

Altar of

T. Diana

The letter T denotes a temple.

A v e n t i n

Hill

*The hatched area denotes the approximate
extent of Nero's Golden House.*

©MMX Steven Saylor

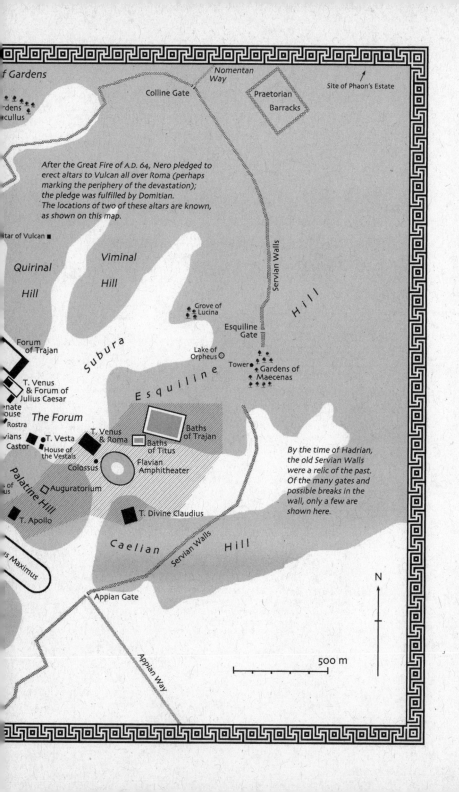

f Gardens

Nomentan Way

Colline Gate

Praetorian Barracks

Site of Phaon's Estate

dens cullus

After the Great Fire of A.D. 64, Nero pledged to
erect altars to Vulcan all over Roma (perhaps
marking the periphery of the devastation);
the pledge was fulfilled by Domitian.
The locations of two of these altars are known,
as shown on this map.

tar of Vulcan ■

Quirinal Hill

Viminal Hill

Servian Walls

Hill

Grove of Lucina

Esquiline Gate

Forum of Trajan

Subura

Lake of Orpheus ⊙

Tower

Gardens of Maecenas

T. Venus & Forum of Julius Caesar

Esquiline

nate ouse

The Forum

Rostra

vians Castor

T. Vesta

House of the Vestals

T. Venus & Roma

Baths of Titus

Baths of Trajan

By the time of Hadrian,
the old Servian Walls
were a relic of the past.
Of the many gates and
possible breaks in the
wall, only a few are
shown here.

Colossus

Flavian Amphitheater

of us

Palatine Hill

Auguratorium

T. Divine Claudius

T. Apollo

Caelian

Servian Walls

Hill

s Maximus

Appian Gate

N

Appian Way

500 m

ROMAN MONTHS AND DAYS

The names of the Roman months were Januarius, Februarius, Martius, Aprilis, Maius, Junius, Julius (to honor Julius Caesar), Augustus (to honor Caesar Augustus), September, October, November, and December.

The first day of each month was called the Kalends. The Ides fell on the fifteenth day of Martius, Maius, Julius, and October, and on the thirteenth day of the other months. The Nones fell nine days before the Ides. The Romans reckoned dates by counting backward, inclusively, from the Kalends, Ides, or Nones. Thus, for example, the date we would call June 9 was called by the Romans the fifth day before the Ides of Junius.

PART I

LUCIUS
The Lightning Reader

A.D. 14

Lucius woke with a start.

He had been dreaming. In his dream there was no earth, only a dark, empty sky, and beyond the sky, unimaginably vast, the crystalline firmament in which the stars shone brightly. No clouds obscured the stars, and yet there was lightning in the dream, lightning without thunder, random flashes of blinding light that illuminated great flocks of birds that suddenly filled the dark sky. There were vultures and eagles, ravens and crows, every sort of bird imaginable, soaring and flapping their wings, yet making no more sound than the silent lightning. The dream had filled him with a sense of urgency and confusion.

Awake now, Lucius heard a faint rumble of thunder in the distance.

He heard other sounds from elsewhere in the house. The slaves were up and beginning to stir, stoking the kitchen fire and opening shutters.

Lucius jumped from his bed. His room, with a small balcony looking west, was on the upper floor of the house. Below him was the slope of the Aventine Hill. The nearer houses, along the crest of the hill, were large and well made, like his family's house. Farther down the hill, humbler houses and tenements and artisans' workshops were crowded close together, and farther yet was a flat expanse with large granaries and warehouses close to the Tiber. At the river the city ended. On the far side of the Tiber, woods and meadows were divided into the private estates of the rich, which extended to the far horizon of hills and mountains.

How his mother hated this view! Born into a wealthy branch of the Cornelius family, she had grown up in a house on the other, more fashionable side of the Aventine Hill, with a view of the vast Circus Maximus below, the Capitoline Hill crowned by temples off to one side, and, directly opposite, the opulent Palatine Hill, where the emperor lived. "Why, from our rooftop, when I was a girl," she would say, "I could see the smoke from sacrifices on the Capitoline, watch the chariot races below, and even catch a glimpse of the emperor himself, strolling on one of his terraces across the way." ("All at the same time, Camilla?" Lucius's father would say, gently mocking her.) But this was the view Lucius had grown up with. For twenty-four years this had been the Roma seen from his room, a jumble of the rich and poor—mostly the poor—where slaves labored endlessly in vast storehouses to accommodate all the goods and grain that arrived day after day, carried up the river from the great world beyond, the world that belonged to Roma.

The month of Maius had been overcast and rainy so far, and this day promised to be no different. By the dim light of dawn beneath an overcast sky, Lucius saw the towering cypress trees along the Tiber sway this way and that. The blustering winds were warm and carried the smell of rain. In the far distance, black storm clouds roiled on the horizon, bristling with lightning.

"Perfect weather for an augury!" whispered Lucius.

His room was sparsely furnished with a narrow bed and a single backless chair, a small pigeonhole bookcase filled with scrolls left over from his childhood education, a mirror on a stand made of burnished copper, and a few trunks to accommodate his clothing. He opened the most ornate of the trunks and carefully removed the special garment it contained.

Ordinarily, he would have waited for a slave to help him dress—arranging the folds correctly was a complicated task—but Lucius could not wait. The garment was not simply a toga, such as the one he had put on when he became a man at the age of seventeen. It was a trabea, the special garment worn only by augurs, the members of the ancient priesthood trained to divine the will of the gods. It was not white but saffron with broad purple stripes. Except for the fitting, when the tailor had made it for him, this was the first time Lucius had even touched the trabea. The never-worn wool was soft and thick and had a fresh smell of murex dye.

He put on the garment and did his best to pull the hanging folds into a proper arrangement. He glanced at himself in the copper mirror, then reached into the trunk again. He picked up a slender ivory wand that ended in a little spiral. The lituus was a family heirloom and a familiar friend; Lucius had spent countless hours practicing with it in preparation for this day. But now he looked at the lituus with fresh eyes, studying the intricate carvings that decorated every part of its surface with images of ravens, crows, owls, eagles, vultures, and chickens, as well as foxes, wolves, horses, and dogs—all the various creatures from whose actions a trained augur could interpret the will of the gods.

He left his room and descended the stairs, crossed the garden surrounded by a peristyle at the center of the house, and stepped into the dining room, where his mother and father reclined together on a couch while a slave served their breakfast.

His mother was wearing a simple stola, with her long hair not yet combed and pinned for the day. She leaped up from her couch. "Lucius! What are you doing dressed in your trabea already? You can't eat breakfast wearing that! What if you get food on it? The ceremony is hours away. We'll be going to the baths first. The barber must shave you and your father—"

Lucius laughed. "Mother, I did it on a whim. Of course I won't wear it to breakfast. But what do you think?"

Camilla sighed. "You look splendid, Lucius. Absolutely splendid! As handsome as ever your father was in his trabea. Don't you think so, dear?"

Lucius's father, who strove always to maintain the restraint proper to a man of his standing—a patrician, a senator, and a cousin of the emperor—merely nodded. "Handsome our boy certainly is. But looking pretty is not the point when a man puts on his trabea. A priest must carry his garment as he carries his lituus, with dignity and authority, as befits the intermediary of the gods."

Lucius drew back his shoulders, raised his chin, and held forth his lituus. "What do you think, father? Do I look properly dignified?"

The elder Lucius Pinarius looked at his son and raised an eyebrow. To him, young Lucius often still looked like a boy, and never more so than at this moment, dressed up in priestly finery but with the folds of his trabea tucked and draped haphazardly, like a child in grown-up costume. Twenty-four was very young for a man to be inducted into the college of augurs. The elder Pinarius had been in his forties before the honor came to him. With his black hair mussed from sleeping, his broad smile, and his smoothly handsome features, young Lucius hardly fit the standard image of the wrinkled, gray-haired augur. Still, the young man came from a long line of augurs, and he had shown great aptitude in his studies.

"You look very fine, my son. Now, go change into a nice tunic. We shall have a bite to eat, then be off to the baths for a wash and a shave, then hurry back home to get ready for the ceremony. Hopefully, the storm will hold off and we won't be drenched with rain."

Having a slave arrange the trabea certainly made a difference, Lucius had to admit, as he studied himself in the copper mirror later that day. The sight of himself freshly groomed and properly outfitted in his trabea filled him with confidence. Of course, he was not an augur quite yet. Preceding the induction ceremony there would be a final examination in which Lucius would be called upon to demonstrate his skills. Lucius frowned. He was a little nervous about the examination.

This time, when he descended from his room, his mother almost swooned at the sight of him. His father, now dressed in his own trabea and carrying his own lituus, gave him a warm smile of approval.

"Shall we be off, father?"

"Not quite yet. You have a visitor."

Across the garden, a young man and a girl were seated on a bench beneath the peristyle.

"Acilia!" Lucius began to run to her, then slowed his pace. A trabea was not made for running, and it would not do to catch the soft wool on a thorn as he passed the rose bushes.

Acilia's older brother rose to his feet, nodded curtly, and discreetly withdrew. Looking over his shoulder, Lucius saw that his parents had also disappeared, to allow him a moment of privacy with his betrothed.

Lucius took her hands in his. "Acilia, you look beautiful today." It was true. Her honey-colored hair was worn long and straight, as befitted an unmarried girl. Her eyes were bright blue. Her cheeks were as smooth as rose petals. Her petite body was largely hidden by her modest, long-sleeved tunica, but during the year that they had been betrothed she had definitely begun to acquire the contours of a woman's body. She was ten years younger than Lucius.

"Look at you, Lucius—so handsome in your trabea!"

"That's what my mother said." As they strolled across the garden, he suddenly felt self-conscious about their surroundings. Lucius was acutely aware that the house of Acilia's father was far grander than that of the Pinarii, more lavishly furnished, tended by more household slaves, and located on the more fashionable side of the Aventine Hill, near the Temple of Diana. The Acilii were plebeians, descended from a family far less ancient than the patrician Pinarii, but the Acilii had a great deal of money, while the fortunes of the Pinarii had dwindled in recent years. Lucius's late grandfather had owned a fine mansion on the Palatine, but his debts had forced the family to move to their current accommodations. To be sure, the vestibule of their house contained the wax masks of many venerable ancestors, but that was not the sort of thing to impress a girl. Had Acilia noticed how overgrown and untended the garden was? Lucius remembered the perfectly trimmed hedges and topiaries, the marble walkways and expensive pieces of bronze statuary in the garden at Acilia's house. The roof of the peristyle behind Acilia was missing more than a few tiles, and the wall was unsightly with peeling plaster and water stains. The slave who was supposed to tend the garden was already overworked with other duties, and there was no money to repair the roof or the wall.

Lack of money: that was the reason they were not yet married. Acilia's father, after the initial excitement of betrothing his daughter to the patrician son of a senator and a cousin of the emperor, had since found one excuse after another to postpone setting a date for the ceremony. Obviously, having discovered more about the Pinarii's finances, Titus Acilius had grown dubious about Lucius's prospects in the world. From the moment Lucius first saw her, at a meeting arranged by their fathers, Lucius had liked Acilia; since then he had fallen hopelessly in love with her, and she seemed to feel the same. But that counted for nothing unless her father could be swayed to approve the union.

Acilia said nothing about the state of the garden or the unsightly wall. She gazed admiringly at the lituus he carried.

"Such ornate carvings! What is it made of?"

"Ivory."

"From the tusk of an elephant?"

"So they say."

"It's very beautiful."

"It's been in the family a long time. You can tell the ivory is very old, because of the color. Many generations of Pinarii have been augurs, taking auspices at state ceremonies, on battlefields, at temple dedications. And at private events, as well, like . . . weddings."

Acilia seemed duly impressed. "And only men from the ancient patrician families can become augurs?"

"That's right." *And I can give you a patrician son,* he thought. Yet even as he basked in her admiration, he heard a scurrying noise and looked up to see a rat running along the roof of the peristyle behind her. With a flick of its long tail, the rat dislodged a loose tile. Hearing Lucius gasp, Acilia looked around just in time to see the tile fall and shatter on a paving stone. She jumped and uttered a little cry. Had she seen the rat?

To distract her, he seized her shoulder, spun her around to face him, and kissed her. It was only a quick kiss, but still she looked astonished.

"Lucius, what if my brother should see?"

"See what? This?"

He kissed her again, not as quickly.

She drew back, blushing but looking pleased. Directly in front of her was the amulet on the necklace that Lucius was wearing. It had slipped from inside his trabea and lay nestled amid the saffron-and-purple folds.

"Is that part of your augur's outfit?" she said.

"No. It's a family heirloom. My grandfather gave it to me when I was ten years old. I wear it only on special occasions."

"May I touch it?"

"Of course."

She reached up to touch the little lump of gold, which was vaguely cruciform in shape.

"I remember the day my grandfather gave it to me. He showed me the proper way to wear a toga, and then took me all around the city, just the two of us. He showed me the exact spot where his great-uncle, Julius Caesar, was murdered. He showed me the Great Altar of Hercules, the most ancient shrine in the city, which was erected by the Pinarius family in the days before Roma even existed. He showed me the fig tree on the Palatine where Romulus and Remus and their friend Pinarius climbed among the branches. And finally he showed me the Temple of Venus that Caesar built, and that was the first time I saw the fantastic golden statue of Cleopatra inside. My grandfather knew Cleopatra very well, and he knew Marcus Antonius, too. Someday . . . someday I want to have a son, and take him to see all those things, and tell him about his ancestors."

Acilia still held the amulet. As he spoke, she had drawn closer to him, until her body pressed gently against his. She gazed at the amulet, then looked up into his eyes.

"But what sort of amulet is this? I can't make out the shape."

Lucius shook his head. "It's funny, my grandfather made such a fuss about giving it to me, but even he wasn't sure what it's supposed to represent or where it came from. He only knew that it had been in the family for many generations. The original shape must have worn away over so many lifetimes."

"There's nothing like that in our family," said Acilia, clearly impressed. She was so close that Lucius felt an urge to put his arms around her and hold her tightly against him, no matter that her brother might appear at any moment. But the sky above them suddenly opened and pelted the garden with rain. The raindrops were warm, and Lucius would have been happy to stand there, holding her, both of them getting soaking wet, but Acilia dropped the amulet, seized his hand, and with a shriek of laughter pulled him through the peristyle and into the house.

They found Lucius's father and Acilia's brother sitting next to each other in a pair of matching ebony chairs with inlays of lapis and abalone. It was no accident that his father had guided their guest to the best two pieces of furniture in the house.

Marcus Acilius was only a few years older than his sister and had the same golden hair and bright blue eyes. "But it's been five years since the disaster that took place in the Teutoberg Forest," he was saying, "and still nothing has been done to settle the score with the Germanic tribes. They're laughing at us. It's a scandal!"

"So, the rain has driven you inside." Lucius's father looked up at the couple and smiled warmly at Acilia. He wanted the marriage to take place as badly as Lucius did. "Marcus and I have been talking about the situation in the north." He turned his attention back to Acilia's brother.

"You're a young man, Marcus. Five years seems to you a very long time. But in the grand scheme of things, it's no more than the blink of an eye. This city was not built in a day, nor was the empire conquered in a lifetime. To be sure, for a long time, Roma seemed unstoppable. Ever outward our legions pushed the limits of the empire, and all obstacles fell before us. To the north, my father's great-uncle Julius Caesar conquered Gaul and set the stage for our cousin Augustus to push beyond the Rhine and conquer the Germans. The wild tribes were pacified. Their leaders were won over with the privileges of Roman citizenship. Cities were built, temples were dedicated to the gods, taxes were collected, and Germania became a province like any other.

"And then came Arminius, or Hermann as the Germans call him, a German who was trained to fight by Romans, who was given all the benefits of Roman hospitality, and who repaid us by the most despicable treachery. On the pretext of stamping out a small uprising, he lured three Roman legions into the Teutoberg Forest—then staged an ambush. Not a single Roman escaped. Arminius's men weren't satisfied with simple slaughter. They desecrated the corpses, chopping them into pieces, hanging their limbs from trees and mounting their heads on stakes. A thoroughly disgusting business, to be sure—but not the end of Roma's interests in Germania. The massacre in the Teutoberg Forest took place because of the ambitions of one man, Arminius, who wants to turn the province we have built into his personal kingdom. The man is nothing more than a thief. I hear he dares to call himself 'Augustus of the North,' if you can believe such effrontery!

"But never fear, young Marcus. Our efforts so far to punish Arminius and bring the situation under control have been thwarted, but not for much longer. As a senator I can assure you that the emperor's attention to this matter is unwavering. Not a day passes that he does not take some action to correct it. And what Augustus sets out to do, Augustus does."

"But the emperor is seventy-five years old," said Marcus.

"True, but there are younger, more vigorous members of his family with military expertise. His stepson Tiberius is a very fit commander; it was Tiberius's late brother, Drusus Germanicus, who conquered the province in the first place. And there's Germanicus's son, who's eager to earn the name his father handed down to him by his own victories. Never fear, Marcus. It will take time and effort and no small amount of bloodshed, but the province of Germania will be pacified. Ah, but listen to me, rambling on about warfare and politics in the presence of one with such tender sensibilities." He smiled again at Acilia.

"Is it true, about the Germans cutting off the soldiers' heads and putting them on stakes?" she whispered, looking pale.

"You've upset her, father," said Lucius, taking advantage of Acilia's distress to put his arm around her. Her brother did not object.

"No more talk of such unpleasant subjects, then," said the elder Pinarius.

"No more talk at all, if you're to be on time for the ceremony," said Lucius's mother, entering the room. "The rain has let up. The two of you must be off, and quickly. But you needn't leave yet, Acilia. I have some spinning to do; nothing is more relaxing than spinning wool. You can help me, if you'd like, and we can have a nice visit." Camilla accompanied Lucius and his father to the vestibule. "Don't be nervous, son. I know you'll perform splendidly. Or is it the presence of Acilia that makes you tremble?" She laughed. "Now off with you!"

"You don't think I laid it on too thickly, do you," said Lucius's father, "reminding young Marcus about our kinship to both the Divine Julius and the emperor?"

They had descended the slope of the Aventine and were walking through the crowded riverfront district, heading for the Stairs of Cacus, which would take them up to the summit of the Palatine.

"I think the Acilii are quite aware of our family connections," said Lucius ruefully. "But I'm not sure that it helps to keep bringing it up. For all that my grandfather was an heir of the Divine Julius, and we're cousins of the great Augustus, what do we have to show for it?"

His father sighed. "What, indeed? Except for the fact that we're still alive."

"What do you mean by that?"

They began to ascend the Stairs of Cacus. As recently as the days of Julius Caesar it had been nothing more than a steep, winding footpath, as it had been since the time of Romulus. Augustus had made it into a stone stairway decorated with flowers and terraces. Lucius's father looked ahead of them and behind, checking that no one was close enough to overhear.

"Have you never noticed, son, how many members of the emperor's family have been sent into exile, and how those dearest to him have a way of dying?"

Lucius frowned. "I know he banished his daughter Julia."

"Her morals disappointed him."

"And his grandson Agrippa."

"Who was also deemed insufficiently upright."

"And I know that his other grandsons, Lucius and Gaius, the ones he intended to make his heirs, both suffered untimely deaths."

"So they did. Being too close to the emperor is not necessarily beneficial, either to one's happiness or to one's health."

"Are you saying—"

"I am saying that the emperor is like a flame. Those around him are like men eager to warm themselves. But no one envies the man who draws so close that he sets himself afire."

Lucius shook his head. "Might things have gone differently, if my grandfather had received more favor from the gods?"

The elder Pinarius sighed. "Like his cousin Augustus, your grandfather was named in the will of Julius Caesar—but little good it did him, since he chose to side with Marcus Antonius and Cleopatra in the civil war. After those two lost everything at the battle of Actium, your grandfather saw sense and went over to Augustus, who graciously forgave him— and forever afterwards showed him not one iota of generosity. Perhaps the victor thought it was enough to spare his errant cousin's life and allow him to keep what remained of his fortune, most of which your grandfather eventually lost anyway, despite all his business concerns in Egypt. Since then, your cousin Augustus has mostly ignored us. We are tolerated but granted little in the way of either favor or disfavor—which is not necessarily a bad thing. Oh yes, to have his favor could be grand. But to suffer his disfavor . . . or the disfavor of those who scheme and plot around him . . . can be fatal."

"You say he grants us few favors, yet he put me in the lists to become an augur."

"That he did. And you have no idea how many favors I had to call in to make that happen. Be grateful for this opportunity, my son."

"I am, father," said Lucius, humbly and sincerely.

At the top of the Stairs of Cacus they were afforded a view of the river; even on an overcast, blustery day, the wharves were bustling and the choppy water was crowded with ships. Above the river loomed the Capitoline Hill with its white temples glistening after the recent shower. A solitary sunbeam broke through the ragged clouds overhead and shone brightly on the gilded statue of Hercules.

In Lucius's short lifetime, he had seen the city of Roma acquire an ever-greater air of prosperity and opulence. Countless shops were filled with goods from all over the world. Ancient temples and monuments had been refurbished, and new, even grander temples had been built. State buildings made of brick had been faced with slabs of travertine and marble. The emperor had once said, "I found Roma built of sun-dried bricks; I will leave her cloaked in marble." Augustus had made good on the promise.

Lucius had never lived anywhere but in Roma and had never traveled farther than Pompeii. But it seemed to him there could be no other place as exciting and beautiful as Roma. He felt proud that he was about to become truly part of the city, to be given a role to play, to act as a mediator between the gods and the city they had favored more than any other on earth.

Amid the grand houses on the Palatine Hill was an open square planted with grass and surrounded by a low stone wall, known as the Auguratorium. On this very spot, almost eight hundred years before, Romulus performed the augury that established the site of the city. Romulus saw twelve vultures; over on the Aventine Hill, his twin brother Remus spotted only six vultures. Thus the gods made known their preference that the new city should be founded on the Palatine, not the Aventine. In time, the city grew to contain the Aventine and all the Seven Hills along the Tiber, but this was the spot where it began. According to family legend, a Pinarius had been present with Romulus on that sacred occasion, and so the induction of a new Pinarius into the college of augurs was always an event that resounded with significance.

As Lucius and his father emerged from a narrow street and approached the Auguratorium, a sea of saffron and purple enveloped them; every man in the crowd was wearing a trabea and clutching a lituus. A tall young man abruptly appeared before them, holding his arms open to give Lucius an embrace.

"L-L-Lucius!" he said. "I thought you'd never get here. The idea of going through the examination all by myself was making me break into a c-cold sweat."

"Surely you jest, cousin Claudius," said Lucius. "Your skills at augury are far greater than mine, and you know it."

"Seeking signs from the gods is one thing. D-doing it in front of an audience is another matter!"

"You'll both do very well, I'm sure," said Lucius's father, beaming proudly at the two of them. Lucius and Claudius were to be the only inductees into the college on this day. Claudius was the grandson of Livia, the emperor's wife, and thus the stepgrandson of Augustus—but was not the emperor's grandson officially by either blood or law, since Augustus had never adopted Claudius's late father, Drusus Germanicus. Nonetheless, Claudius was a blood relative to Augustus. He was the grandson of Marcus Antonius and Octavia, Augustus's sister, and thus the emperor's great-nephew, and also a distant cousin to Lucius.

Claudius and Lucius had been born the same year. In recent months the cousins had been studying the science of augury together. They had become close friends, though to Lucius's father it seemed that their differences were greater than their similarities. Lucius was strikingly handsome, well built, and graceful—that was a plain fact, and not the prejudice of a doting father—while Claudius, though tall and not bad-looking, had a cowed manner, often spoke with a stammer, and suffered from nervous facial tics and jerks of the head. The stammer and the jerking were more pronounced at some times than at others. Some people assumed that the young man was mentally incompetent. In fact, despite his youth, Claudius was an antiquarian scholar more deeply versed in the minutiae of Roma's history than anyone the elder Pinarius had ever met. Of the friendship between his son and Claudius he entirely approved; the danger he had just warned Lucius about—of drawing too near the emperor and his inner circle—seemed hardly to apply to Claudius, whom the emperor, embarrassed by the young man's defects, kept at a distance.

A gong was struck. The augurs stopped their milling and assembled along the four sides of the Auguratorium in order of their age and rank. In the center of the square, the magister of the college called on Lucius and Claudius to stand beside him, then asked, "Who nominates these new members?"

Lucius's father stepped forward and placed his hand on Lucius's shoulder. "I, Lucius Pinarius, an augur, nominate my son, Lucius Pinarius."

Another figure emerged from the crowd, an old man who seemed quite careless of his appearance. His gray hair needed barbering and his threadbare trabea had seen better days. But when he placed his hand on Claudius's shoulder and spoke, his voice carried an undeniable ring of authority. "I, Gaius Julius Caesar Octavianus Augustus, an augur, nominate my nephew, Tiberius Claudius Nero Germanicus."

The magister nodded. "Then I shall begin the examination." A rumble of distant thunder caused him to glance skyward. "Divination is the means by which humankind may determine the will of the gods. The gods make their will known by signs, which we call auspices. Those who know the way may determine whether these auspices are favorable or unfavorable. By augury, the site of Roma was decided. As Ennius began one of his poems, 'After by augury august Roma had been founded . . .'

"As the empire of Roma has grown, we have encountered other peoples with other means of divination. The Etruscans studied the entrails of sacrificial animals; the Babylonians observed the stars; the Greeks listened to blind prophets; the Jews received instruction from a burning bush. But these ways are not Roman ways; these are inferior means of divination, as is made evident by the inferior fortunes of their adherents. The Roman way of divination, handed down to us from our most ancient ancestors, is augury, which was and is and always shall be the best and truest means of divining the will of the gods."

"Hear, hear!" shouted Augustus, prompting others in the crowd to do the same.

"There are five categories of augury," the magister continued, "five means by which the auspices may be obtained. The most powerful auspices are delivered by thunder and lightning, which come directly from Jupiter. Auspices may also be obtained by the observation of certain birds: the raven, the crow, the owl, the eagle, and the vulture. From this second, avian form of augury derives the third form, which our ancestors originally devised for use on military campaigns, where an auspice might be required at any moment to make a critical decision; this third type of augury is performed by releasing a hen from its cage, scattering grain before it, and observing the way the creature pecks or does not peck at the food. Auspices may also be taken from four-footed animals, and this is the fourth form. If a fox, wolf, horse, dog, or any other quadruped should cross a person's path or appear in some unusual setting, only an augur may interpret the meaning; but it is important to remember that this fourth form of augury is never employed on behalf of the state, only as private divination. The fifth class of augury pertains to all signs which do not fall into the other four categories, and may include all manner of unusual events—the birth of a two-headed animal, a strange object that falls from the sky, flames that appear and disappear, leaving no trace. The fifth form of augury may also be derived from common accidents—a sneeze, a stumble, a misspoken name or word."

Claudius suddenly jerked his head from side to side. Lucius barely glimpsed the movement from the corner of his eye, but it must have been quite obvious to the crowd before them. Was this spasm such an accident as the magister had just mentioned, a sign from the gods? Lucius thought not; everyone knew that Claudius had been prone to such twitches from childhood. Sometimes a twitch was merely a twitch. Still, there were uneasy murmurs from the crowd.

The magister pretended to take no notice. "Lucius Pinarius, what form of augury will you demonstrate for us today, to determine whether the gods favor your admission into the college?"

Given that the day was stormy, the answer was obvious. "The first form," said Lucius.

The others stepped back, leaving Lucius alone in the center of the Auguratorium. He slowly turned about in a circle, surveying the sky. The storm clouds were concentrated most thickly to the southwest. He raised his lituus and pointed in that direction. The augurs gathered behind him. With his lituus he drew an invisible square upon the sky. From left to right the square included everything from the top of the Temple of Diana on the Aventine to the top of the Temple of Jupiter on the Capitoline; from bottom to top it included everything from the horizon to the zenith. Having delineated a segment of sky, Lucius lowered his lituus and proceeded to watch and wait.

Lucius was patient at first, keeping his eyes open, trying not to blink; then he began to grow a bit nervous. The gods, including Jupiter, did not always send signs. What if no lightning appeared? The absence of a sign, in such a circumstance, would be taken as an unfavorable auspice. Behind him Lucius thought he heard the sound of murmurs and shuffling feet, as if the augurs were growing as restless as he was. How long was long enough to await a sign? Only the most senior augur present, in this case the emperor, could determine that. They might stand there for hours, until night fell, awaiting the appearance of a lightning bolt—or Augustus might decide to end the examination the next moment.

Lucius's heart pounded in his chest. The wait was maddening! If no sign appeared, what would become of him? What would his father say? He realized that he was clutching his lituus with white knuckles. He took a deep breath and relaxed his grip. He slipped the fingers of his other hand inside his trabea and touched the gold amulet he wore around his neck.

He saw a flash. An instant later, he heard the gasps of the others behind him, and then, a few heartbeats later, he heard the thunder. The distant flash was to the left, just above the Temple of Diana but still within the delineated area. Lightning to the left was favorable, and the more to the left, the more favorable. The auspice was good! Jupiter was clearly pleased. And then, as if to quell any doubt about his approval, several blinding flashes of jagged lightning appeared in the same spot, one after another, followed by rolling peals of thunder. To Lucius, it sounded as if the god were laughing with delight.

"The auspice is favorable!" shouted the magister. "Is there any augur present who disagrees?"

Lucius turned around and sought his father's face amid the crowd. His father was smiling, as were those around him.

Augustus, too, seemed to smile, though Lucius found it hard to read the old man's expression. His eyes looked weary, not joyful, and the baring of his yellow teeth resembled a grimace more than a grin. "I think we are all agreed that the auspice is favorable, are we not?" said the emperor.

There were nods and utterances of agreement from the crowd.

The magister placed his hands on Lucius's shoulder. "Congratulations, Lucius Pinarius. On this day, you have become an augur. May you always use your skills and the power of your priestly office wisely, for the benefit of Roma and with the greatest respect for the gods."

The magister turned to Claudius. "And now you, Tiberius Claudius Nero Germanicus. What form of augury will you demonstrate for us today, to determine whether the gods favor your admission into the college?"

Claudius stepped forward. "I choose to watch for . . ." He came to a complete stop, as he sometimes did when speaking; his stutter was making it difficult for him to say the next word. At last, pressing his lips tightly together, he blurted out, "B-b-birds!"

There were murmurs from the crowd, most of whom, including Lucius, were surprised by the decision. On such a day, with so much lightning about, surely all the birds were in their nests, hiding from the wind and the rain.

Nonetheless, Claudius seemed sure of himself. After carefully scanning the sky, he faced northeast, directly opposite the direction Lucius had chosen. He used his lituus to delineate a segment of sky above the Forum and the Esquiline Hill beyond.

Just as he was finishing the delineation, Claudius dropped his lituus. Lucius groaned, as did several others. Claudius's clumsiness was one thing, but to drop his lituus was surely a bad omen.

If Augustus was embarrassed, he did not show it. "Pick up that lituus," he said, "and let's get to the business at hand, young man, quick as boiled asparagus!"

The tension in the crowd was relieved with laughter. The emperor was known for such homespun metaphors, which from any other speaker would have sounded oafish.

Augustus cleared his throat and spoke. "Back when I first took the auspices, I also chose to watch for birds. I spotted twelve vultures—yes, twelve! The very number Romulus saw when he founded the city. Let us see how Jupiter's feathered emissaries will augur for my nephew today." The old man flashed a smile, or a grimace, Lucius could not tell which.

While they watched and waited for a sign, Lucius considered the daunting complexities of avian augury. To take the auspice, one had to consider not only the types of birds that appeared but how many, and whether they flew in a single direction or doubled back, and whether they called or were silent. Every sound and motion of each bird had a different meaning, according to different circumstances and the time of the year when it was observed. An avian augury was far more likely than a lightning augury to yield an auspice susceptible to differing interpretations—if indeed on such a day any bird would appear.

They waited. Lucius began to grow uneasy, feeling almost as anxious for Claudius as he had felt for himself. It had seemed unthinkable that Lucius might disappoint and embarrass his father. How much greater must be the pressure felt by Claudius with the emperor looming behind him?

Just when Lucius could stand the suspense no longer, Claudius raised his lituus and pointed. "Th-th-there!" he cried. "Two vultures above the Esquiline Gate, flying this way!"

To be sure, two flitting specks had appeared, but they were so distant that Lucius, who had excellent eyesight, was not sure what sort of birds they might be. Apparently Claudius's eyes were even keener than his, for as the birds drew nearer there was general agreement among the squinting augurs that the birds were indeed vultures. The birds wheeled back toward the Esquiline Gate and began to circle above it.

Two more vultures appeared from the same spot, and then two more, and then another, until seven vultures were circling about the Esquiline Gate. Beyond the gate, outside the walls, was the necropolis, the city of the dead, where slaves were buried and the carcasses of executed criminals were left to the birds. It was not surprising that vultures had appeared in that region, but it was surely fortuitous that so many had appeared at once, during Claudius's augury, and on such an inclement day. The pattern of their flight, first toward the Auguratorium and then away, was a favorable auspice as well.

Augustus declared the augury completed. The magister was impressed.

"Seven vultures! To be sure, considerably fewer than the record set by Romulus—and matched by our emperor—but one more than Remus saw! Does anyone here doubt that the auspice is favorable? No? Very well, then, I declare that on this day, Tiberius Claudius Nero Germanicus has shown himself to be a true augur, accepted by his colleagues and, more importantly, by Jupiter himself. May you always use your skills and the power of your priestly office wisely, young man, for the benefit of Roma and with the greatest respect for the gods."

The ceremony was concluded. Lucius and Claudius received the congratulations of their fellow augurs, and then the members began to head to the imperial residence. The banquet following the induction of new augurs was usually held in a private home, but on this occasion Augustus was playing host. He had certainly made a point of reminding everyone of his kinship to Claudius. The fact that Lucius Pinarius was a cousin had not even been mentioned.

During the short walk, which took them past some of the finest houses in the city, Lucius walked beside Claudius and told him how impressed he was by the vulture sightings. "That was very bold of you. I would never have dared to choose an avian augury. I did the safe thing and went with lightning. The smart thing as well, or so I thought, since lightning auguries are usually more highly respected. But you outshone me today, Claudius!"

Claudius pursed his lips, nodded, and hummed thoughtfully. His head twitched to one side. "Yes, well, I suppose I did, even though, as you say, lightning augury is the most highly esteemed of all forms. Why do you suppose that is?" With the examination behind them, his stutter had momentarily abated.

"As the magister taught us, lightning and thunder come directly from Jupiter," said Lucius.

"Ah, but birds are the messengers of Jupiter, so why should avian augury not be as prized? No, I think lightning augury is more impressive because a flash of lightning cannot possibly be fabricated by mortal men, while anyone might arrange to release certain birds from a certain area at a certain time."

Lucius frowned. "Are you saying those vultures were deliberately released?"

"Oh, not for Romulus, surely, and certainly not for Great-Uncle. But for me—who knows?" Claudius shrugged. "Thanks to my obvious short-comings, Great-Uncle can foresee no higher station in life for me than to be an augur. I twitch too much to find glory as a warrior. You saw me drop my lituus today; imagine me dropping a sword on the battlefield! I st-stutter too much to make impressive sp-sp-speeches in the Senate." He flashed a sardonic smile; was he stuttering on purpose? "Since this is as far as I shall go, Great-Uncle is determined that everyone should acknowledge my competence at augury, if at nothing else. Three vultures would have suf-ficed, don't you think? Great-Uncle always overdoes these things! When the two vacancies opened in the college, why do you suppose he chose to allow you to enlist, Lucius?"

"I know my father did everything he could to promote me and to win the emperor's favor. He was surprised he succeeded, considering my youth—"

"Ha! Great-Uncle approved of your admission to the college for only one reason: he wanted to make me an augur, and so be done with me, and he wanted another candidate my age to enter alongside me, so that I shouldn't stand out so much. You weren't made an augur despite your age, Lucius, but because of it! But the important thing, cousin Lucius, is that our examinations are over, and now we are augurs. Augurs for life! But what is that you're wearing?"

Claudius referred to the amulet on Lucius's necklace. It had slipped outside his trabea and the gold shone brightly against the purple wool.

"It's a family talisman."

"Where did it come from? What does it symbolize?"

"I don't really know," Lucius confessed, with some chagrin. Claudius was such a scholar and so steeped in his own family's history that he was never at a loss to explain even the most arcane bits of ancestral lore.

Claudius came to a halt, reached for the amulet, and studied it closely. Lucius had seen such a spark in his friend's eyes before, during their stud-ies together—the excitement of the devoted antiquarian in the presence of an intriguing puzzle. "I think, Lucius—yes, I th-th-think I may have s-some idea of what this is. I'll have to do a bit of research. . . ."

"Come along, my fellow augurs," said Lucius's father, catching up with them. "We're almost there." Like Lucius, he had never been inside the im-perial residence, and he was flushed with excitement.

They entered a courtyard first, no grander than that of any house of moderate wealth, except for the trophies on prominent display in the center of the yard. On a wooden stand was displayed the emperor's personal armor, including his sword, ax, helmet, and shield.

"See how they gleam," whispered Lucius, "as if they've just been freshly burnished!"

"Yes, I believe there is a slave who performs that duty daily," said Claudius.

As the augurs filled the courtyard, waiting for the massive bronze entry doors to open, Lucius looked up at the giant civic crown, a garland of oak leaves and acorns, carved into the marble lintel above the doors.

"The civic crown is traditionally awarded to a soldier who saves a comrade's life in battle," noted Claudius, following his gaze. "Can you guess why the Senate voted to award that stupendous image of a civic crown to my uncle?"

"I suspect you can tell me."

"It was awarded to him in honor of his victory over Cleopatra and my grandfather Marcus Antonius—whom I never knew, of course, since he died by his own sword twenty years before I was b-b-born. By winning that war, you see, Augustus saved us all from being enslaved by the Egyptian queen, the entire citizenry of Roma and all the generations to come— and thus he deserved a civic crown of suitable splendor."

The booming noise of a thrown bolt resounded from within the house, and then the great bronze doors began to slowly open inward.

Flanking the doorway, Lucius noticed, were two flourishing laurel trees. As lightning flashed over their heads and a peal of thunder shook the courtyard, he saw several of the augurs break sprigs from the trees and slip them into their trabeas. It was a well-known fact that the laurel tree was lightning-proof, of all trees the only one never struck. Would carrying a sprig of laurel protect a man from lightning? Many people thought so.

Rather than being opulent or ostentatious, the interior of the imperial house was decorated with great simplicity. The columns were of travertine, not marble. The floors were paved with black-and-white tiles in simple geometric patterns, not decorated with colorful mosaics. The walls were painted in solid colors, not with the amazingly realistic landscapes Lucius had occasionally seen in the houses of his wealthier acquaintances, such as the Acilii. The several dining rooms that opened onto the central garden were spacious enough to accommodate a great many guests, but the dining couches themselves were as humble as those in Lucius's house.

The meal was simple, as well. When asparagus was served as the first course, dipped in boiling water for just a moment so that it was cooked but still crisp, Claudius, reclining next to Lucius, snapped a stalk in two and quipped, " 'Quick as boiled asparagus'—just the way Great-Uncle likes it!"

Lucius had never seen his friend in such high spirits. "I'm a little surprised at how simply the imperial residence is furnished," he said. "Even the house of Acilia's father is more opulent. Are the private quarters equally austere?"

"More so! Great-Uncle sleeps on a bed of straw and will have only backless chairs in the house. 'A Roman's spine should be sufficiently stiff to hold him upright,' he says. He believes in setting an example by practicing old-fashioned virtues of decorum and restraint. He expects his family to do the same. When Julilla, his granddaughter, built a mansion for herself on too grand a scale, Great-Uncle had the whole thing d-d-d-demolished. I can't remember, was that before or after he banished poor Julilla to that island for committing adultery? And then, when she b-b-bore her lover's child, Great-Uncle ordered that the baby be abandoned on a mountainside to die." Claudius bit a stalk of asparagus, chewed loudly, and swallowed. "He's banished Julilla's mother as well, his own daughter, likewise for scandalous conduct. And his only surviving grandson, Agrippa—he, too, failed to meet Great-Uncle's standards and so ended up on an island somewhere. So you see, these Spartan surroundings are not a pretense. They are a genuine reflection of my uncle's temperament."

In each of the dining areas a couch was set aside for the host, who moved across the garden from room to room, allowing all the guests the honor of his presence. To Lucius, it seemed that the emperor was more an observer than a participant in the festivities, saying little and eating nothing. The old man appeared restless and distracted, giving a start whenever there was a peal of thunder. Light rain occasionally swept across the garden, and gusts of wind fanned the braziers that were lit as darkness fell. Hardly an hour after sundown, with several courses yet to be served, Augustus strode to the center of the garden, where all the guests could see him, bade his fellow augurs good night, and excused himself.

With the host gone, the atmosphere became noticeably more relaxed. A few guests dared to drink their wine without water, but no one got drunk. After a final course of carrots in a thick garum sauce, the guests began to disperse, paying their respects to the new inductees before departing. Lucius's father was the last to leave.

"You're not coming with me, son?"

"Claudius has invited me to take a stroll to the Temple of Apollo."

"In this weather?"

"The temple is only a few steps away. And it's not raining now."

"The sky could open at any moment."

"If the storm grows worse, Lucius c-c-can spend the night here in my quarters," offered Claudius.

"I suppose I can hardly object," said the elder Pinarius, looking at once pleased and anxious that his son should become a welcome guest in the house of Augustus.

The Temple of Apollo was surrounded by an ornate colonnade directly adjoining the imperial residence, perched on the crest of the Palatine Hill, directly above the Circus Maximus. Of all Augustus's new constructions, the Temple of Apollo was the most magnificent. Lit by flickering braziers from the surrounding colonnade, with a light mist descending, the temple appeared even more spectacular by night. The glistening walls were made of solid blocks of white Luna marble, and the gilded chariot of the sun atop the roof seemed to be made of flame. Dominating the square in front of the entrance, a marble statue of Apollo loomed above an altar flanked by four bronze oxen. In the flickering light, the oxen seemed almost to be alive. When Lucius said so to Claudius, his friend explained that they were hundreds of years old, the creations of the great Myron, famed for his much-copied statue of the Discus Thrower.

At the top of the steps, past the towering columns, they came to two massive doors, each decorated with reliefs in ivory. By flashes of lightning,

Lucius gazed at a fabulously detailed panel, a riot of figures in violent motion—young men and women running this way and that in a great panic, some pierced by arrows, and in the sky above them, each wielding a bow, the divine siblings Apollo and Artemis.

"The slaying of the Niobids of Thebes," Claudius explained. "When their mother Niobe boasted of having more offspring than Leto, the goddess's children took offense and slew them, every one. Apollo shot the sons; Artemis shot the daughters. Niobe committed hubris—overweening mortal pride—and her children paid the price for it. The d-d-descendants of powerful mortals often seem to pay a price, simply for existing." Claudius looked thoughtful, then turned and pointed with his lituus to the rectangle of sky framed by the nearest columns. "The lightning seems to be drawing closer. Look at that thunderbolt! Have you ever seen one like that? The magister says that every possible manifestation of lightning has been cataloged and categorized over the years, but that implies that lightning repeats itself, as letters and words in a language repeat; but I sometimes wonder if every thunderbolt is not unique to itself. Of course, if that were so, there could be no meaning in lightning at all, or none that men could make sense of."

A great blackness, darker than all the rest of the sky and filled with flashes of lightning, was sweeping toward them from the southwest. It was over the Tiber now, its fury reflected on the water's turbulent face.

Lucius felt steeped in privilege, to be standing with his friend, a member of the imperial household, on the threshold of the emperor's greatest temple; but at the same time he felt a slight thrill of fear, for the approaching storm promised to be violent, and the horrific images of the slaughtered Niobids disturbed him. He was here to pay homage to Apollo, but Apollo could be a vengeful god.

Claudius did not appear to share his anxiety. "Did you know, years ago, this very spot was the site of the imperial residence? Then one day it was blasted by lightning and burned to the ground. Augustus declared that the g-g-gods had marked this as a sacred site, suitable only for a temple, and got the Senate to dedicate the funds to build not just the temple but the new imperial residence next to it. The temple is magnificent, as you can see, and everyone thought Great-Uncle would build himself an equally magnificent palace, but instead he made the new house exactly like the old one, only a little bigger and with annexes to accommodate his growing staff." Claudius chuckled.

"Was Augustus in the house when it was struck by lightning?"

"Yes, he was. And that wasn't Great-Uncle's first encounter with lightning. He was very nearly k-k-killed by a thunderbolt during a night march in the Cantabarian campaign, after my grandfather Antonius was vanquished; a flash of lightning grazed Great-Uncle's litter and struck dead the slave who was carrying a torch before him. After that narrow escape, he dedicated a shrine to Jupiter the Thunderer—there, if you squint you can see it over on the Capitoline, looking very impressive when the lightning illuminates it. Ever since, Great-Uncle's had a morbid fear of lightning. How he hates a thunderstorm! I'm sure that's why he left the b-banquet early, to take shelter under ground. The man fears nothing and no one here on earth, but he thinks that d-d-death from the sky might still claim him, as it did King Romulus. That's why he was wearing that amulet tonight. He always wears it in stormy weather."

"An amulet?"

"Did you not notice, Lucius? He was wearing an amulet made of sealskin, for protection, the way others carry a sprig of laurel."

"Sealskin?"

"Just as the laurel is never struck by lightning, neither is the sea calf. It's a scientific fact, confirmed by all reliable authorities. I myself prefer laurel." He produced a sprig from inside his trabea.

"I suppose I should have taken a sprig," said Lucius. The lightning and thunder were coming closer. The storm was almost upon them.

"Stay close to me; perhaps my sprig will protect you. There's an interesting story about those laurel trees at the entrance to the imperial house. Not long after Livia was first betrothed to Augustus, she was riding in a carriage on a country road and a perfectly white hen dropped from the sky into her lap—with a sprig of laurel in its beak! Livia bred the hen to use its offspring in auguries, and planted the laurel, from which a sacred grove sprang up on the imperial estate along the Tiber, as well as the two specimens that flank the doorway of the imperial house. Augustus wore wreaths from those laurel trees in his triumphal processions. Ah, but I digress. . . ."

"You sometimes do." Lucius smiled, then gave a start at a loud boom of thunder. He heard the hissing of the rain as it swept toward them over the Aventine.

"Well, you did ask about the sealskin amulet. And speaking of amulets, I've been th-th-thinking about the one you wear. I believe I may have an idea of what it is—"

He was interrupted by a flash of blinding light, followed at once by a tremendous thundercrack. Lightning had struck the Palatine, somewhere very close to them.

"Do you think it struck the imperial house?" said Lucius. They ran to the end of the porch and peered toward the residence. There was no sign of fire. Then a sudden downpour obscured everything beyond the temple steps. Wind blew rain onto the porch; the pediment gave no protection. Claudius opened one of the tall doors. They slipped inside the temple and closed the door behind them.

The air smelled of incense. A giant statue of Apollo dominated the sanctuary, lit by flickering lamps mounted on the walls. On this stormy night, it seemed to Lucius that the place had an eerie magic. The air itself carried a charge of excitement. Gazing up at the god, Lucius felt hackles rise on the back of his neck. With an uncanny certainty, he knew that something very important was going to happen that night.

He looked behind him. Claudius was sitting on a marble bench against one wall, already nodding, his jaw hanging open and a bit of drool suspended from his lower lip. Truly, anyone who saw him at that moment would have assumed he was an idiot. Poor Claudius!

The uncanny sensation subsided. Lucius sat beside Claudius, listening to him softly snore, and waited for the raging storm to subside.

When the massive door began to swing inward, he gave a start. Had he been dozing, and for how long? A man entered the temple, dressed in the tunic of an imperial servant and carrying a torch.

"Claudius? Are you here, Claudius?"

Claudius woke. He clutched Lucius's arm and wiped a bit of drool from his chin. "What? Who's there?"

"Euphranor." It was one of the emperor's most trusted freedmen. His hair was black but his beard was almost entirely white. "I've been looking everywhere for you!" He approached and handed Claudius a wax tablet of the sort that could be written on, rubbed flat, and written over.

By the light of the torch Claudius peered at the tablet. In a crabbed, elderly hand was written the quaint phrase "Come, quick as asparagus," with the word *asparagus* marked through and the word *lightning* scrawled above.

"A message written in Great-Uncle's own hand!" declared Claudius, obviously surprised. "The man has an army of scribes to take his dictation at any moment of the day or night. Why in his own hand? What can he want so urgently? And why 'quick as *lightning*'?"

Lucius suddenly felt out of place. "I suppose I should go home now—"

"While the storm still rages? No, no! You'll come with me."

"Are you sure?"

"Great-Uncle didn't say for you *not* to come. Follow me, cousin—quick as asparagus! Euphranor, lead the way."

Pelted by rain, they followed Euphranor back to the house, past the dining rooms and the garden, where rain descended in a torrent, and then through a series of doors and a maze of hallways. At last they came to a narrow doorway that opened onto a flight of stairs leading down.

"I'll stay here," said Euphranor. "You'll find him at the bottom of the steps."

Claudius descended the long, steep, winding flight of stairs with Lucius following. At last they arrived in a lamp-lit, subterranean room. Lucius saw at once that the ceiling and the walls were decorated with mosaics; the thousands of tiny tiles glinted and shimmered. Among the dazzling images he recognized King Romulus with his long beard and iron crown. Another image could only be the infant twins, Romulus and his brother Remus, adrift on the Tiber in a basket. Another image showed Romulus being carried up to the heavens on a ray of light sent by Jupiter. There were many more images, all illustrating stories from the life of the Founder.

"What is *he* doing here?"

Lucius turned to see Augustus, standing closer than Lucius had ever seen the man before. What terrible teeth the emperor had, all yellow and decayed, and how short he was, wearing slippers instead of the thick-soled shoes that usually made him taller. Lucius told himself he should be at least a little awed, but the presence of the emperor was underwhelming. In his younger days, the fair-haired Octavius was said to have been the best-looking boy in Roma, so pretty that his uncle Julius Caesar took him

for a lover (so went the whispered rumor), and in later days, the boy Octavius who became the man Augustus had commanded sufficient authority
to bend whole nations to his will. But at that moment Lucius saw only a
little old man with rotten teeth, unkempt straw-colored hair, tufts of hair
in his nostrils, and bushy eyebrows that met above his nose.

Eye to eye with the ruler of the world, Lucius was buoyed by a curious
sense of confidence, remembering the premonition he had experienced in
the Temple of Apollo that something very important was about to happen.

"Shall I send him away, Great-Uncle?" said Claudius.

Augustus stared at Lucius, so long and hard that Lucius's confidence
began to waver. The old man finally spoke.

"No. Young Lucius Pinarius may stay. He is an augur now, is he not?
And his ancestors were among the very first augurs in Roma. A Pinarius
accompanied Romulus when he took the auspices, and before that the
Pinarii were keepers of the people's first shrine, the Great Altar of Hercules. The state assumed that duty over three hundred years ago; perhaps I
should return the Great Altar to the hereditary keeping of the Pinarii. Re-
viving ancient traditions is pleasing to the gods. And he is a blood relation,
for whatever that's worth. Perhaps, Lucius Pinarius, the gods themselves
delivered you here to me tonight."

Lucius averted his eyes, humbled by the emperor's scrutiny. He stared
at the mosaics above them.

"Images from the life of Romulus, as you no doubt perceive," explained Augustus. "The chamber in which we stand is the Lupercale, the
sacred cave where the foundling twins Romulus and Remus were suckled
by the she-wolf. I myself discovered the cave when the foundations for this
house were being laid, and under my directions it's been decorated as a
sacred shrine."

"The mosaics are exquisite," said Lucius.

"Yes. There you see the twins suckled by the she-wolf, and there, the
rescue of Remus by his brother, the slaying of King Amulius and the taking of his iron crown. There, the sighting of the vultures, and Romulus
plowing a furrow to mark the city boundaries. There, the first triumphal
procession, and the king's ascent to the heavens during a thunderstorm."

Lucius nodded. He recalled something Claudius had told him, that the
emperor had considered taking the name Romulus as a title, rather than

Augustus, but ultimately rejected the name as unlucky; Romulus murdered his brother, after all, and though legend said that Romulus was taken alive by the gods to Olympus, some historians believed he was murdered by conspiring senators.

"Of course, one cannot take the legends too literally," Claudius noted, pointing to the image of the suckling she-wolf. "My tutor Titus Livius says that our ancestors used the same word, *lupa,* to mean either a she-wolf or a whore. Livius suggests that the twins may have been raised not by a wild beast but by a common prostitute."

"Don't be impious, nephew!" snapped Augustus, and seemed about to say more when a crack of thunder shook the room. The emperor frantically reached for the sealskin amulet he wore on a chain around his neck. "Even here, so deep under ground, the earth shakes!" he whispered. "Is it possible the house has been struck by lightning two times in one night?" His rheumy eyes flashed with something Lucius could only interpret as fear.

"Why did you s-s-summon us, Great-Uncle?" asked Claudius quietly.

"I'll show you now—though to do so, we'll have to leave the safety of the Lupercale." Augustus frowned, then braced himself and led the way up the stairs, taking them slowly. Euphranor was waiting for them at the top of the steps. At Augustus's order, the freedman brought each of them a torch to carry.

"When you see the omen, Claudius, you'll understand why no one else must know of this. No one!" Augustus turned to Lucius. "Do you understand as well, young man? Any omen that regards my person is a state secret and must never be divulged. There's no telling how it might be used by those who wish me harm. To divulge such a secret is a crime punishable by death."

He led them to a courtyard. The neatly trimmed hedges and paving stones glistened. The rain had relented; only a light mist descended on them. The courtyard was dominated by a bronze statue of the emperor himself, painted in lifelike colors. *Did he ever look like that?* wondered Lucius, for the statue of the serenely self-assured, handsome young warrior scarcely resembled the shaken old man standing beside him.

As they stepped closer to the statue, Lucius's torch illuminated something on the ground, on the far side of the pedestal. It was the dead body of a young man, dressed in the charred remains of what once had been the tunic of an imperial slave.

"Look there!" cried Augustus. "Wisps of smoke still rise from the corpse. He burns from the inside, like a coal in a brazier."

Claudius pursed his lips. "This slave—he was k-k-killed by the first lightning bolt, the one that struck while Lucius and I were in the Temple of Apollo?"

"Yes. Lightning struck the statue. The slave must have been standing too close. See the damage to the statue—the places where the paint has been scorched, the way the ivory inlays for the whites of the eyes have turned black!" Augustus sucked in his breath. "By Hercules, the statue has been struck again, by that second lightning bolt, the one we felt down in the Lupercale! It's incredible. . . ."

"Impossible!" protested Claudius. "All authorities agree, lightning n-n-never strikes the same spot twice. Such a thing is unheard of."

"And yet, it's true. The bronze plaque on the pedestal wasn't damaged before, I swear to Jupiter it wasn't—but now, see how the letter *C* is missing, blasted into nothing." Augustus swallowed hard. His face was ashen.

Looking closer, Lucius saw that the damage was just as the emperor had described. On the bronze plaque with an embossed inscription, the first letter of CAESAR had been melted away, leaving almost no trace.

"What does it mean, Claudius?" asked Augustus. "Such freaks of nature are always signs from the gods. Useless as you are for most things, skulking in that library of yours, you do know everything there is to know about omens."

Claudius touched his fingertips to the scorched bronze plaque, then quickly drew them back. "Too hot to touch!" he gasped, then stared at the plaque and whispered, *"Aesar."*

"What's that you say?"

Claudius shrugged. "I was simply reading the word that remains, without the letter *C*."

"But *aesar* is not a word."

"I think it might be, in Etruscan. I'm not sure."

"Then find out!"

"T-t-time, Great-Uncle. It will take time to properly interpret such an omen. Do you not agree, Lucius? We must know to the minute the time of the two lightning strikes. We must know the name of the dead slave. Even the name of the sculptor who made this statue might be significant. I must retire to my library to look through the literature, to c-c-consult my Etruscan dictionaries, to study previous omens derived from lightning."

"How long will this take?"

Claudius furrowed his brow, then brightened. "Lucius will help me. As you yourself noted, Great-Uncle, it's no accident that Lucius was with me when you sent that summons. Together, I promise you, Lucius and I will determine the meaning of this omen."

"Do it quickly!"

"Qu-quick as asparagus, Great-Uncle!" Claudius smiled crookedly and wiped a bit of drool from the corner of his mouth.

"Perhaps our fortunes are about to improve, Lucius," said Claudius. "We've just been given a very important task by the emperor himself. That makes us important men. We'd better get started."

They were in Claudius's library. The room was brightly lit by many lamps. Lucius had never seen so many scrolls and scraps of parchment in one place, all neatly, even obsessively, filed and sorted. There were histories, maps, calendars, and genealogies. There were detailed lists of every magistrate who had ever served the Roman state. There were numerous dictionaries, not just of Latin but of Greek, Egyptian, Parthian, the Punic tongue of ruined Carthage, the virtually defunct Etruscan language, and even languages Lucius had never heard of. There were sketches of historic sites Claudius had visited, together with his personal notes and copies of inscriptions taken from statues and other monuments.

Searching among the documents, Claudius found a scroll of heavy parchment, unrolled it on a small table, and placed weights to hold down the corners. A large circle drawn on the parchment was divided into quarters by a vertical line and a horizontal line and surrounded by notations. Though he knew little about astrology, Lucius recognized it as a horoscope.

"And not just any horoscope, but that of the emperor himself," said Claudius. "This is an exact copy of the very horoscope that was cast for the young Octavius by the astrologer Theogenes of Apollonia. Surely you know the story? No? Ah, well, then . . ." Claudius cleared his throat.

"This was back in the days when the Divine Julius was still on earth, though very near the end of his life. He decided to send his nephew to be educated at Apollonia, on the west coast of Greece. For a companion, Octavius took along his dear friend Marcus Agrippa. The boys decided to have their horoscopes cast by the famous Theogenes. Agrippa went first, telling the astrologer the exact time and place of his birth. Theogenes disappeared into his study while the boys waited. The horoscope that resulted was so f-f-favorable—Theogenes swore he had never seen one to match it—that Octavius decided not to have his done after all, for fear that it would pale beside that of his friend. But Agrippa pressed him—teased him mercilessly, I should imagine—until Octavius relented and gave the astrologer the information he needed. Again the boys waited. When Theogenes finally emerged from his study, he fell to his knees before Octavius in awe, and declared that Octavius would become the master of the world. They say—though I have never been able to verify this for certain— that the horoscope was delivered to Octavius at the very moment that his uncle was murdered back in Roma.

"Ever since that day, the emperor has been so sure of his d-d-destiny that he's made no secret of the hour of his birth. He even puts his sign, Capricornus, on his c-coinage. If anything merits classification as a state secret, you'd think it's the emperor's horoscope! Yet here it is, for you and me to study, just as Theogenes cast it. And since we have access to the information, we might as well use it."

"But, Claudius, I know nothing about astrology."

"Then you shall leave this room knowing more than when you entered."

"But the magister says that augury is sufficient for all divinations."

"I suspect the magister is a bit envious of the increasing popularity of astrology. I myself see no conflict between the principles of augury and the study of astral science. Any thoughtful person must perceive that heavenly bodies exert an influence on objects both animate and inanimate.

Certain effects of the sun and moon are obvious: they cause vegetation to grow, determine when animals sleep and rut, and control the tides. Likewise, the stars control storms and floods, which can be observed to come and go according to the rise and fall of certain constellations. This influence is invisible, as is the influence of a magnet. Considering the all-pervasive nature of this invisible influence, it would be irrational to presume that it does not exert an effect on human beings.

"It was the Babylonians who first charted the movements of the stars and created a vocabulary to describe their influence on humankind. After Alexander the Great conquered Persia, the study of astrology spread to Greece and Egypt. It was the Babylonian priest Berossus who moved to Cos, founded the first astrological school in Greece, and translated *The Eye of Bel* into Greek. It was Bolus of Egypt who wrote *Sympathies and Antipathies,* which remains the standard textbook. I've almost worn my copy out."

Lucius stared at the horoscope, puzzling over the mathematical calculations and the notations about houses, signs, and planets. "Do you really think the solution to the lightning omen lies in the emperor's horoscope?"

"I wouldn't be surprised if it has some role to play in our research. But I think we should begin by consulting my Etruscan dictionaries, to see if I'm right about this word *aesar. . . .*"

All night the storm continued, rattling the shutters, pelting the roof with rain, and shaking the ground with thunder, while Lucius and Claudius pored over various texts. From time to time, slaves brought them food and drink and replenished the lamps when the oil ran low. Lucius was not aware that dawn had broken until he heard a cock crow. Claudius opened the shutters. The storm had passed. The sky was clear. But the pale morning sunshine could not dispel the grim mood in the room. They had succeeded in interpreting the omen.

"Perhaps we could tell him that the omen defeated us, that we discovered nothing," said Lucius.

Claudius shook his head. "He won't accept that. He'd be able to tell at once that we were hiding something."

"Then perhaps he'll simply dismiss our interpretation. Why should he believe the two youngest augurs in Roma?"

"Because our interpretation is correct, as he will see for himself. Great-

Uncle has a deep and abiding faith in omens. The outcome of every one of his b-b-battles was foretold by an omen which he himself divined—the eagle that drove away two ravens at Bononia, which foretold his eventual triumph over his fellow triumvirs; the shade of Caesar that appeared before Philippi; the driver and ass he met on the road before the battle of Actium, one named Eutychus and the other Nicon—Greek for 'prosper' and 'victory.'"

"And now, this omen."

"Which we have no choice but to d-d-deliver."

Euphranor accompanied them up several flights of steps to the high, many-windowed chamber where the emperor awaited them. This was the room, as Claudius informed Lucius in a whisper, that Augustus called his Little Syracuse, because the great Syracusan inventor Archimedes had had such a room in his house, isolated from the rest of the building.

Augustus's secluded retreat was cluttered with mementos. There were architect's models of various of his buildings, including a miniature Temple of Apollo in ivory. There were war trophies, including a captured ship's beak from the battle of Actium, where the naval skills of Agrippa had soundly defeated Antonius and Cleopatra. There were exotic Egyptian treasures brought back from Alexandria, where Antonius and Cleopatra had escaped capture only by committing suicide. Draped upon a statue of the Divine Julius was a red cape, a bit faded and moth-eaten, that had been worn by the great man himself at his last great battle, at Munda in Spain.

There were also more-personal mementos, including toy ships and catapults that had belonged to the emperor's deceased grandsons. When Lucius and Claudius entered, Augustus was fiddling with a pair of baby shoes.

"Such tiny feet he has, little Gaius! These just arrived from the German frontier, Claudius, with a note from your brother. Your little nephew has just outgrown these, so Germanicus sends them to me as a keepsake. Charming, aren't they? I suppose Germanicus and Agrippina think they can induce me to name their two-year-old as my heir. Well, your older brother isn't a bad sort, and Agrippina is the only one of my grandchildren who turned out to be not completely useless. Little Gaius *is* my great-grandchild, and they say the boy is healthy, so perhaps there is some hope for the future, after all. . . ."

His voice trailed away. He stared at the tiny shoes for a long time before he finally put them down among the cast-off toys.

The emperor appeared to have suffered as sleepless a night as had the two younger men, and he looked much worse for it. He had changed from his trabea into a tunic so drab and worn that Lucius would not have been surprised to see a slave wearing it. The emperor's voice was hoarse and there was a rattle in his throat.

"So? What have you discovered?"

Claudius stepped forward, but when he opened his mouth to speak, nothing came out. For a moment he was as stiff and silent as a statue, then suddenly he began to twitch and stammer, jerking this way and that and making incoherent noises. Lucius gripped his shoulder to steady him, but the twitching only grew worse. He had never seen Claudius so severely afflicted by his infirmities.

Augustus grunted and rolled his eyes. "Jupiter help me! You, then. Yes, you, Lucius Pinarius! Speak!"

Lucius's heart pounded and he felt something thick pressing inside his throat. For a moment he feared that he was about to have a fit, like Claudius. Then he managed to take a breath and the words tumbled out.

"We believe—that is, Claudius and I—that our examination of the literature and our study of certain precedents—precedents pertaining specifically to lightning and to—to statues—and the Etruscan language—which we found in the literature—"

"By Hercules, you're as useless as my nephew! Say what you have to say."

Lucius felt light-headed and dazed from lack of sleep, but he pressed on. "For example, in the days of Tarquin, the last king, one of his statues was struck by lightning, which did damage only to the inscription, which was written in both Latin and Etruscan; well, you can see how the precedent applies here. In that instance, the numeral X was defaced in four places, as were the Etruscan words *tinia,* meaning days, and *huznatre,* meaning a group of young men. No one could interpret the omen, but its meaning became clear when, forty days later, a company of forty young warriors literally ran Tarquin and his sons from the city, ending the monarchy and establishing the Republic. It became clear then that the four Xs defaced by lightning meant forty, and referred to both the days remaining in Tarquin's reign and the number of warriors who would drive him out. And there is a further example—"

"Enough of this antiquarian drivel! You try my patience, Lucius Pinarius. Deliver the omen clearly, at once."

Lucius took a deep breath. "As Claudius thought, *aesar* is an old Etruscan word. It means a deity or divine spirit. And of course *C*—the letter that was melted away by the lightning—is also the symbol for one hundred. The presence of the dead slave was an indication of mortality, a small death foreshadowing a great one. When these facts are assembled, and the relevant precedents considered—the details of which you would have me omit—then we must conclude that the omen of the two lightning strikes indicates this: that in one hundred days, the person portrayed by the statue will leave the world of mortals and join the gods."

The color abruptly drained from the emperor's face, like wine from a cup. His expression became so strange and his voice so thin that Lucius almost believed the shadow before him was the lemur of a man already dead. "What are you saying, young man? Are you telling me that I have only one hundred days to live?"

"N-n-ninety-nine, actually," said Claudius, suddenly able to speak, but keeping his head down and his eyes averted. "The omen occurred yesterday, so we m-m-must subtract. . . ." He abruptly looked up, as if surprised to hear his own voice, and fell silent.

Augustus was quiet for a long moment. "Will it be an easy death?"

"The omen gives no indication regarding the manner of death," said Lucius.

Augustus nodded slowly. "I've always envied those who died easily. The Greeks have a word for it: *euthanasia,* 'good death.' That is all I hope for: *euthanasia.* I accept that I cannot control the time and place; that will be chosen by others. But I wish to go as quietly and as painlessly as possible, with my dignity intact." He turned away from them, drew himself upright, and composed himself. "You understand that you must repeat this to no one. Now go. You are both dismissed."

As he was leaving the room, Lucius looked back to see the emperor pick up the baby shoes of his great-grandson and stare at them, ashen-faced and with tears in his eyes.

Euphranor was nowhere to be seen. They found their own way down the steps.

"It's almost as if he was expecting it," said Lucius. He felt utterly drained.

"Perhaps he *was* expecting it. P-p-perhaps it was what he *wanted* to hear."

"What do you mean, Claudius? Do you think your great-uncle is contemplating suicide? Or that he fears being murdered? What did Augustus mean, about not being able to control the time and place of his death? 'That will be chosen by others,' he said. What others? The gods?"

Claudius shrugged. "He's an old m-m-man, Lucius. You and I can't begin to imagine all the terrible things he's seen, all the terrible things he's done. Life has brought him a great deal of disappointment, especially in the last few years. So many d-deaths in the family, so much strife." He drew a sharp breath. "Speaking of which . . ."

Coming toward them down the hallway, imposing despite her advanced age and the unassuming nature of her dress, was Claudius's grandmother. The wife of Augustus did nothing to color her hair or mask her wrinkles, and wore a stola simple enough to please even her luxury-hating husband, yet Livia projected an undeniable aura of privilege and power. Walking beside her, in an equally simple tunic, was her son, Claudius's uncle, Tiberius, a robustly built man of middle age with a dour expression. By all accounts, Augustus intended to make Tiberius his heir, despite the fact that his stepson was not a blood relation.

Claudius and Lucius stepped to one side, but, instead of passing by, Livia and her son came to a stop before them. Claudius swallowed hard, then began to introduce Lucius, but he stuttered so badly that Livia cut him short with a wave of her hand.

"Never mind, grandson, I know who this is: young Lucius Pinarius." She looked them up and down and raised an eyebrow. "Curious, that the two of you should still be wearing your trabeas from yesterday. Off to take the auspices, at this early hour? Or did you never go to bed? Yes, from the look of you, I think you've been up all night. But doing what? I wonder. Not celebrating, or else you'd smell of wine."

She stared at Lucius, who was at a loss for an answer. The emperor had explicitly ordered them to speak of the omen to no one.

Livia seemed amused by his discomfort. "Can't you see that I'm teasing you, young man? Nothing that happens in this house is a secret to me. I'm perfectly aware that lightning struck my husband's statue last night, not once, but twice. While I'm amazed that he would entrust the interpretation of such an omen to the likes of you two, I'd be curious to know what you came up with. No answer? Ah, well, I shall simply ask him myself."

Lucius glanced at Claudius. It was obvious that he lived in fear of his grandmother. Tiberius apparently did not frighten him as much, for Claudius dared to reach out and tap the sprig of laurel pinned to the man's tunic.

"From last n-n-night, uncle? The storm is over and you need the laurel's protection no longer. But I should think an atheist like yourself had no f-f-fear of lightning." Claudius turned to Lucius. "Uncle Tiberius has no faith in the gods, and thus no belief in d-divination. If there are no gods, there is no point in trying to discern their will. Uncle Tiberius spurns augury. He puts his faith entirely in astrology."

Tiberius looked at Claudius glumly. "That is correct, nephew. The stars decide when a man is born and when he dies, and the stars determine the course of his life. The logic is undeniable. Some mechanism unimaginably huge must control the movements of the stars, which in turn control our tiny lives. We mortals are many times removed from whatever primal force animates the cosmos."

"Then the stars control humanity rather as the m-m-mechanism of a ballista controls the trajectory of its missile," suggested Claudius, "or the cogs and gears of a water wheel control the m-m-movements of a leaf caught in the channel? Is that all we are, Uncle Tiberius, missiles hurtling through space, or leaves on a torrent?"

"Not bad metaphors, Claudius, especially for someone who believes lightning is an omen." Tiberius sniggered and shook his head. "Only a fool or a child could believe that lightning is a weapon thrown down by some malicious giant in the clouds. Lightning is a natural phenomenon which occurs according to very precise, if very complicated, rules, just like the movement of the stars. I believe in science, Claudius, not superstition."

Livia sighed, bored by the turn of the conversation. She took her son's arm and indicated her desire to move on.

Claudius watched until they disappeared around a corner, gnashing his teeth. "There goes the next emperor."

"Is it certain he'll succeed Augustus?"

"There's always a chance the old man will ch-ch-change his mind about Agrippa. He's Augustus's only surviving grandson, after all. And only two years older than you and me—young enough to enjoy a long reign. Agrippa's banishment was Livia's doing, I suspect: people who stand in her way have a habit of either dying or disappearing. Uncle Tiberius is the last man standing, so Tiberius is the heir apparent. It's probably for the best. The bleeding wound of the German frontier is the biggest problem facing the empire right now, and Tiberius is a c-competent general, even if he is an atheist. I fear, Lucius, that our aptitude for divination will not serve us as well under the next emperor as it has under our present one."

"Served us well? I don't see how I've been well served by any of this!" Lucius snapped, suddenly feeling completely undone by lack of sleep and the strain of meeting the emperor's demands. He lowered his voice to a whisper. "What if our prediction becomes known, and the emperor *doesn't* die in a hundred days? I shall look like a fool!"

"N-n-ninety-nine days, actually—"

"And if he *does* die—"

"Then you shall look like a young fellow wise beyond his years."

"Or will people hold us responsible for his death? What's that old Etruscan saying? 'Men blame the soothsayer.'"

"Oh, no, Lucius, if the emperor dies, it's not you and me whom people will suspect." Claudius glanced toward the spot where they had last seen Livia and Tiberius. "You might do well to take up a new study, Lucius. How much astrology do you think you can learn in n-ninety-nine days?"

"Perhaps, father, we should go to the Temple of Apollo on the Palatine and pray," said Lucius.

By his careful reckoning, exactly 105 days had passed since lightning had struck the emperor's statue. The date on which he and Claudius had predicted that Augustus would be taken by the gods had come and gone, but the accuracy of the prophecy was still uncertain. Augustus was away from Roma, and since news could arrive no faster than the pace of a quick horse, there was no way to know whether something had happened to Augustus or not.

But the latest news, which Lucius and his father went seeking in the Forum each day, was unsettling. Intending to journey to Beneventum, accompanying Tiberius partway on a mission to begin new military operations in Illyria, Augustus had fallen ill. He was said to be recuperating at his retreat on the island of Capri, suffering from a minor irregularity of the bowels. Again, today, Lucius and his father had come to the Forum, anxious for further news of the emperor's condition.

"Prayer is to be commended," said Lucius's father. "But why the Temple of Apollo?"

"Because that was where this all began, the night of the storm." Lucius recalled the uncanny premonition he had experienced just before Euphranor had come to summon Claudius.

"Ah, but what would we pray for?" His father lowered his voice and looked around. They were not far from the Temple of Vesta, on a busy stretch of the Sacred Way. Several Vestals were leaving the round temple with their attendants, and a group of senators in togas was nearby; some of them nodded and hailed the elder Pinarius before passing on. Father and son retreated to a more secluded spot on the far side of the Temple of Castor.

"As I was saying, son, for what would you have us pray? Surely not for the emperor's death; that would be treason. Yet, if we pray that the emperor should not die in accordance with the omen, then are we not praying to thwart the will of the gods?"

Not for the first time, Lucius regretted confiding in his father. If anything, the elder Pinarius was more nervous than Lucius about the omen and its outcome. And had he not put his father in danger by telling him about the omen, against the emperor's explicit orders? Yet, Lucius could hardly have borne the strain of waiting alone.

"Then let us pray for neither of those things, father. Let us pray for the well-being of the Roman state," suggested Lucius.

"Ah, you remind me of your late grandfather!" said the elder Pinarius with a dry laugh. "The old man was a master at finding the middle path. You're right, of course. We shall go to the Senate House and make an offering there."

They crossed the Forum, walking past the massive buildings Augustus had erected to house the imperial bureaucracy. They passed the ancient speaker's platform called the Rostra, decorated by captured-ships' beaks, where the great orators of the Republic had harangued the voters of Roma. The Rostra was little used these days.

The Senate House was relatively new, having been begun by Julius Caesar just before his assassination and completed by Augustus. The exterior was quite austere compared to the elaborately colored and decorated temples nearby. "I was present when the emperor dedicated this building," recalled the elder Pinarius, "still a boy, not yet wearing my manly toga. I practically grew up here, watching debates with your grandfather, taking notes and carrying messages for him long before I became a senator myself."

They ascended the steps and entered. In contrast to the exterior, the chamber was exquisitely finished. Gilded railings and plush red draperies divided the various spaces within the vast room. Polished marble adorned the walls and floors. Windows set high in the walls filled the lofty space with light. The Senate was not meeting on this day, but there were plenty of members about, idly conversing or tending to business with their secretaries. Under the autocratic rule of Augustus, the Senate still performed numerous bureaucratic functions. The continuing survival of the ancient institution helped to maintain the official fiction that Roma was still a republic, and the emperor was merely the first among equals, not the master of his fellow citizens but the devoted servant of all.

Lucius and his father approached the Altar of Victory. The altar itself was made of green marble adorned with elaborate carvings of laurel leaves. Looming beyond and above the altar was a towering statue of the goddess Victory, surrounded by a sampling of the spoils of war taken by Augustus. These displays were changed from time to time. On this day the spoils on exhibit included the iron prow of an Egyptian warship taken at Actium, fashioned in the shape of a crocodile's head. There was also a selection of Queen Cleopatra's royal jewelry, including a carnelian neck-lace, and one of the queen's tall atef crowns made of ivory with inlays of gold and lapis.

The elder Pinarius began the ritual performed by every senator upon entering the chamber. He burned a bit of incense on the altar, poured a libation of wine, and recited a prayer. "Goddess, grant victory to Roma and defeat to her enemies. Watch over the empire which you delivered to Augustus. Protect Roma from all those who would cause her harm, whether from without or from within."

They stepped back from the altar. Lucius's father shook his head as he repeated in a whisper the final words of the prayer. " 'Enemies from with-out . . . or from within.' That last part was meant to apply to people like Marcus Antonius—and your grandfather. What a mess the old man made of his inheritance! He, too, was a great-nephew of the Divine Julius, no less than Augustus. He, too, was named an heir, though he was given a smaller share. He, too, might have risen to greatness. But how he loved that scoundrel Antonius! To please Antonius, he made an enemy of his own cousin. Augustus never quite trusted your grandfather's late conversion to the winning side. The emperor spared him but excluded him from play-ing any role in the new regime. The Pinarii were set to one side, neither persecuted nor rewarded—the forgotten heirs of Julius Caesar." The wist-ful tone of his voice suddenly turned bitter. "And through all our financial difficulties, Augustus has never so much as tossed a sesterce our way!"

He left unspoken the hope that he and Lucius had already discussed, privately and in whispers, that perhaps things would soon change. If the emperor *should* die, Tiberius would almost certainly take his place, and Tiberius had no reason to treat the Pinarii like outcasts. Perhaps the family falling-out between Augustus and Lucius's grandfather could fi-nally be forgotten. If Lucius could please the new emperor, there was no reason why he should not move forward in life. Toward that end, following Claudius's advice and with an aim toward pleasing the future emperor, Lucius had begun to study the Babylonian science of astrology. And though Claudius carried little weight with Tiberius, he was nonetheless a member of the imperial family, and perhaps his growing friendship with Lucius might yet bring some benefit to the Pinarii.

Even as Lucius's thoughts turned to Claudius, his friend appeared at the entrance to the Senate House. Claudius looked this way and that, appearing flustered and confused, then spotted Lucius and hurried to him.

"I thought I s-s-saw you earlier in the Forum. I've been looking everywhere for you."

Lucius raised his eyebrows. "Is there news?"

Claudius shook his head. "Nothing to report. But I do have something else to tell you. Something quite interesting. Perhaps it will at least take your mind off the m-m-matter that is preoccupying us all." He looked around the chamber, at the clusters of senators in hushed conversation and the secretaries scurrying to and fro, and cringed. "I can't stand the atmosphere in this place, all the stuffy formality and self-importance! Come, let's find a more comfortable spot to talk. I know where we can go."

He led them across the Forum, through the valley between the Capitoline and the Palatine, all the way to the waterfront. Their destination was a tavern on the docks. As they stepped inside and their eyes adjusted to the darkness, Lucius wrinkled his nose at the smell, a combination of spilled wine, unwashed humanity, and the effluvia of the Cloaca Maxima, which emptied into the Tiber nearby. The handful of patrons were the types who habituated taverns in the middle of the day—actors, sailors, prostitutes, and gamblers.

Claudius heaved a sigh of relief. "Thank the gods for a place where I can feel at ease! No one staring at me, no one c-c-carping at me, expressing their disapproval and disappointment. Here I can be myself."

"Are you sure it's proper for someone from the imperial household to be seen in such an establishment?" Lucius's father looked askance at the clientele. He hung back for a moment, then sat on a bench beside his son, across from Claudius.

"Why not? Quite a few of Great-Uncle's freedmen patronize this tavern. Why, it was Euphranor who first showed me this place. There's no one more trusted by the emperor. I've seen the m-m-man on this very bench, so drunk on cheap wine he couldn't stand up."

"You said you had something to tell us," said Lucius's father. He looked up at the buxom serving girl who had brought cups and a pitcher of wine. "Just a splash of wine, no more; fill the rest of the cup with water." Lucius gave the same order as his father, but Claudius drank his wine neat. He drained a whole cup, then ordered another before he spoke.

"It's about that amulet, that family heirloom of yours. I see you're wearing it today, Lucius."

Lucius touched the lump of gold at his breast.

"I have been c-c-consulting with my old tutor, Titus Livius," said Claudius, his speech slightly slurred. "Of course you've read his history of the city, from its earliest beginnings. No? Neither of you? Not even the parts about your own family? Most people at least have a slave search through the scrolls to find the mentions of their ancestors." Claudius shook his head. "Well, my conversations with Livius have confirmed my initial belief that this talisman can be identified as a fascinum. In other words, long ago, before the details were worn away, it would have depicted a magical phallus, probably a winged phallus, considering the shape. If you squint and use a bit of imagination, you can visualize the amulet as it originally appeared." Without asking, he reached out and took hold of the talisman, pulling the necklace toward him and Lucius along with it. "Yes, look—here is the shaft, and here the t-testes, and here the two little wings!"

Claudius released the amulet. Lucius took it between his fingers and gazed down at it, feeling profoundly disappointed. A fascinum? Such trinkets were exceedingly common, worn for protection by women in childbirth and put around the necks of infants to protect them from the harmful gaze of the envious, the so-called evil eye. Even slaves wore them.

"So that's all it is?" Lucius said. "Nothing but a common fascinum?"

Claudius wagged his finger. "Ah, hardly c-c-common! No, this fascinum is special, very special. Indeed, if my conjectures are correct, it could be the oldest such amulet in existence. These days, a fascinum is thought of as a mere trinket, a good-luck charm. One sees them made of cheap metal, hanging from the necks of slaves. Hardly anyone remembers the god Fascinus, from whom such amulets take their name, but the winged phallus appears in some of the most ancient stories told by our ancestors. Such a manifestation appeared in the hearthfire to the mother of King Servius Tullius, and even earlier, another such manifestation appeared to one of the kings of Alba, Tarketios, and demanded to have intercourse with his daughter. No god who takes such a form was ever described by the Greeks, or indeed by any of the peoples that Roma has conquered. We may conclude that the god Fascinus appeared exclusively to our ancestors, and must have played some role in the origins of Roma.

"Furthermore, not every fascinum is a mere trinket. One of the holiest objects of the state religion is the sacred fascinum in the keeping of the Vestal virgins. I've seen the thing myself. It's larger than life and very heavy, made of solid g-g-gold. For centuries, the Virgo Maxima has placed it in a hidden spot under the ceremonial chariot driven by generals during their triumphal processions, to ward off the evil eye. You could count on one hand the people who know the origin of this c-c-custom—Titus Livius, the Virgo Maxima, myself . . . and probably no one else, since you Pinarii seem to have neglected to pass the story down through the generations."

"Are you saying a Pinarius was involved in the origin of this custom?" said Lucius's father. He had been distracted earlier by the gambling with dice and certain lewd behavior that was going on in the shadows elsewhere in the tavern, but now Claudius had his full attention.

"I am saying exactly that. The c-c-custom of placing a fascinum beneath the triumphal chariot originated with a Vestal who had a special devotion to Fascinus, and her name was . . . Pinaria! Oh yes, without a doubt, she came from the Pinarius family. This Pinaria served under the Virgo Maxima Foslia in the days when the Gauls captured the city, some four hundred years ago. Back in those days, amulets like your fascinum were not at all common; indeed, I can find only one reference to a fascinum that dates as far back as the time of Pinaria. Now listen closely, because this is where the story gets tricky—especially when you've had as much wine to drink as I have!

"Thanks to the exhaustive history of Roma written by Fabius Pictor, who paid special attention to the contributions of his own family, the Fabii—I don't suppose you've read that, either?—I have discovered a reference to a g-g-gold fascinum worn by a certain Kaeso Fabius Dorso. This Kaeso was the adopted son of the famous warrior Gaius Fabius Dorso, who was trapped atop the Capitoline Hill when the Gauls occupied the city, along with . . . the Vestal Pinaria! They were trapped on the Capitoline for about nine months. Almost immediately after their liberation,

Gaius Fabius Dorso adopted an infant he named Kaeso, whose parentage is unknown. Given these circumstances, it is not hard to imagine that this Kaeso was the love child of the Vestal Pinaria and Gaius Fabius Dorso, and that the gold fascinum he was known to wear was a gift from his mother, the same woman who originated the custom of placing a fascinum under the triumphal chariot." Claudius leaned back against the wall, looking pleased with himself, and waved to the serving girl to bring more wine.

The elder Pinarius frowned. "In the first place, the notion of a Vestal secretly, and criminally, bearing a child is distasteful to any respectable person—"

"But hardly unknown," said Claudius. "I assure you, the history of the Vestals is full of such indiscretions, some made public and punished, but many others covered up. Thus the old joke: show me a Vestal who's a virgin, and I'll show you an ugly Vestal."

Lucius's father did not laugh. "Even so, if one accepts that this Kaeso Fabius Dorso was the love child of the Vestal Pinaria, and that she gave him a gold fascinum, what does that have to do with the amulet handed down by my father and worn by Lucius?"

Claudius gazed at him in drunken disbelief. "You Pinarii! What sort of p-p-patricians are you, not to know every root, branch, and twig of your family tree? You are Kaeso Fabius Dorso's direct descendants! Are you not aware of the Fabia who was your many-times great-grandmother from the era of Scipio Africanus? Oh yes, I am certain of the lineage: I have the genealogical proof in my library. And so we may conjecture that the fascinum you wear, Lucius—an ancient object which has been handed down through many g-g-generations—is the very fascinum that was worn by your ancestor Kaeso Fabius Dorso, which I conjecture came from the Vestal Pinaria. From whom did Pinaria inherit it? Who knows? It may go back much, much further in time. That little lump of g-gold is almost certainly the oldest specimen of a fascinum that I have ever encountered. We might even conjecture that it is *the* fascinum, the original prototype that predates even the fascinum of the Vestal virgins. Perhaps it was created by the god Fascinus himself, or by his first worshippers, the Pinarii, who also founded and tended the Great Altar of Hercules long before the city of Roma was founded."

Claudius opened his eyes wide, overwhelmed by his own erudition. Talking made him thirsty. He swallowed the wine in his cup and ordered more. "The Pinarius family is very ancient, even more ancient than my own. My ancestor, the Sabine warlord Appius Claudius, arrived relatively late in Roma, in the first years of the Republic. But you Pinarii were here before the Republic, before the kings, even before there was a city, in the days when d-d-demigods like Hercules roamed the earth. And that 'little trinket' that hangs from your neck, dear Lucius, is a direct link back to those days."

Lucius looked down at the fascinum, duly impressed but still a bit dubious. "But, Claudius, we're not even sure that this *is* a fascinum."

"Lucius, Lucius! I have an instinct for such things, and my instinct is n-never wrong."

"Is that what history amounts to?" asked Lucius. "Looking through old lists and scraps of parchment, making genealogies, connecting odd facts, and then leaping to conclusions based on guesses or instinct or wishful thinking?"

"Exactly! You put your finger on the very essence of history!" said Claudius with a drunken laugh. Lucius had never seen him so inebriated, or so relaxed. It occurred to him that Claudius had stuttered very little since they had arrived at the tavern.

"To be sure, Lucius, history, unlike divination, is an inexact science. That is because history deals with the past, which is gone forever and which neither gods nor men can alter or revisit. But divination deals with the present and the future, and the will of the gods, which has yet to be revealed. Divining *is* an exact science, provided the diviner has sufficient knowledge and skill."

Claudius glanced at the entrance and gave a start. He sat upright and his eyes grew wide. "Like a messenger in a p-p-play, arriving at the appropriate moment!"

The newcomer was Euphranor. Entering the dark room from the bright outdoors, he did not see them until Claudius called and waved to him.

"Looking for m-m-me, Euphranor?"

"Actually, no. I just arrived in the city and I need a drink."

"Then j-j-join us." Claudius made room on the bench and patted the spot beside him.

Euphranor sat with a wince. "Saddle-sore," he explained. "I'd prefer to stand, but I'm too exhausted." His cloak and tunic were covered with dust.

"What n-news, Euphranor?"

"For the love of Venus, man, let me have a drink first!" Euphranor called for the serving girl and downed two cups in rapid succession. He stared blearily at Lucius and his father and seemed reluctant to speak.

"Go on, Euphranor," said Claudius. "You can speak freely. Surely you remember Lucius Pinarius. The other fellow is his father."

Euphranor closed his eyes for a long moment, then spoke in a voice just above a whisper. "I'm the first to arrive with the news, so not a man in Roma knows this yet. The emperor is dead."

"Numa's balls!" whispered Claudius. "Now we *all* need another drink!" He waved to the serving girl. "When, Euphranor?"

"Five days ago."

Claudius and Lucius exchanged glances. Augustus had died exactly one hundred days after the lightning strike.

"Where?"

"In the town of Nola."

"That's just east of Mount Vesuvius. Why has it taken so long for the n-n-news to reach Roma?"

"The delay was by order of Tiberius."

"But why?"

Euphranor grunted. "I can only tell you the sequence of events. Augustus died. Tiberius gave strict orders that no one was to make the news public until he allowed it. Some days later, a messenger arrived with news that young Agrippa is dead—"

"The emperor's grandson?" said Lucius's father.

"Killed by the soldiers guarding him on the island where he was in exile. After that message arrived, Tiberius told me to ride to Roma as fast as I could and deliver the news to the imperial staff."

"I see," whispered Claudius. "Uncle Tiberius held off making Augustus's death public until Agrippa was disposed of, that's what you m-m-mean. Poor Agrippa!"

"I've only told you the sequence of events. I won't speculate on the whys or wherefores," said Euphranor, with the blank expression so often assumed by imperial servants. "When he received the message about Agrippa's death, Tiberius immediately and publicly disavowed any responsibility."

Claudius nodded. "It's possible that Augustus left instructions that Agrippa be killed upon his death. Or that Livia forged such instructions. Technically, Uncle Tiberius may be innocent of Agrippa's m-m-murder."

"But, Claudius, what will become of *you?*" said Lucius.

"Me? Harmless, stuttering, half-witted Claudius? I shall be left to my b-books and my lituus, I imagine."

The serving girl came to pour more wine. Lucius's father waved aside her offer of water and took his cup full-strength. Lucius did likewise.

"How did the emperor die?" said Claudius.

Euphranor suddenly seemed to fade, done in by exhaustion and wine. His shoulders slumped and his face went slack. "We'd left Capri and were on our way back to Roma. The emperor had been unwell—weakness, a pain in his stomach, loose bowels—but he seemed to have gotten better. But on the road he took a turn for the worse. We made a detour to the family house at Nola. The emperor took to bed in the very room where his father died. He was lucid almost until the end. He seemed resigned to his death. He even seemed a bit . . . amused. He assembled his family and traveling companions, including Livia and Tiberius and myself, and he quoted a line from some play, like an actor seeking approval. 'If I have played my role in this farce with convincing ease, then applaud me, please. Applaud! Applaud!' And we did. That seemed to please him. But at the very end he became restless and frightened. He saw things no one else could see. He cried out a word in Etruscan, '*Huznatre!*' And then, 'They're carrying me off! Forty young men are carrying me off!' And then it was over."

Claudius and Lucius exchanged knowing looks.

"A dying man's delusion," said Lucius's father.

"Not a delusion but a prophecy," said Euphranor. "Tiberius has arranged for forty Praetorians to form an honor guard that will carry the emperor's body back into the city."

A.D. 16

It was a bright morning in the month of Maius. On this day, so long awaited, Lucius Pinarius and Acilia would become husband and wife.

Their marriage had finally been made possible thanks to the generosity of the late Augustus. In his will, besides naming Livia and Tiberius as his chief heirs, Augustus had made numerous smaller but still very generous bequests. Among these was a large sum left to Lucius Pinarius. The gossips of Roma, who pored over the details of the will like Etruscan soothsayers scrutinizing entrails, assumed that this bequest was the emperor's way of making amends after a lifetime of ignoring his cousins the Pinarii, and perhaps it was; but Lucius assumed that the inheritance was also a kind of fee paid posthumously to him for his role in divining the lightning omen. For whatever reason, Augustus had made Lucius a wealthy man.

Yet, even with Lucius's new wealth, Acilia's father had insisted on a lengthy engagement. This gave Lucius time to pay off the family's debts, to invest the money left over in the Egyptian grain trade, renewing his grandfather's old business associations, and to buy and furnish a house for himself and his bride-to-be. He could not afford property on the Palatine, but he was able to buy a house on the more fashionable side of the Aventine, with views from the upper story of the Tiber and the Capitoline and just a glimpse of the Circus Maximus. This pleased his mother greatly.

At sundown, the wedding party departed from the house of Acilius. The procession was led by the youngest boy in the household, Acilia's little brother, who carried a pine torch lit from the family's hearthfire. Its flame would be added to the hearthfire of the bridegroom when they arrived at the house of Lucius Pinarius.

Following the torchbearer was a Vestal virgin. She wore linen vestments with a narrow headband of twined red and white wool called a vitta across her forehead, a headdress called a suffibulum that concealed her closely shorn hair, and a mantle that covered her head and shoulders. The Vestal carried a cake made from consecrated grain and sprinkled with holy salt; a few bites would be taken by the couple during the ceremony, after which the cake would be shared with their guests.

Next came the bride. Acilia's golden hair was pulled back from her face, elaborately coiled and secured with pins of ivory. She wore a yellow veil and yellow shoes. Her long white robe was cinched at the waist with a purple sash tied at the back in a special configuration called the Hercules knot; later, it would be Lucius's privilege to untie the knot. Acilia carried a distaff for spinning and a spindle with wool. Flanking her were two of the bride's cousins, little boys hardly older than the torchbearer.

Following the bride were her mother and father and the rest of the bridal party, who sang the ancient wedding song. It was called "Tallasius" and recalled the taking of the Sabine women by Romulus and his men. According to legend, the most beautiful of the Sabines was captured by the henchmen of a certain Tallasius. As she was carried off, the Sabine begged to know where the men were taking her. The women in the wedding party sang the questions, and the men sang the responses.

> *Where do you take me?*
> *To Tallasius the dutiful!*
> *Why do you take me?*
> *Because he thinks you're beautiful!*
> *What will my fate be?*
> *To marry him, to be his mate!*
> *What god will save me?*
> *All the gods have blessed this date!*

The wedding party arrived at the home of Lucius Pinarius. In the street, under the open sky, a sheep was skinned and sacrificed on an altar. Its pelt was thrown over two chairs, upon which the bride and groom sat. Claudius, as augur, asked the gods to bless the union and took the auspices; the flight of two sparrows from right to left across the darkling sky he declared to be a very favorable omen.

Carrying her distaff and spindle, Acilia rose from her chair and stood before the door to the house, which was decorated with garlands of flowers. Her mother embraced her. Everyone knew what was to come next, and there was a thrill of nervous excitement in the crowd. When Lucius, still seated, seemed to hesitate, his father shouted, "Go on, son, do it!"

"Yes, Lucius, d-d-do it!" shouted Claudius.

Smiling and laughing and clapping their hands, others took up the chant: "Do it! Do it! Do it!"

Blushing and laughing, Lucius sprang from his chair and pulled Acilia from her mother's arms. She shrieked as Lucius swept her off her feet, kicked open the door, and carried her like a captive Sabine over the threshold. The wedding party cheered and applauded and crowded around the open door to witness the final act of the ceremony.

Inside the house, Lucius set Acilia down on a sheepskin rug. She put aside her distaff and spindle. He handed her the keys to the house. "Who is this newcomer in my house?" he said, his heart pounding.

"When and where you are Lucius, then and there I shall be Lucia," she replied. The ceremony gave Acilia something no unmarried woman possessed, a first name; it was a feminine form of her husband's first name, and would be used only in private between the two of them.

Amid the feasting that followed, Lucius sought out Claudius. They strolled to a quiet spot away from the others, under the portico that surrounded the garden. The moon was full. The air was fragrant with night-blooming jasmine.

"You have a l-l-lovely house, Lucius."

"Thank you, Claudius. And thank you for taking the auspices today."

"It was my pleasure to serve as augur, Lucius. But with this house and your lovely bride, you hardly needed m-me to confirm that Fortune is smiling on you."

"Fortune, or Fate?"

Claudius laughed. "I see you've followed my advice and taken up the study of astrology. As Bolus writes in *Sympathies and Antipathies,* every student of astrology must sooner or later confront the paradox of Fate versus Fortune. If Fate is an inexorable path laid before us by the stars, from which no divergence is possible, then what good is a prayer to Fortune or any other deity? Yet men call upon Fortune all the time and in every circumstance. It is our nature to propitiate the g-g-gods and ask their blessing, so there must be some utility in doing so, despite the inescapable nature of Fate. It is my opinion that our personal destiny is like a broad pathway. We cannot go backward or leave the path or change the destination, but within the pathway we can execute small twists and turns. In those circumstances we are able to exercise choice, and the favor of the gods can make a difference."

Lucius stared into the middle distance and nodded.

Claudius sighed. "I see by your face, Lucius, that not one word I've said makes sense to you."

Lucius laughed. "To be candid, Claudius, my study of astrology has not gone especially well. It's not like augury. I didn't particularly like spending all that time with the magister, but I did enjoy the instruction he gave us, because the science of augury makes perfect sense to me. Augury was perfected by our ancestors, it served them well, and it's our duty to continue the practice, so as to maintain the gods' favor for ourselves and our descendants. But astrology . . ." Lucius shook his head. "Naming the planets, categorizing their effects on human behavior, and the rest—it all seems rather arbitrary to me, as if some long-dead Babylonian simply made it up. And as you say, if Fate exists, what point is there in knowing what the future will bring? Unlike you, Claudius, I'm not sure that augury and astrology can be reconciled. I think a man must believe in one or the other."

"In that respect, at least, you are in agreement with Uncle Tiberius."

"It was thoughtful of you, Claudius, to obtain the emperor's birth information for me, as well as those two horoscopes. The older one, cast by Scribonius at Tiberius's birth, I was able to decipher fairly well. But the more recent horoscope, by Thrasyllus—well, it made no sense to me at all. I simply couldn't follow his calculations. And his description of Tiberius's character—a humble man, reluctant but compelled by Fate to assume great responsibility—may be accurate, but I couldn't see how it followed from the casting."

"It could be that Thrasyllus, sifting among the d-d-data, delivered a reading in accordance with the image Uncle Tiberius wishes to project."

"You mean he told the emperor what the emperor wanted to hear."

"The fact that an astrologer may be devious does not negate the science itself, Lucius. Uncle Tiberius is probably as great a puzzle to Thrasyllus as he is to the rest of us. We have an emperor who refuses to wear the laurel crown, or to take any of Great-Uncle's titles—no Augustus, no Father of His Country, no Imperator after his name. But neither d-d-does he seem likely to restore the Republic—he says the whole lot of senators are 'fit to be slaves.' Is Uncle Tiberius truly a humble man, thrust into prominence by circumstance, not to mention the ambitions of my grandmother? Or is he merely striking a pose, as Great-Uncle did when he styled himself the humble public servant who wanted nothing more than to serve the state?"

"Studying the stars may give an answer to Thrasyllus, but not to me," said Lucius. "I simply have no aptitude for astrology."

"Ah, well, I had thought to set you on the p-p-path, but it was not to be. Smile, Lucius! I just made a joke about Fate."

"And you had no choice but to make it."

Claudius nodded and looked across the garden, where Acilia was speaking to her mother. "If free will exists, then you certainly made a fine choice for a bride. Acilia is very b-b-beautiful."

"She is. And I love her. It's a curious thing: my father chose to court the Acilii because they had money, but now that's irrelevant, thanks to the fortune I inherited from your uncle. I am free to marry for love."

"Lucky man! Nowadays, most people marry for the tax advantages. Great-Uncle was determined that everyone should pair up, settle down, and breed, so he punished the unmarried and childless with taxes. He made life easier for the married man, and easier still for the man with children. You can get started on that tonight!"

Lucius joined him in gazing at Acilia. In her white robe and yellow veil, lit by moonlight and lamplight, she seemed to glow softly.

"At this time next year, I could have a son," he said, awed by the enormity of it. "Do you remember, Claudius, when Augustus showed us those baby shoes?"

"Baby shoes?"

"When we spoke to him in that upstairs study, he showed us a pair of your nephew's shoes."

"Ah, yes, the baby shoes my brother sent as a keepsake. Little Gaius has grown since then. He's big for a four-year-old, and quite the warrior. Germanicus tells me the boy has his own pair of miniature army boots, the caliga worn by soldiers. How the troops love to see the boy on parade. Caligula, they call him, 'Little Boots.' "

"Your older brother has done well. He's lived up to his name."

"He has, indeed. His first task was quelling the unrest in the ranks when Uncle Tiberius reneged on the bonuses promised by Augustus; only Germanicus's popularity with the troops prevented a wholesale uprising. We learned a lesson there, about where the real p-p-power behind the emperor lies—not with the Senate, but with the legions. Germanicus not only rallied the troops on the Rhine, he led an invasion deep into German territory and avenged the disaster of the Teutoberg Forest. Two of the lost eagle standards were retrieved, and he's vowed to take back the other as well, even if he has to pry it from the dead hand of Arminius."

"Everyone in Roma is talking about his success."

"The people now love him as much as his troops do. Almost certainly Tiberius will have to award Germanicus a triumph when he returns to Roma. Imagine the pomp and glory, all the German slaves and captured b-b-booty on display, the acclamation of the legions, and little Caligula riding beside his father in the chariot, wearing his tiny army boots!"

Lucius touched the fascinum at his breast. "And beneath the chariot will be the sacred fascinum of the Vestals, to ward off the gaze of the envious."

"The envious in this case being Tiberius," said Claudius under his breath.

Lucius lowered his voice. "Does he see Germanicus as a rival?"

"Who c-c-can say?"

"If Tiberius feels threatened by your brother, what does that mean for you, Claudius?"

"Perhaps I should c-consult my horoscope."

Lucius suddenly felt uneasy. For many years, under Augustus, power in Roma had been a settled affair; whether a man liked it or not, everyone knew his place. But in the aftermath of Augustus's death, the future of the city and the individual destinies of its people seemed uncertain.

But for himself, at least in the short term, Lucius could foresee only happiness. The opportunity to serve Augustus had made him a wealthy man and delivered to him the bride he had longed for. His friendship with Claudius had brought him into the outer circles of the imperial family, close enough to enjoy certain privileges but not so close as to provoke the fear and jealousy of powerful men. To be sure, his study of astrology had led him to a dead end, but his love of augury was greater than ever. What did it matter that the new emperor placed his trust entirely in astrology?

The current fascination with Babylonian stargazing might be only a passing fashion, while augurs would always be needed and respected in Roma.

At last, after much celebration, the last of the guests departed. The slaves disappeared into their rooms for the night. While Acilia withdrew to the bedchamber to make ready, Lucius walked alone from room to room, taking inventory of his surroundings. Claudius had said the house was lovely, and it was. Lamplight softly illuminated the walls, freshly painted with images of peacocks and gardens, and fell softly on all the beautiful objects Lucius had purchased to make the house worthy of Acilia: the lamps and tables, the chairs and rugs, the dining couches and draperies. What a great deal of furniture was required to fill a house, and how expensive it all was! How could anyone who had not received an inheritance afford it? Lucius knew he was a very lucky man.

He entered the bedroom where Acilia awaited him. With trembling fingers, he untied the Hercules knot that secured the purple sash around her waist and removed her bridal robe. Beneath, she wore a brief gown made of shimmering fabric so sheer that he could see right through it. She unpinned her hair, and the honey-colored tresses fell almost to her waist. He stood rooted to the spot, simply gazing at her, wishing he could stop time. What moment could be more perfect than this, balanced between the deep satisfaction the day had brought him and the exquisite pleasures of the night to come?

He stroked the golden hair that framed her face, then he touched the shimmering fabric and felt the warmth and solidity of her flesh.

"My Lucia!" he whispered, uttering the name only he was allowed to speak as he covered her mouth with his.

A.D. 19

To walk across the Forum on a crisp October day, dressed in his trabea and carrying his lituus, gave Lucius a wonderful sense of belonging and self-worth. At the age of twenty-nine he was not just a citizen of the greatest city on earth, he was a husband and the father of twin boys (how Augustus would have approved!) and a highly respected member of the community.

The augury he had just performed had gone very well. A new tavern was about to open on one of the less disreputable streets in the Subura and the owner wanted to determine the best day to begin serving customers. The to-and-fro flight of a seagull, a bird seldom seen so far inland, had clearly indicated the day after tomorrow. The ceremony was hardly a momentous occasion, but part of an augur's duty was to make the auspices available to all citizens, for all sorts of purposes. The tavern owner had paid him the standard fee; Lucius patted the full coin purse tucked inside his trabea. The man had also offered to supply Lucius with food and drink free of charge anytime he wished to drop in. Lucius had feigned gratitude, but it was unlikely that he would ever take up the offer. He had grown used to vintages superior to any the humble tavern had to offer, and except for official purposes he rarely visited the teeming, noisome streets of the bustling Subura. His usual places to dine and drink were located on the lower slopes of the Aventine and the Palatine, in neighborhoods where men of a better class tended to congregate.

He was considering a visit to his local favorite, a charming hideaway just down the street from his house, when he ran into Claudius. He was about to invite Claudius to come along, then saw the look on his friend's face.

"Claudius, what's happened?"

"T-t-terrible news. T-t-terrible!" There were tears in his eyes. He seemed unable to speak for a moment, caught on some stubborn consonant, then he blurted it out: "G-Germanicus is dead! My dear brother. Dead!"

"Oh, Claudius, this *is* terrible news." Lucius wrinkled his nose at the smell of stale wine. His friend was drunk. Lucius took his arm, but Claudius was rooted to the spot, trembling and blinking back tears.

A year before, Lucius's father had died. The elder Pinarius had not suffered much; he developed a terrible headache one day, fell into a coma that night, and two days later was dead, without ever regaining consciousness. The sudden loss had shaken Lucius. Claudius had been a comfort to him in the days of mourning, and Lucius would do his best to return the favor to his distraught friend.

"Did he fall in battle?" asked Lucius. After his grand triumph in Roma, Germanicus had been posted by Tiberius to Asia, where he had enjoyed even greater success, defeating the kingdoms of Cappadocia and

Commagene and turning them into Roman provinces. Lately there had been talk of granting Germanicus a second triumph. Only the greatest commanders in Roma's history had received more than one.

"No, he died in his b-b-bed."

"But Germanicus was so young."

"Barely thirty-five—and in the b-b-best of health until he fell ill. The physicians blame some mysterious wasting disease—but there are rumors of p-p-poison, and m-m-magic spells scrawled on lead tablets."

"But who would have dared to murder Germanicus?"

Claudius took a deep breath and steadied himself. "In the days of Augustus, we wondered who might p-p-poison the emperor. Now we wonder whom the emperor might p-poison! And in both cases, the culprit is the same."

Lucius looked up and down the street. There were few people in sight, and no one close enough to overhear them. Still, Lucius lowered his voice. "You mustn't say such a thing, Claudius."

"At least my nephew is well, as far as we know. P-p-poor little Caligula, an orphan! Surely no one would p-poison a seven-year-old boy."

"Surely not," agreed Lucius, thinking of his own sons, who were barely a year old. He reached up to touch the vacant spot at his breast; on this day he was not wearing the fascinum. He felt an urge to hurry home. "Come with me, Claudius. Acilia will want to hear the news. My mother will cook us dinner. You can spend the night with us."

"No, no, no. I have too much to do. P-p-people to tell. Arrangements to m-make."

"Then I'll come with you," said Lucius, trying to hide his reluctance.

"No, no, Lucius, you belong with your family. Go to them now. I shall be quite alright. No one would ever want to p-poison or put a spell on p-p-poor Claudius." He turned away and hurried down the street.

Lucius looked after him until he disappeared around a corner, then headed home.

Even before he entered the house, he knew something was wrong. The door stood wide open. Where was the slave who minded the entrance? From within he heard the twins, Titus and Kaeso, crying loudly. Then he heard more-disturbing sounds: a man barking orders, the stamp of booted feet, the sound of furniture being overturned, a shriek from Acilia.

Lucius rushed inside. In the vestibule, the wax effigies of his ancestors were askew in their niches, as if someone had been rifling among them; the effigy of his father had fallen to the floor. He ran into the reception hall, from which he could see into the surrounding rooms. Soldiers had invaded his house and were busy ransacking it. From their imperial insignia he knew that they were Praetorians, the elite corps of centurions stationed in a fortified garrison just outside the city. The Praetorians were charged with guarding the emperor's person and with apprehending the emperor's enemies. What were they doing in his house, tearing the furniture apart, shaking out rugs, knocking holes in the walls?

"Stop this at once!" Lucius shouted.

The soldiers looked at him and paused. Two of them ran to him. While one held his shoulders, the other searched his person.

"No weapons!" the soldier shouted. They released him and carried on with what they were doing.

Acilia appeared, carrying Kaeso and Titus, one in each arm. The boys were red-faced and wailing. Their mother was ashen. She ran to Lucius's side.

Following closely behind her was a tall man with a commanding presence. At his approach, the twins fell silent. Lucius recognized him: Sejanus, prefect of the Praetorians and right-hand man to Tiberius. The man's steely gaze made Lucius's blood run cold.

"What is the meaning of this?" said Lucius. "Why are these men looting my house?"

"Looting?" Sejanus smiled grimly. "Later, if an order of confiscation is issued, your possessions will be removed in an orderly fashion. But for now, Lucius Pinarius, my men are not here to rob you. They are here to search for evidence."

"Evidence of what?"

"We shall know that when we find it."

One of the soldiers approached. He held an unrolled scroll in his hands. "Prefect, I found this among the documents in that room over there." He nodded toward Lucius's study.

Sejanus took the scroll, blew dust off it, and studied it. His face grew long. "What have we here? By Hercules, I believe this is a horoscope that was cast for the emperor. What possible excuse can you give me for possessing such a document, Lucius Pinarius?"

Lucius opened his mouth but did not speak. Sejanus held the copy of a horoscope cast by Thrasyllus that Claudius had given him years ago as an example for him to study, when Lucius had tried and failed to master the science of astrology.

"No answer?" snapped Sejanus. "Where did you obtain this?"

Should he tell the man that the emperor's own nephew had given it to him? Surely that would absolve him of whatever suspicion Sejanus harbored. Or would it? Claudius's brother had just died, and Claudius clearly thought that Tiberius was responsible. Doddering, stuttering Claudius had always been considered outside the circle of those who might pose some threat to the emperor, but Claudius now had more motive than ever to hate his uncle. Telling Sejanus that Claudius had given him the horoscope might endanger Claudius. It might also endanger Lucius, making it look as if he were conspiring with his friend.

"I bought it from a vendor in the Subura, years ago, when I made a stab at learning astrology. I had no idea what it was. Look in my study, you'll see a few works about astrology, and some other horoscopes as well, none of any importance. I haven't looked at them in years. You saw yourself that this one was covered with dust."

Sejanus glared at him. "I didn't become prefect of the Praetorians without learning to tell when a man is lying to me. No matter. A new imperial order decrees that all practicing astrologers, except those expressly retained by the emperor himself, are to be exiled from Italy. I would say that this document and the others you admit to possessing are ample evidence that you are among the class of persons to be banished."

"But that's ridiculous! I just told you, I haven't even looked at those documents in years."

"And if I examine these materials closely, will I find astrological calculations and horoscopes executed in your own handwriting?"

Lucius's face became hot. "Perhaps. Years ago, I cast a few horoscopes, simply as exercises. But I am not and have never been an astrologer. I am an augur, as you can see by what I'm wearing." Lucius impotently waved his lituus in the air.

Sejanus stepped closer, looming over him and looking down his nose. He was so close that Lucius could feel the man's breath on his forehead.

"What sort of fool are you, Lucius Pinarius? Can't you see that I'm offering you a way out?"

"I don't understand."

"Most enemies of the emperor have no choice about the charges brought against them, but I am giving you a choice."

"Why?"

"Because I'm a nice fellow," said Sejanus sweetly. "Because I love babies." He glanced at the twins, who stared back at him in wide-eyed silence. "Because one way is more work for me, and the other way is less, you fool! Now, here are your choices.

"First choice: a charge of unauthorized possession of the emperor's horoscope—a treasonable offense. If I bring that charge against you, there will necessarily be a very extensive investigation, and no one can say where that might lead; think of your friends, Pinarius. And the penalty is not only death for you, but confiscation of your estate; think of your wife and sons.

"Second choice: a simple charge of practicing astrology without the emperor's knowledge. In that case, you will be exiled from Italy, your destination to be determined by me, and only those materials that relate to the practice of astrology will be confiscated from you."

Lucius looked at Acilia. She gazed back at him, trembling and terrified. Titus and Kaeso, sensing her distress, began to wail again.

"This is outrageous!" Lucius whispered. "My father was a senator. My grandfather was a nephew and heir to the Divine Julius, a cousin of the Divine Augustus—"

"While Tiberius was merely the stepson of Augustus? Is that what you're saying? Are you questioning the legitimacy of the emperor's claim to power? Are you asserting that you have a better claim?"

"No!"

"Is that why you possess a copy of the emperor's horoscope? To discover on which days he is most vulnerable, so that you can plot his downfall and take his place?"

"Of course not! I told you already . . ." Lucius fought to control his shaking. "I've never been disloyal. I've never spoken against the emperor.

Never! Why did you come here today? What made you think you'd find something incriminating?"

"You were on the list," said Sejanus.

"What list?"

"The list of men to be watched."

"But why? For what reason?"

"For knowing too much, I suspect. That's usually the reason. And sure enough, here in your house we have found the means for gaining knowledge that might be used against the emperor."

"But this is madness. I told you, I'm not an astrologer. I am a respected member of the college of augurs, a public servant of the Roman state. I loyally serve Tiberius, just as I served Augustus—"

Lucius fell silent. Suddenly he understood. He had answered his own question. Why was this happening? Because he was an augur; because he had served Augustus; *because of the lightning omen.* His role in that singular event had seemed to bring Lucius a happy destiny—confirmation of his skills as an augur, closer friendship with Claudius, an inheritance from the emperor that had changed his life. But now his part in that singular event had led to this catastrophe. Had Augustus died on the appointed day because of Fate—or because of human intervention? Livia and Tiberius must have known of the prediction: they knew everything that happened in the imperial house. Lucius had long suspected that one of them, or both, had a hand in Augustus's death. He had never spoken of such a possibility, not even to Claudius. But Tiberius was no fool. The emperor was taking drastic action to eliminate every possible threat to his rule—his rival Germanicus, every astrologer in Italy, the unfortunate men on the mysterious list mentioned by Sejanus—and Lucius was among those who might know too much.

Sejanus was right: Lucius should consider himself lucky if he could escape with his life and his fortune intact.

He stared at the document that Sejanus clutched in his hands. Why had he not burned the incriminating horoscope of Tiberius long ago? Lucius had been a fool to keep it. But would burning it have made any difference? If Sejanus had not discovered the astrological documents, he would have found some other way to incriminate Lucius.

"You finally seem to have run out of words," said Sejanus. "Have you anything more to say? No?" He raised his voice. "Lucius Pinarius, you are guilty of practicing astrology without the authorization of the emperor. You have ten days to settle your affairs in Roma. After that, you will board a ship and leave Italy, under penalty of death. If you wish, you may take your wife and children."

"And my mother?" Lucius looked about. Where was his mother? Probably in her bed; she had been in poor health ever since Lucius's father had died.

"And your mother," said Sejanus sweetly. "Do you have a preference for your destination?"

Lucius felt numb with shock. The twins wailed. "My grandfather had friends in Egypt. I have investments in Alexandria," he said dully.

Sejanus nodded. "Egypt is good. Egypt is a possession of the emperor, rather than a province under senatorial jurisdiction. It will be easier for my agents to keep an eye on you there."

Sejanus rolled the scroll tightly and handed the horoscope back to the Praetorian who had brought it to him. "Burn this immediately. Collect all the other documents and take them with you. Call off the search. We're finished here."

In moments, the soldiers were gone. Except for the crying twins, the house was silent. Gradually, the slaves began to emerge from their hiding places. The women surrounded Acilia, trying to comfort her and the babies. The men approached Lucius, but he waved them away.

Lucius walked into his study. The room had been stripped of every scroll and scrap of parchment, not just the few items pertaining to astrology but all his business documents as well. How was he to settle his affairs without his financial records? Even his small collection of plays and poetry had been taken. He found himself staring at the row of empty pigeonholes that had contained the many scrolls that made up his copy of Titus Livius's history, a gift from Claudius, which he had never read. How was he ever to read it now? Of course, there would be copies of Livius's work in Egypt. Alexandria was famous for its books; Alexandria was the home of the Great Library. . . .

He shook his head in disbelief. The last few moments had destroyed his life, yet already he had begun to accept his Fate.

He walked through the house like a man in a dream. He found himself in his bedroom—the place where he had first coupled with Acilia, where Kaeso and Titus had been conceived, where Acilia had given birth. Even this room had been ransacked. The trunks and cabinets had been thrown open, the clothing scattered across the floor. The bed had been overturned. The cushions—into which he had sighed with pleasure when coupling with Acilia, wept with joy at the birth of his sons, breathed the essence of his dreams while he slept—had been cut open, as if Sejanus thought they might contain some terrible secret.

On the floor lay a silver box with its lid pried open. Among the scattered pieces of jewelry was the gold fascinum.

Lucius knelt and picked it up. He clutched it tightly. He whispered a prayer to the ancient god who had watched over his family from its very beginnings.

"Fascinus, god of my ancestors, watch over me. Watch over my sons. Bring us back someday to Roma."

Ten frantic, tormented, sleepless days later, Lucius was ready to leave the city.

True to his word, Sejanus had not confiscated his property, but had insisted that Lucius sell his beloved house. Lucius had done so at a considerable loss. His financial records, after being thoroughly scrutinized, had been returned to him, as had his copy of Titus Livius's history, along with several other valuable scrolls. The documents had all been tightly rolled and carefully packed away in round leather book-boxes of the sort called capsae.

Lucius stood with his family and the slaves they were taking with them on a dock at the riverfront, waiting to board the boat that would take them down the Tiber to Ostia, where he had secured passage on a trading vessel bound for Alexandria. The smell of the waterfront reminded him of the tavern where Euphranor had arrived with news of Augustus's death. Where was that tavern? Not far, he thought. Turning around and looking beyond a stack of crates filled with his family's belongings, he saw the entrance to the tavern from where he stood. How long ago that day seemed! Even as he looked at the tavern, the door opened. A figure emerged and began walking toward the dock, weaving this way and that and nearly colliding with the stack of crates. It was Claudius.

Claudius averted his eyes as he approached. Lucius stepped forward to meet him and opened his arms. The two men embraced.

"Lucius, I'm so sorry. If only I had never g-g-given you those horoscopes!"

"No, Claudius, this is not your fault."

"But it was I who insisted that you c-come with me that night, when lightning struck Great-Uncle's statue—"

"No, Claudius, you're not to blame. Nor is Sejanus; nor is Tiberius. If Fate exists and cannot be altered, then this moment had to arrive, and the next step in my life's journey is already predetermined, as is the next, and the next, and the next, until the moment I die."

"And if there is no Fate? If chance and free will rule the cosmos?"

"Then it was I who failed to win the favor of the goddess Fortune. It was I who made the wrong choices."

"What a philosopher you've b-b-become!"

"Sometimes the consolations of philosophy are all that a man has," said Lucius bitterly. He shut his eyes, took a deep breath, and shook his head. "No, that's wrong. I have Acilia. I have the twins. I have my mother." He looked at Camilla, who was holding one of the boys—Kaeso, he thought, though it was hard to be sure—cooing and clucking her tongue. She looked very old. She had been in low spirits and poor health since his father had died; the disaster had dealt her a tremendous blow. A sea voyage in October was no place for a woman of her years, but she had insisted on coming, to stay close to her grandchildren.

Acilia was holding the other twin. How miserable she looked! Through all the agony of the last ten days, she had not said a word against him. Her father and brother had not been so kind. The two of them had arrived at the house the morning after Sejanus's visit, first anxious and alarmed at the rumors they had heard, then furious and full of recriminations against Lucius. Acilius said hurtful words of the sort that could never be taken back, about the worthlessness of Lucius's patrician blood and the shame he had brought upon the Acilii. He had argued that his daughter and grandsons should remain in Roma with him, and Lucius had wavered, trying to imagine his exile in Alexandria without them. It was Acilia who had silenced her father, saying that she had no intention of abandoning her husband or of taking her sons from their father. Acilius had left in a rage and they had not seen him since. He had not even come to see them off.

No one had come. No one wanted to be seen saying farewell to an exiled enemy of the imperial house—no one except Claudius.

The twin held by his mother began to cry. Yes, it was Kaeso, as Lucius had thought; he could recognize the boys more readily by their cries than by their faces, which were truly identical.

Slaves began to load the crates into the cargo hold of the boat. Lucius and Claudius were in the way. They stepped to the edge of the dock and stood side by side, staring at their distorted reflections in the water.

"It may be that your exile is a g-good thing. Who can say?"

"A good thing? To leave the only city I know, the only home I've ever had? The idea of raising my sons anywhere else is unspeakably bitter to me, almost unbearable."

"No, Lucius, hear me out. Tiberius is increasingly detached. He gives more and more authority to Sejanus. The situation in Roma can only grow worse. For the first time in my life, I've begun to fear for my own survival. The atmosphere around Tiberius is so clouded with suspicion, even a fellow as harmless as myself m-m-might become a target."

"What will you do, Claudius?"

"I intend to disengage from public life as much as p-p-possible. Grow root vegetables at my country house. P-p-pursue my antiquarian studies. Get drunk with my low-life friends. As soon as you leave, I intend to head back to the tavern and get even drunker than I already am."

The stack of crates had vanished. Packed inside one of them was Lucius's trabea and his lituus.

The boat was ready to cast off.

His mother stumbled on the gangplank. When Lucius caught her, he was shocked at how little she weighed. He wondered how she could survive the journey.

Claudius stood alone on the dock and waved as they departed, then turned around and went back to the tavern.

Lucius gazed at the buildings passing by. He knew every street and rooftop of this part of the city, between the Tiber and the Aventine, though he was more used to looking down from the top of the hill; the view was strange, looking up from the river.

Scanning the skyline, he happened to spot his house, high on the crest of the Aventine. But it was not his house any longer; the new owners were standing on one of the balconies, waving to their neighbors across the way. Lucius gazed at the sight and knew how the lemures of the dead must feel, watching the living from the shadows.

Titus and Kaeso both began to cry. Would they cry all the way to Alexandria?

The boat sailed on. On the shore, temples and houses gave way to warehouses and rubbish heaps, and then to open fields. The city disappeared from view.

As clearly as if a god had whispered the knowledge in his ear, Lucius knew he would never see Roma again.

PART II
TITUS AND KAESO
The Twins

A.D. 40

"Impressive? I suppose. But so is Alexandria," said Kaeso Pinarius, sur-veying the heart of Roma from the summit of the Capitoline Hill.

The Temple of Apollo atop the Palatine dominated the skyline; adja-cent to the temple, the imperial complex had been much built up since the time of Augustus and presented a jumble of tile rooftops, aerial gar-dens, and colonnaded terraces. Directly below was the Forum with its procession of grand edifices along the Sacred Way, from the Senate House to the round Temple of Vesta and beyond. To the north and east lay the other hills of Roma, and nestled among them the concentration of towering tenements, some as tall as seven stories, in the crowded Subura.

"Impressive? It's incredible! Alexandria simply can't compare. Nor can any other place I've seen." Kaeso's twin brother, Titus, could hardly con-tain his enthusiasm. At the age of twenty-two, Titus could not claim to have traveled the world, but their late father had once taken them on a trip to Antioch, and he and Kaeso had stopped in several cities, including Ath-ens, on their journey to Roma. "In Alexandria, all the streets are laid out in a grid. Every corner is like every other. It's so regular and boring. But Roma is all hills and valleys and streets as jumbled as a pile of serpents, and huge buildings everywhere you look."

Kaeso nodded. "Yes, it's a mess."

"It's magnificent!"

" 'Magnificent' would describe the Temple of Serapis in Alexandria, or the Great Library, or the Pharos lighthouse, or perhaps the Museum—"

"But none of those can rival the Temple of Jupiter," said Titus. He looked over his shoulder and up at the grand structure with its immense columns and pediment roof surmounted by a gilded statue of the greatest of the gods in his quadriga, glimmering under the slanting light of a bright November sun. Titus turned in a slow circle, taking in the view in every direction, enchanted by the sinuous course of the shimmering Tiber, awed by the sheer immensity of the city. "Surely, brother, this is the most magnificent sight on earth."

"Father certainly thought so. How he loved to reminisce about his beloved Roma!" Kacso sighed. "If only he were still alive, to be here with us today."

Titus nodded. "He was supposed to be here. He *would* be here, and so would mother, if the fever hadn't taken them last year. Fate was cruel to our parents, Kaeso. More than anything, they wanted to return to this city. At last the opportunity came—and then Fortune snatched it away. But Fate has been kinder to us, eh, brother? We are finally home."

"Home?" Kaeso shook his head. "We were babies when father and mother fled from the city. We have no close kin here, except the Acilii, who severed all ties with our mother. Father's parents died before we were born—"

"Not Grandmother Camilla. She died on the journey to Alexandria. Don't you remember?"

"I remember father telling us that, but I have no memories of *her*."

"I do, I think." Titus frowned.

"I don't. And I have no memories of Roma, do you? We were babies when we left. We grew up in Alexandria. Alexandria is our home."

"*Was* our home, Kaeso. We were born Romans, we have always been citizens of Roma, and now we are truly Romans again. It's what our father wanted. Thanks to Claudius—"

"Did I hear my name? Being spoken k-k-kindly, I hope." Claudius was nearby, stooping over to peer at the sculptor's mark on a statue of Hercules. He straightened, groaning a bit—at fifty, his back was stiffer than it once had been—and ambled toward them. One of his toes had developed a blister from walking, but he bore the pain with a smile. The sons of Lucius Pinarius and their wives were taking their first tour of the city, and it was his pleasure to act as their guide.

"I was reminding Kaeso of how grateful we should be for all you've done," said Titus.

"I only wish I could have arranged for you and your father to return to Roma long ago. I thought it might be possible when Tiberius p-p-put Sejanus to death. Can that have been nine years ago? How the time flies! But getting rid of that treacherous viper didn't make Tiberius any less unreasonable; if anything, Uncle became more suspicious and fearful than ever. Two of my nephews he put to death for plotting against him, locking them away and letting them starve to death, even as he indulged his every appetite—and not just for food."

"What do you mean?" said Kaeso.

"In his declining years, Uncle decided to follow his impulses, no m-m-matter where they might lead."

"His impulses?" said Titus.

Claudius glanced over his shoulder. His young wife and the wives of the twins were taking a rest, sitting on the steps of the Temple of Jupiter while their attendant slaves stood by. The three women smiled and waved, then went on with their conversation. No one else was close enough to hear. Why had he brought up the subject of Tiberius and his appetites? The fact was, Claudius needed to unburden himself. For years, he had had no one to whom he could speak in an unguarded way, not even his slaves, who either could not be trusted or upon whom he did not wish to thrust the responsibility of keeping his secrets. Looking back, he realized that there had never been anyone to whom he could speak with utter freedom except his dear friend and cousin Lucius Pinarius. Since the twins had arrived in Roma, Claudius found himself confiding in them more and more, as once he had confided in their father.

"Tiberius's behavior in his last years was truly shocking. The m-m-man indulged every desire, without the least restraint. What must Augustus have thought, looking down from Olympus?"

"What sort of desires?" asked Titus, curious to know more.

"How I dreaded my visits to that debauched retreat of his at Capri. At least he had the sense to confine his excesses to his private island! All those n-n-naked children wandering about. Not just nubile boys and girls, I tell you, and not just slaves, but freeborn children! Tiberius coined his own terms for them. In bed they were his spintriae—his tight little sphincters. In his bath, they were his little minnows. Uncle said there was no greater pleasure for an old man than to settle in a warm p-pool and be nibbled and suckled under water by tiny mouths while he gazed up at the pornographic mosaics on the ceiling."

"Mosaics with pictures of people having sex?" Titus laughed. "I've never seen such a thing! What do you make of that, Kaeso?"

Kaeso shook his head. Claudius frowned, a bit flustered by Titus's lack of proper outrage, but he was encouraged to see that Kaeso appeared to share his disdain.

"Oh, how Tiberius loved his p-p-pornography! The whole place was like a museum of sex, filled with the most salacious paintings and statues imaginable. I thought to find escape in the library, but the shelves contained nothing but smut—scroll upon scroll of the most salacious stories, especially written for Tiberius by slaves acquired solely for their skill at spinning such tales. Bedtime stories, he called them. Since most of his bedmates were too ill-educated or too young to read, Tiberius had artists illustrate the texts, so that he could use the pictures to show his partners exactly what he wanted them to do."

Titus elbowed his brother. "What do you think of that, Kaeso? I never saw such books at the Great Library in Alexandria!" Kaeso made a sour face.

Claudius blinked. "But what started me on this dreadful subject? Ah, yes, my efforts to bring your father back to Roma. Well, eventually Tiberius lost all interest in running the state; he left that to his underlings and retired full-time to Capri. But every so often, when I could get Uncle to discuss something other than the gratification of his p-p-penis, I would bring up the case of your father. I pointed out that Lucius was my cousin, and that Sejanus's agents had kept him under surveillance for years, and not once had he been heard to utter a treasonable sentiment, or to practice astrology, for that m-m-matter. I begged Tiberius to rescind your father's banishment. But Uncle was not a forgiving sort. He wouldn't hear of it. He wouldn't even listen to me—except once, when I made the mistake of mentioning that Lucius had twin sons, trying to wring some pity from him, and do you know what Tiberius said? 'How old are they? Are they pretty?' By that time you were old enough to wear togas, and I told him so, whereupon he lost all interest and ordered me never to m-m-mention my cousin Lucius Pinarius again."

Claudius sighed. "So, we simply had to wait for Tiberius to die. How the people detested him, by the end. When word of his death at Capri reached Roma, there was d-d-dancing in the streets. You should have seen the jubilation that swept through this city when my nephew was named his successor—the only son of Germanicus whom Tiberius hadn't managed to kill. . . ." His voice trailed away. He blinked and twitched.

"There were celebrations in Alexandria, too," said Titus. "Back in Egypt, everyone says Gaius Caligula will make an ideal ruler. The legions love him. He's young, energetic, sure of himself."

"Yes, very sure of himself, as only a g-g-god can be," muttered Claudius, averting his eyes. "At any rate, amid all the celebration, our new emperor expressed his willingness to hear pleas for amnesty, including mine for your father. It was granted. But the wheels of state turn slowly—you wouldn't believe the layers of bureaucracy in this city—and of course your f-f-father needed time to settle his affairs in Alexandria before he could leave. In the last letter I received from him, he was finally making preparations for the journey. How happy Lucius was that he had convinced the two of you and your wives to come along with him. And then—a fever took both him and Acilia. So sad! But you two are here now, along with those lovely wives of yours. One always hears that Alexandrian women are the world's most beautiful; Artemisia and Chrysanthe are proof. But here, what's this?"

Sunlight glinted across the gold amulet that Kaeso was wearing on a chain around his neck. With a bemused expression, Claudius reached out to touch it. Kaeso smiled. "It's a fascinum, according to our father, though you wouldn't know to look at it. He told us it was very old, maybe even older than Roma itself."

"Ah, yes, I thought it looked familiar. By Hercules, I had forgotten all about it! It was I who informed your father about this amulet's history, before you boys were born. So, when he died, he p-p-passed the fascinum to you, Kaeso? I can use it to tell the two of you apart. I never knew twins who looked more alike!"

"I'm afraid you'll need to learn some other trick to distinguish us, then," said Kaeso. "Father's will didn't specify which of us should inherit it, but since his estate was split equally between us, we've agreed to share the fascinum. Sometimes I wear it. Sometimes Titus does."

"Then twins *can* get along. You have improved upon the example of Romulus and Remus! I'll wager your father never told you that it was I who came up with names for the two of you. No? It's true. When he learned that Acilia had given b-b-birth to twins, he was in a quandary over which of you to give his own name, since Lucius had long been the traditional name bestowed on the firstborn male Pinarius. But the midwife made such a jumble of things that there was no way to tell which of you had come first. Besides, you were so identical in every way, it seemed unfair, perhaps even unlucky, to honor one of you with the firstborn's name and slight the other. So your father decided to break with tradition and name neither of you Lucius. He asked for my advice. We decided to name one of you Kaeso, after a famous ancestor of yours from the Fabius family, a man who wore that very fascinum about four hundred years ago, if my theory is correct."

"What about my name?" asked Titus.

"That was in memory of my mentor, the great scholar Titus Livius. Surely you've read his history of Roma? No? Not even the p-p-parts about the ancient Pinarii?" Claudius shook his head. "I'm sure I gave your father a copy, long ago."

"I think it's among the books we brought with us from Alexandria," said Titus.

"I wonder if your father ever read it. Ah well, neither he nor his father had much interest in the past. But a man must honor his ancestors. Who else made us, and how else did we come to exist?"

"I'd prefer to live for the future," said Kaeso with a faraway look, fingering the fascinum at his throat.

"And I'd prefer to live in the present!" Titus laughed. "But speaking of the future, how soon might we have the honor of meeting the emperor? We should like to thank him in person, not just for allowing us to return, but for restoring the honor of our father's name. With our full rights as citizens and patricians restored, someday we might even be able to gain admission to the college of augurs."

"How that would please the shade of your father!" said Claudius. "Of course I'd be proud to oversee your studies, and to sponsor one or b-b-both of you for admission."

Kaeso made a face. "It's Titus who dreams of becoming an augur, not I."

"I brought father's old trabea and lituus with me, from Alexandria," said Titus. "But what about meeting the emperor?"

Claudius averted his eyes. "Yes, well, if the emperor should summon you for an audience, of course you must go. But in the great press of affairs—Caligula is so generous to so many of his subjects—it's entirely p-possible he will forget all about this particular instance of generosity, and if that should happen, well, perhaps it's best if you don't remind him. Indeed, it might be b-b-best if you do nothing at all to call attention to yourselves."

Titus furrowed his brow. "What do you mean, cousin Claudius?"

"How can I explain? Exile is a curse, but it can also b-be a blessing. Despite his sorrow at being sent so far from the city he loved, your father was fortunate to miss the terror visited on this city by Sejanus, and all the casual cruelties of Tiberius. Then, when my nephew succeeded Tiberius, it seemed that a new era was dawning, a time of hope and fresh confidence. I was eager for your father to return. So was he. P-p-perhaps we were too eager. P-p-perhaps we should have been less optimistic, and waited a little longer." He shook his head. "It was Caligula's father, my brother Germanicus, who should have become emperor. Everyone says so. My brother's military skills were first-rate. His temperament was ideal. Germanicus was loved by the legions, by the people, even by the Senate. But not so loved by the gods, who saw fit to take him from us—the gods, or else Sejanus, or Livia, or Tiberius. What does it matter? They're all dead now. All dead."

Kaeso put his hand on the older man's shoulder. "What are you trying to tell us, Claudius?"

"Unlike his father, my nephew was always a bit . . . unsound." Claudius twitched. He wiped away a bit of drool. "I suppose that sounds judgmental, even absurd, coming from the likes of me, but it's true. As a b-b-boy, little Gaius was troubled with the falling sickness."

"So was the Divine Julius," said Titus.

"Perhaps, but I suspect Caligula's case was rather more severe than that of Julius Caesar. All through his youth he was struck by spells that rendered him b-b-barely able to walk, or to stand, or even to hold up his head. He would be dazed afterwards, unable to collect his thoughts, but he always recovered. As he grew to manhood, he seemed to outgrow the affliction, and that gave us hope. We certainly never had cause to worry about his . . . sanity."

"And now?" said Kaeso.

Claudius hesitated, but once again he could not resist the need to unburden himself. "The change occurred suddenly—overnight, in fact. It was caused by a love p-p-potion given to him by that horrible wife of his, Caesonia. She's much older; she was already a mother of three when they began carrying on. If you ask me, it's unnatural for a young man to take an older partner; it should be the other way around, don't you think? As it is with m-m-myself and Messalina."

"Quite," agreed Titus. "But you were telling us about the emperor."

"Yes. Well, apparently Caligula's lovemaking was a disappointment to Caesonia—a harlot of such vast experience—so Caesonia decided to remedy the situation by giving the boy an aphrodisiac. The gossips say she fed him the substance the Greeks call *hippomanes*—a fleshy mass sometimes found on the forehead of a newborn foal."

Kaeso wrinkled his nose. "It sounds disgusting."

"Does it work?" asked Titus.

"One m-mixes it with wine and herbs to make it palatable," said Claudius. "It's a well-known aphrodisiac—various scholars mention it—but in all my research I can find no other case where it drove a man m-m-mad. I suspect Caesonia adulterated it with some other ingredient."

"She deliberately poisoned him?" said Titus.

"No. Whatever ingredient she added was probably harmless by itself, but when mixed with the *hippomanes* created a combination that was toxic. That at least is my theory. I have a suspicion that Caesonia may have duplicated the very love p-p-potion that drove Lucretius mad."

The twins looked at him blankly.

"The p-p-poet Lucretius," he explained, "who lived in the days of the Divine Julius. They say Lucretius's madness came and went. In his lucid moments he was able to write his great work, *On the Nature of Things,* but eventually he was driven to suicide."

"Are you afraid Caligula may kill himself?" said Kaeso.

Claudius shivered, hugged himself, and whinnied like a horse. The twins feared he was having a fit, but he was only laughing. "Oh, no, Kaeso, that is *not* what I'm afraid of! Caligula's behavior makes even the worst excesses of Tiberius seem trivial. The stories I could tell you—but look, here's Messalina, and your lovely wives."

The women rejoined their husbands. In all of Roma, it was unlikely that one could find three more beautiful women standing side by side. The twins had chosen wives who might have passed for siblings themselves; Artemisia and Chrysanthe both had buxom figures and wore their thick black hair in long plaits, after the Egyptian fashion. Messalina was the youngest of the three, but she affected a matronly look, with her black hair pulled back from her face and pinned in an elaborate coiffure, and a voluminous stola that covered her from head to foot and concealed her arms as well. At a distance, the loose stola concealed her condition; seen closer, her swollen breasts and protruding belly made it obvious that she was pregnant.

"What have you lovely females been talking about all this time?" said Titus, glancing at Messalina's breasts even as he took Chrysanthe's hand.

"This and that," his wife said. "Hairstyles, mostly. Artemisia and I look terribly provincial. Messalina promises to send the slave who dresses her hair, to give us instruction on the latest Roman styles."

"Don't complicate your b-b-beauty too much," said Claudius. "You're lovely as you are." He kissed Messalina on the forehead and gently, dotingly touched her just above the navel.

Kaeso scowled and furrowed his brow. Titus pulled him aside and whispered in his ear, "What's wrong with you, brother? You've been in a foul mood all day."

"That girl is young enough to be his granddaughter!"

"That's not our business. Try not to show your disapproval so openly."

"Back in Alexandria—"

"We're in Roma now. Things are different here." Titus sighed. Back in Alexandria, his brother had taken up with some strange people and acquired some very intolerant ideas. It was their father's fault, for having given his sons too much freedom when they were young. Both Titus and

Kaeso had received traditional instruction at the academy near the Temple of Serapis, and had pursued the usual curriculum of philosophy, rhetoric, and athletics. But when the school day was done, Kaeso had spent his free time in the Jewish Quarter, drawn there by a fascination with mysticism, and the so-called scholars in the Jewish Quarter had filled his head with all sorts of bizarre ideas that were neither Greek nor Roman. Their father, too busy with business, had never sought to divert Kaeso from these dubious influences. That role would have suited a grandfather, thought Titus, an older, wiser man with patience and time to spare, but Fate had robbed them of their grandfather. They had grown up knowing no grandparents at all, a most unRoman circumstance for young patricians.

But they were in Roma now, at last, and they could ask for no better friend and guide than their cousin Claudius.

"Shall we press on to the Palatine?" said Claudius. "We can see the Hut of Romulus, the Temple of Apollo—"

Messalina rolled her eyes. "Husband, you can't expect them to see all of Roma in a single day!"

"But what am I thinking? You must be weary, my d-d-dear. It was brave of you to come out at all."

"I could hardly miss this opportunity to welcome your dear cousins." Messalina looked from face to face. Her eyes lingered first on Kaeso, then on Titus.

"But you mustn't overexert yourself. I'll fetch the l-l-litter and send you straight home."

The litter arrived, borne by a team of brawny slaves. Two of them lifted Messalina into the cushioned box. Claudius kissed her farewell, then closed the richly embroidered curtains so that she could travel home in privacy. As the litter was departing, Messalina parted the curtains with her forefinger and looked out. Her gaze fell on Titus, who gazed back at her.

Claudius and the women were discussing the rest of the day's itinerary and did not see, but Kaeso saw and heard everything—the penetrating look that darted back and forth between his brother and Messalina, the way she narrowed her eyes and parted her lips, and the grunt from Titus, followed by a sigh.

The curtain closed. The litter receded from sight. Titus turned to face Kaeso, who scowled and shook his head.

Titus raised an eyebrow and flashed a crooked smile. "We are in Roma now, brother."

A.D. 41

Kaeso shook the three ivory dice in his hand and tossed them onto the table. The engraved pips that landed uppermost were two fours and a one.

"Rabbits for you, brother. Too bad!" Titus scooped up the dice and threw them. The pips were all different: a one, a six, and a three. "A Venus Throw for me. I win! Today, I shall wear the fascinum."

"No one will see it under your toga, anyway."

"But it will be there, nonetheless, lying close to my heart on the occasion of our audience with the emperor. We've waited a long time for this day, Kaeso."

Three months had passed since their arrival in Roma. They had settled into a house on the Aventine not far from the one in which they had been born. It was not a particularly elegant house, and it was too far down the hill to offer much of a view, but it was large enough for the four of them and their slaves, with room to accommodate new additions to the family.

While the twins put on their best togas, their wives dressed in their finest stolas and put finishing touches to their newly styled hair. It had not taken them long to adopt Roman fashions, though Artemisia remained the more conservative of the two, in deference to Kaeso's distaste for ostentation. Secretly, she envied Chrysanthe's more daring coiffure, which towered atop her head like a Subura tenement.

Carried in a pair of exquisitely crafted litters hired especially for the occasion, the two couples set out for the emperor's house on the Palatine. The Januarius day was mild, with pale yellow sunshine peeking through thin, high clouds. As they passed the ancient Ara Maxima, the Great Altar of Hercules, Titus insisted that they stop and get out. At Claudius's behest, he had at last started reading Livius's history; an early chapter recounted the dedication of the Ara Maxima. It seemed fitting to Titus that on this of all days they should have a look at it.

The altar was made of massive stone blocks, roughly hewn, that looked very ancient. A bronze statue of Hercules stood nearby, a magnificent figure bearing a club and dressed only in a headdress made from a lion's skin. At their approach, a priest offered his services. For a few coins, the priest spilled some wine and burned some incense on the altar while Titus said a prayer that their audience with the emperor would go well.

Titus explained to Artemisia and Chrysanthe why the altar had special significance to the Pinarii. "Long before there was a city on the Tiber, and only shepherds and a few traders lived among the Seven Hills, Hercules paid a visit, passing through with a herd of oxen. A monster called Cacus was living in a cave on the Palatine, just over there, terrorizing the local inhabitants. Cacus made the mistake of trying to steal one of the stranger's oxen—he didn't know who he was dealing with!—and after a terrific struggle, Hercules killed the monster Cacus on this very spot. The Pinarii were living here even then, for Livius tells us that it was a Pinarius who established this place of worship—the very first altar to a god in the whole region of the Seven Hills."

Kaeso, who had remained silent since they had stepped from the litters, finally spoke. "Hercules was not a god, brother."

Titus looked sidelong at his brother. "Strictly speaking, while he lived he was a demigod, since Jupiter sired him on a mortal woman. But after he died, he joined the gods in Olympus."

Kaeso snorted softly. "If you believe such nonsense."

"Kaeso!" Titus ground his teeth. This was not the first time his brother had expressed such atheistic sentiments, but to do so in a public place, where someone might overhear, and in this of all places, with its ancient, sacred ties to their own family, was beyond decency. Titus asked Artemisia and Chrysanthe to return to the litters, then spoke to Kaeso through clenched teeth.

"You should learn when to speak, brother, and when to keep your thoughts to yourself."

"Why? If Jupiter overhears me, will he strike me down with a thunderbolt?"

"He might do just that! Am I mistaken, brother, or has this impious attitude of yours grown worse since we arrived in Roma? I had hoped that coming here, leaving the influence of those Jewish mystics in Alexandria behind, would bring you closer to the gods. I know that was father's hope as well."

"Don't bring father into this."

"Why not? When a man honors his father, he honors the gods, and vice versa. You seem disinclined to do either. The Alexandrians have a long tradition of allowing all manner of outlandish and even dangerous ideas to be taught, and we've seen the result: one has the feeling the gods abandoned that city long ago. But we are in Roma now, the heart of the world, the center of the world's religion. This is the home of our emperor, who is also the Pontifex Maximus, the highest of all priests. The gods make Roma their home when they choose to be on earth. Why? Because no other city offers them so many splendid temples to reside in, or provides so many altars where the pious may sacrifice in their honor. And in return, Roma above all other cities has been divinely blessed. Here in Roma, you must learn to keep unholy thoughts to yourself and to pay proper respect to the gods. It's not I who demand this, but the gods."

"No, it's you, Titus. Your gods demand nothing, because they don't exist."

"Blasphemy, Kaeso! Even your Jewish mystics in Alexandria believe in the gods, even if they favor one above all others. Didn't their god Jehovah say to them, 'You shall have no other gods *before me*'? You see, Kaeso, I do know something about these ideas you picked up in Alexandria, though I can't imagine what sort of god demands his worshippers to spurn his fellow gods."

Kaeso shook his head. "You know nothing about it, Titus. I've tried to explain to you—"

"I know that when a man denies the gods, he's asking to be punished by them."

Kaeso sighed. "I suppose we shall meet one of your so-called gods today."

"What do you mean?"

"They say Caligula believes himself to be a god. Or a goddess, on the days he dresses up as Venus. Shall we fall to our knees and worship him?"

Kaeso's tone was sarcastic, but Titus gave him a serious answer: "In fact, before we enter his presence, we may be required to make some acknowledgment of the emperor's divine origins. It won't kill you to murmur a prayer and burn a bit of incense. Shall we rejoin our wives and get on with it?"

As the bearers made their way up the slope of the Palatine, Chrysanthe tried to lighten Titus's mood with inconsequential speculations. Would the emperor be accompanied by his wife, Caesonia? What would she be wearing? Would their young daughter make an appearance? Titus occasionally grunted in response, but was not listening. The argument with Kaeso had unsettled his nerves. He fell prey to unwelcome thoughts. For days, ever since the summons had arrived, Titus had been telling himself that an imperial audience was a singular honor and a golden opportunity, something to be longed for, not feared. Suddenly he felt nervous and uncertain about what to expect. He had heard a great many strange rumors about the emperor.

Caligula had once set sail for Britannia on a mission of conquest, then suddenly turned back and ordered his troops to collect seashells instead, which he paraded before the people and the Senate of Roma as spoils of war, claiming he had conquered the ocean itself; a tavern keeper in the Subura had told Titus this tale, and every man in the tavern had backed him up. An architect's wife at the market told Chrysanthe that her husband had helped to build a magnificent marble stall and an ivory manger for the emperor's favorite horse, which Caligula decked out in purple blankets and a collar of precious stones, invited to dinner parties, and addressed as "Consul."

These stories could almost be laughed at, but others were more disturbing. Caligula had once arranged an oratory competition, and made the losers erase their wax tablets with their tongues. When Caligula fell ill, a man declared that he would gladly sacrifice his own life to save the emperor's; when Caligula recovered, he reminded the man of his pledge and forced him to commit suicide. At a gladiator show, the number of condemned men to be slain by wild beasts fell short of expectations, and to make up the number Caligula ordered some of the spectators to be thrown into the arena. All these tales were widely told and attested to be true.

Equally widespread was the rumor that Caligula had slept with all three of his sisters, openly practicing incest and proudly claiming that he himself was the product of incest between his grandmother Julia and her father, the Divine Augustus.

Titus did not know what to think. Claudius might have helped him make sense of such stories, but Titus and Kaeso had not seen their cousin for over a month. As Messalina's delivery drew nearer, Claudius had become increasingly reticent and withdrawn, finally confining himself to the imperial residence and accepting no visitors, not even over the Saturnalia holidays. When the twins had received the summons to an audience with Caligula, Titus had dispatched a message to Claudius at once, telling him the news and asking to meet, hoping to receive his cousin's advice. In response, Claudius sent only a cryptic message: "May Fortune be with you!"

The litters arrived in the gravel forecourt of the imperial house, where numerous other litters had been parked. The courtyard was crowded with idle bearers as well as messengers and slaves whose masters had business within. Though the palace had been greatly expanded since the time of Augustus, the entry for guests was still the doorway flanked by laurel trees, and the courtyard still displayed the armor of the Divine Augustus. As they walked by, Titus dared to touch his fingers to the bronze breastplate. The thrill of excitement at being in this place was so great that it almost dispelled his anxieties.

They had to present themselves to a great many retainers and pass through a great many doors on their way to being received by the emperor. Titus soon lost all sense of direction and had no idea where they were inside the sprawling complex. At last they were shown into a small but exquisitely decorated room with a black marble floor, red drapes, and gilded furniture. The mood was informal. A servant announced the two couples, then invited them to relax on couches opposite that of the emperor, who reclined on his own couch with his wife Caesonia.

As all the stories had indicated, Caesonia was of middle age, but with her large breasts and sumptuous hips she exuded a certain overripe appeal. Her henna-stained hair was coiffed to frame her face like a peacock's fan. With a forefinger she idly toyed with her necklace of amber and lapis. Her unblinking gaze made Titus nervous.

The sight of the emperor was reassuring, at least at first. At twenty-nine, Caligula was only seven years older than Titus and Kaeso, but his fair hair was already beginning to thin a bit. His features were plain but regular, and his expression was mild, almost vacant. He looked quite normal, Titus thought, except for his eccentric dress. Caligula appeared to be wearing not the boots for which he was named but a woman's slippers, and the feminine gown called a cyclas embroidered with purple and gold and made of silk. In the days of the Divine Augustus, legislation had been passed outlawing the wearing of silk by men. Yet here was the emperor himself wrapped in the stuff.

"You will address him as Dominus," the retainer had instructed them in a whisper before they entered the room. This was another way Caligula differed from his predecessors. Both Augustus and Tiberius had explicitly rejected using as a title the word by which slaves addressed their master.

The conversation began well. The twins thanked the emperor for lifting their father's banishment. Caligula accepted their thanks and demonstrated his acquaintance with their family history and their current circumstances, noting their success in the Alexandrian grain trade despite the unfortunate treatment of their father by Tiberius.

"And so the wheel of time rolls on," said Caligula, "and here you both are, visitors to the imperial presence as was your father before you. Welcome."

Titus began to relax. The emperor himself was treating them with friendship and respect. What could be better? He glanced sidelong and caught his brother's eye. Kaeso looked tense and anxious. His brother needed to learn to relax and to enjoy the benefits that Fortune had bestowed on them.

The audience was interrupted by the appearance of the emperor's daughter. Little Julia Drusilla was followed by a harried-looking nurse who wore the vestments of a priestess of Minerva. The girl ran shrieking to her father. Titus wondered if something was wrong with the child, but Caligula seemed unperturbed. He opened his mouth and shrieked back at her, then took her in his arms as the two of them screamed with laughter. Father and daughter seemed to be playing a noisy, familiar game. Titus saw his wife and his sister-in-law smile and take an interest, as they tended to do in the presence of any child.

Little Julia Drusilla was thoroughly disheveled, with her golden hair mussed and her gown askew, and once her laughter subsided her petulant mood returned. With a look of alarm, Caligula noted a spot of blood on her tunic.

"What's this?" he cried.

"It's another child's blood," the priestess quickly explained. "She was playing with some other children—"

"And what happened?" asked Caesonia sharply.

"They looked at me funny, so I scratched their faces!" The little girl made a fearsome face and mimicked the clawing of a cat.

"I was afraid she might blind one of them," whispered the priestess.

Caligula examined the girl's hands. "Look at that—she has blood under her tiny fingernails!" He sat back on the couch and clapped his hands. "Good girl! A little she-lion, you are! Well, if ever there was any need for proof that the child is mine—as was doubted by certain gossips now deceased—there's your proof. Like father, like daughter! By all means, if the other children should offend you, don't stand for it. Scratch their eyes out! There's quite a thrill in drawing blood, isn't there, little one?"

"Yes, papa."

"Run and say hello to my guests. I'm sure the ladies want to meet you."

Julia first approached Artemisia, who shrank back. The little girl then turned to Chrysanthe, who managed a crooked smile and held out her hand. Julia stared at the hand for a moment, then snarled and snapped at it. Chrysanthe pulled back her hand with a cry. Julia turned and ran, laughing, to her father, who seemed as amused as his daughter at the women's discomfort. He gave Julia a parting kiss, then sent the child and her nurse on their way.

Caesonia looked at her guests and shrugged. "Children—such a distraction! Yet they bring so much joy. Does either of you have children yet?"

Artemisia blushed and looked to Chrysanthe, who had regained her composure. "No, not yet. But as my husband says, perhaps the waiting has been a blessing, since our firstborn can now be conceived here in the city of his ancestors."

"So young, and not yet mothers," said Caesonia. "So you both must be very tight still."

Chrysanthe's smile wavered. "I'm not sure what you mean."

Caesonia giggled and crooked her finger at Caligula, who leaned close so that she could whisper in his ear.

While the imperial couple conversed in a hush, Kaeso leaned toward Titus. "Let me have the amulet," he whispered.

Titus frowned and shook his head. He defensively touched the fascinum where it lay hidden under his toga. He had won the toss of the dice that morning, as Kaeso was well aware.

But Kaeso was insistent. "Please, brother! Give it to me!"

"Why?"

"For protection."

"From what?"

"Can't you feel his presence?"

"Who?"

"The devil himself!"

Titus rolled his eyes, unable to believe that Kaeso was spouting yet another of the impious notions he had picked up in Alexandria, and in the very presence of the emperor. He gave a start when he realized that Caligula was addressing him in a sharp voice.

Titus's face turned hot. "A thousand pardons, Dominus. I didn't hear you."

"Then listen more attentively, Titus Pinarius. I don't ask unimportant questions, and I hate to repeat myself. But I will ask again, because Caesonia wants to know: are the two of you identical in every way?"

Titus raised an eyebrow. "We certainly have differences of opinion, Dominus."

"I mean physically, you fool!" Caligula smiled, baring a bit more of his teeth than seemed normal.

"Yes, Dominus, we're identical twins, as you can see. People remark on our similarity all the time."

"Truly identical, in every way?"

"Yes."

"Show us."

"I beg your pardon?"

"Show us. Caesonia wants to see, and so do I."

"I don't understand," said Titus, his heart sinking.

"I think you do. Stand up and take off your togas, both of you."

Titus and Kaeso exchanged pained glances. Neither moved.

Caligula sighed. "Please don't be tiresome. You really have no choice. It is a god who asks this of you."

"This is most improper," said Kaeso.

"Improper?" Caligula seemed more amused than angry. "Do you see the armed men standing over there, beside the pillars? Why do you think they're there? Well?"

"To protect the emperor," said Titus, his mouth dry.

Caligula laughed. "The emperor is a god and needs no protection. Those men are here to enforce the emperor's will, when those in the emperor's presence are slow to obey him. Do I need to call on them now? They will use whatever force is necessary."

Titus glanced at the faces of the guards. Perhaps this was all a game, a test of some sort, he thought, until he saw the looks on their faces. His blood turned cold.

Titus was so light-headed that he could hardly stand. He gestured for Kaeso to do likewise. When Kaeso hesitated, Titus grabbed his shoulder and pulled him to his feet. Trying to maintain an air of unconcern, as if he were alone in his own room, Titus began to unwind his toga. Normally a slave helped a master to put on his toga and to take it off as well. Titus's hands were clumsy; the soft wool seemed determined to thwart him. He tripped over the toga and almost fell before he managed to extract himself from it, and in the process lost any pretense of dignity. Pulling the tunic over his head was easier. He stood upright, wearing only his loincloth.

Caligula and Caesonia stared at Titus intently, then turned their attention to Kaeso, who lagged behind. Eventually Kaeso stood in only his loincloth, next to his brother. At the far ends of the two couches, Artemisia and Chrysanthe were so still and quiet that they might have turned to stone.

"Go on," said Caligula. "We must see everything."

His face flushed, his hands trembling, Titus undid his loincloth and let it fall. Except for his shoes and the fascinum at his breast, he stood naked. From the corner of his eye he saw Kaeso drop his loincloth as well.

"Extraordinary!" Caligula rose from his couch and examined them more closely, peering at them as if they were statues, or slaves for purchase. "It is said that the gods never make two pearls, or even two peas in a pod, so alike that a man cannot tell them apart, and yet I would defy any-one to distinguish between the two of you. What do you think, Caesonia?"

"All shriveled up like that, any two members might look alike. I think we will have to see them in a state of arousal."

"Dominus, this is not right!" said Titus, his voice cracking. "Send away our wives, at least."

"But your wives are essential to the experiment."

Caesonia stood facing the brothers. She reached out and began to fon-dle them both at once. Titus gasped and closed his eyes. Though he would not have thought it possible, he began to respond. He felt the blood en-gorging his member, and little thrills of pleasure from Caesonia's touch.

Apparently Kaeso had responded as well, for Caligula clapped his hands and laughed with delight. "Still exactly the same! Identical in every respect! Can you detect any difference, Caesonia? Weigh them each in your hand. Measure the girth and the length. Examine them carefully for blemishes or other distinguishing marks."

Titus opened his eyes. Caesonia looked very pleased with herself and with the effect she was having on them. His head felt lighter than air and his legs were weak, but there was no denying the pleasure she was induc-ing in him.

"No difference at all!" Caesonia announced.

"Ah, but the hand, delicate as it may be, is an insensitive instrument compared to the lips and the tongue. Is that not true, Caesonia, based on your experience?"

"Dominus, please!" Titus begged, his voice weak. "For the emperor's wife to do what you suggest—"

"Shut your filthy mouth!" shouted Caligula. His sudden rage made Ti-tus blanch, yet he felt himself grow even stiffer in Caesonia's hand. "How dare you suggest such a thing? Caesonia is mine and mine alone. The very idea that she would lower herself to such an act with a mortal like you is disgusting."

"Dominus, if I misunderstood—"

"You certainly did! Guards, bring blindfolds for these two women. And bring gags for their husbands, to keep them quiet during the experiment."

"Dominus, what experiment?"

Caligula rolled his eyes, like a tutor with a stupid pupil. "We are going to see if your own wives can tell you apart, of course! First, we shall blindfold the women. Then we shall stand the two of you back to back. Next, we will spin your blindfolded wives around until they lose all sense of direction, then push them to their knees. Finally, your wives will show us if they can tell the difference—using only their mouths—between one twin and the other."

The events unfolded exactly as Caligula desired. Moment by moment, Titus's fear and humiliation were matched only by his unflagging excitement. At times he felt as if he had left his body and was floating above the scene, a mere observer of the degrading spectacle taking place below. Drawing close to form a cordon around them, the guards observed everything. Occasionally one of them snickered or grunted, and several times, when Titus was slow to cooperate, something sharp jabbed his throat or his chest or some exposed part of his body normally hidden from sight. Caesonia frequently giggled and whispered to the emperor, who oversaw the experiment with childlike delight.

A curious fact struck Titus. After all his scrutiny, Caligula had failed to notice the one thing that distinguished him from his brother, even in their nakedness: the fascinum. The little lump of gold felt alternately freezing cold and burning hot against Titus's naked, sweaty flesh; it seemed at times to move and palpitate, as if it were alive.

As Titus reached a climax, the experiment reached a conclusion. Blindfolded, even their wives could not tell Titus and Kaeso apart.

An hour after their audience began, Titus and Kaeso and their wives were allowed to leave the palace—alive, unmarked and to all appearances unscathed. But as the elegant litters bore them back to the house they shared, the women wept and the brothers kept their eyes downcast.

❖

"You should have given me the amulet when I asked for it," said Kaeso.

Night had fallen. Their distraught wives had withdrawn to their bedrooms. The sleepless brothers sat some distance apart in their moonlit garden, shivering under heavy blankets.

Titus shook his head and scowled, amazed that this was how his brother should break the silence that had been uninterrupted between them since they had left the imperial house. "I should have given you the fascinum? What possible difference would that have made?"

"It might have protected Artemisia and me."

"But it failed to protect any of us, you fool! A fascinum is meant to avert the gaze of the envious. But the emperor is a god, or something close to a god. His gaze was too powerful—"

"Caligula is not a god, and that object is not a fascinum."

Titus shook his head. "Must you contradict everything I say, brother?"

"There is only one god—"

"No! Stop this impious talk."

"And the thing around your neck may well be a holy talisman, but it isn't a fascinum."

"What is it, then?"

"Have you ever actually looked at it? Carefully? Do so now."

Titus lifted the chain over his neck and reached for a lamp. The amulet glittered between his fingers. "I see a bit of gold, probably alloyed with some baser metal to make it more durable. Even so, it's worn down to a shapeless lump—"

"Not shapeless, brother. It has a shape. Describe it."

"A bit taller than it is wide, with little nubs projecting from each side. You can see how once it was a phallus with wings—"

"You see it as a winged phallus, brother, because that's what you're looking to see. But if you forget what you've been told, and simply look at it, what does it resemble?"

Titus shrugged. "A cross, I suppose."

"Exactly! A cross—the crucifix upon which criminals and escaped slaves are hung to die."

Titus made a face. "Crucifixion is the most disgraceful sort of death. Who would make an amulet of a crucifix? Unless they wanted to bring a curse on the wearer instead of a blessing."

"I'm not saying our amulet began as a cross, Titus. Perhaps it *is* ancient, as ancient as our father thought. And perhaps it did begin as a fascinum, as Claudius believes. But it has become something entirely different. Time and divine will have transformed it."

"I think it was transformed by a gradual wearing away, over many generations."

"How it happened, here in this material world, is of no importance. What matters is the shape it has come to assume and what that shape symbolizes."

"And what is that?"

"There are those who believe that the one true god, the creator of all things, manifested himself on earth as a man, and that man was put to death on a cross in Jerusalem during the reign of Tiberius."

"Who believes such a thing? Your Jewish mystics in Alexandria?"

"They're not the only ones."

"Oh, Kaeso, don't say these things to me! It's too distressing. We've all suffered enough today—"

"We suffered because we fell into the hands of Satan himself—"

"Satan?"

"The Lord of Evil."

"I thought you believed there was only one god."

"There is, and he is all that is good."

"But you've just told me there's a god of evil called Satan—"

"Satan is not a god. Only God is god."

Titus covered his ears. "Stop babbling, Kaeso!"

"How it happened, I don't know, Titus. But we have been given an amulet in the form of a cross, a holy symbol, because it was on a cross that our Savior, Jesus Christ, was killed."

"Is that the name of your god, Jesus Christ? How could he possibly be killed? A god by definition is immortal. Are you saying there was ever only one god, and now he's dead?" Titus trembled and began to weep. He fell from his chair onto his knees. "O Hercules, whose altar we founded! O Fascinus, worshipped by our family before the city was founded! O Jupiter, father and greatest of all the gods! My brother has been most cruelly treated today. His mind is unhinged! Let this madness pass from him quickly, let him come back to his senses, for the sake of his poor wife, for the sake of us all!"

Kaeso stood. His posture was defiant. "I've never spoken to you openly about these things, brother, because I feared this was how you would react. Someday I hope to bring you to the true knowledge of God, which I received in Alexandria, and which is known even here in Roma, if only by a few. The reward for enlightenment is eternal life, brother."

"And this?" Titus, still on his knees, clutched the fascinum and shook his fist. "That was how this mad conversation began, with your claim that the amulet might have saved you. How might that have happened?"

"There must be a reason that this crucifix was given to us. Had I, as a believer, been wearing it, the power of Jesus Christ might have shielded us from the hateful gaze of Satan himself. True believers have witnessed many such miracles—"

"But you just said that your god was dead!" In anger and disgust, Titus hurled the amulet at his brother. "Here, take it! I never want to see it again. The thing is useless, not even worth the gold it's made of. Keep it, Kaeso. Wear it every day if you like, and see what good it does you!"

※

"Terrible!" said Claudius, shaking his head. "T-t-truly appalling. It's brave of you, T-Titus, to confide in me."

They were in Claudius's private apartment in the imperial complex. Some rumor about the twins' ordeal must have reached him, for when Titus sent a message, asking again for a meeting, Claudius responded at once.

His invitation was addressed to both brothers, but Kaeso had refused to come, saying he would never set foot in any part of the palace again. It was just as well that Titus came alone; since the day of the audience and the argument that followed, the brothers had hardly spoken.

Titus had intended to conceal the more humiliating aspects of their audience with the emperor, but soon found himself telling the older man everything.

"It will g-g-give you no comfort," said Claudius, "but you should know that I myself have been treated almost as shamefully by my nephew. He's seen fit to kill many of those around him, and not from fear or suspicion, as Tiberius and even Augustus occasionally did; he seems to do it from sheer spite. He's spared me so far, but he's made it clear that I could d-d-die at any moment. He keeps me alive solely for the pleasure of making me squirm every now and then. More than once he's reduced me to tears and made me b-beg for my life. I speak of this to no one, but I'm telling you, Titus, because you have been so honest with me."

"But why didn't you warn us, cousin? We'd heard rumors about his eccentric behavior, but nothing prepared us for what happened."

Claudius shrugged. "His unpredictable nature is a p-p-part of his madness. Sometimes he behaves with perfect decency. I hoped you might be lucky. I kept my distance for fear of attracting attention to you. And if I had warned you of the danger, would you have refused the audience? That would have invited something even worse—and believe me, as awful as it was, what Caligula did to you was not the most horrible atrocity he's committed against an unsuspecting innocent."

Titus shuddered. "He's like a monstrous child."

"Caligula was twenty-four when he was made emperor, only a little older than you are now. His youth seemed quite attractive, after enduring Tiberius's unseemly d-d-decrepitude. Now it seems a curse. Caligula could rule for the rest of our lifetimes. He could still be emperor when your grandchildren are grown." Claudius shook his head. "Augustus and Tiberius left us no mechanism for the removal of an emperor. They ruled for life, and we must assume Caligula will do the same. In retrospect, perhaps such a young person should never have been made emperor. For someone so young to be given so much power—"

"You're not talking about me, are you, my dear?" Messalina stepped into the room. Her pregnancy was now in the eighth month. Her sheer gown, more suitable for the bedchamber than the street, showed off not only her round belly but also her greatly enlarged breasts. Titus tried not to stare at her, but she swayed as she circled the room, seeming deliberately to flaunt herself.

"Messalina, you should be in b-bed."

She sighed. "I can't spend every hour of every day lying down. And I'm as hungry as a horse. I thought Caligula was hosting some sort of banquet today."

Claudius nodded and explained to Titus. "My nephew is hosting a private festival. Here, step onto the balcony with me." Below them was a colonnaded walkway that led to a nearby courtyard surrounded by a portico and high shrubs. "It's being held in that courtyard over there. You can see a b-b-bit of the stage that's been assembled for the occasion. The festivities should commence at any moment. Boys from the best families of Greece and Ionia will be singing a hymn which the emperor composed to his own divinity. You can hear them practicing." He turned to Messalina. "But, darling, you know why we're not g-g-going. I was told that the emperor is out of sorts, suffering from indigestion, and wants to be attended only by his wife and daughter. A good thing we're not going, if you ask me. When Augustus had indigestion, we worried for his health; when Caligula suffers, it's our own lives we have to worry about! The shame of it, that once-proud Romans should quake in fear when another man passes wind!"

"Who told you the emperor didn't want us to come?" Messalina put her hands on her hips, causing her breasts to project before her.

"Didn't I say? It was Cassius Chaerea, the Praetorian t-t-tribune."

Messalina grinned. "That prude whom the emperor teases so mercilessly?" She looked at Titus archly. "Caligula thinks it's quite hilarious to give Chaerea naughty pet names, as if he were some old man's spintria—'honey-mouth,' 'pleasure-bottom,' that sort of thing." She laughed. "Well, if you could see iron-jawed, grizzled old Chaerea, you'd understand how absurd it is. And, knowing how Chaerea is so squeamish about words, for the daily password Caligula deliberately comes up with the most obscene phrases he can think of, so Chaerea has to say naughty words over and over, all day long. And funniest of all is when Caligula passes by and offers Chaerea his ring to kiss, and then at the last instant, sticks up his middle finger and makes Chaerea—"

"Messalina, d-d-darling, enough of that!" Claudius shook his head. "The child is so innocent, she has no idea what she's saying. Now go back to your rooms, my dear, and rest. If you're hungry, tell Narcissus to send for something."

Messalina made a show of pouting but did as her husband had told her, flashing a last, lingering look at Titus and brushing her fingertips over her swollen breasts as she departed.

Titus tore his eyes from Messalina and returned his gaze to the view from the balcony. He pricked up his ears and frowned. "Did you hear that, Claudius?"

"My ears are not what they were. I don't hear anything."

"Exactly. The singing stopped. Someone's shouting. Are they sacrificing an animal?"

"Why do you ask?"

"I thought I heard the formula that precedes a sacrifice. You know, when one priest says, 'Shall I do the deed?' and the other says, 'Strike now!' But this sounded odd, somehow, not like priests at all. . . ."

From the distant courtyard they heard a sudden uproar—shouts, the clanging of metal, and then shrill cries. Claudius frowned. "What's going on over there?"

A servant ran headlong from the courtyard, followed by more servants and then a group of screaming young boys. They rushed past on the walkway beneath the balcony, some of them tripping and falling and getting up again.

Claudius leaned over the balustrade. "What's g-g-going on?" he shouted.

They all ignored him except a little boy who paused for a moment and looked up. His eyes were wide with terror. Another boy bumped into him, almost knocking him down, and he hurried on.

"What in Hades?" muttered Claudius. He suddenly stiffened.

The servants and boy singers had all vanished. A group of armed men came striding out of the courtyard. Their swords were drawn. Their faces were grim. Leading them was a Praetorian tribune.

"Cassius Chaerea!" whispered Claudius.

Titus sucked in a breath. "Look at his sword."

The blade was covered with blood. Spatters of blood glistened on Chaerea's breastplate.

Another tribune appeared, walking quickly to catch up with Chaerea. "Cornelius Sabinus," whispered Claudius. His voice cracked.

"Carrying another bloody sword," whispered Titus. He glanced at Claudius, who had gone pale and was gripping the balustrade with white knuckles. Titus's heart pounded.

Chaerea saw them looking down from the balcony. He came to a halt. Sabinus caught up with him. The tribunes exchanged hushed words, then together looked up at Claudius and raised their bloody swords.

"Today we have a new password!" Chaerea shouted. "The password is *Jupiter*. God of the thunderbolt! God of sudden death!"

More Praetorians emerged from the courtyard. They were in two groups. Each group carried a makeshift litter. At first, Titus could make no sense of the lumpy, shapeless forms on the litters. Then, with a start, he realized that they were corpses. One of the bodies, from the mass of disarranged hair and the elegant stola covered with bloodstains, appeared to be that of a woman. As the men drew nearer, Titus was able to see her face. Caesonia's eyes were wide open. Her lips were drawn back and her teeth were clenched.

The other body was much smaller. It was a little girl. Her golden hair was clotted with blood. Her face was unrecognizable; her head had been crushed. Even at such a distance, Titus could smell the gore. The sight made him nauseated.

"Caesonia—and l-l-little Julia!" Claudius swayed and steadied himself against the balustrade, then pushed himself back and staggered from the balcony. "By Hercules, they intend to kill us all! Help me, Titus, I b-b-beg you. Hide me!"

"But they saluted you, Claudius. They gave you the password—"

"They brandished their swords and m-m-mocked me! Didn't you see the look in their eyes? Cold-blooded assassins! Woman-killers! Child-killers! Once upon a time, men like those murdered the Divine Julius, and now they've dared to m-m-murder Caligula. If they mean to restore the Republic, they'll slaughter my whole family. Not just me, but Messalina and the unborn baby! I'm a dead man, Titus!"

Titus did his best to calm him, but Claudius only became more hysterical. He ran back and forth across the room, unable to decide whether to stay or to leave. His head began to twitch uncontrollably and he made no effort to wipe away the drool that ran from the corner of his mouth. At last he ran to the door, determined to flee, then froze at the sound of stamping feet in the hallway. Claudius grabbed Titus by the arm and pulled him back to the balcony. He huddled behind the drapes at one end, pulling Titus close, trying to conceal them both.

The stamping feet reached the doorway. A group of men entered the room.

"He's not here, sir," said a deep voice.

"But the tribunes said they saw him in this room, standing on that balcony."

"Well, he's not here now."

"We didn't pass him in the hallway. . . ."

"Think he jumped from the balcony? Ha! Shirking his duty!"

"Quiet, you fool! Use your eyes. Do you see what I see?"

Claudius and Titus both looked down. Claudius's feet were protruding beyond the hem of the drapes. He drew them back, but it was too late.

Footsteps approached. The drapes were pulled aside.

Titus braced himself. Next to him, Claudius dropped, quivering, to his knees. He began to babble, unable to speak because of his stutter, then covered his face with his arms and let out a shriek.

The soldiers drew back. If they were amused or startled, their emotionless faces did not show it. Having served Caligula, thought Titus, there was probably not much that could shock or titillate them.

The small company of Praetorians threw back their shoulders and stiffly saluted. "Hail, Dominus!" they shouted in unison.

Claudius slowly lowered his arms. He blinked and wiped the drool from his chin. "What did you c-c-call me?"

Titus helped him to his feet. Claudius was so shaky that he could barely stand. He gave a start when more Praetorians entered the room, but the men kept their distance, drew to attention, and saluted.

"Hail, Dominus!"

Whispering a prayer of relief, Titus reached up to touch the fascinum, but it was not there. At such a moment—a moment he would never forget, a moment he would talk about to his children and their children—he should have been wearing the fascinum of the Pinarii. What a fool he had been to spurn the amulet and give it to Kaeso! What a fool he had been not to trust in the gods and in his own good fortune! One moment he had been plunged in despair, a humiliated subject at the mercy of a mad emperor, and then, in the blink of an eye, he found himself standing next to his late father's dear cousin, his own friend and confidant, the new emperor of the world.

Titus backed away from Claudius, leaving the emperor alone on the balcony. He joined the soldiers and bowed his head respectfully.

"Hail, Dominus!" he shouted.

A.D. 47

"What do you think, father?" whispered Titus Pinarius.

He stood in the vestibule of his house on the Aventine, before the rows of niches that housed the wax effigies of his ancestors. Among them was the death mask of his father, which had been cast in Alexandria. Its placement in the vestibule, along with all the other effigies, had been among their first duties when Titus and Kaeso moved into this house.

Titus was wearing the trabea he had inherited from his father. He held the elegantly carved ivory lituus that had been in the family for generations. At twenty-four—the same young age at which his father had been inducted—Titus had become an augur, thanks to the sponsorship of his cousin, the emperor Claudius. Now, at twenty-nine, Titus was an experienced and highly respected member of the college. Chrysanthe, noting that the saffron-stained wool with its broad purple stripe had begun to fade a bit, had recently suggested that Titus acquire a new trabea, but he would not hear of it. Instead, the best fullers in Roma had thoroughly cleaned it and applied fresh dye so that the garment was as soft and bright as the first day his father wore it.

Titus gazed at the effigy of his father—it was a good likeness, just as Titus remembered him—and he felt that his father approved. "When I wear this trabea, I honor the gods," Titus said quietly, "but I also honor you, father."

He felt a twinge of guilt, and it was almost as if his father had spoken aloud: *But where is your brother, Kaeso? He should be here, as well.*

Titus could not remember the last time his brother had stood with him in this vestibule and paid homage to their ancestors. As soon as he could after the incident with Caligula—about which no one ever spoke—Kaeso had moved out of the house. He had taken the fascinum with him, despite Titus's request that they share it again, but he had been happy to leave the wax effigies with Titus; Kaeso seemed to care nothing at all about their ancestors, not even about their father. Kaeso never sought any favors from

Claudius, and spurned Titus's repeated suggestions that he, too, should become an augur, or secure some other respectable position worthy of his patrician status. Instead, Kaeso sold to Titus his half of their interests in the Alexandrian grain trade, saying he had no desire for possessions. What had become of Kaeso's share of the family fortune? Apparently he had dispersed it among fellow members of his cult, of whom there were more than Titus would have thought in Roma. Kaeso and Artemisia were living in a squalid apartment in the Subura. Kaeso seemed unconcerned that he had descended into poverty, and his behavior and beliefs had become more bizarre with each passing year.

"You look splendid!" said Chrysanthe, joining Titus in the vestibule to see him off. In her arms she carried their newborn son, Lucius. The boy had a remarkably full head of hair for an infant and bore a striking resemblance to his grandfather.

To stand before the image of his father, dressed in his father's trabea, with his wife and new son beside him—this seemed to Titus as fine a moment as a man could hope for. Why had Kaeso turned his back on a proper life? Kaeso and Artemisia did not even enjoy the blessing of a child, and apparently this was not by chance but by choice. "Why bring a new life into such a foul world," Kaeso had once said to him, "especially when this world is about to come to an end?" That had been another of their conversations that did not go well.

"What sort of augury will you perform today?" asked Chrysanthe. "Some public event with the emperor present?"

"No, nothing like that. It's a request for a private augury. A family matter, I imagine. The house is over on the Esquiline."

"Will you take the sedan?" She referred to the newly fashionable conveyance carried by slaves in which the occupant sat upright, rather than reclining as one did in an old-fashioned litter.

"No. It's a beautiful autumn day. I'll walk."

"You should take one of the slaves for a bodyguard."

"No need. I'll go alone."

"Are you sure? Walking down to the Forum is one thing, but through the Subura—"

"No one interferes with an augur going about his official duties," Titus assured her. He kissed his wife and his son and set out.

In fact, he had chosen to go alone because he wished to pay a call without the risk that his wife would find out about it later from a loose-lipped slave. On his way to his appointment on the Esquiline, he was going to visit Kaeso.

Passing by the Circus Maximus, Titus ducked inside to have a look at the large-scale refurbishments that had been finished just in time for the recent Secular Games. Among many other improvements, the tufa barriers at the starting area had been replaced with marble and the conical, wooden posts at each end of the spine with pillars of gilded bronze. Only a few chariot drivers were practicing on this day, putting their horses through easy paces around the huge track. How different it was to see the place empty, instead of filled to capacity with eighty thousand cheering spectators.

Crossing the Forum, he wore his trabea proudly and nodded to acquaintances in their togas, and paused for a moment to watch the Vestal virgins on their way to the temple of the sacred hearthfire.

Beyond the Forum, a neighborhood of respectable shops and eateries quickly gave way to increasingly less-reputable venues. Dogs and children played in the narrow streets outside gambling dens, taverns, and brothels. Tall tenements shut out the sunlight. The stifled air grew thick with an assortment of unpleasant odors that Titus could not remember ever smelling on the airy slopes of the Aventine.

He found the five-story tenement where Kaeso lived. The place looked as if it might fall down at any moment. A long section of one wall, made of crumbling brick and mortar, was propped up with wooden planks. The wooden stairway inside was rickety and missing some of the steps. Listening to the building creak and groan around him, Titus cautiously ascended to the uppermost floor and tapped on a thin door.

Kaeso opened the door. He was bearded now and wore a tunic so threadbare that Titus could see the fascinum through the cloth. The necklace upon which it hung was made of twine, not gold.

Kaeso greeted Titus politely but without much warmth. "Come in, brother," he said.

Once inside, Titus shook his head, unable to conceal his dismay at the squalor of Kaeso's living conditions. Sleeping mats were crowded together on the floor. Gathered in the next room were several disreputable-looking men and women whom he could only assume were sharing the apartment. The members of Kaeso's cult seemed to celebrate poverty, living communally and indiscriminately sharing what little they possessed.

One of the strangers, a white-bearded man in a tattered robe, joined them. His eyes fixed on Titus's trabea. "This fellow is a brother? An augur?"

Kaeso smiled. "No, brother, he's not one of us. This is my twin, Titus Pinarius."

The stranger gave Titus another look and laughed. "Well, I should have known! Yes, I see the resemblance now. Shall we give you some time alone, then? The brothers and sisters will leave you for a while."

The men and women shambled out of the apartment. To Titus, each one looked shabbier and more disheveled than the last. The stairway creaked under their weight.

"Do we look that different now?" said Kaeso, when they were alone. Certainly, to a casual observer, the twins no longer resembled each other as closely as they once had. Kaeso had long hair and an unkempt beard and did nothing to make himself presentable, while Titus, conscious of the public nature of his work and fastidious by nature, was shaved by his barber daily and was regularly groomed by his slaves at the public baths. When was the last time Kaeso had visited the baths? Titus wrinkled his nose.

Kaeso sensed his disapproval. His tone was sharp. "So, brother, why have you come to see me?"

Titus was equally sharp. " 'Brother,' you call me? It seems you've found others more worthy of being called your brother." When Kaeso made no answer, Titus regretted his harsh tone. "Does there have to be a reason for me to visit you?"

"Brother, we see each other so seldom, I suspect you must have some cause to be here."

Titus sighed. "In fact, I do have a reason. I suppose it's too much to ask that you keep this to yourself. The decree will become public soon enough, but I'd rather it didn't get out that I gave anyone advance notice."

"What are you talking about?"

"Do you still call yourself a follower of Christ?"

"It's not what I call myself. It is what I am."

Titus shook his head. "You must know how much trouble your people have been causing in the city. Last month there was a riot in one of the Jewish neighborhoods—"

"Caused by the intolerance of certain Jews who do not approve of those among them who follow Christ."

"All this squabbling among the Jews! Can Jews do nothing else? In Jerusalem, people say there are stonings every day, because these Jews slaughter each other over the least religious disagreement. If indeed any of them can be called religious, since they refuse to acknowledge the gods—"

"The Jews worship the one and only god, as do I and the other followers of Christ."

"But if you are not a Jew, Kaeso, how can you be a Christian?"

"Brother, I have explained all this to you before. While there are some who argue to the contrary, it is my belief that a follower of Christ does not need to be a Jew, and therefore does not need to be circumcised."

Titus winced. "Don't tell Claudius that. He's convinced that all this fighting is strictly a matter of internecine squabbling among the Jews, with no Romans involved. That's why he's decided to ban the Jews from the city. That's what I came to tell you."

"What?" Kaeso was aghast. "Where does he expect them to go?"

"Back to Judaea, I suppose. Let them take with them all this squabbling about one god and circumcision and Christ, and leave the good people of Roma in peace."

"Why are you telling me this, Titus?"

"Because I would hate to see you and your wife mistakenly rounded up and deported to Judaea, you fool! Which just might happen, if you insist on spouting impious ideas and keeping company with fanatical Jews."

"But surely if I offer proof of my Roman citizenship—"

"That should be enough to protect you. Or you can always demonstrate that you haven't been circumcised," Titus added, with a shudder of disgust. He looked sidelong at his brother. "You aren't . . . circumcised . . . are you, Kaeso?"

Kaeso raised an eyebrow. "No, brother. In that respect, we are still identical."

Whether it was intended to or not, the remark recalled to Titus their audience with Caligula. He could think of nothing more to say. It was Kaeso who broke the uncomfortable silence.

"Thank you for telling me, Titus. At least I can warn some of my Jewish brothers about the emperor's intentions and give them time to prepare. It may lessen their hardship."

"I thought you welcomed hardship." Titus surveyed the squalid surroundings—the filthy sleeping mats, the threadbare coverlets, the scraps of food on the floor, a cracked clay lamp that smelled of rancid oil.

Kaeso shrugged. "In the kingdom of the wicked, it is inevitable that men must suffer—for a little longer, anyway."

"Please, Kaeso, don't start talking about the end of the world again."

"It's not too late for you, Titus—if you act quickly. The end is very near. Christ taught that his second coming would be sooner rather than later, and to those who have eyes to see, the signs of the approaching end of days are all around us. The veil of this suffering world will be ripped away. The Heavenly City will be revealed. If your so-called science of augury and that useless stick you carry had any power at all, you would see this yourself."

"Don't insult me, Kaeso. And don't insult the gods. I came here as a favor to you. I may no longer think of you as my brother, but I honor the memory of my father, and you are my father's son—"

With a high-pitched squeal, a rat scurried out of the bedding and over Titus's feet, so quickly that he didn't have time to jump back. His heart leaped to his throat. He had had enough.

"I have to go now, Kaeso."

"Off to perform an augury? Every time you deceive others by waving that stick and counting birds, you do the work of Satan."

Titus could barely contain his anger. Why had he bothered to come? He turned his back on Kaeso and left without saying another word.

The house where he had been called to perform an augury was on a quiet street in one of the better parts of the Esquiline Hill. Like many Roman houses, this one presented little more than a blank wall to the street, but the entrance was quite elegant, with white marble steps and an elaborately carved door. Titus had been promised a substantial fee, and it looked as if the occupant could well afford it.

But, from the moment he stepped inside, Titus felt uneasy. The slave who opened the door for him gave him a wolfish leer, which hardly seemed appropriate, then vanished. The vestibule had no niches for the ancestors, but instead displayed a small shrine to Venus with a little statue of the goddess surrounded by smoking incense. Peering into the house from the vestibule, Titus caught a glimpse of a laughing girl as she ran across the atrium. The girl was blond and almost naked, wearing only a sort of loincloth about her hips.

He was left alone in the vestibule for what seemed a long time. At last a female slave arrived, saying she would escort him to her mistress. Titus was almost certain it was the same girl he had seen run across the atrium, now attired in a sleeveless blue tunica that fitted her rather tightly and left most of her legs exposed.

He followed the girl, not sure what to think. They passed through a beautifully furnished room decorated with statues of Eros and Venus. The wall paintings depicted stories of famous lovers, and some of the images were quite explicit. The slave led him down a long hallway, past several closed doors. From the rooms beyond, Titus heard what could only be the sounds of people making love—sighs, groans, whispers, a slap, and a high-pitched giggle.

He had been told that this was a private residence. Could he possibly have arrived by mistake at a brothel?

"This is the house of Lycisca, is it not?" he asked the girl.

"It certainly is," she said, leading him into a dimly lit room decorated in shades of orange and red. "That is my mistress's name. And here she is."

Amid the deep shadows and the amber glow of lamps, reclining on an elegant couch, dressed in a gown so sheer that it appeared to be made of gossamer, was the emperor's wife.

Titus was speechless. He had seen Messalina occasionally over the years, but always in the presence of her husband and usually at some official event. Claudius's sudden elevation had been followed a month later by the birth of their son, Britannicus, and since then Messalina had presented herself as a model Roman wife and mother, doting on her child, wearing modest stolas, presiding at the religious rites that celebrated motherhood, and comporting herself at the games and in the circus in a manner above reproach. So restrained was her demeanor that people had ceased to gossip about the difference in age between Claudius and Messalina. Though still in her twenties, she was the exemplar of a staid Roman matron.

The woman who lounged on the couch before Titus seemed to be a very different person. Her face had been made even more beautiful by the application of subtle cosmetics. Her hair was swept into a vortex atop her head, baring completely her long white neck, which was adorned with a silver necklace hung with tiny pearls. Larger pearls hung from the silver clasps on her earlobes, and the silver bangles at her wrists made a kind of music when she picked up a wine cup. Her gown covered her body with a silvery sheen, concealing nothing.

Sharing the couch with Messalina was someone else Titus recognized—indeed, almost anyone in Roma would have recognized Mnester, who had been Caligula's favorite actor and had continued to enjoy imperial favor under Claudius. The fair-haired Greek was a ubiquitous figure at banquets and public ceremonies. With his bright blue eyes and Apollo-like features, his chiseled torso and long, elegant limbs, Mnester was probably more famous for his good looks than for his theatrical skills, though Titus had once seen him perform a memorable Ajax. On this occasion the actor wore nothing but a loincloth that appeared to be made of the same sheer fabric as Messalina's gown. The two of them reclined head to head and passed the wine cup back and forth. They both appeared to have drunk quite a bit of wine already.

Unnerved by the way the two of them openly stared at him without speaking, Titus felt obliged to say something. "Domina," he began, addressing the empress formally, but she cut him off at once.

"Lycisca. That's my name in this house."

"Lycisca?"

"I was inspired to take the name when I saw Mnester perform in a play about Actaeon. Did you see that performance, Titus?"

"I don't think so."

"But you must know the story. Actaeon the hunter with his pack of hounds came upon Diana bathing in a pool in the woods. The virgin goddess didn't like having a mortal see her naked, and didn't want him bragging about it. So, to keep Actaeon quiet, she turned him into a stag. She didn't intend what happened next. In the blink of an eye, the hunter became the hunted. The dogs fell upon Actaeon in a frenzy and tore him to pieces. I always thought that was a bit harsh, that a fellow should be destroyed just because he saw a goddess naked. You'd think Diana might have invited him to bathe with her instead, especially if Actaeon was as young and handsome as all the statues show him to be—or as handsome as Mnester, who drew tears from the audience with his performance. Even my husband wept."

"And the name Lycisca?" said Titus, trying not to stare at the way Messalina's breasts rose and fell while she spoke, causing the sheer fabric to appear transparent one moment, opaque the next.

"Lycisca was the leader of Actaeon's hunting pack, a half-wolf, half-canine bitch. Under this roof, you must call me nothing else."

"But why would you call yourself such a thing?"

"Let's hope you never find out, Titus Pinarius! Now come here and join us on the couch," she said, patting a spot between them, "and share some of this fine Falernian wine."

"I came here to perform an augury."

Messalina shrugged. "It seemed the best way to get you here. Sorry, but we have no use for your lituus today. Perhaps you possess some other staff that might be of use to me?"

Her intention was all too clear. Titus felt an impulse to turn and leave the room at once. He felt another impulse, equally strong, to pause and consider the opportunity that was being offered to him, curious to see where it might lead. He was not opposed to enjoying a bit of sexual pleasure when it came his way; every man succumbed to temptation now and then, though not usually with the emperor's wife. Titus stalled for time by asking a question.

"There are others in this house; I heard a lot of moaning and groaning through the doors. What sort of place is this?"

"It's not a brothel, if that's what you're thinking!" Messalina laughed. "And the women here are not prostitutes. Some of the most high-born women in Roma come to this house, to enjoy a degree of freedom they cannot exercise elsewhere."

"And the men who come here?"

"They are the sort of men whose company gives pleasure to those high-born women. Most of them are young, handsome, virile. Men like you, perhaps."

"You flatter me, Messalina."

"Lycisca!"

"Very well: Lycisca. But it occurs to me that if I were to stay here much longer, I might commit an act that could be construed as disloyal, not just to my emperor but to my cousin, a man who has been a good friend to me."

Mnester snorted. "That means he's afraid of being caught."

That was true, but it was not the entire truth. Certainly, Titus felt a quiver of apprehension, considering the consequences that might arise from betraying the emperor's trust, but he also felt genuinely grateful to Claudius, and even admired him, despite his flaws. As emperor, the old fellow had proven to be a disappointment to many people; he had ordered numerous executions and often showed poor judgment, and was said to be easily led by those around him, most notably Messalina and his trusted freedman Narcissus. But all in all, most people agreed Claudius, doddering as he might be, was an improvement over the cruelties of Tiberius and the madness of Caligula. Certainly Titus thought so; Claudius had done a great deal to help him and his family, and had never harmed them.

"The consequence you should worry about is the consequence of disappointing *me*," said Messalina. "Does the name Gaius Julius Polybius mean anything to you?"

"The literary scholar and friend of the emperor who was executed for treason?"

"That was the official charge. The fact is, Polybius stood right where you're standing, and refused to do what I wished. Later, I told my husband he had made unseemly advances and I insisted that he be punished."

"Surely Polybius protested his innocence?"

"When it comes to a choice between believing me or believing anyone else—including even you, Titus Pinarius—my dear husband will side with me every time. We can put it to the test, if you insist; but do you really want to risk suffering the fate of Actaeon? Think how much more enjoyable it would be to lie beside me on this couch and sip a bit of wine."

"It's very good wine," said Mnester, raising the cup in invitation.

Torn by indecision, Titus continued to hesitate.

Mnester laughed. "I understand your dilemma, friend. I tried to resist her myself, at first—to no avail. Like you, my fear of offending Claudius outweighed my desire for Lycisca, desirable as she is. She made promises; she made threats; she used all her seductive wiles. Still I refused. Then, one day, Claudius summoned me for a private meeting, just the two of us. He told me that his wife was complaining that I had refused to perform for her, and that this had made her very unhappy. He ordered me in no uncertain terms to do whatever she demanded. 'Must I submit to *anything* she asks?' I said. 'Yes, anything!' So here I am, merely doing my emperor's bidding."

"But Claudius couldn't have known what you were talking about! He couldn't approve of this."

"No? Most husbands give themselves the freedom to seek pleasure outside their marriage, and some husbands are enlightened enough to allow their wives the same freedom, especially if the wife is much younger and possessed of strong appetites, and has already produced a healthy heir."

Little Britannicus would be close to seven years old now, thought Titus. There was nothing maternal in Messalina's appearance at this moment. "Are you suggesting that Claudius wouldn't object if I were to join you? I hardly think he would agree to such a thing if I asked him."

"Not if you asked him explicitly, and performed the deed under his nose, giving him no way to retain his dignity. That's not how the game is played. It all happens with a wink and a nod, and out of sight, don't you see? The important thing is that Messalina should be happy. Don't you want to make her happy, Titus?" Mnester moved closer to Messalina and slipped his fingers inside the sheer gown, cupping his hand around one breast, squeezing it so that the nipple pressed against the fabric. Messalina sighed. "She's very responsive," whispered Mnester. "I've never made love to another woman like her. You really owe it to yourself to join us, Titus."

The last of Titus's resistance faded. They were both young and beautiful and appeared to be completely without inhibitions. The duty would hardly be onerous, as long as Titus could keep his thoughts from leaping to all the fearsome outcomes that might ensue. He was suddenly extremely aroused. Could it be that the element of danger, even more than Messalina, was exciting to him?

"Well, if I really have no choice," he muttered, taking a step forward. "And if Claudius does not object," he added, not believing this lie for a moment. He soon found himself between the two of them, no longer standing but horizontal. The couch was firm, the cushions soft. They took turns refilling the cup with wine and putting it to his lips. They pulled off his shoes and his trabea, and undid the loincloth underneath. Warm hands stroked his flesh. Someone was kissing him—he was not sure which, but the lips were soft and pliant, the tongue eager. It was Messalina who kissed him. Mnester was doing something with his mouth elsewhere. Messalina pulled back so that Titus could see.

"Isn't he beautiful?" she whispered. "I love him and I hate him for the same reason—because he's prettier than I am!" From somewhere she produced a thin leather whip with an ivory handle. With a crack that made Titus jump, she wielded it with surprising strength against Mnester's broad shoulders. He moaned but did not stop what he was doing. If anything, he performed more avidly, making Titus writhe with pleasure.

"Mnester is so pretty, even Claudius has been known to kiss him after a particularly fine performance," said Messalina. "Do you know, I think he's the only man my husband has ever kissed. Claudius has no interest in either men or boys, the silly old fool!"

Messalina kissed Titus again, taking his breath away. "And what interests you, Titus Pinarius? No, don't answer. Between the two of us, Mnester and I will discover everything that gives you pleasure."

After everyone had been satisfied, and satisfied again, there was a long, languid hour of utter indolence as the three of them lay close together, naked and silent and drained of desire.

It was Messalina who finally spoke. "Don't you have a brother, Titus?"

He was almost dozing. It took him a moment to answer. "Yes."

"A twin brother?"

"Yes."

"I thought so. I remember meeting the two of you when you first came to Roma. I could tell you apart, though. I knew *you* were the playful one."

"You were certainly right about that!" said Mnester sleepily. Titus smiled, enjoying the praise.

"But one never sees him about. He's still alive, isn't he, your twin brother?"

"Yes."

"And still in the city?"

"Yes." Titus shifted uneasily. He was wide awake now.

"Then where are you hiding him, Titus? You must bring him to meet me. One of you is delightful; two of you would be divine. Can you imagine, Mnester? Identical twins."

Mnester made a growling sound.

Titus squirmed a bit, not liking the drift of the conversation. "Actually, we're not as alike as we used to be. Kaeso . . . doesn't look after his appearance. He's rather unkempt these days."

"A wild man? All the better!" Messalina purred. "I can catalog the differences and similarities between the two of you."

Titus was now acutely uncomfortable, reminded for the second time that day of his long-ago audience with Caligula. That occasion had been a torment, the stuff of nightmares. Today's tryst, equally unexpected and to some extent coerced, had delivered him to a state of bliss. It was a curious thing, how the same acts, resulting in the same physical release, could bring either misery or joy, depending on the circumstances and the people involved.

Messalina was quiet for the moment, and Titus deliberately tried to think of other things.

"At the Secular Games," he said, "That's where it was."

"What are you talking about?" said Messalina.

"That's where I saw Mnester play Ajax, at one of the plays put on during the Secular Games last summer. I've been trying to remember ever since I stepped into this room and recognized him. I could remember the performance, but not the venue."

"At least I was memorable," murmured Mnester.

"More than memorable," said Titus. "You were brilliant. I believed every moment that you were the world's greatest warrior, wearing that magnificent armor. When Athena put you under a spell, I really thought you were sleepwalking. And when you woke up covered in blood and realized you'd killed a herd of sheep instead of your enemies, well, I had to laugh and shudder at the same time. And your suicide scene—truly, you had me in tears."

Mnester made a contented noise.

"Now that I think of it," Titus went on, "the whole festival was remarkable. Everything about the Secular Games was first-rate—the gladiator matches, the races, the plays, the banquets, the concerts in the temples. The panther-hunt in the Circus Maximus—that was spectacular! Though I think I was even more impressed by the Thessalian horsemen, the way they drove that herd of bulls in a stampede around the track, then dismounted and wrestled them to the ground. Amazing stuff! I think those games were the highlight of Claudius's reign so far. And why not? They say the Secular Games are held only once in a lifetime, and these marked the eight hundredth anniversary of the founding of the city, quite a grand occasion—"

He stopped abruptly. Mnester was kicking him under the thin coverlet. He turned to see that Mnester was frowning and shaking his head, as if to warn Titus away from the subject.

But it was too late. Messalina sat upright and crossed her arms. Her pretty face was twisted by a vexed expression. "The Secular Games—that was where *she* made her move!"

"She?" said Titus.

"Agrippina, Claudius's niece. The bitch!"

Mnester cringed and shifted toward the far side of the couch. "Now you've set her off," he whispered.

"It was during the Troy Pageant," Messalina said. "Were you there that afternoon in the Circus Maximus, Titus? Did you see?"

"The Troy Pageant? No, I missed that." Watching patrician boys dressed up as Trojan warriors perform maneuvers on horseback was a pastime he considered more suitable for doting mothers and grandparents.

"Then you missed Agrippina's triumph. I was there, of course, with Claudius and little Britannicus in the imperial box. Before the pageant commenced I stood with Britannicus and we waved to the crowd. There was hardly any applause at all. What were people thinking, to pay so little honor to the wife, and more especially to the son of the emperor? Eventually I sat down, thoroughly disgusted.

"In the box with us was Agrippina. Claudius invites her to everything. He says it's his duty as her uncle, since both her parents are dead and Agrippina is a widow again, raising her son alone. After I sat, Claudius called on her to stand, along with that spotty-faced brat of hers, little Nero. Numa's balls! I couldn't hear myself think over the applause and the cheering. It went on and on. Why? All I could think was that people had been reading that insipid memoir of hers, in which she paints such a puffed-up portrait of herself and all her suffering. Have you read it, Titus?"

"No, I haven't," he said. Strictly speaking, this was true, but Titus knew most of the stories in Agrippina's book because his wife had read it. Chrysanthe had been greatly inspired by the tale of a woman born into privilege but forced by Fate to fend for herself and her young one. At bedtime, after finishing a chapter, she had breathlessly repeated the stirring details for Titus's edification.

Messalina clearly had a different impression of Agrippina's story. "You'd think she was Cassandra at the burning of Troy, the way she goes on about her woes. Daughter of the great Germanicus and an irreproachable mother, both struck down in their prime—well, everyone's parents die sooner or later. Sister of Caligula, who turned against her, confiscated her possessions, and exiled her to the Pontine Islands, where she was forced to dive for sponges to support herself. Of course she doesn't mention her incest with Caligula, or the fact that she plotted to do away with him. Widowed twice and forced to raise the Divine Augustus's one and only great-great-grandson all by herself—though the suspicious death of her last husband left her very wealthy indeed. Poor, long-suffering Agrippina! Her campaign to endear herself to the people certainly seems to be working, to judge by their reaction at the Troy Pageant. And once the cheering started, the spotty-faced brat stepped in front of his mother and began turning this way and that, smiling and making gestures to the crowd—what do you actors call it, Mnester, 'milking' the audience for applause?"

Mnester grunted, trying to stay out of the conversation.

"Then Agrippina announced that Nero would be participating in the Troy Pageant, despite the fact that he was only nine and the other boys were all older, and down he went to put on his mock armor and take up a wooden sword and mount his pony. More cheering! Though I must admit, for a nine-year-old, he handled himself rather well on horseback."

"Born to ride," muttered Mnester.

Messalina snorted. "What a little showman! Precocious, Claudius calls him, as if that were a compliment. Some people find his affectations charming; I think there's something repulsive about the boy. And about his mother as well. Parading one's sorrows in public and seeking accolades from the mob is terribly vulgar, don't you think?"

Her gaze demanded a response. Mnester gave Titus another surreptitious kick, and Titus vigorously nodded his head.

"It's so obvious what the scheming vixen has in mind," said Messalina. "She thinks her little Nero should be the next emperor."

"Surely not," said Titus.

"Claudius isn't getting any younger, and Nero will reach his toga day ahead of Britannicus, and the brat *is* a direct descendant of Augustus. Of course, so was Caligula, and we all know how that ended."

"Do you really think Agrippina is thinking that far ahead?"

"Of course! The maudlin memoir, the way she grooms Nero and presents him in public, her fawning deference to Claudius, her calculated role as the virtuous widow—oh yes, with Agrippina everything is a means to an end. She and that whelp of hers need to be carefully watched."

Mnester rolled farther away. The coverlet slipped and exposed his meaty buttocks. Messalina abruptly picked up the whip with the ivory handle and gave him a cracking lash across his backside. "What are you smirking at?"

"I wasn't smirking, Lycisca!" Mnester hid his face in a cushion and his whole body trembled. Titus thought he was quaking with fear until he realized that the actor was trying to hide his laughter.

"You lout!" Messalina gave him another lash.

"Please, Lycisca!" cried Mnester, though to Titus it appeared that he made no effort to avoid the blow, but instead raised his hips and wriggled them a bit. So far, Messalina had spared Titus the whip, and though it was stimulating to see a naked, well-built fellow like Mnester take a thrashing, he did not care to receive one himself, not even from Messalina. Also, he was tired. If this was the prelude to more lovemaking, Titus was not sure he was up for it.

He need not have worried. The conversation had put Messalina in a foul mood, and Mnester's giggling had cooled her ardor. She told Titus to dress, and when he was again in his trabea, she handed him a little sack of coins.

"What's this?" he said.

"Your fee. Isn't it customary to pay an augur for his services?"

"But I performed no augury."

"Nonetheless, you performed. And your wife will be expecting you to bring home a little something to add to the household coffers, won't she? Now off with you."

"Will you want to see me again?" Titus asked.

"Who knows? No, don't pout! I hate it when men pout. You were a raging stallion, you were an elemental force of nature, you made me melt with ecstasy—honestly. Of course I'll want to see you again. But now get out!"

Titus left the house on the Esquiline with mixed feelings. An afternoon of debauched lovemaking was the last thing he had expected that day, and to be paid for his services made him feel a bit like a spintria, as people had taken to calling the male prostitutes of the city, adapting the word that Tiberius had coined. Still, his performance must have been superior, for Messalina, who clearly could have any man she wanted, said she would want to see him again.

The autumn day was short. Shadows were gathering; it was the hour for lighting lamps in the streets. Tripping lightly down the slope of the Esquiline and passing through the Subura, Titus passed the alley that led to the shabby tenement where Kaeso lived. What a dreadfully dull existence his brother led, compared to his own eventful life.

A.D. 48

Days passed, and then months, and Titus received no further summons from Messalina. He felt a bit piqued that she seemed to have forgotten him, but it was probably for the best. His afternoon as Lycisca's plaything had been a novel experience, but when he thought of the danger, it took his breath away. Besides, Titus was quite happy with his home life. No man had ever had a more loving wife than his Chrysanthe.

It was from Chrysanthe, of all people, that Titus heard the rumor that explained why Messalina had lost interest in him. "You won't believe what I heard from the neighbor's wife this morning," she said one day when Titus returned home from performing an augury at a temple on the Quirinal Hill.

"Try me."

"It's about the emperor's wife."

"Oh?" Titus attempted to look only mildly curious.

"Everyone knows she's a wanton woman."

"Really? I've always heard that Messalina is a steadfast wife and mother."

Chrysanthe made a rude sound. "That would describe the emperor's niece, Agrippina, but hardly his wife. You are clearly in the dark about that woman, husband, as is your friend the emperor. Of course it's no surprise that Messalina should have taken an occasional lover. Claudius is so much older, and based on the behavior of previous members of the ruling family, starting with the Divine Augustus's daughter, it seems these imperial women are incapable of behaving decently. But now Messalina may have gone too far. They say she's settled on a single lover, the senator Gaius Silius. That was how Silius got himself appointed consul this year, through Messalina's influence."

Titus had met the man. He was young for a consul, broad shouldered, undeniably handsome, vain, and ambitious—just the sort of man Messalina might take for a lover. "Go on."

"The shocking thing is, she calls Silius 'husband.' Can you imagine? As if Claudius didn't exist. Or soon might not exist."

"How could the neighbor's wife possibly know such a thing?"

"Slaves talk," Chrysanthe said. This was her standard explanation for the otherwise inexplicable transmission of certain rumors. She raised her eyebrows. "They say Claudius is so addled, he truly knows nothing about it."

Titus was briefly struck by the irony that Chrysanthe, who was young and had all her faculties, had never suspected Titus's infidelity. The omniscient slaves had stayed quiet about that, at least!

Titus frowned. Chrysanthe's news, if it was true, posed a dilemma. Could Messalina seriously be thinking of doing away with Claudius? Had she carried her playacting as Lycisca to a stage beyond harmless dalliance, to the point that she was considering murder and a palace revolt? If so, surely Titus had an obligation to warn his old friend and mentor about Messalina's seditious behavior, but how could he do so without compromising himself?

He would have to sleep on the matter.

Titus lost no sleep that night over the question of Messalina and her new "husband." He simply pushed the matter to the back of his mind. Why had he thought that some action was called for on his part? If even the neighbor's wife knew such a rumor, then everyone knew it, so it hardly fell to Titus to run to Claudius to warn him that his unfaithful wife might or might not be plotting against him.

The next morning, Titus received a summons to the imperial residence, in the form of a message from the emperor himself. The courier handed him a little wax tablet bound in elaborately decorated bronze plates and tied with a purple ribbon. Inside was written, in a crabbed hand that must have been that of Claudius himself, "Come, my young friend, quick as asparagus! I require a very private augury."

The reference to asparagus meant nothing to Titus, but he quickly put on his trabea and fetched his lituus.

It had been some time since Titus had been inside the imperial residence. As the courier led him through various rooms and corridors, he noticed changes in the decor—new mosaics on the floors, freshly painted images of flowers and peacocks on the walls, gleaming new statues of marble and bronze. Since Claudius cared little about decoration, Titus assumed it was the hand of Messalina that he saw at work.

He and the courier were made to wait in a room where two statues faced each other across a green marble floor. The marble statue of Messalina presented a familiar image. There were several statues of her around the city, all depicting her as a dutiful mother. Her body was wrapped in a voluminous stola with one fold draped over her head like a mantle. With a serene expression she gazed upon the naked baby Britannicus cradled in her arms.

Across from the Messalina was a bronze statue that Titus had never seen before, depicting a nude, heroic figure. Gold covered the naked flesh, while the Greek helmet cradled in the left arm, the upraised sword in the right hand, and the nipples on the muscular chest were chased with silver. The precious metals shone with fiery brilliance in the slanting rays of morning sunlight. The shoulders were so broad and the hips so narrow that one might have thought the artist had taken liberties, but Titus could attest that the portrayal was accurate. The inscription on the pedestal said AJAX, but the model had clearly been Mnester.

"Beautiful, isn't it?" said the courier.

"Stunning. It must have cost a fortune."

The courier smiled. "There's an interesting story about that. After Caligula was gotten rid of, the Senate voted to have every one of the coins that bore his likeness taken out of circulation and melted down. They never wanted to see his face again! The bullion sat for a long time, until the emperor gave instructions to use the silver and gold to decorate this statue. The emperor is certainly fond of Mnester, but they say it was his wife's idea to make this statue."

"Is that right?"

"She said it was proper to use Caligula's coinage to honor Caligula's favorite actor."

"I see." The two statues had been situated so that they faced each other across the room; the eyes of the two figures appeared to meet, as if exchanging knowing looks. It was cruel of Messalina, thought Titus, to flaunt her affair, even in this covert manner, in the very heart of the palace, under her husband's nose and in front of his visitors.

At last Titus was called for.

A thorough inspection was required of anyone entering the emperor's presence. Not even women or children were exempt from the indignity of being searched for weapons, and even the lowliest scribe was made to empty his stylus box. Titus had been through the process before and was ready to have his lituus examined and the folds of his trabea shaken. But on this day the examination was more thorough than ever. He was taken to a private room and politely asked by a hulking Praetorian to remove his trabea.

"Surely that's not necessary."

"It is," said the Praetorian.

"And if I refuse?"

"You're here at the emperor's request. This is the prescribed procedure. You can't refuse." The guard crossed his arms. Titus saw that the man had positioned himself to block the door. He felt a tremor of uneasiness.

As he removed the trabea, he was reminded of his first visit to the imperial residence, long ago, and the audience with Caligula. He drove the memory from his mind with thoughts of how Caligula had met his end, bleeding from thirty stab wounds. That was the reason, after all, for this indignity: Claudius had never forgotten the violent manner of his predecessor's death, and had no intention of meeting a similar fate.

Once upon a time, it had seemed that the emperor was invulnerable and untouchable, protected by the gods; the beloved Augustus and the detested Tiberius both lived to be old men and died in bed. But the violent end of Caligula changed all that. His murder proved that an emperor could be made to bleed and to die just like any other mortal. Caligula's assassination rid the world of a monster but set a terrible precedent; that was why Claudius, instead of rewarding the tribune Cassius Chaerea, eventually had the assassin put to death. No man could be allowed to kill an emperor and get away with it, not even by the man who had benefited most by becoming the next emperor.

At last the indignity was done with, and Titus was allowed to dress. Clutching his lituus, he was shown not into a formal reception room but into the emperor's private study. The shelves were crammed with scrolls and the tables covered with scraps of parchment. Maps, genealogical charts, and lists of magistrates were hung on the walls. The dust in the air made Titus sneeze.

Claudius was fifty-eight but looked older. His purple toga was askew, the way one sometimes saw togas on old men who could not look after their appearance and had no one to do it for them. There was a dark spot just above his chest; while Titus watched, Claudius clutched that bit of cloth and used it to wipe the spittle from the corner of his mouth. He seemed fretful and distracted, shuffling through piles of scrolls and glancing this way and that before looking at Titus.

"You must p-p-perform an augury for me, Titus."

"Certainly, Caesar." This was the title Claudius preferred to Dominus. "What is the occasion?"

"The occasion?" Claudius put his fist to his mouth and made a strange noise. "The occasion is a decision that I have to m-make."

"Can you tell me more?"

"No, not yet. But I can say this: someone will d-d-die, Titus. If I make the wrong decision, people will die, and for no reason. Or I could d-die. I could die!" Claudius gripped the folds of Titus's trabea. Titus saw fear in his cousin's eyes, such as he had seen on the day of Caligula's murder.

"People have died already, of course, because of *her*. Because I was an old fool and believed everything she told me. Polybius, with whom I spent many happy hours in this room, reading b-b-books no one but the two of us had ever heard of . . . and my good friend Asiaticus, whom I would have acquitted of treason except for her meddling . . . and young Gnaeus Pompeius, the last descendant of the triumvir, stabbed to death in his b-b-bed in the arms of a b-b-boy—all dead, because she wanted them dead! And when I think of the family members and old friends I've sent into exile, because of her scheming—oh, Titus, you are a lucky man, that you never crossed her!"

Titus nodded, his mouth dry.

"But before I say another word, you m-m-must take the auspices. I'm afraid to do it myself."

"But I still don't understand the purpose of the augury."

"You needn't know. The gods know my mind. They know what I intend to do. You must merely ask if they favor my intentions—yes or no. Here, we can do it in the garden off the study. There's a clear patch of sky to the north."

With Claudius standing behind him, Titus marked a section of the sky. For long, tense moments the two men watched in silence, until finally two sparrows appeared, flying from right to left. Titus was ready to declare that the auspice was negative, when from nowhere a hawk descended on the sparrows, seizing one of them in its talons. The hawk with its prey flew in one direction, the surviving sparrow in the other. From the empty sky a single sparrow feather drifted down and landed on the far side of the garden.

Behind Titus, Claudius sucked in his breath. "Without question, a favorable omen! Do you agree?"

Titus's heart pounded. "Yes," he finally said. "The gods favor your action. What do you intend to do, Caesar?"

Titus felt his cousin's hand on his shoulder and flinched. Claudius seemed not to notice his reaction. "Thank the gods for the Pinarii! I could always unburden myself to your father, and though the gods took him from me, they gave me you in his stead."

Claudius shambled across the garden and picked up the feather, groaning as he bent and straightened. There were flecks of blood on the vane. "For years, I've b-b-been an utter fool, allowing Messalina and her lovers to make a cuckold of me. I believed all her lies, accepted all her evasions, trusted her above all those who tried to warn me. But now the truth has finally c-c-come out, and it's worse than anything I could have imagined. Messalina has behaved like a whore. She kept a house on the Esquiline under an assumed name and she ran the place like a b-b-brothel, allowing other highborn women to meet their lovers there, staging all manner of orgies. They say that once she gathered prostitutes from the Subura and held a c-competition to see who could satisfy the most customers in a night—and she was the winner! Can you imagine, the wife of the emperor took p-p-payment to have sex with any man who wanted her, one after another! What would Great-Uncle make of such a thing?"

He turned to look at Titus. Titus could think of nothing to say.

"I see you're too shocked to speak, Titus. No words can express your outrage, I'm sure. And what could you possibly say that would bring me comfort? But I haven't told you the worst of it yet. Messalina has entered into a b-b-bigamous marriage with the consul Gaius Silius. They even held a ceremony, with witnesses, as if the marriage were a legal union, blessed by the gods. I suppose they intended to stage my funeral next!"

Titus at last found his voice. "But, Caesar, how can you know these things?"

Claudius's answer was the same as Chrysanthe's. "Slaves talk," he said. "And so d-d-do free men, under torture."

"Does Messalina know you've discovered her secrets?"

"A slave warned her. She fled to her house in the Gardens of Lucullus—the love nest she acquired from Asiaticus, when she tricked me into executing the poor fellow. Praetorians have surrounded the grounds. She awaits her fate."

"Gaius Silius?"

"Dead, by his own hand."

"And . . . her lovers?"

"Yes, her lovers. Her many, many lovers!" Claudius toyed with the feather, pulling his fingers down the shaft to tatter the vane. The blood on his fingertips he wiped on his toga, where the purple wool absorbed it without a trace. "Come with me, Titus. I need at least one p-p-person in the room whom I can trust."

One by one the lovers were paraded before Claudius to make their confessions and receive his judgment.

Claudius sat on a thronelike chair on a raised dais. Praetorian guards were stationed at either side of him and at various places around the room. Titus stood on the dais beside Claudius and next to one of the Praetorians, a hulking brute who stank of garlic. Physicians claimed that eating garlic gave a man strength, and to judge by the muscles on this specimen, they were right.

Claudius's most trusted freedman, Narcissus, oversaw the proceedings. He was a quintessential imperial bureaucrat, fussy about his appearance, snappish with underlings, wheedling but insistent with his master. As each of the accused men was shown into the chamber, it was Narcissus who read the charges and conducted the interrogation.

Some of the men complained that they had been blackmailed into submission by Messalina. Others openly admitted that they had sought her sexual favors. Some begged for mercy, while others said nothing. It made no difference; when the moment came for Narcissus to ask the emperor for his judgment, Claudius looked each man in the eye and declared, "G-g-guilty!"

Most of the men were citizens, and had the right to die by beheading, the fastest, least painful, and most dignified form of execution. But a few of the accused were foreign-born; they could expect to be beaten to death, strangled, or perhaps thrown to wild animals. There were also slaves among the accused, most of them from the imperial household but some belonging to outsiders; rather than charge them with committing adultery—the idea that another man's slave might have copulated with the emperor's wife was too scandalous to contemplate—Narcissus accused the slaves of colluding with Messalina and assisting her conspiracy. Their punishment would be crucifixion. *They'll die like Kaeso's so-called god, on a cross,* thought Titus, touching his breast and wishing he had the fascinum to protect him.

The number of Messalina's lovers was staggering, and the repetition of the process was numbing. Titus would gladly have fled, but he had no choice but to see and hear everything. His cousin wanted him to act as mute witness to an ordeal that was almost as painful and degrading for Claudius as it was for the accused.

Or was Claudius playing a cruel game with him? If Narcissus and his agents had uncovered Messalina's dalliances with all these other men, how had they failed to identify Titus? At any moment, Titus half expected to hear Narcissus call his name, to feel the hands of the garlic-stinking Praetorian upon him, and to be thrust before Claudius to beg for his life.

Could Claudius be that devious? He seemed to have become more simpleminded as he had grown older, but perhaps that was merely the ruse of a truly ingenious mind. Titus looked sidelong at his cousin, who was wiping a bit of drool from his mouth, and tried to imagine him not as the rather sad fool he appeared to be but as a master manipulator. Claudius not only had outlived virtually everyone else in his family but had managed to become emperor. Was his survival the result of blind chance, or careful design?

Yet if any proof of Claudius's blindness was required, surely it was the spectacle taking place before them, as one lover after another was produced to demonstrate just how unaware Claudius had been.

Narcissus called out the name of the next man to face judgment: "Bring forth Mnester!"

Titus's heart skipped a beat. Claudius groaned.

Mnester's golden hair was mussed and he wore only a brief, sleeveless sleeping tunic, as if he had just been pulled from his bed. His eyes were wide with fright as he peered around the room. Titus took a couple of steps back and to the side, concealing himself as best he could behind the hulking Praetorian. Had Mnester seen him already? Titus thought not. He held his breath.

Narcissus read the charges: numerous counts of adultery with the emperor's wife and taking part in a criminal conspiracy to kill the emperor.

Claudius was close to tears. "Mnester, how c-c-could you?"

"But, Caesar, you yourself ordered me to submit to her."

Claudius looked baffled. "Did I?"

"Do you not recall? I tried to resist her, and I begged you to take my side, but you ordered me to do whatever she commanded, no matter how degrading. You said those very words to me: 'You must do anything she asks.' And as a result you can see for yourself how I've suffered!"

Mnester lurched forward and dropped to his knees. Titus gave a jerk, for suddenly he was visible to Mnester, but the actor kept his face down and his eyes averted as he pulled his tunic over his head. He was not wearing a loincloth. Naked, he prostrated himself before Claudius, showing the lash marks across his broad back.

Mnester was racked by sobs. "Do you see how she mistreats me, Caesar? Many times, I wanted to come to you and complain, but I was too afraid of her. Afraid for my very life, Caesar!"

Mnester had not seemed very frightened when Titus had last seen him naked; indeed, the actor had seemed an eager participant in everything that had happened. But even though Titus saw through the lie, he was moved by the man's lament. Mnester was a superb actor, and this was the performance of his life. The tears that streamed from his eyes were real, and so were the fiery red lash marks across the rippling muscles of his back.

Claudius was unnerved. He put one hand to his mouth and shook his head. His eyes glistened with tears.

Mnester glanced up. Titus saw the flash of hope in his eyes. "Please, Caesar, I have been foully used, degraded, humiliated, made the plaything of a woman who had the power of life and death over me. Have pity on me, I beg you! Banish me from Roma, send me to the wilderness, but spare my life!"

"She used you, yes," muttered Claudius, "just as she used me."

Titus looked sidelong at Claudius and saw that his cousin was completely dazzled by the performance. Titus saw the contrast between the two men and at the same time he grasped the connection between them: the aging, hunched emperor gazed raptly at Mnester as if the handsome, prostrate figure before him were the idealized personification of his own suffering. Was this not the highest achievement an actor could attain?

Titus stepped farther behind the Praetorian, but not before Mnester's eyes met his. It was only a brief look, but Titus was certain that Mnester recognized him, and in the other man's eyes Titus saw his own doom. Mnester began to raise one hand, as if to point in accusation. Titus felt as if the floor lurched beneath him. His face turned hot and his heart pounded.

"Remember the auspices!" Titus whispered.

Claudius twitched his head to one side. "What's that?"

"Remember the auspices, Caesar. The gods demand justice."

Claudius slowly nodded his head. He called Narcissus to him and spoke in his ear. Narcissus crossed the room and spoke to the Praetorians at the door.

Mnester remained on the floor, his face and chest wet with tears but with the faint intimation of a smile at the corner of his mouth. It was the face of an actor at the end of a tragic play, exhausted by the role and still immersed in the cathartic moment, but ready to receive the accolades of the audience. He thought he had won Claudius's pardon.

In the next moment he was made aware of his mistake. Praetorians surrounded him. One of them produced a leather strap attached at both ends to an iron rod. While two men held Mnester to keep him from struggling free, the strangling device was slipped over his head. Only two twists of the rod were required to sufficiently tighten the strap. Mnester's face turned a vivid shade of red, then purple. His eyes bulged. Mucus erupted from his nose. His tongue protruded from his mouth. The only noise he made sounded disconcertingly like the squeaking of a mouse.

The man holding the rod gave it another full twist. Every part of Mnester's body convulsed, so violently that the Praetorians barely maintained their hold. Then Mnester went limp.

His body was dragged from the room. Narcissus called a slave to clean the floor where Mnester had emptied his bladder. The slave used Mnester's discarded sleeping tunic as a mop.

"Are there m-m-more?" said Claudius in a hollow voice.

"Yes," said Narcissus. "Several more."

Claudius shook his head. "No more today. I'm tired. And hungry."

"As you wish, Caesar. I'll see that your dinner is made ready."

"Cousin Titus will d-d-dine with me."

Titus suppressed a groan. "If you'd rather be alone—"

"Oh, no, I insist. Run along, Narcissus. We'll catch up." He turned to Titus. "Thank you, cousin."

"For what?"

"For helping me keep my nerve. I almost lost it. Mnester had to be p-p-punished."

"Still, Caesar, there was no need for you to witness the unpleasant-ness."

"No? Mnester betrayed me. He deserved to d-d-die. But his acting gave me great pleasure over the years. I owed it to him to witness his final performance."

At dinner, Titus was the only guest. He said little. It was Claudius who filled the silence as he rambled from one topic to another, from the mili-tary situation in Britannia—conquered but still undergoing pacification by the general Vespasian—to his anger at the Jews, and all the trouble their religious fanaticism was causing, not just in their homeland but in Roma and Alexandria and every other city where their numbers were sig-nificant.

Claudius seemed completely disconnected from the events of the day. Titus could think of nothing else. A part of him remained braced for some terrible surprise.

He kept seeing Mnester's face at the end. If Titus had said nothing, would Mnester still be alive? Titus had merely reminded Claudius of the auspices. Why did he feel a need to justify himself? Everyone else ma-nipulated Claudius to gain his own ends. Titus had done so to save his own life.

Narcissus announced that a messenger had arrived with news about Messalina.

"Yes, where is she?" said Claudius, his voice slurred by wine. "Why is she not here for d-d-dinner?"

Titus felt a sinking sensation.

Claudius continued to eat. Chewing on a chicken bone, he said, "Well, Narcissus?"

"Messalina is dead, Caesar."

Claudius sat back, looking baffled. He blinked a few times, gave a twitch of his head, then shrugged. He reached for his cup and drank more wine. He picked up another piece of chicken.

Narcissus waited, ready to be asked for more information. Claudius said nothing. Eventually, Narcissus cleared his throat and recounted the details. "Caesar's agents surrounded her apartments in the Gardens of Lucullus. Her slaves offered no resistance. She was given a knife and offered the opportunity to take her own life. She announced that she would do so, but she lacked the courage. When she faltered, one of Caesar's agents took the knife from her and finished the job."

Messalina, stabbed to death! Titus was stunned by the enormity of it.

Claudius took a bite of chicken and chewed for a long time, staring into the distance.

"Does Caesar have any further orders?" asked Narcissus.

"Orders? Yes. Tell the b-b-boy to bring more wine." He turned to Titus. "You are a good man, cousin. A man I can trust! Do you know, I think I shall make you a senator. Your grandfather was a senator, wasn't he? We lost a few senators today and they'll need to be replaced. How would you like that?" Claudius nodded thoughtfully. "I shall make you a senator on one condition: if I should ever think of m-m-marrying again, you must stop me. You will put it to a vote and have me stripped of my office. If I should ever so much as m-m-mention m-m-marriage, I give you and the other senators permission to kill me on the spot and put an old fool out of his misery!"

After dinner, Claudius bade Titus good night and retired.

The same courier who had fetched Titus earlier reappeared to escort him out of the imperial house. They passed through the room where Titus had waited. Something was different.

"The statues," he said. "Where are they?"

"What statues?" said the courier, looking straight ahead.

"The statues of Messalina and Mnester."

"I don't recall any such statues in this room," said the courier.

"But you told me that story, about how the coins of Caligula had been melted down. . . ."

The courier shrugged and quickened his pace.

Even the pedestals were gone, and the green marble floor beneath had been polished to show no trace. The images of Messalina and Mnester had vanished as if they had never existed.

A.D. 51

The weather was mild for mid-December. A crowd of dignitaries and members of the imperial household stood around the perimeter of the Auguratorium on the Palatine. The occasion was the fourteenth birthday of young Nero, the son of Agrippina, grandson of Germanicus, great-great-grandson of Augustus, and great-nephew and now adopted son of Claudius. Titus Pinarius was present, wearing his trabea rather than his purple-bordered senatorial toga and carrying his lituus. He was to perform the augury for the young man's toga day, his passage to manhood.

Chrysanthe was among the guests, looking beautiful as always and only slightly uncomfortable in the company of the Roman-born matrons, who would always think of her as an Alexandrian. She devoted most of her attention to their son, Lucius, who at four was deemed by Titus to be old enough and sufficiently well behaved to attend such a ceremony and watch his father at work.

While he waited to be called upon, Titus surveyed the crowd. Many of the women were dazzling in their finery, but none stood out more than Nero's mother. At thirty-six, Agrippina was still a strikingly attractive woman. Her hair was parted in the middle; long curls streamed like ribbons on either side and were gathered by a purple-and-gold fillet at the back of her head. Her stola was a garment of numerous layers and folds,

woven of a fabric of many colors. Her beaming smile showed her prominent canine teeth—a sign of good luck, many believed. Fortune had certainly smiled on Agrippina in recent years.

Despite his vow never to marry again after his humiliation by Messalina,
Claudius almost immediately married Agrippina. It seemed the widower
felt incomplete without a strong-willed and beautiful woman to manipulate
him. Claudius's choice of a bride had scandalized the city, since marriage
between an uncle and a niece was incest. To forestall the fears of the populace that some supernatural calamity might result, Claudius had called on
Titus to look for omens and precedents that favored his marriage to Agrippina, and Titus had obliged. Agrippina was grateful for this service. Titus's
prestigious role at this day's event was the latest proof of her favor.

Fortune had not always smiled on Agrippina. The untimely deaths of her
parents, her humiliating exile under Caligula, the loss of two husbands—
she had endured all these trials and emerged triumphant. She had even
outwitted the machinations of Messalina—for most people now agreed that
it was Agrippina and her son who had been threatened by the jealousy of
Messalina, and not the reverse. It was said that Messalina had once sent an
assassin to kill Nero in his crib, but the man had been frightened off by
a snake in the baby's bed—actually the skin of a snake, placed there by his
clever and vigilant mother. Agrippina had become a stirring exemplar of
Roman womanhood. She had survived every setback, and her marriage to
her uncle Claudius had made her the most powerful woman in Roma.

Also in attendance was the nine-year-old son of Claudius and Messalina, Britannicus. He was dressed in the old-fashioned long-sleeved tunic
still worn by many patrician boys. His hair was long and unkempt. He
seemed a bit shy and standoffish, observing the proceedings with a lowered brow and sidelong glances. What sort of fellow would he grow up to
be? wondered Titus, trying to imagine a combination of his wildly different parents. What must the boy's life be like these days, three years after
the terrible death of his disgraced mother? Claudius had once been a doting father, but it seemed to Titus that he now neglected the boy. No doubt
Britannicus reminded Claudius of Messalina. How did Claudius feel
about a son who looked so much like the woman who had made a fool of
him, and had been put to death on his orders?

Certainly Agrippina had no love for Britannicus. She had not only persuaded Claudius to adopt Nero, making him first in line of inheritance
ahead of Britannicus, but had arranged for Nero to be recognized as an
adult a full year earlier than was traditional—a young man's toga day was
usually between his fifteenth and seventeenth years—so that he could
begin accumulating the honors and rewards of a public career. This was
clearly in service to her agenda of elevating her son, but there was also a
sound political argument for advancing Nero as quickly as possible. As
long as Claudius had no adult heir, potential rivals might be encouraged
to plot against him. And if Claudius should die, an orphaned Britannicus
would be highly vulnerable, while Nero was just old enough, especially
with his mother behind him, to act as a plausible ruler. Also to his advantage was the fact that Nero was the direct descendant of the Divine Augustus.

Neglected though he might be, young Britannicus was not alone. With
him was his constant companion, a boy a year or so older, Titus Flavius
Vespasian, son of the general of the same name. Titus had been brought
up alongside Britannicus, with the same teachers and athletic instructors.
The boy's bright smile and outgoing personality presented a contrast to
Britannicus's withdrawn, almost furtive manner.

The elder Vespasian was also present, along with his wife, who held
their newborn son. In his early forties, Vespasian was a veteran of thirty
battles in the newly conquered province of Britannia. His victories had
earned him a public triumph in which young Titus had ridden alongside
him in the chariot, and he had been rewarded with a consulship, the highest office to which a citizen could aspire. With a large nose, a mouth too
small for his fleshy face, and a heavy, furrowed brow, Vespasian was not
handsome; he had the perpetual expression of a man straining to empty his
bowels. His family fortune had started with his father, a tax collector in
the province of Asia, but the Flavians were otherwise obscure. Behind his
back, members of the imperial court complained of Vespasian's uncouth
manners and flagrant social climbing. To Titus Pinarius, on the few occasions when they had spoken, Vespasian had seemed forthright and without pretense, as befitted a military man. It did not seem quite proper that
Vespasian should have brought his two-month-old infant to such a ceremony,

but clearly the general was eager to show the child off. To everyone who greeted him he insisted on introducing "the newest addition to the Flavians, my little Domitian."

Titus's gaze returned to the youth who was donning the toga of manhood that day. He found Nero to be quite charming and surprisingly self-possessed for his age. At fourteen, he was a connoisseur of painting and sculpture, wrote poetry, and loved horses. He was tall but had an ungainly physique. A boy's long-sleeved tunic had not been flattering to Nero's thick neck, stocky trunk, and bony legs; he looked better in his purple-and-gold toga. His blond hair glinted in the sunlight, and his flashing blue eyes were wide, taking in the scene. Nero enjoyed being the center of attention.

Standing beside him was the young man's adoptive father. Claudius looked more decrepit than ever. The poor fellow had never been the same after his discovery of Messalina's bigamy and the bloodbath that followed. Titus still felt a chill when he remembered how Claudius had expected Messalina at dinner on the very night that he ordered her death. And on the morning that followed, Claudius sent messages to some of the executed men inviting them to play dice, and complained when they didn't come. He sent petulant messages accusing them of staying abed and being too lazy to reply. "Sleepy-heads," he called them, forgetting that by his order they had lost their heads altogether.

On the other side of Nero stood his tutor, Lucius Annaeus Seneca, a bearded man in his forties, wearing a senator's purple-bordered toga. Seneca was an accomplished man of letters, famous for his many books and plays. Messalina had talked Claudius into exiling Seneca, but Agrippina had arranged for his return, and had charged Seneca with giving Nero the most refined education possible.

The ceremony commenced. When the time arrived for the taking of the auspices, all eyes turned to Titus. He began with a short speech about the subject of his augury, whose full name, since his adoption by the emperor, was Nero Claudius Caesar Drusus Germanicus.

"As many of you know, the name Nero comes from an old Sabine word meaning 'strong and valiant,' and those who have seen this young man perform on horseback and wield arms in the Troy Pageant know that he is worthy of his name," said Titus. The appreciative applause for this pretty turn of phrase was cut short by a sudden outburst of crying from Vespasian's newborn. Titus frowned. The baby's wailing grew louder, until at last his mother carried little Domitian away. Vespasian, who seemed unperturbed by the interruption, wriggled his fingers at the departing infant.

Titus loudly cleared his throat and proceeded.

With his lituus he marked a segment of the sky. At midwinter, with few birds in Roma, patience might be required for the observation, but almost at once Titus saw a pair of vultures. They were quite far away, circling above the private racetrack Caligula had built for himself beyond the Tiber on the Vatican Hill. Titus waited, hoping to see more, but eventually he felt the crowd grow restive. He declared the auspices well and truly taken and announced that they were very good. In fact, the auspices had been only mildly favorable, almost noncommittal. Claudius, standing behind him and able to see what Titus saw, would have known this, had he been watching; but when Titus glanced over his shoulder, he saw the emperor staring at the ground.

There were more speeches, and then Nero was called on to parade before the assembly wearing his toga. He did so with a swagger that was almost comical. (Titus was reminded of Messalina's derisive comment: "What a little showman!") No one laughed, though it seemed to Titus that Vespasian might have smirked; with his expression of perpetual constipation, it was hard to tell. At last the company retired to the imperial residence for the banquet, passing the armor of the Divine Augustus in the forecourt and the ancient laurel trees that flanked the massive bronze doors.

"Just how old is the emperor?" Chrysanthe asked Titus, after they had settled onto their couches and been served the first course of olives stuffed with anchovies. She was gazing at Claudius, who shared a couch with Agrippina across the room.

Titus calculated in his head. "Sixty-one, I think. Why do you ask?"

"When we first came to Roma ten years ago, I thought he was old then, but he was so much more alive. Remember how excited he was to show us the city? Now he seems withered, like a tree that's had its roots cut and might fall at any moment."

"All his drinking doesn't help," noted Titus as he watched a serving boy refill the emperor's cup. Chrysanthe was right. His cousin was more doddering than ever. What a contrast Agrippina presented. She was positively effervescent, smiling and laughing and entertaining everyone in earshot with a very witty anecdote, to judge by the laughter she elicited. Nero reclined on his own couch nearby and gazed at his mother adoringly.

While Titus watched, Agrippina gestured to Nero. Obeying her request, the young man pulled back a fold of his purple toga to bare his right arm. Coiled like a snake around his biceps was a golden bracelet. Agrippina's listeners nodded and made appreciative sounds.

"What's that about?" asked Titus.

"He's showing off his snake bracelet," explained Chrysanthe. "Half the children in the city wear a bracelet like that now, though not made of solid gold. Inside that bracelet is the snakeskin that scared off an assassin sent by Messalina when Nero was in his crib. He wears the bracelet to show gratitude and devotion to his mother, and they say the snakeskin still protects him. Do you think we should have such a bracelet made for little Lucius?" Their son was in another room with his nurse, eating with the other children.

"Perhaps," said Titus, though it occurred to him that a more appropriate talisman for his son would be the fascinum of their ancestors. Why had he allowed Kaeso to take it? Titus realized that he was clenching his teeth. He drove thoughts of his brother from his mind, refusing to let them spoil such a joyous occasion.

As the meal progressed and more wine flowed, guests began to move about the room, standing in small groups or sharing couches while they conversed. Titus worked his way to Nero's couch. Agrippina stood nearby, as did Seneca. Standing next to Seneca was a woman about half his age, his wife, Pompeia Paulina.

"Teach my son all the poetry and rhetoric and history you want, I told Seneca, but no philosophy!" Agrippina was saying. "All those notions about Fate and free will and the slippery nature of reality—perhaps they're amusing for people who have nothing better to think about, but they can be nothing but a handicap to a person like my son, who must be ready to assume such a heavy burden of responsibility."

"It's true," said Seneca. He had grown a beard in exile and kept it on his return; it made him look more like a philosopher than a senator. "Poetry gives consolation to the powerful—"

"While philosophy gives consolation to the powerless?" said Titus.

Seneca smiled. "Greetings, Titus Pinarius. Though I suppose I should address you as Senator Pinarius now."

"Or address him as augur; that's Pinarius's special calling, and the one he performed today was splendid," said Agrippina. "But you must excuse me while I attend to another matter. There's to be an entertainment later, and I'm told the flute player and the dancing girl have both gone missing."

Titus watched her leave, then turned to Seneca and his wife. "Speaking of entertainment, is it true that Nero will be singing a song which he composed especially for the occasion?"

"Of course not!" Seneca made a face. "Nero composed a song, to be sure; it's a meditation on the virtues of his great-great-grandfather, the Divine Augustus, entirely appropriate for the occasion. But the song will be sung by a young freedman, a trained performer."

"Is Nero a poor singer, then?"

Seneca and his young wife exchanged glances. He had married Paulina when she was very young and she had shared the years of his exile. Having no other student at hand, it was said that Seneca had taught his wife philosophy. Despite her youth, Paulina was probably the best-educated woman in Roma.

"Nero's voice is not . . . unpleasant," said Paulina. She was evidently being generous.

"But his talent as a singer is irrelevant," added Seneca. "It would never do for a son of the emperor to perform as a mere actor before an audience. The very idea is vulgar."

"Then I suppose I shall never have the pleasure of hearing Nero sing," said Titus. "Still, I'll look forward to hearing his composition. When it comes to writing, he certainly couldn't ask for a better teacher than you. I was present at the recent gathering where your play about Oedipus was read aloud. Such powerful language! Such unforgettable images!"

"Thank you, Senator Pinarius." Seneca beamed. "Nero also appreciated that play. His tastes are quite sophisticated. But he still requires instruction in matters of . . . propriety. The boy wanted to recite the role of Oedipus, if you can imagine that. The son of an emperor, playing the role of an incestuous parricide! I've tried to explain to him that emperors simply cannot be actors, yet he still talks about taking a part in the new play

I'm working on, about Thyestes. I hope to have it ready for a recitation during the upcoming festivities attending Nero's election to the consulship."

"Doesn't a consul have to be at least twenty years old?"

"Yes, but there is no law that says a man cannot be elected at fourteen and enjoy the privileges of a consul-elect until he reaches the age of twenty. I'm sure we can count on your vote to ratify his selection, Senator Pinarius?"

Titus nodded, acquiescing to this slippery bit of constitutional logic. Seneca was a politician after all, not just a philosopher.

"Anyway," Seneca went on, "during the play to celebrate his election, I can assure you the consul-elect will be in the audience, *not* on the stage."

Titus nodded. "A play about Thyestes, you say? Wasn't he the Greek king tricked into eating his own sons?"

Seneca was about to bite into a pastry, but lowered the delicacy from his lips. "Yes. Thyestes' brother, King Atreus, baked the boys in a pie, fed them to their unsuspecting father, then showed their heads to poor Thyestes. But Thyestes exacted a terrible revenge."

"As they always do in these Greek tales," added his wife. Paulina gave Titus a quizzical look. "Thyestes and Atreus were twins, they say. You have a twin brother, don't you, Senator Pinarius?"

Titus frowned. After a long spell of not thinking about Kaeso, twice within an hour his brother had been called to his mind. He changed the subject back to Seneca's work. "Oedipus and Thyestes—such grim stories."

"I draw inspiration from the old Greek playwrights, especially Euripides. Despite the antiquity of his subject matter, his outlook is remarkably modern; the darkness and violence of his stories resonate with present-day Romans. Then there is my own experience of life, which has not been without tribulation. I was forced into a premature retirement by Caligula, thanks to his insane suspicions. I was brought back to favor by Claudius, and then sent into exile again for eight years, thanks to Messalina's scheming. Now I'm back again, thanks to Agrippina, and I've been welcomed in the very heart of the imperial household. Agrippina is my deus ex machina, my Athena appearing at the last moment in the play, descending from the sky to restore harmony to the cosmos."

"The empress is your muse, then?"

"My savior, certainly." Seneca cocked his head. "And then, of course, there are dreams."

"Dreams?"

"As a source of inspiration. Do you not dream, Titus Pinarius?"

Titus shrugged. "Hardly ever."

"Perhaps that's a blessing. My dreams are very vivid, full of noise and blood and violence—louder and brighter and more startling than anything in the waking world. Sometimes I can scarcely stand my dreams. I wake in a cold sweat, then reach for the wax tablet at my bedside and scribble notes for a scene—Oedipus tripping blindly over the body of his mother, or Thyestes agape at the sight of his sons' severed heads."

Seneca raised an eyebrow. "Do you know, a dream has just come back to me. I'd forgotten it until this moment. I had it the night after Claudius told me I would have the honor of tutoring Nero. Odd, how one can forget a dream completely, and then it suddenly comes back. I dreamed I appeared at the imperial house, in this very room, ready for my first day, but when my young pupil turned to face me—it was Caligula! What a shock! And so nonsensical, since Nero is nothing like his uncle. Caligula was raised in army boots and had hardly any education, while Nero loves learning." Seneca shivered. "Did you ever meet Caligula face-to-face?"

"Only once," said Titus.

"Lucky you!"

Vespasian strolled over to join them. His wife, Domitilla, was beside him, still carrying the newborn Domitian, who had quieted down. Paulina left her husband's side to have a closer look at the baby.

"Did I hear you mention the departed Caligula?" Vespasian said.

Seneca eyed the general condescendingly. "Yes, I was telling Senator Pinarius a story about—"

"Who doesn't have a Caligula story to tell?" said Vespasian. The general was more used to talking than to listening. "I suppose my tale is pretty harmless compared to most. Caligula was emperor; I couldn't have been more than thirty—that's right, because my Titus had just been born—and I'd just been elected aedile. One of my responsibilities was keeping the city clean. I thought I was doing a pretty good job, until one day Caligula summoned me to meet him on a muddy little back road on the far side of the Aventine—not a paved road, mind you, but a narrow dirt alley behind some warehouses. He asked me why the street was so dirty. 'Because it's made of dirt?' I said." Vespasian laughed. "Caligula was not amused. He was furious. By Hercules, it's a miracle I didn't lose my head on the spot! He ordered his lictors to scoop up handfuls of mud and to cram it inside my toga, until I was covered all over with mud and loaded with the stuff like a bursting wineskin. Then Caligula laughed until he wept, and off he went. Mind you, later, a soothsayer told me the incident was actually a good omen, something about the very soil of my homeland being next to my skin and under the protection of my toga. Ha! But these soothsayers can turn anything to a fellow's advantage, can't they?" He laughed, then stopped himself. "Oh dear, is that a rude thing to say to an augur?" He laughed again, louder. "Ah, but have you met my son Titus, Senator Pinarius? He was just here, with his friend Britannicus—oh, there they are, having a laugh with Nero."

The boys were indeed nearby, but they were no longer laughing. Something had gone wrong. Nero's face, naturally ruddy and prone to blemishes, turned a darker shade of red and was twisted by a sudden fury. He hurled his wine cup at Britannicus. The boy dodged and the cup went hurtling past Vespasian's nose. Startled, the baby Domitian began to wail again.

Britannicus put on an exaggerated expression of shock. "But, Lucius Domitius," he said, addressing Nero by his birth name rather than his adopted name, "I merely wished you a happy birthday—"

"You will address me by my proper name, brat!" cried Nero. His ringing voice penetrated every corner of the room. The guests fell silent.

Britannicus raised an eyebrow. "But how can I do that, big brother? Earlier today, the augur explained that 'Nero' means 'strong and valiant'— and you, Lucius Domitius, are weak and cowardly."

Britannicus's friend Titus stifled a giggle.

"That's a lie, you little bastard!" said Nero. "What are you doing here, anyway? Shouldn't you be eating in the other room with the children?"

Agrippina approached the boys to stop the row. Claudius remained on his couch and seemed hardly to notice what was happening.

Britannicus left the room, followed by a small coterie of freedmen and attendants, the remnants of Messalina's faction in the imperial household. He carried himself with remarkable poise for a nine-year-old.

Young Titus looked to his father. Vespasian nodded, and the boy left the room with Britannicus. Vespasian shook his head. "That Britannicus—willful and wayward, just like his mother! I should go after the boy. Perhaps I can persuade him to apologize to Nero. I managed to broker a peace between those Celtic tribes up in Britannia, you know. Maybe I can do the same thing here." He departed along with Domitilla and the infant, who continued to wail.

Paulina returned to her husband's side. Agrippina joined them. "What *am* I going to do about that boy?"

"I suppose you mean Britannicus," said Seneca. "But more to the point, what are we going to do about Nero? He can't call the emperor's son a bastard in public. It won't do."

Agrippina nodded. "And yet . . . one does hear rumors about Britannicus."

"Rumors?" said Paulina.

Agrippina looked sidelong at Titus, as if deciding whether to confide in him, then went on. "Not that the child is a bastard—though we all know what a whore Messalina was. No, there are some who believe that Britannicus is the child of neither Messalina nor Claudius, that their baby was stillborn and Messalina substituted some other child in the crib, eager to present Claudius with an heir. I ask you, does Britannicus look like either of his purported parents?"

"A changeling, you mean?" Seneca snorted. "That's the sort of thing that happens in old Greek comedies."

"When it happens in real life, the results are far from comic." Agrippina turned to Titus. "Senator Pinarius, I make no secret of the fact that I favor astrology and know little about augury. But I wonder, in this case, could augury be of help?"

"I'm not sure what you mean."

"Might there be a way to interpret the auspices so as to determine the true identity of a particular child? Your skills at divination are so great, and Claudius has such complete confidence in you. . . ." Agrippina peered at him intently.

Unnerved by her scrutiny, Titus glanced at Claudius. His cousin had sunken deep into his couch and was gazing slack-jawed at his wine cup. Then Titus looked at the young Nero, who was over his tantrum and was flirting with one of the younger female guests. Claudius was the past; Nero was the future. Agrippina seemed to be asking for Titus's help on behalf of the young man who would almost surely be emperor one day, perhaps sooner rather than later. Titus's first loyalty would always be to his calling as an augur, to strive for the correct interpretation of the will of the gods; but could he not do that and please Agrippina at the same time?

"To determine whether a given individual is a changeling, traditional augury might be of little use," said Titus carefully, "but there are other forms of divination to which one might draw the attention of the emperor, who is interested in all forms of prognostication. Cousin Claudius recently charged me with compiling a list of every omen and portent reported in Italy, and together we review that list at regular intervals. Only yesterday, in Ostia, a pig was born with the talons of a hawk. Such an occurrence is invariably a message from the gods. Freakish weather, swarms of bees, rumblings in the earth, strange lights in the sky—all require careful interpretation. I have a secretary who closely examines the registry of deaths, looking for any unusual patterns; on a given day, perhaps every man who dies in Roma has the same first name, for instance. You'd be amazed at all the connections you begin to see, when you look for them."

"Remarkable!" said Agrippina. "But how does one correctly decipher these signs?"

Titus smiled. "The judgment of an augur begins with training but grows with experience. I've spent many years studying manifestations of the divine will." He looked at Nero, noting his large head and prominent brow. "Tell me, has a physiognomist ever examined Britannicus?"

"Not to my knowledge," said Agrippina.

"Nor to mine," said Seneca.

"Their branch of science is very specialized. Based on precepts laid down by Aristotle and Pythagoras, they examine the face and the shape of the head for indications of a person's destiny. Physiognomists talk mostly about the future, but perhaps they can see the past as well. If there is, as you suspect, something . . . untoward . . . about the origin of Britannicus, the truth might yet be revealed to the emperor. Yes, I think the first step to discovering the truth might be to summon a physiognomist. I know an Egyptian practitioner—ah, but here comes your son."

Nero, having sufficiently charmed the young female guest, gathered the folds of his purple-and-gold toga and approached them.

"Brothers!" he said, rolling his eyes, as if to explain his altercation with Britannicus. "You have a brother, don't you?" he asked Titus. "A twin, Seneca told me."

"Yes." Titus sighed. Yet again, Kaeso was being forced into his thoughts.

"Are you *identical* twins?" asked Nero. The young man's curiosity appeared to be entirely innocent, but Titus still cringed.

"In appearance, at least when we were younger. Otherwise, we were so different that I should like to think he was . . . a changeling." Titus glanced at Agrippina.

"Why do we never see him?" said Nero. "You're always coming by to see the emperor in his study. Yet we never see your twin."

"My brother is . . ." This was not the first time Kaeso's unsavory behavior had caused Titus embarrassment, yet he had never come up with a good way to explain his brother's complete withdrawal not just from public life but from decent society. How could anyone in the imperial household possibly understand Kaeso's bizarre beliefs and perverse behavior? What excuse could Titus make this time for Kaeso? Should he say that his brother was insane? A drunkard? Crippled by illness?

"My brother is . . ."

Seneca finished the sentence for him: "A Christian."

Titus turned pale. "How did you know?"

Seneca laughed. "The tutor of the emperor's son must know a great many things, Senator Pinarius."

Agrippina frowned. "How can a Roman patrician be a Christian? I thought that was the name for a sect of the Jews."

"So it is," said Seneca. "But here in Roma, as in many other cities around the empire, they have recruited others to join their cult. Mostly slaves, one presumes. The Christians actually welcome slaves, and you can imagine why the less reputable sort of slaves find such a cult attractive—Christ-worship is yet another activity they can carry on in secret behind their masters' backs. But they are not all slaves. I'm told there are a few Roman citizens among the Christians. They teach that this world is a terrible place, dominated by evil men—indeed, they believe that Roma and all it stands for is evil—but they also think this world will soon end, to be replaced by another world, in which their dead god shall come back to life and rule for eternity. A suitable religion, if one can call it that, for disgruntled slaves, but hardly for citizens of the city whose destiny is to maintain order in the world and uphold respect for the gods."

"It sounds seditious," said Nero. "If these Christians hate Roma so much, let them go back to dusty Judaea and await the end of the world there. Didn't Claudius banish the Jews?"

"That edict proved to be impractical," said Seneca. "It was short-lived and only haphazardly carried out, but it did serve as a warning to the Jewish sects in the city to keep the peace. They no longer stone each other in public, much less riot in the streets. They've learned to keep their feuds to themselves, at least here in the city. As a result, you don't hear much about the Christians these days."

"And that includes this mysterious Christian brother of Senator Pinarius," said Nero. "But of Titus Pinarius I suspect we will be seeing much more in the years to come." Nero bestowed on Titus his most charming smile.

A.D. 59

On the day late in the month of Martius that news reached Roma of the death of the young emperor's mother, Titus Pinarius lit candles in the vestibule of his house and whispered a prayer before each of the wax masks of his ancestors, thanking them for his good fortune.

Long ago, his late cousin Claudius had scolded him for knowing so little of his family's past. "A man must honor his ancestors," Claudius had said. "Who else made us, and how else did we come to exist?" Since that time, Titus had devoted himself to studying his ancestors, discovering all he could about them, learning from their examples, and paying homage to them like a dutiful Roman, trying to make his own life something of which his forebears would be proud.

At the age of forty-one, Titus was more prosperous and well regarded than ever—and glad to still be alive. It had not been easy in the six years since Claudius had died, navigating the treacherous politics of an imperial court split between a ruthless mother and a young son struggling to break free of her.

But now Agrippina was dead. In some ways, her death was a more profound event than the death of Claudius, for Claudius seemed to fade gradually away, while Agrippina still had her wits about her and might yet have regained control of Nero and the court. What a woman she was, and how little she allowed her womanhood to limit her ambitions! Titus recalled the incident when Armenian envoys had pleaded their cause before Nero, and Agrippina emerged from behind the screen where she customarily remained hidden and actually seemed about to mount the emperor's tribunal and preside along with him; while the whole court was paralyzed with alarm, Seneca hissed at Nero to intercept his mother, and so a scandalous scene was averted.

Agrippina! The world would not be the same without her. A new age would begin.

So deeply did Titus feel the impact of the news that he found himself unable to contemplate the activities of a normal day. Only some unplanned and irregular activity would be suitable to such a strange day. Following this impulse, he decided to discharge an onerous duty that had long been weighing on him. On this day, he would visit his brother.

Once every year or two he forced himself to see Kaeso, to offer his brother yet another chance to return to a normal, respectable way of life. Titus felt he owed that duty to the shade of their father, if not to Kaeso, who always refused him.

He left his house with a small retinue, as befitted a senator of his standing. There was a scribe with a wax tablet to take down memoranda. There was another slave who was versed in all the streets and byways of the city, so that Titus need never wonder where the closest tavern or silver shop or eatery might be. There was another slave who knew the names not just of every senator and magistrate in the city but of every person Titus was likely to meet, no matter how important or inconsequential, so that Titus need never search his memory in vain for a name or a title. And of course there were a number of brawny bodyguards, well-behaved fellows whose sheer size was so intimidating that they seldom had to use force to defend their master or to clear a way for him through a crowd.

The day was typical of late Martius, bright and springlike one moment, blustery and overcast the next. Titus found the changeable weather invigorating and walked with a spring in his step. Agrippina was dead! The news had not taken Titus completely by surprise. Recently, Nero had summoned Titus to consult him about omens regarding his mother's and his own immediate future; the young emperor said nothing of what he had in mind, but he was clearly desperate to finally rid himself of Agrippina. Thank the gods it was Nero who trusted and consulted Titus at that precarious stage of the power struggle, and not Agrippina! Like many in the court, Titus had walked a tightrope between mother and son for years, afraid to offend either party or to irrevocably throw his lot with one or the other.

The story of Agrippina's demise had played out like a comedy of errors. According to rumors, Nero had tried on more than one occasion to poison her, but each time Agrippina had either been forewarned or had taken an antidote to save herself. Then the ceiling had fallen in above her bed—surely not by accident—and Agrippina escaped being crushed only because she happened to have been lying next to the headboard.

Then, saying that he wanted to patch things up with her, Nero invited Agrippina to his seaside villa at Baiae to celebrate the feast of Minerva. There he presented her with a splendid pleasure barge and persuaded her to take a cruise on the bay despite the blustery weather. But this was not an ordinary ship: one of Nero's engineers had devised it to collapse on itself and sink without a trace, a circumstance that could be blamed on the choppy waves or a sudden squall but surely not on the young emperor. The ship duly collapsed and sank, but Agrippina—who had once supported herself by diving for sponges—was such a strong swimmer that she made her way to shore. Nero decided that his desperate mother, like a wounded tigress, needed to be disposed of straightaway. In the beach house where the bedraggled Agrippina took refuge, assassins arrived and did away with her once and for all.

An astrologer had once told Agrippina that her son would become emperor, but that she would have to pay for his greatness with her own life. Agrippina had flippantly replied, "Let him kill his mother, then, so long as he is emperor." So it had come to pass.

Walking along the riverfront and through the Forum, Titus let himself be distracted by the sights and sounds of the city. Despite the constant tension and turmoil within the imperial household, for Roma and the empire the last few years had been a golden age. Seneca had taken charge of the actual running of the empire and had done a splendid job. Taxes had been reduced even as the services of the state had been improved. Nero's love of music and poetry, his youthful enthusiasm, his theatrical personality, and his love of spectacle pervaded the culture. He had devised extraordinary entertainments for the populace, made all the more extraordinary by the fact that they were bloodless; though gladiator games were still a part of many holidays and festivals, Nero had decreed that no one should be put to death in the arena, not even criminals.

Roma thrived. It seemed to Titus that the world had never known a better moment. And now that the discord in the imperial house had come to an end with Agrippina's death, who could say to what glorious heights Nero might ascend?

Titus left behind the gleaming marble and travertine monuments of the Forum and entered the Subura with its narrow, filthy streets. He was glad to have his retinue around him, especially his bodyguards. As a younger man he had dared to walk through the Subura at all hours alone and unarmed, but those days were long past. Yet even here, he thought, conditions had improved since Nero had taken power, thanks to the general prosperity of the empire and Seneca's efficient city administration.

It occurred to Titus that the general well-being of the world made his brother's hateful attitude toward existence all the more perverse and inexplicable. How could Kaeso detest the world so much when there was such joy and beauty in it? And of all places on earth, surely Roma was the most beautiful—though as he stood before the tenement where Kaeso lived, Titus had to admit that this was a gloomy-looking place, even worse than his brother's last residence. If Titus had been reduced to living in such squalor and, like Kaeso, had to make his living as a common laborer—back-breaking work for a man of forty-one!—perhaps he would hate the world, too.

Titus left his retinue in the street, gave the bodyguards permission to play dice, and ascended the stairs to the highest floor. Why did Kaeso always live up so many flights of stairs? The stairway itself was littered with debris and filth—a discarded shoe, broken bits of pottery, a child's wooden doll with its limbs missing, and at one landing not one but two rats, whom Titus interrupted in the act of copulation. How could Kaeso stand to live in such a place?

Titus knocked on the door. He heard movement within; in such places, the walls were so thin that one could hear everything. Kaeso opened the door. He smiled broadly. "Greetings, brother!"

Kaeso was as ill-groomed as ever—a bird's nest could have been concealed inside his bushy beard—but in high spirits. Titus took this for a good sign. Perhaps their meeting would go well. He noticed that Kaeso was wearing the fascinum on a bit of twine around his neck.

"Greetings, brother," he said.

"Come inside."

Artemisia briefly looked in from the other room and perfunctorily greeted him, then disappeared. How plump and plain she looked, without makeup and with her hair unwashed. Chrysanthe was holding up much better, despite having given birth to their son and three daughters. Poor Artemisia had not even become a mother because her husband saw no point in bringing new life into the world.

"You seem happy, Kaeso."

"I am."

"May I ask why?"

"You won't like the answer."

"Probably not. But try me."

"I am happy because the end of the world is very close now. Very close! Perhaps it will happen within the year."

Titus groaned. "And this idea makes you happy?"

"Of course. It's what we long for, to shed the trappings of this foul place and be reunited with Christ, to see the naked face of God revealed in all his glory."

Titus sighed. "And how will the world end, Kaeso? How could such a thing even happen? What fire could be big enough, what earthquake terrible enough, what tidal wave high enough to wipe out all of creation? Will the stars come crashing down? Will the sun burn out, and the moon explode like a dandelion? The very idea of the world ending is nonsense!"

"The one God is omnipotent. He made all of creation in six days, and he can destroy it all in the blink of an eye."

"If this god is omnipotent—and if there are no other gods to stand in his way—why does he not simply fix this world to his liking, likewise in the blink of an eye, and put an end to the evil and suffering you say is all around us? What sort of god is this you worship, who plays a cruel waiting game with his worshippers?"

"You simply don't understand, Titus. It's my fault; I lack the power to explain it to you. If you would come to one of our gatherings, there are men far wiser than I—"

"No, Kaeso, Senator Titus Pinarius will not be seen at a gathering of Christians!" The idea was so ludicrous, Titus laughed out loud.

"You mock me, brother, but of what are you so proud? Of your special status in the world, your friendship with the emperor? You were friends with the last emperor, too. Yet you did nothing, said nothing, when cousin Claudius was murdered."

Titus felt the blood drain from his face. "You don't know that Claudius was murdered."

"Of course I do. Everyone knows. Ask your senator friends. Or ask my neighbors. The niece he took in his incestuous marriage—violating even Roman standards of decency—put poison in his mushrooms, and when that failed to act quickly enough, Agrippina called for a physician to treat him, and the physician put a feather down Claudius's throat to make him vomit. But the feather was dabbed with an even more potent poison, and that was the end of poor Claudius. Did you even mourn for him, brother?"

Titus was taken aback. That the common people had some vague notion of how Claudius had met his end did not surprise him, but Kaeso knew the actual details, and if Kaeso knew, then everyone in the city must know.

Perhaps, Titus thought, that was not such a bad thing. If people believed that Agrippina was a poisoner, that would make her violent death more acceptable, once they learned of it.

"No one knows for certain if that feather had poison on it or not," said Titus. "It may be true that Agrippina, as a devoted mother, took extreme measures to promote her son—"

"Her son, who turned his hand to murder with just as much enthusiasm. Or will you claim that young Britannicus met a natural end? He was poisoned as well, wasn't he, only a few months after Nero's ascension? The poor boy! And did you, as Claudius's friend and cousin, lift a finger to protect Claudius's orphaned son?"

The jab was well aimed. Far from protecting Britannicus, Titus, at

Agrippina's bidding, had done his share to promote the notion that the boy was a changeling, so as to discredit any claim he might have to rule.

"I had nothing to do with either the death of Claudius or the death of Britannicus," said Titus.

"But you know who murdered them."

"*If* they were murdered."

"Titus, my poor, deluded brother! You move among these people as an Egyptian snake handler moves among serpents. They may not have bitten you yet, but their venom has poisoned you nonetheless. Nero's venom has seeped into you, polluted you—"

"You dare to call Nero a snake? In five years, that remarkable young man has done more for this city than any emperor since Augustus. If you ever left this hovel and took a walk through the decent neighborhoods of Roma, where decent people live, you'd see how happy those people are. Those are the people who don't want the world to end, because Nero has made this world a better place."

"And what do all Nero's earthly achievements count for, when you consider that he murdered his own mother?"

Titus was stunned. He himself had only just been informed of Agrippina's death by a messenger who came directly from Baiae.

"How can you know about Agrippina? Living in this hole, a nobody among nobodies?" A dark suspicion struck him. "Is there some network of spies among the Christian slaves? Does that network reach even to the imperial household?"

Kaeso laughed. "You think all Christians are Jews, slaves, outcasts, or beggars. If you only knew the truth, Titus! There are people of every rank among us, even fine, upstanding Roman ladies. Not all can aspire to Jesus's example of poverty, but all can look forward to the day when we shall be redeemed and united in the afterlife—"

"Then there *is* a network of Christian spies, even in the imperial household?" Titus recalled something Nero had once said, that the Christians might be seditious. Titus had long ago decided that his brother's obsessions were maddening but harmless, but could it be that the Christian cult was more sinister than he had thought?

"Tell me something, Kaeso. Every so often I come across some bit of information about your cult, whether I want to or not. Someone recently drew my attention to a purported holy text which contained a quotation from Christ himself. When I read it, I found it so alarming I memorized it: 'If any man comes to me, and hates not his father, and his mother, and his wife, and his children, and his brother and sisters, and even his own life, he cannot be my disciple.' Did your god actually say such a terrible thing?"

Kaeso nodded. "A follower of Christ must be ready to reject all the attachments of the material world in favor of spiritual rebirth—"

"You don't have to explain the words to me. I understand them well enough," said Titus in disgust.

A bit of light happened to reflect off the fascinum, drawing Titus's attention to it. "You dare to wear the fascinum of our ancestors—you, who do nothing to honor our ancestors, who profess to despise all they accomplished and handed down to us! You, who would profess to hate our father and to hate me, merely to please your god?"

Kaeso smiled and touched the fascinum. "This amulet is not what you think it is, Titus. It is a symbol of Christ's suffering and a promise of his future resurrection, of the resurrection of all who believe—"

"No, Kaeso, it's a link to the past, a talisman handed down to us from a time before Roma was founded. You would pervert it into something else entirely, with your hatred of the gods and your hatred of Roma!"

"The gods you worship are not gods, Titus. If anything, they're demons, though I tend to believe that in fact they do not exist at all, that they never did exist—"

"Fool! Atheist! The gods have always been and always will be. They are of the world and in the world. They made the world. They *are* the world. If mortals fail to comprehend them, it is because we are so small and they are so vast. What a tiny world you imagine, the plaything of a single god who wants his worshippers to be as poor and stunted and miserable as he is! Can you not see the beauty, the majesty, the mystery of the gods all around you? Yes, they baffle and confound us, and their will is difficult to discern. But I do what I can. I practice the rituals of our ancestors, who were here before us and encountered the gods before we did. I revere their wisdom. You spurn it! You never visit my house. You never come to pay respect to the wax effigies of the Pinarii. You turn your back on our ancestors. You are disrespectful, impious, unworthy to be called a Roman!"

"But I don't call myself a Roman, Titus. I call myself a Christian, and what you call the wisdom of our ancestors means nothing to me. I have no use for the sins and follies of the past. I look ahead to the bright, perfect future."

"A future in which you will be utterly forgotten, because you have created no descendants. All memory of you will vanish, Kaeso, because you have broken the link passed down from one generation to the next. The only immortality a man can achieve is to be remembered, to have those who come after him recall his accomplishments and speak his name with honor."

"Just as you imagine men of some future age will speak of Nero? The fratricide, the matricide? And if you're lucky, they'll mention that Senator Titus Pinarius was Nero's friend—the friend of a mother-killer! Is that your idea of immortality, brother?"

Titus stared at the fascinum. He could barely resist ripping it from his brother's neck.

"I came here today out of respect to our father. I feel a duty to his shade, to do what I can to look after you. But this is the final stroke, Kaeso. I won't come to see you again."

A.D. 61

Titus stayed true to his word: he did not call on his brother again. When next the brothers met, two years later, it was because Kaeso came to call on Titus.

Titus was in his study, completely absorbed in an old text on augury given him years ago by Claudius, when a slave tapped on the doorframe to get his attention.

"What is it?" said Titus without looking up.

"You have a visitor, Master."

Titus looked up, squinting a bit. Reading had begun to tire his eyes, a complaint not uncommon for a man of forty-three. "Do I know you?"

"I'm Hilarion, Master. The new doorkeeper."

"Ah, yes." Titus peered at the boy, who seemed hardly old enough to serve as a doorkeeper. There were so many slaves in the household these days, Titus couldn't keep them straight. Chrysanthe insisted that they were all needed to run the place, but it seemed to Titus he would soon need to buy a larger house just to accommodate so many slaves. To be sure, he was at all times well attended and never had to do anything for himself: slaves tended to his chamber pot in the morning, carried his things to and from the baths, washed him, massaged him, shaved him, dressed him, took his dictation, fetched whatever he needed, carried messages to friends and business associates, taught his children, read aloud to him when his eyes were tired, did all the shopping, prepared and served his food, sang to him during dinner, and turned down his bed at night. Slaves tended to his sexual needs as well. After more than twenty years of marriage and four children, he and Chrysanthe seldom performed the act anymore, but he loved her and had no intention of taking another wife, so he felt no compunction about using the comeliest slaves when he felt the urge. They never seemed to mind, since Titus was not the sort to take pleasure from violence or abuse, and he took his enjoyment discreetly, never in a vulgar, public way that caused a slave shame or embarrassment. Not all masters were so considerate.

"Who is it?" said Titus.

"The visitor says he's your brother." Hilarion sounded doubtful.

Titus stared into the middle distance for a long moment. "Show him in. No, wait. I'll go to the vestibule to meet him."

Titus rose and walked through the house, past the lush garden with a newly installed marble statue of Venus, across the reception hall with its newly laid mosaic floor, and into the vestibule. Sure enough, there was Kaeso, looking like a ragged beggar off the street. He was standing face-to-face with the wax effigy of their father.

"Have you come to pay your respects at last?" said Titus.

Kaeso jumped a bit, taken by surprise, and looked at him blankly.

"If you wish to burn a bit of incense before his effigy, and perhaps say a prayer, I would be happy to join you," said Titus. "And I'm sure our ancestors would be delighted." He gestured to the other effigies in their niches.

"You know that's not why I've come," said Kaeso quietly.

"I have no idea why you've come," said Titus. He noticed that Kaeso was wearing the fascinum. The effrontery, to flaunt his possession of the family talisman in front of the ancestors! Titus took a deep breath, determined to be civil.

"I have a request to make of you," said Kaeso. He sounded almost meek.

Titus nodded curtly. "I'm expecting visitors soon—a senator receives so many callers asking for favors—but I suppose I have time to see you now. Follow me to my study."

As he led his brother through the house, he wondered what Kaeso must make of the place. Since Kaeso had moved out years ago, Titus had made continual improvements, investing in costly furnishings and exquisite works of art. His study was one of the loveliest rooms of all, with beautiful images from the *Metamorphoses* of Ovid painted on the walls and custom bookshelves made of oak. A mosaic on the floor depicted Prometheus giving light to mankind; the naked Titan carried a giant fennel stalk containing a glowing ember stolen from the fiery chariot of Sol, with a circle of awestruck mortals surrounding him. Titus imagined Kaeso must be quite impressed, but his brother's only reaction was to shake his head and mutter, "So many slaves you have!"

"Slaves?"

"All over the house. We passed at least ten between the vestibule and this room."

"Did we? I hardly notice them. Except when I need one and can't find him!" Titus laughed.

Kaeso looked grim.

"Would you like some wine?" Titus was determined to treat his brother no differently than any other visitor. He clapped his hands. A passing slave girl at once stepped into the doorway, awaiting instructions. Titus smiled at her. She was a lovely young redhead, one of his favorites. What was her name? Eutropia? Euthalia?

"No wine," said Kaeso quickly. "It would cloud my thinking. I need to be able to speak clearly."

Titus gestured to the girl to move on. "What's this about, Kaeso?"

"What do you know about the murder of a city prefect, an ex-consul named Lucius Pedanius Secundus?"

Titus sat in an old-fashioned folding chair, an antique the dealer claimed had originally belonged to Cato the Younger. Kaeso remained standing. It was not unusual for Titus to sit while his visitors stood.

"Pedanius was killed by one of his own slaves," said Titus. "A nasty business. Slaves rarely kill a master, but when they do, it always causes a stir. People still speak of the Spartacus revolt, when slaves all over Italy turned on their owners and committed one atrocity after another. Farms were burned. Citizens were crucified. Women were raped and murdered."

"That was over a hundred years ago," said Kaeso.

"A hundred and thirty-two years ago, to be precise. And such a tragedy has not occurred again in the last century because extreme measures were taken at the time, and extreme measures continue to be taken whenever any crime is committed by a slave against his master. The alternative is chaos. Why are you asking about this matter, Kaeso?"

"Do you know the facts of the crime?"

"As a senator, I've been briefed on all the details." Titus pressed his fingertips together. He should have asked the girl to bring some wine, whether Kaeso wanted any or not. Talking about scandal made a man thirsty. "An unseemly affair. It seems that Pedanius had owned the slave, a man called Anacletus, for many years, and Anacletus had risen in the household to a high station. After many years of obedient service, Pedanius agreed to allow Anacletus to purchase his freedom. But the slave wanted more than that: the fellow was in love with a pretty new slave boy in the household and wanted to be allowed to purchase the boy and take him with him. Pedanius, in a generous mood, agreed. But then Pedanius changed his mind; apparently he took another look at the new slave and decided he wanted the boy for his own pleasure. The next thing you know, master and slave were rivals for the boy's affections—an absurd situation for any citizen—and there the trouble started. Pedanius not only reneged on his promise to free Anacletus, but he took to sleeping with the boy every night."

"And then?"

Titus hesitated to continue with the seamy details. They would be common knowledge soon enough. "One night, Anacletus obtained a knife and, holding a lamp to light his way, he snuck past the night watchman and broke into his master's bedroom. He says he only meant to threaten Pedanius. But he caught them in the act. Pedanius was unfazed. Apparently he made quite a show of flaunting his power over the boy, showing

Anacletus that he could and would do anything he desired with a boy who was, after all, his property. This drove Anacletus into a fury. He stabbed Pedanius to death while the boy screamed and wept."

"Disgusting," muttered Kaeso. "All of it, disgusting. So there's no doubt about the slave's guilt?"

"None whatsoever."

"Anacletus will be put to death?"

"Of course. He'll be crucified."

"And the boy?"

"The boy witnessed the crime and did nothing to stop it. The law is very clear."

"And the night watchman?"

"He egregiously failed in his duty. Of course he must die."

"And the rest of the household slaves—what will become of them?"

"As I said, the law is very clear. All the slaves in the household of Pedanius must be interrogated under torture—that's happened already—and then be put to death."

"Surely not!" protested Kaeso. "I know that our ancestors enacted such terrible penalties, but surely the law is more lenient nowadays. Such a crime is so rare—"

"It's rare precisely because the law is so harsh. All the more reason, when such a crime occurs, that the full penalty of the law must be exacted. The common law dates from time immemorial, but it was codified by the Senate under Augustus."

Kaeso shook his head. "Do you know how many slaves are in the household of Pedanius?"

"No."

"I do. There are over four hundred of them. Four hundred, Titus!"

Titus pursed his lips. "That *is* a great many slaves, to be crucified all at once. I hadn't known there were quite so many."

"Some of them are old, Titus. Some of them are children."

"I suppose." Titus shifted uneasily in the chair. Antique furniture was always so uncomfortable; no wonder Cato was famous for a foul temper. Titus was parched. Why had he not told the girl to bring some wine?

"Can you remember such a slaughter of a household of slaves happening in Roma, ever in our lifetime?" said Kaeso.

"No, I suppose not. These crimes usually happen in the countryside, or in some distant province. And I suppose the number of slaves involved is usually not quite so large."

"Think about it, Titus. For a crime of passion committed by a single slave, four hundred human beings must die. People who were elsewhere, going about their work, or probably fast asleep, completely unaware of what was happening. Surely that doesn't make sense to you, Titus."

"If they weren't aware of Anacletus's intentions, then they should have been. That's what the law says. The statute is clear: it is the responsibility of a slave at all times and under all circumstances to protect his master, with his own life if necessary, from any harm from outside the household or from any other slave within the household."

"But Anacletus acted alone. There was no plot. How could the other slaves have prevented the crime?"

"I will admit, sometimes, on a case-by-case basis, the law does not perfectly fit every situation. But the law is the law, and must be obeyed. Bend it in one case, and the next time a slave wants to kill his master, he'll be thinking he can get away with it."

"That makes no sense at all, Titus."

"What is your interest in this matter, anyway? No, don't tell me—there must be some Christians among those four hundred slaves."

Kaeso took a deep breath. "Yes, I have brothers and sisters in the household of Pedanius."

"Ah! You can drop your pretense of moral outrage, then. You simply don't want to see your fellow cult members receive their just punishment. Am I right? But what do you care about their earthly fate? Isn't the world coming to an end at any moment?"

"That's cruel, Titus. Surely you must be moved by the suffering of so many innocent people. Have you ever thought what it must be like, to die on a cross?"

"The law—"

"How can you countenance such cruelty and call it justice, simply because 'this is the way our ancestors did it'? How can the gods you worship endorse such wickedness? Do you feel no pity, no shame at the injustice of it? Do you not feel some impulse to do whatever you can, as a senator, as a friend of the emperor, to alter the course of events?"

"Is that why you're here, Kaeso? To petition me to take action as a senator to pervert the course of justice?"

"Is there nothing you can do?"

Titus shrugged. "There's to be a discussion in the Senate tomorrow. I suppose the logistics of staging four hundred crucifixions will require special planning, if nothing else."

"Then you *could* make a proposal for leniency?"

"I suppose I could, if I were so inclined. And if I didn't think the other senators would laugh me out of the Senate House."

"Surely not every senator will be in favor of the strict penalty of the law. Surely some of them possess a shred of mercy. If not the senators, then perhaps Nero might be persuaded—"

"Or perhaps your omnipotent god might be persuaded to save his followers. How about that, Kaeso? Is he not all-knowing and all-powerful? Why don't you petition your god to change the law? He could do it in the blink of an eye."

"Don't mock God, Titus."

"Then go pray to him, Kaeso, and leave me out of this."

Kaeso trembled with anger. "Have you considered that Pedanius got what he deserved? Taunting a slave with false promises, raping that boy while the slave watched—"

"Stop there, Kaeso! If you mean to suggest that the murder of a citizen by a slave could ever be justified, under any circumstances, leave my house at once. I will not have that sort of talk under my roof. I won't have my family and my slaves exposed to such an obscene notion."

Clenching his jaw, Kaeso left the room without another word.

Titus sat in silence for a long time, staring at nothing.

His throat was parched. He raised his hands to clap them, then saw that the slave Hilarion was already standing in the doorway, watching him with an inscrutable expression.

✻

Titus slept uneasily that night. He was up before cockcrow.

He left Chrysanthe sleeping and went to the garden. He had no appetite, and it was too early to go to the baths. He sat on a stone bench. In the vague light before dawn, everything around him was indistinct. The house was quiet. Even the slaves were still asleep, except for the watchman who stayed up all night, and he was probably asleep as well. What a joke it was to trust one's safety to a watchman, if there was no one to watch the watchman and make sure he was vigilant! The watchman of Pedanius had slept through his master's murder.

It had been a long time since Titus had simply sat alone in silence, with no distractions and no one around him, not even a slave waiting out of sight for his summons.

The Senate would meet later that morning, after its members had time to go to the baths to groom themselves and put on their togas, or, more precisely, after they had been groomed and dressed by their slaves. Titus decided to attend the session. He decided that he might even take part in the debate, something he rarely did.

If he intended to speak, he should probably prepare some notes, he thought. His first impulse was to rouse one of his secretaries, dictate his thoughts, and let the fellow put his random ideas into some sort of order; an old slave called Antigonus was good at that sort of thing. Then it occurred to Titus that he might be saying some things in his speech that he did not care to share with a slave, since the punishment of the four hundred slaves of Pedanius would be the subject of the debate. What a peculiar circumstance, that a senator should wish to hide his thoughts from a slave!

Titus fetched a lamp himself and figured out how to light it from the sconce that stayed lit all night. He rummaged in his study until he found a wax tablet and a stylus, and, squinting under the dim light, began to scribble some notes. Within moments his hand began to cramp; he had not written anything with his own hand in a long time. He was also uncertain of some of his spellings; when a man always dictated to a trained scribe, he did not need to know how to spell.

Writing something worthy of being delivered in the Senate House, without a slave to transcribe and edit, was rather hard work, he realized. But it was also quite absorbing, as he found himself rubbing out awkward sentences and reworking them, coming up with new ideas that needed to be inserted inside other ideas, and rearranging the order of his arguments. Before he knew it, dawn had broken and the house had come to life around him. Slaves were scurrying up and down the hallway, some of them clearly surprised to see their master awake so early. The smell of breakfast farina wafted from the kitchen.

Titus was suddenly very hungry and in the mood for something sweet. He called to one of the girls and told her to bring him a bowl of steaming-hot farina with honey and dates and pine nuts. "You know how I like it," he said.

After breakfast, he summoned his usual retinue of slaves and headed for the baths. Often he patronized a small establishment on the slope of the Aventine above the Circus Maximus. The place was old and small, and a bit drafty, but conveniently close to his house. But on this day Titus decided to go to the Baths of Agrippa. He was in the mood for a bit of luxury and spectacle, and the Baths of Agrippa always provided that. As well, there was plenty of space in the galleries to do a bit of work, in case he wanted to polish his notes a bit more.

The baths were out on the Field of Mars, a fair distance from his house. He considered taking a sedan or a litter, but decided to walk instead. Titus did not want to become one of those effeminate fellows who never stepped outside his house without being carried by slaves.

As he strode through the markets along the Tiber and then through the busy neighborhood around the old Circus Flaminius and the Theater of Pompeius, it seemed to Titus that there were a great many people headed the other way, toward the Forum, and that they all looked rather serious. There was a mood in the air, an atmosphere of tension. His bodyguards noticed it, too. Titus saw them draw more closely together, looking this way and that with more than their usual wariness.

Titus could not think what was happening, and forgot all about it once he arrived at the baths. He never ceased to marvel at the grandiose beauty of the place, with its high ceilings, splendid marble columns, and galleries of famous paintings and statues. The sheer luxury of the hot plunge, the cool plunge, the warm plunge, and then a thorough massage did much to rejuvenate him after his restless night. He watched the swimmers in the long pool for a while, narrowing his eyes at the glimmer of the morning sun reflected off the water and feeling its warmth on his face. He nibbled some dried figs and almonds and sipped a much-watered cup of wine, and forgot all his cares for a while. He even forgot his speech, and did no more work on his notes. When he was finally ready to be dressed in his toga, he saw by the sundial next to the long pool that if he did not hurry he would be late for the taking of the auspices—not his duty on this occasion—and the opening of the day's business in the Senate.

He decided to hire a sedan and told the bearers to move at a fast pace. His bodyguards trotted alongside, but the other slaves lagged a bit; they would catch up and wait outside the Senate House in case Titus needed them. The ride was so smooth that he was able to take out the wax tablet and review his notes. Taking a sedan was not such an indulgence, he decided, if one used the time to do a bit of work.

The bearers took the most direct route, between the north side of the Capitoline Hill and the Temple of Venus built by the Divine Julius. Before Titus knew it, they were approaching the Senate House from the back side. He looked up from his notes, distracted by a strange noise that came from the direction of the Forum: it sounded like the roar of the ocean, or the crowd at the Circus Maximus. As the sedan rounded a corner, Titus saw something he had never seen before: the area before the steps of the Senate House was thronged with people. There were hundreds of them, perhaps even thousands. There was no reason for them to be there; this was not a festival day, and there was no public ceremony requiring their attendance. What were all these people doing here?

The sedan came to a stop at one end of the steps. Hitching up his toga, Titus ascended a few steps, then turned to take a closer look at the crowd. It was made up mostly of men of the common sort, ill-groomed and dressed in drab tunics—the citizen rabble of Roma. He looked at their faces. They did not look happy. Some of them seemed to be drunk, but that was inevitable in any large gathering. Some were clustered in smaller groups, talking among themselves or listening to a speaker. What were they talking about? Why did they appear so angry and agitated?

Titus threw a few coins to the sedan bearers, who disappeared at once. "Wait for me here, at this spot," he told his bodyguards, feeling an unaccustomed uneasiness. Usually he allowed his bodyguards to loiter around the Forum while he was in the Senate House, rather like dogs let off a leash, but on this day he wanted to know that they would be exactly where he had left them when he came out.

Halfway up the steps he ran into a fellow senator, Gaius Cassius

Longinus. Under Claudius, as governor of Syria, Cassius had amassed a great fortune. His learned commentaries on the law had established him as the Senate's leading expert on all matters judicial. Still, Titus could never forget that Cassius's ancestor and namesake had been one of the assassins of the Divine Julius. Cassius's eyesight had begun to fail; he was often in a foul mood, and today was no exception. Titus, who was much junior to Cassius in the Senate, usually would have given the older man a nod and no more, but he could not resist asking Cassius if he knew anything about the crowd before the Senate House.

Cassius squinted at the throng and scowled. "They're here to plead for mercy for those slaves," he said.

"Really? There are so many of them."

"Are there? Then it's a blessing that I can barely see them. I'm told they've been arriving all morning, and more are arriving every moment. You know, our ancestors saw this sort of thing all the time—mobs gathering to demonstrate in the Forum whenever there was a debate in the Senate. Sometimes the mobs would riot. Sometimes it was like this every day in the Republic, especially toward the end. Can you imagine the chaos?"

Titus gazed out at the crowd. So this was an old-fashioned Roman mob! "They look unhappy, but they're not that badly behaved."

"Not yet!" Cassius shuddered. "What I find so appalling is the reason they're here. When their ancestors broke a few patrician heads for plebeian rights, or rioted at the behest of the Gracchi brothers to help the small landowners, or even when they burned down the Senate House after the rabble-rouser Clodius was killed, at least they were fighting for their own self-interest as citizens. But this shameless assembly of freedmen and citizens are here to argue for the benefit of slaves. It's disgusting! Imagine, during the Spartacus revolt, if the rabble had gathered to tell the Senate, 'Stop what you're doing! Perhaps this gladiator fellow has a point!' "

"It's not quite the same thing," said Titus cautiously.

"Isn't it? The law is the law, and these people are here to spit on the law—for the sake of slaves! Nero should summon his Praetorians and drive them all into the Tiber."

"I think there might be too many of them to do that," said Titus. Truly, outside the Circus Maximus, he had never seen such a large gathering.

Was he imagining it, or had the crowd grown more unruly in the last few moments? He gathered the folds of his toga and hurried up the steps.

He was just in time to join his fellow senators on the crowded porch for the taking of the auspices. They were favorable, though Titus thought the augur was being rather generous in his interpretation of a crow's flight. Then the senators filed inside, pausing to light a bit of incense and say a prayer at the Altar of Victory before filling the tiers of seats that faced each other across the long chamber. There was a large turnout. Titus thought there must be more than two hundred senators present.

Once all the senators were seated, Nero arrived. Followed by Seneca and a retinue of scribes and secretaries, he strode up the length of the hall to take his chair on the dais at the far end. To Titus, it seemed that the young emperor did not walk with his usual self-confident swagger; had the sight of the gathering outside unnerved him as much as it had the senators? Titus also took note of the emperor's appearance. Nero had grown a beard, or at least a partial beard, something no emperor had worn before him; the hair was trimmed to leave only the growth beneath his jaw, while his cheeks and chin were clean-shaven. The effect was to provide a golden frame for his square face.

Even more striking was the emperor's costume. Since the death of Agrippina, Nero's mode of dress had grown more eccentric. On this occasion he was outfitted in his customary purple and gold, but his garment was not a toga but a gown of the sort either a man or woman might wear at home in the evening, and on his feet were what looked like slippers rather than proper shoes.

The garment left much of Nero's arms bare. Gone, Titus noticed, was the golden arm bracelet encasing the lucky snakeskin that Nero had long worn to honor his mother. After Agrippina's death, Nero had declared that he could no longer stand the touch of the bracelet on his skin, indeed could not stand even to look at it, and had thrown it into the sea from the terrace of his villa at Baiae. *The emperor no longer has his amulet,* thought Titus, *and nor do I,* wishing as he often did that he still possessed the fascinum of his ancestors. He could have used a bit of luck on this day.

The preliminary business of the Senate was dispensed with quickly so that the members could deal at once with the pressing issue of the murder of Lucius Pedanius Secundus and the punishment of his household slaves. The facts of the case were read aloud by a scribe. The man's delivery, even when reading the most salacious details, was completely without emotion, but at various points some of the senators made rude, mocking noises. To be killed by a slave was shocking but also shameful, and to have it happen under such circumstances—a rivalry over yet another slave—was the stuff of scandal. If Pedanius had escaped death, he would have been a laughingstock. Instead, he was a victim of the most frightening crime imaginable, a deliberate act of violence perpetrated in his own house by one of his own possessions.

The texts of the relevant laws were then read aloud. The statutes were just as Titus had remembered and recited to his brother the day before. If a slave should murder his master, all the slaves in the household must be interrogated under torture and punished with death, without exception. The four hundred slaves had already been interrogated. Now they were confined under guard in the house of Pedanius to await the judgment of the Senate. Meanwhile, in preparation for immediate executions, crucifixes were being prepared along the Appian Way outside the city.

Nero, on his dais, said nothing and merely observed the proceedings, as he often did when the Senate was carrying out its routine business.

The members were invited to rise and address the question at hand: on this occasion, was the law to be carried out fully and faithfully, without amendment or mitigation?

Without waiting to be called on, many of the senators simply shouted their opinions, and a general clamor filled the hall. Titus heard cries of "Kill them now, at once!" and "The law is the law!" But he also heard a substantial number of voices shouting, "Too harsh!" and "Mercy!" and "There should be exceptions!"

Nero covered his ears, as if the cacophony caused him pain. He gestured to Seneca, who stepped forward and called for order. "Will anyone speak formally in favor of rescinding or mitigating the penalty?" said Seneca.

There was a hubbub in the hall and a great many heads turned, but no one stood. Seneca was opening his mouth to speak again when Titus loudly cleared his throat and rose to his feet.

Seneca looked at him in surprise. "Do you wish to speak, Senator Pinarius?"

"I do."

All eyes turned to Titus. His face grew hot. He felt light-headed. His palms were suddenly sweaty. If he wasn't careful, the wax tablet containing his notes would slip right out of his hands—

He realized that his hands were empty. The tablet! Where was it? Titus looked around and saw it nowhere. Had he been holding it earlier, during the taking of the auspices? He couldn't remember. Could he have left it in the hired sedan? Titus felt completely at a loss. Meanwhile, the eyes of the entire Senate were boring into him. The room was utterly silent.

He would either have to sit down without saying a word, and look a complete fool, or he would have to speak without his notes. Could he do that? He had pored over them so intently, surely he could remember at least the major points, if not all the elegant phrases he had laboriously worked out. Titus cleared his throat again and took a deep breath.

"Caesar," he began, nodding to Nero, "and my esteemed fellow senators, we are all aware of the crowd that's gathered outside our front door. I must say it took me quite by surprise when I arrived here. I think it's taken us all by surprise. I've never seen anything like it, have you?"

"No, but I've never seen a herd of giraffes, either," shouted one of the senators. "What has either to do with the law?" This was met with scattered guffaws and a few cries of "Hear, hear!"

"Well," said Titus, feeling flustered, "once upon a time the common people had their own assembly, and they did have some say in the making of laws. . . ." Titus realized that he was straying far from his notes.

"What sort of talk is this?" someone shouted

"Seditious talk!" someone said. "Rabble-rousing!"

Titus raised his hands to quiet the clamor. "I'm merely saying that something has stirred up all those people. Every one of you in this chamber is stirred up, as well. Perhaps we should at least state the case of those who are asking for mercy, so that we can examine the argument clearly." There, that was better, he thought, feeling that he had quieted his listeners and regained their full attention. He noticed that a scribe was taking down his words, no doubt using the shorthand famously invented by Cicero's secretary, Tiro.

"Given the circumstance of this atrocious crime," he went on, "who can doubt that the vast majority of slaves in the household of Pedanius are completely innocent of any wrongdoing? This appears to be a crime of passion, not a conspiracy involving other slaves and hatched over time. Unless a slave was actually in the room, or at least close enough to overhear what was happening, how could that slave possibly have prevented the crime? There is also the fact that in such a large household—four hundred or more slaves—there must be a great many who are old and infirm, or young and frail, or women, some of whom may be pregnant. Shall all those slaves die, despite their innocence? What if a slave is blind? What if he is deaf, or mute—"

"And what if a slave is blind, deaf, *and* mute?" shouted someone.

"Then put him to death for sure, since he's no good to anyone!" shouted another, prompting a gale of laughter.

"Unless he's as pretty as that boy Pedanius was diddling," said someone else. This went too far. The offending senator received boos and angry looks.

"Senators!" shouted Titus, trying to regain their attention. "I have asked myself, why has this proceeding elicited such an unprecedented response from so many common citizens? I think I know some of the reasons. First, there has been no crime like this in recent memory, nor has there been the prospect of a slaughter of slaves on such a massive scale, at least not here in Roma. If such crimes occurred, and such massive punishments were exacted, it must have happened at a farm or country villa, where those slaves were unknown to anyone outside their own household. But this household of slaves is different. They reside here in the city, where they live and work and move about freely. These slaves must be known not only to fellow slaves in other households, but to shopkeepers and artisans and all sorts of citizens who have dealings with them. Some are errand boys and messengers, some are seamstresses and hairdressers, some are cooks and cleaners, some are bookkeepers and scribes, highly educated and valuable slaves deserving a degree of respect. Some are near the age of death. Some are newborn, just beginning life. Some are in the prime of life, at the peak of their usefulness and value. Some are pregnant and about to bring forth new life. These victims of the law are not a faceless crowd but are human beings known to their neighbors, and so we cannot be surprised if there are murmurs throughout the city that the law is too harsh.

When there is such an outcry, even here in the Senate, can no exception to the law be made?"

Well, thought Titus, *that was not so hard after all.* He felt rather pleased with himself. In his fantasies, this was the point at which the entire chamber erupted in applause, even from those who opposed him but admired his courage for taking a stand. Instead, after a few scattered cries of "Hear! Hear!" and some desultory murmurs of assent, the end of his speech was met by a silence almost as deep as that which preceded it.

Gaius Cassius Longinus rose to speak.

"Caesar, and esteemed fellow senators," he said, "often have I been present in this assembly when demands were made to alter or dilute or do away entirely with the customs and laws of our ancestors. In every single instance, those changes were for the worse. Yes, in every instance the laws made by our ancestors were superior to the innovations proposed to replace them. Yet often I've kept my mouth shut and let the majority have its way, wishing not to become known as one of those stalwarts of the law who grows wearisome by always exalting ancient precedent. I was holding my fire, if you will, for a time when my voice truly would be needed to prevent a terrible error by the state. That time is now!

"An ex-consul has been deliberately murdered in his house by one of his own slaves. Not one of the other slaves did a thing to prevent this crime, though the law is clear that this was their duty. Vote to spare them, if you like. But if a city prefect is not safe in his own home, who among us will be? Who will have enough slaves to protect him, if the four hundred of Pedanius were not enough? Who can rely on a slave's help, if even the threat of death is not enough to make a slave help you?

"I have sat here in silence and listened to the account of the 'facts' in this matter, which impute various unseemly behaviors on the part of Pedanius. I ask you, since the dead man cannot speak for himself, how and from whom were these 'facts' obtained? From the two slaves present at his murder, of course—the killer himself and the killer's young paramour. No doubt this 'evidence' was obtained as the law prescribes, under torture, but I think we can discount their story as an utter fabrication, concocted to blacken the name of their victim and to elicit sympathy for themselves. Next we will be hearing that this murder was justifiable homicide, and

Pedanius got what he deserved! Dust has been thrown in your eyes, senators, and not by a skilled advocate, but by slaves. Shame on you!

"We also hear the argument that the other household slaves could not have known that their master was threatened. I don't believe this for a moment. Do you seriously think that a slave plotted to kill his master without uttering a single rash or menacing word beforehand, to someone in the household? Even if this insanely jealous lover kept silent about his intention, how did he obtain a knife without anyone noticing and wondering what he meant to use it for? How did he penetrate to his master's bedroom, past the watchman, and carrying a lamp, mind you, without anyone seeing?

"But even if some of the slaves suspected that their master was in danger, you may say, surely most of the slaves were ignorant of the fact. Perhaps. But I say that every slave in that household, whatever his degree of complicity, is irrevocably contaminated by the crime. Even a slave born into the household that very morning is contaminated and must be destroyed, like a rabid dog. Imagine a slave growing up, knowing that his first master was brutally murdered by one of his own kind and that slaves like himself went unpunished. Would such a slave have an understanding of his place in the world and of the immutable respect he owes to his owner? Would you want that slave in your household, growing up with the knowledge of a murdered master in his head, inevitably spreading that knowledge to others? I think not!

"Some of you act as if we are encountering such a crime for the very first time and must come to some momentous decision never made before. Even if a similar crime occurred in the past, you argue, this case is somehow unique and requires our special consideration. Nonsense! There is nothing new here, no novel and unprecedented situation that must be debated and settled. Our ancestors saw situations no different from this, dealt with those situations in the best possible manner, and handed their precedents down to us. Are you so ungrateful that you spurn their gifts? Are you so vain that you consider yourselves wiser than they?

"Our ancestors were distrustful of their slaves, even though those slaves were born on the same estates, sometimes even in the same house, as their masters. Lifelong familiarity did not reduce their suspicion of their slaves or induce them to treat those slaves with greater leniency. The situation we face today is far more perilous. Nowadays our huge households are filled with slaves from all over the world. Those slaves speak all sorts of languages—who knows what they say behind our backs? They practice all sorts of religions—or none at all. They form all sorts of cliques among themselves, and even join foreign, secret cults without our knowledge. We must be on our guard inside our own households now more than ever. The only way to deal with this motley rabble is by intimidation and a strict adherence to the law.

"Innocent people will die, you say. But the law has long recognized that the suffering of individuals is justified by the benefit to all. When a Roman legion suffers defeat and every tenth man is clubbed to death for shame, brave men may die along with cowards, but by such strict measures our ancestors built armies that have conquered the world. Those same ancestors gave us the law which we discuss today. Think long and hard before you trifle with it. Dismiss the law, and who knows what terrible consequences will follow. Uphold the law, and your children will sleep more safely in their beds tonight."

Titus had dreamed of a rousing ovation, but it was Cassius who received it. Amid the cheering and applause, Titus overheard a nearby senator comment to another, "And that's why Cassius is the best jurist alive!"

"The finest master of the law since Cicero," said the other senator.

Rebuttals were invited. No one stepped forth.

The Senate voted by dividing the chamber. Those in favor of upholding the law without mitigation were to sit in the seats to the emperor's right; those who wished to make some exception to the law were to sit on the emperor's left.

Titus, who was already to Nero's left, stayed where he was. The senators he had just overheard rose to their feet at once and crossed the chamber, as did Cassius, whose poor eyesight required him to seek assistance; numerous admirers rushed forward to claim the privilege of helping him. There was a great deal of movement back and forth, with groups of senators lingering in the middle of the room, engaged in last-moment discussions.

As always, Titus was amused to see which senators remained undecided until the last possible moment, standing in the middle of the chamber and looking anxiously from side to side to see which way the vote was trending. It was the same senators every time, the ones who had no opinions of their own and invariably voted with the majority, once they could determine which side the majority had taken.

When everyone was finally settled, there was no need for a count. Although a substantial number of senators had voted for leniency—far more than Titus had expected after Cassius's rousing speech—the clear majority was in favor of the law. Without exception, all the slaves in the household of Pedanius were condemned to death by crucifixion. Preparations had already been made, and the sentence would be carried out that very day.

Nero had stayed out of the argument. It was his prerogative to speak at any time, but though he had listened attentively, he had said nothing. But after the session was formally closed, and the senators began to rise from their seats, a messenger ran to the dais and whispered in Nero's ear, whereupon he rose to his feet.

Seneca banged a staff on the floor. All eyes turned to the emperor.

"Senators," said Nero, "I am told that the crowd outside has grown more numerous, and that many among them are now brandishing torches and clubs. It seems they have been informed of your judgment, and they are not pleased."

"But the announcement hasn't yet been made," said a senator near Titus. "Who told them?"

"Probably one of the imperial slaves," said another. "They're constantly running in and out of the chamber."

Shouting was audible from the Forum, even though the Senate House doors were closed. When the bronze doors were opened, moving slowly on their massive hinges, the muffled clamor from outside rose to a roar.

Titus followed the other senators onto the porch. He was shocked by what he saw.

The crowd had grown much bigger. The Forum was a sea of angry, shouting faces. Men stood alongside statues, on their pedestals, and on the steps and porches of every building in sight. The crowd had even overrun the venerated speaker's platform, the Rostra, where men waving torches sat astride the famous ships' beaks that projected over the crowd.

At the sight of the senators emerging from the Senate House, the crowd surged forward, rushing halfway up the steps before Nero's Praetorian guards formed a cordon to stop them. They shouted, shook their fists, and brandished clubs. Some farther back in the crowd dared to throw stones at the Praetorians, who raised their shields to protect themselves. The clatter was deafening.

Titus anxiously scanned the crowd and was relieved to see that his body-guards were right where he had left them. But he would not rejoin them yet; Titus had no intention of attempting to pass through such an angry mob. It was a sad day, when wearing a senatorial toga in the heart of Roma could make a man feel like a target!

"This is madness," whispered Titus.

"This is exactly the sort of behavior a speech like yours encourages," said Senator Cassius, drawing alongside him.

"That's absurd," said Titus. "These people weren't present in the chamber to hear my speech."

"Nor were they present to see the result of the vote, yet they knew of it quickly enough. Slaves talk. And knowing that there are senators who sympathize with their cause, indeed are willing to argue for it on the floor of the Senate, however recklessly, only encourages such people to think they may obtain what they want by agitation."

"What's to be done?" asked Titus.

"Since this rabble lacks the self-discipline of their betters, they can be dispersed only by force."

Nero apparently thought otherwise. While the senators continued to huddle on the porch, seeing no safe way to leave, an imperial herald pushed through their ranks and took up a position at the top of the steps. He blew a horn repeatedly until the mob grew quiet enough for him to be heard.

Such heralds were chosen for their ringing voices. This one was able to project sufficiently to fill the vast space, so that his words echoed back from buildings across the way. "Citizens, Caesar has proclaimed an edict! Listen well!"

Amid the hush there were shouts of "Nero! Nero will show mercy! Caesar will save us from the unjustness of the Senate!"

Was such a thing possible? Nero had the power to override the Senate on many matters, but would he choose to do so on this occasion? In the ancient days of the city, when Roma was ruled by kings, it was said that the monarch often took the side of the common people against the rich nobles. Kings had as much cause to fear the nobility as did commoners, so kings and commoners made natural allies. Would Nero take this opportunity to reach out to the people, over the heads of the Senate, and make himself the hero of the rabble? Could even Nero afford to flout the law and make enemies of so many in the Senate?

When the herald spoke, the crowd's hopes were dashed. "The Senate has debated the issue which concerns you. The Senate has reached its judgment. The law will be upheld. The sentence will be carried out. Caesar admonishes you for this unseemly and threatening behavior. This gathering is declared unlawful. You are hereby ordered to disperse at once!"

The mob reacted with howls of protest. More stones were hurled. Some landed near the herald, who quickly retreated.

More torches were passed through the crowd and set alight. The sight of so many flames was alarming. What were these people thinking, to use fire as a threat? An open flame was a force no man could control; fire could sweep anywhere, destroy anything if its power was unchecked. In the last years of the Republic, the Senate House itself had been incinerated by an angry mob. The Divine Augustus had rebuilt it in greater splendor. Was it now to be burned again?

Scanning the crowd, Titus suddenly spotted a familiar face. Hackles rose on the back of his neck. It was Kaeso. His brother was part of the mob. No, not a mere participant, but some sort of ringleader! Kaeso was brandishing a torch in the very faces of the Praetorians protecting the Senate steps, waving with his other arm and yelling encouragement to those around him.

Titus shook his head. Just as he had harbored the false hope of receiving the accolades of his fellow senators for making a fine speech, so he had been looking forward to telling Kaeso what he had done, to let his brother know that he was not such an unfeeling fellow after all, in fact that he had done something rather courageous, especially considering his position in society. What a change that would have been, to receive some approval, even praise from Kaeso! But here was Kaeso, spoiling things, as always, not just taking part in the demonstration but yelling louder than anyone else and making a spectacle of himself. Titus cringed; what if one of his fellow senators noticed Kaeso in the crowd, took a good look at him, and despite the shaggy beard and wild-eyed expression noted his resemblance to Titus and realized who he was? If the other senators knew that his brother was one of the leaders of the mob, Titus would be mortified.

Suddenly his brother looked back at him. Kaeso's reaction at seeing him exactly matched that of Titus on seeing Kaeso. He blanched, looked shocked and appalled, then disgusted and angry. The twins stared at each other for a long moment, as if looking into a distorting mirror. Then, as neither could bear to look at the other a moment longer, at the same instant they turned their gazes elsewhere.

Soon the tramp of marching feet echoed through the Forum. Having failed to quell the mob with his edict, Nero had summoned more Praetorians from their garrison outside the city. As the ranks of grim-faced soldiers converged with swords drawn, many in the crowd panicked and fled at once. Others pulled back reluctantly, throwing rocks as they withdrew. A few dared to stand up to the Praetorians, wielding their bludgeons and torches.

Titus looked for Kaeso, but he had disappeared in the surging crowd.

To reinforce the Praetorians, Nero also called up the vigiles, the troop of trained firefighters first organized by Augustus. The vigiles also acted as night watchmen and sometimes apprehended runaway slaves. They wore leather helmets instead of armor and carried firefighter's pickaxes, not swords, but their discipline made them more than a match for the shopkeepers and laborers in the crowd.

A few heads were broken and some blood was spilled, but soon the mob dispersed. While the vigiles extinguished the abandoned torches scattered around the Forum, the Praetorians regrouped and headed for the house of Pedanius, where the slaves were being kept under guard.

Within the hour, the slaves were driven to the place of execution outside the city, with Praetorians lining the entire route to forestall any interference. Normally the crucifixions would have been a public event—the larger the crowd, the better, for the purpose of moral instruction—but once the slaves were outside the walls, the Praetorians closed the Appian Gate and diverted all traffic from the Appian Way.

The crucifixions were carried out with no spectators. The work went on through the day and into the night.

The next morning, with Praetorians still patrolling the area, the Appian

Gate and the Appian Way were reopened for traffic. For travelers arriving from the south, their first view of the city's outskirts was the grisly display of Roman justice that lined the road. From within the city a steady stream of citizens came to witness the fate of the four hundred slaves of Pedanius. Some gawked, speechless. Some muttered angry words. Some wept.

The crucified bodies remained on display for many days. Most of the senators found time to go and take a look at their handiwork, including Gaius Cassius Longinus, who cursed the failing eyesight that prevented him from beholding the full splendor of Roman justice.

Titus Pinarius did not go to see the crucifixions. He tried to forget everything that had happened that terrible day in the Senate House.

A.D. 64

Before dawn on a warm morning in the month of the Divine Julius, in his house on the Aventine Hill, Titus Pinarius awoke with the smell of smoke in his nostrils.

"Hilarion!" he called.

Chrysanthe stirred beside him. "What's happening?"

"I'm sure it's nothing, my dear. Go back to sleep."

Young Hilarion appeared at the door. The former doorkeeper had become one of Titus's favorite slaves; that was why Titus called for Hilarion by name, rather than simply clapping his hands to summon whichever slave was nearest.

Over the last three years or so—since the Pedanius affair—Titus had made a point of actually looking at his slaves, learning to tell them apart, paying attention to their idiosyncrasies, and even learning all their names. Every slave owner in Roma had taken a closer look at his human possessions in the aftermath of Pedanius's murder, and Titus had made a conscious decision to treat his slaves with more care. He told himself this was not a sign that he was growing soft with age (he was only forty-six, after all); he was simply being prudent. Did not a well-treated horse or dog return the investment of its master's kindness with better and longer service? Why should it not be so with the people one owned?

Among his slaves, Titus had taken special notice of Hilarion. The young man was not only presentable, being easy to look at and always well groomed, but was quick-witted and uncannily deft at anticipating his master's needs. Titus had taken to calling on Hilarion for almost everything, and so, waking with the smell of smoke in his nostrils, it was Hilarion's name that sprang to his lips.

"Yes, Master?" Hilarion spoke softly, in deference to his dozing mistress.

"Do you smell it, too?" Titus whispered

"Yes, Master. Smoke. It's not coming from inside the house. I woke some of the other slaves and we checked everywhere. It's not from close-by, either. I sent two of the messenger boys to circle the neighborhood, and they saw no signs of fire."

"That's a relief. Good for you, Hilarion. That was very responsible of you."

"Thank you, Master."

"Still, there's definitely smoke in the air. I think the smell is getting stronger."

"I think you're right, Master."

"Did you go on the roof?"

"Not yet, Master." Hilarion averted his eyes. The young man seemed to have a fear of heights. Ah well, no slave was perfect.

"Bring the ladder to the garden." Titus rose from his bed, groaning as he stretched his limbs. "I shall climb up myself."

Chrysanthe, keeping her eyes shut, murmured, "Make one of the slave boys do it."

"I think not, my dear. If there's something to be seen, I want to see it with my own eyes. But I'm sure I'll see nothing. Go back to sleep."

The climb up the ladder, even by the dim light of dawn, did not frighten Titus, but the possibility of slipping on a loose or broken tile did. He trod very cautiously across the roof, feeling the dry wind on his face. The wind came from the east and carried the smell of smoke. The sunlight just breaking over the distant hills to the east illuminated a small cloud of smoke that appeared to be rising from the far end of the Circus Maximus, down in the valley between the Palatine and the Aventine. As the cloud rose, it was tattered and dispersed by the wind, but lower down it was dense and black, and within it Titus fancied he could see the glow of flames and bits of whirling cinder.

What was burning? There was a shopping arcade at that end of the circus, with a large fabric storehouse Chrysanthe sometimes visited. Burning wool and linen would account for such a dense volume of smoke rising from such a small area. Ascertaining the source of the flames reassured him. The fire was a long way off, and undoubtedly the vigiles were already moving to contain it.

What wisdom and foresight the Divine Augustus had displayed when he established the vigiles! Before that, there had been only privately operated fire brigades in the city, composed of slaves hired out by their masters to fight fires. That system had never worked very well; the slaves had little incentive to risk their lives, and not everyone could afford to pay the exorbitant fees demanded by the brigade owners. Augustus levied a tax on the sale of slaves to establish the state-run vigiles, put military men in charge of their training, and induced slaves to take on the hazardous duty by offering them freedom and citizenship after a six-year term of service.

Climbing carefully down from the roof, Titus decided to get on with his day. He would send some slaves to keep watch on the fire, but unless there was some unexpected development, he would simply try to ignore the acrid smell. He would have a quick bite to eat, then bathe at his local establishment—but no, those baths were located not far from the source of the flames, so perhaps that was not a good idea. He would hire a sedan and go to the Baths of Agrippa instead; out on the Field of Mars the air would almost certainly be clearer. Titus had a number of letters to dictate to business associates in Alexandria, and that was best done after a relaxing soak in the hot plunge. There were also arrangements to be made for young Lucius's upcoming toga day. How was it possible that his son was almost seventeen?

But even at the Baths of Agrippa the smell of smoke was strong, and everyone was talking about the fire. Titus, who had seen the source, overheard so many obviously false rumors that he dismissed them all. But on his way home, he saw that the fire was now producing a great deal of smoke. The black cloud filled a quarter of the sky.

Hilarion greeted him with alarming news. Far from being contained, the fire had spread to the Circus Maximus, engulfing the entire eastern end. The flames had begun to work their way up the slope of the Palatine and were threatening the imperial residence.

Titus happened to know that Nero was away from Roma, down at his villa at Antium. At least the emperor was safe.

Titus found Chrysanthe in their bedroom. He was going to tell her to begin packing her more valuable jewelry, but she was already doing so. He ordered Hilarion to fetch a specially designed trunk from the storage room and bring it to the vestibule. Tending to the task himself, Titus began to take the wax masks of his ancestors from their niches, wrapping each one in linen and stacking them carefully in the trunk.

Lucius appeared. "Can I help, father?"

"Of course, son," said Titus, glad to see the boy take an interest in his ancestors. Lucius took the mask of his namesake in his hands. Looking from the mask of his father to the face of his son, Titus smiled to see how closely Lucius resembled his grandfather.

"Are we leaving the house, father?"

"I don't think it will come to that. Still, it never hurts to be prepared." Titus meant what he said. He was not seriously worried, at least not yet, but already in the back of his mind he was calculating the time it would take to reach their country house on the far side of the Tiber. It was usually only half a day's journey, but the roads might be crowded with others fleeing the city.

"There, that's the last of the ancestors, carefully packed away," he said. "Now I think I shall go and take a look at the fire myself."

"May I go with you, father?" said Lucius.

Titus hesitated. His impulse was to say no, but Lucius was nearly a man, after all. In some families, he would already have received his manly toga. Titus could hardly order him to stay at home with his mother.

"Of course, son. You'll come with me, and together we will see what there is to see."

Taking only a pair of bodyguards with them, father and son set out. Smoke was thick in the air, stinging their eyes and making Titus cough. The streets were full of people. Some seemed to be going about their normal business, conversing and even laughing as if nothing untoward was taking place. Many more were heading away from the fire, toward the Tiber, looking anxious. Common people pushed carts piled high with their meager possessions. Groaning under the weight, slaves carried litters and sedans normally used for passengers but instead loaded with trunks and precious objects. One of the most bizarre sights was a gilded litter carried by an elegantly outfitted troupe of Nubian slaves, in which the passenger was a bronze statue of Aphrodite reclining. Young Lucius laughed aloud at the strangeness of it.

People were on their knees, praying before the Ara Maxima. A huge throng had gathered in front of the Temple of Fortune, where harried-looking priests were trying to calm the wailing women on the temple steps.

Titus and Lucius passed a cart loaded with scores of round leather boxes. No doubt the capsae contained the prized scrolls of some devoted bibliophile. Titus had not even thought of what would become of his small library in a fire. Did he own enough capsae to stuff them all into, if he needed to carry them to safety? Some of his books were quite old and valuable, like the history of Livius that had been a gift from Claudius to Titus's father.

The entrances to the Circus Maximus were open, so they went inside and ascended the steps to the highest tier of seats in the curve at the far western end. A number of others had done the same thing. It was as if they were spectators at a play staged by Vulcan himself. The far end of the circus was a bowl of flame that reached as far as the spine down the middle of the track. To their left, much of the slope of the Palatine above the circus was aflame, including a small part of the imperial complex. The fire had also engulfed the farthest slope of the Aventine. With a gasp, Titus realized that his local baths, the place he had considered visiting that morning, must be completely lost to the fire. He thought of the little man who always greeted him at the entrance and the Egyptian slave boy who performed massage and flirted so outrageously with the customers. Had they been trapped by the fire? What if Titus had gone there earlier this morning? Would he still be alive?

A hot wind blew down the length of the Circus Maximus, stinging Titus's eyes and filling his mouth with the taste of ash. He wiped his hand across his face and saw that his fingers were black with soot.

Titus had seen enough and was ready to leave, but Lucius pointed to a distant group of vigiles who could be seen at work on the Aventine. A small group of spectators inside the circus had gathered, leaning over the upper parapet of the viewing stands to watch them.

"Father, let's go see!"

"We should head back. Your mother will be worried—"

"But others are watching. It must be safe. Please?"

In truth, Titus was curious himself to see the vigiles at work. They walked along the upper parapet until they reached the crowd and could go no farther. It was just as well; this was as close to the flames at the end of the circus as Titus cared to go. Leaning over the parapet, they had a clear view of the vigiles below.

Flames had just been sighted on the roof of a building of three stories just across the street from the circus. The vigiles were using all their tools to fight the fire before it could claim the building. A portable pump with a tank of water had been rolled as close as possible. While two of the men aimed the huge metal nozzle, four others worked the seesaw pump that sent a jet of water streaming all the way to the roof of the building. More vigiles, calling on citizens to help them, had formed a bucket brigade to continuously replenish the tank with water from a neighborhood fountain.

Farther away, another group of vigiles was attempting to demolish a building already lost to the flames. A ballista of the sort the legions used to hurl missiles—essentially a huge crossbow with a hand-cranked ratchet to set the tension—was used to launch three-pronged iron hooks attached to chains. Aimed with uncanny precision, one hook after another landed inside a window frame and caught fast. When five of the hooks were in place, the vigiles formed teams, seized the chains, and heaved in unison. The burned-out wall gave way and collapsed with a shower of sparks. The vigiles dropped the chains, took up picks and axes, and ran to break up the fallen debris.

"What they're doing must be incredibly dangerous!" said Lucius. "But look there, farther up the hill. Aren't they actually setting a fire?"

With their prefect barking orders at them, some of the vigiles took up firebrands, lit them from the smoldering embers of the demolished building, and set fire to a long, narrow, one-story building at the periphery of the conflagration.

"I think that must be what's called a fire break," said Titus. "If they can destroy that building quickly, you see, the gap they'll create may put an end to the fire's progress, as least in that direction."

Lucius nodded, fascinated by both the fire and the techniques used to combat it. "Could I join the vigiles someday?"

Titus laughed, and quickly looked around, thankful that no one in the crowd seemed to have overheard. Tradition and the law said that Lucius was almost a man, but he still had some boyish ideas about the world. "The vigiles are all slaves and freedmen, Lucius. Such labor is not for free-born men, not even those of the lowest social rank."

"But who commands them? Like that fellow there, shouting orders?"

"Men of the equestrian class are eligible to serve as prefects of the vig-iles. But no patrician would ever stoop to such a prefecture. If you're look-ing for adventure, for a young man of your social rank there's always a military career—"

"But soldiers don't put out fires. They burn down cities on purpose."

Titus pursed his lips. "Yes, sometimes fire is a weapon used by the le-gions. But I'm sure the troops are trained to put out flames, as well, when the enemy uses fire against us." He thought of an example. "When your many-times-great-uncle the Divine Julius was trapped with his army in Cleopatra's palace at Alexandria, the Egyptians tried to burn him out. They set fire to a warehouse attached to the Great Library. I imagine Cae-sar's men were responsible for putting out that fire before it spread out of control."

Lucius nodded thoughtfully. He gazed at the vigiles below. "Just a group of slaves and freedmen, then. Still, one has to admire their bravery and their skill."

Not long after noon, the wind abruptly ceased. The cinder-filled smoke rose straight into the air, like a vast column. Thanks to the calm air and the hard work of the vigiles, the fires appeared to be under control, at least on the Aventine.

Titus decided not to leave the city. Before he went to bed, he instructed Hilarion and several other slaves to keep watch through the night and to wake him at once if the need arose.

That night he and Chrysanthe made love, something they had not done in a long time. Perhaps it was the air of crisis that aroused him, and her as well, for she seemed to enjoy herself immensely. Certainly the act relieved a great deal of tension and helped Titus fall asleep.

He had a strange dream. He was taking an augury on the Palatine, but there were no spectators; the whole city was empty. He was watching for birds when suddenly, one by one, every cloud in the sky burst into flame, like tufts of white fleece set afire. The flaming clouds began to loose raindrops of fire on the city, setting everything alight.

That was when Chrysanthe and Lucius woke him. Titus bolted upright, drenched with sweat. He found it hard to breathe, and his throat was sore. The air was thick with smoke.

"Father, come to the garden. Look at the sky!"

He followed his wife and son, wondering if he was still dreaming, for in the middle of the night the starless sky was aglow with a dull red illumination. Titus climbed the ladder to the roof, with Lucius following him. From his rooftop, he witnessed a horrific sight: the entire Circus Maximus was in flames. The long valley between the Aventine and the Palatine was a lake of fire. Indeed, below a certain level, the entire city appeared to be a sea of flames, with the hills rising like islands from the conflagration. Even on the hilltops, here and there he saw spots of flame or the glow of orange embers amid the charred remains of areas already burned. The imperial complex on the Palatine was almost entirely engulfed.

"Why was I not awakened sooner?" he shouted. "I told Hilarion to wake me at once if the fire grew worse."

"They say it happened very quickly, father. The fire seemed to spread everywhere all at once—"

"We must leave immediately, and pray we're not too late!"

The trunk with the wax effigies and other essential valuables, packed and loaded onto carts earlier in the day, were wheeled into the street by his strongest slaves. His three young daughters were roused by their mother. By the time they were all ready to leave, everyone was in a near panic.

Titus summoned the slaves and gave them instructions. They were all to come with the family, each carrying something of value, except for two of the youngest and strongest bodyguards. "You two will stay here as long as possible. If the flames fail to reach this street, it will be your job to protect the house against looters. If the flames do come, and if vigiles are here to fight it, you will help them save this house."

"But, Master," said one of the slaves, "what if the house catches fire, and there's no one to help, and we have no choice but to flee?"

Titus realized that both slaves were hardly more than overgrown boys, ill-equipped to make such a decision. "Hilarion will stay with you. He'll decide if you're to leave or stay. Do you understand? Hilarion has authority to give you orders while I'm gone."

Titus looked at Hilarion and felt an unaccustomed twinge of some unpleasant emotion. Was it guilt? Before he could think about it, Hilarion stepped forward and took his master's hand.

"Thank you, Master. You honor me with your trust."

Titus nodded but found it difficult to look the slave in the eye. He gathered the household and set out.

The route Titus intended to take was blocked, and they were forced to double back and seek another. The dark streets, filled with terrified people, were lit only by a dull vermilion glow from the sky. Amid the chaotic crush of bodies, Titus overheard an outrageous statement. A man nearby said, "It was set by the emperor, you know! It was Nero's own agents who started the fire, and then kept starting more fires, all over the city!"

Titus grabbed the man by the arm. "That's a filthy lie!"

"It's the truth," said the man. "I saw it happen with my own eyes. Uniformed men in leather caps demolished the wall of a granary, using some sort of battering ram—a good stone wall that would never have caught fire—and then they deliberately set fire to the contents. I know arson when I see it!"

"What you saw were the vigiles, you fool, setting fire to a warehouse full of highly flammable grain before the greater fire could reach it and cause the grain dust to explode. Tearing down walls and setting small fires is a part of the vigiles' work—"

"Setting fires to stop a fire? How stupid do you think I am?" shouted the man. "This fire was set by Nero's men. I've seen the evidence, and so have plenty of others. As for the vigiles you talk about, they're doing nothing to stop the fire. They've joined in the looting."

There was no time to argue. Titus roughly shoved the man aside and pressed on.

The streets were like something from a nightmare, littered with rubble and overturned carts. Abandoned children huddled in corners and wept.

Confused elders wandered aimlessly, looking lost. There were also a great many dead bodies blocking the way. Some had died from inhaling smoke, perhaps, for their bodies were unmarked. Others had died from burns, and others appeared to have been trampled by the crowd.

Finally, Titus and his household reached the nearest bridge across the Tiber. The area in front of the bridge that funneled into the narrow road-way was jammed with people, animals, and carts. It would take a long time to cross. Some people, in desperation, were swimming across the river instead. At last Titus and his household set foot on the bridge, with the crowd pushing them forward. He counted heads. By some miracle, they had all managed to stay in a group, even the oldest and weakest of the slaves.

But not everyone in his family was accounted for.

He called to his son, "Lucius, you know the way to the villa. You can lead the others there, can't you?"

"Of course I know the way, father. But what are you talking about? You'll lead us there."

Titus sighed. "No. I have to go back."

Chrysanthe heard him and spun around. "Don't be ridiculous, husband! What could you possibly have forgotten that's worth going back for?"

"I'll join you later tonight, or perhaps in the morning. Don't worry about me. The gods will look after me."

Titus stopped in his tracks. The crowd surged past him, carrying his household onto the bridge and quickly out of sight.

It was a struggle to move against the current. He was jostled and poked and cursed at, and several times he was almost knocked down. At last he cleared the thickest part of the crowd and was able to move more freely.

He made his way to the Forum. Here the flames were haphazard, with some buildings alight and others as yet unscathed. Had the holy hearth-fire, which must never go out, been transferred to a sacred vessel by the Vestals and taken to safety, as in the days when the Gauls invaded the city? How strange, to worry about a fire going out in the middle of an inferno!

Above the Forum, the whole Palatine appeared to be aflame. The Au-guratorium, the ancient Hut of Romulus, the temples, the houses of the rich, the imperial residence—was everything destroyed? The catastrophe was beyond comprehension.

He pressed on and reached the Subura. There were large areas here where the flames had not yet reached. What a conflagration that would make, if all these towering tenements, built so closely together, should catch fire! He tried to remember the streets that would take him to Kaeso's latest residence, but found himself lost in the darkness and the unfamiliar maze of alleys. What a fool's mission he had undertaken! What mad impulse had driven him back into the city to look for his brother? What were the chances he could possibly find Kaeso amid so much confusion?

Titus rounded a corner and came upon a large area where a tenement had recently been demolished. In the open space, a small group of people had gathered and were watching a burning building nearby. In the middle of the group were Kaeso and Artemisia, holding hands.

While all the other people around were in frantic motion, Kaeso and his friends stood perfectly still. With their faces turned toward the fire, they seemed to be in a kind of trance. Some stood in silence with linked hands. Others clapped or sang or shouted prayers to their god. Some seemed to be weeping with joy.

"The end has come! The end has finally come! Praise God!" cried one of the women, raising her hands.

"This is judgment day! Roma has been judged and found wanting!" cried a man in a tattered tunic with a long white beard. "Fools call on their false gods to save Roma, but I say God has cursed Roma! God has damned Roma! Praise God and all his works! And of all his works, this is the mightiest, to smite this wicked city and destroy it!"

Some passersby overheard the man's ranting and were outraged. They shook their fists, shouted curses, and threw stones at the Christians, then hurried on.

Titus strode into the gathering. He walked up to Kaeso. His brother had a blissful expression, lit by the flames. He did not notice Titus at first. Finally he lowered his eyes and looked at his brother in surprise.

"Titus! Why are you here?" Kaeso looked perplexed, then smiled. "Have you come to join us at last?"

"I came to see that you were alright, Kaeso."

Kaeso grinned and nodded. "Words can't describe my joy!"

"At what? Seeing the city of our ancestors burned to the ground?"

"This is the end of the world, Titus. The day we've been waiting for, longing for."

"Don't be absurd! Come with me, before it's too late."

" 'Too late'? Those words have no meaning now. This is the end of all things, the end of time itself. Praise God!"

Suddenly the burning building collapsed. The Christians let out a collective sigh of ecstasy at the awesome sight, but as showers of cinders and bits of flaming debris swept toward them, they retreated in confusion. Even Kaeso gave a start and staggered back from the fiery blast. The golden amulet at his breast glittered bright red in the firelight, like a flaming cross.

Without thinking, Titus reached out, grabbed the fascinum, and gave it a hard yank. The twine necklace snapped. Titus turned and ran back the way he had come, clutching the talisman in his fist, desperate to return to the bridge and be reunited with his family.

Let Kaeso perish in the flames, if that was his desire. Titus would not allow the fascinum of his ancestors to be lost in the conflagration.

For days the fires continued to rage.

From his country estate on the far side of the Tiber, Titus could see the distant glow of the flames at night. During the day he could see great columns of smoke.

Eventually the glow grew dimmer and the smoke diminished. Had the fires been extinguished?

The news he received from neighbors and passersby was confusing and contradictory. The fires had been contained but continued to burn in isolated areas; the fires had spread all the way across the Field of Mars to the Tiber, consuming the whole city, so that nothing was left to burn; the fires had been put out several times, but someone kept setting more fires. It was impossible to know what to believe.

Was his house still standing? If the house was lost, Hilarion and the two slaves should have come to join him, but they had not. Was the house destroyed, then, and were all three slaves dead?

At last Titus decided to venture back to the city. Lucius wanted to come with him. Feeling anxious and uncertain about what he might find, Titus was glad to have his son for company. They took bodyguards with them. Who knew what degree of order prevailed in the city?

As they neared the Tiber, the smell of smoke grew stronger. That was not a good sign. But no vast clouds of smoke loomed over the city. There was very little traffic on the road, and they crossed the bridge with almost no other people in sight. It was as if Roma had been completely abandoned. But this was a temporary illusion. The fire had not reached the waterfront, leaving the wharves and warehouses intact, and here and there they saw sailors and dockworkers going about their business. Nor had the fire consumed the Capitoline Hill. Above them, the great temple precinct, including the most ancient and sacred Temple of Jupiter, appeared to be unscathed.

Titus had intended to head directly to the house, but Lucius suggested they scale the Capitoline first; from its summit they could see virtually the entire city and ascertain the state of things. Titus acquiesced, in part because he dreaded finding his house in ruins and was willing to postpone the discovery a little longer.

Long ago, when he first came to Roma, Titus had stood on the Capitoline and gazed out over the city, marveling at the view. Now he stood with his son in the same spot and was aghast at the extent of the damage. To be sure, while small fires still burned in a few scattered locations, in most places the flames had been extinguished. And the extent of the damage was not as great as he had feared. The worst of the devastation was on the Aventine and the Palatine and in the low area between the Palatine and the Esquiline. Much of the Forum was undamaged, the Field of Mars had largely escaped the ravages of the fire, and only a few areas of the Subura had been destroyed. Looking toward the Aventine, he could not tell whether his house still stood or not. Some parts of the neighborhood looked blackened and charred but others appeared unscathed.

When Titus had first stood on this spot to take in the view, Kaeso had been beside him. Where was his brother now? Titus touched the fascinum at his breast and whispered a prayer to Jupiter, greatest and most powerful of gods, that his brother was still alive, and—since the world had not ended, as Kaeso had so joyfully predicted—that he had seen the foolishness of his beliefs and was ready to repent of his atheism and return to the worship of the gods.

They descended from the Capitoline and headed to the house. As they drew nearer, they saw that some houses had been burned and others had not; the caprice of the fire followed no discernible pattern. They rounded a corner, and Titus saw the house of his nearest neighbor. The place was a pile of smoldering rubble. His heart leaped to his throat. He could hardly breathe. He took a few more steps, and his own home came into view.

The house still stood. The wall adjacent to his neighbor had been scorched and blackened, but there was no other sign of damage.

Lucius cried out with joy and ran ahead. He reached the entrance, hesitated for a moment, then disappeared. Were the doors standing open? Surely Hilarion had the sense to keep them shut and bolted. Titus quickened his pace. Before he reached the house, Lucius reappeared. The boy looked stunned.

Titus reached the entrance and saw the cause of his son's distress. The doors had been smashed and ripped from their hinges. In the vestibule lay two mangled bodies. By their tunics, Titus recognized the two young bodyguards he had left to protect the house.

He walked slowly through the house, from room to room, speechless.

His home had been ransacked. Every portable object of value left behind when the family had fled had been taken—vases, lamps, rugs, even some of the larger pieces of furniture. Gone was the antique chair in which Cato the Younger had once sat.

What the thieves could not take they had destroyed. The marble statue of Venus in his garden had been overturned and broken into pieces—an act of wanton desecration. Floor mosaics had been shattered, as if beaten with a hammer. Wall paintings had been smeared with excrement. In the room where Titus slept, the bed he shared with Chrysanthe had been destroyed, the wooden frame broken and the bedding ripped apart.

It was as if the rampant destructiveness of the fire had infected the looters with an insane desire to cause as much damage as possible. Or was this the envy of the poor for the rich, allowed by chaos to manifest itself unchecked? Titus was appalled at the hatefulness of those who had done such a thing to his home. He had never realized that he lived among such people. He thought of the angry mob that had gathered outside the Senate House when the fate of Pedanius's slaves was decided. Were those the sort of people who had done this? Perhaps men like Gaius Cassius Longinus were right to be so suspicious and disdainful of the Roman rabble.

Titus entered the slave quarters. These small rooms, furnished with simple pallets for sleeping, were largely unmolested; there was little of value in them to be stolen or damaged. From the next room he heard a faint scuffling sound. It occurred to him that the thieves or some other vagrants might have taken refuge in this part of the house. He was about to call for the bodyguards to join him when a familiar face peered around the corner.

It was Hilarion.

The young slave looked at first fearful, then relieved, then ashamed. He ran to Titus and dropped to his knees.

"Forgive me, Master! The day after you left, men broke into the house. We had no way to stop them. There were too many. They killed the bodyguards. They would have killed me, too, if I hadn't managed to hide myself. Please, Master, don't punish me!"

"Hilarion! Of course I won't punish you. But why didn't you come to the country estate and bring me the news?"

"You told me to stay here, Master. And it was a good thing I did, because that night the neighbor's house caught fire. I ran and found some vigiles, and they managed to stop the flames from spreading to this house. There was always the chance the fire might come back, so I couldn't leave. Oh, Master, I've been so frightened here, all alone, especially at night. There's been so much violence—people killed, boys and women raped, horrible crimes!"

Titus pulled the slave to his feet. "You did very well, Hilarion. Thank the gods you're still alive!"

They managed to find a bit of food in the pantry. Titus sat with Lucius and Hilarion in the garden. The sight of the broken Venus made him lose his appetite.

Titus stood. "I'm going for a walk. Alone."

"But, father, surely you should take one of the bodyguards with you," said Lucius.

"No, they'll stay here with you and Hilarion. I am a Roman senator, a patrician, and a blood relation of the Divine Augustus. I will not be so intimidated that I cannot take a walk around my city without armed men to protect me!" Titus strode to the vestibule and left the house.

He wandered through the city, awed by the scale of the destruction. In once-familiar areas he became hopelessly lost; streets had been filled with rubble and landmarks had vanished. On a slope of the Esquiline he came upon a troop of vigiles working to put out one of the remaining fires. The vigiles were covered with mud and soot and looked utterly exhausted, yet still they labored. What a foul slander, that anyone should have accused such men of arson and looting!

As twilight began to fall, there was a terrible beauty in the way the blanket of clouds reflected the somber glow of the still-smoldering city, as if the sky were a vast, mottled bruise above the wounded earth. Roma was like a beautiful woman who had been terribly scarred. She was still recognizable, however damaged, and still beloved. Titus would never abandon her.

Above him on the Esquiline a slender tower rose like a finger pointing to the sky. The tower was located in the Gardens of Maecenas, one of the imperial properties where Nero sometimes resided; the gardens appeared to have escaped the devastation. It was the hour of twilight, and all was still. From the tower, Titus heard the music of a lyre and a man singing. The voice was thin and reedy, but strangely poignant.

The song was about the burning of Troy—Troy, most glorious of the ancient cities, more beautiful than Memphis or Tyre, which the Greeks had conquered by deceit and burned to the ground; Troy, from which the warrior Aeneas had fled to Italy and founded the Roman race. Troy had burned; now Roma burned. The song seemed to come from a half-forgotten dream. The melody, slowly strummed upon the lyre, cast an eerie spell.

Titus suddenly realized that it was the voice of Nero he heard. Stepping back and gazing up, Titus saw a figure in purple and gold standing at the parapet of the tower, strumming a lyre and gazing at the city. The young emperor had returned to Roma and found the smoldering ruins of Troy.

Nero reached the end of a verse. The music stopped. There must have been others with him on the parapet, for the silence was followed by quiet applause and voices urging him to sing another verse. Nero obliged. Titus listened, enthralled, but one of the vigiles, his face black with soot, put his hands on his hips and spat on the ground.

"This fire is the most terrible thing to happen to Roma since the Gauls sacked the city," the man muttered, "and what does the emperor do? He sings a pretty song. Can't hit a note, can he?"

Titus had no idea what the man was talking about. To him, the song was unspeakably beautiful, strange and mysterious, unbearably sad yet filled with hope. It did not matter that Nero was not a great singer; he had the soul of a great poet. What a contrast Nero presented to Kaeso, who had stared at the flames and grinned like an idiot. Nero responded with a lament that would wring tears from a god.

Gazing up, listening raptly to each word of Nero's song, transported by each note, Titus clutched the fascinum in his hand, glad to have it back in his possession at last. At that moment he felt that all his ancestors were watching him, just as all the gods were surely watching Nero.

A.D. 65

With his wife and son beside him, Titus Pinarius stood before the wax effigies of his ancestors in the vestibule of his house. As he looked from face to face and recited each of their names to honor them, Chrysanthe lit small candles and Lucius set one candle in each niche. Were his son's hands shaking? They were all nervous and excited about the day's upcoming events.

Titus was thankful that he had taken the wax effigies when he fled the city; unlike the objects the looters had stolen or destroyed, the masks of the ancestors were truly irreplaceable. Returning them to their niches had been the first step in restoring the house to its former glory. Titus had not yet found a skilled artisan to repair the floor mosaics—such artisans were in tremendous demand—but the wall paintings had been meticulously cleaned, the broken statue of Venus had been reassembled and patched and painted so that one could hardly tell it had been damaged, and many of the stolen or destroyed furnishings had been replaced. He had even found an antique folding chair almost identical to the one Cato had owned. In the months since the fire, thanks to a great deal of hard work and at considerable expense, Titus's household had gradually returned to normal. Many people in Roma had not been so fortunate.

Titus had looked after the images of his ancestors, and they had looked after him; of that he had no doubt. That was one of the reasons he honored them on this special day, when the emperor was about to pay him and his family a great honor.

Titus wore his senatorial toga with a purple stripe. His son also wore a toga, a garment he was still not used to. His wife was in her finest stola, a gown of beautifully embroidered ocher linen. Her hair was arranged in the style made fashionable by the emperor's strikingly beautiful young wife, Poppaea Sabina, with multitudes of ringlets framing her face.

The ceremony was concluded. They retired to the garden to await the day's events. Nothing in the garden was as beautiful as Chrysanthe, thought Titus, feeling proud, as he often did, of the choice he had made for a bride so many years ago. Nor was anything in the garden as fragrant as Chrysanthe. "You smell of rose petals and milk," he whispered in her ear.

She smiled. "Credit the emperor's wife. Poppaea has made it fashionable for the best women in Roma to bathe in milk."

"And will you become a Jewess, like the empress?" asked Titus, teasing her. It was widely known that Poppaea had shown favor to the Jews in Roma and had regularly received their scholars and holy men. Some claimed she had secretly converted to the religion.

"No more than you have become a Christian," said his wife, teasing him back. She gestured to the fascinum, which Titus was wearing to mark the special occasion. Titus did not find this jest particularly funny. It seemed to him that Kaeso must have altered the amulet in some way to make it look even more like a cross. Nevertheless, Titus wore the fascinum openly and proudly, refusing to hide it inside his toga.

There was a knock at the door, followed by a flurry of excitement in the house. Even the slaves were excited, and with good cause. It was not every day that the emperor himself came calling.

Hilarion rushed into the garden. "They're here, Master!"

"Are they coming in?"

"I think not, Master. The man at the door says you're to come out and join them."

"Then we mustn't keep them waiting." Titus took his wife by the hand and allowed his son to lead the way.

The retinue in the street was even larger than Titus had expected. There were secretaries and scribes, a troop of Praetorians, several senators in togas, and even a colorful group of actors and acrobats. In the middle of the retinue, carried by some of the brawniest slaves Titus had ever seen, was a large litter set on gilded poles and decorated to look like a giant swan. A hand adorned by many rings pulled back a purple curtain. Smiling broadly, Nero made a gesture of welcome. Sitting next to him was the beautiful Poppaea, her blond hair done up in an elaborate fashion that Titus had never seen before.

Portable steps were produced. Chrysanthe entered the litter first, followed by Titus and Lucius. They settled amid plush cushions across from the emperor and his wife. Titus felt Chrysanthe tremble and he took her hand. Poppaea smiled at this gesture of intimacy and likewise took one of Nero's bejeweled hands in hers.

"We're not pressed for time. I thought we might take a little tour of the city on the way to our destination," said Nero.

"Certainly," said Titus. "There's so much construction going on, all over Roma, I can't keep up with it." Actually, Titus was well aware of almost every building project in the city, but the tour would be a treat for Chrysanthe and Lucius, and he was enormously flattered by the emperor's offer to spend time with his family.

Nero smiled. "My great-great-grandfather famously said that he found Roma a city of bricks and left her clad in marble. I found a city of scorched marble but shall leave her covered in gold."

As they were carried aloft through the city, Nero proudly pointed out the rapid progress that had been made on reconstructing various temples and public structures. The rebuilding of the Circus Maximus was one of the largest projects; it would be some time before it was ready to reopen, but Nero had plans to make it more splendid and beautiful than before. There were also curiosities to be seen. Up on the Palatine, the ancient Hut of Romulus had been spared by the fire, and though most of the oldest parts of the imperial residence had been burned, the laurel trees flanking the original entrance had survived and remained intact.

"Surely that's an omen, father," declared Lucius, overcoming his shyness in front of the imperial couple, especially Poppaea, whose beauty could have intimidated any man.

"It certainly is," said Titus. "Those trees appear to be indestructible, immune to both fire and lightning. I believe those two laurel trees will survive as long as there are descendants of the Divine Augustus."

This comment was clearly appreciated by the imperial couple, who gave each other a loving glance. Poppaea, though not showing it yet, was rumored to be pregnant. Her first child with Nero, a daughter, had died in infancy; Nero had been grief-stricken. Now there was again hope for a new generation directly descended from the Divine Augustus, and an heir for the emperor, who was not yet thirty.

"So many beautiful old houses were lost," said Nero, pressing his fingertips together while he gazed at the passing view. "But the fire displaced not just the wealthy who lived on the Palatine, but a great many other people as well. I'm told many of those citizens lived in appalling squalor, stacked atop one another with hardly enough room to turn around. Well, we shall build shiny new tenements for them, better than those rattraps they lived in before. That will take time, of course. For now, sadly, many of the homeless are still in temporary shelters on the Field of Mars and at my own gardens across the Tiber. To give the citizens work, I've hired a veritable army of bricklayers and day laborers for construction projects all over the city. To feed their families, I've repeatedly lowered the price of grain. And to make sure such a catastrophe never occurs again, I've introduced new building codes that the experts assure me will reduce the danger of fire—buildings set farther apart, limitations on their height, requirements to keep firefighting implements such as picks and buckets on the premises, that sort of thing. Oh, look there," he said, pointing to an aqueduct covered with scaffolding. "We're also repairing and extending the aqueducts that were damaged. There must be cisterns and fountains to ensure an adequate water supply to fight any fire that may occur in the future."

"Caesar's swift and steady response to the crisis has been an inspiration to us all," said Titus.

"Ah, now we're passing through the very heart of what will become the new imperial complex," said Nero, grinning with excitement. "This entire side of the Palatine has been cleared and claimed for the new imperial apartments. And down there, in that cleared area that used to be crammed with hideous old buildings, there will be a rather large lake, entirely enclosed within the imperial complex. Won't that be charming? A private lake in the heart of the city, surrounded by vineyards and gardens and a little forest stocked with wild deer, so that Poppaea and I may retreat for a stroll in the countryside, or even go hunting, without ever stepping outside the imperial palace, much less the city walls. Of course, the lake will have a practical purpose as well. It will serve as a reservoir, a source of water in the event of fire."

The creation of the artificial lake was well under way. Hundreds of workers were raking and shoveling great piles of excavated earth, shaping them into the rolling hills that would become the man-made woodland surrounding the lake.

"Along here, on this side of the lake, there will be a vast pavilion with a covered walkway a mile long," said Nero. "The rooms will be very spacious and finished with the best of everything—imported marbles, fine statuary, ivory screens, and the most sumptuous fabrics. You must see the sketches the designers have made for me. The ceilings will be decorated with gleaming gems and mother-of-pearl, so that at night, by lamplight, it will seem that the starry sky itself has descended to gaze with envy at such splendid rooms. And gold—there must be a great deal of gold everywhere. We shall cover the whole facade with tiles of golden glass, so that it dazzles the eye. The only color that truly pleases me is purple, and the only metal is gold. How I love the weight of it, and the mellow color, like sunlight on water. Like that lovely little golden amulet you're always wearing, Senator Pinarius."

Titus touched the fascinum and smiled. "A gift from my ancestors."

"Yes, I know. Curious-looking thing," said Nero. He flashed a quizzical smile, then returned his attention to the construction work going on around them. "When the time comes, there shall be a grand ceremony to mark the day that Poppaea and the baby and I move in. I think I shall call it the Golden House. What do you say to that, Senator Pinarius?"

"A splendid name for a splendid house."

"The only house fit for a person such as myself to live in," mused Nero. "Ah, we've come to the site of the grand courtyard. This will be the main entrance for visitors who come from the Forum. The Sacred Way will terminate at a stairway that ascends to the door of the Golden House. There'll be other entrances, of course, including Augustus's old entry on the Palatine, flanked by those ancient laurel trees, but that will be a sort of back door. The grand courtyard is going to be enormous, surrounded by a portico with hundreds of marble columns. You can't really appreciate the enormity of it now, cluttered as it is with all these workmen's shacks. The centerpiece will be that colossal bronze statue going up in the middle, depicting myself. We haven't yet decided in what guise I should appear. Poppaea thinks I should pose as Hercules, but Zenodorus, the sculptor, thinks I should be Sol, wearing a crown of sunbeams. When it's finished, the statue will be over a hundred and twenty feet tall—the largest statue since the Colossus that once stood at Rhodes. And unlike that statue, this one will be covered in gold. Can you imagine the splendor of it on a sunny day? People will be able to see it from miles away, and the closer they come, the more dazzled they'll be. On a sunny day, it will be positively blinding."

"Truly, Caesar, the new Colossus will be a stupendous monument," said Titus, amazed anew not just at the extent of Nero's imagination but at the enormity of his expenditures. A great deal of private property had been seized by the state to allow for the massive expansion of the imperial palace, and a great many temple treasuries from all over the empire had been appropriated to pay for construction and to provide decorations.

In this ambitious enterprise, Titus had played an invaluable role. Auspices had to be taken to seek divine approval for many of Nero's actions, and religious ceremonies had to be conducted to propitiate the gods whose treasuries were depleted. Titus had faithfully served as Nero's augur, just as he had once performed the same duties for Claudius. He had volunteered to do so and had performed eagerly and with unswerving loyalty. Since the night he had been transfixed by Nero's song about the burning of Troy, Titus has become one of the emperor's most fervent adherents.

The emperor was thankful for his loyal service. The invitation to Titus and his family to accompany the emperor and his wife in the imperial litter was one of Nero's ways of thanking him.

"I am grateful, as always, to play any part, however small, in Caesar's grand enterprises," said Titus.

"Unfortunately, Senator Pinarius, not everyone seems to feel as you do," said Poppaea. She had been quiet throughout the tour and had even been looking a bit bored; no doubt she had heard Nero speak the same words many times before. Titus, who had met her on several occasions but had never spoken to her privately, was not quite sure what to make of Poppaea, who always seemed distant and self-absorbed and tended to speak in riddles. Nero was not her first husband; previously she had been married to Nero's friend Otho. Rumor had it that the three young people had become so intimate that they formed, as one wag put it, "a three-headed love monster." But ultimately Nero wanted Poppaea all to himself. He forced Otho to divorce her, appointed Otho governor of Lusitania to get him out of Roma, and made Poppaea his wife.

Her remark probably referred to the increasingly widespread rumors of a conspiracy against the emperor. Despite Nero's energetic response to the crisis and his optimistic plans for the future, a simmering discontent reached across all classes. The fire had been followed by a pestilence that had killed tens of thousands of people, especially among the homeless poor, and the loss of so many religious and historical treasures had thoroughly demoralized the populace. Nero's vast building projects were intended to replace those lost treasures, but among the wealthy there was a fear that his profligate spending would precipitate a financial crisis. Hostile senators were said to be plotting against him, and among the common citizens, vile rumors claimed that Nero himself had deliberately started the fire so that he could claim vast tracts of ruined real estate for the imperial house and rebuild the city to suit himself.

Unfortunately, and with obvious regret, Nero had found it necessary to banish a number of senators whom he suspected of disloyalty. Among these had been Gaius Cassius Longinus, the senator who had made an impassioned speech to crucify the slaves of Pedanius. Nero had ordered him to remove from his ancestral effigies the wax mask of the Cassius who had assassinated the Divine Julius—a perfectly reasonable request, Titus thought. The senator had refused. Cassius's exile to Sardinia had caused an outcry among his colleagues, who argued that pity should be shown to a jurist of such renown, especially since he was now completely blind.

Next to him, Titus heard Chrysanthe groan, and then he saw the reason. On a scorched wall, all that remained of a destroyed building, a message had been scrawled in black paint:

> *Strong and valiant,*
> *He killed his mother*
> *And set my house on fire!*

More and more frequently in recent days, Titus had seen such ugly graffiti on walls and in latrinae all over the city. Fortunately, a group of men was in the process of painting over this message and adding their own. Titus craned his neck to see what they were writing, but as the litter moved on all he could make out were the words *Christians* and *burn*.

"My loyal freedmen, hard at work," said Nero, pulling at the rings on his fingers. "I don't even have to ask them. They go about the city and clean up such slander wherever they see it."

"Gossip is a terrible thing," muttered Poppaea.

"It certainly is," agreed Chrysanthe, nodding sympathetically.

"But on this day, all those nasty rumors will be put to rest, and the true culprits will be brought to justice," said Nero, regaining his good humor. "The people will see that their emperor is dedicated to protecting Roma and destroying those who harm her. I shall give them a show they will never forget!"

They proceeded toward their destination, the imperial gardens on the far side of the Tiber, where Caligula had built a large racetrack for his private amusement at the foot of the Vatican Hill. Nero used the track frequently, for he loved to race chariots, and Seneca had convinced him that it was unsuitable for the emperor to race in public. Since the Circus Maximus was not yet rebuilt, Nero had decided to open the Circus Vaticanus to the public; it was one of the few spaces large enough to accommodate the spectacular entertainments he had devised for the punishment of the condemned arsonists.

As the litter bearers carried them across an undeveloped area of the Field of Mars, Titus saw the sea of makeshift shelters where much of the populace was living. These dwellings were little more than lean-tos built from scrap lumber, or makeshift tents stitched together from bits of cloth. On this day, no one stayed inside the shelters. Excited by the impending spectacle, everyone in Roma seemed to be heading in a great mass toward the imperial gardens across the Tiber.

As the litter passed through the crowd, with the Praetorians clearing the way, people flocked to have a look at the emperor and his wife. There were cheers and shouts of "Hail, Caesar!" and "Hail the beautiful Poppaea!" But some in the crowd shrugged and turned away, or gave the imperial couple hostile looks, or even muttered curses. Poppaea frowned and whispered in Nero's ear. He called to one of the Praetorians to tighten the cordon around the litter, then unhooked the chains holding back the drapes so that they could proceed in relative privacy; the gauzy drapes allowed Nero and his guests to see out but appeared opaque from the outside.

A new bridge crossed the Tiber, allowing direct access from the Field of Mars to the Vatican meadows. At Nero's orders, the bridge had been built with amazing speed for the purpose of allowing the homeless of Roma to cross easily from the city to the shelters provided for them on the far side. On this day, the new bridge served as a means for the multitudes of Roma to attend the spectacle in the Circus Vaticanus. Already such a crowd had gathered that the bridge and the area before it were packed with people, but the Praetorians quickly cleared a path for the litter to pass through and cross the river.

Spread across the Vatican meadows was a veritable city of makeshift shelters; some people even appeared to be living in the trees. Beyond the meadows they came to the formal gardens that had been planted by Caligula. These were entered through an iron gate. The Praetorians pushed back the crowd so that Nero could pass. The gardens to either side of the wide gravel path were splendid, with beds of roses and other fragrant flowers and fine statues, including a particularly striking fountain in which the nude Diana stood ankle-deep in shimmering water while the unfortunate Actaeon, transformed into a rearing stag, was attacked by his hounds.

They arrived at the circus. The permanent viewing stands, built of travertine, were elegantly appointed but quite small. These had been supplemented by the erection of temporary wooden stands that completely encircled the track and could accommodate tens of thousands of spectators. The stands were already about half filled, and more people were arriving at every moment.

The litter came to a halt before the travertine structure adjoining the circus. Nero and his party stepped out. The emperor and Poppaea abruptly disappeared—Titus was not sure where they went—while Titus and his family were escorted directly to the imperial box. Titus was flushed with excitement. He could see that his wife and wide-eyed son were equally elated. Never before had the Pinarii been invited to be the personal guests of the emperor at a public entertainment. Not only would they view the proceedings side by side with the emperor, but they would be seen beside him, in his company, perceived to be among the most elite of the imperial circle. This was an important day for the Pinarii—not just for Titus and his immediate family, but for all who had borne the name Pinarius in the past or would bear it in the future.

The box was lined with purple draperies bordered with gold and surrounded by a cordon of Praetorians. Titus and his family were the first guests to arrive and were shown to couches at one corner of the box. A slave offered them a choice of wines and set out a tray of delicacies for them.

Directly before them, in the center of the spine that bisected the oval racing track, loomed a towering Egyptian obelisk made from solid red granite. The obelisk had been brought to Roma by Caligula from the city of Heliopolis in Egypt. The four sides were strikingly plain, without hieroglyphs. A gilded ball was set atop the obelisk, balanced on the very tip. The obelisk was a landmark visible from many places in the city. Titus had previously seen it only from a distance and was awed by its height.

The Vestal virgins and members of various priesthoods had been seated in the front rows to the left of the imperial box. To the right of the box was a large section reserved for senators. Out in the arena, to warm up the crowd, musicians played while acrobats tumbled, walked on their hands, and formed human pyramids. Laughter and applause swept through the stands, but many people continued to talk and move about while waiting for the main event.

More guests arrived in the imperial box. Leading the party was Seneca. Since the death of Agrippina, he had become more powerful than ever, though Titus had heard rumors of growing discord between the emperor and his chief adviser; the strains of dealing with the aftermath of the fire were taking a toll on everyone. Arriving with Seneca was his wife, Paulina; now that he was in his sixties and she was nearly forty, the gap in their ages was not as striking as it once had been.

Also with Seneca was his handsome nephew. Lucan was two years younger than Nero and their shared love of poetry had made them close friends. Like Nero, Lucan had bloomed early. At the age of eleven he had created a sensation with his first poem, about the combat between Hector and Achilles, and at twenty-five he was the city's most famous poet. On this occasion, he wore an augur's trabea. Nero had seen fit to induct Lucan into the college well ahead of the prescribed age, just as previous emperors had done for Titus and his father.

Lucan was accompanied by his wife. Polla Argentaria was almost as famous as her husband, thanks to the verses he had written praising her. She was the daughter of a wealthy senator and, like Seneca's wife, had received an unusually extensive education for a woman. Argentaria was said to be her husband's muse and amanuensis, and perhaps even his collaborator, as she tirelessly helped him revise and perfect his verses.

Gaius Petronius was next to arrive. The emperor's arbiter of elegance was not quite forty and had flecks of silver in his hair. Titus found it impossible to put his finger on what set the man apart from all others; Petronius wore a toga about which there was nothing extraordinary, and his grooming, while impeccable, was not in any way unusual. Still, the man cast a spell by his very presence. Perhaps it was the effortless grace with which he moved, or his inscrutable expression. Even when he was most serious, there were flashes of amusement in his pale gray eyes.

Titus felt privileged to be in such illustrious company, but he also found it rather stressful, since he had difficulty keeping up with the conversation, which revolved largely around the three men's literary projects and was full of puns and allusions and double entendres, many of which Titus couldn't decipher. Lucan, he gathered, was about to publish the next volume of his epic poem about the civil war between Caesar and Pompeius, a work full of violent action and scenes of epic grandeur. Seneca, who had been reading the work in progress, thought that his nephew sided perhaps too much with Pompeius and the Republican cause against the Divine Julius, a point of view sure to stir controversy.

Petronius was working on something very different, a long work in which his narrator recounted a series of erotic misadventures and comical disasters, all related, to heighten the irony, in the most elegant and rarefied prose. Knowing how Nero relied on Petronius for advice on all matters to do with good taste, Titus asked him if he was responsible for staging the spectacles they were about to witness.

Petronius narrowed his eyes. "I contributed very little. Caesar devised most of the entertainments. The emperor threw himself into this project as he enters into all his endeavors, with extraordinary energy and enthusiasm. But what about you, Seneca—what are you working on these days, when you're not out mining gold to build the emperor's new house?"

Seneca smiled. "I've finally finished the play about Pasiphae." He noted the blank look on Lucius's face. "Do you know the tale, young Pinarius?"

"I'm afraid not," admitted Lucius. Titus winced. His son's education reflected on himself.

"Pasiphae was the wife of King Minos of Crete," said Seneca. "She was cursed by Neptune to crave intercourse with a bull."

"What woman has not?" said Petronius. Chrysanthe blushed, Lucius giggled nervously, and Titus himself was startled by the comment, but the others seemed to find it quite amusing.

"Just so," conceded Seneca with a wry smile, "but Pasiphae did something about it. She ordered the inventor Daedalus to construct an effigy of a heifer so realistic that even a bull would find it convincing, then she concealed herself inside the mock heifer and seduced the bull into gratifying her. Nine months later, Pasiphae gave birth to a child with a bull's head—the minotaur."

"Who but Seneca would bring such material to the stage?" said Petronius. It was impossible to tell whether his tone was respectful or sardonic. "Has the emperor read it yet?"

"The emperor is always my first reader, and invariably the most astute. I'm happy to say that Caesar seemed quite fascinated by the tragedy of Pasiphae. Ah, here he is now!"

They rose to their feet as Nero entered the box with Poppaea beside him. People in the crowd saw him enter, and a thrill ran up and down the stands. But the response was mixed. Just as earlier Titus had heard shouts of "Hail Caesar!" in the streets, so many in the crowd now shouted accolades, but there was a low grumbling as well, and scattered hisses.

Nero escorted Poppaea to her seat, then stepped forward and raised his hands. With his fair hair and purple-and-gold robes, he was visible and instantly recognizable to everyone in the circus. The crowd fell silent. For a moment, it appeared that Nero might address the crowd. Indeed, Nero had wanted to deliver the opening speech, but Seneca had persuaded him not to do so: there were simply too many problems that might arise when an emperor directly addressed such a large and unpredictable gathering.

Instead, Nero gestured to a public crier, who stepped forward. With his powerful, trained voice, the man was able to make himself heard from end to end of the circus. While he spoke, Titus could see that Nero moved his lips along with the crier, like a proud author in the theater mouthing lines spoken by an actor.

"Senators and people of Roma, you are here today at Caesar's invitation. Welcome! But if you have come expecting a mere entertainment, you may be surprised at what you are about to witness. Today you will not see charioteers race. You will not see gladiators fight to the death. You will not see wild animals hunted. You will not see captives of war made to re-enact a famous battle for your amusement. You will not see actors perform a comedy or a drama. What you will see is an act of justice, carried out under the open sky so that all the gods and the people of Roma may witness the proceedings.

"The criminals you will see punished today are guilty of arson and murder. They have conspired against the Roman state. They have plotted the destruction of the Roman people. Even those not directly guilty of setting fires must be punished. Their notorious hatred of the gods, of mankind, and of life itself makes them a menace to us all.

"Because of the fire, many of you are still without proper homes. Because of the fire, many of you lost your most cherished possessions. Because of the fire, many of you lost loved ones, whose cries of anguish still ring in your ears. Our city—the most beloved by the gods of all cities on earth—has been devastated. The gods themselves weep at the destruction of Roma and the suffering of the Roman people.

"Thanks to the vigilance of your emperor, the arsonists who perpetrated this misery have been apprehended. They call themselves Christians. The name comes from Christus, the founder of their sect, a criminal who suffered the extreme penalty at the hands of Pontius Pilatus, one of our procurators in Judaea during the reign of Tiberius. Thanks to Pilatus, the insidious superstition propagated by this Christus was checked—but only for a short while, because it quickly broke out again, not only in Judaea, the first source of this evil, but in many places across the empire, even here in Roma. Lurking among us, the followers of Christus have plotted our destruction.

"Thanks to Caesar's vigilance, the Christians were apprehended. Under interrogation, they revealed their accomplices and confessed their crime. More than confessed it, they proclaimed it, without remorse. The Christians are proud of what they did. They are gratified by your suffering!"

The crowd erupted in boos and jeers.

Initially, Titus had been dubious when the mass arrest of Christians began; they struck him as an ineffectual group of lay-abouts. But when he remembered the jubilant reactions of the Christians watching the flames, it was not hard to imagine that some of them had deliberately started the fire. Such a crime was almost unthinkable, but the fanaticism of all the Jewish sects was well known, and the unyielding atheism of the Christians and their loathing of all things Roman was particularly virulent. That their abhorrence of the gods had led them to such a monstrous crime was shocking, but perhaps not surprising.

The jeering of the crowd continued until Nero himself gestured for silence. The crier continued.

"But what punishment, you may ask, could possibly fit so terrible a crime? For offenses so hideous, so foul, so wicked, what retribution can possibly be adequate? That is what we are here to see.

"Senators and people of Roma, this is a holy day. We call on the gods to pay witness to what happens in this place. What we do, we do in honor of the gods, and in gratitude for the favor they have shown us."

The crier stepped back. Lucan stepped forward. From the folds of his trabea he produced a beautiful ivory lituus. While the young poet took the auspices, Titus felt a twinge of envy, wishing he had been chosen for the honor. But as high as Titus had risen in the emperor's favor, he knew he could not compete with Lucan, with whom Nero felt a special intimacy because they were so close in age and shared such a deep love of poetry.

The auspices were favorable. The emperor pulled a white mantle over his head to assume his role as Pontifex Maximus, stepped forward, and raised his hand. Every head in the circus was bowed as Nero uttered the invocation to Jupiter, Best and Greatest of the Gods.

The spectacle commenced.

At gladiator games and other public events, the punishment of criminals was often part of the program, but usually only a very small part, worked into the proceedings by making the condemned fight against gladiators or act as bait for wild animals. On this occasion, the punishment of criminals, because there were so many of them, and because their crime was so great, would make up the entire program. The stagers, with Nero guiding them, had faced great challenges both logistical and artistic. How could so many criminals of all ages be made to suffer and die in ways that were not only sure and efficient but also meaningful and satisfying to those who were watching?

From a cell beneath the newly erected stands a large number of men, women, and children were driven to the racetrack. They were dressed in rags. Most looked confused and frightened, but some had the same serene, glassy-eyed stare as Titus had seen on the faces of the Christians watching the fire. They seemed oblivious of what was about to happen, or perhaps they even looked forward to it.

"So many!" muttered Chrysanthe, leaning forward.

"Oh, this is only a small portion of the arsonists," said Nero. "There are many more to come. The punishments will go on for quite some time."

"How could we have had so many of them among us?" wondered Lucan. "What drew these terrible people to Roma in the first place, and how did they seduce decent Romans to join their ranks?"

"All things hideous and shameful from every part of the world eventually find their way to Roma, and inevitably attract a following," said Petronius. "As a flame attracts insects, as a whirlpool attracts flotsam, so Roma attracts the vermin and filth of the world."

"Yet, a flame is beautiful," said Nero, "once the charred insects are brushed aside. And a whirlpool is beautiful, once the flotsam is flushed away. Just so, Roma will be beautiful again, once it has been purified of these vile criminals." He gazed raptly at the arena below.

Next to him, Poppaea also sat forward in eager anticipation. While it might be true that she had played hostess to Jewish scholars and wise men, she detested the Christians, as Jewish heretics if nothing else.

Lucan looked sidelong at Titus. "My uncle tells me that you had a brother who called himself a Christian."

Titus stiffened. It was inevitable that the subject would come up, and he was prepared for it. "I have no brother," he said stiffly. Self-consciously, he touched the fascinum that nestled amid the folds of his toga.

From storage rooms under the stands, an army of stagehands produced a multitude of crosses and laid them on the sand. The Christians were made to circle the racetrack, driven with scourges, then were seized and thrown on the crosses. While they screamed in terror, their hands and feet were nailed in place. Then the crosses were set upright into holes that had been dug ahead of time.

Suddenly the circus was filled with a forest of crucifixes. The crowd jeered at the Christians. Spectators with strong arms and good aim competed to pelt them with stones and other objects. Some in the stands had brought eggs especially for this purpose.

"These crucifixions are in imitation of the dead god they profess to worship, who likewise ended up on a cross," explained Nero in a hushed voice. "While this batch hangs from the crosses, they will witness what happens to their accomplices."

More Christians were driven into the arena. Their arms were bound and they were wrapped in bloody animal skins, but their heads were uncovered so that their faces could be seen and their screams heard. At the two far ends of the circus, packs of vicious dogs were released. The animals sniffed the air. Within moments, they began racing toward the Christians.

The dogs had a long way to go. The Christians staggered first one way, then the other, trapped between the packs bounding toward them from both sides. The crowd went wild. People jumped to their feet with excitement, anticipating the moment the hounds would reach their prey. Nero smiled. This was exactly the reaction he had hoped for.

The dogs attacked without hesitation and tore their victims to pieces. The barking and screaming and the sight of so much blood and gore excited the crowd to an even higher pitch. Some of the Christians provided considerable sport as they squealed and whimpered for mercy and darted this way and that, trying to elude the dogs. Those among the Christians who died with a degree of dignity, muttering prayers or even singing songs, ignited the fury of the crowd. Such behavior made a mockery of justice; how dare such criminals continue to taunt their victims even as they were punished?

More Christians were driven onto the racetrack. More hounds were released. Each death was as bloody as the last, but the crowd began to grow restless, bored by the repetition. Nero had anticipated this. At his signal, a new phase of the spectacle began. To revive the spectators' interest, various familiar stories were reenacted, using the Christians as props.

For the story of Icarus, boys with wings attached to their arms were driven to the top of a portable tower and made to jump off. One after another they plummeted to earth and lay twitching on the sand. Those who survived were carried to the top of the tower and thrown off again.

To illustrate the story of Laocoön and his sons, tanks filled with deadly eels were wheeled onto the sand and groups of fathers and sons were thrown into the water, where they died screaming and thrashing.

For Titus, the most striking of the tableaux was the tale of Pasiphae, perhaps because Seneca had just related it. A naked Christian girl was first paraded around the track while the crowd jeered and shouted obscenities, then she was forced inside a wooden effigy of a heifer. By some trickery, the animal trainers induced a white bull to mount the effigy. The device was constructed to amplify the girl's cries rather than muffle them; her bloodcurdling screams could be heard from one end of the circus to the other. The crowd was transfixed. Eventually her screams stopped.

When the bull was finished, the trainers led it away. A few moments later, from a concealed compartment in the bottom of the effigy, a naked boy wearing a calf's head jumped out and performed a lively dance.

"The minotaur!" people cried. "She's given birth to the minotaur!"

The crowd went wild with applause and cheering. Nero beamed with pride.

Such tableaux, one after another, took place all up and down the length of the circus.

Eventually, for a climax, men with torches appeared, and all the Christians who lay lifeless or near to death on the sand and all the wooden props were set afire, though the crucifixes were left untouched. The sight of the flames was alarming, as was the stench of the smoke. Some in the audience, reliving the trauma of the conflagration, wept with grief. Others laughed uncontrollably. There were gasps and shrieks from the crowd, but also cheering and applause. The Christians were convicted arsonists, and the legally prescribed punishment for arson was death by fire.

As the scattered flames died down and night began to fall, sturdy poles twice the height of a man were erected in the spaces between the crucifixes. The poles had been soaked in pitch, as was evident from their strong smell. Obviously, another spectacle involving fire was about to be presented. The crowd reacted with cries of mingled dread and fascination. To the top of each pitch-soaked pole a kind of iron basket was affixed, large enough to hold a human body.

Thus far, Titus had watched the spectacle with grim detachment. The auspices had been unequivocally favorable for this event—Titus had watched closely as Lucan performed the augury—and that was a clear indication that the gods were pleased. Watching the gruesome punishments of the arsonists gave Titus no pleasure, but it was his somber duty as a citizen and as a friend of the emperor to witness the event.

Titus felt the need to empty his bladder. The moment seemed opportune, as there appeared to be an interlude before the next event, so he rose and excused himself. Looking over his shoulder, Nero told him where to find the nearest latrina and then giggled, as if at some secret joke. Titus left the imperial box, glad that the spectacle had put the emperor in such a buoyant mood.

The latrina was in a small building some distance from the stands. A few other men were inside, talking about the spectacle as they went about their business. They were in general agreement that, while some of the punishments had been too repetitious, others had been quite remarkable. There was an enthusiastic consensus that the rape of Pasiphae had been by far the most impressive of the tableaux.

"Not something you see every day!" quipped one man.

"Unless you're a god, like Neptune, and can make such things happen with a wave of your trident."

"Or unless you're Nero!"

Titus headed back to the stands. The sky had grown darker. The stars were coming out. Torches had been placed here and there to light the grounds. As he neared the stands, a pair of Praetorians abruptly blocked his way.

"What's that?" said one of them. The man was big and brutish but had perfect teeth, which glinted in the torchlight. He pointed at the fascinum at Titus's breast. "Isn't that a cross, like some of those Christians wear?"

"What I wear around my neck is none of your business," said Titus curtly. He tried to step past the two men, but they barred his way.

"You'll come with us," said the Praetorian with perfect teeth.

"I most certainly will not. Can you not see that I wear a senator's toga? I'm returning to the imperial box."

"Sure you are! A Christian, in the emperor's box!"

Each of them grabbed an arm and together they led him, despite his efforts to resist, to a small room under the newly built wooden stands. A third Praetorian, apparently their superior, sat at a table piled high with scrolls.

"Problem?" he asked.

"An escaped Christian, sir," said the Praetorian with perfect teeth.

"This is ridiculous!" snapped Titus.

"What's your name, Christian?" said the officer

"My name is Pinarius. Senator Titus Pinarius."

The officer consulted a list. "Ah, yes, we do indeed have a Pinarius among those scheduled to be punished in the circus today. A male citizen, age forty-seven. This must be him."

Titus clenched his jaw. All day he had avoided thinking about his brother, telling himself he had no brother. "That would be Kaeso Pinarius, not Titus—"

"*Now* I recognize you!" said the officer. "You were one of the first arsonists we arrested. You certainly look different now! How did you manage to clean yourself up like that, and escape from the cell? And where in Hades did you get that toga? I'll bet you murdered a senator to get your hands on that!"

"This is absurd," said Titus. "I am a senator, an augur, and a friend of the emperor."

The Praetorians laughed.

Titus felt a sinking sensation. The situation was getting out of hand. He told himself to remain calm.

"Let me explain something," he said, speaking through gritted teeth. "I have a brother . . . a twin brother . . . who is a Christian—"

The Praetorians only laughed harder.

"An identical twin?" shouted the Praetorian with perfect teeth. "That's rich!"

"With your imagination, you should be writing comedies for the stage, not setting fires," said the officer, who abruptly ceased laughing and looked grim. "Such a preposterous story only confirms what I suspected. What do you fellows think? How do we treat a lying, murdering Christian?"

The Praetorians roughly shoved Titus back and forth between them, yanked at his toga until they pulled it off him, then ripped his undertunic until it hung in tatters and he was left wearing nothing but his loincloth. When one of them reached for the fascinum Titus tried to fight back, but he felt like a child flailing at giants. The Praetorian with perfect teeth struck him hard across the face, jarring his teeth and leaving him dazed and unsteady and with the taste of blood in his mouth.

They grabbed him by the arms, pulled him out of the little room, and began taking him somewhere else. In the open space behind the stands, they passed two men in senatorial togas. Titus tried to raise his arms, but the Praetorians restrained him.

"Help me!" he shouted.

The senators glanced at him. One of them muttered, "Filthy arsonist!"

The Praetorians struck Titus across the face to silence him and shoved him to a gate. The gate opened and Titus was forced into a dimly lit enclosure. Above him he could hear the murmur of the crowd. All around him echoed the creaking of the wooden stands as people moved about overhead. As his eyes adjusted to the darkness, he saw that the cell was quite large and full of people, most of them in rags or wearing little more than he was. They were filthy and unkempt and stank of urine and sweat. He passed among them, staring at their faces. Some were trembling with fear and muttering prayers with their eyes tightly shut. Others were oddly calm, speaking to their companions in low, reassuring voices.

"In such a wicked world, death is a release to be longed for," said a man with a long white beard. Titus had seen him once in Kaeso's rooms. "Even a death under circumstances as horrible as this is better than life in such a world. Death will deliver us to a better place."

A harried stage manager scurried by, followed by a group of Praetorians. "I am *trying* to maintain order here; I am *trying* to keep to the emperor's schedule of events!" the man shouted. "Now, I need you fellows to divide the prisoners into groups—"

Titus ran toward the man. "Listen to me!" he said. "A mistake has been made. I shouldn't be here—"

The man started back, as if a wild dog had jumped at him. Before Titus could say another word, one of the Praetorians raised a shield and used it to shove him back. By a flicker of torchlight Titus caught a glimpse of his reflection in the highly polished metal. He was shocked at what he saw.

Staring back at him was a nearly naked man with a crazed look in his eyes, his face bruised, his lips bleeding. How quickly his dignified, untouchable identity as a Roman senator had been stripped from him!

Titus looked this way and that, desperate to find someone to whom he could explain his situation.

Suddenly he was face-to-face with Kaeso.

He had never before seen his brother look so wretched. Like Titus, Kaeso wore only a loincloth. The body Titus saw before him was familiar but distorted, like a mockery of his own, covered with bruises and wounds and bloody patches. Kaeso had been beaten and tortured. From his gaunt appearance, he had been starved as well. There was nothing aloof about his manner, as was the case with some of the Christians; Kaeso looked utterly broken and unnerved. Titus saw a pitiful, frightened man.

As the arrest and interrogation of the Christians had proceeded and the day of their punishment approached, Titus had forced himself not to think about his brother. He had told himself so many times that he had no brother that he almost believed it. Now Kaeso stood before him, a shadow of the man he once had been, but still undeniably the son of Lucius Pinarius, Titus's twin brother. Titus felt an unbearable sadness, remembering their boyhood together in Alexandria and the years before they became strangers to each other. How had they grown so far apart? How had Kaeso ended up among these mad death-worshippers?

"It's alright, brother," whispered Kaeso. "I forgive you."

Titus's sadness faded. He felt a quiver of anger. What had he done to require forgiveness? Why did Kaeso always have to be so smug and self-righteous?

He tried to think of something to say, but there was no time. Suddenly a line of Praetorians was between them, forcing Kaeso into one group and Titus into another. With the Praetorians barking orders at them, the people in Kaeso's group were forced to put on tunics soaked in pitch, then their arms were tied behind them.

A door opened. From the arena came the roar of the crowd. The stage manager screamed at the prisoners to hurry into the arena. "Quickly, quickly, quickly!" Guards with spears herded them through the opening.

Titus suddenly realized that his meeting with Kaeso had not been accidental. The gods had given him a last chance to save himself. He stepped away from his group and tried to get the attention of the stage manager. "We're twins! That's my twin brother! Look at us! Do you see? There are two of us, but it's my twin brother who's the Christian, not I! I'm not supposed to be here!"

The stage manager gave him an exasperated look and rolled his eyes. One of the guards used the butt of his spear to knock Titus to the ground.

Kaeso managed to break away from the group and ran to Titus. Stinking of pitch, with his arms bound behind him, he dropped to his knees beside his brother.

"Give me the crucifix," he whispered. "Please, Titus! It's the only thing that can give me strength to face the end."

Lying on his back, Titus clutched the fascinum at his chest and shook his head.

"Titus, I beg you! Titus, I'm about to be burned alive! Please, brother, grant me this one small favor!"

Reluctantly, Titus removed the necklace and put it over Kaeso's head. Even as he did so, he knew it was wrong to give it up. He reached desperately to grab the fascinum and take it back, but a guard pulled Kaeso to his feet and the fascinum eluded Titus's grasp.

Kaeso was the last of his group to be herded onto the track. Titus scrambled to his feet. Through the opened door, he saw that the prisoners were being lifted up and placed in the iron baskets atop the pitch-soaked poles. Guards carrying torches ran onto the track and stationed themselves by the poles, ready to set the human torches alight.

As Titus watched, Kaeso was driven to the nearest of the poles; he was the last to be lifted into a basket. Titus caught a glimpse of something bright and glittering at his brother's breast—the fascinum—then averted his eyes. He could not bear to watch.

He heard a low murmur run through the crowd, a rush of indrawn breath like wind passing through tall grass. This was followed by a cheer that started at one end of the circus, then gradually rose to a roar. From the stands above came the deafening noise of spectators stamping their feet in excitement.

Titus stepped to the doorway and peered outside. At the far end of the circus, a lone charioteer had driven onto the track. He was dressed in the leather racing outfit and helmet of the green faction favored by the emperor. The charioteer was driving his white steeds at a slow canter as he waved to the crowd.

There were charioteers whose popularity rivaled that of the most famous gladiators, but what charioteer could be so high in the emperor's esteem that Nero would select him to play this majestic, even godlike role? As the charioteer drove past each human torch, he raised his arm, pointed an accusing finger at the prisoner, and the torch burst into flame. The effect was uncanny, as if the charioteer had the power to cast thunderbolts.

As more torches were lit, the arena grew brighter, and Titus at last saw what the crowd in the stands had already perceived: the charioteer was Nero.

As the emperor continued his slow progress, he drew nearer and nearer to the doorway where Titus stood, and to the pole on which Kaeso had been hoisted. With a gesture from Nero, the torch next to Kaeso was set alight. Kaeso would be next.

Suddenly, Titus felt hands on him. The guards had seen that he was at the opening and were pulling him back. Summoning all his strength, Titus managed to break free. He ran onto the track.

He slipped on a slick, wet spot and tumbled forward. Scrambling to his feet, he touched something and screamed in revulsion. It was a mangled human ear. He staggered to his feet and looked at himself. Wherever his naked flesh had touched the ground he was covered in a gritty paste of sand and blood. He heard the guards shouting behind him and ran.

How different it was, to be here on the arena floor, rather than in the imperial box! He had watched the day's proceedings from the stands with a mixture of grim determination and exalted privilege, comfortably remote from what was taking place in the arena below. Now he found himself in a bizarre landscape of towering crucifixes and human torches, surrounded by flames and carnage. The blood, urine, and feces of dogs and humans littered the sand. Everywhere he looked he saw fingers and toes and other scraps of flesh left behind by the ravenous hounds. A nauseating stench filled his nostrils, and hot smoke burned his lungs. Above the roar of the crowd he heard the screams of those set alight, the crackling of burning bodies, and the moans of the crucified.

With the guards at his heels, Titus rushed headlong toward Nero. He reached the chariot and threw himself on the ground.

Basking in the approval of the crowd, his eyes glittering in the firelight, Nero registered no surprise at Titus's sudden appearance. He grinned broadly, then threw back his head and laughed. He pulled at the reins to stop the horses and waved at the guards to draw back. He stepped from the chariot, strode to the spot where Titus lay gasping on the sand, and stooped over to pat him on the head.

"Never fear, Senator Pinarius," he said. "Caesar will save you!"

Weeping with relief, Titus clutched Nero's spindly legs. "Thank you! Thank you, Caesar!"

The spectators assumed this exchange was part of the entertainment. They applauded and roared with laughter at Nero's satirical demonstration of clemency amid such overwhelming carnage.

"Nero is merciful! Merciful Nero!" someone shouted, and the crowd took up the chant: "Nero is merciful! Merciful Nero! Nero is merciful! Merciful Nero!" The chant mingled with the shrieking of the human torches.

Titus trembled so violently that he thought he might fly to pieces. He wept uncontrollably. He had no choice but to remain on his knees. He could not stand.

Nero shook his head and clucked his tongue. "Poor Pinarius! Did you not realize your predicament was all a practical joke?"

Titus stared up at him, baffled.

"A practical joke, Pinarius! That ridiculous family heirloom you insist on wearing gave me the idea. Where is it, by the way? Don't tell me you've lost it."

Titus pointed mutely to Kaeso, trapped in the basket atop the nearby pole.

Nero nodded. "I see. You gave it to your twin. How appropriate! Petronius always said it was in very poor taste for you to wear something that looked like a crucifix, since everyone knows you have a Christian brother. How amusing, I thought, if Pinarius should find himself among the Christians."

"You . . . you planned for this to happen?"

"Well, not all of it. I had no idea you'd run out to greet me like this. But how perfect! Truly, this is one of those rare, fortuitous moments that sometimes happen in the theater, when everything comes together as if by magic."

"But I could have been killed. I could have been burned alive!"

"Oh, no, you were never in danger. I instructed the guards to lay in wait and apprehend you outside the latrina—you had to go there sooner or later—but not to harm you. Well, no more than they had to, to convince you to go with them. You've had quite a scare, haven't you? But inducing terror is one of the functions of the theater; Aristotle himself says so. Terror, and pity—which you will feel soon enough. Was it not delicious, to feel the hot breath of Pluto on you, and then, when all hope was lost, to escape unscathed? I fear your arsonist brother shall have a different fate."

Cupping Titus's chin, Nero directed his gaze to Kaeso. With his other arm, Nero mimed the act of hurling a thunderbolt. The pole on which Kaeso was trapped burst into flames.

Titus was unable to look away. He watched—horrified, spellbound, stupefied.

Never before had he felt the presence of the gods as powerfully as he did in that moment. What he felt was beyond words, almost too intense to bear. This was the place, unlike any other, where the characters in a tragedy arrived; this was the moment of utmost revelation, so terrible that a mere mortal could barely endure it. What Titus felt was wonderful and horrible, bursting with meaning and yet utterly absurd. It was Nero who had brought him to this moment—Nero, who loomed above him, smiling, serene, godlike. To have devised this moment, Nero was without question the greatest of all the poets or playwrights who had ever lived among humankind. Titus felt again, now magnified beyond measure, the awe he had experienced when he heard Nero sing of burning Troy. Truly, Nero was divine. Who but a god could have brought Titus to this supreme moment?

Nero gazed down at him and nodded knowingly. "And when this is done, Pinarius—when the smoke clears and the embers die down—we shall retrieve that amulet of yours from your brother's ashes, and you must wear it every day. Yes, every hour of every day, so that you may never forget this moment."

A.D. 68

"You are a man now, my son. You are the heir of the Pinarii. Sometimes the passing of the fascinum has taken place at the death of its wearer, sometimes while the wearer is still alive. It is my decision to pass it to you now. From this moment, the fascinum of our ancestors belongs to you."

, Titus Pinarius was repeating a ceremony that had been enacted by countless generations of the Pinarii since a time before history. He lifted the necklace with the fascinum over his head and placed it around the neck of his son. Titus was fifty. Lucius was twenty-one.

But the mood in the household was not jubilant. Chrysanthe averted her eyes. Their three daughters wept. Hilarion lowered his face, and the other slaves followed his example. Even the wax masks of the ancestors, brought into the garden to witness the ceremony, seemed melancholy.

The garden itself was full of color and fragrance, surrounding them with roses and flowering vines. Like every other part of their splendid new home on the Palatine, the garden was remarkably spacious and exquisitely maintained, a place of beauty and elegance, especially on a warm day in the month of Junius.

As one of the emperor's most loyal subjects, always ready to take the auspices, to give him trusted advice, and to encourage his endeavors, Titus had prospered greatly in the last few years. Thanks to Nero's generosity, he had acquired a considerable fortune and owned properties all over Italy. The old house on the Aventine had begun to seem cramped and antiquated. It was a proud day when the Pinarii moved into a newly built mansion only a few steps away from the Palatine wing of Nero's Golden House.

Titus made ready to leave the house. He wore his trabea—the same one he had worn long ago when he first joined the college at the invitation of his cousin Claudius—but the lituus he selected was his second-best. The ancient ivory lituus he had inherited from his father he decided to leave behind.

"Are you sure I can't come with you, father?" said Lucius. There were tears in his eyes.

"No, son. I want you to stay here. Your mother and sisters will need you."

Lucius nodded. "I understand. Goodbye, father."

"Goodbye, son." They embraced, then Titus embraced and said farewell to each of his three daughters. The youngest was ten, the eldest sixteen. How like their mother they all looked!

Chrysanthe and Hilarion followed him to the vestibule. Hilarion opened the door for him. Chrysanthe took his hand.

Her voice was choked with emotion. "Is there no chance—?"

Titus shook his head. "Who can say? Who knows where the gods will lead me this day?"

He kissed her, then drew back and took a deep breath. Quickly, not daring to hesitate, he strode out of the house and into the street.

The last member of his household he saw was Hilarion, who looked after him from the doorway. Titus paused and turned back.

"You've served me well, Hilarion."

"Thank you, Master."

"How old are you, Hilarion?"

"I've never been entirely certain, Master."

Titus shook his head and smiled. "However old you are, you still look like a boy to me. Still, I suppose, if you were a freedman, this would be the time for you to think of starting your own family. You know that I've left instructions to Lucius that you should be manumitted, in the event . . ."

Hilarion nodded. "Yes, Master, I know. Thank you, Master."

"Of course, I would expect you to continue to serve Lucius. He'll need a slave—a freedman—he can trust. Someone loyal, like you, with intelligence and good judgment."

"I'll always be loyal to the Pinarii, Master."

"Good." Titus cleared his throat. "Well, then . . ."

"Shall I close the door now, Master?"

"Yes, Hilarion. Close the door and bar it."

The door closed. Titus heard the heavy bar drop into place. He turned and walked quickly up the street.

He passed no one. The street was deserted. Perhaps that was a good sign.

He reached the nearest entrance to the Golden House, the one he was accustomed to using almost every day, but found it blocked by a massive bronze door. Titus had never seen the door closed before; invariably, at any hour, he had found the entrance open and guarded by Praetorians. Today there were no guards in sight.

He raised the heavy bronze knocker on the door and let it drop. The sound reverberated up and down the street. There was no response.

He used the knocker several times, self-conscious about the noise he was making. No one answered.

He would have to try another entrance. Probably the closest was the original entrance to the old imperial house, the one built by Augustus, which was now essentially the back entrance, the farthest from the grand vestibule of the Golden House at the south end of the Forum. Titus had not used that entrance in a long time.

Not all of the rebuilt Palatine was taken up by the Golden House or by private residences. His route took him through an area of shops and taverns that normally catered to a very exclusive clientele. The shops were all closed and shuttered, but one of the taverns was open and seemed to be doing a good business, especially for so early in the day. Passing by, Titus heard the drunken patrons inside singing a song:

> *Mother-killer,*
> *Wife-kicker,*
> *Who's sicker than Nero?*
> *Burned his city,*
> *Killed his baby.*
> *Crazy maybe? Nero!*

Suddenly a group of men rushed by. They looked panic-stricken. One of them Titus recognized as a fellow senator, a staunch supporter of the emperor, like himself, but the man was wearing a common tunic instead of his senatorial toga. The man recognized Titus and grabbed his arm.

"What in Hades are you doing in the street, Pinarius? You should be home with your family. Or better yet, get out of town. Don't you have a country estate to go to?"

The man hurried on without another word.

Titus saw more people coming up the street. They were brandishing clubs and chanting a slogan. Titus did not stay to hear what they were saying. He quickly headed in the opposite direction.

He passed through empty streets and came to a small square with a public fountain. A marble statute of the emperor stood nearby. Titus groaned. Someone had put a crude stage wig on the head, tilting it askew, and tied a sack and a sign around the neck. The sign read: THIS ACTOR HAS EARNED THE SACK!

Titus shuddered. The sack was the sort into which a convicted parricide was sewn up before being thrown into the Tiber to drown.

It had come to this. When had it all gone wrong?

Was it when Nero, tired of Seneca's advice, dismissed his old tutor and replaced him with the cold-blooded, insanely suspicious prefect of the Praetorian Guards, Tigellinus? Things had certainly taken a turn for the worse after that.

Or was it when the senatorial conspiracy against Nero came to light? The bloodshed that followed tore the city apart, but what choice did Nero have but to ruthlessly suppress the plotters? To be sure, Nero might have flung his net too wide. The senator Piso and a handful of others were certainly guilty, but what about Seneca, Petronius, Lucan, and so many others who had made the court of Nero such a vibrant place? All were gone now, either executed or forced to commit suicide. Their deaths had been as memorable as their lives, and were already the stuff of legend.

Petronius held a lavish banquet, then cut his wrists and bound them up so that he could slowly bleed to death while he conversed with his closest friends. He was said to be as witty and outspoken as ever that night, thumbing his nose at Nero by dictating a letter in which he listed all the emperor's sexual partners and the intimate details of their couplings. His final act as the arbiter of elegance was to seal the letter and send it to Nero.

Shortly after the punishment of the Christians, Lucan fell out with Nero and was forbidden to publish more poems. Nevertheless, verses attributed to him were widely circulated, in which he accused Nero of starting the Great Fire. When he was arrested for conspiring with Piso, Lucan was pressed to name accomplices and shamed himself by implicating his mother, then took his own life. While he bled to death he recited the words of a dying soldier from his poem about the civil war:

My eyes are opened wide by death's mark.
You who go on living do so in the dark.

> *The gods keep you blind so that you may endure,*
> *But I see the truth: death is the cure.*

Seneca, whom many suspected of wanting to replace his protégé as emperor, spoke bitter words when Nero's Praetorians came for him. "Is this how all my efforts to educate him end? All my teaching, for this? He killed his brother and his mother, and now he kills his tutor!"

Seneca's wife decided to die with him. They cut their wrists and lay side by side. But death was slow to come. Seneca took poison—hemlock, in emulation of Socrates—but that did not work either. Finally he was placed in a hot bath to quicken his bleeding and was suffocated by the steam.

When Nero was told that Paulina still lived, he declared that she had done nothing to harm him and ordered that her wrists should be bandaged. Paulina survived. Following the dictates of her husband's will, she cremated Seneca without funeral rites.

Tigellinus's investigation of the conspiracy became so far-flung that Titus began to fear suspicion might fall even on him. But no one was more loyal to Nero than Titus. The emperor never doubted him.

As each conspirator was convicted, Nero confiscated the guilty man's assets. By Roman law, traitors always forfeited their property to the state. Still, the confiscations caused a great deal of grumbling. People said that Nero convicted wealthy men simply to lay his hands on their estates. It was true that Nero needed all the money he could get. The lavish construction of the Golden House and the massive rebuilding of monuments and temples all over Roma had sent the emperor deeply into debt. People complained when he proposed that the resurrected city should be called Neropolis, but had he not purchased the right to rename it?

Money—that was the problem, thought Titus. If Nero still had money, he might yet be in control of the city, the Senate, and the empire. But all Nero's money was gone. The treasury was empty. When Titus realized the severity of the situation, he had offered to donate his own property to the public coffers, a token of his gratitude for all the blessings Nero had showered on him. Nero only laughed. Even Titus's considerable wealth was a pittance compared to Nero's debts, a drop of water in the ocean.

Trouble in the provinces had also taken a toll. The bloody uprising of

Boudica in Britannia, earlier in Nero's reign, had been summarily dealt with, but the revolt that had been going on in Judaea for the last two years was more vexatious. Nero had appointed Vespasian to put down the Jewish rebellion. Resistance along the coast and in the northern part of Judaea had been quelled, but the city of Jerusalem, a hornet's nest of fanatics, had so far resisted the Roman siege. It was in Jerusalem that the cult of the Christians had originated, Titus recalled. Why was that part of the world such a breeding ground for dangerous ideas and so resistant to Roman rule?

There had also been a revolt led by Vindex, the governor of Gaul, ostensibly against Nero's exorbitant taxes. The revolt had been suppressed, but not before Vindex's slanders about Nero's personal life incited a great deal of prurient speculation across the empire.

Titus sighed. As crushing as events in the public sphere had been—the Pisonian conspiracy, the rise of Tigellinus and the loss of Seneca, the decimation of Nero's inner circle, the vast expenditures required by the rebuilding of the burned city, the troubles in Britannia and Judaea and Gaul—perhaps the most pivotal event of all was the death of Poppaea Sabina. Was that when the trouble really began?

Poor Nero! With his own eyes, Titus had seen the emperor's remorse after the death of Poppaea. Nero had been drinking heavily that night. The imperial couple were heard shouting at each other. Nero flew into a rage. No one witnessed what happened, but the physician who examined Poppaea later told Titus that only a kick in the belly could have caused the bleeding that killed both her and her unborn child.

Nero was inconsolable. Instead of cremating Poppaea in the Roman way, he had her body filled with fragrant spices and embalmed. Some said that this was in deference to her peculiar religious beliefs, but Titus thought it was because Nero could not bear to see her beauty consumed by flames.

It was purely by chance one day that Titus noticed a boy who might have been Poppaea's double. The boy's name was Sporus and he was a servant in the imperial household. When Titus drew Nero's attention to the uncanny resemblance, Nero was instantly infatuated. But his attraction was not merely sexual or even romantic; Nero seemed to think that Sporus was linked in some mystical way to Poppaea, that his dead wife had returned to him in the form of a boy. This strange notion became such an obsession that Nero induced Sporus to undergo castration. Nero declared that by an act of divine will he had transformed the boy into a girl. He called his creation Sabina, which was Poppaea's cognomen.

In a ceremony that exactly duplicated his wedding with Poppaea, Nero took Sporus, now Sabina, as his wife. Such a thing could never have happened when Agrippina or Seneca held sway. Titus took the auspices and Tigellinus performed the ritual, and from that day forward Nero dressed Sporus in Poppaea's gowns and treated the eunuch in every way as his wife. Seeing the two of them quarrel at a banquet and then make up and dote on each other, Titus was sometimes startled by the illusion that Poppaea was still among them.

It seemed to Titus that Nero's transcendence of male and female was yet another manifestation of the emperor's divine nature. Nero's appetites were not to be proscribed by the presumed limitations of the mortal body. The god-emperor could remake a boy into a girl, and could even, after a fashion, resurrect the dead.

But not everyone possessed Titus's delicate insight. Inevitably, cruder minds made the unconventional relationship the butt of jokes. "If only his father had taken such a wife," went one, "there would never have been a Nero!"

Titus gazed for a long moment at the desecrated statue of Nero beside the little fountain. He climbed onto the pedestal, intending to remove the ridiculous wig and the parricide's sack, then heard a group of men coming toward him. They sounded drunk and were singing another verse from the ditty he had heard from the tavern:

> *Performed in Greece*
> *And took a crown.*
> *Winning clown: Nero!*
> *Fit for gods is*
> *The Golden House.*
> *Or fit for a louse: Nero!*

The men carried clubs of some sort; Titus could tell because he heard them banging the clubs against the walls of the buildings they passed.

Titus jumped from the pedestal and hurried on.

It was no use now, raking over the past, trying to understand how Nero had landed in such a mess. Titus tried to remember the good times. The Golden House was surely the greatest architectural wonder of the age, even if parts of it were still unfinished. Nero had dared to build a house truly fit for a god to live in, a place so beautiful that every vantage point offered a delight to the eye and each of its hundreds of rooms invited visitors to indulge in boundless luxury. What parties Nero had held there, presenting the best and most beautiful performers from every corner of the world, offering the most sumptuous banquets, and making available the most refined and esoteric of sensual pleasures. "Pain is for mortals," Nero had said. "Pleasure is divine." To be a guest in the Golden House was to be a demigod, if only for a night.

The good times in the Golden House had been unforgettable, but no times had been better than the days of Nero's grand tour through Greece. Away from the censorious gaze of fusty Roman senators and their wives, the emperor had performed publicly in the legendary theaters of Greece, playing the great roles—Oedipus, Medea, Hecuba, Agamemnon—always with Titus to take the auspices before his appearances. Some churlish critics complained that the emperor's skills as a singer and actor were mediocre at best, despite the many prizes he won. Vespasian, who went along on the tour, actually fell asleep during one of Nero's recitals. Only a select few, like Titus, were able to appreciate the full range of the emperor's brilliance.

Wherever Nero appeared, the theater was filled to capacity; everyone wanted to see an emperor on the stage. For the classic dramas, Nero declaimed while holding a tragic mask, in the ancient Greek style. For more modern productions, when the other actors went bare-faced, for propriety's sake Nero still wore a mask, not of a character but of his own face. The effect, to Titus, only heightened the drama. How strange it was, to see a mask of the emperor and to know that the emperor himself was behind it. And how strikingly the whole logic of the theater was reversed by having an emperor on the stage. Normally the audience felt invisible, with the power of their collective gaze focused on one man, but who in the audience could feel invisible when the emperor himself might be gazing back at him? Spectators became spectacle, actor became observer. Theater had begun as a sacred institution, and once upon a time plays were religious rites. Nero had restored the sanctified power of the theater, making it a truly transcendent experience. Over and over again, Titus was awed by the god-emperor's genius.

Titus at last arrived at the entrance he was seeking, the original forecourt built by Augustus. The armor of the Divine Augustus was still in place, as were the original bronze doors and the marble lintel above them with its relief carving of a civic crown. But, to Titus's dismay, the two laurel trees that flanked the doors, which had been there since Livia had planted them and had miraculously escaped the Great Fire, were naked and withered. He reached for one of the branches. The brittle, black wood snapped off in his hand.

A comment Titus had once made to Nero and Poppaea echoed in his head: "I believe those two laurel trees will survive as long as there are descendants of the Divine Augustus." Now the trees were dead. Titus shuddered, more unnerved by the sight of the withered trees than by the roving gangs in the streets.

The huge bronze doors were shut. Titus pushed on one of them. It was very heavy and at first refused to budge, but at last he managed to push it open just far enough to slip through the gap.

What had once been the vestibule of Augustus's modest home was now a garden open to the sky. There were cherry trees and grapevines, roses and other fragrant flowers, and shrubberies shaped to look like animals. Beyond this garden lay a meadow planted with grass, where an artificial stream cascaded down to rocky waterfalls. Hallways and rooms lay beyond, and then more gardens, and more rooms.

As he rambled through the house, seeing and hearing no one, Titus was sometimes inside and sometimes outside; to pass from interior to exterior was a kind of magical act in the Golden House, so perfectly did its design bring the two together. Inside, Titus often felt that he was in the heart of nature, surrounded by lush paintings of greenery, shimmering green mosaic floors, bubbling fountains, and high windows open to the blue sky. Outside, Titus often felt as if he were in the most beautifully furnished room imaginable, surrounded by marble columns and ivory lattices, sumptuous draperies, and furniture made of stone and elegantly wrought metal and strewn with plush cushions.

Decorating both the gardens and the rooms were a great many statues.

Nero had plundered the whole empire to find enough pieces to decorate his vast house; from Delphi alone he had taken five hundred statues. Some depicted the gods and some mortals, some were quaint and some erotic, some were remarkably realistic and others boldly heroic. Some were new and some old, but all were freshly painted, so convincingly that they looked as if they might move or speak at any moment.

The painters who had decorated the Golden House were the best in the world. Along with the statues, virtually every wall was painted, as were the enormously high ceilings. To create borders and frames, the painters had used geometric patterns and medallions and images from nature—leaves, shells, flowers—while they filled the larger spaces with illustrations that depicted the great stories of mankind and the gods. The colors were incredibly rich and vibrant; the compositions were exquisite. There were so many rooms—hundreds of them—that Titus, though a frequent visitor, had never been in the Golden House without finding himself in a room he had never seen before, filled with paintings entirely new to him, each more beautiful than the last.

Equally dazzling were the floors and walls covered in marble and the soaring marble columns. There was rich green marble from Sparta, yellow marble veined with purple from Numidia, and regal porphyry from Egypt, but these were only the more common types. There were colors and patterns of marble in the Golden House that Titus had never seen anywhere else, brought to Roma in great quantities and at enormous expense from all over the world.

Many of the floors, inside and out, were decorated with mosaics. Beautiful pictures were framed by multiple borders made from dizzying geometric designs. The mosaics showed sailors catching fish, harvesters at work in fields of grain, gladiators in the arena, charioteers in the circus, scholars in their libraries, women dancing, priests offering sacrifices, children at play. The tiles shimmered, catching the light at many different angles, so that the images seemed to live and breathe beneath one's feet.

As Titus moved from garden to garden, from building to building, from room to room, he was struck by the utter stillness. The entire palace seemed deserted. The quiet was unnerving. At last, after descending the stepped terraces on the Forum side of the Palatine, he entered a building and heard a noise from the next room. Before Titus could decide whether to conceal himself, a lion came striding toward him through the doorway.

Nero kept an extensive menagerie in one of the gardens at the far side of the Golden House, at the foot of the Esquiline. Evidently the beast keepers had fled along with everyone else, and someone had left the cages open.

The big cat paused for a moment. It stared at Titus, twitched its whiskers, and flicked its tail. It was a superb specimen, with a fine tawny pelt and a magnificent mane.

Titus stood frozen to the spot. He felt a bead of sweat trickle down his spine. He reached reflexively to touch the fascinum, which was not there. He had given it to Lucius.

The lion cocked its head, shook its mane, then appeared to reach a decision. It sauntered straight toward him.

Titus resisted the urge to run. He had seen condemned criminals run from lions in the arena. The result was never good. It occurred to him that he might try shouting at the animal, to see if he could frighten it, but he found himself unable to speak.

The lion reached him, tilted its head forward, and rubbed its face against Titus's thigh. The beast emitted a noise that Titus first took for a growl, then realized was a purr. The lion looked up at him with large eyes, then rubbed its face against his other thigh.

His hand trembling, Titus dared to touch the lion's mane. The creature stuck out its long, rough tongue and licked his hand.

Slowly, Titus turned and backed through the doorway, keeping his eyes on the lion. The creature watched him with a quizzical expression but made no move to follow. It threw back its head, opened a mouth full of sharp fangs, and yawned.

As soon as he was out of the lion's sight, Titus began to walk very quickly, and then to run.

Rounding a corner, he collided with a pair of middle-aged household slaves, the first people he had seen since he had entered the Golden House. The male slave tumbled onto his backside and dropped the bulging sack he was carrying. The sack burst open. There was a great deal of clanging as silver cups and plates and serving implements went flying across the marble floor.

The female slave steadied herself and clutched the bulging, makeshift sack she was carrying, which appeared to be a bedsheet gathered at the corners. The woman stared at Titus, her eyes wide.

Titus caught his breath. Before he could speak, the female slave blushed a deep red and blurted out, "Polished! We were taking them . . . to be polished!"

All the scattered pieces had come to rest except for a small plate. With a ringing noise of metal against marble, the plate rolled on its edge in an ever-decreasing spiral. At last it tipped to one side and settled with a rhythmic clatter. The pieces of silver gleamed brightly on the floor, unsullied by the least hint of tarnish.

Titus ignored the slave's obvious lie. "Where is everyone?" he asked.

The woman shrugged. "Gone their separate ways."

"And your master? Where is the emperor?"

"We saw him in the grand courtyard a while back. Sitting at the foot of the Colossus. It's straight ahead—"

"I know where it is," said Titus. He hurried on. Behind him he heard the two slaves squabbling as they gathered up the scattered silver.

Entering the grand courtyard, whether for the first time or for the hundredth, inevitably produced a sensation of awe and vertigo. Everything was beyond human scale. The surrounding portico was suitable for giants, with soaring marble columns that alternated between black and white, as did the oversized marble paving stones underfoot. Zenodorus had convinced Nero that simple black and white would make the most striking yet at the same time the most harmonious showcase for the gigantic gilded statue that stood in the center of the courtyard, towering higher than any other object in sight.

From the neck down, the naked statue, with its ideal physique, certainly did not resemble Nero, who had a protruding belly and spindly legs. But Zenodorus had done a splendid job of capturing Nero's face, which was instantly recognizable even at a great distance. The statue represented the emperor in the guise of Sol, with sunbeams radiating from his head.

Titus spotted four tiny figures at the base of the Colossus. One of them, recognizable by his purple-and-gold robes, was Nero, who seemed to be lying flat on his back. He was also singing, if it could be called that, emitting long notes that echoed across the vast courtyard.

Of the three other figures, one, apparently male, was pacing back and forth, while the other two, a male and a female, stood close together, talking. All three stopped what they were doing and looked up as Titus approached, peering at him with trepidation. Eventually Titus drew close enough to recognize Epaphroditus, Nero's personal secretary, and Sporus, with whom he had been conferring. The pacing figure was one of Nero's most trusted freedman, Phaon. The three of them recognized Titus and sighed with relief.

At their feet lay Nero. Two metal plates, fastened together by leather straps, lay across his chest. He was holding a note for as long as he could, practicing a lung-strengthening exercise. His breath smelled of onions. When Nero was in training for a singing contest he ate a special diet consisting of olive oil for his throat and onions to clear his nose and open his lungs.

Titus looked up at the Colossus and then down at the prostrate Nero. How large one was, and how small the other! The note Nero was singing went on and on, until at last his lungs gave out and he drew a deep breath, defying the metal plates on his chest. When his lungs were full, with his chest raised high in the air, Nero began to sing another note, higher than the last.

Titus looked at Nero's companions. Epaphroditus was a highly educated Greek freedman, clean shaven with a touch of gray at his temples. As a reward for his key role in uncovering the conspiracy of Piso, Epaphroditus had been made Nero's personal secretary and chamberlain of the court. No one knew more about the day-to-day operations of the Golden House than Epaphroditus, and within the immensely complex imperial bureaucracy, nothing of consequence could be accomplished without his knowledge and approval. He was a student of philosophy and famous for remaining calm in a crisis.

Sporus's hair and makeup and elegant stola made him look uncannily like Poppaea. So did his posture, as he stood with one foot slightly in front of the other, hands on hips and chin held high. But when Sporus turned his head, Titus saw that the eunuch had an ugly bruise across one cheek. Sporus saw Titus looking, touched the bruise, and averted his face.

Pacing rapidly back and forth, the freedman Phaon seemed to be at his wit's end. He was younger than Epaphroditus, but his rise under Nero had been rapid. For his loyal services, Nero had rewarded Phaon with many choice properties, including an estate near the city off the road to Nomentum.

The long-held note trailed into silence as Nero's lungs were once again exhausted. Titus thought the emperor might pause in his exercises to give him some sign of acknowledgment, but instead Nero took a deep breath, heaving against the metal plates, and produced another note, this one very low.

Titus heard someone running toward them. Even before he turned to look, he knew from the irregular footsteps that it must be Epictetus, a slave owned by Epaphroditus. Epictetus was lame in one leg and walked with a limp; compelled to run, he assumed an awkward, loping gait. The slave was barely old enough to grow a beard, which he wore long and un-trimmed in the manner of philosophers and pedagogues.

Epictetus reached them and struggled to catch his breath. He was not used to running. Nero appeared to take no notice. He finished the note and began to fill his lungs again.

"Caesar!" said Epaphroditus. "The slave may have news. Perhaps you should take a break from your exercises."

Nero rolled his eyes up to look at Epaphroditus. He undid the leather fasteners holding the metal plates, which fell to the marble paving stones with a clatter. He sprang to his feet. His eyes glittered. He grinned broadly. Titus did not know what to make of the emperor's ebullient mood. Per-haps it was a side effect of his breathing exercises.

"Well then, what news?" said Nero. "Has someone chopped off the old goat's head yet?"

The old goat he referred to was Servius Sulpicius Galba, the governor of Spain, who was marching on Roma with his legions. Galba was in his sixties, tall, blue-eyed, craggy-faced, and completely bald. In many ways he was the exact opposite of Nero, a parsimonious military man with a dis-like of pomp and ostentation and a reputation as a ruthless disciplinarian. When Caligula was murdered, some in the Senate had favored Galba, then an energetic military man in his prime, as his successor; but Galba had de-clined to put himself forward and loyally served Claudius. Then, as Nero's authority had crumbled, with no one from Augustus's family in line for suc-cession, Galba's supporters convinced him that his time had come. His open bid for power and the news that he was marching on the city had caused chaos in Roma.

Epictetus leaned on his walking stick. He reached down to massage his lame leg. "I've come from the Senate, Caesar. They're debating what to do about Galba. I listened to some of the speeches. . . ."

"Yes?" Nero raised an eyebrow.

"The news is not good, Caesar."

"What do you mean? Is there no one who supports me?"

"Some. But your supporters were drowned out by the rest. The sentiment for Galba is strong."

Nero shook his head. "And what about my Praetorians? What is Tigellinus doing to deal with the situation? Tigellinus is loyal to me, and the Praetorians are loyal to Tigellinus."

Epictetus exchanged uncomfortable looks with his master. Epaphroditus pursed his lips and spoke. "We don't know where Tigellinus is, Caesar. I've sent messengers—"

"And the messengers can't find him?"

"We don't know; the messengers don't come back. Caesar, we talked about all this yesterday—"

"Yes, yes, I remember. Well, if Tigellinus has run off, where is his fellow prefect, Nymphidius Sabinus?"

Epaphroditus looked to Epictetus, who reluctantly spoke again. "Nymphidius has openly declared his support for Galba. The Praetorians seem willing to follow his lead—"

"What? Impossible! Nymphidius is a kinsman of Poppaea. He would never betray her. What can he be thinking . . . ?" Nero looked at Sporus and appeared confused. Titus frowned. Had the emperor come to believe that the eunuch was literally his dead wife?

Nero abruptly began to weep. "My Praetorians! So brave, so loyal! How have they been corrupted? What is to become of Neropolis with no one to defend it? What will become of the Golden House?"

Nero turned his back on them, drew back his shoulders, and took a deep breath. When he turned back, his smile had returned. "It's a good thing that I've been strengthening my voice. One way or another, I shall be called on to use it." He looked from one long face to the next. "Why do you all have such sour expressions? Why are you staring at me like that?"

"We are waiting to hear what Caesar plans to do next," said Epaphroditus.

"Isn't it obvious? I must appear before the common people, the citizens of Neropolis, for whom I've built new homes and baths and theaters, my beloved children, upon whom I've showered so many lavish festivals and entertainments. The people love me. They're grateful for all I've done for them. They delight in the beauty and joy I've given them as an artist. It's only the senators who hate me, all those little Galbas with their narrow minds and their spiteful jealousy and their hatred for beauty and culture. What do you think? Should I send out criers to call a public meeting? I'll dress myself all in black and mount the Rostra to address the people. I'll tear my hair, weep and wail, remind them of all the love I've shown them, plead for their help in my hour of need. I shall have to call upon all my skills as a tragic actor; perhaps I shall model my performance on Antigone, or Andromache. I shall move them to terror and pity. Terror and pity—that will rally the people to my side!"

"I think," said Epaphroditus, speaking carefully, "that the mood in the city is far too uncertain to be sure of the people's reaction to such an address."

"What he's trying to say is that the mob is likely to tear you limb from limb," said Sporus, speaking at last. He stood apart from the rest and kept the bruised side of his face turned from them. Even the intonation of his voice was uncannily like that of Poppaea.

Nero blanched, then stiffened his jaw and glared at Sporus, who stared back at him. Nero blinked first. He swallowed hard. "Tear me . . . limb from limb?" he whispered. "Very well, if I can't count on the people to protect me, then I'll negotiate with the Senate. Not directly, of course. Caesar does not deal directly with his inferiors." He furrowed his brow, then looked at Titus and smiled. "You're awfully good at this sort of thing, Pinarius! I remember that day you spoke before the Senate on behalf of all those slaves. It took nerve to do that! You were so eloquent, so passionate. If you were to speak for me—"

Titus flushed. His mouth was dry. "Caesar, the slaves for whom I begged mercy were all crucified," he said.

Nero blinked. "Ah, yes, so they were. Well, I suppose the negotiations can be done by letter. You can frame the terms for me, Epaphroditus.

What if I were to agree to step down as emperor, without protest, and in return the Senate makes me governor of Egypt? The Egyptians love the Greek culture handed down to them by the Ptolemies. The Egyptians would appreciate my talents. That's where I should go, to Alexandria. They'll love me there. What do you think, Sabina?" He turned to Sporus. "How would you like to sail up the Nile with me on a barge, as Cleopatra did with the Divine Julius?"

Sporus kept his face in profile, staring into the middle distance.

Epaphroditus assumed a pained expression. "Caesar, even if the Senate could be persuaded to grant you the prefecture of Egypt, which I doubt, I find it highly unlikely that Galba would agree to such an arrangement. The Nile grain trade is essential to the Roman economy, and the prefecture of Egypt has always been under the direct control of the emperor—"

"Yes, yes, I see your point," said Nero. "Well then, what if I simply ask for safe passage to Alexandria? I don't have to be the governor, I suppose. I can make my living as an actor, or playing the lyre."

Epaphroditus grimaced. "Caesar cannot seriously suggest—"

"But I would no longer *be* Caesar," shouted Nero, more exasperated than angry. "That's the point! I would be free of all these endless, tedious rules of decorum. I would be my own man at last. Or do you doubt that I could support myself by my talents? Is that your worry? Are you forgetting all the garlands and prizes I won in Greece? Almost two thousand, Epaphroditus! No other performer in the history of the world ever achieved such a thing. And it wasn't just the judges who loved me. Do you remember how they applauded me at Olympia, and the ovation I received at the Isthmian Games? Sweet memories!" Nero sighed and wiped a tear from his eye. "I should think the Alexandrians would be quite excited to receive the most famous actor in the world into their midst. The whole city will turn out for my debut. What should I perform? Something to please the locals, I think. What is that play where Odysseus is shipwrecked and finds Helen living in a palace up the Nile? We could perform it on the actual locations. But which of the leading roles would suit me best? Everyone loves wily Odysseus, but Helen is the one who flees from a burning city and finds herself in a strange land, a goddess among crocodiles, so perhaps I should play Helen—"

Sporus let out a shriek of nervous laughter and slapped his hand over his mouth. Epaphroditus groaned. Epictetus fretfully rubbed his lame leg. The freedman Phaon recommenced his nervous pacing. Titus averted his eyes and found himself gazing up at the Colossus. From such a low angle, the immense statue was hardly recognizable as a human figure; it loomed like a weird, monstrous image from a nightmare.

Nero observed their reactions and frowned. He was quiet for a long moment, then threw up his hands. "Very well, then! I'll abandon my art and rely on statecraft. Shall we proceed directly to the last resort? I'll go to the Parthians as a suppliant. Why not? I shall give myself up to the only other empire on earth that can rival that of Roma. The Greeks and Persians used to do that sort of thing, didn't they? When one of their leaders was deposed, he'd flee across the border and throw himself on the mercy of his enemy. Who better than a foreign rival to understand and sympathize with my plight? If I'm lucky, the Parthians may even help me return to power. That would make me beholden to a foreign king, not an ideal circumstance, but if it means I can return to the Golden House, I'll do it. What do you think, Epaphroditus?"

Titus expected the chamberlain to deliver another pained objection, but Epaphroditus seemed to take this notion more seriously than the others. "If Caesar is finally ready to leave Roma and the Golden House for some safer destination, then yes, I would advise Caesar to consider approaching the Parthians. But there's very little time. We have no reliable intelligence about Galba's position; he may be only days away. The Senate even now may be voting on a resolution to proclaim Galba emperor. And if Nymphidius and the Praetorians decide to support such a move, they may take action at any time."

"Action?" said Nero.

Epaphroditus cleared his throat. "Caesar, I am thinking of the fate of your uncle."

The words sent a chill through them all. The death of Caligula at the hands of treacherous Praetorians had been much on everyone's mind lately.

"But such a journey would require a great deal of preparation," said Nero, tapping a forefinger against his lips. "Do you remember the size of my retinue when we traveled through Greece? You kept advising me to cut back, Epaphroditus, yet we found it was impossible for me to travel with fewer than a thousand attendants. Feeding and providing accommodations for all those people—"

"But that was because you were performing almost every night, and providing banquets to the festival organizers," said Epaphroditus. "The journey we're now contemplating would be a very different affair. The fewer the people who accompany you, the better. Indeed, it may be advisable for Caesar to travel incognito."

"Incognito? Unknown?" said Nero. "I don't like the sound of that."

"Think of it as a role, Caesar. Think of wily Odysseus on the occasion of his homecoming, when he assumed the guise of a lowly vagrant to outsmart the suitors of Penelope."

Nero nodded thoughtfully. "Ah, yes, I see your point. Dressed in tatters, even Caesar will be invisible to his enemies." Suddenly he broke into song.

> *And to Odysseus in his rags Athena came.*
> *"Why do you fret? Here is your home,*
> *And there your lady, and your son,*
> *As fine a son as any son could be . . ."*

While the emperor sang lines from Homer, Titus took Epaphroditus by the arm and spoke in his ear. "Has it come to this? Is there no choice but to flee?"

The chamberlain grunted. "I've been trying to steer him to this choice for days! So far he's refused to leave the Golden House. He says he'd rather die, and he seems to mean it, at least sometimes. Yesterday he actually sent for one of his favorite gladiators to put an end to him, but the man disappeared when he heard what Caesar wanted. Then he called for some poison which he apparently obtained behind my back, but the slaves ran off with the stuff rather than bring it to him."

"But is it possible to flee?" said Titus. "Are there horses available? Is there a ship for him at Ostia?"

"Not at Ostia, not anymore, but it might be possible to cross the mountains and make our way down to Brundisium and hire a ship there, taking the route Pompeius took when the Divine Julius crossed the Rubicon. He would need to be incognito, as I said; we would all need to disguise ourselves. If Caesar can be made to see the necessity, and if he can endure the hardships—"

"But is his life truly in danger? Has it come to this?" Titus suddenly felt as Nero must have felt, pushed to the limit and desperate to defy Epaphroditus's unassailable logic. "I realize that Caligula was killed by Praetorians, but those were conspirators who plotted in secret. And Claudius later put those conspirators to death! Would anyone dare to do the same to Nero?"

"They won't have to plot in secret. Caesar's fate is being discussed openly in the Senate right now."

"And do you seriously believe the Senate would dare to impose a death sentence on the rightful emperor, the heir of Augustus? Would a majority of senators vote to set such a precedent?"

Epaphroditus shook his head. "The problem is that we have no precedent for an emperor to voluntarily relinquish his position. Augustus, Tiberius, Caligula, Claudius—all of them died in power. Yes, Caesar has his adherents among the senators, and some of those men are attempting even now to negotiate a way for Caesar to cede his office to Galba without bloodshed. But the prospects are slim. Even if the debate should produce an acceptable outcome, Caesar should flee to some safe haven in the meantime—"

"Eureka!" cried Nero, abruptly abandoning his song, "if I may quote Archimedes."

"We know how he ended," mumbled Phaon, still fretfully pacing. "In a pool of blood on the beach at Syracuse."

Nero did not hear. "It occurs to me that we are overlooking the obvious. I should make my appeal not to the Senate, not to the people, but directly to the legions."

Epaphroditus sighed. "Unfortunately, Caesar, we have lost the allegiance of the troops in Gaul and of those in Greece as well. You may recall that we discussed this earlier—"

"I mean the legions under Galba, the ones marching this way from Spain."

Epaphroditus cocked his head and raised an eyebrow.

"Just because those troops are obeying orders from a rebel commander," said Nero, "that is no reason to assume that the soldiers themselves no longer love their emperor. What if I were to make my appeal directly to them? Yes, what if we gather a theatrical troupe, go out to meet the legions, put up a stage . . . and I deliver the performance of my life? When they see me next to that shriveled corpse Galba, the choice will be obvious. What do you say?"

Nero looked from face to face. No one responded, but his enthusiasm was undaunted.

"The soldiers will want to see me play a warrior, naturally. What do you think, would they prefer to see me as Hercules or as Ajax? Hercules is more majestic, of course, but Ajax is more tragic, and thus more sympathetic. And it's a better singing role; nine times out of ten it's the voice that wins over the audience. Ah, but as Hercules I could kill the Nemean lion! As you know, Epaphroditus, I've been training for that performance for quite a while. The last time I rehearsed with the tame lion, everything came off without a hitch. The beast was practically licking my nose! It will be a shame to kill it, but it's the authenticity of such a performance that makes it so riveting. I pretend to wrestle the lion, I release a bit of fake blood to make it look as though I've been scratched across the back and the face, the spectators gasp, convinced that I may be mauled to death at any moment, and then, in a glorious turnabout, I slay the creature and raise my arms in triumph. Killing it with my bare hands would be best, but I don't think even that tame beast would allow me to crush it between my arms; I suppose I shall have to use a club. Well, what do you all think? I invoke the divine spirit of Hercules, place my life in his keeping, engage in a death-defying struggle, and then, right before the soldiers' eyes, I kill the most dangerous creature on earth. Well, does anyone here seriously think those soldiers are going to raise a hand against me?"

The others exchanged uncertain glances. The idea was absurd. And yet, Nero's enthusiasm was compelling. Could such a mad gamble actually turn the tide of events?

Titus cleared his throat. "There may be a problem," he said quietly. "I think the lion you're referring to may have escaped."

"Escaped?" cried Nero.

"I saw such a creature wandering through the Golden House. He licked my hand."

Sporus nodded. "Someone opened all the cages in the menagerie this

morning. Zebras and monkeys are wandering all over the place. Crocodiles are loose in the lake."

"Then we shall have to catch the lion and put it back in its cage!" insisted Nero. "Where is the lion trainer? And how many stagehands will
we need to transport the stage props and put on a show? Oh, and there
must be someone to help me select my wardrobe—"

"Caesar, I think we should revert to your previous idea," said Epaphroditus, quietly but firmly. "We must escape the city at once."

The fire in Nero's eyes flickered, then went out. His shoulders slumped.
He let out a low moan and lowered his face.

Sporus sighed and smiled sadly. He stepped to Nero and moved to
embrace him. Nero jerked back and slapped the eunuch across the face.

Sporus touched his stinging cheek and broke into tears. He staggered
back. The slave Epictetus rushed to him, almost falling, but managed to
catch him and steady him with an arm around his shoulders.

Phaon abruptly stopped pacing. "Epaphroditus is right. We must flee
the city at once. No more hesitation, no more crazy ideas."

"But where will we go?" said Nero quietly.

"To start, we can go to my estate off the road to Nomentum," said
Phaon. "It's only a few miles past the Colline Gate."

Nero brightened. "That will take us right by the Praetorian barracks!
When the soldiers see me, we can gauge their reaction. Almost certainly—"

"But Caesar will be incognito," Epaphroditus reminded him.

"Ah, yes." Nero was crestfallen. Again, he seemed to hesitate.

Epaphroditus groaned. Phaon threw up his arms. Epictetus was still
comforting Sporus.

"Pinarius!" cried Nero, startling them all. "It's up to you now."

Titus shook his head. "Caesar? I don't understand."

"You've taken the auspices for me on many occasions. You must take
them once again. Shall I stay or shall I go? We must seek the judgment of
the gods."

Titus reached into his trabea and brought forth his lituus. He was
afraid Nero would see that it was his second-best, but the emperor seemed
not to notice. Within the vast courtyard, Titus had a great deal of open
sky to choose from. He stepped a little away from the others, into the long

shadow cast by the towering Colossus, and delineated a portion of the heavens with his lituus.

The simple dignity and the lifelong familiarity of the act calmed him and steadied his nerves. He remembered who and what he was: a citizen of Roma; a patrician; the descendant of one of the city's most ancient families, blood kin to the Divine Julius and the Divine Augustus; an augur trained to divine the will of the gods; the son of Lucius Pinarius and the father of Lucius Pinarius; the bearer, for most of his life, of the ancient fascinum; the friend and confidant of the emperor.

Titus watched the sky. He saw nothing: not a bird, not a cloud, not a leaf carried on the faint breeze. The gods were mute.

To Titus, it seemed that the silence of the heavens was itself a message. The gods had abandoned Nero.

Titus felt a chill, followed by a flush of anger, then a surge of pride. The gods in their fickleness might betray their favorite, but Titus never would!

He turned to Nero. "You must do as Epaphroditus and Phaon suggest. You must flee the city at once."

Nero gazed at the terraces and rooftops of the Golden House, then looked up at the Colossus. He squinted. The light glinting off the radiant crown of gilded sunbeams was blinding.

"You'll come with me, Pinarius?"

It was a question, not an order. Titus was touched. "Of course, Caesar."

"And you, Epaphroditus? And you, Phaon? And of course you, Sabina. Dear Sabina!" Nero opened his arms wide.

Sporus hesitated for a moment, then extricated himself from the encircling arm of Epictetus. He walked to Nero with eyes downcast and allowed himself to be embraced. Nero tenderly touched his fingertips to the bruises on the eunuch's face and stroked his golden hair.

Epictetus went to the slave quarters to fetch clothing. The others retired to a private chamber off the courtyard. Behind a screen, Nero stripped off his purple-and-gold robes and removed his jewel-encrusted slippers. Titus took off his trabea. Epaphroditus and Phaon shed the elegant robes that marked them as freedmen of the imperial household. Sporus, with a woman's modesty, went to another room to remove his stola and makeup and to let down his hair.

Epictetus arrived with their clothing. Nero made a face at the sight of the patched tunic, the faded cloak, and the flimsy shoes he was expected to wear, and seemed about to change his mind. Then he laughed.

"I shall pretend we're doing Plautus—*The Pot of Gold,* perhaps?— with myself as the downtrodden slave. Comedy is a stretch for me; tragedy is my strength. But an artist must be willing to expand his repertoire."

The coarse woolen tunic felt scratchy against Titus's skin. He shuddered at the thought that Nero was being subjected to the indignity of wearing such clothes, but took strength from the emperor's indomitable sense of humor.

Sporus appeared. In a plain tunic and with the makeup scrubbed from his face and the pins removed from his hair, he looked as much like a boy as a girl, despite his long blond tresses. Epictetus put a hooded cloak over the eunuch's shoulders. Sporus pulled the hood over his head, concealing his hair and obscuring his face.

Epictetus brought horses from the stable. The best had been taken already, and others had wandered off. Titus's heart sank at the sight of the nag he was expected to ride, but Nero laughed.

"Mounts to suit our disguises!" he said. "Who would recognize the world's greatest charioteer sitting astride such a pathetic creature?"

"Still, Caesar, I think you should hide your face," said Epaphroditus. Epictetus produced a cloth and tied it around Nero's head, pulling it low over his forehead to shadow his eyes.

"You'll have me wearing an eye patch next!" said Nero.

Epictetus had also brought daggers for each of them. When the slave handed one of the weapons to Nero, careful to select the best, the emperor stared at the dagger with a strange expression, then threw it to the ground and refused to look at it again.

Epaphroditus gave orders to Epictetus to stay behind and listen for news of Galba's progress and the outcome of the Senate's debate. "As soon as you know anything of importance, follow after us as quickly as you can. Come yourself. No one else can be trusted."

The slave shambled off, limping badly. Nero barked out a laugh. "A lame messenger! Surely this is a comedy, for no tragic playwright would resort to such a stale device. Well, let us be off!"

They mounted their horses, such as they were, and set out with Phaon leading the way. Titus decided to bring up the rear. He had to wait for Sporus, who lingered behind, looking over his shoulder at Epictetus until the limping slave disappeared from sight.

The streets were deserted except for a few skulking loners and roving groups of drunkards whom they saw at a distance. Titus frequently looked over his shoulder but saw no sign that they were being followed. Behind them, the colossal statue of Nero dominated the skyline but grew smaller and smaller as they made their way to the Colline Gate. A few soldiers were manning the wall but paid no attention to the ragged group as they rode out of the city.

The route took them past the Praetorian garrison outside the walls. Discipline had vanished. Outside the garrison, soldiers sat on the ground in small groups, some in full armor and others stripped to their tunics, talking, drinking, and throwing dice. The men looked up as Nero's little entourage passed by but took no notice.

Suddenly the earth beneath them shook. Titus's mount shied and whinnied. The soldiers sitting on the ground felt the tremor more acutely than the party on horseback. Some of them scrambled to their feet, only to be thrown down again by the violent shaking.

As abruptly as it had begun, the earthquake ended. Titus regained control of his mount. He saw that Sporus was having trouble with his horse and rode alongside to help him.

One of the nearby soldiers cursed. "Numa's balls! Look at the dice! I swear the ones I just threw were all different, but now they're all ones!"

Another soldier laughed. "What a fool you are, Marcus! Do you think the gods sent an earthquake just to turn your Venus Throw to Dogs? That was a sign from the heavens, alright, but it wasn't meant for you."

"Who for, then?"

"For Nero, I reckon. They've had enough of that scoundrel. Maybe that tremor sent that huge statue of him tumbling to the ground, and the rest of the so-called Golden House with it!"

"Quiet, Gnaeus! You're talking about the emperor."

"Not emperor for much longer, I reckon." The soldier drew the edge of his hand across his throat and made a slicing noise.

Titus looked at Nero, who was still struggling to calm his mount. The emperor's face was obscured by the rag around his head, but for an instant Titus glimpsed Nero's eyes, wide with alarm, and knew that he must have overheard.

"Galba's emperor now, or as good as," the soldier went on, addressing his comrades. "I say, screw the mother killer, and screw that pretty boy whose balls he cut off."

"Ha! You'd like to, I bet!" someone yelled, and the men all laughed.

Nero regained control of his mount. Phaon rode on, leading them at a quicker pace.

A little later they met a rough-looking group of twenty or so men on horseback heading toward the city. Nero's party pulled to one side of the road to allow the larger group to pass. The horses were as gaunt as their own and the men were even more shabbily dressed. One of them, taking Phaon to be their leader, called to him, "What news from the city?"

Phaon did not answer.

"Well, stranger?" said the man. "Is Nero still alive?"

"The emperor lives," Phaon said.

"Good! Then we're still in time to join the hunt!" The man and his companions laughed. Some brandished daggers. Others held up clubs and lengths of rope. "They say there'll be good sport when the Senate outlaws Nero and all his rotten crew. You fellows are riding the wrong way. You'll miss the fun!"

Nero swayed on his horse, as if he might faint. Titus reached out to steady him with a hand on his shoulder. The group passed by. Phaon set out again, leading them onward.

They came to the Anio River. Coming toward them across the bridge was a single Praetorian guard. From his sleek horse, the satchels he carried, and the fact that he rode alone, Titus took him to be a messenger. Just as the Praetorian cleared the bridge and passed them, Nero's mount took fright at a dead body that lay by the road.

The corpse was fresh. Blood streamed from a wound on the head. "That gang heading into the city must have just killed him," whispered Titus, appalled.

The emperor's horse reared. Nero managed to control the beast, but the cloth around his head came undone and fell to the ground. The Praetorian, pausing to see what was the matter, took a look at him and went pale. The young soldier looked utterly confused for a moment, then stiffened, gave Nero a salute, and shouted, "Caesar!"

Nero gazed back at him, reflexively raising his arm to acknowledge the salute.

The Praetorian reined his horse. He stared at the body on the ground, then at Nero and his ragtag entourage, then again at the dead body.

"Ride on, Praetorian!" said Nero. His voice shook.

The man hesitated. "If Caesar needs assistance—"

"Ride on, I said!"

The Praetorian kicked his heels against his mount and departed.

"He's headed toward the garrison," said Epaphroditus. "We should have asked to see the messages he carries. He might have news about Galba—"

"He recognized me!" said Nero, his voice shrill. "We should have killed him."

"There's not a man among us capable of taking on an armed Praetorian," said Sporus under his breath.

Nero looked down at the dead body. The man had been of middle age and was well dressed. "If that wretched gang murdered him, did they do it just to rob him . . . or did they kill him because he spoke up for me?"

"We're not far from my estate, Caesar," said Phaon. "We should ride on at once."

They crossed the bridge. Phaon led them off the main road and onto a narrow, wooded path, saying he thought it best if they approached the estate from the back way and took shelter in one of the remote outbuildings, so that even his slaves wouldn't know they were there.

Eventually they came to the doorless, windowless back wall of a building.

Turning around to take in the view, Titus saw why Phaon had chosen this property as one of his rewards from the emperor. The site was pleasant, secluded, and quiet, with a lovely view over the wooded plains of the

Tiber. The skyline of the city could be seen in the distance. Despite the earthquake, the Colossus still stood, its radiant crown glinting in the afternoon sunlight, looking at this distance like a child's toy.

Phaon told them to stay behind while he took a look around the corner of the building. After a moment he returned.

"It's as I thought," he said. "This is the old, disused slave quarters. It's some distance from the rest of the estate up the hill, but the ground has been cleared from here on and the front of the building is completely exposed. There's no way to enter through the front door without the risk of being seen by someone from the main house, higher up."

"I need to rest!" cried Nero.

Phaon thought for a moment. "This is an old building. The walls are thin. We can break through the back wall. It may take a while, and we might make some noise. In case someone hears and comes to have a look, it's best if they don't see you, Caesar. There's an old sandpit just over there, with shade. If Caesar would like to rest there—"

"No! Not a pit! I won't be under ground. Not yet . . ."

While the others found a loose plank and pulled at it, Nero wandered down the hill to a little pond. He knelt, scooped up some brackish water, and sipped it. Titus heard him cry out, "Is this my special water?" In the Golden House, the emperor was used to drinking only distilled water cooled in snow. Nero sat on the ground. From the expression on his face, Titus might have thought he was weeping, but no tears ran down the emperor's ruddy cheeks. It was almost as if Nero were feigning despondency, like a mime practicing a facial expression.

The plank came loose and without too much effort they managed to make a hole in the rear wall. Phaon went through to have a look, then gestured for the others to follow. Nero went first, getting on all fours to crawl through the passage.

They found themselves in a dusty little room with only a few stools for furniture and a sack stuffed with moldering old straw for a bed. A short hallway led to a little vestibule. Not surprisingly for slave quarters, the door had no lock on the inside, not even a bar that could be dropped into place.

A small window, covered by a tattered cloth, provided light. Looking through a hole in the cloth, Titus saw a dirt courtyard, a grassy slope, and a bit of the main house, farther up the hill. How elegant the place looked, with its red-tile roof and its yellow-marble columns, surrounded by stately cypress trees and blooming rose bushes and hedges pruned in the shapes of obelisks, cubes, and spheres.

Nero sat on the bed with his back against the wall. He began to weep in earnest, sobbing until his face was wet with tears. "Weep with me, Sabina!" he cried. "Lament for me and tear out your hair, like a good wife!"

Sporus obligingly began to sweep the filthy floor with his unbound tresses and to make a keening noise.

"Caesar, there's no need to give up hope," said Epaphroditus quietly. "Not yet."

"You think I weep for myself, but I don't," said Nero. "I weep for those who will never see me on the stage. What an artist the world is losing!"

Titus sat on one of the stools. He leaned against the wall and closed his eyes, exhausted. His consciousness came and went. The afternoon wore on, but time seemed to come to a stop. The whole world contracted to the dismal little room in which he found himself.

Phaon produced some bread and water. Nero sipped a bit of the water but did not eat. He told them that they should begin to dig a grave for him, so as to hide his body from his enemies. "Otherwise they'll cut off my head and take it back to Roma to prove to everyone I'm dead. Don't let them cut off my head, Epaphroditus!"

"That will not happen, Caesar. I swear to you, that will not happen."

"Better yet, you must burn me. Bring water to wash my corpse. Gather firewood to make the pyre!"

"Not yet, Caesar," whispered Epaphroditus, wearily closing his eyes. "Not yet. Rest. Sleep if you can. Night will come, and then another day. . . ."

Titus dozed.

He was awakened by a stirring in the room. The others were crowded together at the window, gazing out in alarm.

The room was dim. It was the last hour before sunset. Titus joined the others and peered with bleary eyes beyond the torn curtain. Long shadows lay across the dirt courtyard in front of the building. Slanting sunlight pierced the clouds of dust stirred by a lone horseman. By his long, full beard, Titus saw that the horseman was Epictetus.

Before anyone else could react, Sporus rushed to the front door, opened it, and went outside. The eunuch ran up to Epictetus while he was still on horseback. The two exchanged words. From the window, Titus strained to hear what they were saying, but he could not make out the words.

Epictetus dismounted. His bad leg failed him and he fell. Grimacing, he got to his feet, looked about for a place to tie his mount, then clutched his leg, stumbled, and fell again.

Meanwhile, Sporus ran inside.

"How did he find us?" asked Phaon.

"He asked at the main house. The slaves knew nothing, but someone suggested he try this building."

"What news?" said Epaphroditus.

Sporus looked at Nero and seemed afraid to speak.

"What news?" cried Nero.

"The Senate took a vote."

"Yes?" Nero's voice was shrill.

"They declared Galba emperor."

Nero gasped. "And me? What of me?"

"The Senate declared you to be a public enemy." Sporus averted his eyes. "They say . . . they say you're to be put to death in the ancient manner."

"The ancient manner?" said Nero.

"That's what Epictetus told me."

"What in Hades does that mean? What does it mean, Epaphroditus?" cried Nero.

Epaphroditus did not answer.

It was Titus who spoke. His voice sounded hollow in his ears. "The ancient manner refers to a specific means of execution devised by our ancestors. The victim is paraded before the people and publicly stripped—"

Nero let out a cry.

"When he is naked, his neck is fastened in a two-pronged pitchfork, so that he can be driven this way and that or held in place," continued Titus. "Men with rods beat him until—"

"No!" Nero trembled from head to foot. His eyes were wide with terror.

Strangely, Titus did not share the emperor's fear. He felt something very different. He was experiencing the extreme sense of wonder and revelation that had come to him when he heard Nero sing of Troy above the burning ruins of Roma, and again when he was made to witness his brother set aflame.

"Caesar, do you not see? This is the fate the gods have intended for you all along."

"What are you saying, Pinarius?"

"What greater role could there be for the greatest of all actors? You will be the fallen hero, the god-emperor made to suffer the most terrible and disgraceful of deaths. Your execution will take place with all Roma watching. Everyone in the city will see you naked. Everyone will see you suffer and bleed. Everyone will see you soil yourself and weep and beg for mercy. Everyone will see you die. No one will ever forget the end of Nero. Your public execution will be the crowning performance of a lifetime!"

Nero stared back at him, his mouth agape. For a moment he seemed to seriously consider what Titus had said. He slowly nodded. Then he shuddered and staggered back, shaking his head and waving his hands before his face. "Madness! What you say is madness, Pinarius!"

Suddenly Nero froze. He looked down at his right arm, and gripped it with his left hand. "Where is it?" he shrieked.

"What, Caesar?" said Epaphroditus.

"My bracelet! Where is the golden bracelet my mother gave me, the amulet that holds my lucky snakeskin?"

"Do you not remember?" said Epaphroditus. "Caesar cast it away long ago. Caesar declared it was hateful to him, after the death of his mother."

Nero gazed at Epaphroditus, baffled, then gave a start. From the dusty courtyard came the sound of rumbling hoofbeats.

They gazed out the window. The men arriving on horseback were armed Praetorians.

"They must have followed Epictetus," whispered Phaon. He set about gathering up the stools and bits of debris from the hole in the wall, stacking everything he could find against the door in an effort to block it.

The Praetorians quickly dismounted. Some of them seized Epictetus as he tried to limp away from them. One of them studied the building for a moment, then drew his sword and began to walk toward the entrance.

Sporus pulled at his hair and wailed. His shrill cries caused hackles to rise on the back of Titus's neck. He gazed at Nero. Suddenly he saw not a god, not a genius, but a mere mortal, pitiful and afraid.

Nero ran to Epaphroditus. "Give me your dagger! Quickly!"

Epaphroditus handed him the knife.

Nero held the point to his breast, then hesitated. He looked at the others. "Will one of you not kill yourself first, to give me courage?"

Sporus continued to wail. The others stood frozen to the spot. From the vestibule, they heard the Praetorian bang the pommel of his sword against the door.

"Jupiter, what an artist perishes in me!" cried Nero. He pushed the dagger into his belly, but he could not drive it all the way. Blood stained his coarse tunic as he fell to the ground. He writhed in agony.

"Help me!" he whimpered.

Epaphroditus knelt beside him. His eyes glistened with tears but his hands were steady. He rolled Nero onto his back and pulled the dagger from his belly. He placed the dagger above Nero's heart, gathered his strength, and drove the blade deep into the flesh.

Nero convulsed. Blood flowed from his mouth and his nostrils.

The Praetorian pushed open the door, scattering the stools stacked against it. He paused for a moment in the vestibule to let his eyes adjust to the dim light, then rushed into the room. Titus recognized the young messenger they had met at the bridge. The shocked expression on his face made him look almost childlike. The Praetorian pulled off his cloak and threw it over Nero's bleeding wounds. He knelt beside the emperor.

"Too late!" Nero gasped, taking the soldier's hand. "Too late, my faithful warrior!"

The emperor writhed, vomited more blood, clenched his teeth, and then suddenly went stiff. His glassy eyes were wide open. His mouth was fixed in a bloody grimace so awful that even the Praetorian shuddered and everyone in the room looked away—everyone except Titus, who stared spellbound at the agonized face of Nero.

To Titus, the horror of the moment was exquisite beyond bearing. Even Seneca at his goriest had never contrived a scene to rival this. Nero's end had been unspeakably tawdry and pathetic. Watching, Titus had been moved to uttermost terror and pity. Even in the instant of death Nero had played the actor, making his face into a mask that could have made a strong man faint.

Nero had been right and Titus had been wrong. A public execution in the ancient manner would have been gaudy and overstated, an unseemly waste of Nero's talents before an audience unworthy of his genius. Instead, Nero's end had been a private performance played out before the eyes of a privileged few. Titus felt honored beyond measure to have witnessed the final scene of the greatest artist who had ever lived.

Titus looked at the others in the room. Epaphroditus, Phaon, and Sporus were mere freedmen and courtiers and might yet hope to escape execution. But Titus was a senator, and as an augur he had declared divine approval for Nero's every action. With Nero dead, Titus had no doubt that he would be tried and executed. If that were to happen, his family would be disinherited, disgraced, and driven from Roma. Only if Titus were to die by his own hand might his wife and son and daughters hope to escape retribution.

Titus gripped Epaphroditus by the wrist.

"Make a vow, Epaphroditus! Swear by Nero's shade! If you survive this day, promise me you'll do all you can to look after Lucius, my son."

Overwhelmed by emotion and unable to speak, Epaphroditus could only nod.

More Praetorians came rushing into the little room, their swords drawn. Before they could reach him, Titus pulled out his dagger and plunged it into his chest.

PART III

LUCIUS
The Seeker

A.D. 69

Lucius Pinarius sighed. "If only Otho were still alive, and emperor. You were able to twist Otho around your little finger."

Sporus, wearing an elegant silk robe, made only a grunt for an answer. She—for Lucius always thought of Sporus as "she," and Sporus preferred to be addressed as a woman—stretched with feline grace on the couch next to Lucius. Side by side, the two friends gazed up at the elaborate scene painted on the ceiling, its vivid colors softened by the slanting winter sunlight. The scene depicted the abduction of Ganymede by Jupiter; the naked, beautiful youth was clutching a toy hoop in one hand and a cockerel, Jupiter's courtship gift, in the other, while the king of the gods stood with muscular arms spread, ready to make himself into an eagle to carry the object of his desire to Olympus.

"Is there a prettier room in all the Golden House?" said Sporus. "I love these apartments, don't you?"

"I'd love them more if I were only a visitor, and Epaphroditus would agree to let me return to my own house and family," said Lucius.

"He's only doing what he thinks is best for you. He made a promise to your father to look after you; I witnessed the vow. If Epaphroditus says you're safer living here, then you should be glad he still has these apartments, despite all the changes, and gladder still that he has space for you.

Besides, if you were no longer here, I should grow awfully lonely without you, Lucius."

Lucius smiled. "A year and a half ago, we hardly knew each other."

"A year and a half ago, many things were different. Nero still lived. Imagine that—a world grand enough to contain Nero in it! Nero was too big for this world. Galba was too little."

"Galba might still be emperor, if he had paid the Praetorians what he owed them."

"Galba was a bore!" declared Sporus. "A miser and a bore. His reign was seven months of misery for everyone, including himself. The soldiers were right to kill the old fool. And right to make Otho emperor in his place. It was almost as if Nero had come back to us." Sporus sighed. "Once upon a time, back in the golden days, Otho and Nero were best friends, you know. Their parties and drinking bouts were legendary. Nero told me Otho was like an older brother to him—though he flattered himself if he thought there was any physical resemblance. Otho was so good-looking. And what a body he had! It was Poppaea who came between them. Otho was married to her; Nero had to have her. Poor Otho was forced to divorce Poppaea and head off to Spain."

"And when the soldiers got rid of Galba, Otho was their choice to succeed him."

"Because the people were already nostalgic for Nero, and Otho was the closest thing to Nero they could find. He was only thirty-seven; he could have ruled for a long, long time. He took Nero's name. He restored the statues of Nero that had been pulled down. He announced his intention to complete the parts of the Golden House still under construction, on an even grander scale than Nero intended."

"The bricklayers and artisans in Roma loved hearing that!" said Lucius.

"In every way, Otho seemed ready to rule just as Nero had done."

"And ready to love as Nero had loved."

Sporus sighed and nodded. "Yes. Dear Otho! Because I looked like *her*, of course. I remember the first time he saw me. It was in these apartments. He came to see Epaphroditus with some question about the household staff. Otho saw me across the room. He looked as if he'd been struck, as if he might fall. I could see his knees trembling."

"His tunic was short enough to show his knees?"

"Otho loved to show off his legs, and with good reason. He had the legs of a mountaineer, as smooth and firm as if they'd been carved from marble. Thighs like tree trunks. Calves like—"

"Please, Sporus, that's enough about Otho's legs!" Lucius laughed.

Sporus smiled. "It didn't take us long to get acquainted."

"You dragged him straight to your bed, you mean!"

"It was his bed we slept in, though I don't recall sleeping. It was like the night the Divine Julius met Queen Cleopatra in Alexandria—love at first sight."

"Or lust!"

"Perhaps. Sometimes lust comes first, and love later. In private he called me Sabina, just as Nero did." Sporus frowned. "Sometimes I wonder what my life would have been like if I hadn't looked so much like *her*. What a strange destiny the gods laid out for me. Ah, well, it doesn't bear thinking about."

A wistful expression crossed the eunuch's face. Lucius had seen it before, and Epaphroditus had once explained it to him: "That is the look Sporus gets when she thinks about her long-lost testes."

Otho had reigned for only ninety-five days. Many of those days had been spent away from Roma, mustering troops and preparing for the invasion of Aulus Vitellius, the governor of Lower Germania, who had been proclaimed emperor by his own troops. Otho took to the field against Vitellius in northern Italy, but before the campaign could begin in earnest, Otho killed himself.

Why? Everyone in Roma had asked that question. Otho had every chance of winning against Vitellius, but instead chose to die in his tent on the eve of battle. His friends said that Otho killed himself to save Roma from civil war. Lucius could hardly imagine such an act of self-sacrifice, especially from a man who had been hailed as a second Nero. But the story was repeated so often and so fervently that Otho's suicide for the sake of Roma had already become the stuff of legend.

Otho might have hoped to give the city a respite from bloodshed and upheaval, but his death and the unopposed succession of Vitellius accomplished just the opposite. The new emperor arrived in Roma at the head of a licentious and bloodthirsty army, and the city became the scene of riot and massacre, gladiator shows and extravagant feasting. To reward his victorious legionaries, Vitellius disbanded the existing Praetorian Guard and installed his own men. Under Galba and Otho, a few brave voices in the Senate had spoken up for a return to Republican government; Vitellius's reign of terror silenced all opposition.

Physically, the new emperor was the opposite of the statuesque Otho. He was grotesquely obese. Apparently he had not always been unattractive; rumor had it that the young Vitellius had been one of Tiberius's spintriae at Capri, where his services to the debauched emperor had advanced his father's career. Titus found it hard to imagine Vitellius as a pleasingly plump boy when gazing at the man in his late fifties.

The death of Otho had left Sporus without a role in the imperial household. As she had done in the confusion after Nero's death and under Galba, Sporus again looked to Epaphroditus for protection. That was how Lucius and Sporus had been thrown together. Lucius was already residing with Epaphroditus, seldom stirring beyond his suite of rooms, trying to draw as little attention as possible to himself or to the personal fortune he had inherited from his father. There was plenty of space in Epaphroditus's apartments to accommodate both Lucius and Sporus, but the two wards inevitably found themselves spending time together. They were about the same age: Lucius was twenty-two and Sporus a bit younger. Otherwise they had little in common, yet they never quarreled and often talked for hours, sharing gossip, laughing at each other's jokes, and reminiscing about the dead—not only Lucius's father and Otho, but all the others who had passed into oblivion in the tumult that had begun with Nero's death.

So far, Lucius had remained beneath the new emperor's notice, and so had Sporus. Epaphroditus told them that this was a good thing, but inevitably they grew restless shut up in Epaphroditus's apartments.

Now change was again in the air. According to Epaphroditus, Vitellius might not be emperor much longer. The general Vespasian, vastly enriched by his war against the Jews and anticipating even greater riches from the sack of their capital, Jerusalem, had been proclaimed emperor by his troops in the East and by the legions on the Danube. While Vespasian and his son Titus remained in the East, commanders loyal to him were marching on Italy. Another struggle for control of the empire was imminent. The mood in the city had become increasingly unsettled and anxious. There was a sense that anything might happen, and fear of a bloodbath. Astrologers had predicted the end of Vitellius. Vitellius's response, besides ordering every astrologer in Roma to be killed on the spot, was to throw one lavish party after another.

There were even rumors that Nero had not died after all—that he had staged his death as a hoax—and the heir of Augustus would return at any moment at the head of a Parthian army. Sporus and Epaphroditus knew better, of course, though neither of them would tell Lucius exactly what had transpired in the last moments of Nero's life, which had also been the last moments of his father's life. "The emperor chose the moment and the method of his death, and he died with dignity," was all that Epaphroditus would say, "and so did your father, who bravely decided to follow him into death."

Lying back on the couch, Lucius gazed up at the painting of the broad-shouldered Jupiter and the slender but elegantly muscled Ganymede, who looked a bit too mature and developed to be carrying a boy's hoop.

"I can see why Ganymede is as smooth as a baby," said Lucius, "but you'd think a brawny fellow like Jupiter would be shown with a bit more hair on his chest, wouldn't you? Yet the painters never seem to show hair on a man's chest, and neither do the sculptors. Is it true that Otho didn't have a hair on his body?"

Sporus laughed. "True: Otho had not a hair on his body. Or on his head. When he took off that hairpiece—"

"Otho wore a hairpiece? You never told me that!"

"He made me take a vow to tell no one, even if he should die in battle. Well, he didn't die in battle, did he? He chose to abandon me by his own hand! So I'll tell you anyway. Yes, Otho wore a hairpiece. It was a very good one, I must admit. It fooled you, obviously!" Sporus laughed. "As for the rest of him, even *I* have more hair on my body than did Otho. He went to great lengths to remove every strand. He shaved here, plucked there, and in certain delicate areas he used a wax poultice to depilate himself. He was so vain about his physique, you see. When he was naked, he wanted nothing to obscure the sight of all those muscles. And of course he liked the touch of silk against his hairless flesh. What a wardrobe the man had! This robe I'm wearing belonged to Otho. . . ." Sporus's voice trailed off.

Lucius thought of another thing that Epaphroditus had said: "That is the look of Sporus remembering those who have died and left her behind."

There was a quiet knock at the door. Epictetus entered.

For a long time, Lucius had been confused by the lame slave's furtive, almost cringing demeanor whenever he was in Sporus's presence. Epaphroditus treated Epictetus with respect, acknowledging and even deferring to his young slave's immense erudition, and allowed Epictetus considerable freedom to do and say whatever he pleased. Epictetus was no cowed underling, yet around Sporus he behaved awkwardly and averted his eyes; even his limp became more pronounced. Eventually, Lucius realized that the slave was in love with Sporus and painfully aware that his love could never be requited. Sporus had been the consort of two of the most powerful men on earth; she could hardly be expected to take notice of a lame slave who hid his homely face behind a shaggy beard. To be sure, Epictetus was clever; Epaphroditus declared that he had never known any man who was better read or more thoroughly versed in philosophy, which was quite remarkable considering that Epictetus was the same age as Lucius. But what good was all his learning to Epictetus when the object of his affection was more interested in muscular legs and depilating poultices than in Stoic discourse?

"There's a visitor in the vestibule," said Epictetus, glancing at Sporus and then at the floor.

"Epaphroditus is out for the afternoon," said Lucius. "The visitor will have to come back later."

"I failed to make myself clear," said Epictetus, daring to look up again. "The visitor is here to see Sporus."

Sporus sat upright. "Me? No one ever comes to see me anymore. A friend of Otho's, perhaps?"

"No. He comes from the emperor Vitellius," said Epictetus. "He calls himself Asiaticus."

Sporus raised an eyebrow. "Not a big, muscular fellow, rakishly handsome? Struts like a gladiator but grins like a spintria?"

Epictetus frowned. "That might describe him."

"Who is this Asiaticus?" asked Lucius. "How do you know him?"

"I *don't* know him," said Sporus, "but it looks as if I soon shall. Really, Lucius, you don't know the stories about Vitellius and Asiaticus?"

"I'm afraid not."

"What a sheltered existence your father imposed on you, sparing your delicate ears from the gossip of the court. Nero loved telling tales about Vitellius and his stud horse. The relationship between those two made Nero's bedroom antics seem quite tame."

"My ears are open," said Lucius, rolling onto his stomach and propping his chin on his fists.

"Quickly, then: Asiaticus was born a slave, no different from any other slave, until in adolescence a certain appendage became rather prominent. When Vitellius saw the boy standing naked on the auction block one day, he didn't buy him for his brains. Like a racing master who'd acquired a new stud, Vitellius took him home and tried him out right away. Vitellius was happy with his purchase.

"But as you know, in these relationships it's not always clear who is the master and who the slave, and desire isn't always mutual. Asiaticus grew tired of Vitellius, and who could blame him? They say Vitellius is actually rather skilled at lovemaking, but really, can you imagine having that mass of quivering flesh on top of you? Or under you, I should imagine, since I suspect that to be his preferred position. Anyway, at some point, young Asiaticus had quite enough and ran off. Vitellius wept and tore out his hair! He was heartbroken. Then, one day, Vitellius was down in Puteoli and who should he come across at a little stand on the waterfront, flirting with the sailors and selling cheap wine hardly better than vinegar, but Asiaticus. Vitellius burst into tears and moved to embrace him, but Asiaticus was off like an arrow. Vitellius's men gave chase, knocking down half the market stalls along the waterfront, and finally caught Asiaticus and brought him back in irons. A happy ending—the lovers were reunited!"

Lucius laughed. "Something tells me there's more to this story."

"Much more! So, it's back to Roma, where all goes well—for a while. This time it's Vitellius who decides he's had enough of Asiaticus—the insolence, the lying, the thieving, the cavorting behind his master's back. Vitellius stamps his feet and rants and pulls out his whip, but eventually he makes good on a longstanding threat and sells Asiaticus to a new master, a fellow who keeps a traveling band of gladiators. Again the lovers are separated. Vitellius thinks he's seen the last of Asiaticus, who's gone from spilling seed in his master's bedroom to spilling blood in the arena."

Standing in the doorway, Epictetus cleared his throat. "The man is just outside, still waiting—"

"Don't worry, I won't keep him much longer," said Sporus. "Well, to make a long story short, one day Vitellius is invited to be the guest of honor at the games being put on by a local magistrate in some country town.

Who should be scheduled for the final match but Asiaticus! Vitellius goes pale when the love of his life enters the arena, but he puts on a brave face and tells himself he's long since gotten over that scoundrel and would be happy to see him suffer an agonizing death. Then the match begins, and things go badly for Asiaticus from the start. He's wounded once, twice, and ends up flat on his back with his opponent's sword at his throat. The crowd screams for his death, and the magistrate is ready to give the signal, when Vitellius leaps to his feet and cries out, 'Spare him! Spare my sweet Asiaticus!' Vitellius buys him back on the spot, paying an outrageous sum, and down in the gladiators' quarters the two are reunited. Imagine the tears and kisses and whispers of forgiveness! I know this sounds like a tawdry Greek novel, but I swear I didn't make it up."

Epictetus cleared his throat again.

"And the rest of the story?" said Lucius.

"Vitellius took Asiaticus with him when he went to govern Germania. He ruled there the way he's ruled in Roma—wild banquets and gladiator shows to amuse the local chieftains while his soldiers raped and plundered the citizenry. To make amends for having made him a gladiator, Vitellius freed Asiaticus and gave him an official post. Asiaticus turned out to be rather useful, apparently; living by wits and brawn had trained him to be just the sort of factotum a governor like Vitellius needed. Few were the troublemakers Asiaticus couldn't bully or seduce into submission. And now he's here in Roma, helping his old master run the show. Not just a freedman any longer, but a respected member of the equestrian order."

"No!" said Lucius.

"Yes. Not long after Vitellius became emperor, some of his fawning supporters urged him to elevate Asiaticus to equestrian rank, since he possessed the requisite wealth. Vitellius laughed and told them not to be ridiculous, that the appointment of a rascal like Asiaticus would bring disgrace to the order. When Asiaticus got wind of this, you can imagine his reaction. Quick as asparagus, Vitellius threw a banquet where he presented Asiaticus with the gold ring to mark his new status as an equestrian. He'll make the fellow a senator next!"

Lucius laughed, then frowned. "And now Asiaticus has come to call on you. This can't be good."

"No? I'm eager to have a look at him," said Sporus. "Epictetus, tell my visitor he can come in now. Have one of the serving girls bring suitable refreshments."

Even as Epictetus nodded and turned, he was confronted by a figure coming through the doorway. The visitor pushed Epictetus aside and swaggered into the room.

In Lucius's experience, men who craved the company of youths tended to look for the Greek ideal of beauty. The sight of Asiaticus surprised him. The man had a round head set atop a squat neck and an almost piggish face—an upturned nose, heavy lips, and squinting eyes. Even allowing for a coarsening of his features due to debauched living, it was hard to imagine that he had ever possessed the kind of beauty the old Greek masters immortalized in marble. Nor was he any longer a boy: there were flecks of gray in his wiry black hair. His equestrian's tunic, with its narrow red stripes running up and over each massive shoulder, seemed barely to contain him, leaving his brawny arms and more of his hairy thighs exposed than was decent, and straining to contain the breadth of his bull-like chest. On his left hand, pushed onto a thick, stubby finger, Lucius saw the gold equestrian's ring that had been placed there by Vitellius.

Lucius rose from the couch. He drew back his shoulders. Asiaticus gave him a glance, then settled his gaze on Sporus. He twisted his lips into a smirk.

"You must be Sporus," said Asiaticus. His voice was not what Lucius had expected, either, tinged with what Lucius's father had called the gutter accent of uneducated slaves and freedmen.

"And you must be Asiaticus." Sporus continued to recline on the couch. With one hand she smoothed a fold of her silk gown over her hips.

"This is for you." Asiaticus stepped forward and held forth a scroll.

"What's this?" Sporus untied the ribbon.

"A new play, written by the emperor himself."

"By Jupiter, another one who thinks he's Nero!" muttered Epictetus from the doorway.

"*The Rape of Lucretia by the Son of King Tarquinius and the Subsequent Fall of the Last Dynasty of Kings,*" read Sporus. "The title is certainly a mouthful, though the play seems hardly more than a sketch."

"Short and sweet," said Asiaticus. "It's mostly action. The emperor doesn't want to bore his audience."

"Audience? Is there to be a performance? Are we invited?" Sporus cast a quick, wide-eyed glance at Lucius, then smiled graciously at Asiaticus.

"The audience will consist of the emperor's closest friends and advisers. Men of high rank and exquisite taste."

"Will you be there?" said Lucius. He kept a straight face. Sporus covered her laugh with a cough.

Asiaticus stared at Lucius for a moment, then grinned. "Oh, yes, I'll be there. And so will you, young Pinarius. And so will your host, Epaphroditus. The emperor wouldn't want either of you to miss Sporus's performance."

"Performance?" Sporus brightened.

"Did I not explain? You'll play Lucretia."

"I?" Sporus sprang to her feet and perused the scroll with greater interest.

"There'll be a rehearsal tonight for the performance at the banquet tomorrow."

"Tomorrow! But I can't possibly—"

"You don't have that many lines." Asiaticus stepped closer. Lucius was struck by how slender and delicate Sporus looked face-to-face with Asiaticus, who was only a little taller but massively broader. "If you forget a line, don't worry. I shall be there to whisper it in your ear. Like this." Asiaticus drew closer and blew into Sporus's ear.

Sporus flinched and stepped back. "You?"

"Did I not explain? I'm to play Sextus Tarquinius, the son of the king. The villain who rapes Lucretia."

Sporus took another step back. She opened the scroll with both hands, interposing it between herself and Asiaticus. "I see. You and I are to act in the emperor's play together, performing opposite each other?"

"Exactly. I'll leave you now. Try to get those lines into your pretty head, and do whatever else you need to prepare yourself. We'll stage a private rehearsal for the emperor tonight while he dines." Asiaticus looked Sporus up and down. The smirk vanished, replaced by a vacant, slack-jawed expression that Lucius found even more disturbing. Then he swaggered out of the room.

"This is ridiculous!" said Lucius.

"Ridiculous?" Sporus stood erect. "Do you think me incapable? I didn't spend all that time at Nero's side without picking up some knowledge of acting. Here, Epictetus, you and I will read the play together, and you'll help me with my lines."

As Asiaticus had noted, the so-called play was quite short. It could hardly be intended as the main part of an evening's entertainment. It was more likely a vignette to fill out the program; Vitellius's parties typically included dancing boys and girls and gladiators fighting to the death along with declaiming poets and comic actors.

The story required little in the way of background. Everyone in the audience would know the tale already. When a friend of the king's son boasted of his wife's virtue, the reckless Sextus Tarquinius felt obliged to take it from her; arriving while her husband was away, he took advantage of Lucretia's hospitality and raped her. Unable to bear her shame, Lucretia used a dagger to kill herself. When her body was shown to an angry crowd in the Forum, King Tarquinius and his wicked son were driven from Roma and the Republic was founded.

Epictetus quickly scanned the text. He wrinkled his nose in disgust. "Hardly more than a vulgar mime show," he declared. "According to the stage instructions, the rape takes place right on stage, and so does Lucretia's suicide."

"Seneca saw fit to include all sorts of shock effects in his plays," noted Sporus. "Thyestes eats his roasted children right in front of the audience, and Oedipus gouges out his eyes. They use hidden bladders and pig's blood."

"If Vitellius thinks he's another Seneca, he's completely deluded," said Lucius, taking his turn at scanning the text. "This dialogue is utter drivel."

Sporus shrugged. "Still, if this is the sort of thing Vitellius likes, it's a chance for me to please him."

Lucius shook his head. "I didn't like Asiaticus's manner. What an oily fellow!"

"Yes, he wasn't quite what I expected, either," said Sporus. "Men seldom are. Still, he has a certain beastlike appeal. If you imagine him outfitted as a gladiator—"

"I'll let you get on with it, then," said Lucius, glad that Sporus had chosen Epictetus to practice with her and not him. Asiaticus's visit had put him in a foul mood. He needed to take a walk. Epaphroditus's apartments were off the long portico that fronted the meadows and the man-made lake at the heart of the Golden House. Perhaps he would walk all the way around the lake.

He fetched a cloak, though for such a mild winter day he probably wouldn't need it. As he made ready to leave, he heard Sporus and Epictetus declaiming their lines.

"Who is at the door?"

"It is I, Sextus Tarquinius, your husband's friend and the son of the king."

"But my husband is not home tonight."

"I know. But would you deny me your hospitality? Open your door to me, Lucretia. Let me in!"

Lucius smiled. Epictetus seemed to be getting into the spirit of the thing, despite his avowed disdain for the material. It occurred to Lucius that the slave might be taking a certain vicarious pleasure in playing such a role opposite the unobtainable object of his affection.

It also occurred to Lucius that Sporus might be imagining yet another return to imperial favor. Why not? Nero had married her. Otho had made her his mistress. Vitellius might be oblivious to her charms, preferring a more "beastlike" partner (to use Sporus's word), but Asiaticus had blatantly displayed his attraction, and Asiaticus was a powerful man.

Lucius sighed. As he left the apartments he heard a last exchange of dialogue.

"No! Unhand me, brute! I am faithful to my husband!"

"Yield to me, Lucretia! I will have my way with you!" Epictetus declaimed with such vigor that his voice broke. He cleared his throat, then spoke again, sounding rather chagrined. "And then the stage directions say that we struggle a bit, and then I tear your gown. . . ."

At sundown, a group of Praetorians arrived to escort them to the emperor's private quarters. Sporus walked ahead of the others, conscious of her special status. Lucius and Epaphroditus followed. Epictetus came along as well, ostensibly to attend to his master.

They were shown to a large, octagonal banquet room. The walls were of dazzling multicolored marble and there was a splashing fountain at the entrance. Lucius had never seen the room, but it was obviously quite familiar to Sporus, who must have spent many happy hours in this room, first with Nero, then with Otho. Lucius heard her sigh as she gazed about, assessing the changes wrought by Vitellius and his wife, Galeria, who was said to find Nero's taste too understated. A great many statues, decorative lamps, bronze vases, ivory screens, and woven hangings had been crowded into the room, filling the spaces against the walls and between the dining couches.

The only part of the room not cluttered with precious objects was a raised dais against one wall. The dais's sole decoration was a larger-than-life marble statue of Nero, who was depicted in Greek dress with a laurel crown on his head. It appeared that this dais was to serve as the stage for the play, since the dining couches were arrayed before it in a semicircle.

All the couches were empty except for two in the center of the front row. Upon one reclined the emperor's wife, Galeria, and their seven-year-old son, Germanicus. Upon the other couch, occupying the entire space, lay the emperor. A Molossian mastiff almost as big as a man lay curled before his couch. The dog sprang up and growled when Lucius and the others entered, then came to heel when its master made a shushing sound.

As Vitellius roused himself and stood, Lucius pondered the considerable energy required to set in motion such an imposing mass of flesh. The emperor was very tall, with big arms and a huge belly and the flushed face of a heavy drinker. As he took a few steps toward them, he limped slightly. Vitellius's lameness was said to be the result of a long-ago chariot accident in the days of his debauched youth; Caligula had been driving.

Vitellius held a sword, clutching the handle in his right fist and fondling the blade with the fingertips of his left hand. The pommel was ornately decorated and the blade was covered with gold. Lucius let out a little gasp when he realized what he was seeing: the sword of the Divine Julius. One of Vitellius's followers had stolen Caesar's sword from its sacred place in the Shrine of Mars and presented it to Vitellius when he was first proclaimed emperor. Vitellius carried it in place of the traditional dagger that his predecessors kept on their person as a symbol of the power of life and death they wielded over their subjects. He kept it always at his side like a lucky talisman. He even slept with it.

Beneath the folds of his toga, Lucius touched his own talisman, the fascinum he had been given on the last day of his father's life. Like his father, he wore it for special occasions and in times of danger.

Vitellius stared openly at Sporus. Unlike Asiaticus, he did not leer. His gaze was curious, but not lustful. If anything, to judge by the way he curled his upper lip, he was disgusted by what he saw.

"So you're the one who gave up his balls to please Nero, eh? Ah well, plenty of boys have lost their balls for less reason than that." Vitellius slowly circled Sporus, fondling the sword in his hands. "Then along came Otho. He took a fancy to you, as well. I suppose he looked at you and thought: there's a bargain, the work's already been done! Rather like a quality piece of real estate already refurbished by the previous owner."

The emperor completed his circuit and stood before Sporus, looming over her. She stared up at him for a moment, then lowered her eyes.

"That Otho!" Vitellius clucked his tongue. "Never knew what to make of the fellow. So amenable! Avoided confrontation at all costs. Supposedly he was Nero's best friend, but when Nero wanted his Poppaea, Otho gave her up without a fight. I certainly wouldn't give up my wife, just because a friend asked for her. Would I, my sweet?"

The empress Galeria, reclining next to her son, smiled sweetly. She was Vitellius's second wife and considerably younger than her husband. She was wearing one of Poppaea's gowns, a magnificent confection of red-and-purple silk to which she had added a great deal of silver embroidery and strings of pearls. Her son reclined beside her, staring vacantly at Sporus. Germanicus was large for his age. Lucius could see that the boy resembled his father, with his chubby cheeks and fleshy limbs, and realized with a shiver that Germanicus was probably the age his father had been when Tiberius inducted him into the debaucheries at Capri. The boy was said to have a stutter so severe that he could hardly speak at all.

"As long as Nero reigned, Otho seemed quite content to live in exile," continued Vitellius, fondling the sword and gazing at Sporus. "Never joined in any of the plots against the man who stole his wife, not even after Nero kicked poor Poppaea to death." He glanced over his shoulder at Galeria. "If anyone kicked you to death, my dear, I would certainly take steps to avenge you."

Galeria laughed quietly. Germanicus made a braying noise.

"Perhaps Otho was just biding his time," said Vitellius, "waiting for his chance. It did seem that he was going to have the last laugh, at least for a while; he ended up living here in Nero's Golden House, having his way with Nero's new version of Poppaea. Poppaea with a penis, if you like!" He stepped closer to Sporus, towering over her. "But along I came, and poof! Otho vanished like a candle in the wind. In the taverns, they sing a song about him: 'Gave up his wife, gave up his life, all without strife.' I can't have any respect for a fellow like that. I wonder what sort of lover he made. How did he compare to Nero? Poppaea could have told us, but Poppaea is dead. Perhaps you can enlighten us, eunuch. But not yet. We have a play to rehearse!"

The emperor clapped his hands. Lucius and Epaphroditus were shown to couches and offered food and wine. Epictetus stood behind his master. The fare was exquisite, but with Praetorians stationed against each wall, Lucius did not find the atmosphere relaxing. Little Germanicus made a great deal of noise when he ate, snorting and drooling and chewing with his mouth open.

Vitellius took Sporus's hand and escorted her onto the dais. With his sword, he gestured to the statue of Nero. "This is one of the statues that was pulled down after Nero's death, then restored by Otho. If you look closely, you can see where the head was reattached to the neck. It's fitting the statue should be here, because tomorrow's banquet will be in honor of Nero. First, there will be a sacrifice at his tomb on the Hill of Gardens, followed by gladiator games and then a feast for everyone in the city. Only very special guests will be invited to the banquet in this room."

Vespasian's supporters were marching on the city, Lucius thought, and the response of Vitellius was to invoke the spirit of Nero and to treat the people of Roma to yet another feast. The man knew only one way to rule, by throwing parties; the graver the crisis, the grander the party.

"The highlight of the menu will be a dish of my own devising," said Vitellius. "I call it the Shield of Minerva. If I am remembered for nothing else a thousand years from now, I hope that men will still speak of this dish. No vessel of pottery large enough to contain it could be fired, so a gigantic shield made of solid silver has been cast for the presentation. The shield will be carried into the room by a group of slaves. Upon it will be arranged an exquisite confabulation of pike livers, pheasant brains, pea-cock brains, and flamingo tongues, all sprinkled with lamprey milt. The total cost will be more than a million sesterces. My guests will have seen and tasted nothing like it in their entire lives.

"While we eat, we must be entertained. For the occasion, I wrote a little play about Lucretia. When I began to consider whom to cast in the title role, it was Asiaticus who suggested you, Sporus. I swear, that fellow can go for years without expressing a single intelligent thought, and then he produces a stroke of genius! To honor Nero's memory, who else but Nero's widow could play the role of Lucretia? Are you ready to show me what you can do?"

Sporus nodded. "I shall do my best to please you, Caesar."

"Oh, you shall please me, I have no doubt." Vitellius smiled. "The props will all be imaginary, except for Lucretia's distaff and spindle and her bed. The stagehands will bring those on at the proper time. A piper will play whenever the scene changes, and to underscore the more dra-matic moments."

The emperor descended from the dais and reclined on his couch.

The rehearsal commenced. A chorus of three actors stepped onto the stage first, to declaim the prologue. The chorus then became the entou-rage of Sextus Tarquinius, played by Asiaticus, who engaged in a debate with an actor playing Lucretia's husband concerning which man had the more virtuous wife. To settle the argument, the husbands decided to drop in on their wives unexpectedly. The chorus became the female atten-dants of Sextus's wife, who was caught gossiping and drinking wine with her slaves. The chorus then became the female slaves of Lucretia; when the husbands dropped in, they found her spinning and overheard her deliver a soliloquy about the duties of a wife. Sporus's first lines were a bit shaky, Lucius thought, but she seemed to gain confidence as she went on.

The chorus vanished. Lucretia's gloating husband sang his wife's praises. Vexed, Sextus ordered him to leave the city on a military mission, then delivered a speech expressing his fury at the man who had made a fool of him and declaring his intention to destroy Lucretia's virtue.

Sextus paid a call on Lucretia. The hour was late. The slaves were all abed. Lucretia, spinning by candlelight, looked up at a sudden noise.

"Who is at the door?" Sporus cried, with a convincingly nervous quaver.

"It is I, Sextus Tarquinius, your husband's friend and the son of the king," said Asiaticus in a booming voice.

Standing behind his master, Epictetus snorted quietly, trying not to laugh out loud. Lucius likewise bit his tongue. Asiaticus was a terrible actor, though physically he fit the part. Had Vitellius written a comedy or a tragedy? It was hard to tell. How would the audience react the next day, besotted by wine and stuffed with the delicacies from the Shield of Minerva? The emperor's guests would be thinking as much about the actors as about the play, titillated by the novelty of seeing Vitellius's stud and Nero's eunuch bride together on the stage.

The rehearsal continued with the determined Sextus forcing his way into Lucretia's bedroom. He knocked aside her spindle. He threw her onto the bed. Above them loomed the statue of Nero.

Lucius recalled the stage directions, which read, "He tears her clothes and has his way with her; she resists and weeps."

Perhaps Sporus and Asiaticus were merely acting, but to Lucius it seemed that the activity on the stage suddenly looked quite real, and became more so as the mock rape continued. Sporus seemed quite genuinely to struggle; Asiaticus seemed genuinely to overpower her, handling her very roughly, even slapping her face. Sporus let out a cry that did not sound like acting.

Epictetus stiffened. Epaphroditus, hearing the slave's indrawn breath and sensing his agitation, shook his head and raised his hand. But Epictetus could not be still. He began to move toward the stage. Epaphroditus seized him by the wrist.

Vitellius was excited by the scene. So was Germanicus, who screeched and clapped his hands at the display of violence. Father and son both sat upright and leaned forward on their couches. Vitellius toyed nervously with the sword of the Divine Julius and began to direct the action.

"Come on, Asiaticus, you can do better than that! Tear her clothes, as it says in the script. Don't just pretend—I want to hear the fabric rip. Yes, that's it. And again! But not too much—we mustn't see that the eunuch has no breasts. It's the sound that will thrill the audience.

"Now slap her face again. Gather her hair in your fist, pull back her head, and give her a good, hard slap. Oh, harder than that! This is Lucretia you're violating, the bitch who made a fool of you by parading her virtue. This is every patrician lady with her nose in the air who ever said no to you. You despise her self-righteousness, you want to see her disgraced, humbled, completely humiliated. I want to hear her squeal like a pig, Asiaticus. That's better. Louder! The music must be louder, too, and more frantic."

The piper, who stood offstage, was performing a piece called "Lucretia's Tears," one of Nero's best-known compositions. He played louder and faster.

Held down on the bed by Asiaticus, Sporus made such a plaintive cry that Epictetus pulled free of his master and began limping toward the stage. One of the Praetorians immediately blocked his way.

Lucius watched in dismay as Asiaticus knocked Sporus about and turned her this way and that. Throwing back his head and laughing, Asiaticus positioned Sporus on all fours, facing the audience. He hitched up her tattered gown, exposing her thighs, and pretended to mount her from behind. He was clearly enjoying himself, grinning broadly as he raised his hand to slap the eunuch's buttocks. Sporus looked so terrified that for a moment Lucius thought an actual rape was taking place before his eyes.

But no—when Asiaticus, after a great deal of thrusting and grunting, finally feigned a climax and drew back, smirking and sticking out his tongue, and Sporus, disheveled and shaken, crumpled to the bed, Lucius could see that the act was simulated after all.

Vitellius applauded. Mimicking his father, Germanicus likewise clapped his hands and made a braying noise. Galeria toyed with the pearls on her gown and looked bored.

"Very good," said Vitellius. "Very good, indeed! Very much what I had in mind. But tomorrow night, I want it to last rather longer than that, Asiaticus. I know how excited you'll be, but draw it out as long as you can. Take your time. Enjoy yourself. Relish the punishment you're inflicting on Lucretia. And you must be *much* more violent—I know you're capable of that! Remember that you are the brutal, merciless Sextus Tarquinius and this is the rape of Lucretia; her suffering is every schoolboy's fantasy. Also, make sure you hold the eunuch's face to the light at the critical moment, so that we can have a good look at her when she gasps and cries out. Let my guests see for themselves what Nero and Otho saw when they mounted the creature. Alright, then, on to the next scene!"

Asiaticus left the stage. Sporus lay motionless on the bed, hiding her face.

"On with it, I said!" Vitellius impatiently slapped the flat side of the sword against the palm of his hand. "Yes, yes, you're miserable; quite convincing. So miserable that you reach for the dagger under the bed. Go on, reach for the dagger."

Sporus looked up with a dazed expression. She straightened her twisted gown, pushed back her disheveled hair, and reached under the bed. The dagger was a stage device made of soft wood. Sporus stared at it. Her brow became twisted and her jaw trembled. A trickle of blood from her swollen lower lip ran down her chin.

"Can you not remember the lines?" barked Vitellius. " 'I have been violated—' "

"I have been violated," Sporus whispered, staring at the dagger.

"Louder!"

"I have been violated!" Sporus shouted. After a moment, she went on, speaking in a hollow, dull voice. "I cannot bear the shame. The king's son had taken his vengeance on me for no other crime than my virtue. I call on the gods to witness my suffering. Avenge my death with the fall of the house of Tarquinius—"

"No good! You've learned the lines, but you speak without conviction and your voice keeps trailing away. This is the pivotal moment of the play; this is how everyone will remember you. Don't you care? You'll have to do better than that tomorrow night. Well, then, we know what happens next. If you need courage, look up at that statue and think of Nero. What was it the last Praetorian to desert the Golden House said to Nero when he begged the man to stay? 'Is it so hard to die, then?' Ha! Good words to keep in mind these days."

Sporus clutched the mock dagger in both hands and pointed it at her breast, staring at it.

"Alright, then," said Vitellius, "enough of this. Lucretia is dead. The audience is thrilled. Her lifeless body remains on the bed during the rest of the play, while her grief-stricken husband rouses the people to revolt.

Sextus Tarquinius gets his comeuppance, and the chorus delivers the final lines. You needn't stay for this part, eunuch. You and your friends are dismissed. Go back to your quarters. And practice your lines!"

Her gown torn and her hair in disarray, Sporus managed to stumble across the stage and step down from the dais. The Praetorian who had been blocking Epictetus stepped aside and allowed him to join her. Lucius and Epaphroditus rose from their couches and made their way across the room.

As they stepped into the hallway, Asiaticus suddenly blocked their way. He seized Sporus's chin in a viselike grip and flashed a lascivious grin. "Did you enjoy that?" he said. "I know I did."

Sporus tried to draw back, but Asiaticus held her fast. "Tomorrow night, we do it for real, for everyone to see."

"Not . . . in front of an audience!" whispered Sporus

"Of course in front of the audience. That's the whole point. Exciting, isn't it? Here, feel how excited I am, just thinking about the things I'll do to you while everyone watches." Asiaticus pressed one of her hands between his legs and whispered in her ear, "Feels like a dagger, doesn't it? And when I'm done with you tomorrow night, when you reach under the bed, you'll find a real dagger waiting for you, not a toy." He thrust his tongue into Sporus's ear. She wriggled and squealed. He bit her earlobe, sinking his teeth into the flesh.

Sporus pulled free. She ran weeping down the hallway.

Lucius and his companions stood speechless. Asiaticus threw back his head and laughed.

Vitellius called to him from the banquet chamber, "Asiaticus! Leave the eunuch alone. You'll have your way with that disgusting creature soon enough. Get back in here. We need to rehearse your exit speech!"

The Praetorians who escorted them back to Epaphroditus's apartments did not depart but took up stations in the hallway outside.

Sporus resisted all attempts to comfort her. She withdrew to her bedroom and closed the door.

On a terrace overlooking Nero's meadows and the lake, Epaphroditus sat and covered his face with his hands. Epictetus muttered and paced, tugging at his beard.

"Can this really be happening?" said Lucius. "Does Vitellius really expect—"

"It's quite clear what he expects," said Epaphroditus. "Tomorrow night, before an audience, Sporus will be publicly raped—the consort of two emperors degraded like the lowest prostitute! Then she'll be given a dagger to commit suicide for the amusement of Vitellius and his friends."

"Seneca and Nero are responsible for this," said Epictetus.

"How do you arrive at that conclusion?" Epaphroditus looked up at him wearily.

"Vitellius is merely taking their work one step further. Seneca debased the whole idea of stage plays with those obscene dramas he wrote, playing up the prurient interest and the meaningless horror, making hopelessness and horror the whole point of the play. Nero took the tradition of execution as a public spectacle and raised it to what he and his depraved friends considered art—burning people alive and inducing bulls to rape young girls while the audience in the stands applauded and cheered. Now Vitellius intends to make his vile fantasies take place on a stage while his friends stuff themselves with pike livers and pheasant tongues."

"Is there no way to prevent this from happening?" Lucius said. "Perhaps Sporus can flee the city."

Epaphroditus shook his head. "The Praetorians stationed outside the door are there for a reason. If you look below this terrace, you'll see more guards. Vitellius has no intention of letting his Lucretia run off before tomorrow's banquet."

Lucius left them on the terrace and went to Sporus's room. Through the door, he heard her weeping. He called her name. She did not answer, but after a while the weeping stopped. He called her again and heard only silence. Lucius pushed against the door. It was locked, but the lock was flimsy, intended only to keep slaves from entering when they were unwanted. He pushed against the door with his shoulder. The lock gave way and he stumbled into the room.

Sporus lay on the bed, no longer in disarray but dressed in one of her finest garments, a gown of green silk with gold embroidery inherited from Poppaea. Her hair had been combed and pinned. Makeup hid the bruises on her face. Her hands lay crossed on her breast. She no longer looked distraught but seemed composed—too composed, Lucius realized. On the floor beside the bed, lying on its side, was an empty silver cup.

Sporus stared at the ceiling with glassy eyes. Her words were slurred. "Lucius, you've been such a good friend to me these last few months."

He knelt beside the bed. "Sporus, what have you done?"

"Don't pester me with questions, Lucius. There's no time. But I'm glad you came. Glad it was you, not one of the others. Because I have to tell you something. I need to confess."

"What are you talking about?"

"I was responsible . . ."

"For what?"

"It was my fault Nero died."

"No, Sporus. You don't know what you're saying."

"Listen to me, Lucius! It was my fault Nero died—and my fault your father killed himself."

Lucius drew a sharp breath.

"I was responsible for everything, for all the horrors since Nero died . . . all my fault. . . ."

Lucius picked up the empty cup. "What did you drink, Sporus? Why is it making you say such things?"

"I know what I'm saying, Lucius. It's been so hard to keep it a secret . . . all these months. . . ."

"I don't understand."

"You weren't there, Lucius . . . at the end . . . with Nero . . . and your father. You didn't see . . . or hear. You've only been told what happened by Epaphroditus, but he doesn't know the truth. Epictetus must know, but he's never told anyone . . . because he loves me. But you should know."

Sporus's voice was very weak. Lucius leaned closer, putting his ear to her lips.

"When Epictetus arrived from the city with news . . . I ran out to meet him . . . while the others stayed inside. Then I took the message to Nero, before Epictetus could do it. I told Nero a lie. I told him the Senate . . . had voted to put him to death."

"But that's what happened."

"No! The message Epictetus brought was that the Senate had failed to vote. They were still deliberating. They balked at the prospect of putting Augustus's heir to death. There was still hope . . . for Nero. Praetorians had been sent from Roma to bring him back, but only so that the senators could address him face-to-face, to try to come to some . . . resolution. They wanted to negotiate. But that was not the message I gave to Nero. I lied. I made him think there was no hope left."

"But why, Sporus?"

"Because I wanted him to die!" Sporus convulsed on the bed. Her brow was suddenly covered with beads of sweat. She gasped for breath.

"Only later, after Nero's body was brought back to Roma . . . did the Senate pass the resolution calling for his death. But that was after the fact. They did it just to please Galba, to make him think they had taken the initiative to make him emperor. Don't you see, that's why there are so many rumors . . . that Nero must still be alive. All those senators couldn't understand why Nero would kill himself, when they were ready to negotiate. They think he must still be alive, that his death was a hoax, that he'll yet return . . . and have his revenge."

Sporus gripped his arm. "But Nero *is* dead, Lucius. I saw him die with my own eyes. And I saw your father die. He wouldn't have killed himself . . . if Nero hadn't done so first. It was my fault. I didn't understand . . . that so many people would die . . . because of what I did . . . to Nero."

"But why, Sporus? Why did you want Nero to die?"

"I hated him . . . at the end. I think I loved him . . . once. I don't know. I was always so confused . . . by what he did to me . . . by what he wanted from me. Who am I, Lucius? Am I the boy your father noticed one day in the Golden House and took to meet Nero? Am I Poppaea? Or am I . . . Lucretia? Why do they all want me to be someone else?"

Sporus convulsed again and grimaced. Her eyes glittered like broken glass. "I caused Nero to die. That means I caused all the suffering that followed. I created Vitellius, don't you see? I've brought about my own destruction. Would you hold my hand, Lucius? I can't see any longer. I can't hear. I'm cold. If you hold my hand, it means you forgive me."

Lucius took Sporus's slender hand in his. Her flesh was like ice. She shuddered and went rigid. She opened her mouth wide, trying to draw a breath. A rattling sound came from her throat. The fascinum slipped from inside Lucius's toga and dangled before her. She reached for it and gripped it tightly, pulling him closer.

Her grip slackened. The fascinum slipped from her fingers. The light went out of her eyes.

Lucius stared down at her for a long moment, then looked around the room. On a dresser nearby he saw the mirror she must have used when she combed her hair and put on her makeup, a round silver mirror with an ebony handle. The mirror had belonged to Poppaea. Poppaea and Sporus had looked in the same mirror and had seen the same face reflected there.

He held the mirror to Sporus's nostrils. No trace of mist fogged the polished silver. Sporus was dead.

Epaphroditus sent a messenger to inform Vitellius of the death. Asiaticus came to confirm the news. He left in a fury. The Praetorians keeping watch on Epaphroditus's apartments withdrew.

The next day, the citywide feast in honor of Nero went on as scheduled. Even without the presentation of Vitellius's play at his banquet, his guests were impressed. For many days the Shield of Minerva was the talk of the city—until news arrived that Vitellius's troops to the north had been destroyed and Vespasian's forces were marching unopposed on Roma.

From the terrace of Epaphroditus's apartments, Lucius watched and listened to the signs of panic in the Golden House. Various residents installed by the emperor—friends, relatives, supporters, sycophants—were hastily gathering whatever precious objects they could carry and making ready to flee.

Epaphroditus joined Lucius on the terrace. "Vitellius is preparing an abdication speech. He sent a messenger to ask me to help him draft it."

"And will you?"

"I sent the messenger away without a reply."

Lucius frowned. "Abdication? No emperor has ever done such a thing. The man who becomes emperor dies as emperor."

"Nero considered abdication. I suppose that's why Vitellius wanted my advice, though my efforts to help Nero abdicate were fruitless."

Lucius nodded but made no reply. He had not told Epaphroditus, or anyone else, what Sporus had confessed to him.

They heard the sounds of a scuffle and looked over the parapet. In the courtyard below, two well-dressed women were fighting over an antique Greek vase. The vessel slipped from their hands and shattered on the paving stones. The enraged women flew at each other.

"Apparently," said Epaphroditus, "Vitellius will ask for safe conduct out of the city for himself and his wife and child, along with one million sesterces from the treasury."

"One million sesterces? So little—the cost of his precious Shield of Minerva!"

"The Flavians, Vespasian's relatives in the city, will attend the speech. If they give their approval, a bloodless transition of power may yet be accomplished."

Below them, the women tumbled on the ground. One of them grabbed a shard from the broken vase and slashed the other's cheek.

Lucius looked away, sickened by the sight of blood.

Lucius and Epaphroditus stood amid the crowd at the south end of the Forum. Before them, a vast flight of marble steps led up to the main entrance to the Golden House, with its highly ornamented facade of golden tiles and colored marble. Beyond the entrance, above the roofline, Lucius saw the head and shoulders of the towering Colossus of Nero, gleaming dully against the leaden December sky. The gigantic statue formed a backdrop that threw everything before it bizarrely out of scale. How small Vitellius looked, standing at the top of the steps to address the crowd, with that gigantic head looming behind him. The man who had seemed so large when Lucius encountered him in the octagonal dining room now appeared no bigger than an insect, a trifling creature that could easily be crushed on the palm of one's hand. Even the ranks of Praetorians flanking him looked tiny.

"Look over there." Epaphroditus pointed to a group of men in togas who had just arrived and were making their way to the front of the crowd. "See how everyone falls back to make way for them? The Flavians."

Vespasian's relatives were surrounded by a vast entourage of slaves, freedmen, and freeborn supporters. Their arrival elicited various emotions from the others in the Forum—fear, hope, resentment, curiosity.

"Look there, in the center," said Epaphroditus, "the one all the others defer to, though he's only nineteen years old—that's Vespasian's younger son, Domitian. The older son, Titus, is his father's right-hand man in Judaea, but Domitian is in charge of things here in Roma."

Lucius spotted the young man, who had the typical features of a Flavian, with his round face, prominent nose, and ruddy complexion. Domitian was notoriously vain about his luxurious head of chestnut hair, which he wore longer than was currently fashionable for young Romans. Even as Lucius watched, Domitian reached up and swept both hands through his wavy mane, combing it back, then gave a practiced toss of his head to make his tresses fall into place.

"What a preener!" Lucius laughed.

"Maybe so, but he's a young man whose time has come. The Flavians all feel it. This is their moment."

Apparently, not everyone in the crowd agreed. As Vitellius stepped forward to speak, voices rose from the crowd crying, "Stand firm, Caesar! Stand firm!"

The Flavians responded with their own shouts: "Abdicate! Step down! Leave the city now!"

Vitellius seemed to hesitate. Was he reconsidering his decision? He exchanged glances with Galeria, who stood nearby with little Germanicus beside her. He called Asiaticus to his side. While the two of them conferred, the competing shouts from the crowd grew louder and more vociferous.

"Step down!"

"Stay where you are!"

"Abdicate!"

"Hold firm, Caesar! Stay the course!"

Asiaticus stepped back. Vitellius still did not speak. He crossed his fleshy arms and peered down at the crowd.

"Numa's balls, what is he waiting for?" whispered Lucius.

The shouts grew more vehement and more threatening.

"Give way to Vespasian, you fool! Get out of the city now, while you can!"

"To Hades with the Flavians! Cut off their heads and send them to Vespasian with a catapult!"

Vitellius came to a decision. He turned to Asiaticus and said something. Asiaticus turned to the prefect of the Praetorians and pointed at the Flavians in the crowd below.

"No!" whispered Epaphroditus. "This can't be happening! What is Vitellius thinking?"

The Praetorians drew their swords and rushed down the steps. The Flavians had come prepared for a fight; almost all of them carried daggers or cudgels inside their togas. Vitellius's supporters were also armed.

Amid the screams and shouts, Lucius and Epaphroditus looked for a way to escape, but the crowd surged around them, knocking them this way and that. They were soon separated. Screams came from all around and from underfoot: men were being trampled to death by the mob. Lucius frantically searched for Epaphroditus, without success, but some distance away he caught a glimpse of Domitian. His long hair was now in disarray, hanging in tangles over his eyes and making him look like a wild man. Domitian was shouting, but amid the uproar Lucius couldn't make out his words. The Flavians rallied to shield him on all sides.

From the corner of his eye, Lucius caught sight of Epaphroditus, who had reached the steps of a nearby temple and was fleeing inside for safety.

He looked again at Domitian, who was waving a sword with one hand and pointing with the other. Lucius still couldn't hear him, but the gesture was unmistakable. Domitian was signaling a retreat. The battle was going badly for the Flavians.

An elbow struck Lucius hard in the back and he staggered forward. He turned and saw Asiaticus. The man's face was covered with blood— whether his own or someone else's, Lucius couldn't tell. He brandished a bloody sword.

"Either fight or get out of the way, Pinarius!"

Lucius managed to stagger to the edge of the crowd and looked up at the entrance of the Golden House. Vitellius was peering down, pressing his fingertips together as he assessed the progress of the battle. Galeria stood beside him, shaking her head. Germanicus was jumping up and down, clapping his hands in excitement.

Above and beyond them loomed the gigantic statue of Nero. Crowned by sunbeams, his face looked utterly serene.

❄

"Do you realize where we are?" said Epictetus.

The slave stroked his long beard and gazed at the amazing collection of precious objects that cluttered the vast room—Galeria's doing, no doubt—then limped across the black marble floor and onto the broad balcony. He shaded his eyes against the bright, milky sunlight. "This must be the place where Vitellius watched the Temple of Jupiter burn, the day he unleashed his guards on the Flavians. You can see the whole of the Capitoline Hill from here. The ruins are still smoldering."

They were high on the Palatine Hill in a part of the imperial complex Lucius had never before visited; this wing had originally been built by Tiberius and was later refurbished and incorporated into the Golden House by Nero. Between Epaphroditus's apartments and these chambers they had encountered not a single armed guard. Except for a few looters seen at a distance and some panic-stricken slaves, the only people they had encountered were a gang of street urchins who had broken into a storeroom and gorged themselves on Vitellius's private stock of wine. Lucius had been briefly alarmed when the boys brandished daggers and shouted threats, then fell in a drunken heap on the floor, giggling helplessly.

Lucius and Epaphroditus joined Epictetus on the balcony. Over on the Capitoline, the columns of the Temple of Jupiter still stood, but the roof was gone and the walls had collapsed. Smoke rose from the jumble of charred beams and fallen stones.

"The Flavians thought they'd be safe there, barricaded inside with Jupiter to protect them," said Epaphroditus. "At worst, they must have thought Vitellius would surround the temple and hold them for ransom. That would have been a logical thing for him to do, to keep Vespasian's son and the other Flavians hostage while he bargained for his own survival. I'm sure they never imagined that Vitellius would set the temple on fire. His own men balked at the order. They say Vitellius took a torch and some kindling and started the fire himself."

"So Vitellius did what Nero was accused of doing: he set fire to his own city!" said Lucius.

"Thank the gods the fire didn't spread," said Epaphroditus. "In this chaos there'd be no one to put it out. Who knows what's become of the vigiles?"

"They're probably rioting and looting like everyone else in the city," said Epictetus. He reached down to rub his bad leg. It seemed to Lucius that the slave's limp was growing worse and that he was often in pain, yet he never said a word of complaint.

Epaphroditus gazed at the ruins. "While the temple went up in flames, Vitellius came here to watch the spectacle, and enjoyed yet another banquet. The burning of the temple and the slaughter of the Flavians was just another entertainment for him. The fire went on all night, as did the screams from inside."

"I heard Domitian was killed in the fire along with the others," said Lucius.

"I heard otherwise," said Epictetus. "One of Vitellius's scribes swore to me that he saw Domitian escape from the flames disguised as a priest of Isis. The mantle of his linen robe fell back for a moment and showed his hair; that's how the slave recognized him. But before the scribe could tell Vitellius, Domitian lost himself in the crowd, so the slave kept his mouth shut. Vitellius thinks Domitian is dead."

"He almost certainly is," said Epaphroditus. "I wouldn't put much store by the scribe's story. Disguised as a priest of Isis, indeed! It's rather far-fetched."

"Not as far-fetched as an emperor of Roma setting fire to the Temple of Jupiter," said Epictetus.

To that his master had no answer.

"Vitellius must regret that decision now," said Lucius. "What's that line from Seneca? 'Such a deed, once done, can never be called back.'"

Epaphroditus nodded. "Yesterday he sent the Vestal virgins out to meet the approaching army, to plead for peace. They came back empty-handed. Then he assembled the senators, made a tearful speech, and offered the sword of the Divine Julius to them, one by one, to show his willingness to abdicate. No one would accept it."

"Not one of them had the courage to take that sword and put an end to Vitellius!" said Epictetus bitterly.

"Like the rest of us, the senators are waiting to see how the thing plays out," said Epaphroditus. "The last of Vitellius's troops have defected. He may have some supporters left, but they're hardly better than street gangs. Vespasian's men crossed the Milvian Bridge this morning. The advance guard must be in the city already."

"Today is the holiday of Saturnalia," said Lucius, "but instead of slaves and masters changing places and everyone getting stinking drunk, we have a conquering army and the lowest rabble in Roma in a competition to ransack the city. Look over there, at the shopping arcade on the far side of the Forum. You can see dead bodies in the street."

"And a woman being raped on a rooftop," whispered Epictetus.

"And over there, toward the Subura, some sort of street battle is going on. People are watching from the tenement windows. They're actually cheering, as if they were spectators at a gladiator show."

"Probably gambling on the outcome," said Epictetus.

The view from the balcony was like a scene from a nightmare. The more they watched, the more violence and bloodshed they saw. Chaos seemed to have spread everywhere. Lucius leaned over the parapet and saw with alarm that a group of armed soldiers was directly below them.

"We should leave the Golden House," he said. "Anyone found here will be subject to retribution from Vespasian's troops."

"We'll hardly be safer in the streets," said Epaphroditus.

"We'll take a cue from Domitian and disguise ourselves."

"As priests of Isis?" Epaphroditus raised an eyebrow.

"We'll put on common tunics, to make ourselves less conspicuous."

"I fled the Golden House once before in such a disguise, with Nero. That day had a bad ending."

"What choice do we have? It's madness to stay here. We'll make our way to my family's house on the Palatine. It's not far. Hilarion will have barricaded the door, but we'll find some way to get in."

Finding tunics to wear was not difficult. Finding a way to leave the Golden House proved more challenging. Vespasian's men seemed to have converged on all the Palatine entrances at once. From every hallway that led south, east, or west they heard shouts and sounds of fighting.

They turned and headed north, taking one flight of stairs after another, heading for the courtyard of the Colossus. If they left by the main entrance, they would almost certainly be seen when they descended the broad steps to the Forum, but Lucius hoped that amid such grand spaces three men in simple tunics might escape notice. He touched the fascinum at this throat, then tucked it inside his tunic to hide the gleam of gold.

They reached the courtyard. With the Colossus of Nero looming over them, they hurried along the covered portico to the grand vestibule. They rounded a corner, only to discover that soldiers had already arrived at the entrance.

The soldiers glanced at them but took little notice. They were busy trying to break down a small door just inside the main entrance.

"That leads to the doorkeeper's quarters," said Epaphroditus. "What do they want in there?"

"It's been barricaded from the inside," shouted one of the soldiers, reporting to a superior officer. "But my men will break down the door any moment."

The hinges gave way. The door was pulled outward and thrown into the vestibule. Pieces of furniture—a couch, a mattress, a chair—had been stacked against it. These were pulled out into the vestibule as well. The way was clear.

The first soldier through the doorway was met by a huge dog. The snarling Molossian mastiff leaped onto the man's chest, knocked him to the ground, and sank its fangs into his throat.

Blood was suddenly everywhere. Some of the soldiers slipped on it. The dog's victim, unable to scream with his throat torn open, made a strange hissing sound. The growling mastiff refused to release him even when one of the soldiers poked a sword at its ribs. The officer pushed the men aside, raised his fist, and struck the dog's head with the pommel of his sword, killing it with a single blow. The soldier on the ground was already dead.

The soldiers rushed into the doorkeeper's quarters. A few moments later they brought out a man dressed as an imperial slave. The man was very tall and immensely fat. His hair was filthy and he had not shaved for several days, but Lucius recognized Vitellius at once.

"Who are you? What are you doing here?" asked the officer.

Epictetus began to step forward. Epaphroditus pulled him back.

"I'm the doorkeeper," said Vitellius, trying to pull free from the soldiers who gripped his fleshy arms. The motion caused a jingling noise. The officer ripped open Vitellius's tunic. Underneath his protruding belly, an equally protruding girdle was cinched around his hips. The officer poked at it with his sword. The girdle burst open and golden coins poured out.

Some of the soldiers fell to their knees, scrambling for the coins.

The officer laughed. "Grovel for those coins if you want to, men, but I think we have something far more valuable here. This is the emperor Vitellius."

"No! That's not true!" Vitellius was drenched with sweat. He quivered from head to foot. He presented such a pathetic sight that the officer was suddenly doubtful.

Lucius stepped forward. Epaphroditus moved to stop him, but Lucius shook him off.

"This is Vitellius," he said.

"Who are you, and how would you know?" said the officer.

"I'm Lucius Pinarius, the son of Senator Titus Pinarius, but that doesn't matter. This craven mass of flesh is Aulus Vitellius and I can prove it."

"How?"

"There's something strapped to his leg."

"So there is. Men, undo those wrappings. I suppose you can tell me what we'll find, Lucius Pinarius?"

"Vitellius's most precious possession, a relic he stole from the Shrine of Mars. Something he has no right to. Something he would never willingly be parted from."

"It's a sword, sir," announced one of the men. "But not a regular sword. The blade's covered with gold!"

"The sword of the Divine Julius!" The awestruck officer took the blade from the soldier. "So you *are* Vitellius. Deny it again and I'll slice open your throat." He pressed the edge of the sword against Vitellius's neck.

Vitellius looked at the blade cross-eyed. "I have a secret," he said. "A secret I can only reveal to Vespasian! Do you understand?"

"Oh, I think we understand," said the officer. "Tie his arms behind his back. I'll put the noose around his neck myself."

The torn tunic clung to Vitellius's flesh but the girdle had fallen away, so that only the folds of fat hanging from his belly shielded his genitals from view. The men laughed at his jiggling nakedness and the way he limped as they pulled him down the steps toward the Forum. The officer, elated by his catch, paid no more attention to Lucius or his companions.

Lucius felt that he had done enough and seen enough, but Epictetus would not be denied the chance to see what happened next. Lucius and Epaphroditus followed the lame slave, who followed the soldiers pulling Vitellius down the Sacred Way.

Word spread quickly. A mob gathered to watch, cheering and shouting, "Hail, Imperator!" as if they were witnessing a grotesque parody of a triumphal procession through the Forum.

"Hold up your head!" shouted the officer. "Look at the people when they salute you!" He pressed the point of the Divine Julius's sword under Vitellius's chin, forcing him to hold his head high. Criminals were taken to be punished in the same way, with their heads forced back so that they could not hide their faces. The point of the sword repeatedly jabbed the soft flesh. Streams of blood trickled down Vitellius's throat and ran over his fleshy chest.

The mob pelted him with dung and garbage and hurled insults.

"Look how ugly you are!"

"As fat as a pig!"

"And see how he limps? One of his legs is bent."

"Arsonist!"

"Pig!"

"You're a dead man now!"

They arrived at the Capitoline Hill. Vitellius was dragged up the Gemonian Stairs to the Tullianum, the traditional place of execution for the enemies of Roma. While Vitellius blubbered and wept and begged for mercy, a fire was kindled.

"Have you no respect?" he cried out. "I was your emperor!"

In a fit of loyalty, one of Vitellius's former soldiers broke from the crowd and rushed forward with his sword drawn. He stabbed Vitellius in the belly, meaning to put a quick end to him. The soldier was attacked by the mob and thrown down the stairs.

Vitellius's wound was bound up to stop the bleeding. Men whose relatives had died in the temple conflagration were invited to heat irons and press them against Vitellius's body. At first, he thrashed and screamed each time he was burned, but eventually the strength left his body and his screams turned to blubbering squeals, then to moans. Others preferred to prick him with knives, making small cuts so as not to kill him too quickly. The torture went on for a long time.

In the crowd, Lucius saw Domitian. The son of Vespasian was alive, after all. For a long time Domitian stayed back and watched, showing no emotion. Finally, when it seemed that everyone who wished to inflict punishment on Vitellius had been allowed to do so, Domitian stepped forward.

A soldier grabbed Vitellius's hair and pulled his head back, shaking him until he opened his eyes. Vitellius gazed up at Domitian and opened his mouth, stupefied. The officer who had taken the sword of the Divine Julius handed it to Domitian, who gripped it with both hands. While soldiers held Vitellius in place, Domitian swung the sword.

Vitellius's head flew through the air and tumbled down the Gemonian Stairs. The crowd cheered.

Clutching the bloody sword, Domitian was lifted onto the crowd's shoulders. The head of Vitellius was placed on a pike and paraded through the Forum. The body of Vitellius—so burned and bloody that it was hardly recognizable as human—was dragged by a hook through the streets and thrown into the Tiber.

Lucius and his companions made their way to his house on the Palatine, where Hilarion and Lucius's mother and sisters shed tears of joy at the sight of them.

Lucius tossed and turned all through the long midwinter night, unable to sleep. At the first glimmer of dawn he put on a tunic and left the house. The dim, chilly streets were deserted. He passed the ancient Hut of

Romulus and descended the Stairs of Cacus. He stood for a while before the Great Altar of Hercules, thinking of his father and trying to make sense of all that had happened since his father had died.

He walked aimlessly for a while, then he found himself at the river-front. He followed the Tiber downstream, walking past the granaries and warehouses at the foot of the Aventine Hill. He came to the old Servian Wall and walked beside it all the way to the Appian Gate. He set out on the Appian Way, walking away from the city.

The rising sun sent slanting rays of red light across the tombs and shrines that lined the road, casting deep shadows. A short distance up the Appian Way, silhouetted by the rays of the sun, a cross had been erected near the road.

Crucifixion was the means of executing slaves. Amid the chaos of the previous day, who had bothered to carry out a crucifixion?

Lucius stepped closer. A man with a gladiator's build was nailed to the cross. Lucius saw no movement, heard no sound. It could take days for a man to die on a cross. The gods had blessed this victim with a speedy death.

Lucius looked at the man's face. Despite the uncertain light and the grimace that contorted the features, Titus recognized Asiaticus, the freed-man of Vitellius.

Asiaticus had been a member of the equestrian order, legally immune from crucifixion. Those who had killed him in such a manner deliberately meant to degrade him. Lucius glanced at Asiaticus's hand. The gold ring had been taken from his finger.

Lucius saw something in the grass nearby. He stepped closer. It was the lifeless body of a child dressed in a shabby tunic and a threadbare cloak. The head was twisted at an unnatural angle: the child's neck had been bro-ken. Lucius circled the body and looked at the face. It was Vitellius's son, Germanicus. The boy must have been fleeing the city in disguise, with Asi-aticus as his protector.

The sunlight grew stronger. The gray, shapeless world began to take on color and substance, but Lucius still felt surrounded by darkness.

Vitellius had been the most despicable man Lucius had ever met. Asi-aticus had been a vile creature, and Lucius certainly had felt no affection for Vitellius's son. Yet none of these deaths gave him pleasure. His reaction was the opposite. Witnessing the end of Vitellius had filled him with horror. Discovering the dead bodies of Asiaticus and Germanicus made him feel a dull ache of sorrow.

Why did he feel so empty, and so unsatisfied? Sporus had been his friend. Now the death of Sporus was avenged. Was that not what Lucius wanted?

And yet, Sporus herself had not been innocent in the long chain of horrors leading to this moment. If her confession was true, she had been responsible to some degree for the death of Lucius's father. And Lucius's father had not been innocent, either. As a senator and an augur, Titus Pinarius had been complicit in the acts that had led so many to clamor for the death of Nero.

The events of the previous day were as appalling as anything Lucius had ever witnessed. Yet, as far as he could see, the chain of crimes and atrocities that had led to this day had no beginning and would have no end.

He realized that he was clutching the fascinum. He held it so that it caught the sunlight. The gold glittered so brightly that it hurt Lucius's eyes to look at it.

Did the god Fascinus exist? Had he ever existed?

Lucius's glimmer of doubt was followed by a quiver of superstitious fear. The protection of Fascinus might be the only reason why Lucius was still alive, and not hanging on a cross like Asiaticus.

Lucius was alive, but toward what end? What was the point of living in such a world?

He returned to the road and walked back to the city.

A.D. 79

"Your father was a very religious man," said Epaphroditus. "Indeed, I never knew a man more pious in his respect for his ancestors, or more devout in his belief in the revelation of divine will. Of course, like his own father, Titus became an augur at a very early age, younger than you are now, I imagine. How old are you, Lucius?"

"Thirty-two." Lucius Pinarius sipped wine from his cup. Epaphroditus always served very fine wine, and the shady garden terrace of his house on the Esquiline Hill had a splendid view of the city. It was a cloudless day in the month of Augustus. The heat was relieved by an occasional breeze from the west.

Having kept his fortune intact throughout the tumult that followed the death of Nero, Epaphroditus had retired from the imperial service, happy to recede into anonymity in the relatively quiet decade of Vespasian's reign. Lucius, too, had done little these past ten years, at least in the eyes of society; he had not even married and started a family, and while he possessed numerous properties and business interests, he had no proper career. His mother lived with one of his sisters, all three of whom were married and running their own households. Living alone, Lucius avoided politics and public service and pursued simple pleasures like sitting in his friend's hillside garden, enjoying good wine and taking in the view.

"Thirty-two!" exclaimed Epaphroditus. "Where do the years go? Well, it seems you have reached an age at which you might consider following in the footsteps of your father and grandfather."

"Become an augur, you mean?"

"For a start. Nowadays the augurate is usually a reward from the emperor to men who have given long years of service to the state, but there are always exceptions, especially for those with hereditary ties to the priesthood. I know that you never established any relationship with the late Vespasian, but now that his son Titus has succeeded him, it's a new day in Roma. The men around Titus are closer to your own age. If you were to seek the emperor's favor—"

Lucius shook his head. "I used to watch my father perform auguries. I never felt drawn to the art."

This was not the first time they had discussed augury. Why did Epaphroditus keep bringing up the subject? Probably because Lucius would not speak his true thoughts aloud.

Lucius's feelings about his father were very mixed. The more Lucius learned about Nero, the more he wondered at his father's unshakable loyalty to the man. As a freedman, Epaphroditus's service had been compulsory, but what had drawn Titus Pinarius to Nero? Was it merely the opportunity for advancement and wealth? Had he not been appalled when his own brother was put to death by Nero?

Kaeso, the uncle Lucius had never known, was another source of consternation. How had a Pinarius, a relative of Augustus and the descendant of one of the city's most ancient families, become a Christian? Lucius wished he had been given the chance to talk to his uncle Kaeso, instead of being kept away from him. Had his father made a genuine effort to understand Kaeso, or to bring him back to the worship of the gods? Since both men were dead, Lucius would never know the truth of their relationship.

Lucius took pride in his family's ancient heritage but felt deeply puzzled by the preceding generation. He would never say a word against his father, especially to Epaphroditus, but the idea of following in his father's footsteps did not appeal to Lucius.

"Granted, Lucius, you may feel no particular affinity for augury, but consider the benefits. The priesthood would give you a vocation, a focus for your talents, a connection with others of your class—"

"Fortunately, I need none of those things." Lucius flashed a wry smile. "The last time I sat here in your garden, Epaphroditus, you put forth very similar arguments, only then the subject was family and marriage. You said I should finally take a wife and make some sons—to enjoy the tax exemptions, if for no other reason. But I have no worries about money; my father left me a very wealthy man. Yes, I could fritter away my time in the so-called service of the state, either as a priest or a magistrate—but why should I bother? And I could marry a fine patrician girl and produce some fine patrician sons—but again, why bother? The state is the emperor; the emperor is the state. The rest of us are like grains of sand on a beach: interchangeable, indistinguishable, inconsequential. A Roman citizen has no importance whatsoever, no matter how much some of us would like to pretend otherwise."

Epaphroditus drew a sharp breath. He looked around the garden to make sure there were no slaves to overhear. "Lucius, you must be more careful about what you say, even to me. That kind of talk is not only defeatist, but dangerously close to sedition."

Lucius shrugged. "You prove my point. If a citizen has no more freedom of speech than a slave, why serve the state?"

"How old did you say you were, Lucius? Thirty-two?" Epaphroditus shook his head. "A dangerous age for a man—old enough to feel that he should be in charge of his destiny and to chafe against the constraints of living under an absolute ruler, but perhaps not yet old enough to discern the fine line that a man must tread if he's to survive the whims of Fortune."

"By which you mean the whims of the imperial family?"

"Roma could have fallen into worse hands than those of the Flavians."

Epaphroditus expressed the prevailing consensus. Vespasian had been a competent and levelheaded ruler, his reign made smoother by a vast infusion of wealth provided by the sack of Jerusalem, which had filled the Roman treasury with gold; the enslavement of the Jewish insurgents had provided thousands of slaves to build Roma's roads and grand new monuments. Nero and his immediate successors had failed largely because they ran out of money. Vespasian had never had to worry about that.

Increasingly confident as his reign progressed, Vespasian gradually abandoned the fiction, steadfastly maintained by the dynasty of Augustus, that the emperor and Senate were equal partners, with the emperor merely the first among citizens. By the time of his death from natural causes, there was no doubt that Vespasian was absolute ruler of the state. He became so confident of his popularity that he put a stop to the practice, begun by Claudius, of searching every person admitted to the imperial presence for weapons. He also abandoned Claudius's practice of staffing the bureaucracy with imperial freedman, making state service a professional career open to citizens of merit, or at least ambition.

In the last ten years there had been a radical shift in the way people thought about the "good old days" of the long-ago Republic. Where once people sentimentalized the Republic and senators spoke wistfully of its return, it was more common now for people to refer to the era of Caesar and Pompeius as the "bad old days," when unbridled competition between ruthless warlords resulted in bloody civil war. The Year of Four Emperors that followed Nero had been a throwback to the end of the Republic, a reminder of the chaos that could reign when there was no clear successor to command the legions and run the empire. How much better it was to bow to an emperor whose legitimacy was beyond question and to enjoy the stability of a ruling dynasty.

If Vespasian had a vice, it was greed. The emperor and his favorites had shamelessly exploited their positions to accrue enormous wealth, treating the Roman state as a moneymaking scheme for insiders. Vespasian famously put a tax on the city's latrinae, claiming a share of the money made by the sale of urine to fullers, who used it to clean wool. Thus the saying, "Even when you piss, the emperor takes a percentage."

A year after Vespasian's death, people still wondered at his dying words: "Oh, damn! I think I'm becoming a god." The Senate duly voted to honor him in death as the Divine Vespasian.

His elder son, Titus, succeeded him. He had served under Vespasian in Judaea, taking part in the plunder of Jerusalem and the enslavement of the Jews. Titus had been an active partner in his father's reign—his father's henchman, some called him, since as prefect of the Praetorian Guards he ruthlessly protected his father's interests. But as emperor, Titus had so far displayed an even milder temperament than his father's. With the transition of power, the new dynasty was firmly established, making it clear that Roma was destined to be ruled by hereditary kings, even if no one called them that.

Epaphroditus returned to the subject of Lucius's future. "If you have no inclination for augury or state service, perhaps it's not too late for you to consider a military career. I don't know anyone more skillful with a bow and arrow. Last year at your Etrurian estate I saw you bring down a charging boar with a spear. Not every man can do such a thing; that took nerves as well as skill. I suspect you could handle yourself quite well on a battlefield."

Lucius shook his head. "I learned to use weapons because I own land in the countryside, and hunting amuses me. It also puts meat on my table. But why should I wish to kill my fellow mortals?"

"To defend Roma."

Lucius laughed. "No one serves in the military to defend Roma: Roma is not under attack. Men join the legions to head for the outskirts of the empire and look for fresh lands to plunder. It's all about looting, isn't it? All the successful emperors looted something and brought the booty back to Roma."

"For glory, then?"

"If one finds it glorious to kill strangers and rape their women and then brag about it. If I wanted to loot, I could become a magistrate and collect taxes. That would be far less dangerous for me, and would kill my victims much more slowly; one wants to keep them alive so they can keep paying taxes."

Epaphroditus shook his head. "Our emperor collects taxes to make the state function, for the benefit of us all. Consider the grand public projects—"

"Like that monstrosity that's ruined the view?"

Lucius referred to the massive structure that now dominated the skyline of the city from all directions, but especially as seen from Epaphroditus's garden. The architects called it an amphitheater—two semicircular theaters put together to form a complete circle. It was by far the largest and tallest building in Roma.

In the days of the first emperors, the valley between the Caelian, Esquiline, and Palatine hills had filled up with tenements. After the Great Fire, Nero razed the charred tenements and made the area into his private hunting meadow in the heart of the Golden House, complete with a large manmade lake. Determined to get rid of the Golden House bit by bit, Vespasian started by filling in the lake and clearing the meadow. On the huge, flat site that resulted, using money looted from Jerusalem to purchase materials and twelve thousand Jewish slaves captured in the war for labor, Vespasian began constructing an immense, elaborately decorated amphitheater. The Divine Augustus had first expressed the idea of building such a structure in the middle of the city for the presentation of gladiator combats, hunting exhibitions, and other spectacles; Vespasian would make Augustus's dream a reality. Construction went on throughout Vespasian's reign, but he did not live to see it finished. It was left to Titus to complete the structure.

From Epaphroditus's garden, the enormous scale of the Flavian Amphitheater was somewhat deceptive, due to its proximity to the giant statue of Nero: seeing the huge amphitheater next to the Colossus played tricks with the viewer's grasp of perspective. The towering statue was no longer enclosed by a courtyard; Vespasian had demolished the grand entrance of the Golden House but left the statue intact. For a while the Colossus had been surrounded by scaffolds, and from Epaphroditus's garden one could hear the sound of artisans wielding hammers and chisels and crowbars. When the scaffolding came down, the face of the Colossus no longer resembled that of Nero; henceforth it would simply be the sun god, Sol.

"Monstrosity?" said Epaphroditus. "I think the Flavian Amphitheater is not only an amazing feat of engineering, but also quite beautiful to look at. I'll admit I was dubious when the foundation was laid and one began to realize just how big it would be. But once it began to take shape, and the decorations and architectural details were filled in, I thought to myself: *I shall never tire of looking at that.* It's been a joy, sitting here in the garden day by day, season after season, watching the thing go up. I haven't even minded the noise, though I suppose there'll be even more noise once the thing opens in a year or so. Imagine the roar of fifty thousand spectators! It's quite impressive on the inside, as well. One of the architects is an old friend of mine and let me have a look. You feel as if you're in a gigantic bowl, with all those rows upon rows of seats rising around you. There's never been anything like it."

Lucius was not convinced. "How will so many people get in and out without waiting for hours on end? And once they're inside, how will they avoid being crushed to death?"

"The engineers have planned for that. The place has eighty entrances— vomitoria, they're called—and each has a number; people will enter and exit by the vomitorium specified on their ticket. The stairways, corridors, and landings are architectural marvels in themselves. Since it was built on the site of Nero's lake, the area was already plumbed, so there's no lack of running water. The place has over a hundred drinking fountains, and the two largest latrinae I've ever seen."

"Marvelous! Fifty thousand Romans can all take a piss at the same time."

Epaphroditus ignored him. "The arena is immense, able to accommodate whole armies of gladiators. Or navies; using the plumbing that maintained Nero's artificial lake, the arena can be flooded and drained at will. The challenge will be staging spectacles large enough to fill the space."

Lucius and Epaphroditus sat in silence for a while, watching the slaves and artisans scurry like insects inside the massive network of scaffolding that surrounded the amphitheater. More construction was going on at a vast bathing complex not far from the amphitheater, and on a huge triumphal arch that would serve as a ceremonial gateway between the amphitheater and the Forum. The gigantic stone plaques being installed on the arch could be seen even from Epaphroditus's garden; the images celebrated the victory of Vespasian and Titus over the rebellious Jews and the sack of Jerusalem. The Jewish slaves working on the arch wore ragged loincloths and glistened with sweat.

The sun had moved, and with it the patch of shade. Lucius moved his chair and Epaphroditus nodded to the serving girl, who brought more wine. The breeze had died. The day was growing quite hot.

"These antisocial ideas, Lucius—where do they come from?" Epaphroditus shook his head. "I worry that someone in our little circle of friends has been a bad influence on you. But which one? The Stoic, the poet, or the sophist?"

Lucius smiled. "You certainly can't blame Epictetus. How could a Stoic ever be a bad influence? I can't say the same about Martial or Dio. Ah, but here they all are, arriving together."

A slave showed the three newcomers into the garden. Chairs were rearranged to take advantage of the shade. More cups and more wine were brought.

Epictetus was no longer a slave. Epaphroditus had freed him some years ago, and the two had become close friends. His limp had grown more pronounced; he never went anywhere now without a crutch to lean on. In all the years he had known him, Lucius had never once heard the man complain about his infirmity. Epictetus was a living example of the Stoic philosophy he embraced, which placed great value on the dignity of the self and a graceful acquiescence to those things over which the self had no control. In the years since his manumission, he had gained a considerable reputation as a teacher. Epictetus looked the part: his long beard was flecked with the first touches of gray and he wore the customary garment of philosophers, the Greek cloak called a himation.

Dio of Prusa also wore a beard and a himation. He was a Greek sophist, a writer who popularized philosophical ideas with clever essays and discourses. At forty, he was a few years older than Epictetus.

The third visitor, about the same age as Dio, was also a writer, though of a very different sort. The Spanish-born Martial was a poet. Among the most fervent admirers of his work was the new emperor. Martial was clean-shaven and immaculately groomed, and dressed formally in a toga, as befitted a poet paying a visit to an important patron of the arts.

After they each had a cup of wine and exchanged casual conversation about the weather—could anyone recall a month of Augustus so hot?—Epaphroditus got to his feet and stood before the object that he had invited them to see. A new statue had been installed in the garden, occupying a spot at the very center, with the Flavian Amphitheater as a backdrop. The statue was covered by a large sheet of canvas.

"First," said Epaphroditus, "let me say that obtaining this statue was not easy. The new amphitheater has claimed the best available work of every sculptor from the Pillars of Hercules to Lake Maotis. Count all those niches and archways in the amphitheater facade, and imagine a statue in every available spot—that's a great many statues. But this is the one I wanted, and I got it. I won't tell you how much I paid for it, but when you see it, I think you'll agree it was worth whatever I paid, and more."

"Please, keep us in suspense no longer!" Martial laughed. "Let us see this masterpiece in marble."

Epaphroditus nodded to two slaves waiting nearby. They pulled the billowing canvas up and away from the statue.

"Extraordinary!" whispered Epictetus.

"Splendid!" said Martial.

"Do you recognize the subject?" asked Epaphroditus.

"It's Melancomas, of course," said Dio. "Was it done from life?"

"Yes. Melancomas modeled for the sculptor just a few months before he died. This is the original, not a copy. The hands that molded this marble were guided by eyes that beheld Melancomas in the flesh. The statue and the man himself occupied the same room in the same moment. The painting was also done from life, so the delicate colors of the flesh and the hair are as accurate as possible. What you see before you may be the most true-to-life image of Melancomas that exists. You can understand why I was so excited to obtain this piece."

During his brief but remarkable career, the Greek boxer Melancomas had become the most famous athlete in the world. The life-size statue depicted a naked youth with his broad shoulders thrown back, his brawny chest lifted, and one muscular leg firmly planted before the other. His shapely arms were extended before him. Wavy blond tresses framed his strikingly handsome face, which expressed serene concentration as he used one hand to wind a leather strap around the other. The statue was so realistically rendered and colored that it seemed almost to breathe. Epaphroditus had chosen to install it not on a pedestal but at ground level, so that instead of looming above them, Melancomas seemed to be standing among them. The effect was uncanny.

Melancomas had become famous for his unique fighting technique: he hardly touched his opponents, and on a few occasions won matches without landing a single blow. Using remarkable dexterity and stamina, he could duck punches and dance around his opponents until they fell from exhaustion. His bouts became legendary. Men came from great distances to see him compete. There had never been another boxer like him.

An equal claim to fame had been his extraordinary beauty. Some said that Melancomas's face was the reason why so few blows were ever landed against him: seeing such perfection, no man had the heart to spoil it. Five years ago, when Titus, then thirty-three, presided at the Augustan Games in Neapolis, he took Melancomas for a lover. When the boxer died suddenly and unexpectedly, Titus had grieved, and so had many others.

"You wrote an elegy for Melancomas, did you not, Dio?" said Epaphroditus.

The sophist needed no further encouragement to quote from his work. He rose from his chair and stood before the statue. " 'When Melancomas was naked, nobody would look at anything else; the human eye was drawn to his perfection as iron is drawn to the lodestone. When we count the vast number of his admirers, and when we consider that there have been many famous men and many beautiful men, but none was ever more famous for being beautiful, then we see that Melancomas was blessed with a beauty that we may truly call divine.' "

Dio inclined his head. The others rewarded him with applause. "I saw Melancomas myself on a few occasions," he went on. "Truly, the statue does him justice. What a dazzling throwback he was; what a splendid anachronism!"

"Why do you say that?" said Lucius.

"Because nowadays, the ideal of male beauty has become so very confused. I blame the Persians and their influence. Just as they gave the world astrology, which has found its way into every corner of our culture, so they introduced to us an ideal of male beauty very different from that handed down to us by our ancestors.

"Melancomas embodies the old ideal. As long as there are young men like him, we are reminded of that perfection which the old Greeks quite literally put on a pedestal, capturing it in stone for the world, and for their descendants, to witness and aspire to. They believed that nothing in the world was more beautiful than the physical splendor of the masculine form, which found its most sublime embodiment in the young athlete: a runner's legs and backside, arms fit to throw a discus, a lean and well-proportioned torso, a face that radiates calm intelligence and the potential for wisdom. Such a youth is a model for other youths to aspire to; he is a worthy protégé to whom older men are drawn because he offers such great hope for the future.

"The ideal offered by the Persians is quite different. They find women more beautiful than men, and as a result they think the most beautiful young men are those who look most like girls. They find beauty in pliable eunuchs and boys with slender limbs and soft bottoms. More and more you see this taste for feminine beauty embraced by the Greeks and Romans. As a result, fewer and fewer young men aspire to the old ideal; instead of hardening their muscles with exercise, they pluck their eyebrows and put on cosmetics. So a specimen like Melancomas—a youth whose splendor can be compared to the most famous of the old statues—stands out all the more. He is the exception that proves the rule: our standard of male beauty now, sadly, is the Persian standard."

"And to think, Titus actually had the fellow," said Martial, gazing at the statue over the brim of his cup and pursing his lips. "No wonder my dear patron was so heartbroken when the young man died. Frankly, I'd settle for a boy one-tenth as pretty as Melancomas—if the boy would simply show up!"

"Have you been stood up again, Martial?" Lucius smiled. This was the poet's perennial complaint.

"Yes, again! And this boy was so promising. Lygdus, his name was. He picked the place, he picked the time . . . and never appeared. I was abandoned, but not seduced—left to consort with my left hand yet again."

The others laughed. No matter how abstruse or rarefied the arguments put forward by the philosophers, Martial could always be counted on to bring the conversation back down to earth.

"But can a boy be *too* beautiful?" asked Dio. "Can beauty pose a danger to its possessor, especially the Persian style of beauty?"

"What sort of danger?" said Martial.

"I'm thinking of writing a discourse on the question, using as my subject the eunuch whom Nero married. Sporus, he was called. His story fascinates me. You knew Sporus, didn't you, Epaphroditus?"

"Yes," said Epaphroditus quietly. "So did Lucius. Epictetus also knew her." The three of them exchanged thoughtful glances.

"Good. Perhaps the three of you can give me further details to advance my argument. Everybody knows Nero castrated the youth and took him for a wife precisely because of the boy's resemblance to the beautiful Poppaea. Nero dressed Sporus in Poppaea's clothing, made hairdressers style his hair in the fashion of the day, and surrounded the boy with female attendants, just as if he were a woman. Otho was drawn to Sporus for the same reason, his resemblance to Poppaea. And then came Vitellius, who drove the poor eunuch to suicide out of a desire to exploit the boy's beauty for his own depraved amusement. What a strange and finally tragic path the boy's life took, all because of his resemblance to a beautiful woman. Had the boy been plain, or had he been beautiful in the manner of Melancomas, one imagines his life would have been very different."

Lucius looked at Epictetus to see his reaction. The Stoic's face was turned away from the others, as if something at the far corner of the garden had drawn his interest. When Epictetus turned back, his face showed no emotion.

Martial laughed. "Sporus was pretty but had an ugly end. Vitellius was ugly, and had an uglier end! Perhaps you should write a discourse comparing those two, Dio."

Dio shook his head. "As a rule, I avoid discussing the lives of our emperors, even those who came to a bad end. My object is to deliver morals, not debate politics."

"But haven't you heard?" said Martial. "Our enlightened new emperor has declared free speech for all. No subject or person is off-limits, not even Titus himself. Allow me to quote my patron: 'It is impossible for me to be insulted or abused in any way, since I do nothing that deserves censure, and falsehoods are beneath my notice. As for emperors dead and gone, they can avenge themselves if anyone should slander them, if in fact they are demigods and possess divine power.' "

"Did you write that speech for him?" asked Lucius.

"I most certainly did not," said Martial. "Titus is quite capable of writing his own speeches. And what he says, he means. There'll be no more payments to those who turn in others for seditious talk, as happened under his father. We all know Vespasian had an army of paid informers, and there are whole rooms in the imperial library filled with dossiers about perfectly innocuous citizens. I suspect there's a file on every one of us here. But Titus has pledged to burn those documents, and to put the informers out of work. He'll even punish the most notorious of them, who maliciously spread lies about innocent men."

Lucius sighed. "The subject shifts to politics—at last!"

"I thought politics bored you," said Martial.

"Yes, but only one thing bores me more: talk about pretty boys." The others laughed. "No, hear me out," said Lucius. "Every one of us here is a bachelor, true, but we are not all boy-lovers. I think I must suffer from the emperor Claudius's complaint. My father, who knew him quite well, told me for a fact that cousin Claudius was aroused only by girls or women; he had no interest in boys or men. The beauty of Melancomas would have been lost on him. A discussion of male beauty, no matter how grandiose, would have bored him to tears."

Martial laughed "As it b-b-bores you, Lucius? I think your cousin Claudius simply never met the right b-b-boy!"

"Our reigning emperor certainly doesn't suffer from Claudius's complaint," observed Dio. "Titus buried his first wife, divorced the second, and, despite his reputed dalliance with the beautiful queen of the Jews—and with brawny Melancomas here—he seems to like eunuchs best of all. Is it true, Martial, that Titus keeps a whole stable of pretty eunuchs in the palace?"

"It's true. Each is prettier than the last."

"A fact which provides yet more evidence for my thesis regarding the triumph of Persian standards," said Dio. "You'd think the emperor would seek another Melancomas. Instead, he surrounds himself with castrated boys."

Lucius laughed and threw up his hands. "Do you see what's happened?

The conversation veered briefly to politics, then circled directly back to sex."

"The subject is eunuchs, who have no sex," said Martial.

"Enough!" declared their host. "To please Lucius Pinarius, we will talk about something else. Surely there must be some other topic worthy of discussion, in a world so enormous."

"We could talk about the world itself," suggested Lucius. "Did you know that the general Agricola has discovered that Britannia is an island? It's true. The land mass to the uttermost north doesn't go on forever, as people thought. It ends in a stormy, frigid sea."

Dio laughed. "That information might be of some interest, if anyone had a reason to go to Britannia. I'd much prefer to travel south. Epictetus, you've hardly said a word. Didn't you just come back from Campania?"

"Yes. I took a brief trip down to Herculaneum and Pompeii, and then across the bay to Baiae. I may have found a rather lucrative position in the home of a very wealthy garum maker. His villa is built right next to the manufactory, which stinks of fermenting fish, but the house has a spectacular view of the bay, and the brat I'll be teaching is not a complete barbarian."

"But how could you bear to leave the city?" asked Martial.

"Granted, Campania isn't Roma," said Epictetus, "but anyone who's anyone in Roma has a second home on the bay, so interesting people are always coming and going. The social scene is the same as in Roma, but along with dinner parties they have boating excursions and banquets on the beach. Some people live there year-round, like your friend Pliny."

"You dropped in on him, as I suggested?" said Martial. "Good old Pliny, a bit of a bore but always good for a drop of wine and a bed for the night."

"I didn't find him boring at all. In fact, he told me about some rather odd things going on down there."

"What sorts of things?" said Lucius.

"Strange phenomena," said Epictetus.

"Oh, Pliny loves that sort of thing," said Martial. "Collects every odd fact in the world and puts them in a book."

"He's rather worried about the earthquakes they've been having."

"You'll have to get used to earthquakes if you move to Campania," noted Epaphroditus. "There were a couple of big ones back in Nero's reign. You must remember, Epictetus, you were there with me when Nero performed for the very first time in public, in Neapolis. An earthquake struck the theater in the middle of his song—the ground surged like a stormy sea—but Nero just kept singing. No one dared to get up! Afterward, he told me that he considered the earthquake a *good* omen, because the gods were applauding him by shaking the ground. The moment he was finished, everyone got up and ran for the exits. And no sooner was the place emptied than the whole building collapsed! And what did Nero do? He composed a new song, an ode of thanks to the gods, since they saw fit to stave off the catastrophe until after he finished his performance, and not a single person was injured. Ah, Nero!" Epaphroditus wiped a nostalgic tear from his eye.

Epictetus responded to the story with a brittle smile. Now that he was a freedman, he no longer needed to pretend to share his former master's fond memories of Nero, but he was discreet enough to keep his opinions about the late emperor to himself. "Yes, earthquakes are common in Campania," he said, "but lately they've been having two or three tremors every day. It was nerve-rattling, let me tell you. And earlier this month, a great many springs and wells in the vicinity ran dry, sources of water that have always been reliable in the past. Pliny says that something must be happening deep in the earth. It has people worried. They say . . ." He lowered his voice. "They say that gigantic beings have been seen, walking through the cities by night. They skulk in the forests. They even fly through the air."

"Giants?" said Lucius.

"Titans, one presumes. The gods of Olympus defeated them aeons ago and imprisoned them in Tartarus, the deepest caverns of the underworld. The people in Campania are afraid the Titans have broken free and made their way to the surface. That would explain the tremors and the divergence of the subterranean water channels. These Titans are always seen coming from the direction of Mount Vesuvius."

"Aren't there caves at the summit of Vesuvius?" said Lucius. "I know there's a circular valley with steep sides at the top. The rebel slave Spartacus camped there with his army of gladiators."

Epaphroditus cocked his head. "You've been reading Titus Livius."

Lucius nodded. "I take down the scrolls I inherited from my father and dip into his history every so often."

Epictetus continued. "To the locals, Vesuvius is best known for the vineyards and gardens on the slopes. The soil is amazingly fertile. But yes, Spartacus did hide his army there, in the early days of the great slave revolt. It's a substantial mountain, visible for miles around and far out to sea, but not too difficult to scale because the slope is so gradual. At the top there's a kind of hollowed-out depression, a desolate, rocky, flat place surrounded by steep, craggy walls—a perfect place for Spartacus to make his camp, since it's hidden from sight and the walls form a kind of natural parapet all around. It occurs to me that the summit of Vesuvius is not unlike the new amphitheater over there, if you imagine the amphitheater set atop a great mountain with the slopes coming up to its rim—though of course the crater atop Vesuvius is much larger. Among the rocks there are fissures that appear to have been singed by flame, as if they once spat fire. You see that sort of phenomenon still active in places all around Campania, but on Vesuvius the fuel long ago gave out and the fissures closed up."

"Unless they've opened up again because these Titans are breaking out," said Martial.

Epaphroditus shook his head. "I wouldn't put too much store in these supposed sightings of Titans. It's my opinion, and I suspect Pliny would agree, that the Titans have long been extinct. Certainly, they once existed: occasionally, excavating deep holes for foundations or canals, people find bones so enormous they can only have belonged to the Titans. But the fact that one finds only bones would indicate that such beings must be extinct."

"I should think that makes their appearance now all the more disturbing," said Lucius. "Epictetus just told us that people have reported seeing these giant creatures—in the cities, in the woods, even in the sky. All these rumblings in the earth may be the portents of some terrible event."

Epaphroditus gave him a quizzical look. Lucius knew what he was thinking. Despite his disavowal of any interest in augury, Lucius had just expressed a belief in divination. Without realizing it, he had slipped a hand inside his toga and was touching the fascinum of his ancestors. He often wore the talisman, though never outside his clothes, where it could be seen.

There was a sudden gust of wind. It was not the mild westerly breeze that had provided some relief from the heat earlier in the day but a stronger, warmer wind from the south. The light changed as well. Though there was not a cloud in the sky, the sun abruptly grew dim, then dimmer still. The sky grew dark. The five friends stopped talking and exchanged uncertain glances.

An eerie silence descended. The laborers at the amphitheater stopped working. The whole city was suddenly quiet.

Epaphroditus began to cough. So did Lucius. He moved to cover his mouth and found himself looking at the back of his hands. They appeared to be covered with a fine white powder, like marble dust. He looked up and blinked; the same white powder clotted his eyelashes. He puckered and spat, tasting ashes in his mouth. Pale dust fell from the sky, not in drifts but evenly and steadily, everywhere at once, like snow falling in the mountains.

Without a word, all of them rose from their chairs and made their way to the shelter of the portico that bordered the garden on three sides. As they watched, the dust continued to descend. The light of the sun was reduced to a faint glow. The fall of dust was so thick that they could no longer see the amphitheater.

"What is it?" whispered Lucius.

"I have no idea," said Epaphroditus. "I've never seen anything like it."

"It's like something from a nightmare," said Dio.

From somewhere beyond the garden walls, a voice cried out, "It's the end of the world!"

The shrill cry of panic ignited others. From the neighbors all around they heard shouts of alarm. The cries sounded strangely muted and faraway.

The fall of ash grew so heavy that they could see nothing at all beyond the garden. It was as if the world around them had utterly vanished. At the center of the garden, dust piled high atop the wavy hair of the statue of Melancomas, frosting his ears and covering his muscular shoulders and arms with a thick mantle of white.

A.D. 80

"What a year, what a terrible, terrible year!" said Epaphroditus. "First, the fiery eruption of Vesuvius and the complete loss of Pompeii and Herculaneum—whole cities buried as if they never existed."

A year to the day after the fall of ash on Roma, Epaphroditus was again playing host to Lucius and the others in his garden.

"And then, the outbreak of plague here in Roma—the plague that claimed your mother, Lucius. Chrysanthe was such a lovely woman. She died before her time."

Lucius nodded, acknowledging his friend's words of condolence. His mother's death had been quick, but not painless. Chrysanthe had suffered a great deal, racked by fever and coughing up blood. Lucius had been with her at the end, along with his three sisters. He was not close to his siblings. It was the first time in years that they had all been together.

"That plague," Epaphroditus continued, "was caused, so everyone assumes, by that bizarre dust that fell on us after Vesuvius erupted. There must have been something toxic in that dust. Remember, for a couple of days, until word of the disaster at Pompeii arrived, we had no idea what the dust was or where it came from. People thought the firmament itself was crumbling, signaling the end of the universe. Who could imagine that a volcano could throw up so much debris? They say the ash from Vesuvius fell as far away as Africa, Egypt, and even Syria.

"Then, yet another disaster. While the emperor was down in Campania, comforting the survivors, that terrible fire broke out in Roma—three days and nights of conflagration that seemed to strike precisely those areas that were *not* burned during the Great Fire under Nero. The devastation extended from the Temple of Jupiter on the Capitoline—just repaired after the arson of Vitellius!—all the way to the Theater of Pompeius on the Field of Mars and Agrippa's lovely temple called the Pantheon, which was totally gutted."

Lucius Pinarius nodded somberly. "Cities lost, plague and fire in Roma—truly, it's been a terrible year. And yet here are the five of us, all alive and well."

"The six of us, if you count Melancomas." Dio cast an appreciative glance at the statue.

"Melancomas will be here long after the rest of us are gone," said Epaphroditus.

"Terrible disasters," agreed Martial, "but no one can fault the emperor. Titus made quick restitution to the citizens in Campania and began rebuilding the remaining cities around the bay, then turned to restoring the burned areas of Roma—and without raising taxes, mind you, or making special appeals to the wealthy. He did it all himself, even stripping his own properties of ornaments to redecorate the temples and public buildings, like a true father of the Roman state. To combat the plague, Titus did all that any man could, seeking counsel from the priests and offering the appropriate sacrifices to the gods."

"The emperor's leadership in these times of crisis cannot be faulted," said Epaphroditus. "Still, people are badly shaken and fearful of the future."

"Which is why the opening of the amphitheater could not have come at a more propitious time," said Martial.

They turned their gaze to the massive structure across the way. The last of the scaffolds had been removed. The curved travertine walls gleamed in the morning sunlight; the niches formed by the multiple arches were filled with brightly painted statues of gods and heroes. Colorful pennants streamed from poles affixed to the rim. The open space between the amphitheater and the new baths was thronged with people on holiday. This was the opening day of Vespasian's great dream, the Flavian Amphitheater.

"Are we ready to set out?" said Lucius.

"I think so," said Epaphroditus. "Should I bring along a slave?"

"Of course," said Martial. "We'll be there all day. The slave can fetch food for us. Alas, if only he could go to the latrina for us as well! But there are still some tasks that cannot be delegated to a slave."

"Where will we put him?" said Epaphroditus.

"I imagine it's like the theater," said Martial. "There's bound to be a section at the back of the tier for everyone's slaves."

"You have the tokens?" said Epaphroditus.

Martial held up three tiny clay tablets upon which were stamped numerals and letters. "For yours truly—the poet charged with witnessing the inaugural games and composing an official tribute in verse—three excellent seats in the lowest tier. We're right next to the imperial box, just behind the Vestal virgins. Take good care of your ticket. You'll want it for a souvenir."

"Only three?" said Lucius.

"I'm not going," said Epictetus.

"Nor am I," said Dio.

"But why not?"

"Lucius, I haven't attended a gladiator show since I became a freedman," said Epictetus. "I certainly don't intend to see this one simply because it promises to be bigger and bloodier than any that's come before."

"And you, Dio?"

"Perhaps you've never noticed, Lucius, but philosophers are seldom seen at gladiator shows, unless they wish to stand up and address the crowd about the evils of such spectacles. I don't think even our free-speech-loving emperor would welcome such an interruption on this occasion."

"But the gladiators won't even appear until later in the day," said Martial. "Before that there'll be a whole program of spectacles—"

"I am well aware of the typical entertainment offered at such events," said Dio. "There will be the public punishment of criminals by various ingenious means, intended, ostensibly, for the edification of the crowd. But take a look at the faces in the stands; are the spectators uplifted by the moral lesson, or titillated by the humiliation and destruction of another mortal? And there will undoubtedly be animal exhibitions; these, too, are educational, or so we are told, since they give us a chance to see exotic creatures from faraway places. But the animals are never simply paraded for our perusal; they're made to fight one another, or hunted down by armed men and killed. Yes, yes, Lucius, I know: you're a hunter yourself, so you appreciate an exhibition of fine marksmanship. But again, is it the hunter's skills the spectators applaud, or the sight of an animal being wounded and slaughtered? And all that bloodshed is merely prelude to the gladiator matches, where human beings are forced to fight for their lives for the amusement of strangers. Since at least the time of Cicero there have been those of us who object to the spectacles of the arena, which debase rather than elevate the audience. The fact that such games have now been given a grander venue than ever before may be cause for the poet to celebrate, but not the philosopher."

"But don't you want to see the building?" said Lucius.

"You yourself have called it a monstrosity."

"I'm not in love with it, as Epaphroditus is. The thing is too big and too garish for my taste. Still, there's never been a place like it, and this is the opening day. All of Roma will be there."

"All the more reason for a philosopher to stay away," said Dio. "It's one thing when a city holds its gladiator shows at some rustic spot outside the gates, in a natural setting where there's no pretense about what's taking place—men sitting in the dirt, watching other men kill each other. But to take these blood sports and display them in a palatial setting, surrounded by beautiful statues and fine architecture, as if killing were simply another artistic endeavor to be appreciated and enjoyed by sophisticated people— that in itself is offensive. No man who considers himself a philosopher can lend his presence to such an event. Epictetus and I will find something better to do. You're welcome to join us, Lucius."

"Ha!" Martial waved back the philosophers and put his arm about Lucius's shoulder. "You won't lure Pinarius away from the most exciting event of the year to go sit on a hilltop and listen to you grumble about your bunions and how they must have been sent by the gods to test your endur- ance!" He pressed one of the tokens into Lucius's hand. "Now take that, my friend, and hold on to it tightly, and don't let any philosopher talk you out of using it. Come along, then, everyone who's coming."

They parted ways in the street outside the house. Lucius watched the philosophers walk up the hill. Epictetus used his crutch. Dio took small steps and walked slowly to match the younger man's pace. Lucius felt an urge to join them, but Martial grabbed his toga and pulled him in the op- posite direction.

The open space around the Flavian Amphitheater was thronged with people. A small crowd had gathered to watch a mime troupe perform a parody about a brawny gladiator and a senator's wife who lusted after him behind her husband's back. Street vendors moved through the crowd, of- fering good-luck charms, freshly cooked bits of meat and fish on skewers, little clay lamps with images of gladiators, and tickets for excellent seats so crudely stamped that they had to be counterfeit.

Long lines began to form at the entrances, radiating outward from the amphitheater, but there was no waiting at the gate to which Martial led them. The finely dressed men and women going in were clearly of a higher class than the citizens in ragged tunics queuing up at the other gates.

Once through the entrance, they found themselves in a finely appointed vestibule with a marble floor and elegant furniture. The railings had ivory fittings and the walls were exquisitely painted with pictures of gods and heroes.

"It reminds me of the Golden House," said Epaphroditus. "See that mosaic of Diana in front of the steps? I'm almost certain that was lifted stone by stone from the anteroom to Nero's bedchamber."

"It makes sense that the Flavians would have stripped the Golden House to decorate their amphitheater," said Lucius. "But surely the entire structure isn't decorated this elaborately."

"Of course not," said Martial. "This is the section for important people—magistrates, visiting dignitaries, Vestal virgins, and friends of the emperor, such as yours truly. Only the best for my companions! And look, just as I promised, there's a splendid buffet laid out for us right here in the vestibule, and free wine. What a privileged existence is the life of the poet!"

They mingled in the vestibule for a while, eating and drinking, until a horn sounded and a crier came through the room, calling for all to find their seats. The men in togas and the women in elegant stolas began to drift to a marble stairway that led up to bright daylight. Lucius and his friends followed the crowd.

Epaphroditus had described the scale of the amphitheater and the way it was laid out; Epictetus had compared it to the circular valley, now vanished, at the summit of Vesuvius. But no amount of mere description could have prepared Lucius for what he beheld from the top of the steps. For a moment his mind could not take it in; as the sound of fifty thousand people created a single dull roar, so the sight of so many people in one place registered as a kind of blur, an undifferentiated mass of humanity in which no individuals could be perceived. But, little by little, as he stood on the landing, he began to regain his bearings, and his mind began to perceive what was near and what was far.

Lucius had never experienced anything like that first moment inside the Flavian Amphitheater. That instant alone, so disorienting that it was almost frightening, yet so unique and thrilling, was worth the excursion. Dio and Epictetus were fools, he thought, to deprive themselves of such an experience, which was surely to be had in no other place on earth.

He realized that he was standing not in full sunlight but in brightly filtered shade, and looked up to see awnings like sails that extended from the uppermost parapet all around the building. As he peered upward, squinting, he saw that men were working the complicated rigging, adjusting the angle of the awnings to block the sunlight.

Martial pulled at his toga. "Stop gawking like a bumpkin. You're hold-ing up the crowd. Come along."

They found their seats. The great bowl of the amphitheater encircled them. Below, jugglers, tumblers, and acrobats of both sexes, wearing scanty but brightly colored costumes, were already in the arena. Some were so close that Lucius could see their faces. Others were small in the distance. The scale of the place confounded him. Somewhere nearby, a water organ was playing a lively tune.

"Have we missed the beginning of the show?"

"Oh, this isn't the show," said Martial. "This is just a trifle to keep the crowd amused while they file into their seats. Numa's balls, look how high they've strung that tightrope! Can you imagine walking across that thing with another fellow on your shoulders? It always gives me the shivers when they perform without a net."

"Why are the seats in front of us empty?"

"Because the Vestals haven't yet arrived. They're often the last to show up at any public event, even after the emperor. Ah, but here he comes now."

Titus and his retinue began to file into the imperial box. The em-peror was forty but looked younger, thanks to his genial expression and a full head of hair not yet touched by gray. He had married early and been widowed, then remarried and almost as quickly divorced his second wife, whose family was too closely associated with the Pisonian conspiracy against Nero. He had not remarried since. For female consorts he was flanked on one side by his grown daughter, Julia, and on the other by his younger sister, Flavia Domitilla. Several of his favorite eunuchs also attended him, beauti-ful and exquisitely dressed creatures who at a glance seemed neither female nor male; they exemplified what Dio called the Persian ideal of beauty.

The last members of the imperial family to enter the box were the em-peror's younger brother, Domitian, with his wife and their seven-year-old son. At twenty-eight, Domitian looked almost as old as Titus, thanks to his dour expression and the fact that he had lost much of his hair; gone was the glorious chestnut mane that had made him so conspicuous amid the Flavian entourage during the last days of Vitellius. While Titus smiled and waved enthusiastically to the crowd, Domitian hung back, looking glum. The brothers were known to have a stormy relationship. After Ves-pasian died, Domitian had publicly complained that their father's will specified that the brothers should rule jointly, but that the document had been deliberately altered; the implication was that Titus himself had tampered with it. Some people believed Domitian, but most did not. For one thing, Vespasian had always favored his elder son; for another, he had expressed the opinion that one of the reasons why Caligula and Nero had come to a bad end was the fact that they rose to power at too young an age. Domitian was twelve years younger than Titus and clearly lacked his brother's experience.

No one was quite sure of the proper etiquette in the new amphitheater. As the emperor continued to wave, many in the crowd rose to their feet and waved back. Some cheered and applauded. Others remained seated. Epaphroditus was among those who stood and clapped his hands. "Now there you see the head of an emperor," he said to his companions. They looked at him quizzically. "Have I never told you the story of Agrippina and the physiognomist?"

"I think I should have remembered that," said Martial. "It sounds quite naughty."

"It's not that kind of story. Long ago, when Nero was a boy and his mother was desperate to make him Claudius's heir, Agrippina called on an Egyptian physiognomist to examine the head of Claudius's son, Britannicus. Do you know, Lucius, I think it was your father who suggested the examination."

Lucius shrugged. "I've never heard the story."

"Perhaps because it had a rather embarrassing outcome. The Egyptian was unable to draw any conclusions from Britannicus's head, but since Britannicus's constant companion happened to be present, the man took a look at his head, as well. That boy was none other than Vespasian's son Titus. The physiognomist declared he had never seen a head more fit to rule over other men. People forgot about that incident for a long time, but as you can see, the Egyptian turned out to be right."

"Where was Domitian when this examination took place?" said Lucius.

"Oh, he was a baby. He'd only just been born."

"What could be easier to read than a baby's head, since it has no hair?" said Martial. "Although Domitian probably had more hair then than he does now!"

There was a stirring in the crowd around them. The Vestal virgins had arrived and were taking their seats in the front row. No one had been sure whether to stand for the emperor, but everyone did so for the Vestals. They walked with such grace and poise that their linen mantles seemed to float atop their heads.

As the six women passed by, Lucius looked at their faces. He had seen the Vestals at public events but had never been this close to them before. The badge of their office was the vitta, a red-and-white band worn across their foreheads. Their closely shorn hair was hidden by a distinctive headdress called a suffibulum, and their linen gowns obscured the shapes of their bodies, so that all one could really see of them were their unadorned faces. They were of various ages, some old and wrinkled but some no more than girls. Vestals began their mandatory thirty years of service between the ages of six and ten, and most remained Vestals until they died. It seemed to Lucius they kept their eyes straight ahead and deliberately avoided making eye contact—until one of them turned her head as she passed and looked straight at him.

The Vestal was beautiful. The fact that every feature except her face was hidden only accentuated her beauty. Two green eyes flashed beneath delicate eyebrows of dark blond. Her full lips favored him with a faint smile. Lucius felt a quiver run down his spine, like a trickle of warm water.

"Her name is Cornelia Cossa," whispered Epaphroditus in his ear.

"How old is she?"

"Let me think. She was only six when she was inducted into the sisterhood in the eighth year of Nero's reign; that would make her twenty-four."

"She's beautiful."

"Everyone says so."

The acrobats and jugglers dispersed. The official ceremonies commenced with a series of religious rites. An augury was taken, and the auspices were declared highly favorable. The priests of Mars paraded around the arena, chanting and burning incense. An altar was erected in the center of the arena. The priests sacrificed a sheep to the war god and dedicated the amphitheater in his honor. The blood of the sacrificed animal was sprinkled in all directions onto the sand of the arena.

A proclamation by the emperor was read aloud, in which he paid homage to his father, whose military success, architectural genius, and love of the city had given birth to the amphitheater; the structure in which they had all gathered was the Divine Vespasian's posthumous gift to the people of Roma. Jewish warriors—filthy, naked, and shackled with chains—were driven at sword point around the arena by armed legionaries as a reminder of the great victory that had brought peace to the eastern provinces of the empire and secured the treasure that had paid for the amphitheater, the new baths, and many other improvements all over the city. Vespasian had joined the gods, but his legacy in stone, the Flavian Amphitheater, would endure for all time.

The proclamation went on for some time. Lucius's mind began to wander. He noticed that Martial had pulled out a stylus and a wax tablet and was busy scribbling. He assumed that his friend was taking down the words of the proclamation, but the notes he was able to read had nothing to do with what they were hearing. Martial saw him scanning his notes.

"Random impressions," he whispered. "You never know what might become a poem. Look at all these people. How many races and nationalities do you think are represented here today?"

Lucius looked around them. "I have no idea."

"Nor do I, but it seems to me the whole world is here, in microcosm. Look at those black-skinned Ethiopians over there. And that group over there—what sort of people have blond hair and wear it twisted into knots like that?"

"Sicambri, I think they're called. A Germanic tribe that lives at the mouth of the Rhine River."

"And before we took our seats, in the vestibule I saw men in Arabian headdresses, and Sabaeans from the Red Sea, who wear black from head to foot. And I smelled Cilicians."

"Smelled them?"

"The women and boys and even the grown men of Cilicia wear a very distinctive perfume, made from a flower that grows only on the highest peaks of the Taurus Mountains. You'd know that, Pinarius, if you'd ever had a Cilician boy—"

He was interrupted by a shushing noise. One of the Vestals had turned around in her seat and was glaring at them. She was old and wrinkled, with a severe expression that intimidated even Martial. The Vestal sitting next to her also turned and looked up at them. It was Cornelia Cossa. Her calm smile and radiant beauty was in such contrast to her fellow priestess that Lucius laughed out loud, then regretted doing so at once, fearing he had offended her. But if anything, Cornelia's smile widened a bit, and there was a twinkle in her eye as she returned her attention to the crier who was reading the proclamation.

"Did you see that?" whispered Martial. "She looked right at you."

Lucius shrugged. "What of it?"

"She looked at you the way a woman looks at a man."

"Martial, you are incorrigible! Go back to sniffing your Cilician boys."

At last the various proclamations and invocations were finished. The Flavian Amphitheater was officially opened. The spectacles began.

The first event was the scourging of the informers. Titus had promised to round up the worst offenders—liars and scoundrels who made a living off the public purse by accusing innocent men of conspiring against the emperor or defrauding the state. Such creatures had been a blight on every reign since that of Augustus. No matter how sensible and confident an emperor might be at the beginning of his reign, with each year that passed, he and his ministers invariably grew more susceptible to baseless rumors and more fearful of imaginary enemies. The hardheaded Vespasian had been no more immune to poisonous slander than had his predecessors. By the end of his reign, many a man had suffered punishment based on groundless suspicion and many an unscrupulous informer had grown rich. Titus intended to make a clean break with the past.

The crowd murmured in anticipation as a large number of men were driven at spear point into the arena. Most wore togas and looked like respectable businessmen and property owners. They were stripped first of their togas, then of their tunics, so that they wore nothing but loincloths, like slaves, though one seldom saw slaves as fat as most of these men. In groups of ten, the men were secured by the neck with two-pronged pitchforks and forced to stand in place while they were beaten with whips and rods. The beatings were severe: bits of flesh and showers of blood were scattered across the sand. Even when the men collapsed to their knees, they were forced by the pitchforks to hold their heads up.

"Do you see who's delivering the punishment?" said Martial. "Titus chose a corps of officers made up entirely of nomadic Gaetulians from North Africa."

"Why the Gaetulians?" said Lucius.

"For one thing, they're outsiders with no connection to the victims or to anyone else in the city. More importantly, they're famous for their cruelty."

It certainly seemed to Lucius that the Gaetulians enjoyed their work. So did the audience. Many of the victims, more used to handing out such treatment to slaves than to receiving it, reacted with a great deal of screaming and blubbering. The more undignified the victim's behavior, the more boisterous was the crowd's reaction. Rather than tiring as the punishments proceeded, the Gaetulians were urged on by the cheering of the spectators and grew increasingly violent. The later victims were more severely beaten than the first ones; to even the punishment, and to the delight of the crowd, the first victims were scourged again.

Many of the informers lost consciousness or could not stand after being scourged and had to be dragged from the arena. A few of them died from the punishment. ("Not from scourging, but from shame!" whispered Martial, taking notes.) Those who survived would be sent into exile to live out their days on remote islands or, in the worst cases, would be sold into slavery at public auction.

More punishments followed. The victims were all condemned criminals, guilty of a capital offense—murder, arson, or theft of sacred treasure from a temple.

The organizers of the games outdid themselves in the creation of special tableaux for the various ordeals, staging several of them at once around the vast arena so that there was always something dramatic or suspenseful to engage the spectators. The punishments were based on myths and legends, with the victims playing parts, like actors. The fact that each victim's suffering and death were not imaginary but real made their performances all the more riveting to watch.

In one of the tableaux, the naked victim was chained to an elaborate stage set made to appear as a craggy cliff. A crier proclaimed that the victim was a murderer who had killed his own father. The audience booed and hurled curses at him. He was a muscular man of middle age with a bristling beard, a suitable candidate to play Prometheus, the Titan who gave fire to mankind in defiance of Jupiter. To remind the audience of the story, dancers dressed in animal skins circled the shackled Titan, waved torches, and chanted a primitive song of thanksgiving. The song was suddenly drowned out by a stage device hidden inside the rock face, which loudly reproduced the sound of thunder. At this sign of Jupiter's wrath, the worshippers of Prometheus dispersed in panic. As soon as they were out of the way, two bears were unleashed. The animals headed straight for the bound Prometheus, who began to scream and struggle frantically against his chains.

"Bears?" Epaphroditus wrinkled his nose. "Everyone knows Prometheus was tormented by vultures. Every day they tore out his entrails, and every night he was miraculously healed, so that the ordeal was endlessly repeated."

Martial laughed. "The trainer who can induce vultures to attack on command will be able to name any price! I suspect we'll see a lot of bears today. The emperor's beast trainer tells me that bears are by far the best choice when it comes to attacking human victims. Hounds are too common, elephants too squeamish, lions and tigers too unpredictable. Bears, on the other hand, are not only terrifying but extremely reliable. These come from Caledonia, the northernmost part of the island of Britannia."

The bears who converged on the helpless Prometheus lived up to their trainer's expectations. They concentrated their furious attack on the man's midsection, ripping out his entrails just as the vultures were said to have done in the ancient story. Martial voiced the opinion that the bears had been trained especially to attack that part of the man's body; Epaphroditus suspected that honey had been smeared on the man's belly. The victim's screams were bloodcurdling.

At length the bears' trainer appeared and shooed them away. The stage set was wheeled about in a circle so that the gory sight of the disemboweled Prometheus could be seen by everyone in the stands. Then the dancers reappeared, pirouetting and lamenting before Prometheus, waving their torches so that they produced a great deal of smoke. Only after they ran off did Lucius realize that the purpose of their dance and the smoke was to distract the audience from a bit of stagecraft being performed on the victim. As if by magic, his entrails had been stuffed back inside him and his belly had been stitched up. Even the blood on his legs had been wiped clean. The man was extremely pale, but apparently conscious; his lips moved and his eyelids flickered. Just as the punishment of Prometheus was said to be repeated in an endless cycle, so this victim had been made ready for yet another assault by the bears. Again they came loping toward him. The man opened his mouth to scream, but no sound came out. Instead of struggling against his chains, he twitched and convulsed as the bears proceeded to disembowel him again. Eventually even the twitching stopped.

The dancers reappeared. They cast aside their torches, flinging them onto the stage set. The mock cliff went up in flames, consuming the body of the victim with it. The dancers circled the bonfire, joined hands, and sang a song of jubilation, praising the wisdom and justice of Jupiter.

Lucius found himself wondering what Epictetus and Dio would have made of the tableau. The victim was not just a murderer but the very worst sort of murderer, a parricide. Surely he deserved to be punished, and why should his death not be used to educate the public? The tableau taught a double lesson. First, while men might sympathize with a rebel like Prometheus, the authority of the king of the gods—and by extension the authority of the emperor—must be respected, and would always triumph in the end. Second, on a more basic level, no man should dare to kill his own father, for fear of suffering such a terrible fate. Lucius suspected that his philosopher friends would be unmoved by such arguments. He himself was left feeling more queasy than uplifted by the spectacle.

There were a great many other such tableaux. As Martial had predicted, bears featured prominently in most of them. A temple thief was made to reenact the role of the robber Laureolus, made famous by the ancient plays of Ennius and Naevius; he was nailed to a cross and then subjected to the attack of the bears. A freedman who had killed his former master was made to put on a Greek chlamys and go walking through a stage forest populated by cavorting satyrs and nymphs, like Orpheus lost in the woods; when one of the satyrs played a shrill tune on his pipes, the trees dispersed and the man was subject to an attack by bears. An arsonist was made to strap on wings in imitation of Daedalus, ascend a high platform, and then leap off; the wings actually carried him aloft for a short distance, a remarkable sight, until he plunged into an enclosure full of bears and was torn to pieces.

"A bit repetitious, isn't it, ending all the tableaux with bears?" said Epaphroditus.

"Ah, but those are Lucanian bears, not Caledonian," said Martial. "Good Italian beasts, not exotic stock from beyond the sea. See how the people cheer them on? Poor Daedalus never stood a chance."

After the punishments, there was an intermission. Acrobats once again ran onto the sand floor of the arena. Lucius and his friends went to the vestibule for refreshments and then to relieve themselves at the nearest latrina, where the quality of the bronze and marble fixtures was the finest Lucius had ever seen in a public facility. Martial joked that he felt unworthy to relieve himself amid such splendor.

While his friends lingered in the vestibule, Lucius returned to his seat. Down in the arena, the lifeless body of an acrobat was being carried off.

"What that's about?" he wondered aloud.

"The poor fellow was walking across a tightrope when he lost his balance and fell." The voice came from the row in front of him. All the Vestals had left for the intermission except one. She turned in her seat and looked straight at him.

Lucius stared back at Cornelia. He could think of nothing to say.

The Vestal finally broke the silence. "He was hardly more than a child. I think they should use nets, don't you?"

"I believe they practice with nets," Lucius said. "But they never perform with them. That would eliminate the suspense."

"It would still display their skill. I for one have no desire to see a tightrope walker die. What's the point? Such a death is simply an accident, not a punishment or the outcome of a ritual combat. They're acrobats, not murderers or gladiators. What's your name?"

The question was so abrupt, he simply stared at her.

"It's not a difficult question, surely." She laughed. There was nothing malicious in her laugh. The sound of it gave him pleasure.

"Lucius Pinarius," he said. "My father was Titus Pinarius."

"Ah, yes, I know the name, though there don't seem to be a great many of you about these days."

"There was a time when the Pinarii were quite prominent," said Lucius. "More than one Pinaria was a Vestal. One was rather famous. But that was a long time ago."

She nodded. "That's right, the Vestal Pinaria was among those trapped atop the Capitoline Hill when the Gauls sacked the city. We still talk about her, and pass down the story to the new sisters. That's why your name is so familiar." She looked him up and down. "You're not wearing a senator's toga. Not a politician, then. Nor are you a military man, I think. How did you merit such a choice seat on opening day?"

"You're awfully forthright," said Lucius.

"When you're a Vestal, there's really no point in being circumspect. I say what I mean and I ask what I want to know. Perhaps it's different for other women."

"I don't know a lot about women," he admitted.

"Now who's being forthright?"

"Here come my friends," he said. "One of them is a poet. The emperor likes his work; that's why we have such good seats. Martial will write verses to celebrate the inaugural games."

"Ah, I wondered who that fellow was, constantly chattering and scribbling on his wax tablet."

"I'll introduce you, if you like." Lucius stood to let Martial pass. When he looked back, Cornelia had turned away. The other Vestals had returned to their seats.

The program recommenced with a series of animal exhibitions. First, a brightly decorated elephant with a trainer on its back ascended a ramp to a platform, then walked down a tightrope. While the spectators were still crying out in amazement, the elephant sauntered toward the imperial box, emitted a trumpetlike cry from its trunk, then folded its forelegs and dropped forward, making a very dignified bow to the emperor. The spectators responded with the first standing ovation of the day.

Hunting exhibitions followed. All manner of creatures were released, chased, and slain—boars, gazelles, antelopes, ostriches, the huge wild bulls of the Germanic lands called aurochs, and even the spindly-legged, long-necked creatures from farthest Africa called cameleopards, because they had a face like a camel and spots like a leopard. The hunters stalked their prey on foot and on horseback, using various weapons—bows and arrows, spears, knives, nets, and even nooses. Lucius, who enjoyed hunting boars and stags on his country estates, watched the exhibitions with interest and a bit of envy, especially when the hunters pursued the rarer or more dangerous animals, since he himself would probably never have the opportunity to bring down a cameleopard or an aurochs. As the slaughter continued, attendants with wheelbarrows and rakes covered the pools of blood with fresh sand.

There were also exhibitions in which animals were pitted against each other. The audience thrilled to see a leopard stalk and fell a cameleopard by leaping onto its huge neck. "Like a siege tower brought down by a catapult," muttered Martial, searching for a metaphor.

A tigress had less luck pursuing an ostrich. The absurdity of a bird unable to fly was obvious, but the creature could run with amazing speed. The tigress eventually gave up the chase and crouched, panting, on the sand. The spectators laughed and shouted mockery at the feline, disgusted by a cat unable to catch a flightless bird. But when the tigress's mate was unleashed, the same spectators fell silent and watched in fascination as the two cats appeared to use a coordinated strategy to trap the ostrich. The bird ran this way and that as the cats closed in.

"My old friend Pliny, not long before Vesuvius put an end to him, wrote that the ostrich hides its head in a bush when attacked and thinks its whole body is concealed," said Martial. "See how the attendants have placed bits of shrubbery all around the arena, so that the bird may demonstrate its foolish behavior?"

But the ostrich did not hide its head. Eventually, in desperation, it used its long, powerful legs to kick furiously at the nearest tiger. This gained the ostrich a brief respite, but the bird was quickly exhausted, while the tigers seemed to find fresh strength. The ostrich at last resorted to lying flat on the ground with its long neck and head pressed against the earth. In the rippling haze of heat that rose from the sand, the bird looked like a lifeless mound of earth, and for a while the cats were confounded. They circled the prostrate, motionless bird, sniffing the air and growling. At last the tigress began to paw at the ostrich, which gave a twitch, whereupon the feline pounced and seized the ostrich's long neck in its powerful jaws. The two cats hissed at each other and fought over the carcass for a while, much to the amusement of the audience, then settled down to share the feast. When they were done, attendants plucked the huge feathers from the dead bird and handed them out as souvenirs to the nearest spectators, who used them to decorate their clothing or fan themselves.

To see an animal hunted, whether by a man or by another animal, thrilled the audience. But far more exciting was the spectacle of seeing one fearsome beast pitted against another in equal combat. For the inaugural games, the emperor had arranged a pairing that had never been seen before. First a wild aurochs was released into the arena. The gigantic bull had huge horns and a fiery temper, as was demonstrated when trainers behind wooden enclosures taunted the creature by throwing red balls at it. The aurochs charged at the cloth balls and managed to spear one of them on his right horn. The clinging ball angered the creature even more. He snorted and tossed his head furiously until the ball went flying into the stands. Spectators leaped to their feet, shoving and struggling against one another to claim it.

Next, a creature that many of those present had never seen before was released into the arena. This was the rare rhinoceros, a beast whose iron-colored flesh appeared to be made of plated armor and whose enormous nose terminated in a formidable pair of horns, one large and one small. As fearsome as the aurochs might be, it was clearly a relative of the domesticated bull familiar even to the city-dwellers of Roma, and was a creature of grace and beauty, but the rhinoceros was like no other animal, an exotic being from the ends of the earth.

By taunting both animals with balls, prods, and torches, driving them closer and closer together, the trainers eventually induced them to fight. Their methods of combat were so similar that one seemed to be the distorted mirror image of the other. They stood their ground, stamped their feet, shook their haunches, lowered their heads, and finally charged. On the first clash, they only grazed each other, as if each were merely testing his opponent. They drew apart, faced each other, then charged again. This time the aurochs delivered a glancing blow against the rhinoceros, which snorted in pain. The wagering in the stands, which had been heavily against the aurochs, was suddenly reversed.

On the third charge, the rhinoceros demonstrated its brute strength and the sheer power of its horn. The creature landed a shuddering blow against the aurochs's head. The bull was dazed. While it staggered and stumbled, the rhinoceros backed away just enough to reposition itself for a fresh charge, then struck the aurochs with such power that the beast was thrown clear into the air before it plummeted to the ground, landing on its side. The aurochs beat its hooves against the ground but was unable to stand. Again the rhinoceros charged, sinking its horn into the aurochs's vulnerable flank and throwing it into the air again. The aurochs bellowed out in pain. When it struck the ground, it thrashed its limbs for a moment, then threw back its head and expired.

The rhinoceros goaded the carcass for a while, then appeared to realize that its opponent was no longer a threat. It charged one of the attendants, who ducked behind a wooden enclosure. The rhinoceros struck the enclosure with such force that its horn became stuck in the wood.

This provoked laughter in the audience but also posed a problem for the trainers. How could the rhinoceros be pulled free? While the animal was in such a fury, no one dared get close to it. Finally, someone decided to make the best of the situation by improvising yet another combat. A bear was released and driven toward the rhinoceros.

The audience spontaneously rose to its feet in excitement. No one could imagine how this unscheduled, unprecedented combat would proceed. If the rhinoceros remained trapped and unable to move, it would be completely at the mercy of the bear, unless its armorlike flesh offered adequate protection against the bear's sharp claws.

The bear landed a few blows against the rhinoceros's haunches, drawing blood, but these served only to incite the beast to exert the effort necessary to free itself. To the sound of splintering wood, the rhinoceros at last extricated its horn.

Once the rhinoceros was mobile again, the bear stood no chance. Just as the aurochs had been tossed into the air, so was the bear, which landed with a gaping wound in its belly and did not get up again.

Trainers moved in to corral the rhinoceros, which was surprisingly docile once its fury was expended. The spectators remained on their feet and enthusiastically cheered the beast, which had triumphed in not one but two death matches, without even pausing to rest. One of the acrobats ran up to touch the horn for luck. The startled rhinoceros jerked its head, and the small but powerful movement knocked the man flat on his back. The audience gasped, then roared with laughter when the acrobat sprang to his feet and made his exit by executing a series of nimble cartwheels and backflips.

Passing the acrobat on his way out, a massively muscled man strode into the arena. He wore only the briefest of loincloths and a hooded cloak made from a lion's pelt. Clearly he was meant to be Hercules, about to perform one of his famous labors.

A bull was released into the arena. Streamers of yellow, blue, and red on its horns identified it as the Cretan bull, the creature that sired the monstrous minotaur on Queen Pasiphae.

The man playing Hercules flexed and preened for the crowd, looking supremely confident even as the bull snorted and stamped its feet. When the bull charged, the man grabbed its horns and vaulted onto its back. Crouching as he held the horns, he managed to stay on the bull's back even as it furiously bucked and kicked its hind legs. When the bull at last began to tire, the man leaped off. In a remarkable show of strength, he seized the bull by the horns, twisting them this way and that until he forced the bull to kneel before him.

The sight of a man overcoming a bull with his bare hands would have been amazing enough, but this contest was only the first stage of the spectacle. While the bull wrestler held the beast immobile in the very center of the arena, a team of men ran onto the field and fitted a harness on the bull. A rope descended from the sky. It seemed to have appeared from nowhere, but in fact it was part of a system of ropes and winches that stretched from one side of the amphitheater to the other across its highest point, from rim to rim above the canvas awnings. The hoisting mechanism had been put in place while all eyes were on Hercules wrestling the bull.

The dangling rope was hooked to the harness on the bull. The man playing Hercules mounted the beast. The rope drew taut and the bull began to rise into the air. When its hooves lost contact with the ground the bull panicked and began to buck violently, spinning wildly in midair. The rider clutched the rope with one arm and waved the other. He threw back his head with a raucous shout.

Higher and higher the bull rose. Looking upward to follow its ascent, the spectators were dazzled by the sun. The bull and its rider became a silhouette, and the thin rope seemed to vanish. The bull appeared to be running through the air, flying without wings.

Small, brightly colored objects showered down on the audience from above. The little squares of parchment flitted and skipped on the air like butterflies. Blinded by the sun, no one could tell where the little tokens came from as they descended by the thousands. As they landed amid the crowd, there were cries of joy and excitement.

"A loaf of bread! My token says I receive a free loaf of bread!"

"Ha! Mine's a lot better than that. I get a silver bracelet!"

"And I get a basket of sausages and cheese. That'll feed my family for a month!"

People began to compete for the little squares of parchment, jumping for them as they descended or scrambling for those that fell underfoot. The scene was chaotic but jubilant.

"Titus manipulates them as if they were children," said Epaphroditus with a sigh, looking at the token in his hand, which promised a jar of garum.

"You sound wistful," said Lucius.

"I'm thinking of the old days. What might Nero have achieved if he'd built this amphitheater instead of the Golden House, and if he'd known how to please the people? They don't want to see an emperor play Oedipus on the stage. They want to see a bull fly through the air!"

"Speaking of the bull . . . where did it go?" said Martial.

Lucius looked up, squinting at the sunlight. The bull and its rider were nowhere to be seen. Nor was the contraption that had hoisted them into the air. Bull, rider, and rigging had all vanished somehow while everyone was distracted by the shower of tokens, creating the illusion that the bull had carried Hercules to Olympus, melting into the ether. As others in the audience began to realize what had happened, another tumultuous round of acclamations rang through the amphitheater.

Amid the jubilation, a second intermission was announced.

While Lucius and his friends stood and stretched themselves, a well-dressed messenger appeared and spoke in Martial's ear.

Martial's eyes grew wide. "All three of us?" he said.

The man nodded.

Martial turned to his friends. "A humble poet's dream come true! Follow me, both of you." Without waiting, he hurried off.

"Where is he taking us?" said Lucius to Epaphroditus.

"I imagine one of his patrons is hosting a private party during the intermission," said Epaphroditus. "More food, more wine."

Lucius glanced over his shoulder. Cornelia was standing and conversing with one of her fellow Vestals. She turned her face in his direction. He tried to hang back, hoping to exchange parting glances, but Epaphroditus grabbed his arm and pulled him along.

They followed Martial and the courier through the vestibule, then past a cordon of Praetorians and down a splendidly decorated hallway that terminated in a flight of porphyry steps. The purple marble shone with veins of crimson under the filtered sunlight.

Martial skipped up the steps, following the courier. He looked back and saw that his friends were hesitating. "Don't just stand there, you two. Come along!"

Lucius ascended the marble steps into the imperial box, his heart racing. He looked at Epaphroditus for reassurance, but the older man, normally so calm and self-possessed, appeared to be as flustered as Lucius himself.

What was Epaphroditus feeling? Once he had lived at the very center of power, but for more than ten years he had been retired from imperial service, living a modest, quiet existence, occasionally waxing nostalgic for his glory days under Nero but more often content to sit in his garden and talk about philosophy and literature with Epictetus and Dio. Nero was long gone. The Golden House had been demolished and dismantled. Epaphroditus had survived, but in the new world of the Flavians, he was a forgotten man.

They were led before the emperor, who remained seated, with his sister on one side and his daughter on the other. His brother stood nearby. The courier presented Martial and Epaphroditus, and then Lucius heard his own name spoken aloud and had the presence of mind to step forward. The emperor gave each of them a gracious nod.

Titus's cheeks and forehead were flushed. His eyes glittered with excitement. "So, Martial, these fellows are members of your little circle, the friendly critics who have the privilege of hearing your poems even before I do."

"Yes, Caesar. And a good thing that is, or else Caesar's ears would be subjected to some very bad poems."

"That other writer fellow you consort with, the one who wrote that lovely elegy for Melancomas—"

"Dio of Prusa?"

"Yes, that's the one. Is Dio not with you?"

"Alas, Caesar, Dio is indisposed."

"What a liar you are, Martial! I know Dio's philosophical bent. Admit that the man is not here today because he objects to such games on principle."

"I may have heard him utter some such nonsense."

Titus nodded. "Well, the world shall be deprived of Dio's impressions of the day's spectacles, but I do look forward to reading yours. Have the proceedings inspired you?"

"Exceedingly, Caesar. To enter the Amphitheater of the Flavians is to be transported into a world where perfect justice reigns and the gods walk among us. I wish I never had to leave."

Titus laughed. "See if you feel the same after sitting through the next few hours. I have the best seat in the house, and my backside is already numb. Oh, I'm not complaining. The animal hunts were splendid, truly first-rate. Though on such a fine day I'd rather be out hunting, myself. Hadn't you, Lucius Pinarius? I'm told you're a hunter."

Lucius was taken aback, surprised that the emperor knew anything at all about him, much less such a personal detail. Had Titus gleaned the information from one of Vespasian's old dossiers? "Yes, Caesar, I do enjoy hunting. But there are no cameleopards or aurochs on my estate."

"No? You really should get some. The thing with the bull—that was really quite something, wasn't it? The engineers assured me they could pull it off, but I was biting my lip there for a while, let me tell you. What a mess if the rope had broken! But I should never have doubted my trusty engineers. Just give those fellows a winch and some rope and then get out of their way, as my father used to say. If they can hurl a missile over the walls of Jerusalem and hit the forehead of a Jewish priest on the dome of the temple, why shouldn't they be able to make a bull fly?

"But I fear the best of the day is over, at least for me. I'd go home right now if I had the option. Nothing left but the bestiarii and the gladiators. Carpophorus is on the bill—the best bestiarius in the world, able to kill any animal he's matched against with his bare hands if he has to. Fun to watch, but expect no surprises. And then the gladiators. Who wants to see a lot of fat, sweaty men spill each other's blood? I saw enough gore in Jerusalem to last a lifetime, but I suppose it's a novelty to these lay-abouts in Roma who never venture farther than the Appian Gate. Of course my brother loves that sort of thing, don't you, Domitian? He could watch gladiators strut and stab each other all day long. He gets quite excited by a good match. Nero was bored by gladiator shows, wasn't he, Epaphroditus?"

Epaphroditus blinked. "I suppose he was, Caesar."

Domitian stepped forward with his arms crossed and an unpleasant expression on his face. His young son, watching him intently, likewise crossed his arms and glowered.

"You only suppose?" said Domitian. "I thought you knew Nero quite well. With him to the bitter end, weren't you?"

Titus had been making conversation with his guests, playing the role of the congenial emperor, which his father had perfected; his brother's aggressive tone made everyone uncomfortable, including his family members.

"Epaphroditus is not here to be questioned," said Domitilla. Like her brothers, she had the broad face and prominent nose typical of the Flavians; her temperament seemed closer to that of the affable Titus than to the dour Domitian.

Epaphroditus cleared his throat. "I suppose I knew Nero as well as anyone, especially in his last days. Caesar is quite correct: Nero was not much interested in blood sports."

"Preferred plays and poetry and that sort of thing, didn't he?" said Titus helpfully. "My versatile brother likes both gladiators *and* poetry, don't you, Domitian? Quite a poet himself. Wrote a rather good one about the battle on the Capitoline Hill, when that fiend Vitellius set the Temple of Jupiter on fire. Domitian saw it all with his own eyes; came up with some verses so vivid I feel I was there myself—I smell the smoke and hear the screams. Just the sort of thing I want you to do, Martial, for the games today."

"No one who sees these games will have need of my verses, Caesar, for they shall never forget them," said Martial. "But to the unfortunate few who miss this occasion, I will strive to convey some small hint of the glorious sights and sounds I've witnessed, however inadequate my words may be."

Domitian snorted. "The 'unfortunate few' who aren't here today—including your friend Dio. Who are these philosophers, to think they're so much better than everyone else? It was our father's dream to see this amphitheater opened. He died before that could happen, but we persevered without him. Titus put a great deal of work into these games, we all did, more care and effort than a do-nothing like your friend Dio could possibly imagine, yet the philosopher thinks himself too good to accept this generous gift to the people of Roma."

"Some men are simply squeamish," said Titus charitably. "Cicero had no stomach for gladiator shows. Nor did Seneca."

"But they attended them, nonetheless," said Domitian. "These games are as much a solemn duty as they are a celebration, brother. Those who don't attend—indeed, who make a show of their absence—disparage the memory of our father."

"I wouldn't go that far, little brother. But you make an excellent point. Gladiator games began as a way to honor the dead. Our ancestors forced prisoners to fight to the death at the funeral games to mark the passing of great men. We've come a long way from those early days, as the building of this amphitheater demonstrates—what would Romulus with his thatched hut make of this place? Nonetheless, the gladiator games today hearken back to the very first such games, because they honor the passing of a great man, our father. Every drop of blood spilled today will be shed in his honor."

"And every drop of wine poured today should be drunk in his honor," said Martial. The words were risky, breaking the somber mood created by the emperor, but the risk paid off. Titus smiled at Martial's turn of phrase and raised his cup.

"Let us drink, then, to the Divine Vespasian," said Titus.

Wine was poured for the guests. As Lucius raised his cup, he was suddenly conscious of the extraordinary nature of the moment. He stood in the imperial box, close enough to touch all three children of the Divine Vespasian, sharing wine with Caesar himself—and all because of his friendship with a poet!

Lucius and his friends returned to their seats.

The games resumed with a series of matches between men and beasts, culminating in the appearance of the famed Carpophorus, who was in excellent form, uncannily nimble for a man so heavily muscled and apparently able to read an animal's thoughts as he anticipated his opponent's every movement.

Lulled by the afternoon heat and too much wine, Lucius dozed during Carpophorus's long performance, waking intermittently to witness the bestiarius armed with a dagger to fight a bear, armed with a club to fight a lion, and taking on not one but two bison with his bare hands. Each time he killed a beast, Carpophorus slung the carcass over his brawny shoulders and paraded around the arena to show it off. Waking and dozing and seeing nothing but Carpophorus in combat, over and over again, Lucius seemed trapped in an endlessly repeating dream of slaughter.

At last Lucius was roused by a thunderous ovation as the multitude rose to its feet to acclaim the bestiarius after his final match.

Lucius stood with the rest. He blinked, yawned, and rubbed his eyes. "How many animals did the fellow kill?" he asked Martial.

"What! Weren't you counting along with everyone else?"

"I dozed."

"You and the emperor both, I imagine. Carpophorus took on a total of twenty animals, one after another. That must be a record. And he suffered hardly a scratch. The man's invincible. If they want to find an even match for him, they shall have to bring in a hydra, or maybe one of those fire-breathing bulls that Jason encountered in the land of Colchis."

The gladiator matches followed. Lucius was glad that Epictetus and Dio had not come; the contests were bloodier than any he could recall, and seemed endless, stretching on for hour after hour. Long before the final match between two of the most famous gladiators, Priscus and Verus, Lucius thought that even the most ardent lover of the games must be sated. But as Priscus and Verus engaged, Lucius looked at the imperial box and saw Domitian standing at the parapet, clutching the railing with white knuckles, watching the contest with rapt attention and responding with his whole body, jerking, scowling, grunting, clenching his teeth, and exclaiming under his breath. His little boy stood beside him, mimicking everything his father did. Meanwhile, the emperor remained seated, watching the match without emotion, occasionally casting a sardonic glance at his agitated brother and nephew.

Priscus was a gladiator of the Thracian type, wearing a broad-brimmed helmet with a grille that covered his face and a griffin ornament; greaves covered his legs up to the thighs, and he carried a small round shield and curved sword. Verus was a Murmillo, the traditional opponent of a Thracian, so called for the *mormylos,* a fish, that decorated his helmet; his right leg was padded with a thick gaiter and he was armed like a Roman legionary with a short sword and a tall, oblong shield.

The two fighters were so evenly matched that neither seemed able to draw blood from the other, but the gracefulness of their movements was so striking and the violence of their sudden clashes so thrilling that theirs was by far the most exciting contest of the day. Even Titus stopped chatting with his sister and daughter and sat forward in his chair, while his brother became increasingly animated. There was no doubt which gladiator Domitian favored; he kept shouting the name of Verus, and when a senator seated nearby began to yell encouragement to the Thracian, Domitian hurled a cup at the man and told him to shut up.

Titus rolled his eyes at the sudden outburst but made light of it. "Perhaps the Murmillo should add a wine cup to his weaponry. My brother draws more blood than does Verus today."

The senator, who was using a fold of his toga to stanch the bleeding from a cut on his forehead, flashed a crooked smile to acknowledge the emperor's wit.

The match had many high points and suspenseful moments, eliciting gasps and shrieks and even some outbursts of weeping from the exhausted, sun-dazed spectators. At last Titus put an end to it. He rose to his feet and gave a signal to the master of the games to stop the contest. Priscus and Verus removed their helmets. Faces covered with sweat, chests heaving, they gazed up at the emperor, awaiting his judgment.

In one hand, Titus held a wooden sword, the traditional gift to a gladiator who had earned his freedom. After such a closely fought match, with no clear victor, to which gladiator would he grant the sword?

The partisans of the two gladiators began to chant their names—"Priscus! Priscus!" and, "Verus, Verus!" The two groups were so evenly dispersed throughout the stands that the names merged into a jumbled shout of two syllables.

The emperor disappeared from the imperial box. The crowd grew confused and the chanting trailed off, until a gate beneath the imperial box opened and Titus strode into the arena. His appearance on the blood-strewn sand thrilled the crowd, which gave a deafening roar as Titus approached the two waiting gladiators, holding the wooden sword before him.

Titus reached the gladiators. His back was to Lucius, who found himself wishing he could see the emperor's expression. The crowd began to chant the names of their favorites again.

Titus stepped forward. The crowd fell silent. Titus paused. Instead of awarding the wooden sword, he raised his left arm to show that he was carrying a second sword. Stepping forward, he presented the wooden swords to both gladiators at once. Verus and Priscus were both declared victors; both were rewarded with freedom. Such a thing had never been done before.

As the grinning gladiators lifted their wooden swords high in the air, the spectators rose to their feet in the last and most thunderous ovation of the day. At first they shouted the names of the gladiators, but gradually the mingled roar resolved into a single word repeated over and over: "Caesar! Caesar! Caesar!"

Lucius scanned the vast bowl of the amphitheater. He had never seen so many people in one place, or so vast an outpouring of emotion. At the very center of it all was the emperor.

Titus was still a young man. With luck, he might reign for many years, until Lucius himself was old. He had certainly made an auspicious beginning. All the disasters and trials of the last year—the destruction of Pompeii, the plague in Roma, the fire that had devastated the city—were eclipsed by the stunning success of the inaugural games. Titus had not merely distracted the citizens, he had inspired them with a sense of unity and restored confidence. More feasting and plays and spectacles would follow in the days ahead, at venues all over the city, but it was hard to imagine anything that could match the splendor of the opening day of the Flavian Amphitheater.

The two gladiators made their exit. The emperor gave a final salute to the people and left the arena. The imperial box was empty. The arena was deserted. There were no more acrobats, no more contests, no more spectacles to behold.

As he gazed at the thousands of spectators around him, it occurred to

Lucius that the crowd itself was the true spectacle. Seated in a circle, with everyone visible to everyone else, the spectators had spent as much time watching one another as they had watching the games. The sound of the gathering, whether a murmur or a roar, was intoxicating; the acoustics of the place could capture a whisper or a laugh from across the way or amplify the roar of the crowd to superhuman volume. Already the great amphitheater had taken on a life of its own: from that day forward, this would be the gathering place for all Roma, rich and poor, great and small, the living embodiment of the spirit of the city and the will of its people. The world outside the amphitheater might pose dangers beyond human control—plague, earthquake, fire, flood, all the perils of war—but within the protective shell of the amphitheater existed a cosmos in miniature where the people of Roma were like gods, gazing down at the little world of the arena where mortals and beasts lived and died at their whim.

Perhaps Epictetus and Dio should have come, Lucius thought; how else could they understand the collective grandeur experienced by the spectators? And who but his philosopher friends could help Lucius make sense of the curious feeling of detachment that cast a cold shadow over his enjoyment of that moment, that drained the experience of its glamour and made it seem hollow and empty? Amid the blur of so many faces and the dull, throbbing roar of so many voices, Lucius suddenly felt more alone than he had ever felt before in his life.

But he was not alone. Amid the vast crowd, two eyes looked back at him. Surrounded by her fellow Vestals, close enough to touch if he had dared to do so, Cornelia was smiling at him. She said nothing, nor did she need to. Lucius knew he would see her again.

A.D. 84

Lucius made ready to set out from his house on the Palatine, dressed not in his toga but in a worn, brown tunic borrowed from one of his household slaves. No Roman wife, married to a man of property, would have allowed her husband to leave the house looking so drab and nondescript; but at thirty-seven, Lucius still had no wife, nor had he any intention of acquiring one. He came and went as he pleased, unconstrained by concerns of family or by most of the societal obligations that applied to men of his age and wealth.

As he stepped out the front door, his heart began to race. How absurd, he thought, that a man his age should feel such adolescent excitement at the prospect of a sexual tryst, and with a woman who had been his lover for more than three years. Yet the thrill he felt at seeing her never diminished; it grew stronger. Was it the danger that excited him? Or was it because they were able to meet so seldom, which made each occasion special?

He looked up at the cloudless sky. He would have preferred the anonymity of a hooded cloak, but on a hot summer day such a garment might attract more attention than it deflected. He took a few steps down the narrow street, then looked back at his house. How absurdly big the place was, for a single man to dwell in. A huge staff of slaves was required just to keep the place running. Sometimes he felt that the slaves were the true inhabitants and he was simply an occupant.

How he preferred the tiny house on the Esquiline that was his destination, the place he had purchased for the sole purpose of meeting his lover.

He made his way down the slope of the Palatine and across the heart of the city, passing the Arch of Titus and the Flavian Amphitheater, glancing up at the towering Colossus of Sol. He passed through the crowded Subura, hardly conscious of the noise and the odors. He ascended the steep, winding path up a spur of the Esquiline Hill and paused for breath at the little reservoir called the Lake of Orpheus, so named because the splashing fountain was decorated by a charming statue of Orpheus with his lyre surrounded by listening beasts. The house of Epaphroditus was nearby, but Lucius turned in a different direction.

At last he arrived at his destination. The house was small and unassuming, with nothing to distinguish it. The door was made of unpainted wood without even a knocker for ornament. He pulled a key from his tunic and let himself in. There was no doorkeeper to admit him; there were no slaves at all in the house. That in itself made the house a special place. Where did a man ever go in Roma where he could be truly alone, without even slaves present?

She was waiting for him in the tiny garden at the center of the house, reclining on a couch. She must have only just arrived, for she was still dressed in the hooded cloak she had worn to cross the city. Unlike Lucius, she could not possibly go out in public without hiding her face, even on a day as hot as this.

He sat beside her without saying a word. He pulled back the hood. The sight of her short blond hair excited him. It gave her a curiously boy-ish look and made her different from other women. Only the other Vestals and their female servants ever saw her like this, without her headdress; the sight of her cropped hair, like the sight of her naked body, was his alone, a privilege both sacred and profane that was enjoyed by no other man on earth. He ran his fingers through her hair, intoxicated by a sense of pos-session.

He put his mouth on hers and tasted her sweet breath. He slid his hands inside the cloak and touched warm, sleek flesh. He gasped. Beneath the cloak, she was wearing nothing at all, not even a sleeping gown or a simple tunic. She had crossed the city like this, naked except for slippers and a hooded cloak.

"Madness!" he whispered. He pushed back the cloak and buried his face against her neck. She laughed softly, touching her lips to the inner folds of his ear, nipping gently at the earlobe with her teeth. She opened the cloak and let it fall, so that she was suddenly naked in his arms.

He threw off his tunic and made love to her, as quickly and desper-ately as a boy. It was selfish of him, because he knew she preferred a much slower rhythm. But she indulged him, and seemed to draw pleasure from his trembling, uncontrollable excitement. All his emotions crested at once and poured from him in a flood. He wept, which aroused her; as if to draw more tears from him she dug her fingernails into his back and drew him closer to her, exerting a strength that never failed to surprise him, wrap-ping her limbs around him as the tendrils of a vine embrace a stone.

He did not have to work to reach the climax: it came upon him un-bidden, like a fire that consumes all before it. It consumed her as well, for he felt her shudder against his sweating flesh and clench the part of him inside her. She cried out so long and so loudly that people in the neighboring houses must have heard. *Let them hear,* he thought; they would know they heard a woman in ecstasy, but they could not know she was a Vestal.

❈

When it was over, they lay close together, their naked bodies touching, saying nothing and savoring the afterglow.

When he had first met her, he was struck at once by the beauty of her face, but he could not have imagined how beautiful her body was. It took his breath away the first time he saw her naked; it still took his breath away. Over the years he had paid to take his pleasure with some of the most accomplished and alluring courtesans in Roma, but he had never known any woman with more beautiful breasts or more sensual hips than Cornelia; the voluptuous curves and the pale, marmoreal perfection of her flesh induced him to explore every part of her with his hands, eager to discover the most secret and sensitive parts of her body. Her breasts and hips were like those of Venus, ripe and womanly; her slender calves, her small hands, and the hollows of her neck and throat were as smooth and delicate as those of a child.

She was beautiful. She was also passionate. Not even the most skilled courtesan had ever responded to his touches with so much vitality, or touched him so lewdly and shamelessly in return. At times he felt he was the more vulnerable partner, a quivering slave of pleasure at the mercy of a completely uninhibited lover able to give or withhold ecstasy with the merest brush of her fingers or the soft caress of her breath.

She was beautiful, passionate—and dangerous. What he did with Cornelia was not only illicit and irreverent, it was illegal. Their lovemaking was a crime as serious as murder. He took no perverse pleasure in that fact, or so he told himself. Yet why had he chosen Cornelia, of all women? Deep down, he sensed that the forbidden nature of their relationship played some role in his excitement, but like a leaf caught on the flood he did not question how he had come to be in such a situation, or make any attempt to resist the force that carried him along. He simply accepted that he was at the mercy of a power greater than himself and submitted to it.

Cornelia gave him the greatest physical pleasure he had ever experienced, but she also fascinated him in ways that had nothing to do with her body. He had never known a woman who could converse so knowledgeably about the world; she was as educated as Epictetus, as witty as Martial, as worldly as Dio. As a Vestal, she knew everyone of importance and was in a position to follow everything of significance that happened in the city. She was far more connected than was Lucius to the spheres of politics and society; she opened a window to those worlds through which he could gaze from a comfortable distance, maintaining his customary detachment. She was not only the best possible bedmate but the most interesting conversationalist he knew. He could talk to Cornelia about anything, and what she had to say was always of interest.

As the glow of their frenzied lovemaking subsided and the sweat of their bodies cooled, they gradually drew apart. They lay side by side, touching at the hips and shoulders, staring at the ceiling above.

"What excuse did you give this time?" he said.

"For my absence from the House of the Vestals? I've assumed responsibility for looking after the lotus tree in the sacred grove attached to the Temple of Lucina here on the Esquiline."

"How much care does a lotus tree need?"

"This one is over five hundred years old. We tend it very lovingly."

"And what makes it special to the Vestals?"

"All lotus trees are sacred. There's a lotus tree in the grove next to the House of the Vestals. When a girl is inducted, her hair is cut for the first time and the locks are hung on the tree as an offering to the goddess. It's a beautiful ceremony."

"I'm sure it is."

"Something's troubling you. What is it, Lucius?"

He sighed. "A messenger came to my house yesterday. He delivered a letter from Dio of Prusa."

"Ah, your dear friend who was exiled by the emperor. Where is the famous sophist now?"

"In Dacia, if you can believe it's possible for a letter to travel all the way to Roma from beyond the Danube."

"They say that Dacia is one of the few civilized lands that the Romans have yet to conquer."

"One of the few wealthy lands we've not yet looted, you mean."

"How cynical you are, Lucius. Do you not accept the notion that Roma has a special role given to her by the gods, to bring Roman religion and Roman law to the rest of the world, one province at a time?"

He was never quite sure how seriously to take Cornelia when she spoke in a patriotic vein. When all was said and done, despite her disregard for her vow of chastity, she considered herself a devoted priestess of the state religion.

"They say the Dacians have been crossing the Danube and making incursions into Roman territory," she said, "enslaving farmers on the frontier, looting villages, raping women and boys. It's almost as if King Decebalus is deliberately provoking Domitian to attack him."

"Or at least that's what the emperor wants us to think. It's an old Roman ploy, pretending that an enemy is responsible for the start of a war we greatly desire to wage. Titus spent the last of the treasure their father looted from the Jews, so Domitian needs money. If he wants to get his hands on King Decabalus's gold, a war to revenge outrages against Roman citizens will serve his purposes nicely."

She made a dismissive gesture with her hand. "Enough of that! I won't waste our time together debating the Dacian question. You were talking about your friend Dio. Is he terribly despondent?"

"Not at all. His letter was actually quite cheerful. Still, his exile weighs heavily on me."

She sighed. "Men cross Domitian at their peril—even a harmless sophist like Dio."

"But philosophers aren't harmless, or so Dio says. He believes the power of words and ideas is as great as the power of armies. Apparently, Domitian believes that, too. What a contrast to his brother, who proclaimed that he had no fear of words and let people say whatever they wished. The reign of Titus is beginning to look like a golden age."

"Curious, how golden ages are always so brief," said Cornelia. "I wonder if Titus's reign in retrospect seems so golden precisely because it lasted for only a few years. 'He put not a single senator to death,' they say. Perhaps he simply didn't live long enough. When he died of that sudden illness—no one ever suggested there was foul play—Domitian took over without bloodshed. Right away he banished some of Titus's most fervent supporters, men he felt he couldn't rely on. But when brother succeeded brother, what really changed? Very little. Still, people were at once nostalgic for Titus, because he died young and handsome and beloved, so Domitian started at a disadvantage. He was never as personable or even-tempered as his brother—"

"That's an understatement! You've seen Domitian's behavior at the amphitheater—his apoplectic fits during gladiator matches, the way he shouts encouragement to one fighter and yells threats at anybody who favors the other. He lowers the tone of the whole place. Spectators emulate him. Fights break out. Some days there's more blood in the stands than on the sand."

"You exaggerate, Lucius. Like you, I would prefer to see more decorum in the amphitheater—the place is dedicated to Mars, and the spectacles are religious rituals—but the sight of so much bloodshed releases powerful emotions in people, even in the emperor, it seems. More disturbing to me are the maneuverings in the imperial court. I suppose trouble must develop in every reign, sooner or later—factions form, rivalries emerge, intrigues simmer. It was all made worse when Domitian's son died."

"How he loved that little boy! The child was the mirror image of his father, always with him at the games, emulating his every movement."

"The boy wasn't just a beloved child. For an emperor, an heir is insurance, because the very existence of a son discourages rivals. When the boy died, Domitian was not only grief stricken, he became acutely suspicious of everyone around him. His courtiers in turn became suspicious of him. Once such an atmosphere develops, even the smallest action by the emperor sets people's nerves on edge."

"Exile is hardly a 'small action' if you're the one who's banished."

"True," she said.

"Nor is losing your head."

"You're talking about Flavius Sabinus, the husband of Domitian's niece. That was most unfortunate, and almost certainly uncalled for. My friends in the imperial court tell me Domitian had no real cause to believe Flavius was conspiring against him; the man was arrested and beheaded nonetheless. Unfortunately for your friend, Dio was often seen in the company of Flavius Sabinus."

"Was that a crime?"

"Perhaps not, but if Domitian had accused Dio of conspiring against him, your friend would have lost his head along with Flavius. Instead, Domitian banished him. Dio is lucky to be alive."

"Alive, but exiled from Italy, and forbidden to return to his native Bythinia. That's a steep price to pay for having been a welcome visitor to the home of Titus's daughter and son-in-law. Do you know the first thing Dio did after he fled Roma? He went to Greece to consult the oracle at Delphi. The oracle is famous for giving ambiguous guidance, but not this time. 'Put on beggar's rags,' Dio was told, 'and head for the farthest reaches of the empire and beyond.' So off he went, beyond the Danube."

"For a man with Dio's curiosity," said Cornelia, "travel to far-off lands must offer a splendid chance to learn more about the world. Think of all the obscure metaphors and allusions he'll be able to work into those learned discourses of his."

Lucius smiled. "He used just such a metaphor in his letter, referring to the funeral practices of the Scythians. 'Just as these barbarians bury cup-bearers, cooks, and concubines along with a dead king, so it is a Roman custom to punish friends, family, and advisers for no good reason when a good man is executed.' "

Cornelia drew a sharp breath. "Did you burn the letter?"

"Of course, after I read it aloud to Epaphroditus and Epictetus."

"Did you read it to anyone else?"

"To Martial, you mean? How he would have loved it! But no, I didn't share it with him. Dear Martial—Titus's fawning poet one day, Domitian's lapdog the next. He was still working on those poems about the inaugural games when Titus died. What to do with all that hard work? Rewrite the verses to suit the new emperor, of course. The book's just been published. Domitian is apparently quite pleased, and that pleases Martial, because he says Domitian is a more discerning critic than his brother ever was. But Martial would say that. A poet has to eat."

"While philosophers starve?" Cornelia stretched her arms above her head and extended her toes. Her body rubbed against his, and Lucius felt a stirring of renewed excitement.

"Dio isn't starving," he said. "He says the Dacians are actually quite civilized, despite the fact that they worship only one god. The temples and libraries of Sarmizegetusa can't have much to offer compared to those of Roma, but King Decebalus is reputed to have one of the largest hoards of gold in the world. Where there's that much wealth, a celebrated philosopher from Roma needn't go hungry. There'll always be some Dacian nobleman willing to feed a man who can bring a bit of wit and erudition to his table."

Lucius rolled onto his side, facing her. He ran his hand over the sinuous curve of her hip, then trailed his fingers across the delta formed by her thighs. "His letter was actually rather inspiring. Nothing seems to dampen his spirits; he always looks for the good in the bad. Dio says his exile may actually be a blessing, despite the trouble it's caused him. That's what the Stoics teach. Every misfortune that befalls a man—poverty, illness, a broken heart, old age, exile—is simply another opportunity for a lesson to be learned."

"Is that what you believe, Lucius?"

"I don't know. I listen to my philosopher friends and I try to make sense of what they tell me. Epictetus says it isn't a given event that disturbs us, but the view we take of it. Nothing is intrinsically good or bad, only thinking makes it so. Therefore, think good thoughts, and find contentment in the moment."

"Even if you're ill or hungry or in pain, or far from home?"

"Epictetus would say that even an affront to one's body, like illness or torture, is an external event, outside our true selves. The self of a man is not his body, but the intelligence that inhabits his body. That self is the one thing no one else can touch, the only thing we truly possess. The operation of our own will is the one thing in all the universe over which we have control. The man who learns to accept this is content, no matter what his physical circumstances, while the man who imagines he can control the world around him is invariably confused and embittered. So you see men who are oppressed by the worst sort of misfortunes, yet who are happy nonetheless, and you see men who are surrounded by luxury and have slaves to carry out their every wish, yet who are miserable."

"But what if a man is oppressed by others? What if his exercise of free will is constrained by the brute strength of another?"

"Epictetus would say that such a thing is impossible. Other men can have power over one's body and possessions, but never over the will. The self is always free, if we are but conscious of it."

"And what about the act of love, or the other pleasures of the body?"

"Epictetus disparages what he calls 'appetite,' the drive to satisfy the cravings of the body. Too often appetite controls a man, rather than being controlled by him."

"But since we have a body, and its bare requirements must be met if we are to exist at all in this world, clearly appetite serves a purpose. A man must eat, so why not take pleasure in food? And what you and I do together, Lucius—does it not give you pleasure?"

"Perhaps too much. There are moments when I'm with you that I forget where I am, even who I am. I lose myself in the moment."

She smiled. "And isn't that delicious?"

"Dangerous, Epictetus would say. To lose one's self in ecstasy is a trap, an exaltation of the body over the will, a capitulation to appetite, an invitation to heartbreak and disappointment, because we have no control whatsoever over the passions and appetites of another. A person may love us one day and forget us the next. Pleasure can turn to pain. But I believe a man needs to touch and be touched, to find union with another, to feel sometimes that he is an animal with a body and cravings and nothing more. I experience that with you, Cornelia. I wouldn't give up what I share with you for anything."

"So, do you embrace the Stoic view or not, Lucius?"

"Much of it makes sense to me. But I have my doubts. Is that all there is to wisdom—an acceptance of fate, an acknowledgment that we're essentially powerless? If the pains and pleasures of the body are separate from the self, and if nothing precedes or follows life, why bother to live at all? But look at me—talking philosophy with a Vestal virgin! Do the gods look down and laugh at us, Cornelia? Do they despise us?"

"If Vesta were displeased with me, she would let me know."

He shook his head. "Sometimes I can't believe the risk you take by meeting me." He ran the tip of his forefinger over her breast and watched the nipple grow erect. "Sometimes I can't believe the risk I'm taking."

They both knew the law. A Vestal convicted of breaking her vow of chastity was to be buried alive. Her lover was to be hung on a cross and beaten to death.

Cornelia shrugged. "At least since the days of Nero—all through my tenure as a Vestal—our vow of chastity has never been enforced. Some

Vestals remain virgins, some do not. We don't flaunt what we do, and the priests of the state religion don't look too closely into our lives. They take their cue from the Pontifex Maximus, who is also the emperor. Vespasian never cared what we got up to. Titus also looked the other way. They knew what truly mattered. As long as we keep Vesta's hearthfire burning without interruption and perform the rituals correctly, Roma will continue to receive the goddess's blessing."

"Do you truly believe in Vesta and her protection?"

"Of course I do. Don't tell me you're an atheist, Lucius. You haven't converted to Judaism?"

"You know my foreskin is intact."

"Or worse, become a follower of Christ, a hater of the gods and mankind?"

"No. I am neither a Jew nor a Christian. But . . ."

"Yes?"

He hesitated. What he was about to say he had never said aloud to anyone. "My uncle Kaeso was a Christian."

"Really?"

"Yes. He was burned alive by Nero, along with the other Christians who were punished for starting the Great Fire."

She pursed her lips. "How terrible for you."

"How terrible for him. I never knew the man. My father kept me away from him."

"Terrible for him, yes . . ." Cornelia left something unspoken, but he could read her thoughts: if the man was a Christian and an arsonist, perhaps he deserved his punishment. "Your uncle didn't give you that, did he?" She gestured to the amulet that hung from the chain around his neck.

"Why do you ask?" Lucius had never worn the fascinum when he went to see her. Today was the first time he had forgotten to leave it at home.

"I saw you touch it when you mentioned him. It looks a bit like a cross. The Christians boast that their god died by crucifixion—as if that were something to be proud of!"

"As a matter of fact, my uncle Kaeso did wear this amulet during his lifetime; he was wearing it when he died. So my father once told me. But the resemblance to a cross is only a coincidence. It's a family talisman, a fascinum."

"It doesn't look like a fascinum."

"That's because it's so very old and worn. If you look at it from a certain angle, you can make out the original shape. Do you see? Here is the phallus, and here are the wings."

"Yes, I see."

"You're one of the few people who's ever seen it. When I wear it, I keep it beneath my clothes, out of sight."

"And when you go to the baths?"

"I leave it at home, for fear of losing it."

"Then I am indeed privileged to see Lucius Pinarius naked, wearing only his family heirloom."

He lowered his eyes. "I've also never talked about my uncle before. Not to anyone, ever."

"Is it a secret, then?"

"Some people know about him, I imagine—Epaphroditus must know, since he knew my father quite well—but it's never spoken of."

"I understand. In every family there are certain events that are never talked about, relatives who are never mentioned."

He realized that he was touching the fascinum, turning it this way and that between his forefinger and thumb. He stared at it for a moment, then released it with a grunt. "How in Hades did we end up talking about my uncle Kaeso?"

"We were talking about Vesta and the sacred hearthfire, and atheists like the Christians who don't believe in the gods."

"I'm not sure what I think about the gods. Lately I've been reading Euhemerus. Do you know him?"

"No."

"Euhemerus served at the court of Cassander, who was king of Macedonia after Alexander. Euhemerus believed that our tales of gods are simply stories about mortal men and women who lived long ago, made larger than life by the storytellers and given supernatural powers."

"Then I think this Euhemerus was most certainly an atheist."

"I've also been studying Epicurus. He thought the gods existed, but believed they must have withdrawn from our world, growing so distant from mankind that their effect on mortals is only very faint, hardly perceptible, like a shadow cast by a feeble lamp."

"The light cast by the hearthfire of Vesta is not feeble, I can assure you," said Cornelia. "The goddess is with me every day. I attend her with joy and thanksgiving. But the common belief that she demands virginity of her priestesses, and punishes impurity by visiting catastrophes on the city, is a fallacy, a mistaken notion that has been proved false many times. I know for a fact that many Vestals have been unchaste with no bad consequence whatsoever. Otherwise, Roma would have suffered multiple disasters virtually every year that I've been a Vestal."

"We lost Pompeii—"

"That was far from Roma."

"There was a terrible fire—"

"The Temple of Vesta and the House of the Vestals were untouched."

"And a plague—"

"Not a single Vestal died, or even became ill. Does talking about disasters always make you so hard?"

"Only with you."

They made love again. They had never met without making love more than once, perhaps to make up for the infrequency of their meetings. To Lucius, the second time was always better than the first—less hurried and more relaxed, with a greater sense of union between them and a more satisfying climax for both. For the duration of their lovemaking, all his questions about existence were suspended. Each moment was sufficient in itself.

He held her tightly as she reached the crisis. He had never felt closer to her. But afterward, she slipped out of his embrace and turned her back to him.

"This is the last time we'll meet for a while," she said. "For several months, at least."

"Why?"

"I'm going away. I won't come back until the spring."

"It'll be a long winter without you. Where are you going?"

"To the House of the Vestals at Alba Longa." The town was a day's journey down the Appian Way, in a hilly region of quaint villages, luxurious villas, and hunting estates.

"That's only a few hours from Roma. I could come to see you—"

"No. I'll be in seclusion. The rules are stricter in Alba. The Vestals there belong to the oldest of all the orders, established even before Roma was founded."

"I thought the worship of Vesta originated here in Roma."

She smiled ruefully and shook her head. "And you, a patrician with a name going back to the days of Hercules!"

"The history of religion is not my strong point."

"I thought you read Titus Livius."

"Only the parts about my family."

"Even so, every Roman child should know that Rhea Silvia, the mother of Romulus and Remus, was a Vestal."

"Imagine that—another Vestal who was not a virgin!"

"Rhea's father was King Numitor of Alba. He was murdered by his brother, Amulius. Her wicked uncle feared that Rhea might someday produce a rival for the throne, so he forced her to become a Vestal and go into seclusion. But Rhea became pregnant nevertheless. Some say Mars ravished her. Others say her uncle Amulius raped her. However it happened, Rhea kept her condition secret until the twins were born. . . ." Cornelia's voice trailed off.

"Even I know this part," said Lucius. "Their mother put the newborn twins in a basket, then a slave took the babies out to a rocky hillside and left them there to die. That was a terrible thing to do, don't you think?"

"But what choice did Rhea Silvia have? A lot of women do the same thing nowadays. It's common practice."

"But what sort of mother could abandon her child to die?"

"Slave women, poor women, girls who've been raped. Rhea Silvia faced death if the evidence of her crime was discovered."

Lucius shook his head. He had never approved of the common practice of abandoning babies, but he did not care to argue with her. "Ah, well, I know the rest of the story. Jupiter raised a tremendous storm, and there was a great flood, and the twins were carried all the way to Roma, where their basket foundered on a hillside. A she-wolf found them, took them to her cave, called the Lupercale, and suckled them. Eventually, Romulus and Remus were adopted by a pig farmer and his wife, grew up to become fearsome warriors, killed the wicked Amulius, rescued their mother, Rhea Silvia, and founded Roma. And the rest is history. But why must you go to Alba, Cornelia? And why for so long?"

"The decision isn't mine. The Virgo Maxima has ordered me to go. It's my duty to obey her." There was something evasive in Cornelia's tone, but he sensed that there would be no point in pressing her.

"I'll miss you. I'll miss this." He pulled her close. "But even more, I'll miss *this*—the thing we do after making love. The banter. The teasing. The serious talk. Will you take another lover, while you're in Alba?"

"No." She answered without hesitation.

"Then neither will I," he said.

"Don't be ridiculous. You're a man."

"And you are a woman—the only one I want. To whom else might I turn? The bored wife of some acquaintance looking for an hour's distraction? A slave, counting the cracks in the ceiling until I'm finished? A whore, with one eye on the coins in my purse? Or perhaps I should look for some doe-eyed young girl fresh on the marriage market whose father is willing to settle for a suitor with a worn-out patrician name, a reputation for keeping company with exiled philosophers, and a family fortune only a little tainted by association with Nero. Not one of those women would be able to discuss philosophy and religion with me afterward."

"You might be surprised."

"I suppose I'll do what Martial does when one of his boys fails to show up—learn to love my left hand. Or I suppose I could turn to another of the Vestals—"

"You wouldn't dare!"

"Varronilla isn't bad-looking, and she's even younger than you; maybe too young for my taste. What about the Oculata sisters? I once enjoyed the attentions of a pair of sisters, years ago—and how many men have had sisters who were also Vestals? The sheer novelty of it—"

"Don't even think about it!" Cornelia gave him a pinch, playful but painful enough to make him yelp. "You and I take precautions, Lucius. We're discreet. When our paths cross in public—at the Flavian Amphitheater, in the Forum—we greet each other briefly, as is perfectly natural and acceptable, then we move on. We give no one cause for suspicion. But if you gain a reputation for deliberately seeking the company of Vestals, if you seem to be too familiar with our comings and goings—"

"Cornelia, I was only joking. I was teasing you—the way a man teases the woman he loves when she's just told him that for months and months he won't be able to talk to her, or touch her, or do this to her. . . ."

His passion reignited hers. Their lovemaking was fiercer than ever, fired by the knowledge of their coming separation.

A.D. 85

"And you've been faithful to her the entire time, Lucius? Even though you haven't been alone with her for over a year?" said Martial. They were in the garden of Epaphroditus, along with their host and Epictetus.

"Just as I vowed to her," said Lucius.

"Let me make sure I understand. This woman went away for several months, then finally returned, and now she refuses to meet with you again, except in public and in passing. Yet still you remain chaste, having no intercourse with either women or boys?"

"That is correct."

"But, Lucius, this is madness! If the woman's lost carnal interest in you, you must move on. Oh, I understand the heartache, the longing, the period of grief when a love affair ends. But while you're waiting for that to pass, you still must attend to your physical needs. If you don't feel ready yet to take pleasure with another woman, then take a boy, since you have no real interest in boys. That way you can experience all the physical pleasure with none of the regret you might feel for betraying this woman— though how you can betray a woman when it was she who abandoned you is beyond me."

"Martial, you simply don't understand. She hasn't betrayed me. She's as chaste as I am."

"Oh, really? How can you believe that? Of course, you won't even tell us if this woman is married, or a widow, or some other man's slave, or a common whore in the Subura."

She is none of those things, thought Lucius, but he could think of no way to explain that fact without giving away Cornelia's identity.

"Personally," said Epictetus, "I think there's nothing perverse or unnatural or even unusual about remaining chaste, if the body and mind are in harmony with such a choice. This mad rage to deflower virgins and sample every available prostitute and carry on illicit affairs with other men's wives, and meanwhile to give equal attention to fawning boys and compliant eunuchs—the sort of topic so fashionable nowadays in poetry—seems only to make a man constantly agitated and dissatisfied. Such a surrender to lust yields very little contentment in the long run."

"Ah, but it yields so much pleasure in the short run," said Martial. "Though it can be quite exhausting, I'll grant you. Our emperor used to be quite the sexual athlete, you know. In his younger days, before his father became emperor, they say the young Domitian was on a first-name basis with every prostitute in Roma; he'd go swimming naked in the Tiber by moonlight with a whole group of lovelies. And he was quite the seducer of respectable matrons as well. He called his activities 'bed wrestling.' I like that, don't you? It shows that our emperor in his younger days didn't take lovemaking too seriously. It was just another way of keeping fit and working up a good sweat, like horseback riding or a bit of exercise at the gymnasium. Of course, once our emperor married—a true love match— there was never a more devoted husband and father. Ah, the death of that precious little boy! What a blow that was. And his wife's subsequent affair with that actor, Paris—the irrational act of a grieving mother, surely—was yet another disappointment. Our emperor did what any self-respecting Roman would do—divorced his wife—and Paris just happened to be murdered in the street one night. But so devoted was our emperor to his chosen spouse that he forgave and took back the empress, and their marital bliss continues. My fondest wish is that they will soon produce another heir. Indeed, I have a poem already prepared for that occasion: 'Be born, great child, to whom your father may entrust the everlasting reins of empire—' "

"And yet, does Domitian look happy?" said Epictetus. "Was he ever happy, even in his younger days, when he was so proficient at this so-called bed wrestling? No. Always, he displays that same dour, constipated look that one saw on his father's face. Yet behold our friend Lucius here. Have you ever seen a man who appeared more contented? Yet Lucius has but one lover, and that lover makes no demands on him at all. He remembers the pleasures he once experienced with her, which are perfect and inviolable in retrospect, and contemplates her from afar, with some suffering but also with the bittersweet satisfaction that she longs for him as well. Clearly there is some danger or impropriety attached to their relationship, either for her or for him, or else I think he would tell us her name; but that element of risk must only add spice to his longing. He loves this woman as certain men are said to have loved a goddess—from afar, with utmost devotion, and at their peril. See how satisfied he appears—his eyes gleam, his movements are sure and graceful, his whole bearing is that of a man at peace with the world and with himself. I think our friend Lucius has discovered a secret happiness that the rest of us can only guess at."

"We're certainly left guessing at the name of his lover," said Martial.

Lucius smiled. "It's strange, but somehow this relationship—irregular as it may be—has filled a need in my life. As grateful as I am for the gift of friendship from each of you, there was a vacant place inside me, an emptiness that remained unamused by your wit, Martial, unsatisfied by your philosophy, Epictetus, insecure despite all your fatherly concern for me, Epaphroditus. She fills that emptiness."

"So poetry, philosophy, and friendship cannot compete with unrequited love?" said Martial.

"Not unrequited love, only unfulfilled—for the time being, anyway."

Epictetus nodded. "If you've found contentment in a chaste love affair, you should strive to maintain the relationship just as it is. The happiness that comes from physical consummation is fleeting."

"All happiness is fleeting," said Martial. "Life is precarious. Everything changes. Look at the four of us, growing older year by year."

"Yet we've all managed to remain unmarried," said Epaphroditus with a laugh.

"Only that fellow never changes." Epictetus nodded toward the statue of Melancomas. "The young boxer is as perfect now as he was the day Epaphroditus unveiled him."

"And as empty of all desires!" Martial laughed. "Perhaps we should be envious of Melancomas here. While everything around him changes, he never ages, and he is never troubled by hunger or sorrow or longing. Perhaps Medusa wasn't such a monster after all, when she turned men into stone. Maybe she was doing those men a favor by freeing them from suffering and decay. On the other hand, Pygmalion lusted for a statue and brought her to life, and that went rather well; according to Ovid, they lived happily ever after. So we are left with a puzzle: is it better to turn a man to stone, or bring stone to life?"

"I think you may have found a subject worthy of a poem," said Epaphroditus.

"No, the paradox is too subtle for my audiences. Rich patrons want a quick setup, a clever allusion or two—preferably obscene—and then a smashing punch line. No, I think my Medusa-versus-Pygmalion idea would be better suited to one of those learned discourses by our friend Dio. Imagine the convoluted argument he could spin, evoking all sorts of metaphors and obscure historical references. Say, has anyone heard from Dio lately?"

"I received a new discourse," said Epaphroditus, "only yesterday. . . ." His voice trailed off.

"What! And you're only just now mentioning it? Come, read it aloud," said Martial.

"I only had time to quickly scan it. I'm not sure . . ."

"Don't tell me it's no good," said Martial. "Has the poor exile lost his wit, stuck in Sarmizegetusa?"

"No, it's not that. To be candid, I'm not sure it's safe to keep the thing. It may be . . . seditious."

"Read it quickly then, and afterward we'll burn it." Martial laughed.

Epaphroditus smiled uneasily. Lucius knew what he was thinking but would not say aloud: none of them completely trusted Martial any longer, because of his favored status with the emperor. Martial hardly seemed the type to betray old friends, but Epaphroditus had learned to be cautious over the years. It was one thing to gossip about the emperor's love life— everyone from saltmongers to senators did that—but it was something else to read aloud a work by a banished philosopher.

"I don't mean that the discourse is overtly seditious," said Epaphroditus. "Dio is far too subtle for that. But this work could be seen as . . . teasing the emperor."

"You've set my curiosity ablaze," said Martial. "What's the subject?"

"Hair."

"What?"

"Hair. A learned discourse on hair and its role in history and literature."

They all laughed. Domitian was notoriously sensitive about his premature baldness. In his younger days he had been famously vain about his chestnut mane, and once, as a gift to a friend, he had even written a monograph on his secrets for hair care. After Domitian's ascension to power, copies of the treatise proliferated overnight; every literate person in Roma had read it, but no one dared to mention it in the author's presence. Was Dio's encomium on hair meant to mock the balding emperor who had exiled him?

"Even the emperor cannot avoid the ravages of time," observed Martial. He rose and circled the statue. "But our friend Melancomas shall never grow bald, or fat, or wrinkled, and if his lustrous hair should fade, it can always be repainted. How I envy his unchanging perfection! Ah, well, if our host is not going to share that new discourse from Dio, I'm off. I should get a bit of work done before the sun sets. Maybe I can make something of that notion about Pygmalion and Medusa after all. Or perhaps I'll write a letter to Dio and give him the idea as a gift."

"I'll come with you." Epictetus reached for his crutch and got to his feet with some difficulty. "I dine tonight with a prospective new patron. He wants to meet at the Baths of Titus, so I'd better be off. Are you leaving as well, Pinarius?"

Lucius began to rise, but Epaphroditus touched his arm.

"No, Lucius, stay a bit longer."

When they were alone, Lucius looked expectantly at his host. "You look worried, Epaphroditus."

"I am." The older man sighed. "By all the gods, Lucius, what do you think you're doing?"

"What are you talking about, Epaphroditus?"

"I know the identity of your mystery woman."

"How?"

"Lucius, Lucius, I've known you since you were a boy! Have you ever been able to keep a secret from me?"

Only about the role that Sporus played in Nero's death, thought Lucius, but he said nothing and let Epaphroditus continue.

"Even before you spoke of her chastity, I knew who she must be. I've seen the two of you when you meet in public—the stiff greeting, the averted gazes, the intentional distance you keep between you. And I happen to know that she was absent from Roma during the period you spoke of. I must admit, I find it ironic that the vow she would not keep for a goddess, she will keep for a man. I won't say her name aloud—what slaves don't overhear, they can't repeat—but you know whom I mean. Am I right?"

Lucius gazed at the Flavian Amphitheater, which was surrounded by scaffolds and cranes; a new tier was being added to accommodate even more spectators. "Yes, you're right."

Epaphroditus shook his head. "Lucius, Lucius! What a terrible risk you're taking. When I think of my promise to your father, to look after you—"

"I'm a grown man now and responsible for myself, Epaphroditus. Your promise to my father was long ago discharged."

"Still, the danger—"

"We were always very careful, very discreet. I'm not even seeing her anymore. We love each other at a distance."

Epaphroditus shut his eyes and took a deep breath. "You don't understand the gravity of the situation. Events are about to take place that will affect us all."

"Events?"

"I didn't want to talk about this in front of . . . the others."

"In front of Martial, you mean?"

"Or Epictetus, either. Or even you, for that matter." Epaphroditus paused to collect his thoughts. To Lucius he suddenly looked quite old, and more worn with cares than Lucius had seen him in many years. "You know I still have friends in the imperial household, even after so many changes and so many years. Sometimes I hear about things before they happen. My sources demand my utmost discretion, so usually I keep what I know to myself. Yes, I keep things even from you, Lucius. But there's no point in shielding you now, seeing the danger you're in. Domitian is about to revive the office of censor. He intends to assume the powers of the magistracy himself, permanently."

"Didn't his father do the same?"

"Yes, for a limited time and for a specific purpose. Vespasian conducted a census. That is one of the traditional functions of the censor, but it is not the function which interests Domitian."

"I don't understand. What else does a censor do?"

"Lucius, Lucius! Did you learn nothing of history when you were growing up? I know your father supplied the very best tutors for you."

Lucius shrugged. "Why bother to learn about the institutions of the long-dead Republic, when all power now resides in the hands of one man and the rest of us count for nothing?"

Epaphroditus stifled his exasperation. "Once upon a time, when Roma was ruled by the Senate, the censor wielded great power—in some ways he was the most powerful man in the Republic, because he was responsible for keeping the official list of citizens, and it was the citizens who elected the magistrates. People didn't vote as individuals, but in various blocks, determined by their wealth and other indicators of status. The censor determined in which block a man voted. That was important, because the voting blocks of the elite counted for more than those of the common rabble. And the censor could strike a citizen from the rolls altogether, which meant that citizen lost his right to vote."

"And why might a censor do such a thing?"

"If a man committed a criminal offense, for example. Or, more to the point, if the man was guilty of offending public morals."

"And who was the judge of that?"

"The censor, of course. And so, stemming from his duty to keep the voting rolls, the censor acquired another duty: to maintain public morals. If the censor declared a man guilty of immorality, he could not only strike that man from the voting rolls, but could deprive him of other rights, even throw him out of the Senate. The censorship began with a high purpose, but quickly devolved into a political tool, a way to punish enemies and destroy careers."

Lucius shook his head. "I still don't understand. Domitian already can install any man he wants in the Senate, or remove any man he pleases. And what do the senators matter, anyway? They have no real power. Never mind that pathetic decree they recently passed—'It is forbidden for the principal officer of the state to put to death any of his peers.' The notion that the emperor is the first among equals is a fantasy, and the idea that they can constrain him with laws is wishful thinking. So why does Domitian want to make himself censor for life?"

"The office will provide him with a new and very powerful tool. Consider: if the emperor wishes to punish an enemy or a rival, and does so for no purpose but to protect his own authority, he acts as a tyrant. Conversely, he could charge his enemy with a real crime, like embezzling or murder, but that would require producing actual evidence. But in his role as censor, Domitian can cast himself as the guardian of public morality, acting for the good of everyone."

"What constitutes an immoral act?"

"A list of offenses is being drawn up even as we speak. I saw an early draft. It includes adultery, which is defined as any sexual act performed by a married person which takes place outside the marriage."

"But that's absurd! Domitian himself slept with married women when he was younger. One of those women was the empress, who divorced her husband to marry him."

"Domitian will also revive the old Scantinian law."

"Refresh my memory.

"It outlaws sexual acts between men in which a freeborn male is the penetrated partner."

"Half the members of the imperial court consort with eunuchs!"

"Ah, but everyone assumes it's the eunuchs who are penetrated, which is perfectly legal, since they're all either slaves or freedmen. It's the Roman citizen who plays the passive role who'll be vulnerable to prosecution."

Lucius frowned. "Domitian seriously intends to police the sexual behavior of every Roman citizen?"

"Augustus had such a proclivity. He was quite ruthless when it came to punishing what he considered immorality within his own family, especially among the women. To be sure, when it came to dictating the morals of the citizenry, Augustus generally preferred to rely on inducements rather than penalties, giving tax benefits to married men with children and so forth. But I fear Domitian will use his power as censor to inflict a great deal of suffering."

Lucius was not convinced. "Perhaps your fears are exaggerated. If Domitian wishes to make an example of a few particularly outrageous people—"

"But, Lucius, don't you see? That's what everyone thinks at the outset of such a crackdown: it will be the *other* people who suffer, the 'outrageous' ones, not me. False hope! Domitian sees enemies everywhere. The very fact that the Senate passed that decree, making it unlawful for the emperor to put a senator to death, makes him think they're plotting against him."

"So Domitian will seek to punish his enemies by accusing them of vice, rather than insurrection?"

"Exactly. A dossier will be kept on everyone of importance, and who in the Senate is such a paragon of virtue that he need never fear the censor's wrath?"

"What else is on the list of immoral acts?"

"Incest, which includes relations between uncles and aunts and nieces and nephews—the so-called 'crime of Claudius.' Also, carnal relations between a free woman and another man's slave—"

"But not between a woman and her own slave? Or between a man and another's man's slave?"

"Those acts were not listed on the draft I saw."

"What about fornication with a Vestal virgin?"

Epaphroditus turned pale. "There's no need for that to be on the list. It's a capital crime already."

Lucius began to pace. "How can anyone know what people get up to behind closed doors?"

"The censor will assume the right to know. Remember the banishment of the informers under Titus? Those days are over. Men and women who sell other people's secrets, even slaves who betray their masters, will flourish under the censor. Citizens arrested for breaking the moral laws can be questioned in whatever manner the censor sees fit, and their slaves will be interrogated under torture. Men found guilty will be encouraged to implicate others."

"Is that Domitian's only motivation for this moral legislation? To give himself a tool to terrorize people?"

"Who can say what's in his mind? He may genuinely believe that he can control the morals of his subjects, and wishes to do so."

"The hypocrite!"

"Yes; he had a wild youth, but licentious young men often become judgmental in later life, like supple reeds that turn brittle. The emperor is a bitter man. Everyone loved his brother; no one loves Domitian. His precious son died. His wife cuckolded him with an actor."

"So all Roma must suffer because of one man's disappointments?"

Epaphroditus sighed. "To be fair, not all the new moral legislation is punitive. Domitian plans to outlaw castration throughout the empire, as well as child prostitution. How strictly such laws can be enforced I don't know, but we can applaud the intent. The practice of buying up young boys, making the prettiest ones into eunuchs, and selling them for the pleasure of others is a cruel business. Domitian's distaste for the practice seems to be sincere. Many a young slave may be spared the loss of his manhood."

Lucius paced from one end of the garden to the other. "Thank you for the warning, Epaphroditus, but I assure you, no one knows about me and . . . the woman I love. Except you. And you would never tell."

"Any witness can be made to talk, Lucius, unless he has a weak heart and dies first."

Lucius felt the blood drain from his face. After a few mumbled words of farewell, he took his leave of Epaphroditus.

He walked aimlessly, his thoughts racing. The sun began to set. Shadows grew long. He found himself in the heart of the Forum, passing the round Temple of Vesta. The doors stood open. The light of the eternal hearthfire illuminated the marble interior with a soft orange glow. A shadow moved across the light; one of the Vestals was tending the flame. Was it Cornelia? He longed to run up the steps and look inside—the merest glimpse of her face would calm his racing heartbeat—but he forced himself to turn and walk on.

"Lucius, could you add more wood to the brazier?" Cornelia shivered inside her heavy cloak and drew it more tightly around her neck.

The little house on the Esquiline was unchanged since the last time they had met there, many months ago. Lucius had considered selling the house but could not bear to do so; nor did he rent it out. He had kept it vacant, and just as it was in the days when they were meeting regularly. A slave came occasionally to tend to the garden and to clear the cobwebs, and every so often Lucius visited the house, alone, to walk through the rooms and the garden, remembering the times he had spent here with Cornelia.

He could hardly believe she was here again.

The winter day was windy and overcast. Even at midday the room was full of shadows. Lucius fetched wood for the brazier. They sat in chairs across from each other, shivering inside their clothes. He could not recall a meeting in this house when they had not been naked and making love within minutes of arriving. But they had not come here for pleasure. The chill in the air matched their moods.

The thing they most feared had come to pass—and yet they were both still alive. It was Cornelia who had contacted him, insisting that they meet again, despite the danger. He could not refuse her.

In anticipation of this meeting, he had passed a sleepless night imagining their reunion. His heart would race at the sight of her; he would embrace her; she would weep and speak of her suffering; he would listen, and share the terror of his own experience. They would find comfort once again in each other's bodies.

But that was not what happened. When he entered the house and found her waiting, with only a feeble fire in the brazier to warm the room, they kept their distance. There seemed to be an invisible barrier between them, not only keeping them apart physically but blunting their emotions. They were not like strangers—that could never happen—but they were not like lovers, either. They were mutual survivors of a disaster, numb with shock. The terror they had experienced eclipsed the passion that had once united them.

They seemed unable to approach each other physically, nor were they able to speak of the reason for their meeting, at least not at first. They began by skirting the subject. They talked as any two acquaintances might, about the latest news, keeping their voices steady and quiet. Of course, all the news was about the emperor and the emperor's schemes.

"Remember what Titus said, about the powerlessness of words to harm the powerful? 'It is impossible for me to be insulted.'" As he spoke, Lucius loaded more pieces of wood onto the brazier, stacking them carefully so that they would ignite quickly and burn with a minimum of smoke. The simple task calmed him. "Domitian has drawn up a list of plays that can no longer be performed, either because they offend the dignity of the emperor or undermine public morals. And all new plays must be read and approved by the censor himself. We have an emperor who scrutinizes comedies as if they were manifestos against the state."

"Surely someone reads the plays for him," said Cornelia. Her tone of voice was almost normal, only slightly strained. She looked not at Lucius but into the fire.

"Domitian has a whole staff dedicated to combing through every play, discourse, and poem produced on the Street of the Scribes, but he himself makes the final judgment. He fancies himself a writer, you know. Only he can judge the seditious intent of other writers. He's mounted a campaign against slander, as well. Apparently there are too many scurrilous lampoons making the rounds. I don't mean ditties that insult the emperor—no one is mad enough to do that—but the kind of verses recited at drunken dinner parties, harmless doggerel making fun of the host or hostess, teasing a man for having skinny legs or a woman for putting too much paint on her face. 'The dignity of distinguished men and women must not be impugned,' says the censor. So we have poets being whipped and then thrown onto ships headed for Ultima Thule."

"And men of importance must not compromise their own dignity," said Cornelia. "Only yesterday he expelled a man from the Senate. The fellow had appeared in a play during one of the festivals and danced in public."

"And to think, we once had an emperor whose highest aspiration was to act on the stage." Lucius attempted a smile, but wondered what his face must look like. She glanced at him only briefly, then looked away, as if it pained her to look at him.

"He's also drawn up a list of 'notorious women'—alleged fortune hunters who prey on rich old men," said Cornelia. "Those women are not only banned from receiving inheritances, they can no longer use a litter to cross the city. 'If they must seduce and rob old men instead of living within their means, let them go about their shameless business on foot,' says the censor. I happen to know a few of the women on the list. They're not harpies or sirens. One is a widow of noble birth whose brothers have all died and whose husband left her destitute. The fact that a certain senator wishes to pay her rent and provide for her in his will shouldn't constitute a crime."

"Soon a man won't be allowed even to give a pair of earrings to his lover," said Lucius. "What will become of the time-honored Roman tradition of keeping a mistress? How are those women supposed to support themselves? And what pleasure remains in life for those rich old men?"

"You sound like your friend Martial." Cornelia managed a semblance of a smile. The room was beginning to grow warmer. She loosened her cloak at the neck and sighed.

"Actually, I *don't* sound like Martial, and that's a sad thing," said Lucius. "He's changed."

"How?"

"We don't see him as often as we used to. He's always at some court function these days, or at home in his little apartment, scribbling his verses. He still shows up at Epaphroditus's house every now and then, but when he does he's very cautious about what he says, just as we're careful what we say around him. Martial used to joke about the emperor's 'bed wrestling,' his sour expression, even his baldness, but no more. Martial has become the emperor's favorite—every poet's dream—only to discover that his role requires an almost impossible balancing act. He must amuse and flatter his patron and produce the cleverest possible poem on whatever topic Domitian chooses, but he must never produce a pun or metaphor or hyperbole that might offend the censor."

"It's too bad Martial has been muzzled," said Cornelia. "We could use a poet with teeth to record the absurdities of these days. Did you hear about the citizen who was struck from the jury rolls? He charged his wife with adultery and divorced her, but then he took her back—just as Domitian did. The censor decreed that a man who couldn't make up his mind about his own wife should never be allowed to judge his fellow men. And so we have a man who divorced his wife and took her back declaring that a man who divorced his wife and took her back is unfit to judge other men."

She laughed, but the laughter caught in her throat. She stared at the fire. Watching flames was a familiar occupation for her.

"Does the flame remind you of Vesta's eternal hearthfire?" he said quietly.

"Yes."

"What of your faith, Cornelia?"

She took a long time to answer. "I remain steadfast in my devotion to Vesta—despite what's happened."

They had finally arrived at the subject they had come to talk about. Lucius moved a few steps closer to her and joined her in gazing at the fire. "What happened to Varronilla and the Oculata sisters was unspeakable," he said.

Cornelia drew a deep breath. "People say Domitian was merciful. The punishments could have been worse. Much, much worse."

Her hollow, emotionless voice seemed to be that of another woman, a stranger. He knelt beside her and took her hand. Her fingers were frigid.

"Cornelia, we don't have to talk about it."

"No, I want to talk. I want to tell you everything. Oh, Lucius, how I longed to speak to you every day, while it was happening—but you were the one man I couldn't possibly talk to." She spoke at last in a normal voice, full of sorrow and pain; the sound of it broke his heart. For the first time, he felt that the woman in the room with him was Cornelia, his Cornelia, the woman he had loved so long and so devotedly.

She wept. He put his arm around her. She fought back her tears.

"It all happened so suddenly. In the middle of the night, armed men appeared at the entrance of the House of the Vestals. They blocked the exits—as if we were criminals and might try to flee. They were led by a man named Catullus, one of the emperor's oldest friends. Remember his name, Lucius! A tall, thin man with pale, mottled skin and a gaunt face. Everything about Catullus is as cold as ice, except his eyes. The way he looked at me, I felt I was made of straw. I thought his gaze would set me on fire."

She shuddered. Lucius held her and said nothing, letting her speak at her own pace.

"They assembled the household slaves and took them into custody, dressed in their nightclothes. I'm not sure where they took them, but we later learned they were tortured—all of them, from the youngest to the oldest, from the accountant who kept records for the Virgo Maxima to the half-witted slave who emptied chamber pots. 'You never know which slaves will yield the most damning evidence'—so Catullus said at the trial. And by law, the testimony of any slave must be obtained by torture, even the slaves of a religious order like the Vestals. Some of the slaves died from the torture; they were too old to endure it. Others were maimed for life.

"Four of us were accused of breaking our vows of chastity: Varronilla, the Oculatae, and myself. I'm not sure why I was accused. They had no evidence against me, as it turned out. But I didn't know that at the time. I racked my brain, trying to imagine what they knew and how they found out. We were always so careful, you and I! Or had they simply invented something, and intended to make their case using false evidence, against which I could offer no possible defense? We were taken to the Regia, the ancient house of the Pontifex Maximus in the Forum, and confined to a small room. I didn't dare say anything to the others for fear that Catullus or one of his henchman was listening from some place of concealment.

"The trial took place in the Regia. Domitian presided, not in his role as censor but as Pontifex Maximus. All the Vestals and a great many priests were there. Catullus presented the evidence.

"Poor Varronilla! There was no question of her guilt. She had been very careless, confiding in one of the slaves, even telling the woman the name of her lover. The Oculata sisters were even more flagrant. They shared the same lover, at the same time, and were seen coming and going outside his house. The lovers of Varronilla and the Oculatae had already confessed, but they were made to appear before the court and repeat their testimony.

"Before Domitian rendered his judgment against those three, the Virgo Maxima begged him to be lenient. He told her she should be ashamed of herself, that she was running the House of the Vestals as if it were a brothel. But he offered conditional clemency: if the accused Vestals would admit their guilt, he would forgo the traditional punishment—being buried alive—and allow them to choose their own form of death. Varronilla and the Oculatae agreed. They confessed before the court, with Catullus asking questions. He forced them not only to name their lovers but to recount each of the occasions on which they broke their vows and to describe the specific acts in which they engaged, no matter how intimate or embarrassing—which parts of their bodies had been touched and penetrated, and in what positions, and what acts they had performed to please their lovers.

"After Catullus had wrung every humiliating detail from Varronilla and the Oculatae, he allowed them to step down. During all this time, no one had questioned me or even mentioned my name, except in the initial reading of the charges. I almost thought they had forgotten me. But they were saving me for last.

"No witnesses were called against me. How could there be witnesses, when not a single slave in the House of the Vestals knew anything of our affair, and no slave of yours had ever seen me in this house? Catullus called on me to name my lover and confess. If I did so, he said, I would be spared like the others from being buried alive and be allowed to choose my own form of death.

"I told him I had nothing to say. Domitian rose from his chair and stood before me. 'If you confess now, at this moment, you will be spared the traditional punishment. But this is your last chance. If subsequent evidence goes against you, and you are pronounced guilty, you will be buried alive. What do you say, Vestal?'

"Still I said nothing. But I thought: they must have Lucius; they must be holding him just outside this room. If I fail to confess, Catullus will parade Lucius before me, and my lover will tell them everything, and I shall be buried alive. How close I came to confessing! I was terrified. The suspense was unbearable. I could have ended it by telling Domitian what he wanted to hear. I had only to utter a few words, and it would be over.

"But I held fast. I said nothing. Catullus took Domitian aside and whispered in his ear. Domitian announced that I was to be taken to a private chamber, stripped, and examined to determine whether or not I was a virgin. He himself, in his role as Pontifex Maximus, would conduct the investigation, with the Virgo Maxima as witness."

Lucius felt physically ill, imagining the scene. He shuddered.

"No, Lucius, it didn't happen. The Virgo Maxima stood up to him. She said that such a procedure, carried out against a Vestal who maintained her innocence and against whom there was no evidence of wrongdoing, would be an offense against Vesta. The priests agreed. As timid as they are, almost all of them stepped forward to object. Even Domitian could see he had gone too far. He backed down. But he was furious. So was Catullus. Every time that man looked at me, I felt naked.

"Domitian dropped the charges against me. The Virgo Maxima counted that as a small victory. I still don't know why I was accused, since they could produce no evidence against me. I think someone must have accused me anonymously, someone who may have suspected me without knowing enough to testify. Perhaps they thought I might confess simply from fear. I very nearly did."

Lucius nodded slowly. "I think this Catullus was your accuser. Had you ever seen him before?"

"I must have, as part of the emperor's entourage. I never took any notice of him."

"But I'll wager he noticed you. A man like that, lusting after a woman he can't have, will use whatever influence he has to get her under his control."

"He very nearly drove me to my death."

"You're a Vestal, Cornelia. Beautiful, aloof, unobtainable. There are men who would take perverse pleasure from destroying a woman like you. That may be exactly what Catullus wanted, to see you stripped naked and humiliated."

"He failed, then. But he did manage to destroy Varronilla and the Oculata sisters. They were returned to their cell. The Virgo Maxima obtained a fast-acting poison for them. They died before sundown."

"And their lovers?"

"Because they freely confessed, Domitian was lenient. Instead of being hung on crosses and being beaten to death with rods, they were stripped of their property and citizenship and sent into exile—a punishment no more severe than those Domitian hands out to slanderers and adulterers. But, Lucius, what of you? When you heard about the arrests, you must have been terrified."

"My suffering was nothing compared to yours, Cornelia."

"Even so—"

"It isn't worth speaking of."

In fact, the days and nights immediately after he learned of the accusations against the Vestals had been the longest of his life. At every moment he had expected a knock at his door. The punishment for a despoiler of a Vestal haunted his nightmares; sleep became impossible. He considered fleeing to one of his country estates, or even taking an outbound ship from Ostia, heading for the Euxine Sea and land of the Dacians to join Dio, but the futility of such an enterprise stopped him; if Domitian wanted to arrest him, there would be no escape, and sudden flight would be as good as a confession. Nor could he abandon Cornelia. If he should be arrested, he would refuse to testify, even if he was tortured—so he told himself—and if he was executed, he would die with the knowledge that he had not betrayed Cornelia.

He talked to no one about the arrests and upcoming trial, not even Epaphroditus. If he was being watched and followed, anyone with whom he had contact might fall under suspicion.

The date for the trial of the Vestals arrived, and still Lucius was a free man. All that day, he expected soldiers to come and arrest him. As he did every day, he dispatched his freedman Hilarion to go down to the Forum to deliver messages and bring back the day's news. Late that afternoon, Hilarion finally returned. He quoted the latest price for grain from Alexandria. He also mentioned that another play had been added to the censor's list, though he could not remember the title.

"Oh, and what else?" said Hilarion, scratching his head. "Oh yes, the Pontifex Maximus has rendered his judgment of the accused Vestals."

"Yes?" Lucius tried to control the quaver in his voice.

"All were pronounced guilty—except one."

"Is that right?" Lucius could hardly breathe. "Which Vestal was that?"

Hilarion thought for a moment. "Cornelia Cossa is her name. She was acquitted."

Lucius could hardly believe his ears. He was as stunned by the news as if Cornelia had been found guilty. He felt faint. Hilarion asked if he was alright.

"I could use a bit of wine. Would you fetch it yourself, Hilarion?"

As soon as Hilarion left the room, Lucius had burst into tears.

He had longed to contact her, but did not dare to. Then one day a message arrived, written on a scrap of parchment and carried by a street urchin. "Meet me tomorrow" was all it said, but Lucius knew who had sent it and what it meant. And so they were together again at last, after so many months apart.

Lucius shook his head. "If Catullus was responsible for your arrest, he won't give up. He'll be watching and waiting for another chance to ruin you. He may be watching even now. He may have seen you come here. It was madness for us to meet again."

"I had to see you, Lucius."

"And I had to see you, Cornelia."

He touched her face. He kissed her.

Both of them had arrived expecting their tryst to be chaste, a meeting to talk and share their suffering, to acknowledge the terrible danger they had escaped and to say a final farewell; but the strain of their ordeal culminated in a physical desire beyond anything they had experienced before. Their union was more than a simple coupling of bodies; it was an affirmation that they were still alive. Lucius was shaken to the core of his being. He experienced a blissful release such as he had never imagined. He knew this would not be the last time they met.

Much later, as he was walking home alone and the haze of lust began to lift and he could think clearly again, the irony of the situation struck him so forcefully that he laughed out loud. Domitian's relentless campaign for public morals had driven him back into the arms of a Vestal virgin.

A.D. 88

It was the fifth day before the Ides of Junius, the twentieth anniversary of the death of Titus Pinarius.

As he did every year on this date, Lucius conducted a simple ritual of remembrance before the wax effigy of his father that occupied a niche in the vestibule of his house on the Palatine. He was attended only by the freedman Hilarion, who had been his father's favorite and who cherished the memory of his old master. In the years since he had been manumitted, Hilarion had married and started his own family, and in many ways was a more devout Roman than Lucius, observing all the holidays and the customary rituals for the benefit of his children. Lucius, since he had little interest in religion and had created no family of his own, observed few ceremonies throughout the year, but he never neglected to note the day of his father's death.

As happened every year, he felt a little guilty as he honored the memory of his father. At the age of forty, Lucius had not produced an heir; after he died, who would continue to honor the memory of his father and all his other ancestors? Two of Lucius's three sisters had children, but they were not Pinarii.

It was also the twentieth anniversary of the death of Nero.

That anniversary was not especially significant for Lucius, except as it related to his own father's death, but it meant a great deal to Epaphroditus.

To observe the occasion, he had asked Lucius to join him at the tomb of Nero on the Hill of Gardens.

It was a mild, clear day. Lucius decided to walk rather than be carried in a sedan. He told Hilarion to spend the rest of the day with his family if he wished, and set out alone.

Leaving his house, Lucius gazed up at the massive new wings that had recently been added to the imperial palace. Domitian had so enlarged the complex that it now occupied not just the whole southern portion of the Palatine but much of the rest of the hill. He had also given the complex a name; as Nero had called his palace the Golden House, so Domitian called his palace the House of the Flavians. The public rooms were said to be enormous, with soaring vaulted ceilings, while the rooms and gardens where the emperor actually resided were said to be surprisingly small and to lie deep within the palace, accessible only by secret doorways and hidden passages.

Lucius descended the Stairs of Cacus and crossed the marketplace and the Forum. He walked along the huge, cordoned-off area where a saddle of land connecting the Quirinal Hill to the Capitoline was being excavated to make room for a grand new forum that would facilitate passage from the center of the city to the Field of Mars. The amount of earth being removed was staggering; the buildings that would fill such a space would have to be constructed on a truly monumental scale. This new forum was without doubt the most ambitious of the emperor's building projects, but it was only one of many. Structures could be seen going up all over the city, and a great many older buildings, still damaged from the fires under Nero and Titus, were at last being restored. Everywhere he went in Roma, Lucius saw cranes and scaffolding and heard foremen shouting orders to their work gangs. The incessant banging of hammers echoed from all directions.

Everywhere, too, he saw the image of the emperor. Monumental statues of Domitian had been placed at every important intersection and in every public square. The statues were of bronze, decorated with gold and silver, and invariably portrayed the emperor in the ornate armor of a triumphing general. Walking across the city, a man was never out of sight of a statue of the emperor; from certain spots, one could see two or even three of them in the distance. There was no place in Roma where a citizen could escape the stern gaze of Domitian.

Along with his statues, Domitian erected commemorative arches all over the city, little replicas of the vast Arch of Titus in the Forum ornamented in the same excessively decorated style. On many of these arches, some brave, seditious wit had scrawled a graffito that consisted of a single word, ARCI—which, when said aloud, could be taken either as the Latin word for "arches" or the Greek word, *arkei*, meaning "enough!"

Almost as ubiquitous as the statues and the arches, and built on a massive scale, were the altars to Vulcan that Domitian had erected all over the city. The altars had been pledged by Nero, who as Pontifex Maximus had promised that propitiations to Vulcan would prevent a reoccurrence of the Great Fire. Nero had poured his energies into the building of the Golden House instead, and in the chaos that followed his death the plans for the altars had been lost. Vespasian had never seen fit to revive the project, and the result, many thought, had been the extensive fire that damaged the city, especially the Field of Mars, under Titus. Titus renewed the vow to build the altars, but he died before he could commence construction. It was Domitian who at last built the altars. They were enormous, carved from solid blocks of travertine more than twenty feet wide. On the days that animals were sacrificed to Vulcan, huge plumes of smoke could be seen all over the city as the priests appealed to the god to prevent another conflagration.

The devastation of the Field of Mars had allowed Domitian to rebuild the area to his liking. As Lucius crossed the flat expanse, he saw the new temples that dominated the skyline, along with a vast stadium for athletic contests and a grand theater called the Odeum, intended for musical performances, not for plays. Domitian had banned the public presentation of plays altogether.

As Lucius began to ascend the Hill of Gardens, he saw that a number of other people were walking in the same direction. He noticed more people, and yet more, all converging on the same spot, the street that ran in front of Nero's family cemetery, which was surrounded by a stone wall. Many in the crowd were dressed in black, as if in mourning. Some carried garlands of flowers.

Most of these people were his age or older—in other words, old enough to remember the days of Nero. Having raised no children, Lucius sometimes forgot that a whole generation had come up behind him that knew only the Flavians. But the predominance of people in their forties or older made the scattered younger faces in the crowd stand out all the more. The older people tended to look serious and somber, while the younger ones exuded a buoyant air of celebration.

Seeing his perplexed expression, a smiling young girl seized Lucius's arm. Her clothes were worn but she looked freshly scrubbed, as if she had just come from the baths. She had shimmering red hair and carried a garland of daffodils, violets, and poppies. "Smile, friend!" she said. "Have you not heard the good news?"

"What news?"

"He's coming back!"

"Who?"

"The Divine Nero, of course."

Lucius cocked his head. "I don't recall the Senate voting divine honors to that particular emperor."

"What does it matter, whether or not a bunch of old fools vote to call a god a god? Nothing the Senate says can change the truth that Nero is a living god."

"*Was* a living god, you mean?"

"No!" She laughed and rolled her eyes. "Didn't you hear what I said? He's coming back, from the East, where he's been living all this time. He'll be here any day now, to reclaim his rightful place as emperor. He shall rebuild the Golden House, and bring about a new Golden Age."

Lucius stared at her blankly. The girl was quite pretty, even if she was deluded.

She laughed and shook her head. "I see you're a doubter. Never mind. Put this on his monument today. When he comes, he will know and be pleased with you." She pulled a daffodil from the garland and handed it to him.

He took the flower from the girl, managed a halfhearted smile, and moved farther into the crowd. Some of the people stood idle and held on to their garlands, waiting for the sepulcher to be opened to the public. Others, who could not stay, were moving as close as they could to lay their garlands against the high wall of stone that surrounded the gravesite. Jostled on all sides, Lucius looked around, hoping to spot Epaphroditus amid the crowd. A wooden gate in the wall opened on creaky hinges and a familiar voice called his name.

Epaphroditus gestured to him from the narrow doorway. Lucius stepped inside. Epaphroditus closed the gate behind him.

"What a crowd!" said Lucius, happy to escape the crush. "Does this happen every year?"

"Yes and no," said Epaphroditus. "Every year people come to deliver garlands and perform ceremonies of remembrance, but I've never seen so many before. It's because it's the twentieth anniversary, I suppose."

They were alone inside the stone enclosure. Nero's was not the only tomb—this was the family plot of his ancestors on his father's side—but it was by far the most impressive. The ornate sepulcher containing his ashes was sculpted from rare white porphyry. Before it stood an altar of Luna marble. The exquisite carvings of horses on all four sides were doubly appropriate, since Nero had loved to ride, and horses were a funerary symbol from the most ancient times. Flowers had been laid on the altar, where a smoldering bit of incense overpowered their fragrance with its cloying scent.

"I see you've already honored the dead," said Lucius.

"I'm sorry I didn't wait for you, Lucius. I have my own key to the gate and let myself in. I wasn't sure when you'd arrive and I wanted to say a prayer before the gate is opened to the public. In a little while, the people out there will be allowed to pass by the sarcophagus and lay their garlands."

"There are hundreds of people out there."

Epaphroditus shook his head. "Like most people, they have the ability to believe two things at once. They will gladly tell you that Nero never died, yet here they are, marking the anniversary of his death and bringing garlands to his tomb. Nero is dead, yet Nero lives."

"And he's on his way to Roma right now. Someone just gave me the news, and told me I should make ready for his arrival."

"A young redhead?"

"Yes, quite pretty and carrying a garland."

"The same girl talked to me earlier. I didn't have the heart to tell her

that I was present when Nero died—much less that he died by my hand."
Epaphroditus frowned. "Curiously enough, my contacts in the imperial
house tell me there actually *is* an impostor claiming to be Nero, somewhere in Syria. He's not the first such pretender, but this one appears to
have serious backing from the Parthians, who may actually give the fellow
some military support and make an incursion. If that happens, Domitian
is worried that this Nero pretender might cause considerable mischief in the
Eastern provinces. There are still a great many people, especially in Judaea,
who hate the Flavians—the ones Vespasian and Titus didn't manage to
kill or enslave. And people in that part of the world are always talking
about the dead coming back to life."

"Who is this impostor?"

"I have no idea. The people who've seen him say he sings like a lark
and looks the very image of Nero."

"But do these people consider that Nero would be in his fifties now?"

Epaphroditus laughed wistfully. "He would be quite fat and bald, I
imagine."

"How can people believe such a thing, so fervently?"

"Because, Lucius, without the discipline of philosophy to give rigor to
their thinking, people can and will believe anything, no matter how absurd. Indeed, the more far-fetched the notion, the more likely they are to
believe it. People have grown weary of Domitian. They enjoy the fantasy
that Nero will return."

"Bringing with him a new Golden Age?"

"Why not? Some of the older people out there actually remember the
reign of Nero, and they'll tell you how wonderful it was—though I suspect the nostalgia they feel is not so much for Nero as for their own lost
youth. And the younger ones have the natural propensity of youth to believe that a Golden Age must have existed somewhere, at some time—
most likely just before they were born—so why not in the days of Nero?"

"Does that mean that a generation from now, people will look back to
a so-called Golden Age of Domitian?"

"That's hard to imagine!"

"I wouldn't be so sure," said Lucius. "On the walk here, I saw the hand of
the emperor everywhere. His statues, his temples and altars and arches—"

"*Arkei!*" said Epaphroditus. "People have had enough of Domitian look-ing over their shoulders."

"Do you think so? He pleased the people greatly when he added that tier to the Flavian Amphitheater. You admired the monstrosity before, Epaphroditus, and now there's more of it to love than ever. No one in Roma need go without a seat."

"But he banned the public performance of plays," said Epaphroditus.

"Every actor must suffer for the sin of Paris! But do the people mind? I think not. Why should they wish to see stodgy old dramas and stale com-edies when Domitian gives them games instead, and not just games, but the most spectacular ever staged. His marvels eclipse even those his brother presented. He floods the amphitheater and stages full-scale naval battles, with convicts and slaves fighting for their lives and drowning before our eyes. What play could possibly match such a spectacle? He gives the people freakish delights, like the gladiator shows he holds at night where naked women and dwarves are forced to fight one another by torchlight. What comedy could make people laugh half that much? And from the sky above, figs, dates, and plums rain down on the audience. The spectators think they've died and awoken in Elysium."

"And all the while the emperor sits in his box," said Epaphroditus, "ac-companied by that creature with a too-small head. Is it a child? A dwarf? Is it even human? The two of them whisper to each other and giggle." He shuddered. "Nero loved beauty and perfection, and his taste in all things was impeccable. Domitian loves excess—too much decoration, too much ornament—and he surrounds himself with human oddities. His behavior at the games is appalling. Do you remember the day the sky turned black and a tremendous storm blew up? The wind and rain were so fierce that the awnings were useless, and people began to leave the amphitheater. Domitian ordered his soldiers to block the exits. People weren't even al-lowed to take shelter in the stairwells and passages. All Roma sat there and endured the deluge. And when a roar of complaint filled the amphi-theater, the emperor angrily demanded silence—and got it, after enough of the offenders had been thrown into the arena to join the convicts about to be gored by a herd of rampaging aurochs."

Lucius nodded. "What a bizarre moment that was, sitting in the pouring rain with fifty thousand others, and no one saying a word, while thunder rumbled and lightning tore the sky and men screamed and died down in the arena. Say what you like, it was unforgettable, a day like no other—just what people crave when they go to the amphitheater. The games are more popular than ever."

"Because Domitian has reduced the Roman people to the level of dogs. They remain faithful even when their master beats them, as long as he also feeds them."

"He has the loyalty of the legions as well," said Lucius, "and that's where true power lies. It was only when Nero lost control of the legions that he came undone. Nero never led the legions into battle, as Domitian has. And those legions are as loyal to Domitian as they were to his father and his brother. He pays the soldiers well and exempts the veterans from paying taxes."

"But his wars in Germania and Dacia have ended in stalemates, at best. The death of his general Fuscus and the loss of an eagle standard to the Dacians was a catastrophe."

"Which Domitian turned to his advantage," said Lucius. "Just when the threat from Germania had grown stale, the Dacians became the new enemy for Romans to fear and despise. And despite his limited success, he still staged triumphs for himself, parading through the Forum as a conqueror."

"Though no one is quite sure what he's conquered. Did you hear the rumor about the supposed captives who were paraded in chains in the German triumph? A source in the imperial household told me they were actually the biggest and brawniest slaves from the palace, dressed in leather pants and blond wigs to look like Germans."

"That's the problem with Domitian, isn't it?" said Lucius. "We never know what's real and what's not. All the city is a stage. Everything that happens is a spectacle put on by the emperor. One wonders if he himself knows any longer what's real."

"He now signs official letters with the title Dominus and Deus," said Epaphroditus. "That makes him the first emperor since Caligula to demand to be addressed as the people's master, and also the first since Caligula to consider himself a living god. He renames months in his honor. We celebrate his birthday not in October but in Domitianus, which is preceded not by September but by Germanicus, in honor of his German triumphs. He goes everywhere accompanied by a huge bodyguard of lictors and wears the costume of a triumphing general on formal occasions, even when he addresses the Senate and should be dressed in a toga, as the first among equals. The laurel wreath hides his baldness."

"But how can he afford all this—the spectacles, the generous pay for his soldiers, the massive construction projects?"

"That's a bit of a mystery," said Epaphroditus. "My sources tell me he manages the treasury himself, obsessively scrutinizing even the smallest expenditures; not a nail is bought without Domitian's approval. As you can imagine, the accountants and bursars are terrified of him. There's a good side to that: Domitian has put an end to the corruption and self-enrichment that were so rampant in the flush, freewheeling years of his father's reign. But my old friends at the treasury believe that the state is headed for bankruptcy, and when that happens, the emperor will hold them to blame. They're like men awaiting a death sentence, watching sand run through the hourglass—only in this case it's sesterces running through the emperor's fingers. They were all hoping that Fuscus might actually conquer Dacia and capture King Decebalus's treasure, but now there seems no likelihood of that happening.

"Master and God he may call himself, but Domitian fears his underlings as much as they fear him. He sees conspiracies everywhere. Senators are put to death for chance remarks that only a madman would find suspicious. He's become deeply superstitious: he fears not just daggers and poisons, but enchantments. Did you hear about the woman who was executed because she was seen undressing before a statuette of the emperor? Presumably she was trying to bewitch him, using sex magic."

Epaphroditus placed his hands upon the sarcophagus of Nero, feeling the coolness of the polished stone. The last bit of incense on the altar had turned to ash, but its fragrance lingered on the air.

"Curiously," he said, "Domitian now has something in common with Nero that none of us expected: he's in love with a eunuch."

"No!"

"Oh yes. Remember the disdain he used to show for his brother's coterie of eunuchs, and the one laudable achievement of his campaign for morality, his ban on castration? Now Domitian has quite openly fallen in love with a eunuch. The boy's name is Earinus and he comes from Pergamum. A slave trader unsexed him here in Italy when he was very young, using the hot-water method."

"What is that?"

"The child sits in a vat of steaming water that softens the scrotum, then his testes are pressed between a finger and thumb until they're crushed. The method leaves no scar, which many owners find pleasing. The boys subjected to this method must be very young, and they subsequently develop fewer masculine attributes than those who are castrated later in life; some owners find that pleasing, also. A few years ago, Earinus was acquired by the imperial household, where all the most beautiful eunuchs end up. He has a face like Cupid. His hair is a very light blond, like white gold. He can sing, as well."

Lucius shook his head. "Imperial eunuchs are always said to have some talent, other than the purpose for which they were made."

"In the case of Earinus, the boy apparently has a true gift. When he sang for the emperor, Domitian fell for him at once. He dotes on Earinus shamelessly, showering him with gifts, dressing him in the costliest garments, anointing him with the rarest perfumes. For his seventeenth birthday, Domitian manumitted him and gave him a very generous endowment. To mark the occasion, Earinus sent a lock of his blond hair to a temple in Pergamum. It's a Greek custom for boys to donate a lock of hair to a temple in their native city when they attain manhood. You may remember that Nero did something of the sort, when he donated a clipping from his first beard to the Temple of Jupiter on the Capitoline.

"When Earinus sent off the lock of his hair, the court poets fell over one another in the rush to commemorate the event. Our dear Martial wrote some lines comparing Domitian to Jupiter and Earinus to Ganymede—no surprise there—but for sheer sycophancy his rival Statius outdid himself. Statius's poem is a veritable *Aeneid* of eunuch-worship. Listen to this."

Epaphroditus cleared his throat and declaimed.

> *All previous favorites and flocks of servants stand back*
> *As the new one carries to the mighty leader*
> *The heavy goblet of crystal and agate,*
> *Making the wine sweeter by the touch of his soft white hands.*

Boy dear to the gods, chosen the first to drink the vintage,
Blessed to touch so often that mighty right hand
Whose sway the Dacians yearn to know—

Epaphroditus broke off and made a retching sound. "Even Martial never stooped to writing anything as awful as that, though he's come perilously close."

"It's curious," said Lucius, "how a man as vicious as Domitian can lavish so much affection on a harmless, mutilated boy. It's almost as if Earinus were a pet."

"Earinus means 'springtime' in Greek. Domitian is almost forty now. Statius says Earinus restores Domitian's youth, though I imagine the boy only reminds him of it. But you put your finger on something, Lucius. They say the empress is quite aware of Domitian's passion and that she, too, is quite fond of Earinus. Why not? Better for her if Domitian spends his time courting a eunuch rather than the wife of some senator, or worse, an unmarried girl of childbearing age who might pester him to divorce his wife. The empress has yet to give Domitian another heir to replace his dead son; as long as he spills his seed with a eunuch, no one else will do so. For dynastic purposes, a eunuch is no rival at all. Earinus is more like a pet, as you say, a pretty creature whose company both of them can enjoy."

"Domitian! What do we make of the man?" said Lucius. "He's obsessed on the one hand with bureaucratic minutiae, but on the other with a morbid fear of plots and magic. He was once a promiscuous adulterer and now dotes on a eunuch, but he's determined to criminalize the 'bed wrestling' of others. And this is the man who shapes every facet of the world we live in. He's in the very air we breathe."

Epaphroditus sighed. "Enough about the emperor. What about you, Lucius?"

Lucius shrugged. "Nothing in my little world ever changes."

"Does that mean you're still seeing her?"

Lucius smiled. "We're like an old married couple nowadays—if you can imagine a couple married in secret who see each other only a few times a year. The passion is still there, but it burns more steadily, with a lower flame."

"Like the flame in Vesta's hearth?"

"If you like. She has even less time to see me, now that she's become the Virgo Maxima."

"At such a young age! How old is she now?"

"Thirty-two. And more beautiful than ever."

Epaphroditus laughed. "You don't sound like a married man to me. You still sound like a lover."

"I'm a very lucky man, to know such a woman. Ah, don't give me that look, Epaphroditus. You need not lecture me again about the risks. I believe I was blessed, not cursed, when Fortune led me to her. I would never have found a love like hers anywhere else."

"Truly, spoken like a lover. How do you spend the rest of your time?"

"When I'm not hunting at one of my estates, enjoying the fresh air and the thrill of the chase, I do what I must to maintain my fortune. Dealings in real estate and trade aren't exactly respectable activities for a patrician—large-scale agriculture or state service would be more suitable—but you know I've never been a status seeker. Hilarion does most of the actual work. He takes so much pleasure in moving numbers from one column to another, dictating letters to merchants, and issuing instructions to lawyers."

"Still no politics or public service for you, then?"

"Certainly not! More than ever, it seems to me that the only sensible strategy for a Roman citizen is to attract as little attention to himself as possible. So far, I've managed to stay beneath the notice of the emperor. I intend to keep it that way." Even as Lucius said these words, he felt that he was tempting Fate. He reached inside his toga and touched the fascinum.

Epaphroditus opened his mouth to say something, then seemed to change his mind.

"What is it?" said Lucius.

"I was wondering if you had heard about Catullus?"

Lucius drew a breath. "The emperor's henchman—the one who led the investigation against the Vestals?"

"And many other investigations in recent years. That seems to be his special gift, an ability to ferret out every secret act and utterance that could bring destruction to another mortal. How Domitian prizes him for it! But now a bit of misfortune has befallen Catullus. He fell gravely ill with a fever and almost died. He's back on his feet, completely recovered, but he's completely blind."

Lucius remembered what Cornelia had said about the man: *Everything about Catullus is as cold as ice, except his eyes. I thought his gaze would set me on fire.*

"But this is happy news," Lucius said, though his expression was grim. "Catullus—blind! You should have told me right away."

Epaphroditus pursed his lips. "Epictetus says that to feel joy at the suffering of another is a sin, like hubris; it invites the retaliation of the gods."

"Really? All Roma watches and applauds when thousands die in the arena, or when captives are strangled at the end of a triumph, and the gods seem to approve. Why should I not take a little satisfaction at the much-deserved downfall of a monster like Catullus?"

"I'm not sure that blindness has put an end to Catullus. Domitian still counts him among his closest advisers. They say the infirmity has only made him more dangerous."

Again Lucius felt a superstitious chill. He was reaching to touch the fascinum when they heard the jangling of a key in the lock. The gate opened and an attendant looked inside.

"I shall allow them to enter in a moment," the man said. "You might want to pay your last respects."

They turned their attention back to the sarcophagus. While Epaphroditus stood in silence with his hands folded and his eyes downcast, Lucius burned a bit of incense and placed the flower the girl had given him on the altar. He was not really thinking of Nero as he prayed, but of his father, and of Sporus.

They made their way to the gate. The attendant shouted at the crowd to make way for them. As Lucius stepped through the crush, surrounded by the smell of flowers, a hand gripped his arm.

It was the red-haired girl. "Don't forget," she cried. "Nero is coming, any day now. Oh, yes, any day now!"

A.D. 91

"Did you enjoy your stay in the country?"

"I did, Hilarion."

"Good hunting?"

"Typical for this time of year. Not much to shoot at but deer and rabbits. Still, beautiful countryside."

"And did you enjoy sleeping late this morning?"

"I did indeed. I was up at dawn every day in the country, but the journey home tired me out. Fortunately, here in the city a man can sleep until noon and miss nothing."

"And your visit to the baths this afternoon?"

"Very pleasant. I prefer the afternoon to the morning, especially at the Baths of Titus. It's less crowded, more relaxed. I actually spent an hour playing some silly board game with a complete stranger in one of the galleries, then took a final hot plunge. I feel quite clean and revived, ready for the rest of the day."

"There's not much of the day left, alas. The sun sets quite early. But we may still have an hour of sunlight in the study. I was hoping you might join me in reviewing the accounts from the granary outside Alexandria. There are a few discrepancies to which I'd like to draw your attention—"

"Not now, Hilarion."

"It won't take long."

"I'm off."

"To where, may I ask?"

"You may not."

"Perhaps this evening, by lamplight?" With a forlorn expression, Hilarion held up a scroll.

"Probably not, Hilarion. I may not be back until quite late."

"I see." Hilarion looked at Lucius's garments. The master of the house was not wearing a toga, but a brightly colored tunic short enough to show off his athletic legs and cinched with a leather belt with silver inlays around his waist, still trim at forty-four thanks to his recent regimen of riding and hunting all day and eating only what he could catch. Hilarion shook his head. It was obvious that the master of the house was going to see *her*— the woman whose existence Lucius had never acknowledged and whose identity Hilarion, very wisely, had never attempted to discover. Hilarion sometimes felt sorry for the old master's son. He himself was only a freedman, yet he had found a suitable woman to marry and together they had made some wonderful children.

As Lucius made ready to leave the house—alone, as he always did when he was going to meet his secret lover—he whistled the tune of an old hunting song. Hilarion went about his business.

It was a brisk autumn afternoon. Lucius took a roundabout route, occasionally glancing over his shoulder and doubling back. Long ago he had adopted such habits to make sure he was not being followed when he set out for the little house on the Esquiline.

As usually happened when he returned to Roma after an extended stay in the country, he found the city disgustingly dirty and noisy and smelly, full of unhappy and dangerous-looking people—and that was just in the Forum. Once he entered the Subura, he actually felt more relaxed, because, although the streets were more crowded and the people were dirtier, there were not quite so many statues of Domitian everywhere. That was the most unnerving thing about the first day or two back in Roma—the ubiquity of Domitian, Master and God, always watching him.

But even the inescapable images of the emperor could not dampen Lucius's mood on this day. Perhaps it was the nip of autumn in the brisk air that made Lucius feel half his age. Or perhaps it was the fact that he had not seen Cornelia in so very long—more than two months—and at last they had both found time to meet. He had received her cryptic message at the baths that afternoon, delivered as always by a street urchin selected at random who could not possibly know the identity of the woman who hired him or the meaning of the words he was told to repeat: "Today. An hour before sunset."

Shops in the better parts of town would already be closed, but many establishments in the Subura stayed open until it was dark, and Lucius had found that the quality of their foodstuffs was often as good as anything to be found in shops on the Aventine that charged four or five times as much. He bought some flatbread with a thick crust, a hard, smoked cheese, a little jar of his favorite garum, and a few other items. There would be wine and olives in the little house on the Esquiline, but no fresh food, and if experience was any guide, they would both have a ravenous appetite later. He left the Subura and ascended the hill, carrying a cloth bag with his provisions and whistling a happy tune.

He stopped whistling when he saw the Praetorians who loitered around the little reservoir called the Lake of Orpheus. The soldiers were armed and in uniform but appeared to be off duty. One of them had climbed amid the bronze statues in the fountain and was leaning against a deer that stood enraptured, ears pricked up to listen to Orpheus play his lyre.

What were Praetorians doing in this mostly residential area, with its mix of elegant homes, like that of Epaphroditus, and more modest but still respectable dwellings, like the little house Lucius kept? The sight of armed men was disturbing. He almost turned back, then thought of Cornelia, patiently waiting for him. He continued up a winding, narrow street. After a sharp turn, he saw the front of his house.

The door was wide open.

He turned around. The soldiers he had seen at the Lake of Orpheus had followed him. The foremost of them looked him in the eye. The man's expression was dispassionate but determined. With a nod and a slight gesture of his hand, the Praetorian made it clear that Lucius was to enter the house.

He passed through the vestibule and entered into the room beyond. Someone was sitting on the couch where he had expected to find Cornelia. The room was dim; it took his eyes a moment to adjust. The man on the couch was dressed like a member of the imperial court, in a lavishly embroidered robe with long sleeves. He wore a necklace with large pieces of carnelian and a ring of the same red stone on one finger. He turned to face Lucius, but there was a disconcerting blankness about his eyes, which seemed to fix on nothing. His face was gaunt. His skin was pale and mottled.

"Are you Lucius Pinarius?" the man said.

"I am."

"My name is also Lucius. I am Lucius Valerius Catullus Messalinus. Perhaps you've heard of me."

"Perhaps."

"Do I hear a quaver in your voice, Lucius Pinarius?"

There appeared to be no one in the room but the two of them. From a shadow on the wall Lucius could see that one of the Praetorians had followed him into the house and was standing in the vestibule.

"Your presence honors me, Catullus."

Catullus laughed. "How polite you are, Pinarius! Decorum would have me now say something complimentary about your home, but alas, I cannot see it. My other senses are quite sensitive, however. Do I smell, very faintly, a woman's perfume in this room? Or do I only imagine it?"

"There's no woman here, Catullus."

"No? And yet, I can almost feel her presence."

In the silence that followed, the items in the cloth bag made a slight rustling sound.

"What's that you carry?" said Catullus.

"Only a bit of food. May I offer you some, Catullus?"

Catullus laughed. "Oh, no, I never eat anything not prepared by my own cook, or that of the emperor, and tasted first by a slave. Such essential precautions are one of the drawbacks of my station in life. I would advise you not to eat any of that food, either."

"Why not?"

"Why spoil your appetite, when shortly you shall be dining in the House of the Flavians?"

"I will?" Lucius's voice cracked like that of a boy.

"That's why I'm here, Lucius Pinarius. To deliver an invitation from our Master and God. You are invited to dine with him. A sedan is waiting outside."

Lucius swallowed. "I'm not properly dressed. I'll need to go home first, to change into my best toga—"

"No need. The emperor will provide your clothing."

"He will?"

"This is to be a special dinner, requiring special dress. You need bring nothing. Shall we be off?"

Lucius looked around the room. Where was Cornelia? Had she arrived before him, seen the Praetorians, and left? Had she not come at all? Or—he could hardly bear the thought—had she been here when Catullus arrived?

Catullus called to the Praetorian, who assisted him as they stepped outside the house. Lucius pulled the door closed and produced his key.

"What are you doing?" said Catullus.

"Locking the door."

Catullus shrugged. "If you wish."

It seemed to Lucius that his meaning was clear: there was little need to lock a house to which a man would never return.

He was carried through the streets in a sedan that seated only himself. He made no attempt to converse with Catullus, who had his own sedan and was carried sometimes alongside him, sometimes in front, depending on the width of the street. Lucius found himself thinking of stories he had heard regarding the cruel games Domitian played with his victims, disarming them with gifts and tokens of friendship before subjecting them to hideous tortures. His favorite interrogation technique was to burn the genitals of his victims. His favorite punishment, short of death, was to cut off their hands.

The shortest route to the palace would have taken them close by the Flavian Amphitheater and the Colossus. Instead, they went through the Forum, passing by the House of the Vestals and the Temple of Vesta. Was this done deliberately to unnerve him? Surely it was, for when they at last ascended the Palatine, the bearers passed directly by Lucius's house. Catullus had to know exactly where they were; as they passed by the house, his sedan fell back alongside that of Lucius, and Catullus turned his head to Lucius and smiled, as if to taunt him with a final glimpse of his home.

The sedans deposited them at one of the entrances to the imperial palace. The reception chamber to which they were led, with its soaring ceiling, was grander than any room Lucius had ever seen before. Even the most ornately decorated temples could not compare with the opulence of the place, which was perhaps best seen at this hour of the day. The last of the fading sunlight from the high windows still lit the far corners, revealing the sheer scale and the astounding attention to detail, while a multitude of newly lit lamps gave a lustrous gleam to the polished surfaces of marble and bronze and caused the monumental statue of Domitian at the center of the chamber, covered with silver and gold, to sparkle with points of fiery light.

From the reception room they were shown through a series of equally opulent but increasingly smaller chambers, until Lucius found himself walking in single file behind Catullus, with a Praetorian directly behind him, through a narrow hallway faced with dark green marble on all sides; even the low ceiling was made of the same marble. If any daylight remained, it could not penetrate here; the way was lit only by feeble lamps set far apart in the walls. Lucius had the sense of having gone under ground, though they had descended no steps. He felt as if he were entering the tomb of some ancient king. The air grew stale and thin. He found it difficult to breathe.

Lucius was shown to a small side chamber, faced all around with the same dark green marble and lit by a single lamp, and was left alone to change his clothes. The garment laid out for him was a robe with long sleeves, not unlike the one Catullus was wearing, but solid black; even the embroidery around the hems was black. Reluctantly, Lucius took off his bright tunic, laid it aside, and picked up the robe. Then he gave a start and let out a stifled cry.

From nowhere, a boy had appeared. He was wearing black and had black hair, and his skin had been painted black as well. In the dimness of the room, Lucius had not seen the boy until he suddenly stepped forward, like an apparition from a nightmare.

"I am to be your cupbearer tonight, Master," said the boy, taking the robe from Lucius. "Allow me to help you dress, Master."

Dumbfounded, Lucius allowed the boy to help him put on the black robe. Then the boy took him by the hand and pushed against a spot on the marble wall. A door opened as if by magic, and the boy led him through.

Lucius found himself in a room without color. Every surface was black. The floor and the walls were of solid black marble. The small tables set about the room were made of black metal, as were the lamps, which emitted only the faintest light. The four dining couches gathered in a square were made of ebony and strewn with black pillows. One of the couches was larger and more ornate than the others.

Lucius detected a movement from the corner of his eye. He thought he had seen a door open in one of the black marble walls, but since no light was admitted from whatever room lay beyond, he was not sure until a figure entered, dressed like himself in black and led by a boy painted black. It was Catullus. Without a word, the man stood before the dining couch opposite the larger couch. He made a gesture to indicate that Lucius should stand before the couch to his right.

Another figure emerged from the doorway, led by another boy. Lucius let out a gasp that echoed sharply in the small room.

It was Cornelia.

She was dressed in a linen gown and a suffibulum headdress, much like the vestments she normally wore, except that these were solid black.

Their eyes met. The fear on her face mirrored his own. She raised a hand toward him; her fingers trembled. The gesture was a plea for help. Neither of them spoke, conscious of the blind Catullus, who indicated with a nod that Cornelia should stand before the couch to his left.

By the dim light, Lucius saw an upright stone marker leaning against the wall behind Cornelia's couch. Letters were engraved on the stone, but he could not make them out. He looked over his shoulder and saw that a similar stone marker was behind his own couch. The decorative engraving and the general shape were those of a grave marker. Chiseled into the stone was his own name.

Lucius saw spots before his eyes. The room seemed to sway and pitch. He thought he might fall, and looked for a way to steady himself. The cupbearer sensed his distress and took his hand. Lucius leaned against the boy, feeling faint and dizzy.

He was in such distress that he did not realize Domitian had entered the room until he saw the emperor half sitting, half reclining on the couch of honor. At first glance, the emperor appeared to be dressed in black, like everyone else, but on closer inspection Lucius saw that Domitian's robes were of a purple so dark as to be very nearly black, decorated with embroidery in the darkest possible shade of red. On his head he wore a black laurel wreath. The lamps cast their light in such a way that his eyes were hidden by deep shadows and could not be seen.

Attending the emperor was the small-headed creature who accompanied him at the games. The creature's face was oddly shaped and his features were wizened. Even seeing him so closely, Lucius could not tell if he was a child or a dwarf. Like the other cupbearers, he was painted entirely black.

Lucius realized that Catullus was reclining as well, and so was Cornelia, and everyone in the room was staring at him. Had he lost consciousness for a moment? His cupbearer hissed at him. The boy tugged his hand, urging him to sit.

Lucius lowered himself onto the couch. The cupbearer made a great fuss of fluffing pillows and arranging them for his comfort. A first course of black olives was served, along with crusts of a moist, black bread sprinkled with black poppy seeds. Wine was poured for him. In the cup, the wine looked pitch-black.

Meanwhile, in the space between the four couches, a group of young male dancers, painted black like the serving boys and wearing very little, performed a dance. The music was funereal, all shrill pipes and rattles. Lucius had no idea where it came from. The musicians were nowhere to be seen.

The dance seemed interminable. Lucius saw that Catullus was eating, but he himself had no appetite, and neither, he noticed, did Cornelia. Amid so much darkness, her face looked very pale. Nor did Domitian eat. He watched the dancers.

At last, with a wild trilling of pipes and a final flourish of rattles, the performance ended and the dancers dispersed. They seemed to vanish into the walls.

"An interesting fact, about funerals," said Domitian. He stared straight ahead. "In the old days, all funerals were performed at night, even those of great men. Nowadays, only the poor are buried at night, because they can afford no funeral procession. Funeral processions, in my view, are overrated, if only because they are all alike. First come the musicians, alerting everyone to the coming event, then the mourning women, usually hired, then the players and buffoons who imitate the deceased. Then come the slaves he freed, showing gratitude with tears and laments for their late master, and then the players who wear the wax masks of his ancestors, as if the dead have come back to life to welcome their descendant into their ranks. And then comes the dead man himself, carried on a bier on the shoulders of his nearest relatives, so that everyone can have a final look before he's laid on a pyre and burned. People throw all sorts of things on the fire—the dead man's clothes, his favorite foods, his most beloved books. Someone makes a speech. And when it's all over, the ashes are scooped up and put in a stone sarcophagus.

"Another interesting fact: in the old days, our ancestors didn't burn the bodies of the dead, but buried them intact. I'm told that the Christians favor this type of burial even today; they place some value on the corpse itself, expecting it to come back to life. But who would wish to come back to life after the body has begun to rot, especially to find oneself trapped in a stone box or buried under ground? Like most of the far-fetched ideas of the Christians, this one seems rather poorly thought out. We Romans no longer practice burial—except in the very special case of the inhumation of a Vestal guilty of breaking her vow of chastity. But in that event, the burial is not of a dead body, but of a body while it still breathes."

Catullus nodded. "That is the ancient penalty. But I recall that Caesar in his wisdom allowed a less severe punishment when the Oculata sisters and Varronilla were condemned a few years ago."

"I have been having second thoughts about that decision," said Domitian. "It is seldom advisable to abandon the wisdom of our ancestors. It was King Numa, the successor to Romulus, who founded the order of Vestals in Roma. The punishment he decreed for an errant Vestal was death by stoning."

"Is that a fact?" Catullus chewed an olive and spat the pit into the waiting palm of his cupbearer. "I never knew that."

"It was a later king, Tarquinius Priscus, who devised the penalty of death by inhumation. His argument was religious. 'Let no mortal kill a priestess of Vesta,' he declared. 'Let that decision be left to Vesta herself.' So the Vestal is alive when she's placed in that little vault under ground, and then the vault is sealed and the opening is covered over with dirt. No man commits the act of killing her, and she is given nothing with which she might commit the act herself. Time and the judgment of Vesta take care of her. I have been thinking that Tarquinius Priscus showed great wisdom in this matter, even exceeding that of Numa."

The first course was taken away. Each of the guests was given a plate of mushrooms and other fungi, all black thanks to the sauce in which they had been simmered. Again, only Catullus showed any signs of appetite. He ate with relish, sucking the sauce from his fingertips.

"As I recall," he said, "when Caesar judged the men who violated Varronilla and the Oculatae, he showed great leniency."

"Yes, I allowed them to live. I have been reconsidering the wisdom of that decision, too. It might have been wiser, I think, to enforce the traditional punishment for the seducer of a Vestal, as a deterrent to others who might be tempted to commit such a crime in the future. As Pontifex Maximus, I must do all I can to preserve the sanctity of those who keep Vesta's fire. Do you not agree, Virgo Maxima?"

For the first time, Domitian acknowledged Cornelia's presence. In a very faint voice, she replied, "Yes, Dominus."

"Tonight, you may address me as Pontifex Maximus," he said.

"Yes, Pontifex Maximus."

"That's better. Would you not agree, Virgo Maxima, that the traditional penalty makes for a powerful deterrent? The man is stripped naked, hung on a cross, and publicly beaten with rods, while the violated Vestal watches, until he is dead. I'm told that can take quite a while, depending on the man's general health. A man with a weak heart might die after the first blow. Others remain alive for hours. The beating can become quite tedious to administer, not to say tiring. Sometimes the lictors charged with the beating become so exhausted that new lictors have to be brought in to continue the punishment."

It seemed to Lucius that the plate of delicacies held before him by his cupbearer contained not fungi but a mixture of viscera and organs, swimming in a nameless fluid. He began to feel nauseated.

Black figs were served next, to all except Domitian. The servers brought him a single apple, together with a silver knife. Domitian set about peeling the apple very slowly and methodically, cutting away thin strips of the skin. He handed these to the small-headed attendant, who gobbled them up as a dog might eat scraps from its master's table. When Domitian bit into the apple, the noise was startling, like the cracking of bones.

Lucius again saw spots before his eyes. He heard a low noise. It was Domitian, whispering to the small-headed creature, who whispered back. The two of them laughed.

"We were wondering how it is, Catullus, that a man who is blind can burn with lust for another. Beauty inspires passion, but how can beauty be perceived without sight?"

Catullus turned his face to Cornelia. "A blind man may possess memories of beauty. A blind man has imagination."

"Ah, but beauty fades, Catullus; it is as short-lived as it is intoxicating. Your memories are surely out-of-date." Domitian stared at Cornelia, who lowered her face. "Beauty exists only in the moment. That is why I asked Earinus to entertain us tonight. Although you cannot see him, Catullus, I assure you that he is beautiful."

The eunuch entered the room, dressed in black. He was small and delicate and moved with such grace that he seemed to float across the floor. His pale hair, the subject of poets, was startlingly bright in the dark room; it seemed to glow with a light of its own. His skin was creamy white.

In the shadowy room, Earinus seemed to be an ethereal being from a realm of dreams. He stood in the center of the room and began to sing. The notes were pure and sweet, but also unsettling; his voice had an uncanny quality, impossible to categorize. The song, like the singer, seemed to emerge from some realm beyond ordinary experience.

> *What has death to frighten man,*
> *If souls can die as bodies can?*
> *When mortal frame shall be disbanded,*
> *This lump of flesh from life unhanded,*
> *From grief and pain we shall be free—*
> *We shall not feel, for we shall not be.*
> *But suppose that after meeting Fate*
> *The soul still feels in its divided state.*
> *What's that to us? For we are only we*
> *While body and soul in one frame agree.*
> *And if our atoms should revolve by chance*
> *And our cast-off matter rejoin the dance*
> *What gain to us would all this bring?*
> *This new-made man would be a new-made thing.*
> *We, dead and gone, would play no part*
> *In all the pleasures, nor feel the smart*
> *Which to that new man shall accrue*
> *Whom of our matter Time molds anew.*
> *Take heart then, listen and hear:*
> *What is there left in death to fear?*
> *After the pause of life has come between,*
> *All's just the same had we never been.*

The last note of the song was followed by a long silence. Watching the eunuch and listening to him, Lucius thought of Sporus. A tear ran down his cheek. Before he could wipe it away, he realized that Domitian had risen from his couch and was walking slowly to him.

The emperor's eyes emerged from the shadows and glittered, reflecting the lamplight. His unblinking gaze was fixed on Lucius's face. As a hunter, Lucius had often wondered at the tendency of certain prey, such as rabbits, to freeze rather than to flee when observed by the hunter. Now he understood. He felt as the rabbit must feel, unable to move a muscle, frantically willing himself to vanish into the darkness around him. It was as if he had turned to stone. Even his heart seemed to stop beating.

Domitian stepped closer. He stared at Lucius intently, his small mouth compressed in an unreadable expression. He stopped directly in front of Lucius and reached out to him. Frozen as he was, Lucius nevertheless feared that he would cry out if Domitian touched his face. He struggled not to flinch, and only a stifled gasp escaped his lips.

Domitian used his forefinger to wipe the moisture from Lucius's cheek. He furrowed his brow, gazed at his finger, then turned and very gently brushed his finger against the parted lips of Earinus.

"Does it taste of salt?" he whispered.

Earinus touched his tongue to his lips. "Yes, Dominus."

"A tear!" said Domitian. "Was it the words of the poet Lucretius that made you weep, Lucius Pinarius?"

Lucius opened his mouth, afraid he had forgotten how to speak, then found his voice. "I'm not sure I heard the words, Dominus. I only know that I heard Earinus sing, and then I felt the tear on my cheek."

Domitian slowly nodded. "I, too, wept the first time I heard Earinus sing." He stared at Lucius for a long time, then turned to Catullus. "The dinner is over," he said.

The emperor left the room without another word. The small-headed creature followed him, as did Earinus.

Lucius stood. He looked at Cornelia across the room and felt an urge to run to her. She raised one hand, beseeching him to keep his distance. As they stared into each other's eyes, with all the power of his will he tried to show her what she meant to him. He had never loved her more.

The serving boy took Cornelia's hand, gently pulled her to her feet, and led her from the room.

The room became even darker. Lucius looked around and saw that all the lamps but one had been extinguished. Catullus had vanished. Except for his cupbearer, Lucius was alone.

The boy led him through a doorway. He was hardly aware of his surroundings, though he sensed that each turning brought him to a hallway that was larger and more brightly lit than the last. Finally he arrived at the vast reception room dominated by the statue of the emperor. He looked up at the statue's face. The sculptor had captured the terrible power of Domitian's gaze. Lucius shut his eyes and reached for the cupbearer, letting the boy lead him like a blind man.

He opened his eyes only when he felt fresh air on his face and realized that they were outside, under a dark and moonless sky. A flight of steps led down to the sedan that had brought him. The boy helped him step inside. Bearers lifted him aloft. Next to him on the seat were the clothes he had changed out of earlier.

The trip to his house was short. He stepped from the sedan. The bearers turned and vanished without a word.

Lucius rapped on the door. Hilarion opened it. His knowing grin vanished when he saw the look on Lucius's face.

"What do you see, Hilarion? No, don't speak. You see a dead man before you."

In the days that followed, Lucius expected Praetorians to arrive at his house at any moment to arrest him. Moving sometimes in a stupor, sometimes in a frantic rush, he put his affairs in order. He wore the fascinum always, so that he would not be without it when they came for him.

Confronted by oblivion, he tried to think about the gods and his ancestors and all the other things a man was supposed to think about in the face of death, but he drew a blank. In the end, did he believe in nothing at all? This revelation was the most disturbing aspect of the ordeal. He had left the House of the Flavians shaken, uncertain, full of dread, as would any man; but more than that, he had emerged with a sense that nothing mattered. In the black room, all illusions had been stripped away. A man and a rabbit were exactly the same, two flashes of consciousness caught for a brief instant in the cycle of life and death that had no beginning, no end, no resolution, no purpose.

In such a frame of mind, he received the news that Cornelia had been arrested. Then he heard that others had been arrested—men accused of being her lovers. That these men were innocent, Lucius had no doubt, for he was certain that he was her only lover; they were simply men who had run afoul of the emperor, and this was Domitian's way of destroying them. Not one of them confessed, though they were interrogated under torture. Nor did Cornelia's slaves from the House of the Vestals produce any evidence against them. The verdict against Cornelia and her alleged lovers was delivered not in Roma but at the emperor's retreat at Alba. Cornelia was not even present at the mockery of a trial. She was condemned in absentia.

There was speculation that the guilty men would be allowed to flee into exile, as had happened after the previous trials of Vestals. But because they had not cooperated with the court—in other words, confessed—it was decreed that the men must suffer the traditional penalty. In the Forum, for all to see, they were stripped naked, tied to crosses, and beaten to death. Cornelia was compelled to be present. Lucius stayed at home. He was not sure which would have been worse, to see the men killed or to see Cornelia as she was forced to watch.

He intended to avoid the spectacle of Cornelia's punishment as well, but on the scheduled day, well publicized by heralds and placards, he found himself unable to stay away.

Starting before dawn, thousands of people began to gather outside the House of the Vestals. No living person had ever before witnessed the traditional punishment of a Vestal. The same spectators who flocked to the Flavian Amphitheater came to see this spectacle as well. They dressed in dark colors appropriate for a funeral. The Forum was a sea of black.

Lucius found himself at the back of the crowd; he could not have pushed his way to the front if he had wanted to. There was nothing to see, at least at first. The beginning of the ceremony took place out of sight,

within the House of the Vestals. That was where Cornelia would be relieved of her vitta and her suffibulum, stripped naked, and scourged with
rods while the Pontifex Maximus, the other Vestals, and the assembled
priests of the state religion watched. Then she would be dressed as a corpse
and placed in a closed, black litter, with restraints on her limbs and a gag
over her mouth, and the litter would be carried aloft, like a funeral bier,
through the streets.

The crowd awaiting the appearance of the funeral litter grew restless.
Some of the women began to keen and tear out their hair. Some of the
men muttered curses against the guilty Vestal. Some made obscene jokes,
smirking and laughing. A few dared to speculate that the Vestal might be
innocent, despite the judgment of the Pontifex Maximus, for it was said
that she had comported herself with utmost dignity throughout her trial
and that not one of the condemned men had spoken against her.

At last, preceded by musicians with rattles and pipes, the funeral litter
appeared. Black curtains concealed the occupant, but the knowledge that
a living woman was inside—the Virgo Maxima herself, known to everyone because of her appearances at religious rites and at the amphitheater—
caused people to shudder and gasp.

The procession passed at a stately pace through the Forum, then entered the Subura, heading for the Colline Gate. This was the very route,
thought Lucius, that his father had taken with Nero on their final journey
out of Roma.

The procession moved slowly down the narrow street. Oppressed by
the crush of people, Lucius left the route and took other streets to arrive
ahead of the procession at an open area just inside the old Servian Walls.
Here the crowd had only begun to gather and Lucius was able to find a
place near the front. There was not much to see—only a hole in the ground
from which a ladder protruded, and next to it a pile of freshly dug earth.
This was the opening, normally covered over, to the underground vault that
had existed since the time of Tarquinius Priscus, in which, for centuries,
condemned Vestals had been interred and left to die.

How large was the chamber, and how deep under ground? No one
knew except the very few officials of the state religion who had seen it. It
was said to contain a cot, a lamp with a little oil, a few scraps of food, and

a pitcher with a bit of water—cruel gestures of welcome and comfort for a victim doomed to starve to death in darkness. Presumably the vault was quite small, but for all Lucius knew it extended under his feet. He might be standing over the very spot where Cornelia would breathe her last.

What became of the previous Vestals who died in this place? Were their remains ever removed, or were they left in the chamber on grisly display for each new victim to see? If that was true, the chamber would house the remains of every Vestal who had been condemned to die there. Cornelia would be made to see exactly what was to become of her and to contemplate the company she was joining, and to realize that her own remains would be there for the next condemned Vestal to see. Lucius found himself imagining the scene in horrifying detail, unable to think of anything else.

At last he heard the sound of horns and rattles, along with cries and moans of lamentation. The procession was approaching.

The crowd grew thick around him, but Lucius stayed where he was, determined to be as close to Cornelia as possible.

At last the funeral litter arrived, surrounded by a great many lictors to hold back the crowd and keep order and followed by the Vestals and numerous priests. Among them was Domitian, wearing the toga of the Pontifex Maximus with its many folds gathered and tucked in a loop just above his waist and the cowl pulled over his head, casting his face in shadow. Near him was Catullus, dressed in black and guided by a boy who held his hand.

The litter was placed on a platform near the opening. The bearers drew back. Priests opened the curtains, undid the straps that held Cornelia in place, and removed the gag from her mouth. They roughly pulled her from the litter onto her feet.

Cornelia stood before the crowd, dressed not in her linen vestments but in a simple stola made of black wool. The sight of a Vestal without her headdress was startling, even shocking. Without her suffibulum, her uncommonly short hair was visible to all. To see her that way, in public, knowing all eyes were on her, made Lucius's face turn hot. The sight of her short hair had been his exclusive privilege; now all Roma saw her that way. The indignity was as obscene as if she had been stripped naked. Some in the crowd dared to jeer at her. Without her vestments she was no longer a priestess but a mere woman, and a fallen woman at that, a wicked creature deserving a horrible death.

Domitian put an end to the jeering. Lictors with rods quickly moved into the crowd, striking anyone who failed to maintain the proper decorum.

Cornelia was expected to walk the short distance from the litter to the opening in the ground by herself. She did so with halting steps. Her body was stiff. She seemed to be in pain. Lucius knew that she had been beaten with rods and wondered what sort of wounds and bruises were concealed by her black stola.

She reached the opening and looked down at the ladder that descended to the vault. She swayed and jerked, like a reed blown by a wind. She looked upward and stared at the sky. She raised her hands.

"Vesta!" she shouted. "You know I never betrayed you. While I served in your temple the sacred flame never wavered."

"Silence!" cried Domitian.

Cornelia lowered her eyes and gazed at the crowd, looking from face to face. "Caesar says I am guilty of impurity, but my conduct of Vesta's rituals was immaculate. Every one of his victories, every triumph he celebrated, is proof of the goddess's favor."

Domitian signaled to one of the lictors, who moved toward Cornelia. If she would not step onto the ladder and begin the descent of her own volition, she would be forced to do so. When the man reached out to grab her arm, she shrugged him off. It was only a slight movement, but the lictor recoiled violently, as if he had been struck.

"Cornelia never touched him!" cried a woman in the crowd. "It was the hand of the goddess that threw him back!"

"See how calm she is, how dignified," said someone else.

His heart racing, Lucius dared to raise his voice. "Perhaps she's innocent after all, if Vesta allows no man to touch her!"

It made no difference. The crowd ignored these scattered protests.

Cornelia stepped onto the ladder and took hold of it with trembling hands. She took a step down, and then another, until she was visible only from the waist up. It was all Lucius could do not to call to her. Despite his silence, she seemed to sense his presence. She paused and turned her head. She looked straight at him.

She moved her lips, mouthing silent words intended only for him: "Forgive me."

Cornelia took another step, and another, then vanished from sight. The crowd let out a collective groan. Men shook their heads and shuddered. Women dropped to their knees and wailed.

While she descended, the ladder moved slightly, relaying the vibration of her steps. Then the ladder was still. Lictors stepped forward and pulled it from the hole. The ladder was a long one; the vault was many feet under ground. A large, flat stone was placed over the opening. The mound of earth was spread over the stone and pounded with mallets until the ground was even and no sign remained of the opening.

The new Virgo Maxima, with averted eyes and a trembling voice, stood on the spot and uttered a prayer to Vesta, asking the goddess to forgive the people of Roma for allowing such a breach of piety and to restore her favor to the city. The Pontifex Maximus and his retinue began to withdraw. Catullus was the last to leave, led off by the boy. It seemed to Lucius that there was a smile on the man's gaunt face.

The crowd gradually dispersed, until only Lucius remained. He stared at the place where the opening had been. There was nothing to see, nothing to hear. Cornelia had been swallowed by the earth. Yet he knew she must be still alive, still breathing.

Why was Lucius still alive?

Lucius knew the answer. He had been saved by a quirk of fate. The Master and God of the world, who saw enemies everywhere and executed men without reason, who watched thousands die in the arena without mercy, had been swayed by a sentimental whim. Earinus was the one human being for whom Domitian felt any semblance of love; when Earinus sang in the black room, Lucius had wept. For that reason alone, Domitian had spared him.

Lucius had been saved by a tear. The absurdity of it only deepened his despair.

He thought of Cornelia's final words: "Forgive me." He was alive and unscathed, a free man. For his affair with Cornelia he had suffered no consequence whatsoever. For what should he forgive Cornelia? It made no sense, yet he was certain that she had mouthed the words *forgive me.*

What did it mean?

A.D. 93

Reclining in the shade of his garden on a hot afternoon in the month of Augustus, Lucius reflected on the unexpected path his life had taken over the last two years.

The punishment of Cornelia had marked a low point in his life. Existence had lost all meaning. His taste for life had vanished. Nothing brought him pleasure. Was he in pain? If so, his pain was not a sharp agony—a reminder that he was alive—but a dull, hollow sensation, like a foretaste of death. He was stripped of all emotion. He did not loathe the world or hate the people in it; he felt nothing.

Now, all that had changed. His time of utmost despair was in the past. Once again he was able to take enjoyment from simple pleasures—the bright colors and sweet fragrances of flowers in his garden, the cheerful songs of birds, the humming of bees, the warm sunshine on his face, the cooling breeze on his fingertips. He was alive again—fully alive, not merely existing, experiencing each moment as it occurred. He was conscious of himself and accepting of the world in which he lived. He had attained a state of contentment that he had never before thought possible.

His newfound peace was due to one man: the Teacher.

What had his life been like before he met the Teacher? Lucius recalled his frequent visits to the house of Epaphroditus over the years. Friendship had been the main reason for those visits, but he had also been seeking wisdom. But after the death of Cornelia, Martial's wit no longer amused him, and Lucius found the poet's ties to the emperor intolerable. The philosophy of Epictetus seemed bland and insubstantial. Nor did the letters Lucius received from Dio convey any sense of enlightenment. Lucius's visits to the house of Epaphroditus grew less and less frequent. The unanswered letters from Dio piled up on the table in his study.

Yet, even at the deepest point of his despair, Lucius had continued to seek comfort and enlightenment. Turning away from his circle of friends, for a while he had studied the more esoteric modes of belief available to a curious man in Roma. Of these, there were a great many; every cult in the empire eventually found adherents and proselytizers in Roma. As Epaphroditus had once told him, people were capable of believing anything; the startling array of religions practiced in the city was proof of that. Lucius even investigated the much-despised cult of the Christians, of which his uncle Kaeso had been a member, but found it no more interesting than any of the other cults.

He had also made a study of astrology, since so many people held such store by it. But the fatalistic nature of it had only made him more despondent. The astrologers taught that every aspect of a man's life was determined in advance by powers unimaginably larger than himself; within that predestined fate a man had very little leeway to affect the course of his life. What was the point of knowing that a certain day was ill-omened if one could do nothing to reverse the tide of events? A man could hope to propitiate a temperamental god, but nothing could be done to alter the influence of the stars—if indeed such an influence existed. For although wiser men than himself considered astrology a science and devoted great study to it, Lucius was unimpressed by all the charts derived from ancient texts and the endless tables full of esoteric symbols. He had an uneasy suspicion that astrology was a fraud. Certainly, astrologers had carefully observed the heavens and had learned to predict the movements of the celestial bodies with considerable accuracy, but the rest of the so-called science—determining precisely how those celestial bodies affected human existence—seemed a mere invention to Lucius, a compendium of nonsense contrived by men who understood no more about the secret workings of the universe than did anyone else.

Philosophy, exotic religions, astrology—Lucius had been open to them all, but none had provided him with any sense of purpose or enlightenment. None had relieved the emptiness he felt at the core of his being.

Then, he met the Teacher, and everything changed.

It happened on the first anniversary of the day Cornelia was buried alive.

For a long time Lucius had been dreading that day, knowing that when it arrived he would be able to think of nothing else. That morning he woke early. He had no appetite. He put on a plain tunic and left his house. For hours he walked aimlessly all over the city, lost in memories. Eventually he found himself standing before the house on the Esquiline where he had met with Cornelia so many times over the years. He had sold the house, quickly and for less than its value, only a few days after her interment, thinking that he would never want to step inside it again. Now he stood before it in the street, longing to go in, to stand in the vestibule and remember the sight of her face across the room, to smell again the jasmine in the small garden where they had made love.

The door of the house opened. A mother and her young daughter stepped out, followed by a slave carrying a basket for a trip to the markets. The spell was broken, and Lucius moved on.

Inevitably, he found himself at the Colline Gate, standing exactly where he had stood when he saw her last, before the entrance to the sealed underground chamber. In his hand he held a single rose, the symbol of love, and also of secrecy. He could not remember where he had gotten it; he must have bought it from a vendor. He clutched it so carelessly that a thorn had pricked his palm; he did not feel the wound, but saw a trickle of blood run down his fingers.

The moment felt unreal, dreamlike. He found himself kneeling at the very spot where the stone had been covered over. As one might place a garland on a sepulcher, he placed the rose on the beaten earth. Blood dripped from his fingers.

A shadow fell across him. He imagined that he had been observed by some disapproving magistrate and that a lictor stood over him. But the outline of the shadow was not that of a soldier. He looked up to see a small man with a long white beard. The sun was directly behind the man's head, making his unruly hair into a wispy halo. His features were surprisingly youthful for a man with snow-white hair, and deeply tanned—the sunburned face of a traveler, or a man without a home. His eyes were bright blue and appeared to sparkle; later, Lucius would realize this was impossible, since the sun was behind the man's head and his face was in shadow. From whence came the light that emanated from his eyes? This was Lucius's first indication that the man who stood over him was more than an ordinary mortal.

"You're suffering, my friend," said the man.

"Yes." Lucius saw no point in denying it.

"Such suffering is like a flower that blooms. It opens all at once and engages all our senses, but soon enough it fades and falls away. You will remember it always, but it will no longer be present before you. Take heart, my friend, for the time when your suffering will fade and fall away is very near."

"Who are you?" Lucius frowned. He was still on his knees. Anyone seeing him now would assume that he was kneeling to honor the man before him, despite the fact that the man was barefoot and dressed like a beggar, wearing a threadbare, ragged tunic. Strangely, the idea did not displease Lucius. He stayed on his knees.

"My name is Apollonius. I come from Tyana. Do you know where that is?"

"In Cappadocia, I think."

"That is correct. Have you heard of me?"

"No."

"Good. Those who have heard of Apollonius of Tyana often have certain preconceptions about me, which I am not interested in fulfilling. What is your name, friend?"

"Lucius Pinarius. Are you some sort of wise man?" Cappadocia, with its weird desert cities carved from rock, was famous for breeding hermits and seers.

The man laughed. The sound was very pleasant. "I am whatever people choose to call me. When you know me better, Lucius Pinarius, you will decide what I am."

"Why are you talking to me?"

"All men suffer, but no man should suffer in secret, as you do."

"What do you know of my suffering?"

"You loved a person whom law and religion decreed you should not love, and her separation from you has caused you much pain."

Lucius gasped. "How can you know this?"

The man smiled. There was no mockery in his smile, only gentleness. "I suppose I could put on airs of mystery and pretend that the stories about me are true—that I can read men's minds, that I have occult means of gaining knowledge—but the truth is much simpler. I'm a visitor to Roma. Before this morning I never passed through this particular neighborhood, but even a casual visitor will quickly be told by the locals what happened on this spot a year ago. When I observed a man standing here, clutching a rose and staring for a long time at the ground, I knew you must have had some relationship with the Vestal who was buried here. When you knelt and placed the rose so carefully, heedless of your own bleeding wound, I knew you must have loved her. Anyone with eyes could have seen this, but in such a busy spot, where everyone is passing by in such a hurry, I alone observed your suffering."

"Who are you?" said Lucius.

"You asked me that already. I am Apollonius of Tyana."

"No, I mean—"

"Here, why don't you stand, my friend?" Apollonius offered his hand. "Let's take a walk."

Lucius said little. He listened to Apollonius, who spoke of his travels. Apollonius talked about these journeys in an offhand way, as if it were the most ordinary thing in the world for a man to have gone to Egypt to learn what the priests there could teach him about the hieroglyphs on the ancient tombs, and to Ethiopia to meet the naked sages who live at the source of the Nile, and even all the way to India to consort with the fabled wise men of the Ganges.

A light rain began to fall. They had wandered into an area of fine homes on the Quirinal Hill. Lucius was looking for a tavern or eatery where they might take refuge when Apollonius noticed that the door of a nearby house was open. He cocked his head.

"Do you hear that?" he said.

"I hear nothing," said Lucius.

"No? I distinctly hear the sound of weeping, coming from that house." Apollonius walked toward the open door.

"What are you doing?" said Lucius.

"Going inside. Where there is weeping, there is need for comfort."

"Do you know these people?"

"I've never been on this street before in my life. But all streets and all people are the same. Once a man knows that, he is a stranger nowhere."

Apollonius stepped inside the house. Against his better judgment, Lucius followed him.

Beyond the vestibule, in the atrium, a drizzling rain fell from the open skylight into a shallow pool. Beyond the pool, on the tile floor, lay the body of a young woman. She wore a white bridal gown with a purple sash around her waist. Gathered around the body were several women, all dressed for a wedding. They looked stunned. Some quietly wept. Farther back stood a group of men who looked helpless and confused.

How had Apollonius heard the sound of the women weeping, when Lucius had not? For an old man, his hearing was very acute, thought Lucius.

Apollonius looked down at the young woman. "Is this her wedding day?" he said.

One of the kneeling women looked up. There was an expression of shock on her face. "Yes. This is my daughter's wedding day—and the gods see fit to strike her down!"

"What happened?" said Apollonius.

The woman shook her head. "We were organizing the procession to set out for the bridegroom's house. We were in her room and I was tying the sash around her waist, and she complained I was pulling too tight. She said she couldn't breathe. But the sash wasn't too tight; I slipped a finger under it to show her. Still, she couldn't catch her breath. She said her face felt hot. A servant told us it was raining. Without a word she pulled away from me and ran here, to the pool. I thought she wanted to cool her face. I told her she mustn't get her gown wet, and then . . . she collapsed. She fell, just as you see her now."

"Perhaps she only sleeps."

"She has no heartbeat! She isn't breathing!"

"Alas," whispered Apollonius. He looked intently at the girl, then at the huddled women. He waved his hands before him—to get their attention, Lucius thought, but then the old man continued to move his hands, making signs in the air. Apollonius had the full attention of everyone in the room, including the men who stood farther back. They all stared at him. The women who had been weeping were now silent.

"Stand back," said Apollonius.

Without a word, the women drew back. Apollonius circled the pool and knelt beside the girl. He put one hand on her forehead and passed the other hand over her body, not touching her. He whispered inaudible words.

Apollonius snapped his fingers. In the quiet room, where the only other sound was the fall of drizzling raindrops on the pool, the noise echoed like the breaking of a small branch. He paused, then snapped his fingers twice more.

The girl shuddered, drew a deep breath, and let out a sigh. She opened her eyes. "Where am I?" she said.

Her mother cried out. The women gasped, uttered exclamations of thanksgiving, and shed tears of relief.

Some of the men began to weep as well. One of them stepped forward.

"Stranger, you brought my daughter back to life!" The man was giddy with joy.

"Your daughter is indeed alive, but I am no stranger. I am Apollonius of Tyana."

"How did you work such a miracle? What god did you call upon?"

Apollonius shrugged. "I merely spoke to your daughter. 'Awake, young woman!' I said. 'The rain is about to stop, and you shall be late for your wedding. Breathe deeply and awake!' And then, as you saw, she woke. What girl wants to be late for her own wedding?"

"But how can I repay you? Here, you must take these." The father fetched a pair of drinking cups. "Solid silver," he said, "decorated with bits of lapis. And not just any lapis, but the special variety flecked with gold that comes only from Bactria."

"The workmanship is exquisite," said Apollonius.

"They were to be a gift to my daughter and her new husband. But here, I want you to have them."

Apollonius laughed. "What use have I for cups, when I never drink wine?"

"Drink water from them, then!" The man grinned. "Or sell them. Buy yourself a tunic with no holes in it!"

Apollonius shrugged. "A few more holes in this garment, and I shall be as splendidly arrayed as the naked sages of Ethiopia."

The man looked puzzled but was so happy that he burst out laughing.

"I see that your daughter is on her feet again," said Apollonius. "Go to her. She won't be yours for much longer. You should enjoy every precious moment."

"Precious, indeed!" said the man. "How precious I never knew until this day. Thank you, Apollonius of Tyana! May the gods bless you!" The man joined his wife, who was making a great fuss over their daughter.

Amid the hubbub, Apollonius discreetly withdrew. Lucius followed. On the way out, they passed a young Vestal who was just arriving to take her place in the procession. The sight of her sent a chill through Lucius. In the street he had to pause to collect himself. Apollonius stood by, observing him with a sympathetic smile.

"I don't understand what happened in there," Lucius finally said. "Was the girl dead or not?"

"Ah, wedding days! They bring out a great deal of emotion in people."

"Are you saying they only imagined she was dead?"

Apollonius shrugged. "I suspect they were less observant than they might have been. People often are. Did you notice, for example, how the women near the misty drizzle exuded a faint but visible vapor with each exhalation?"

"Are you saying you observed such a vapor coming from the girl's nostrils?"

"I saw what there was to see. My eyes see no more and no less than those of other men."

Lucius raised an eyebrow. "You did something with your hands. They all watched. Did you bewitch them somehow?"

"I made them take notice of me, and when I asked them to move aside, they did so. Does that sound like magic to you?"

Lucius crossed his arms. "Those cups he offered you were quite beautiful. Quite valuable, too, I imagine."

"I had no use for them."

"Nonsense! As the man said, you could have sold them. Those cups would have paid for three months' lodging in a nice apartment on the Aventine."

"But I never pay for lodging."

"No?"

"I always stay with friends."

"Who are you staying with now?"

"With you, of course!" Apollonius laughed.

His laughter was infectious. Lucius felt his suspicions of the man fade away. He began to laugh, too, and realized that it was the first time he had done so in more than a year.

So began his relationship with the Teacher.

Apollonius did not ask Lucius to call him the Teacher; that was Lucius's decision. As Apollonius told him at their first meeting, "I am whatever people choose to call me . . . you will decide what I am."

Apollonius was not a teacher in any traditional way. He did not cite authorities and recite from texts, as Lucius's boyhood tutors had done. He did not construct edifices of logic leading to rational conclusions, as Epictetus did. He did not tell stories that led to some moral or theological conclusion, as the man-god of the Christians did. He did not create charts and diagrams or write long treatises, as the astrologers did. And he certainly claimed no special status for himself or any special connection to the gods, as did the priests of the state religion. Apollonius simply rose from his bed each morning and went about his day. He visited old friends and made new ones. By the example of his behavior, he showed that a man could move through the world without vanity or fear, never showing anger or despair, envious of no one, wanting for nothing.

When asked, Apollonius would state his opinions and preferences, but he never expounded on these to offer proof, and he never insisted that others should agree with him. He professed to believe in the gods, but only as shadowy manifestations of a higher, all-encompassing principle, and he claimed no special relationship with this principle beyond that which belonged to all living things, which were equally a part of the Divine Unity and had equal access to the blessings that radiated, like sunshine, from that being. "I am to that deity as I am to the sun, and so are you," he would say. "I am no closer than you; it warms me no more than it warms you; it sheds no more light before me. Its blessings are for all, equally and in endless abundance."

Often, it seemed to Lucius that Apollonius behaved in ways contradictory to what other men called common sense. When Lucius would question these seemingly perverse actions, Apollonius would patiently explain himself; even so, Lucius could not always understand the Teacher's words. But Lucius was ceaselessly amazed by the Teacher's unfailing equanimity, and he came to trust the man implicitly. Even when Lucius could not follow Apollonius's reasoning, he strove to emulate the Teacher as best he could, and to accept on faith that a fuller understanding might someday come to him.

Apollonius did not drink wine. Intoxication did not bring a man closer to the deity, he said, but interposed a veil of illusion. Lucius followed his example.

Apollonius did not eat meat, saying that all life was sacred, including that of animals. Nor did he wear anything made from an animal; there were no scraps of leather, bones, or ivory on his person. Lucius followed this example as well, and, like Apollonius, he came to see the slaying of animals as no different from the slaying of men. Men did not kill other men for food or for hides; nor should they kill animals. And just as civilized men had long ago given up the religious practice of human sacrifice, so it was time for men to give up animal sacrifice; the slaying of a beast could be no more pleasing to the gods than the slaying of a child. As for the killing of animals in the arena for sport, that was sheer cruelty and, if anything, was worse than the killing of humans for sport, for the animals did not possess speech and could not beg for mercy. Lucius, who had enjoyed hunting all his life, gave it up.

Apollonius did not engage in sexual intimacy with others, which he called an illusion and a trap; fleeting moments of pleasure led only to endless agitation and suffering. Lucius asked him if copulation was not a virtue, since it was necessary for procreation. Apollonius, who believed in reincarnation, replied, "What is the virtue of creating more human beings, and thus more mortal life, and thus more suffering? If there were to be no more human beings, eventually the population would vanish, and would that be a bad thing? If we possess spirits, those spirits will still exist; they will simply be freed from the onerous process of transmigrating from body to body, wearing out one after another, endlessly suffering the pains of mortal decay. With or without humanity as we know it, the Divine Unity will continue to exist. This sentimental attachment to creating endless replicas of ourselves is yet another illusion, another trap. Procreation only perpetuates the cycle of suffering. There is no virtue in it. It is a vice."

As far as Lucius could determine, no other wise man, whether philosopher or religious savant, had ever declared universal chastity to be a virtue. At first, Lucius was dubious of following this example, but in fact he was already practicing it. Since the death of Cornelia, he had withdrawn from seeking intimacy with anyone else. It required no real change on his part to emulate Apollonius, and once he made a conscious decision to do so, he felt a great sense of freedom and relief.

Apollonius held the great and powerful in no special esteem. Nor did he fear them. During his first visit to Roma, in the reign of Nero, he had attracted the attention of the emperor's henchman Tigellinus, who had put a watch on him. Apollonius gave the informers no cause to arrest him, until he happened to hear Nero sing one day in a common tavern. The emperor was incognito, wearing a mask, but there was no doubt that it was him. Tigellinus was in the audience, also in disguise, wearing a hooded cloak and an eye patch. After Nero's performance, he asked Apollonius's opinion.

"Was it not fit for the gods?"

"If the gods like it, we must strive not to think less of them," said Apollonius.

Tigellinus was incensed. "Do you realize who that was? You've just heard Caesar sing one of his own compositions. Was it not divine?"

"Now that it is over, I do feel closer to the gods."

"Stop speaking in riddles and say what you mean! I say the singing was wonderful. What do you say?"

"I say I have a higher opinion of the emperor than you do."

"How is that?"

"You think it is wonderful if he sings. I think it is wonderful if he simply remains silent."

Tigellinus charged Apollonius with impugning the dignity of the emperor and arrested him. As the trial approached, he realized that he needed stronger evidence than the ambiguous statements made by Apollonius. He put an informer up to writing a series of charges against Apollonius and had the charges notarized, so that when they were produced in court they would appear to come from an outside witness. All sorts of false statements were imputed to Apollonius, of a nature seditious enough to have him put to death.

In the court, before Nero and the magistrates, Apollonius was called forth. Tigellinus produced the sealed scroll upon which the accusations were written and brandished it like a dagger. But when he unrolled the scroll, his jaw dropped and he stood speechless.

Nero demanded to see the scroll for himself. "Is this a joke?" he asked Tigellinus. The parchment was completely blank. Nero ordered Tigellinus to set Apollonius free, with the stipulation that he should leave Italy at once.

"Nero thought I was a magician," explained Apollonius. "He feared that I would exact a supernatural revenge if I were to be imprisoned or executed."

"But, Teacher," asked Lucius, "how did it happen that the scroll Tigellinus produced was blank? Had the original scroll been taken and another substituted? Had the scribe been given a special ink, which faded away? Or did you call upon some supernatural power to make the lies on the parchment vanish?"

"I can think of another possibility," said Apollonius. "What if those who looked at the scroll simply did not see the writing that was there?"

"But, Teacher, how could that happen?"

"Very often, when a thing is inexplicable, it is simply a matter of seeing or not seeing. Just as it is possible to open a man's eyes to what is before him, simply by directing his attention, so there are ways to make a man blind to what is before him." That was as clear an explanation as Apollonius would give.

Apollonius had also met Vespasian. This was when Vitellius was emperor. Legions supporting Vespasian were marching on Roma, but Vespasian himself was in Alexandria. Uncertain about the future and eager for advice, Vespasian had solicited the counsel of the most prestigious astrologers and philosophers in a city renowned for its learning. In his first meeting with Vespasian, Apollonius described a vision in which he beheld the final days of Vitellius, including the burning of the Temple of Jupiter and the narrow escape of Domitian. Vespasian was dubious, but a messenger brought news of these events to Alexandria the very next day. Vespasian was greatly impressed. "Either this fellow truly has visions of far-off events," he remarked, "or else he has information-gathering capabilities superior to my own. Either way, I want his advice!"

"I took advantage of the opportunity to encourage Vespasian in his ambitions," Apollonius told Lucius. "I could see he was a man of equable temperament, and the most likely candidate to restore peace and order to the chaotic state of the empire. But later, when he wrote me letters beseeching me to come to Roma to advise him, I refused."

"Why, Teacher?"

"Because of his treatment of the Greeks. Nero had many faults, but he loved Greece and Greek culture; he bestowed many privileges on the Greek cities, allowing them a degree of dignity and freedom no emperor had granted them before. But Vespasian saw fit to revoke every one of those privileges. He deliberately and systematically returned the Greeks to their subservient state. He was a great disappointment to me. Whenever he wrote to me, I wrote a scolding letter back to him."

"No!"

"Oh yes."

"What did you say in these letters?"

"This was my final letter to him. 'Apollonius to the Emperor Vespasian: A bad man redeemed himself by freeing the Greeks. A good man tarnished himself by enslaving them. Why should any man desire the company of a counselor to whom he will not listen? Farewell.' "

Given a letter of introduction by Vespasian, Apollonius had also met Titus. This was in Tarsus, after Vespasian returned to Roma as emperor and entrusted affairs in the East to his son.

"I liked Titus," said Apollonius. "He was surprisingly modest and had a wonderful sense of humor. And at thirty, when many fighting men let themselves go, he kept himself very fit. Titus had a very stout neck, like an athlete in training. Once I grabbed him by the back of the neck and said, 'Who could ever force such a sturdy bull neck as this under a yoke?' And Titus laughed and said, 'Only the man who reared me from a calf!' His deference to his father was endearing, yet he had the makings of a better ruler than his father. Alas, we had the father for ten years and the son for only two."

"Is it true that you foretold Titus's early death?" said Lucius.

Apollonius smiled. "Sometimes, I know, I seem to speak in riddles. But about this I shall be as clear as I can. Imagine that you enter a dark cave. You strike a spark, and for just an instant you see the extent of the place. The details are uncertain, and the shape of the cavern is vague, but you grasp at once if the cave is large or small. So it is, sometimes, when I first meet a person. In a flash I sense whether their time on this earth will be long or short. I knew from the moment I met him that Titus would not live to be as old as his father. He was like a lamp that burns more brightly than others but for a shorter time."

"And his brother?"

"I haven't met Domitian. But to me it seems he is not like a lamp at all. He is an extinguisher of lamps. He brings darkness, not light."

"I wonder how much longer his reign of darkness will last."

Apollonius shrugged. "The man is only forty-two."

"That was the age at which Titus died."

"Yes, but Vespasian lived to be sixty-two."

"Twenty more years of Domitian!" exclaimed Lucius.

"Perhaps," said Apollonius. "Or perhaps not."

Lucius reclined on his couch in the garden, his eyes shut, smelling the flowers, thinking of how his life had changed in the year since he had met the Teacher.

He felt the warmth of the sun on his bare feet. Apollonius had taught him to go barefoot. What need had a man for shoes in his own house? Sometimes Lucius even went to the Forum barefoot. Others stared at him as if he were mad.

"Are you dreaming?" said Apollonius. He had excused himself for a moment to empty his bladder in the small latrina off the garden. The Teacher had a body just like those of other men, and was subject to the same needs to ingest and expel as dictated by the endlessly repeating cycles of mortal flesh.

"The others will arrive soon," said Lucius, wishing it were not so. He treasured time alone with the Teacher, listening to his stories, asking him questions, simply enjoying his tranquil presence. But Apollonius had many friends, and it sometimes fell to Lucius to play host to the others in his home. He was expecting perhaps fifty men and women. They would be of all social ranks, from freedmen to patricians like himself. There would probably be a few senators among them, but also shopkeepers and artisans and bricklayers. No one who wished to hear Apollonius speak was turned away.

Lucius looked at the Teacher and smiled. To a careless observer, Apollonius might appear to be nothing more than a doddering old man. But such were the illusions of the material world: appearances meant nothing. Emulating Apollonius, Lucius had begun to eschew the services of his barber. His hair had never been so long, and never before had he sported a beard. At the age of forty-six, Lucius had only a few touches of silver in his hair, but hoped someday to have a beard as fleece-white as that of the Teacher.

"What story will you tell the gathering today?" asked Lucius.

"I was thinking I might talk about my time in Ethiopia."

Lucius nodded. The Teacher's stories about Ethiopia were among Lucius's favorites.

"I thought in particular I might tell the story of my encounter with the satyr, since most people nowadays have never seen a satyr and have various misconceptions about the creatures."

Lucius sat upright. "You met a satyr in Ethiopia? I've never heard that story."

"Could it be that I never told you?"

"Never! I'm sure I would have remembered."

"Well, then. It was during my journey to see the great lake from whence the Nile originates. On its shores one finds a colony of the naked sages, who are wiser than Greek philosophers but not quite so wise as the sages of India, to whom they are kin. They welcomed me heartily, but I could see they were in distress, and I asked the cause.

"Nightly, they were plagued by the visitations of a wild creature, a being that was goatlike from the waist down, with shaggy hind legs and hooves, and manlike from the waist up, but with goat horns and pointed ears. From their description I deduced it was a satyr, a being previously unknown in those parts. This satyr interrupted the sleep of the sages, tramping outside their huts and bleating in the middle of the night. When they confronted the satyr and complained, the creature made rude noises and obscene gestures. When they attempted to apprehend him, he proved to be swifter than even the swiftest among them, leaping and careening and causing them to trip over one another and make fools of themselves.

"The sages took me to a nearby village, where the elders informed me that the satyr's incursions there were far more serious. At least once a month, always by night, he intruded upon the comeliest and most nubile of the women, muttering incantations in their ears while they slept, putting them under a spell and luring them into the woods. A few of the women had awakened from this spell and dared to resist him, whereupon the creature physically attacked them, strangling them and trampling them with his hooves. Two women had been killed in this way, and others had been seriously injured. The villagers were terrified of the satyr."

"What did you do to help those people, Teacher?"

"I recalled my studies of a rare book left to us by King Midas, who was known to have a bit of satyr blood in his own veins, as could be seen by the shape of his ears. Occasionally his satyr relatives imposed on Midas's hospitality, making chaos of his court with their wild behavior. But as a child Midas had been told by his mother of a way to deal with satyrs, which he put to the test. Wine has a peculiar effect on them. When a satyr imbibes, he becomes intoxicated, as men do, and eventually he falls fast asleep, snoring loudly, as men do. But when the satyr awakens from this drunken stupor, his animal nature has departed from him and he is as harmless as a child. Such a tame satyr is capable of being taught to speak and even to reason. The widespread reformation of satyrs is no doubt one reason they are so very rarely seen nowadays, since such satyrs are more afraid of humans than are humans of them.

"But a wild satyr has a great aversion to wine, so the challenge is to trick him into drinking it. The villagers had reason to think this satyr drank at night from a particular cattle trough. The chief of the village had a jar of Egyptian wine left over from a recent festival. At my instruction, every drop of wine was emptied into the trough one night. In the morning it could be seen that a substantial part of the mixture of water and wine had been drunk.

"The satyr was asleep in his lair, no doubt, but where was that? I traversed the area all around the village, pricking up my ears, listening for the sound of snoring. At last I heard a faint noise. I followed it to a place the locals called the Grotto of the Nymphs. There, lying on a mossy stone amid the reeds, snoring loudly, lay the satyr, fast asleep and stinking of wine.

"The villagers were eager to awaken him, but I thought it best that he should be allowed to come to his senses in his own time. An hour later, quite abruptly, he ceased snoring, rubbed his eyes, and stood upright. The villagers were of a mind to stone him, and even began to gather up suitable rocks, but I shielded him with my own body and told the villagers they must do no harm to the creature, for now he was a changed satyr and his days of mischief were behind him. That night, at a blessedly sober festival—for all the wine was gone—the naked sages danced for the villagers, and the satyr joined them, leaping and somersaulting in the air."

Lucius smiled. The scent of jasmine under the hot sun was intoxicating. "If I heard such a tale from any other man, I wouldn't believe it for a moment," he said. "But from you, Teacher—"

Hilarion rushed into the garden. From his look of alarm, he was not there to announce the arrival of the guests.

"Praetorian Guards!" he said. "They refused to wait in the vestibule—"

Armed men entered the garden.

"You must be Apollonius of Tyana," said an officer. "I'd think this hairy fellow was your son, if I didn't know better," he said, smirking at Lucius. "I should think a well-born patrician could find a better teacher to model himself on, or at least one who was better groomed. But don't worry, we'll relieve you both of those ridiculous beards soon enough."

Lucius was snatched up by the guards and dragged from his house. He and Apollonius were marched barefoot through the streets, toward the imperial palace, while his neighbors, alerted by the commotion, looked on. Some were aghast, but others looked smugly pleased. Lucius's disdain for social functions, his eccentric new appearance, and his disreputable-looking visitors had caused a scandal among his well-connected neighbors on the Palatine.

They approached the same entrance to the palace at which Lucius had arrived for his dinner in the black room. He felt a surge of panic and looked to Apollonius for guidance. The Teacher did not appear to be impressed by the grand entryway, or fearful of what might lie beyond.

"Teacher, do you understand what's happening?"

"I think so. At long last, I am to meet the emperor."

"Forgive me, Teacher. If I had been on my guard, if Hilarion had given us more warning—"

"Then what? Would you expect me to avoid the opportunity to meet Domitian? This is why I came to Roma."

"But, Teacher—"

"Let us be grateful that these men arrived when they did. Had they come later, they might have arrested all those visitors you were expecting, and that would have been most inconvenient for everyone concerned. Imagine such a crowd, being herded into the House of the Flavians. This way, we may hope to have the emperor's undivided attention."

They were taken through a maze of corridors, arriving at last in a small but opulently decorated reception room. In an ornate chair atop a dais, Domitian sat with his chin cupped in one hand, looking bored. A eunuch secretary was reading aloud to him from a scroll. When Apollonius entered the room, Domitian waved aside the secretary, who put down the scroll and took up a wax tablet and stylus to take notes.

"I've been listening to the charges against you, magician," said Domitian.

Apollonius looked at him blankly.

"Have you nothing to say?"

"Are you addressing me?" said Apollonius. "I thought you were speaking to some magician, though I see no such person among us."

"Do you deny that you practice magic, Apollonius of Tyana?"

"Does magic exist? Our ancestors believed that there were two means of obtaining favors from the gods. The first is by propitiation, whereby a mortal sacrifices an animal and begs the gods for their blessing. The second is by magic, whereby a mortal casts a spell and compels the gods to do his will. Now, the traditional method of propitiation is surely a mistake, since the gods cannot be expected to delight in the destruction of a creature they themselves imbued with life. As for magic, can it be possible to force the gods to act against their will? Such a thing would violate the order of nature."

"That is why we call it magic, and make it a crime," said Domitian.

Apollonius shrugged. "As I said, I see no magician here."

"Then what do you call yourself? You dress like a beggar. You put on airs and wear long hair and a beard, like a philosopher."

"I call myself Apollonius, which is the name I was given at birth."

"And you, Lucius Pinarius. You would be a dead man today, but for my mercy. What excuse can you make for consorting with this magician?"

Lucius summoned his courage. "I see no magician, Dominus."

Domitian scowled. "I see the magician has turned you into his puppet. Did he cast a spell over you, or are you such a fool that you follow him by your own choice? Never mind. Shave off their beards."

The Praetorians converged on them with shears and blades. Apollonius did not resist. Lucius followed his example. Their hair was roughly shorn and their beards were cut. They were stripped of their tunics but allowed to keep their loincloths. Lucius was wearing the fascinum on a thin chain around his neck. He was touching it when one of the guards seized his hands and pulled them before him. Shackles were fastened around his wrists; the metal was so heavy that Lucius could barely lift his arms. More shackles were fitted around his ankles. Lucius saw that the same thing was being done to Apollonius, who in his unclothed state looked very thin and frail.

"Now this is a curious thing," said Apollonius. "If you think me a magician, what makes you think you can fetter me? And if you can fetter me, what makes you think I practice magic?"

Domitian was not listening. A fly had landed on an arm of his chair. The emperor motioned to the secretary to hand him his stylus. Domitian touched a fingertip to the point of the sharp instrument, held it poised above the fly for several heartbeats, then struck, transfixing the fly. He held up the skewered insect and smiled. "I learned to do that as a boy. Instead of using my stylus to copy Cicero, I spent whole afternoons hunting down the little pests and impaling them. It requires considerable skill."

Apollonius shook his head. "When I met your brother in Tarsus, a fly landed on his finger. Do you know what he did? He blew the fly away, and we both laughed. Any man can end a life with a weapon, but not every man can spare a life with a puff of breath. Which man is more powerful?"

Domitian gritted his teeth. "Lucius Pinarius—you must appreciate the skillful use of a weapon. You're a huntsman, aren't you?"

"Not any longer, Dominus," said Lucius. "All life is sacred. I kill nothing if I can help it."

Domitian shook his head in disgust. He called to the Praetorians. "You, bring me a bow and a quiver of arrows. And you, go stand against that far wall, facing it. Extend your arm parallel with the floor. Press your hand against the wall with your fingers spread wide apart."

Domitian tested the string of the bow, then notched an arrow. "This is another skill I taught myself. Observe, huntsman. I shall fire four arrows. Watch the spaces between the fingers."

Domitian took aim. Lucius saw that neither the Praetorians nor the emperor's secretary appeared apprehensive. This was a feat Domitian had performed many times before.

In sudden quiet, Lucius heard a low murmur. He could not make out the words, or where the sound came from. The murmur faded away. No one else seemed to have noticed. Lucius wondered if he had imagined it.

Domitian let fly four arrows in rapid succession. Each made a sharp sound like the buzzing of a wasp. With a grin of satisfaction, he lowered the bow.

"What do you think of that?" he said. "One arrow in each of the spaces between the man's fingers. Titus could never have done such a thing—"

With a loud groan, the Praetorian collapsed against the wall, slid down, and lay crumpled on the floor. The secretary shrieked and dropped his wax tablet.

All four arrows had landed squarely in the Praetorian's back, shot with such force that they had pierced his armor. Some of his comrades cried out and ran to help him.

"What is this?" shouted Domitian. His voice quavered. "This is your doing, magician!"

"I shot no arrows." Apollonius held forth his shackled wrists to show that his hands were empty.

"Get the magician away from me! Lock them both away!"

"But what is the charge against me?" asked Apollonius.

"The secretary has written down everything you've said. Your own words will condemn you. You blasphemed the gods by ridiculing the practice of animal sacrifice. And you repeatedly offended my majesty by failing to address me as Dominus."

"So a man can now be condemned for what he does not say, as well as for what he says? Your brother punished no man for speaking freely; you would punish a man for saying nothing."

Domitian threw the bow against the floor, so hard that it broke and the string went flying.

Apollonius was unfazed. "And what are the charges against Lucius Pinarius?"

"Is he not your accomplice?"

"I would prefer to call him my friend. I have many friends. Will you arrest them all?"

"Wait and see, magician!"

Apollonius sighed and shook his head as the Praetorians attached chains to their manacles and pulled them from the room. The heavy shackles bit into Lucius's ankles and wrists. The polished marble floor was cold against his bare feet.

They were taken to a subterranean cell lit only by grated openings in the ceiling. The stone walls seemed to sweat. Heaps of straw provided the only bedding. The place had a foul smell. For the disposal of wastes, there was a single bucket attached to a rope that could be pulled upward through one of the openings.

They were not alone. It took Lucius's eyes a long time to adjust to the dimness of the place, but gradually he counted more than fifty fellow prisoners, most of them huddled against the walls. Occasionally, Lucius heard something rustle in the straw and heard the squeak of a mouse.

Lucius felt faint. He steadied himself against a wall. He touched his forehead and found that it was as clammy as the stones against which he was leaning.

"Are you unwell?" said Apollonius.

"This place . . ."

"You're thinking of her, and imagining the hole under ground in which they confined her."

"Yes."

"Push all such imaginings from your mind, Lucius. Think only of this moment, and the place in which you find yourself. See it for what it is, nothing more and nothing less."

"It's horrible!"

"It's certainly not as comfortable as your garden. And yet, we are able to breathe, and to move about. We have enough light by which to see each other, and more importantly, we are together, sharing each other's company, and the company of these new friends with whom we find ourselves. I'm guessing they have many stories to tell. As long as we possess curiosity, we shall not be bored."

Lucius managed a rueful laugh. "Teacher, this is a prison."

"Lucius, we mortals are in a prison every moment we live. The soul is bound inside a perishable body, enslaved by all the cravings which visit humanity. The man who built the first dwelling merely surrounded himself with yet another prison, and made himself a slave to it, for any dwelling must be maintained, just like the human body. I think that the man who lives in a palace is more surely a prisoner than the men he puts in chains. As for the place where we now find ourselves, we must reflect that we are not the first to be confined in this way. Many a wise man, despised by the mob or hated by a despot, has had to endure such a fate, and the best have done so with serene resignation. Let us strive to do the same, so that we may not be inferior to those who set an example before us."

Some of the other prisoners, hearing him speak, drew closer.

"You're Apollonius of Tyana, aren't you?" said one of the men.

"I am."

"I heard you speak once. I recognized your voice. But I'd never have known you otherwise. Your hair's been cut, and so has your beard." The man shook his head. "I never thought to see those snow-white tresses shorn like fleece from a lamb! Who would have thought that Apollonius of Tyana could be put in chains?"

"The person who put me in chains thought of it, for otherwise he wouldn't have done it," said Apollonius.

The man laughed. "Truly, you are Apollonius. But those fetters must be causing you great pain. Look how the rough iron chafes the skin."

"I hadn't noticed. My thoughts are on more important things."

"But how can you be in pain and not think about it? A man can't ignore pain."

"Not so," said Apollonius. "The mind attends to what the self deems important. If there is injury, a man may choose not to feel pain, or order the pain to stop."

The man pursed his lips. "But why are you still here? You're a magician. Why don't you just walk out?"

Apollonius laughed. "Like the man who put me here, you accuse me of being a magician. Well, let us suppose that it's true. In that case, it must be that I am here among you because I wish to be."

"Why would any man wish to be here?" said another man, stepping forward and crossing his arms.

"Perhaps I can serve a purpose. Perhaps my words can give comfort or courage. How did you come to be here, friend?"

"The plain truth? I have too much wealth."

Lucius saw that the speaker was dressed in a fine tunic and cloak, though his clothes were filthy from long confinement in the dank cell. His face was haggard, but folds of flesh hung from his chin, as if he had once been fat but had lost weight very quickly.

"Who put you here?" said Apollonius.

"Who do you think? The same man who put us all here."

"He covets your wealth?"

"He told me to my face, before he sent me here, that an excess of wealth is dangerous for a common citizen. Money makes a man insolent and prideful, he said. As if trumping up charges against me, throwing me in this hole, and trying to extort my money was all for my own good!"

"Did he offer you a way out?"

"As soon as I'll admit to false charges of evading taxes and hand over my fortune, I shall be released."

"Then why are you still here? The money is doing you no good. Its only value is to buy your way out of this place."

"I won't give it up!"

"Your wealth landed you here, my friend, and your wealth will purchase your release. More importantly, paying the ransom will free you from the money itself, for wealth is also a prison. The man who takes it from you will only increase his bondage."

"This is nonsense!" The man mumbled an obscenity and turned away.

Apollonius spoke in a low voice to Lucius. "I think that fellow is not quite ready to receive my message."

"What about me?" said another man, stepping forward. He was tall and solidly built but his hands trembled. "I could use some courage. They're taking me to face the emperor this very afternoon. I think I shall die from fear before that happens."

"Take heart, my friend. I myself just came from the emperor's presence, yet you can see that I emerged unscathed."

"But everyone knows you're fearless. How do you do it?"

"I thought of an example I would not be ashamed to follow. You can do the same."

"But what example did you think of?"

"I remembered Odysseus and the peril he faced when he entered the cave of Polyphemus. The Cyclops was gigantic, and far too strong for even a hundred men to overmaster. With its single eye, the creature was almost too hideous to look at, and its booming voice was like thunder. Strewn all around were human bones, the remains of past meals, for the Cyclops was an eater of human flesh. But did Odysseus take fright? No. He considered his situation and asked himself how to get the better of an opponent too powerful to be overcome by force and too vicious to be reasoned with. Yet, Odysseus left the lair of the Cyclops alive, and with most of his companions alive."

The first man who had spoken, who had asked Apollonius about the shearing of his hair and the pain caused by his shackles, spoke up again. "Are you comparing our emperor to the Cyclops? Are you saying he should be blinded?"

Apollonius whispered in Lucius's ear, "I suspect this fellow is an informer. His previous comments were not to commiserate with me, but to goad me into speaking ill of Domitian." Apollonius answered the man, "What do *you* think, my friend, of the man who put you here among us?"

The man shrugged. "I have nothing good to say about him."

"Would that every man could have such a mild temperament! Have you no harsh words for the man who confines other men to such a foul place, who cuts their hair and puts them in shackles, who extorts their wealth, whose famous cruelty causes them to tremble when they're called before him?"

"Naturally, I feel as the others here must feel."

"And how is that? By all means, speak freely," said Apollonius. "You can say whatever you like in front of me, for I am the last man in the world to inform against another. No? You have nothing to say? As for myself, what I have to say to the emperor, I'll say to his face."

"That's telling him!" said the man who had been fearful of meeting the emperor. There were nods and grunts of agreement. Clearly, many in the cell already suspected the informer.

Apollonius stepped back, as if he were done speaking, but the other prisoners implored him to keep talking. "Tell us more," said one of them. "The worst thing about this place is the boredom. Tell us about your travels. You've been all over the world."

Apollonius sat on the floor. The prisoners gathered around him. He described rivers and mountains and deserts he had seen. He talked about the people he had met and their exotic customs. The men listened with rapt expressions, some closing their eyes, transported by the Teacher's narrative to faraway places, freed from their prison cell by the pictures he painted in their imaginations. Lucius closed his eyes and listened with them.

Apollonius spoke of finding the spot, high in the icy mountains of the Caucasus Indicus, where even Alexander the Great had not ventured, where the gods had chained Prometheus for his crime of giving fire to mortals.

"I discovered the very manacles which had held the Titan. Gigantic they were, so big that a man could stand inside one with his arms outstretched and barely touch the sides. The manacles were set into either side of a narrow gorge—thus, one could see just how enormous Prometheus must have been. The Titan himself was long gone. The locals told me that Hercules, on one of his many journeys, came upon Prometheus even as Jupiter's eagle arrived to perform the daily torment of tearing out the Titan's entrails. Hercules took pity on Prometheus and shot the eagle out of the sky. In the ravine below, I found the bones of an enormous bird, larger than any other bones I had ever seen. Hercules broke the manacles and set Prometheus free. Indeed, I could see that the metal was severed and twisted, but strangely it was not covered with rust. Vulcan must have forged those manacles of some alloy unknown to mortal men."

Exhausted by the day's events and lulled by the Teacher's voice, Lucius was almost dozing. He chanced to open his eyes, just enough to peer through the lashes, and saw that Apollonius was using each hand to rub the wrist of the other, stretching the tendons and massaging the soreness caused by the manacles—*which were gone.*

Lucius's eyes shot open and he uttered an exclamation of amazement. The others, most of whom also seemed to be half dozing, bolted upright and followed his gaze.

"His shackles!" said one of the men. "He's taken off his shackles."

"Have I?" Apollonius looked around absentmindedly, as if he had misplaced something. "So I have. Ah, but it would never do for the guards to see me this way. They'd be terribly upset." He turned his back on them for a moment and engaged in a series of peculiar movements, hunching over and twisting from side to side. When he turned back, the shackles were again around his wrists.

"There, that's better," said Apollonius, shaking his manacles so that they made a dull clang. He began a new story, this one about the time he had spent in Babylon in his younger days, where he met the Parthian king, Vardanes, and his Chaldean astrologers.

Lucius looked down at his own manacles. He turned his hands this way and that and tugged against the shackles. There was no way he could possibly take them off. And yet it seemed that the Teacher had slipped out of his manacles without even thinking, as a man might shuffle off a pair of loose shoes. Or had Apollonius only created the illusion of doing so? Or had he never been placed in the manacles at all?

❖

They passed many days in the cell. The accommodations were foul and the food was poor, but the regimen was not harsh; they were not physically harmed or made to do labor. Lucius received a visit from Hilarion, who assured Lucius that everything was running smoothly in his absence. It occurred to Lucius not for the first time that he was an incidental part of his own household, which was entirely capable of running itself without him.

Apollonius also received visitors, including a delegation of distinguished men headed by Marcus Nerva, an elder statesman of the Senate. Nerva looked the part, with his narrow, ascetic face, his high, broad forehead, and his neatly groomed white hair. Lucius knew the senator to be a friend and correspondent of Dio of Prusa.

Nerva asked after the prisoner's health; Apollonius responded by asking after the senator's health, since Nerva looked considerably more frail than he did. From their easy manner with each other, Lucius realized that the two were old acquaintances. Lucius never ceased to be surprised at the great number and variety of people Apollonius knew. To know Apollonius, it seemed, was to be only a step or two removed from almost anyone in the world.

Nerva and Apollonius conversed about inconsequential matters— prison food, the weather, and which of them had whiter hair. Apollonius asked Nerva about his hometown, the village of Narnia, which was said to be in the exact center of Italy and was one of the few places Apollonius had never visited; Nerva assured him that it was a charming town. It seemed to Lucius that Apollonius must have given Nerva a sign early on that an informer was present, and that their conversation should be guarded. Or were they conversing in code?

After the visitors left, Lucius expressed surprise that Nerva and the others had dared to pay a call on Apollonius. Domitian was always seeing conspiracies among the senators. Did these men not risk arousing the emperor's suspicion by visiting a man arrested for disrespecting the emperor's majesty?

"Not so," said Apollonius. "By coming to see me so openly, those fellows protect themselves from suspicion. If I were indeed seditious, and if they were colluding with me, would they come to chat with me about the weather? They came here as Roman statesmen, to pay a courtesy call on a man who once counseled the Divine Vespasian and the Divine Titus. Conspirators would not come to see me at all, but would lurk in the shadows. Thus, by their boldness they disarm Domitian's fear."

"I see. Nerva didn't look that clever to me."

"Don't let his manner fool you. Nerva is a very canny fellow. I have high hopes for him."

"High hopes for a frail old senator?"

"To all appearances, there was never a more robust man than Titus, yet those who put their hopes for the future in Titus saw those hopes dashed. So why not look to a frail old man to deliver a brighter tomorrow?"

One day passed into another, until one morning a Praetorian arrived and told them they were to be taken before the emperor, who was ready to try them and pronounce judgment.

Lucius had done his best to prepare for this moment, striving to emulate the Teacher's equanimity. Still, he felt a thrill of panic.

"Teacher, what will become of us?"

"Lucius, what do you fear? That we shall be tortured and killed? Every living thing must die, and there are things far worse than the suffering of physical pain. How much more terrible if we should comport ourselves disgracefully and lose our self-respect; then we should truly be damaged, and the harm would have been inflicted by ourselves."

Lucius breathed deeply. "I shall look to you, Teacher. I shall follow your example."

"And I shall do my best to make that example a good one, Lucius. To know that your eyes are on me will give me strength."

They were taken first to an antechamber adjoining the reception room. Their shackles were removed. A group of slaves appeared, charged with making them presentable for the trial. Basins of water were brought. Their faces and hands were scrubbed clean. They were dressed in clean tunics. They were also given shoes, but because these were made of leather, Apollonius would not wear them. Lucius followed the Teacher's example and remained barefoot.

When the attendants were finished cleaning and dressing them, they were put in shackles again.

A figure in the sumptuous robes of an imperial courtier entered the room and approached them. To Lucius's surprise, it was his old friend and protector Epaphroditus. Lucius had seen him very little since the death of Cornelia. His old friend had aged a great deal.

"I'm sorry I didn't come to visit you in prison, Lucius," said Epaphroditus. He kept his distance and maintained a dignified posture, but his voice was thick with emotion. "It wasn't possible, given my new position. To see you like this, in shackles—"

"You serve Domitian now?"

Epaphroditus flashed a crooked smile. "The emperor called me out of retirement. He insisted that the state required my services. I saw no way to decline his request."

"You should be flattered, I suppose," said Lucius. "The emperor could use the help of the man who ran the Golden House." It seemed that

Domitian—who refused to have among his courtiers anyone who had been close to his father or to his brother, and in his fits of suspicion had eliminated many members of his own imperial staff—was now being forced to reach back to the days of Nero to find men of sufficient experience to run the state.

"I would gladly have remained as I was, a retired observer of events," said Epaphroditus. "Still, there are advantages to my new position. I was able, for example, to persuade the emperor to give me the role of preparing you and your friend for your trial."

Epaphroditus turned to Apollonius. "Are you aware of the rules of procedure? The trial will take place before a select audience of senators, magistrates, and imperial dignitaries. The charges against you will be read by a prosecutor. You will have a chance to respond to those charges. Then Caesar will render judgment."

"Caesar will judge me?" said Apollonius.

"Yes."

"But who will judge Caesar?"

Epaphroditus raised an eyebrow. "Caesar is not on trial."

"No? I think he has committed many offenses contrary to the teachings of philosophy."

Epaphroditus sighed. "Caesar is not concerned with philosophy."

"Ah, but philosophy is very much concerned with Caesar, that he should govern as a wise man."

Epaphroditus sighed and exchanged looks with Apollonius that left Lucius perplexed. He had presumed that Epaphroditus and Apollonius were strangers—or did they know each other?

Epaphroditus continued. "You'll have only a short time to give your answers. Look to the water clock. When the water level drops and the lever rises, that means your time is growing short. Finish what you have to say. You won't be allowed to speak longer than the clock permits."

"Then I hope that the Tiber itself is connected to this water clock, for every drop of its water will be needed for me to say all I have to say to the emperor."

"I'm afraid your time will be considerably shorter than that," said Epaphroditus. "Also, you are not allowed to bring anything with you into the chamber from which you might read or with which you might cast a magical spell. So you may not have on your person any scroll or scrap of parchment or anything at all with writing on it, or any amulet or other magical device."

"As we were stripped naked and then dressed by servants of the emperor himself, I think that will not be a problem," said Apollonius.

"Still, it is my duty to make sure there is nothing concealed in your tunics. Raise your arms as high as you can."

Epaphroditus ran his hands over Apollonius, then did the same thing to Lucius.

Lucius stiffened, for he realized that he was wearing the fascinum beneath the thin tunic. He suppressed an urge to touch it. Epaphroditus ran his hands over Lucius's chest. He must have felt the talisman, yet he said nothing and stepped back.

Epaphroditus led them into the judgment chamber, a somber but magnificent room decorated with dark marbles and blood-red curtains. Before a towering statue of Minerva sat Domitian. Seated cross-legged on the dais beside him was his small-headed companion. Epaphroditus joined a group of other courtiers who stood to one side. Next to him was the water clock he had mentioned. The inner workings of the device were hidden behind an ornate bronze covering that depicted images of the sun, moon, and stars.

Among the senators in the room, Lucius saw the white-haired Nerva and several others who had visited Apollonius. There were also some faces he recognized from gatherings of Apollonius's followers—magistrates and even a few imperial courtiers who had dared to attend meetings in private homes where the Teacher spoke. Lucius felt heartened by the sight of these familiar faces, even though not one of them dared to look him in the eye or show any sign of sympathy.

The prosecutor stepped forward. Lucius's heart sank. It was Catullus. The blind man carried a staff and was assisted by a secretary who frequently whispered in his ear.

"Dominus, the magician Apollonius and his accomplice Lucius Pinarius have entered your divine presence," said Catullus. "The time has come for them to submit to your judgment. The magician will be tried first. Step forward, Apollonius of Tyana. Look upon our Master and God, address him as Dominus, and beseech him to be just and merciful to you."

Apollonius stepped forward, but he did not look at Domitian. Instead, he seemed to look everywhere else. He looked at the emperor's small-headed companion and made a whimsical face, as one might at a child, at which the creature seemed to take fright and started back. He gazed curiously at the water clock next to Epaphroditus. He looked over his shoulder at the spectators and smiled.

Catullus's assistant whispered furiously in his ear. Catullus struck his staff against the marble floor. "Magician! You will face and address our Master and God!"

"Very well," said Apollonius with a shrug. He lifted his head and gazed upward, and raised his shackled hands as high as he could. "Divine Singularity, emanation of perfection whom the Romans call Jupiter, greatest of gods!" he cried. "Reveal your wisdom to us. Render your judgment. Make known to us your will. Tell us, we beseech you, who displeases you more—the man who utters profane flattery, or the man who receives it?"

There were gasps from the onlookers.

Catullus struck his staff against the marble floor, demanding silence. "We can dispense with your formal response to the first charge against you, since, by your actions, magician, you have just given us ample reply."

"And what was that charge?"

"That you refuse to show proper respect to Caesar and address him as Dominus."

"You told me to look upon our Master and God, and I did. I looked upward to the Divine Singularity."

"Don't try to throw dust in our eyes with a pretense of piety, magician. Is it not true that you believe yourself to be a god? Is it not true that others have called you a god, and that you accepted their worship without objection?"

"Prosecutor, I am impressed," said Apollonius. "You have done your research. I believe you must be referring to my days in India, when I sought wisdom among the sages of the Ganges. They refer to themselves as gods. When I asked them why, they answered: 'Because we are good men.' All creatures, despite their mortal forms, possess divinity, and to be truly good is to be godly. Before I left them, the Indian sages addressed me as 'god,' and I was honored."

"So a man can become a god simply by being good?"

"To be good is not as simple as you seem to think."

"But if you meet a good man, you gladly call him 'god'?"

"I do. If the man you want me to address as a god were a good man, I would gladly do so."

Again there were gasps from the spectators. Catullus banged his staff repeatedly against the floor.

The small-headed creature was heard to mumble, in a high voice, "He isn't even wearing shoes!"

"What's that?" said Apollonius. "Speak up, little one."

The creature hissed and spat, like a cat with its back up. "You come here barefoot!" he cried. "You show contempt to Caesar!"

"If I had put on the shoes I was offered, I would have shown contempt to the poor animal who provided the hide. I would no more kill a cow, a godly creature, and carve it up, simply to cover my feet, than I would kill and carve you up, my little friend, to make a pair of shoes out of you. The bounty of the soil provides all that I require to eat and clothe myself. If I must protect my feet, I wear shoes made of cloth and bark. I need not resort to the killing of fellow creatures."

The small-headed creature pressed himself against Domitian's leg and covered his face.

Catullus smirked. "Is it true, magician, that in your youth you took a vow of silence and did not speak for five years?"

"That is so. Silence is a language unto itself. There is much to be learned by not speaking."

"Yet it seems that ever since then, you can't keep your mouth shut. You may regret not keeping silent today, magician. The words you spoke just now lead nicely to the second charge against you: that you have profaned against the gods and imperiled the state by preaching against the institution of animal sacrifice. Do you deny this charge?"

Catullus signaled to Epaphroditus, who touched a switch on the water clock. Water gurgled as it flowed from one chamber to another and the lever that indicated the passage of time began to move.

Apollonius cleared his throat. "Have I said that animal sacrifice is unnecessary? Yes. Have I offended the gods and imperiled the state by doing so? No. To show fitting respect to the Divine Singularity we must offer no victim at all, nor kindle a fire, nor burn incense, nor make promises, nor offer up any sort of trinket or amulet or any other material object. For if there is a god who is higher than all else and of such perfection that he is unique and distinguished from every other essence, then what use does this god have of our paltry offerings? Far from giving him nourishment, such material offerings can only pollute his purity. And how dare we attempt to bargain with the Divine Singularity by making promises and pleading? We should approach the Divine Singularity using only our highest faculty, which is our intelligence. By thought alone should we strive to make ourselves known to the Divine Singularity, which itself is pure thought. If we desire to make these thoughts manifest for the benefit of other mortals, then we may employ beautiful speech, which is the imperfect servant of thought. A song or an uttered prayer shared among mortals may be pleasing to the Divine Singularity, but bloody carcasses and charred remains can only be offensive to that which is perfection."

The lever on the water clock reached its upright position, which caused a bell to be struck. The gurgling of water ceased. Apollonius smiled serenely. He had said what he had to say in exactly the allotted time.

Catullus made a face of disgust. "Do I need to state the next charge, Dominus? The accused has already sufficiently incriminated himself. To offer him more opportunities to speak will only subject your majesty to more blasphemy and sedition."

Domitian, who had been watching the proceedings in silence, stared at Apollonius with a quizzical tilt of his head. "That this man is guilty and worthy of death, there can be no doubt. But surely the third charge against him is the most serious. It should be addressed."

Catullus stated the next charge. "It is alleged that Apollonius of Tyana practices magic. Witnesses attest that he has healed sick persons by the use of magical influence, and has even caused the dead to return to life, against the laws of nature. He has used magic to witness faraway events and otherwise obtain knowledge of the movements of others, including even yourself, Dominus. He has used magical powers to look into the minds of others, so that even when they remain silent, his victims cannot conceal their thoughts from him. These uses of magic, which in and of themselves violate the laws of men and gods, also constitute a clear danger to the state and to the person of Caesar. What do you say to the charge, Apollonius of Tyana?"

Again, Epaphroditus touched a switch on the water clock. Its gurgling echoed loudly in the suddenly silent room, for everyone present was intent on hearing what Apollonius had to say.

Apollonius turned to Lucius. His lips did not move, yet Lucius heard him speak. "Do you have the thing Epaphroditus gave you earlier? Give it to me now."

Lucius was puzzled. Nothing in the room had changed and yet everything suddenly seemed unreal, as if he had entered a dream without falling asleep. What was Apollonius talking about? Epaphroditus had given him nothing earlier. And yet, he found himself reaching into his tunic and pulling out a small sphere made of glass. He handed it to Apollonius.

Again without moving his lips, Apollonius spoke to him. "You are a good friend, Lucius Pinarius. I will miss you. Be strong."

Apollonius raised the glass sphere and threw it against the floor. There was a blinding flash of light and a loud blast. A cloud of smoke enveloped Apollonius. There was a loud clatter, as of shackles falling to the floor. A peculiar smell filled Lucius's nostrils. The floor seemed to ripple, as if shaken by an earthquake. Lucius thought that he alone felt these things, but when he looked at the spectators he saw that they, too, were reeling, as if from a blow. Some of them dropped to their knees. Lucius turned and saw that Domitian had risen from his chair. His small-headed companion was clutching the emperor's leg.

The blind Catullus turned his head this way and that. "What's happening?" he cried. "What has the magician done?"

The smoke dispersed. Apollonius was nowhere to be seen. His empty shackles lay on the marble floor.

"What trickery is this?" said Domitian. He ordered the guards to search every corner of the room and make sure that every exit was blocked. Apollonius was not to be found.

Domitian glared at Lucius. "The magician looked at you before he vanished. What happened?"

"I don't know, Dominus."

"Where has he gone?"

"I don't know, Dominus."

"Strip this man!" cried Domitian. Lucius's tunic was torn from him. "What is that?" said Domitian.

"What is it you see, Dominus?" asked Catullus.

"He wears a talisman of some sort."

Catullus raised his eyebrows. "How did this happen, Epaphroditus? You were to make sure the prisoners had no magical devices on their persons."

"I'm as baffled as you," said Epaphroditus.

Domitian stepped from the dais and approached Lucius. Lucius flinched but stood firm. The emperor reached out and took hold of the fascinum. "What is this? Did this amulet play some part in the magician's disappearance?"

"It's a fascinum, Dominus. A family heirloom. I call on it for protection, but I know of no other powers it might possess."

Domitian frowned. "It looks like a cross."

Catullus scurried to them, tapping his staff on the floor before him. "A cross, Dominus?" Domitian put the fascinum into the hand of Catullus, who examined it with his fingertips. Lucius cringed at having the man so close to him. Catullus cringed, as well. He released the fascinum with a show of disgust.

"Most certainly this is a magical amulet. I can feel the sorcery in it! Christian magic, I suspect."

"Christian?" said Domitian.

"They use amulets in the shape of a cross to bewitch their enemies."

"It's a fascinum, Dominus, not a crucifix," said Lucius.

"He lies," said Catullus. "When I was preparing my dossier on this man, I discovered that his uncle was a Christian, one of those punished by Nero for arson. Can it be a coincidence that he wears a Christian amulet?"

Domitian peered down his nose at Lucius. "This man is a follower of Apollonius, and whatever else he might be, Apollonius is not a Christian."

"We cannot expect the enemies of the gods to be consistent in their blasphemy. This secret Christian has just assisted in the escape of a most dangerous magician, and by means of this amulet he may intend to endanger your divine person. Lucius Pinarius has conspired against you, Dominus. He must be punished."

Domitian narrowed his eyes. "Yes, but how?"

"His uncle was burned alive in the Circus Vaticanus."

Lucius felt a sudden prickling sensation all over his body and saw oily spots before his eyes. He tried to emulate the courage of Apollonius, but he swayed and fell to the floor.

Domitian looked down at him. "Are you sure this pitiful wretch poses a threat to me, Catullus?"

Catullus lowered his voice to a whisper. "Dominus, if the magician Apollonius has truly escaped, then this one must be made to suffer in his place. His punishment must be public, and it must be made to fit his crime."

Domitian nodded. "I know what to do with him."

Lucius was taken not to the cell where he had previously been held but through a series of narrow underground passages to a much smaller cell, large enough to hold only one prisoner. He was allowed to keep the fascinum. From the whisperings of the guards, Lucius gathered that they had been instructed to take it from him, but they were all too afraid to touch it.

His cell was a bare, windowless cubicle of dank stone with iron bars on one side. Beyond the bars, set too closely for him to stick his head between them, was a curved hallway, dimly lit by indirect sunlight. From somewhere nearby he heard wild animals—the growling of lions, the snorting of aurochs, the yelping of dogs. The air was heavy with the odors of straw, dung, and urine, and the smell of the raw meat that was fed to the carnivores.

From elsewhere he heard the clashing of swords and gruff voices—the sounds of gladiators training—and realized where he must be: in the cells beneath the Flavian Amphitheater. If he recalled correctly, the next occasion for games in the amphitheater was five days away.

By the alternation of darkness and light he was able to mark the passage of the days. At night the hallway was unlit and the darkness of his cell was absolute. The blackness of the nights terrified him at first, but in his imagination he sought the company of Apollonius and was comforted. It seemed to him sometimes that the Teacher actually spoke to him during the night, but in such complete darkness he could not tell if he was awake or dreaming, or even if he was alive or dead. "Be calm," Apollonius said. "Though my body is far away, I am with you."

On the fifth day, Lucius awoke to a great tumult of sounds from near and far—the blare of trumpets, men shouting and laughing, gates clanging, and the steady hum of a vast crowd, punctuated at intervals by roars of excitement. The amphitheater above him was filled with people, and the games had commenced.

The punishment of criminals was a part of the games. Lucius had watched such exhibits many times, until he had become a follower of Apollonius and ceased to attend the games. Though he had sometimes imagined himself in the role of the hunters in the arena who stalked exotic prey, he had never imagined himself as one of the wretched criminals forced to fight to the death or to become the prey of savage beasts. And yet, that was to be his fate.

Had Apollonius foreseen this outcome? Why had the Teacher fled, saving himself, only to abandon Lucius to a horrible and humiliating death? Why had he not used his magic to take Lucius with him?

For a brief instant, Lucius fell into despair. Then his spirits suddenly lifted. He felt a sense of lightness, as if a great weight had been lifted from him. Even his shackles felt lighter. He decided to surrender himself completely to the Teacher, to trust that Apollonius had foreseen this moment and had sufficiently prepared Lucius to face it calmly and with dignity. All was for the best.

When the guards came for him, they were surprised by his demeanor. They were used to seeing men who cringed, wept, struggled, and begged, or who fell limp or went stiff and stared into space. But Lucius looked them in the eye, nodded to them amiably, and stood up to follow them.

They removed his shackles. His arms and legs felt weak and stiff after such long confinement, but he was glad to be free of the restraints. He stretched out his arms and spread his fingers wide. He kicked out his legs and lifted his knees, testing his control of his body. It was a good thing that in his final moments he would be able to feel like a man again, however briefly.

They took off his tattered tunic so that he wore only his filthy loincloth. Around his waist they fitted a leather belt with a sheath; in the sheath was a knife. He pulled it out for a moment and saw that the blade was very dull. They handed him a bow and a single arrow. The bow was weak and poorly strung, and the head of the arrow was made not of metal but of cork. From a distance, the spectators would not be able to tell that the weapons were useless.

As they proceeded down a hallway, the roar of the crowd grew louder. They arrived at a gate made of iron bars. The gate opened. The guards lowered their spears, but there was no need for them to drive Lucius into the arena. He walked barefoot onto the sun-heated sand, squinting at the brightness of the day.

He had beheld the enormity of the amphitheater from the stands but never from the arena floor. The magnitude of the crowd was staggering. The imperial box looked very small amid the vastness, and the people within it seemed like figures in a picture. Lucius spotted Domitian and the empress, and also the emperor's small-headed companion. The most highly favored members of the imperial family were there, including the emperor's beautiful niece Flavia Domitilla, along with her husband and two of their young sons. Earinus was there, and close to the eunuch, Lucius saw with a slight shock, was Martial. Would he make a poem of what was about to happen? Amid the courtiers, Lucius saw Catullus, and also Epaphroditus.

There was a hush. A crier made an announcement. The words echoed oddly in Lucius's ears. He was unable to make out anything the man said, except his own name: "Lucius Pinarius . . ."

His name sounded strange to him, a collection of sounds that had nothing to do with what he was. "Lucius Pinarius: I am called Lucius Pinarius," he said to himself. "I am in a place called Roma. I am about to die."

Lucius strode to the very center of the arena and turned in a slow circle, gazing around him.

He felt that he was at the precise center of the cosmos, surrounded on all sides by the whole population of Roma, and by the city itself, and by the vast empire and the lands and oceans that lay beyond it. Every eye in the amphitheater was upon him; he was the focus of every gaze. And yet he felt not exposed and vulnerable but strangely isolated and protected. All around him was ceaseless noise and swirling chaos, but in the place where Lucius stood there was silence and stillness. He stood in the pupil of the eye of the Divine Singularity. Had Apollonius known that he would feel this? Was that why the Teacher had guided him to this place and this moment?

He heard the clanging of a gate and turned to see that he was no longer alone in the arena. A lion had been released. The beast looked about, sniffing the air, then spotted Lucius. It crouched for a moment, tensing and flexing its haunches, then sprang forward and ran straight toward Lucius.

Of what use were the bow and arrow? Even if Lucius took aim and struck the beast, he would only aggravate it. Lucius cast them aside.

Of what use was the knife? There was a slim chance that even with such a dull blade Lucius might inflict a wound on the beast; he might even, by some miracle, fatally wound it. But by the time that happened, the lion would have mauled him, and in the best possible outcome they both would die. Lucius felt no desire to kill the lion. He drew the knife from the sheath, which greatly excited the crowd, then cast it away, which elicited cries of derision and mutterings of confusion.

Lucius looked at the belt around his waist. What would Apollonius think if he saw Lucius wearing a garment made of leather? Lucius undid the belt and cast it away.

He suddenly loathed the touch of the filthy loincloth against his flesh. He did not want to die wearing it. He pulled off the loincloth and threw it to the ground.

Lucius stood naked at the center of the cosmos, stripped of all earthly pretense—naked except for the fascinum, which caught the sunlight and glittered brightly.

Where did he find the sense to do what he did next? An old slave, the scarred survivor of many dangerous hunts over a long lifetime, had once advised Lucius on the best way to comport himself should he ever encounter a deadly animal in the wild without the advantage of a weapon: "You must be as wild and fierce as the beast. No—wilder, fiercer! Jump, flail your arms, scream and shout like a madman."

"Pretend to be dangerous?" Lucius had asked.

"No pretending," said the slave. "You must find inside yourself the part of you that truly is as savage as the beast."

"And what if there is no such part of me?" said Lucius.

"There is," the slave had answered.

Lucius had quickly forgotten this exchange, but he remembered it now, as the lion ran toward him.

He heard a shrieking noise so bloodcurdling that even he was unnerved by it, though he knew he must be producing it himself. His body was in motion, but he had no conception of what his movements must look like. Perhaps they were comical, like the writhing of a mime, for he heard laughter from the stands. But the lion did not seem amused by his screaming and stamping and flailing. The beast stopped in its tracks and sprang back, looking startled. Lucius sensed that he had the advantage and pursued it. He did what no sane man would have done: he charged the lion.

What would he do if the lion stood its ground? He would have no choice but to leap onto the beast and wrestle it. The idea was absurd, but there was no turning back.

He heard gasps of disbelief and screams of excitement from the spectators. The lion crouched, flattened its ears, lifted a paw, and bared its fangs. Lucius continued his headlong rush, screaming at the top of his lungs, waving his arms and gaining speed as he drew closer. Just as he was about to leap, the beast turned and began to run.

Lucius chased the lion. The roar from the crowd was deafening. He perceived a vast upward movement all around him. The spectators, in unison, had risen to their feet.

The lion ran for a short distance, then stopped and looked back at him with flattened ears, made ready to fight, then lost its nerve and began to run again, staying low to the ground. The beast seemed as perplexed by its own craven behavior as it was by Lucius's headlong advance. The predator was not used to being pursued.

Lucius could not continue to scream and run for long. He was weak from imprisonment. He had managed to find within himself an unexpected reservoir of energy and had released it in a great burst of noise and action, but already he was flagging.

In the blink of an eye, his strength was gone. He stopped running. He could scream no longer. He gasped for air. He could barely stand.

The lion ran until it reached the far side of the arena. It spun around and peered at Lucius, then sat on the sand like a Sphinx and snapped its tail this way and that.

They stayed like that for a while, man and lion, peering at each other across the sand. Eventually, a gate opened. Attendants with long poles ran onto the sand and poked at the lion, trying to goad it into attacking Lucius again. But the cat turned on the attendants instead, spitting and batting its claws at them. Eventually the attendants retreated. The lion sat on the sand again, panting and showing its tongue.

No longer able to stand, Lucius sat. Nearby he noticed a bloody spot on the sand. Amid the blood lay a lump of flesh. Most likely it was from a human being, one of the day's previous victims, but it was so bloody and torn that it looked like a cut of meat from a butcher's shop. Lucius wrinkled his nose and felt a twinge of nausea.

For a while Lucius and the lion sat on the sand, resting and keeping their distance. Then the cat roused itself. It stood and began to walk very slowly toward Lucius. The crowd murmured in anticipation. A stone's throw from Lucius, the lion came to a stop and sat again, Sphinxlike, staring at him.

Lucius summoned his last vestige of strength to crawl on his hands and knees to the lump of bloody flesh on the sand. What would Apollonius think of his intention? Apollonius believed that men should not eat animals, but Lucius had never heard him express the opinion that animals should not eat men. It was in their nature, and they could not be reasoned out of it.

Grimacing with disgust, Lucius grabbed hold of the lump of flesh and flung it at the lion. The beast scrambled back, then poked its head toward the flesh and sniffed at it. It leaped onto the bloody lump, seized it with both paws, and attacked it with its powerful jaws.

The lion relished its meal. When it was done, it rose to its feet and sauntered toward Lucius, who stayed where he was, too exhausted to do anything except shut his eyes. He breathed deeply and awaited what was to come. As the lion drew nearer, Lucius heard its footsteps on the sand and smelled the gore on its breath.

Something rough and wet touched Lucius's hand. He opened his eyes and saw that the cat was licking the blood from his fingers. The lion took its time and did a very thorough job, then sat beside him and closed its eyes, seemingly content.

From the stands came a strange mixture of sounds—applause and laughter, but also angry jeers and cries of scorn. Some of the spectators were enthralled by the scene they had just witnessed and hailed Lucius's bravery. Others felt cheated of the thrill of seeing a man torn apart, and suspected that some trickery was afoot.

Lucius looked at the imperial box. Domitian was on his feet. Catullus was beside him, speaking into his right ear. Epaphroditus was speaking into his left ear. Domitian waved them both aside and gave an order to another courtier in his retinue. A few moments later, the attendants with long poles again appeared in the arena. One of the poles had a bit of meat tied to the end. They lured the cat to one of the openings and through the gate, which clanged shut after them.

A courtier beckoned to Lucius from the imperial box. Somehow, Lucius rose to his feet and staggered in that direction. Domitian stood at the parapet, looking down at him.

The emperor raised his hand. The spectators fell silent.

Domitian flashed a chilly smile. Thanks to the extraordinary acoustics of the amphitheater, he barely had to raise his voice to be heard by Lucius. "I think, Lucius Pinarius, that you are the luckiest man I have ever met. More than once I have intended to do away with you. More than once I have changed my mind."

"Caesar is merciful," Lucius managed to say. His throat ached and his voice was hoarse from screaming.

"Perhaps. Or perhaps Caesar is mindful of some powerful magic about you. Did the magician from Tyana teach you to cast that spell on the lion?"

"I am always mindful of the Teacher's example, Dominus. But he did not teach me any spells."

"Then perhaps that amulet you wear is responsible for your good fortune. It must possess a powerful magic."

Lucius touched the fascinum.

"You are pardoned and released, Lucius Pinarius. The property that was to be confiscated from you is hereby returned. Epaphroditus, see to the details."

"But, Dominus—" protested Catullus, before Domitian cut him off by pressing a finger to the man's lips.

Attendants assisted Lucius from the arena. They were strong men, and for that Lucius was glad. His legs had turned to water and the attendants practically had to carry him out.

A.D. 96

The weather was unusually stormy all through the summer months and into September—or Germanicus, as the month had been renamed by Domitian. As one violent tempest followed another, even casual observers noted the unprecedented occurrence of lightning. Lightning struck the Temple of Jupiter on the Capitoline. Lightning struck the Temple of the Flavians, causing damage to the statue of Vespasian in the sanctuary. Lightning struck the imperial palace on several occasions, including, it was said, a strike that caused a small fire in the emperor's bedchamber. There was widespread speculation on what so many omens from the sky could mean.

Wrapped in a woolen cloak, Lucius sat on a stone bench in his sodden garden under the threatening morning sky. A bolt of lightning flashed above his head, casting a weird light on the glistening greenery around him, followed a heartbeat later by a thunderclap that caused the leaves to tremble. If there were omens to be perceived in all the lightning, Lucius was oblivious to them. He was again at a low ebb in his life, the lowest he had experienced since the death of Cornelia. How he missed her still, especially at a time like this!

He also missed Apollonius. Since his disappearance from Roma, the Teacher had been constantly on the move, traveling from city to city in the Eastern provinces, staying just ahead of Domitian's agents. For a long time, Lucius had no news of him at all, but eventually the senator Nerva paid Lucius a visit and revealed that he was in contact with Apollonius. Nerva even offered to send messages between the two of them, sharing with Lucius a cipher with which he could encode his letters.

Apollonius's letters to Lucius were encouraging, but brief to the point of being perfunctory. A typical letter, after being decoded, read: "I am in a coastal town which must not be named, among good people. I told them the tale of my friend in Roma who lay beside a lion in the arena. How I wish I had been there to see it. Your courage gives courage to others. Farewell."

When Lucius wrote to Apollonius, he said little about himself—there was little to report about his secluded existence—so he mentioned events in Roma that he thought might be of interest to the Teacher, though he suspected that Nerva already kept Apollonius well informed on that count.

These infrequent exchanges were no substitute for the personal contact Lucius once had enjoyed with the Teacher. With Apollonius no longer present to set a daily example for him, Lucius often felt confused and lost. He still adhered to the Teacher's tenets, abstaining from wine, meat, and sex, but the sense of balance and well-being he had felt at the side of Apollonius often eluded him.

More lightning flashed across the sky, followed by a long rumble of thunder.

Despite the Teacher's belief that one should not dwell on sadness, Lucius found himself brooding over the loss of all the people who had mattered most to him. The suicide of his father had been a terrible blow, and even after all these years, the death of Sporus still haunted him. His mother had died from the plague that followed the fall of ash on Roma after Vesuvius erupted; without her presence to unite the family, he had drifted further and further from his three sisters, and his appearance in the arena, a mark of shame despite his pardon, had completed the estrangement. He had grieved when Domitian banished Dio of Prusa; now the emperor had seen fit to banish Epictetus as well, along with virtually every other philosopher in Roma. And while once Lucius had taken enjoyment from Martial and his wit, the poet's sycophantic loyalty to Domitian had alienated Lucius long ago; to him, Martial might as well have been dead. With Apollonius gone and likely never to return to Roma, Lucius felt forlorn and isolated, the lone survivor of the ongoing catastrophe that was his life.

These morbid thoughts had been set off by the terrible news Lucius had received the day before: Epaphroditus was dead.

No man had ever been a better friend to him. Epaphroditus had kept Lucius safe through the treacherous months that followed the death of Nero, had welcomed Lucius into his circle of learned friends, had been the only person in whom Lucius confided about his love for Cornelia. The intimacy of their friendship had eventually lessened, but only because Lucius's melancholy had driven him to seek inspiration outside Epaphroditus's circle.

Epaphroditus's reappearance in his life, at the trial of Apollonius, had been as brief as it was unexpected. After being spared by Domitian, Lucius arrived home from the arena to find a letter from Epaphroditus, delivered not by imperial courier but by a private messenger. The letter expressed joy at Lucius's good fortune, but also made it clear there could be no further contact between them: "My return to imperial service and your singular history with the emperor make it impossible that we should be as close as we once were. You are a dangerous man to know. So am I. Let us keep a distance between us, for both our sakes. But know, Lucius, that I am forever fond of you, and I wish you well. I trust you will destroy this message after you have read it."

In the years since, Lucius had not seen or communicated with his old friend and mentor. And now Epaphroditus was dead.

Hilarion, gleaning information in the Forum the preceding day, had brought Lucius the news. Hilarion had not been able to discover the cause or the exact circumstances of Epaphroditus's death. Lucius hoped to learn more from the visitor he expected to arrive at any moment.

The cloudy morning sky turned as dark as night. A heavy rain began to fall. Shivering in his woolen cloak, Lucius retreated from the garden to his library, where Hilarion was stoking the fire in the brazier. Above the pelting of rain against the roof and the peals of thunder, Lucius did not hear the knock at the front door, but Hilarion did. The freedman showed the visitor to the library, then discreetly vanished.

Her long, voluminous cloak concealed her gender. The hood concealed her face. Did she wear the cloak to protect herself from the inclement weather, or because it allowed her to traverse the Palatine without being recognized? She stood before the brazier and warmed her hands for a moment, then pushed back the hood and shook her head, freeing tresses of lustrous black hair in which there were a few strands of gray.

Flavia Domitilla was the emperor's niece, the daughter of his sister, Domitilla, but she did not share his typical Flavian features. Her cheekbones were high, her nose was small, her forehead broad. She had dark, flashing eyes and a sensual mouth. The outlines of her cloak hinted at a voluptuous figure giving way to stoutness. Though Flavia's life scarcely resembled that of a Vestal—she had borne seven children—something about her reminded Lucius of Cornelia. Perhaps it was her willfulness and her spirit. Or perhaps it was simply that Flavia was the first woman since

Cornelia who had inspired in Lucius a faint stirring of lust. But it was not to woo him, or even to seek his friendship, that she had come.

"Greetings, Flavia," he said.

"Greetings, Lucius."

"What can you tell me about the death of Epaphroditus?" he said.

She sighed. "I gather the two of you were close friends, back in the days of my grandfather?"

"Yes. I never ceased calling Epaphroditus my friend, though I hadn't seen him in quite some time."

"What have you heard?"

"Only what my freedman was able to pick up from the gossips in the Forum, which wasn't much. It's true that he's dead, then?"

"Yes."

"How did it happen?"

"Domitian condemned him. He took his own life."

"But why? What was the charge?"

"The same charge my uncle always brings against his enemies, whether real or imagined. He was accused of conspiring against Caesar."

"And was he?"

Flavia gazed at the fire. "You're assuming that I would know such a thing—that I know who wants to see the emperor dead."

"I should think that many men desire his death. But only a few would risk everything to make it happen. Was Epaphroditus one of them?"

Flavia pursed her lips. The firelight glinted in her eyes. Lucius found her beauty distracting. What would Apollonius say about her presence in Lucius's house? Certainly, the Teacher would disdain the physical attraction Lucius felt toward her, but Flavia was not here because of that. She was here because they both desired the death of Domitian. What would Apollonius think of that? Would the Teacher ever approve of murder, even the murder of a tyrant?

Flavia shook her head. "I used to see Epaphroditus in the imperial court. His manner was so cowed and timid, I thought to myself: that fellow would make an ideal agent. Who would ever suspect him? So I approached Epaphroditus—cautiously, discreetly. And he rebuffed me. He told me he had seen enough chaos after the death of Nero, and could never be part of any plan that might lead to such chaos again, however well intentioned. His timidity was not an affectation, it was genuine. He wanted no more trouble in his life. Poor thing! Uncle should have left him where he was instead of dragging him out of retirement. His return to court was Epaphroditus's undoing."

"What made Domitian suspect him?"

She sighed. "The story is so pathetic, it pains me to tell it. Domitian heard a rumor that when Nero tried to kill himself, he failed, and it was Epaphroditus who finished the task for him. Out of loyalty and mercy, of course; nonetheless, it was the hand of Epaphroditus that dealt the final blow. Domitian called Epaphroditus before him and demanded that he tell him the truth. Epaphroditus was too frightened to lie. He admitted that he dealt the final blow to Nero. After that, Domitian became obsessed with the story. He made Epaphroditus tell it to him again and again, sometimes in the middle of the night, as if he were trying to trick the man into confessing a crime, letting slip some previously hidden detail. Eventually, Domitian got it into his head that Epaphroditus had murdered Nero. 'And if so, was that such a bad thing?' his courtiers would say. After all, without Nero dead, my grandfather would never have become emperor. But Uncle became convinced that Epaphroditus was a threat to him. 'Once a man dares to kill an emperor, he'll do it again,' he said. Epaphroditus wasn't involved in any conspiracy against Uncle. But he was the man who killed Nero, so he had to die."

"That was almost thirty years ago. It's absurd."

"It's mad. Uncle is mad. That's why I'm here. That's why I need your help."

Her first visit had been a month earlier, and she had come to him twice since then, approaching Lucius as cautiously as she had approached Epaphroditus. Unlike Epaphroditus, Lucius had been receptive to her subtle overtures. Now she was back.

"I can also tell you that Epaphroditus left a will," she said. "It was fetched from the keeping of the Vestals and read this morning. You were named."

"Was I?"

"Yes. Of course, Uncle will probably invalidate the will and claim the estate for himself, since Epaphroditus was condemned as an enemy of the state."

Did she think to incite him against Domitian by telling him that the emperor meant to cheat him out of an inheritance? If so, Lucius was offended. Greed was not his motivation. But what she said next made him realize that he had misjudged her.

"The will didn't leave you much. Almost everything was left to a freedman of his, a philosopher called Epictetus, who's been banished from Italy, with the stipulation that the proceeds should be used to set up a school. 'Let my fortune, such as it is, foster the learning of philosophy.' But to you he left a statue."

"A statue?"

"It's in his garden, apparently. A statue of an athlete, if I recall correctly."

"The boxer Melancomas," whispered Lucius, remembering the first time he had seen the statue, on the day the ash of Vesuvius fell on Roma.

"Yes, that's the one."

Epaphroditus had once remarked, "Melancomas will be here long after the rest of us are gone." The statue had survived its owner.

Lucius stood across the brazier from her, looking at her through the flames. He tried to see her not as a beautiful woman or a grieving widow, nor as the niece of the emperor, but as a potential partner in a very dangerous enterprise. Could she be trusted to keep silent when she needed to? Was she clever enough to hatch a successful plot against a man as suspicious as her uncle, and would she have the courage to see it through?

Her reasons for hating and fearing her uncle were obvious enough. Married to a Flavian cousin and the mother of seven children, she had long been a member of Domitian's inner circle. After the death of the emperor's son, and the subsequent failure of his wife to produce another heir, Domitian had placed two of Flavia's young sons in the line of succession. Her future and that of her family had looked very bright.

Lucius recalled an ancient Etruscan proverb: "Sit too near the flame and your cloak will catch fire." In one of his frequent fits of suspicion, Domitian had turned against Flavia. His pretext was that she and her husband had secretly converted to the religion of the Jews, or else had become Christians; it hardly mattered which, since both cults promoted atheism and a disrespect for the gods, which could not be tolerated within the imperial family. Were the charges true? Lucius had never asked Flavia, nor had she told him.

Whatever the truth, Flavia's husband had been executed, and she and her children had been exiled to the island of Pandateria, off the western coast of Italy. Eventually, Domitian had allowed Flavia to return to Roma—indeed, had compelled her to do so—while her children remained on the island to ensure their mother's loyalty.

Flavia was bitter and desperate. She was motivated by revenge, but also by the desire to see her progeny survive. Every day Domitian lived, she and her children were in danger. A botched attempt to kill him would certainly mean death for them all. Even a successful assassination might lead to their destruction, but it might also free them from fear and allow them to be reunited.

Looking at her across the flames, Lucius made up his mind to trust her.

"You know why I'm here," she said.

"Yes."

"Will you help us?"

He thought of Cornelia. He thought of Epaphroditus. He also thought of Apollonius, but in the present circumstance he could find no inspiration in the precepts of the Teacher. Lucius himself was not truly a philosopher, only a sincere but oft-thwarted seeker. Nor was he a man of action—but he might yet become one. "Yes. I'll help you. But what can I do?"

She flashed a smile of triumph. It marred her beauty. He suddenly saw her as the niece of her uncle, more like him than not—rapacious, unstoppable, murderous. She had made no mention of the danger he would surely face. Probably she did not care whether Lucius survived or not; he was simply a tool to be used. Her questionable motives, the likelihood that he would be killed, the risk of failure—none of these mattered to Lucius. He was determined to cast his lot with hers.

"Uncle will send for you very soon," she said. "Today, perhaps. Perhaps within the hour."

His heart sank. "By all the gods, what have I done to attract his attention this time?"

"It's not what you've done, but who you are. You'll understand when he tells you. He will ask a favor of you."

"What favor?"

She shook her head. "It's better if you know as little as possible. Agree to help him. Do as he asks. Observe and listen. Through you, an opportunity may arise that will lead us to success."

"I don't understand."

"You don't need to, not yet. Just go to him when he summons you."

"That's all you can tell me?"

"One more thing. Within the House of the Flavians, there is one person whom you can trust absolutely. If he should tell you to say or do something, do as he says. I speak of an imperial steward named Stephanus. He's a brave man, and not squeamish. When the moment finally comes, he's the man we're all counting on."

Hilarion appeared in the doorway, looking shaken. "Forgive me for interrupting—"

"What is it, Hilarion?"

"There's a visitor in the vestibule. A courtier from the palace. He says he's come to take you there. Praetorians came with him. They're waiting for him in the street."

"Don't look so glum, Hilarion. It's only when the Praetorians come inside the house that we should worry. This visit was not unexpected." Lucius looked at Flavia and raised an eyebrow.

"I should conceal myself," she said.

Lucius nodded to Hilarion, who stepped to one of the bookcases that appeared to be built into the wall, took hold of a scroll that was not a scroll but a lever, and pulled it. The bookcase opened like a door. Hilarion ushered Flavia into the hidden compartment, then shut the bookcase behind her. Lucius sighed. In such a world, it was a foolish man who did not have at least one concealed room in his house.

For his visit to the palace, he dressed in his finest toga. The rain had abated for a while. A shaft of bright sunlight, unseen for days, broke through the clouds and caused the wet paving stones and puddles to glisten.

He was conducted to a part of the palace he had never seen before. The narrowness of the passages, the small size of the rooms, and the less formal demeanor of the courtiers seemed to indicate that this was a more private, less public area of the imperial complex. At various points he was searched for weapons, not once but three times. At last, after waiting alone for an hour in a small chamber off a small garden, he was joined by Catullus.

"Greetings, Pinarius," said Catullus, in a flat tone of voice that acknowledged nothing of the history between them.

"Greetings, Catullus." Lucius strove to keep his voice steady, though the very sight of the man made his heart beat faster. His palms began to sweat, so profusely that he had to wipe them on his toga. Fortunately, the blind courtier could not see his distress.

"For a man who professes to have no interest in public affairs, your visits to these premises are surprisingly frequent," remarked Catullus. He smiled. Perhaps he was making a joke to set Lucius at ease. Or was he toying with him?

"I came because I was summoned. What is it you want from me?"

Catullus began to pace. He knew the room well. Without hesitation, and apparently without thinking, he could pace from end to end, turning just before he reached a wall.

"What I'm about to tell you, you must never reveal to anyone. Do you understand, Pinarius?"

"Yes."

"On penalty of death."

"I understand."

"Do you? In the past, Caesar has been extraordinarily merciful to you; unduly so, in my opinion. But if you should ever reveal what I'm about to tell you, I shall see to it myself that you're put to death."

"You make yourself clear, Catullus."

"Good. Foul weather we've been having, don't you think?"

"Surely you didn't summon me here to discuss the weather."

"As a matter of fact, I did." Catullus ceased pacing. "You are aware that there have been a great many lightning strikes in the city during recent months?"

"I'm aware of this, yes."

"Regarding these numerous lightning strikes, Caesar is not happy. To be candid, Caesar is in some distress."

"Every man fears lightning."

"It's not the lightning itself that Caesar fears, but what it may portend.

I will explain. Many years ago, when Caesar was only a boy, an astrologer predicted the day of his death—indeed, the very hour. The astrologer also predicted the manner of Caesar's death: by a blade. At the time, the date foretold must have seemed very distant. But time passes. The day is swiftly approaching. And for a boy, 'death by blade' meant death in battle, as a brave warrior; but now when he imagines death by a blade, Caesar thinks of treachery and assassination."

"Does Caesar believe this prediction made so long ago?"

"Whether he takes it seriously or not, a man never forgets such a prediction. Once, Caesar's father made a joke of it. The Divine Vespasian was dining with his two sons; the young Domitian was suspicious of a mushroom he had been served and refused to eat it. The Divine Vespasian laughed. 'Even if that mushroom is of a poisonous variety, you must be immune to it, my son, for we know the day of your death is a long way off, and it isn't mushrooms that will do you in!' "

Lucius shrugged. "Perhaps, if the day predicted draws close, Caesar should summon this astrologer and order him to cast his horoscope again."

"The astrologer is long dead."

"So the man can neither be punished if his prediction proves false, nor rewarded if his prediction proves correct."

Catullus grunted. "You twist words like Apollonius of Tyana!"

"You flatter me, Catullus. But surely there are other astrologers whom Caesar can consult."

"He did so. Ascletarion, whom Caesar had never consulted before, cast Caesar's horoscope afresh. The astrologer made no specific predictions, but what he had to say was unsettling nonetheless. Because of a conjunction of the stars, the beneficent influence of Minerva, the goddess whom Caesar most venerates, is waning. According to Ascletarion, Minerva's protection will be weakest on the very day that was predicted for his death. Naturally, Caesar was alarmed. To relieve his anxiety, he decided to test the man's skill. He asked if Ascletarion could predict the manner of his own end, to which the astrologer replied, 'Yes, Dominus; I will be torn apart by dogs.' "

Lucius almost laughed aloud. "Could it be that Ascletarion feared the ill-tempered emperor was inclined to throw him to the dogs in the arena, and thought to save himself by predicting that very thing, knowing Caesar would then not dare to do so?"

Catullus grimaced. "If the astrologer outwitted anyone, it was himself. Caesar ordered the astrologer to be strangled to death, then and there. I watched him die a most unpleasant death, and thought: *so much for his powers of prediction.* Caesar ordered me to arrange the man's funeral rites that very afternoon, so that his body might be disposed of quickly. But, though the day had been clear, a storm blew up. A deluge extinguished the flames before the body was consumed. A pack of wild dogs appeared. Before anyone could stop them, they bolted onto the pyre and tore the corpse to pieces."

Lucius shook his head. "So Ascletarion's prediction was correct. For their sake, I hope Caesar has sought the advice of no more astrologers."

"His attention is currently fixed upon a soothsayer from one of the Germanic tribes, a man named Eberwig. Caesar summoned him all the way from Colonia Agrippina on the strength of the man's reputed knowledge of lightning. As the art of lightning reading has declined among the Romans, it seems to have been taken up by the Germans. Even now the man is making a thorough study of all the lightning strikes that have taken place in recent months, charting their location and frequency. Eberwig will deliver his report to Caesar today."

"This is all very fascinating," said Lucius. "But what has any of this to do with me? Why am I here?"

"When he cannot sleep at night, Caesar reads; and of late, Caesar hardly sleeps at all, which means he reads a great deal. His current fascination is the reign of Tiberius, whose career he finds of great interest. Far into the night Caesar pores over documents from the reign of his predecessor. Secretaries are sent to fetch this document or that. Among Tiberius's private journals, Caesar has come across a mention of your grandfather, who was also named Lucius Pinarius. You are aware that he was an augur?"

"As was my father."

"Yes. Your father performed auguries for both the Divine Claudius and for Nero. But before that, your grandfather was known to Tiberius, and to Claudius, and even to the Divine Augustus."

Lucius's father had spoken little of his own father, whose exile to Alexandria he considered a chapter of the family's history better forgotten. "I know that my grandfather was a friend of his cousin Claudius. And I know he ran afoul of Tiberius, who banished him from Roma. But that had nothing to do with augury, or with lightning. It's my understanding that my grandfather's troubles stemmed from dabbling in astrology at a time when Tiberius was banning all astrologers."

"Yes, that's correct. But before that, when the Divine Augustus was still alive, he called upon your grandfather to interpret a lightning strike which occurred in the old imperial palace. Did your grandfather never tell you the story?"

"I never knew my grandfather, and my father never mentioned such a story."

"Amazing, how families fail to pass on the most interesting tales about themselves! Yet I assure you, in his private journal, Tiberius gives all the pertinent details. There was a lighting strike. Augustus called upon your grandfather to interpret the omen. Your grandfather told Augustus that the strike meant he had exactly one hundred days to live. And when the hundredth day arrived, Augustus died."

"This has the ring of a legend."

"Tiberius recounts it as a fact, and Domitian accepts it as such."

"Again I ask, what has this to do with me?"

"Just as the Divine Augustus was convinced, correctly, that your grandfather was the man to interpret that lightning strike, so our Caesar has become convinced that you, the grandson of Lucius Pinarius, are the man who can determine the significance of this current plague of lightning. Why else have the gods inspired Caesar to spare your life when he had every reason to snuff it out, not once but twice? Caesar now sees that you were fated for this task."

Lucius was about to dismiss the idea as nonsense, then realized that Flavia must have known that this was the reason Domitian was summoning him to the palace. Catullus was offering Lucius a means to enter the emperor's presence and perhaps even to gain his confidence. How could such a charade lead to the result that he and Flavia mutually desired? That he could not foresee, but he knew that Flavia would want him to cooperate with Catullus.

"You realize that I'm not an augur, like my father and grandfather?" he said.

"Yes. But your father actively practiced the science for Nero while you were growing up. You must have learned something about it simply from observing him."

Just enough, Lucius thought, to perform a mock augury himself, if he had to, without looking completely foolish. "Yes, I saw the ritual performed many times. I know how it's done."

"And your father must have confided certain secrets of the science to you—the tricks of his trade?"

"As a matter of fact, he did. He liked talking about augury. I suppose he had hopes that I would follow his example one day and become an augur myself." Lucius recalled the last time he had seen his father. On the day Titus Pinarius left the house to join Nero on his final flight, he took his second-best lituus with him, and left the family heirloom, the beautiful old ivory lituus of their ancestors, for Lucius, who had hardly looked at it since that day and had done nothing to pursue the study of augury. The old lituus was still in his possession, kept in a chest of keepsakes in the vestibule of his house, just under the niche that held the wax mask of his father.

"Caesar wishes you to take the auspices," said Catullus. "He wants you to observe the skies for lightning and to give him your interpretation, not as a member of the college of augurs but as the grandson and namesake of Lucius Pinarius."

"Here? Now?"

"Why not? The day is stormy, with no lack of lightning."

"This seems most irregular. Isn't Caesar's German soothsayer already at work to interpret the lightning?"

"Caesar will listen to both of you, and compare your findings. Will you do this or not?"

"What if I refuse?"

"That is not the answer I'm looking for."

Lucius took a deep breath. "I'll do what Caesar asks."

Without an assistant to guide him, using only his staff, the blind man led Lucius across the small, sodden garden and then through a series of hallways. Their destination was a gravel courtyard surrounded by a low portico. Lucius recognized the Auguratorium; he had seen his father take the auspices in this place, which had once been situated outside the imperial palace but was now completely enclosed within the House of the Flavians.

Under a nearby portico, shielded from the drizzling rain and surrounded by courtiers, sat Domitian, who looked up at their arrival. Lucius suddenly felt unsure of himself. To perform a religious travesty for a man he wanted dead, Lucius could hardly look to the Teacher for inspiration.

To stall for time, he told Catullus that he would need the lituus of his ancestors.

"Surely any lituus will do," said Catullus.

"No, it must be the ivory lituus I keep with my father's things. I'll have to go home and get it."

"No, you'll stay right here. Someone will fetch it for you."

A nearby courtier, overhearing, stepped forward. He was a middle-aged man with bristling eyebrows and a neatly trimmed beard. "I'll go for it," the man said.

"Very well, Stephanus," said Catullus. Lucius's ears pricked up at the name. "Pinarius will tell you where to find it while I explain the delay to Caesar."

As soon as Catullus was out of earshot, Lucius whispered, "I heard your name spoken earlier today, before I came here."

Stephanus nodded. "Ten days hence," he said quietly, barely moving his lips.

Lucius wrinkled his brow. What was the man talking about?

"Ten days hence," Stephanus repeated. "Fourteen days before the Kalends of Domitianus, at the fifth hour of the day. Can you remember that?"

Lucius stared at him blankly for a moment, then nodded. "Yes," he said, in a normal tone of voice. "I keep it in an antique chest in the vestibule, just under the wax mask of my father. You can't mistake it—a beautiful old thing, made of solid ivory. My freedman Hilarion will help you find it."

"Then I'm off," said Stephanus. "I'll be back as quickly as I can."

Domitian was not pleased by the delay. He strummed his fingers against the arms of his chair. He tapped his foot nervously. He glared at Lucius. He muttered something to Catullus.

Catullus shook his head. "Dominus, surely it would be better to wait until after—"

"Fetch him now!" said Domitian. "And take Pinarius elsewhere, until he's ready for the augury."

As Lucius was led away, he passed a man wearing such an outlandish costume that he looked like a parody of a German, with a huge mane of red hair and a bristling red beard, fur boots on his feet, tanned leggings, and a tightly laced leather vest that left bare much of his broad, hairy chest. His bare arms were decorated with bracelets that were fashioned as coiling dragons and covered with runes.

Lucius was shown to a small waiting room and left alone. He spied a grated window high in one wall. He stood on a chair. If he peered to one side, looking down the length of the portico, he could see most of the imperial party, including Domitian, and he could hear everything that was said.

Catullus spoke to a translator. "You will tell Eberwig that Caesar is ready for him to deliver his report."

The translator spoke to Eberwig. The German replied to the translator at length.

Domitian leaned forward impatiently. "What is he saying?"

The translator looked uneasy. "He says, if he should deliver news to Caesar which displeases Caesar, what will become of him?"

"Tell him to speak," said Domitian. "As long as he tells the truth, he'll receive his reward and remain unharmed. But if he doesn't speak at once, I'll have him strangled."

The translator and Eberwig conferred at length. At last the translator addressed Domitian in a quavering voice. "Dominus, the soothsayer declares that he has examined all the evidence of the lightning strikes most scrupulously and he is convinced that he has reached a correct interpretation. He says that the frequency and location of the strikes foretell an imminent change at the very highest level of power. He says that this can only mean . . . yourself."

"Speak clearly."

"He says that very soon there will be a new emperor in Roma."

Domitian sat back, nervously picking at something on his forehead. "When?"

"He cannot say exactly. But very soon."

"A matter of months?"

The translator questioned Eberwig. "Not months, Dominus. Days."

There was a flash of lightning, followed by thunder.

"Take him away," said Domitian.

Eberwig protested. The translator cleared his throat. "He says, what of his reward?"

"If his prophecy comes true, let him seek his payment from my successor!" snapped Domitian. "Now take him away and keep him under close guard."

An uneasy silence followed. Eventually Stephanus appeared, slightly out of breath from running. Lucius was brought back to the courtyard. Stephanus stepped forward and handed him the lituus.

There could be no more delaying. Lucius took a deep breath. He looked at the lituus in his hands. He had not touched it in many years. What a lovely thing it was, with all its intricate carvings of birds and beasts!

As he had seen his father do many times when he was a boy, Lucius gazed up at the skies and marked out a zone for his augury. The sky was cooperative: almost at once a flash of lightning rent the dark clouds to the north, and then another. Lucius waited a while longer and was rewarded by a third flash of lightning, so close that it illuminated the whole courtyard with a spectral blue light. It was followed by a tremendous clap of thunder that made everyone jump except Lucius, whose thoughts were focused entirely on what he was about to say.

He turned and faced Domitian. "The augury is done, Dominus."

"So quickly?"

"The signs are unmistakable."

"And?"

"There is to be a great change. A change so great it will affect the whole world. The change will be sudden, not gradual. It will happen in a single moment—like a thunderclap."

"When?"

"The signs are very clear about that—unusually so. By counting the branches of all three strikes and observing their relationship to the main trunks of lightning, an exact number of days and hours from this moment can be calculated. The event will take place—"

"Not out loud, you fool!" snapped Domitian. "Whisper it in my ear."

Lucius approached the emperor. He had never been so close to the man before. He was close enough to smell his breath, and to know that he had eaten onions recently. He was close enough to see a black hair that grew out of one nostril, and a wart on the man's forehead. He was close enough to kill him, if he'd had a weapon. He fought back the revulsion he felt and spoke in Domitian's ear.

"Exactly ten days hence, during the fifth hour of the day."

Domitian calculated the date. "Fourteen days before the Kalends, in the hour before noon. You're certain?"

"Absolutely."

Domitian gripped Lucius's wrist, squeezing it painfully hard. "You will return here on that day, Lucius Pinarius. You will be with me during that hour. If your prediction is false—if you're playing some trick on me—I'll see you strangled at my feet. Do you understand?"

"I understand, Dominus."

"You will speak of this to no one."

"As you wish, Dominus."

Domitian released him. The emperor sat back, nervously picking at the wart on his forehead with one hand and making a curt gesture of dismissal with the other. Guards escorted Lucius from the courtyard, through the palace, and all the way back to his house. One of the guards, he noticed, took up a post across the street from his door. His comings and goings were to be carefully watched, and no one could call on him without being observed. He could expect no further visits from Flavia Domitilla.

That night he wrote a coded letter to Apollonius, telling him of the day's events—his summons to the palace, the nervous demeanor of Domitian, and the sham augury, which he described in detail. Where was Apollonius now? Nerva would know. When he was done, Lucius would dispatch Hilarion to take the letter to an intermediary who would take it to Nerva. They never communicated directly.

Lucius finished the letter with the customary closing of "Farewell," and felt a chill as he wrote the word.

On the morning of the fourteenth day before the Kalends of Domitianus, the month previously known as October, Praetorian Guards arrived at the house of Lucius Pinarius.

Lucius was ready for them, dressed in his best toga. He had slept surprisingly well the night before. He rose at daybreak and wrote farewell letters to his old friends Dio and Epictetus, and even an affectionate message to Martial. Hilarion stood by, unsuspecting. Lucius had told him nothing about his visit to the palace; the less Hilarion knew, the better for him. What a dreary morning this would have been, had Hilarion suspected that Lucius would be dead before midday. Instead, Hilarion was in a cheerful mood, and kept exhorting him to eat something, unable to understand why Lucius had no appetite.

Lucius took a stroll through his garden. The sky was overcast but not stormy. The garden was usually dull and dreary at this time of year, but all the recent rain had kept everything quite green. At the center of the garden stood the statue of Melancomas he had inherited from Epaphroditus. It had arrived just the day before, and Lucius had insisted that the workmen install it at once. Like Epaphroditus, he chose to display the statue not on a pedestal but at ground level. It was a pity, Lucius thought, that he would have so little time to enjoy it.

When the Praetorians arrived, Hilarion was quite flustered. Lucius assured him that all would be well, and Hilarion seemed to believe him, until Lucius told him about the letters in his study, to be delivered in the event that he failed to return. Hilarion began to weep. Lucius embraced him, then left with the Praetorians.

He was led farther into the palace than he had ever been led before. The reception room where Domitian awaited him appeared to be attached to the emperor's private bedchamber, for through an open door Lucius glimpsed an unmade bed piled with richly embroidered pillows and coverlets. On this morning, the emperor was not stirring far from the place where he felt most secure.

At the far end of the small reception room was a dais where Domitian sat on a chair, attended only by Catullus and the small-headed creature. There was also a water clock on the dais, a beautifully made device that used a dial to indicate the hours of the day. The dial was very nearly touching the numeral for the fifth hour of the day.

A balcony to one side admitted weak daylight from the overcast sky. Lucius instinctively took a closer look at the balcony, wondering if it might provide a means of escape, but the room was located on one of the palace's uppermost floors. The balcony looked down on a garden several stories below.

"Take off your clothes," said Domitian.

Lucius sighed. "Dominus, I've already been searched for weapons. Your guards did a thorough job."

"I didn't ask if you'd been searched. I told you to take off your clothes. All of them!"

Lucius did as he had been ordered. He felt no embarrassment. Instead, he felt a kind of freedom, as he had felt when he stood naked before the emperor and all of Roma in the amphitheater.

Domitian sent the small-headed creature to look through Lucius's discarded toga and undergarments to make sure they contained no weapons, then sucked in a sharp breath when he noticed the fascinum on the chain around Lucius's neck. "That amulet! You always wear it, don't you? And no harm ever befalls you."

"That is not true, Dominus. I've suffered harm. Those closest to me are all dead or banished, because of you."

"But you still live. Is it because of the amulet? Give it to me!" Domitian's wide eyes were bloodshot and his face was haggard. He looked as if he had not slept for days.

Lucius lifted the chain over his neck. The small-headed creature snatched it from him and scurried to the dais. Domitian put the chain over his head and touched the fascinum, which nestled amid the folds of his purple robes. "Yes," he whispered, "I can feel its power. Let it protect me today, blessed Minerva! And let this man's presence protect me."

"My presence, Dominus?"

"Are you not a magician, Lucius Pinarius, like that accursed teacher of yours? There can be no doubt that some protective magic clings to you. That sort of thing rubs off on others. Today, I intend to keep you close at hand, until the fatal hour passes."

Lucius smiled at the idea that he himself might be a sort of lucky charm. He was also struck by the curious reversal of their roles. Once he had stood before the emperor, a condemned man; now the emperor sat before him, convinced that he was the one facing death. Lucius had found peace when he confronted almost certain destruction, but Domitian was growing more agitated by the moment.

The small-headed creature gave a shriek and pointed to the water clock. The dial had touched the numeral V.

"Make sure the door is locked!" shouted Domitian. Catullus, who could move about the familiar room like a sighted man, stepped from the dais, strode past Lucius, and tested the door.

"Might I put on my clothes, Dominus?" said Lucius. "There's a draft from the balcony."

Domitian grunted and waved his hand.

Time passed with excruciating slowness. Lucius did not know what he had expected, but it was not this endless tedium. Was there not to be an attempt on the emperor's life? What part was Lucius expected to play? Or was he simply to wait here until Domitian did or did not die, and then to die himself? It took all his presence of mind simply to stand in the middle of the room and show no emotion, as the time slowly passed.

Domitian fidgeted and sighed. His stomach growled. "Did you hear that, Lucius Pinarius? I've eaten nothing since yesterday morning."

"Do you fear poison, Dominus?"

"It's not poison that will kill me. I fear some drug that might render me unconscious and vulnerable. I'm hungry!"

"My stomach, too, is empty, Dominus."

"Is it? I set aside some apples I was given yesterday, for my midday meal today—if I should live until then. They're in the bowl on the table by my bed. Fetch one, Catullus, and give it to Lucius Pinarius. We'll see if it makes him sick."

Catullus brought him an apple. Lucius bit into the crisp flesh. Domitian watched him eat and began to salivate, so copiously that he had to wipe the drool from his lips. When Lucius was done, Domitian told him to get rid of the core by tossing it to the garden below. Lucius stepped onto the balcony. He dropped the apple core and watched it fall a great distance. Looking down made Lucius dizzy. The apple core struck and bounced off a large sundial in the garden below. The dial was an iron triangle set in a round stone pedestal. The day was too overcast for the dial to cast a shadow.

Lucius turned and looked at the water clock on the dais. The hour was almost done.

Domitian continued to fidget. He tugged at his chin and cracked his knuckles. He picked at the wart on his forehead. Suddenly, blood appeared on his fingers. He gave a cry of alarm, then realized that it came from the wart. "Minerva, let this be the only blood I spill today!"

His cry brought a knock at the door. "Dominus, is something wrong?"

"Never mind, Parthenius," called Domitian. "All's well. But look, the clock has reached the sixth hour! It's done! The hour has passed, and no harm came to me. Unlock the door and let him in, Catullus."

The chamberlain Parthenius entered the room. Behind him, in chains and flanked by guards, was the German soothsayer, Eberwig.

"What do you say now, soothsayer?" demanded Domitian.

Eberwig muttered something, but there was no one present to translate. The guards pulled him to his knees.

"Strangle the fool," said Domitian.

One of the guards wrapped a chain around the man's neck and twisted it. Eberwig turned a dark shade of crimson. His eyes bulged and his tongue protruded. Domitian sat back in his chair, smiling. He appeared to take great pleasure from watching the man die.

The guards dragged the corpse from the room. Parthenius followed them. Lucius stayed where he was, on the balcony. By a great application of will, he had managed to remain calm for the last hour. Now his body began to exhibit signs of panic. His heart raced. His palms turned clammy. Sweat erupted on his forehead.

Did Domitian intend to kill him, as he had killed the German soothsayer? For the moment, the emperor was distracted. He told Catullus to bring him the bowl of apples from the bedroom. As the blind courtier walked by the balcony, Lucius held his breath, fearful of drawing the man's attention. Catullus returned with the apples and Domitian began to eat ravenously, consuming one after another.

Parthenius reappeared. "The steward Stephanus wishes to see you, Dominus."

"I'll see no one," said Domitian. "As soon as I finish these apples, I'll retire to my private bath."

"Stephanus is most insistent. He says it's very important, Dominus. He says he has urgent information about a plot against you."

"A failed plot, you mean! I'm still alive!" Domitian laughed. "But show him in. Perhaps he has names for me. Wait! Has he been searched for weapons?"

"Of course, Dominus. No one comes before you without being thoroughly searched."

"Go ahead then, show him in."

Lucius's heart sank. The hour predicted for Domitian's death had come and gone, and now he knew why: Stephanus had betrayed them. Poor Flavia; this would be the end of her. Would Domitian allow her children to live? Probably not. Lucius gazed over the parapet of the balcony, wondering if death by falling would be preferable to strangulation. He felt a sudden urge to flee, but the balcony was much too high. If only he could disappear, like Apollonius, in a puff of smoke!

The clouds had begun to break. A warm shaft of sunlight touched his face. The sky itself seemed to be smiling on the emperor's deliverance.

Stephanus entered the room. Before he could speak, Domitian waved him aside. He called to Catullus and pulled him close.

"I'd almost forgotten about Pinarius," Lucius heard the emperor say in a low voice. "What shall I do with him?"

"Whatever pleases you, Dominus," Catullus said.

While waiting to be called on, Stephanus joined Lucius on the balcony. In his right hand he clutched a rolled document. Was this the incriminating list, and was Lucius's name on it? Lucius noticed that the man's left forearm was wrapped in bandages.

"A boar's tusk can inflict a very nasty wound," Stephanus explained, keeping his voice low. "It happened when I was out hunting a few days ago. Would you believe the guards made me unwrap the whole thing the first day I came here wearing it? Once they saw the blood and the oozing gash, they were satisfied. I think it made them a bit queasy. Since then, whenever I come, they search me like everyone else—but they never make me take off the bandages."

Domitian finished his conversation with Catullus and called to Stephanus. The steward hurried to the dais, while Catullus backed away.

"Dominus," said Stephanus, "the moment this document entered my hands, I headed directly here."

"What is it?"

"A list of names, Dominus. When you see them, I think you'll be shocked."

Catullus stepped toward the balcony. Lucius moved as far from the man as he could. Again he gazed over the parapet. A shaft of sunlight struck the sundial far below. Something was not right. Lucius squinted and peered more closely at the sundial. The shadow cast by the dial indicated not the sixth hour of the day—shadowless noon—but the fifth hour.

Lucius looked at the water clock. Without a doubt, the clock indicated the sixth hour. The water clock was in error. Someone had changed its settings.

Stephanus extended the document to Domitian, who unrolled it and stared at it. He scowled. "What is this? All I see is a list of provincial magistrates. What has this to do—"

Quickly, deftly, Stephanus loosened the bandages around his left forearm and reached inside. He pulled out a dagger and lunged for the emperor. Because of Domitian's elevated position on the dais, Stephanus fell short of stabbing the man's heart. His blade struck Domitian's groin.

Domitian bellowed in pain. He struck Stephanus across the face. The steward staggered back, clutching the bloody dagger. Domitian bolted forward. The throne tumbled backward. The small-headed creature shrieked and scrambled out of the way. Domitian grappled with Stephanus.

"My knife!" Domitian cried. "The one I keep beneath my pillow—bring it to me!"

The creature scurried past Catullus, striking him with his elbow and knocking him farther onto the balcony, where he almost collided with Lucius before grabbing the parapet to steady himself. The creature ran into the bedchamber and a moment later emerged with a stricken look on his face. He held a scabbard in one hand and in the other a hilt that had no blade. Someone had substituted a false dagger for the one Domitian kept under his pillow.

Other courtiers entered the room. They swarmed over Domitian, who roared and put up a tremendous struggle, like a lion attacked by dogs.

"What's happening?" cried Catullus. "Dominus, how can I help you?"

Suddenly, the blind man realized that Lucius was next to him. He snarled like an animal and lunged for him. The accuracy of the man's aim and the ferocity of his attack took Lucius by surprise. While Domitian struggled with the courtiers, Lucius and Catullus wrestled on the balcony.

Catullus used his sharp fingernails to gouge at Lucius's eyes and nose, and sank his teeth into Lucius's arm. Lucius seized the man's wrists and tried to immobilize him, but Catullus was too strong. The best Lucius could manage was to push the man to one side, toward the parapet. Almost before Lucius knew what was happening, Catullus went tumbling over. With a bloodcurdling scream, Catullus plummeted to the garden below.

Lucius heard a sickening sound of impact and looked over the parapet. Faceup, with his limbs outstretched, Catullus was impaled on the metal blade of the sundial. His body was broken nearly in two. His mouth gaped open and his eyes glittered. His limbs flailed horribly for a moment, then fell limp.

Lucius realized that the room behind him had fallen silent, except for the sound of men gasping for breath. The struggle was over. Stephanus stepped beside him, throwing back his head to exult in the sunshine on his face. His hair was disheveled and his torn clothes were covered with blood.

The tattered remains of the bandage hung from his left forearm. The gash looked very real. Stephanus saw Lucius looking at it and grinned. "I inflicted the wound myself, using a boar's tusk. There's no substitute for authenticity."

What had Flavia said about Stephanus? *He's a brave man, and not squeamish.*

Blinking and bleary-eyed, Lucius looked over his shoulder. A bloody heap draped in imperial purple lay in the center of the room. Courtiers with knives stood in a circle, gasping for breath and gazing numbly at their handiwork. Blood and gore were smeared all over the floor.

"Is he really . . . ?"

"The tyrant is dead," said Stephanus. He proudly held up the dagger in his right hand. Sunlight glinted on the blood. Then he showed Lucius his left hand, in which he clutched a chain with an amulet. "I think this belongs to you, Lucius Pinarius."

Lucius took back the fascinum, covered with blood.

A.D. 99

The philosophers had returned to Roma.

Three years had passed since the death of Domitian. On a morning in early September—no longer called Germanicus—Lucius played host in his garden to two guests who had long been absent from Roma.

"It's a shame that neither of you intends to move back to the city," said Lucius, sipping a cup of water spiced with dried apple peel, cinnamon, and cloves. Wine had been poured for his guests, but Lucius, as always, abstained.

"There is no city like Roma," said Epictetus, who had arrived the preceding night. "But my life now is the school I've founded in Nicopolis. The students are so bright and eager. They inspire me as much as I inspire them. And there's something to be said for living in an environment where Greek is spoken from dawn to dusk, without a word of Latin being uttered. I feel more at home there than I've ever felt anywhere else."

"And you, Dio? How can you leave Roma now that you've returned?" Looking at the sophist, Lucius was pointedly reminded of the passage of time. Dio was now in his sixties and looked much older than when Lucius had last seen him. Of course, Lucius, at fifty-two, probably looked much older to Dio.

"I was delighted when Nerva became emperor and lifted my banishment," said Dio. "Roma I longed to see again, but I was even more pleased by the fact that I could at last return to Prusa. With so many changes afoot, I feel that my place is in my native land, looking after the interests of my fellow Bithynians. And it's so lovely and quiet in Prusa. I think my long absence from Roma has cured me of it. I couldn't ask for more comfortable accommodations than those you've provided, Lucius, but out there in the streets of Roma, how noisy it is, and how crowded!"

"And how smelly! Don't forget the smells," said Lucius's third guest. It had occurred to Lucius that his visit from the two philosophers was the perfect opportunity to effect a reconciliation with Martial, though "reconciliation" was perhaps too strong a word. Lucius and the poet had never had a falling-out; they had simply grown distant in recent years. Determined to set aside any bitterness he felt about Martial's relationship with Domitian, Lucius had invited the poet to gather with their mutual friends.

"Ah, but you have a good reason to live in Roma," said Dio, "to enjoy all the accolades you're receiving on the publication of your collected poems, which was long overdue. At last your genius is being recognized beyond the—how shall I say it?—the elite circles where it was previously enjoyed."

"Fah!" said Martial. He, too, had aged considerably in recent years. Though he was a bit younger than Dio, he looked older, probably due to the overindulgent style of living he had enjoyed at the court of Domitian. "Accolades? What do I care for accolades? Accolades will not pay my rent, which has just gone up, by the way. Why is it that every time there's a change of emperor, the cost of living goes up? I'm leaving Roma as soon as I can settle my affairs. And why not? I've had all the boys in this city worth having, or at least all the ones in my price range. I'm retiring to Spain, the land of my birth, where both the rents and the boys are said to be very cheap."

"Our new emperor was also born in Spain," noted Lucius. "They say Trajan is the first emperor to be foreign-born."

"And why not?" said Dio. "Having seen a great deal of the empire and the lands beyond in recent years, I think it will be a good thing for Roma to have a emperor who was born outside Italy. Though I must say I was greatly saddened by the death of Nerva. He was a good man, and a true lover of philosophy. How delighted I was when I heard that he took a vow to kill no senators. And I was even more delighted when I heard his declaration that Domitian's so-called House of the Flavians would henceforth be known as the House of the People. That sort of thing sets a tone, if nothing else. To be sure, Nerva was old and frail, and the demands of his office were probably too much for him. We can only hope that his successor will be half as good a man."

"Trajan is a military man," said Lucius, "and widely traveled, with experience in Syria and on the German and Dacian frontiers. Nerva chose him to please the Praetorians, who insisted that he put a capable commander in the line of succession. Since Nerva was childless, he acquiesced and picked Trajan."

"Let's hope that sets a precedent," said Dio. "Succession by bloodline did not prove very successful. From Augustus we descended to Nero; from Vespasian we plummeted to Domitian. Perhaps if we can settle on some more-rational method for choosing an emperor's successor, the empire and everyone in it will be better off."

"Just make sure all the emperors are childless," quipped Martial, "like old Nerva—or like Trajan, for that matter. Poor Plotina! Trajan stays so busy chasing after boys, one wonders if he ever beds that horse-faced wife of his at all."

"From what I've heard about her, Plotina can take care of herself," said Lucius. "She's said to be quite formidable."

"Well, soon enough we shall behold the imperial couple with our own eyes," said Martial. After more than a year of settling affairs on the German and Dacian frontiers, this was the day Trajan was to make his official entry into Roma. "I presume we'll all go down to the Forum together later, to gawk at Trajan's arrival along with everyone else in the city?"

"I wouldn't miss it," said Dio.

"If my leg will allow it," said Epictetus.

"Didn't you write a poem in anticipation of the event?" said Lucius. He asked out of politeness, to allow Martial the opportunity to recite from his work, but the poet reacted with a sour expression.

"I did indeed, and I sent it to the new emperor, hoping to please him. As yet, I've received no reply."

Lucius nodded. In other words, he thought, Martial had attempted to ingratiate himself with the new regime, and had been rebuffed. No wonder he was leaving Roma. "Still, I'm sure we'd all love to hear what you wrote."

"Oh, very well," said Martial, who needed little encouragement. He stood and cleared his throat.

> Happy, happy those blessed by Fortune to behold
> the arrival of the new leader whose brow dazzles
> with the light of northern constellations!
> When will the day come? When will the route be thronged
> with the lovely ladies of Roma perched in every
> tree and window along the Flaminian Way?
> Come soon, longed-for day! Come clouds of distant dust,
> rising from the road to foretell the approach of Caesar!

Then shall every citizen and richly clad foreign delegate go forth
to exclaim as one, with joy, "He comes!"

The others clapped politely as Martial took a bow. He returned to his couch and drank thirstily from his cup. "And now the day has come," he said. "I wonder what sort of chariot Trajan will be riding. Some ornately gilded wonder, or something more austere and warlike, to emphasize his status as a military man? If he wants to look like a general, arriving on horseback would be best, I suppose. Or will he recline in a litter and be borne aloft by the prettiest boys he's collected from the far corners of the empire?"

Lucius sighed. How vacuous and irritating Martial seemed to him. Lucius almost regretted inviting him, but Dio and Epictetus seemed genuinely to be enjoying the poet's company. Perhaps a bit of wine was necessary to appreciate Martial's wit.

"As you say, soon enough we'll see for ourselves," said Lucius. "But it's too early yet. Hilarion will let us know when it's time to go."

"In the meantime, Lucius can tell us more about all the changes in Roma," said Dio. "Simply to have had a sane man like Nerva in charge of the state must have seemed a miracle after the grim years of Domitian."

"That's true," said Lucius. "After fourteen long years, I felt that I could breathe again."

"Breathe all you want, if you can stand the smells of this city!" said Martial, wagging his finger. "Though I must admit, it became much easier to move about after they pulled down all those triumphal arches choking the streets, and got rid of the statues. There's definitely more elbow room without a gilded Domitian on every corner. What happened to all those statues, anyway?"

"Nerva melted them down, to replenish the treasury and pay the Praetorians," said Lucius.

"Speaking of statues," said Dio, "our old friend here looks as magnificent now as the day we first saw him." He gestured to the statue of Melancomas that dominated the garden. "Do the rest of you remember that occasion?"

"The day the ash of Pompeii fell on us?" said Epictetus. "Who could forget that?"

"It seems a lifetime ago," said Dio. "And yet, Melancomas never ages. What a remarkable work of art. Incomparable! It was good and right that Epaphroditus left most of his estate to you, Epictetus, but I'm glad he left the Melancomas to you, Lucius. It looks splendid here in your garden."

Lucius nodded. "I think of Epaphroditus every time I look at the statue, and I look at the statue every day."

"A toast to Epaphroditus!" Martial lifted his cup.

"A toast!" said the others in unison. Lucius quaffed his brew of spiced water and the others drank their wine.

"I don't know how you can stand to drink that," said Martial. "I suppose you abstain from wine to follow the example of your old teacher?"

"I do," said Lucius. "I strive to follow his example in all things, to the extent to which I am able."

"Where is Apollonius these days?" said Dio.

"The last I heard, he was back in his native Tyana," said Lucius. "But he's always traveling. I hoped he would return to Roma to enjoy the brief reign of his friend Nerva, but he's never come back."

Epictetus smiled. "In Ephesus, they tell the most remarkable story about Apollonius. Have you all heard it?"

"Of course," said Dio, and Lucius nodded, but Martial shrugged and said, "Enlighten me, Epictetus."

The Stoic smiled, glad to have a pair of fresh ears for the tale. "On the day Domitian was assassinated by his courtiers, Apollonius happened to be in Ephesus, hundreds of miles from Roma, speaking to a huge crowd. Suddenly, in the middle of his talk, he fell silent and began to stagger and clutch the air, staring into the distance. 'Good for you, Stephanus!' he shouted. 'Hurrah, Stephanus! Do it! Smite the bloodthirsty wretch! That's it! That's it! The deed is done! You have struck, you have wounded, you have slain the tyrant!' There were so many witnesses, there's no doubt whatsoever that this happened—and it occurred *at the very hour* that Domitian was killed. At the time, no one had any idea what Apollonius was talking about, but once the news from Roma arrived, it became clear that Apollonius had witnessed the killing *as it happened.* Truly, the man possesses a remarkable gift for seeing far-off events. Now, wherever he travels, he

attracts more followers than ever. I can assure you that everyone in Nicopolis knows the story."

"They talk of it in Prusa, as well," said Dio. "Apollonius's fame has
spread all over the empire, thanks to that incident. Do you suppose the
tale is true, Lucius?"

"I think it must be," said Lucius, with a wry smile. He remembered the
coded letter he had written to the Teacher ten days before the assassination, thinking it would be his last, in which he told Apollonius not only
the day foretold for the death of Domitian but the hour, and the name of
the man who would kill him. It amused him to think that at the very moment he was grappling with Catullus on the balcony, and Stephanus was
stabbing Domitian, Apollonius was hundreds of miles away in Ephesus,
shouting encouragement.

Hilarion appeared. The time had come for them to head down to the
Forum.

Lucius could not recall ever having seen a more jubilant crowd in the Forum. The new emperor's anticipated arrival had been the talk of Roma
for months. People were giddy with excitement, and everyone in the city
seemed to be present, even old people who usually avoided such crowds
and children held high on their elders' shoulders. The roofs of the buildings sagged under the weight of spectators. At temples and altars, people
formed long queues to pray for the well-being of the new emperor, and the
air was thick with incense. The atmosphere was not of religious awe, as
attended certain festivals, or of the patriotic fervor displayed during triumphal processions, or of the frenzied bloodlust evoked by shows in the
amphitheater. The feeling was lighter, yet equally intense. The atmosphere
was one of joy, of release—of *hope*, thought Lucius, finally putting his finger on it.

As it turned out, Martial was mistaken on all counts about Trajan's
mode of transportation. The new emperor did not arrive in a chariot, or on
horseback, or in a litter. Trajan entered the city on foot, and he wore not a
general's regalia, as Domitian had done on public occasions, but a toga.

The sight of the new emperor simply walking into the city, like any common citizen, evoked spontaneous cheers and applause. Even on foot, Trajan was easy to spot at a distance because of his height. Walking alongside him was his wife, Plotina, who graciously smiled and waved to the crowd. In their forties, the imperial couple were both quite plain, but physically robust. Their relaxed manner seemed completely unpretentious.

Walking a little behind them was Trajan's cousin and ward, Hadrian, who was in his early twenties and also of Spanish birth. Like Trajan, Hadrian was tall and powerfully built. He was handsomer than Trajan, but his clean-shaven cheeks were covered with acne scars. Faced with the cheering crowd, he comported himself much more stiffly than the genial Trajan. The cousins were said to be very close; it was young Hadrian, serving under Trajan on the German frontier, who had delivered to him the news of his acclamation as emperor.

In the heart of the Forum, the entire membership of the Senate gathered in groups to greet the new emperor, beginning with the foremost magistrates and senior members. Lucius and his friends happened to be standing in the crowd nearby. As Trajan began to approach the receiving line, Hadrian, looking in the direction of Lucius and his party, whispered in Trajan's ear. The emperor nodded, turned, and walked directly to them.

Trajan raised his hand in greeting. "Dio of Prusa! Epictetus of Nicopolis! Have you come to welcome this humble citizen to Roma?" His accent was decidedly provincial.

Lucius was startled by Trajan's approach. He was even more surprised by the casual ease with which his philosopher friends responded.

"Caesar has come home, and his people rejoice," said Epictetus.

"The House of the People has been empty too long," said Dio. "Caesar and his wife will fill it with light and happiness."

Trajan laughed. Seen close at hand, he was even larger than Lucius had thought. His face was homely but pleasant, dominated by a long nose and topped by a thick mop of graying hair.

"Since we haven't met before, you must wonder how I recognized you. Thank my cousin over there. Young Hadrian is quite the scholar—I call him the Little Greek. He's too shy to come meet you, but he insisted that I do so. Many a night, in my tent, Hadrian has read your works aloud to me, Dio. I laugh, I cry—if you can imagine tears from a big fellow like me.

Your discourses about Melancomas—delightful! And you, Epictetus—my wife speaks very highly of you, though I think she leans toward the Epicureans rather than you Stoics. I leave the philosophy to Plotina, and believe whatever she tells me to. Much simpler that way. And your companions?" He indicated Lucius and Martial, who stood to one side.

"This is our host in the city," said Dio, "Lucius Pinarius. And this is Martial, the famous poet."

Martial eagerly stepped forward. "Welcome, Caesar! The day of your arrival is finally here. Now every citizen and richly clad foreign delegate steps forth to exclaim as one, with joy, 'He comes!' " He made a small bow.

Trajan looked down his nose for a moment. He worked his large jaw back and forth, then nodded to the philosophers. "Well, I must go say hello to some senators now." He turned around and headed to the receiving line.

"Astounding!" said Lucius. "He greeted you two even ahead of the magistrates."

"A good sign, I think," said Dio. "The new emperor may not be a lover of philosophy, but he acknowledges the contribution of philosophers. I have high hopes for this man."

"Did you hear his accent?" said Martial, making a face. "He sounded like a Spanish fishmonger."

"One might almost wish to remain here in Roma, to see what sort of tone Trajan sets for the social life of the city," said Epictetus.

Martial grunted. "Not me! I can't wait to get out of this stinking dung heap."

After Trajan had received the personal greetings of every senator, embracing and kissing many of them, he and Plotina ascended to the Temple of Jupiter on the Capitoline for a formal ceremony, then returned to the Forum and made their way through the crowd to the grand entrance of the imperial palace. On the steps, Trajan made a brief speech, mostly in praise of Nerva. Like Nerva, he made a vow to kill no senators. He then invited Plotina to say a few words. She made a show of surprise at this and demurred, whereupon a cry went up for her to speak. Without too much prompting, she acquiesced.

"Nerva called this place the House of the People," said Plotina, "and so we shall call it, for that way, every day, we shall be reminded of who put us here and for whom we toil—the people of Roma. Not long ago, people dreaded to enter this house, and some who entered were never seen again. It is my hope that we can make this a place where every citizen feels safe and welcome. I am a simple woman, the wife of a soldier, a daughter of the house of Pompeius. To reside in the House of the People, with your blessings, is the greatest honor of my life. Your respect is the greatest prize I can imagine. I shall strive to earn it and to keep it."

"We love you, Plotina!" shouted someone in the crowd. "Never change!"

Plotina laughed. "I don't intend to. The way I go into this house is the way I hope to be carried out of it."

This prompted a huge cheer, and with that, Trajan and Plotina gave a final wave and disappeared into the palace.

"What a charming couple," said Dio.

"What a couple of actors!" said Martial. "Really, they should start a mime troupe."

"They seem delightful," said Lucius.

Martial grunted. "Pinarius, the man was downright rude to you. He didn't say a word when Dio introduced you."

"That's quite alright by me," said Lucius. "I should prefer to remain beneath the emperor's notice."

"I'm off," said Martial. "I need a drink, and someone to drink with, and I know I won't find that at your house, Pinarius. It was good to finally see you all again."

After a round of farewells, Martial took his leave, as did Dio, who wished to spend the rest of the afternoon at the baths, relaxing and writing his impressions of the day's events. Lucius made his way home, walking slowly to accommodate the lame Epictetus.

Back in Lucius's garden, Epictetus joined him in drinking a cup of spiced water. He grimaced and rubbed his leg.

"If it would help," said Lucius, "I could have one of the slaves give you a massage."

"No, please don't bother. Actually, I've been waiting all day to have a moment alone with you."

"Is there something we need to talk about?" said Lucius. Epictetus had seemed quiet and moody all day. The expression on his face was grave.

"You know that Epaphroditus left his estate to me."

"Yes, for the establishment of your school. A worthy cause."

"His wealth has been put to good use. But among the many objects I inherited, there were some of no monetary value. Among them was this." Epictetus pulled forth a rusty circle of iron.

"What on earth is that?" exclaimed Lucius.

"This note was attached to it." Epictetus handed him a scrap of parchment.

This manacle circled the wrist of a man from Tyana, but could not restrain him. It should be given to the man who appeared beside him that day.

Lucius picked up the manacle and laughed aloud at the wonder of receiving such a memento. "One of the shackles cast off by Apollonius at his final appearance before Domitian! How remarkable, that Epaphroditus managed to get his hands on it. How thoughtful, that he should have intended it for me."

Epictetus nodded but did not smile.

"There's something else?" said Lucius.

"Yes. Epaphroditus's estate included a great many documents, as you might imagine—many capsae full of scrolls and scraps of parchment, some dating back to the days of Nero, some more recent. I've slowly been sorting through them, as time allows. Just before I left for Roma, I came across a document that will be of particular interest to you."

"Yes?"

"It's a letter written in Epaphroditus's own hand—or a draft of a letter, as it appears to be unfinished and has no salutation or signature. At first, I had no idea for whom it was intended, but as I reread it, and saw the documents attached to it, I realized it had to be you. Why Epaphroditus never finished the letter, and why he never sent it, I don't know. Perhaps he intended to wait until Domitian was dead. Perhaps he changed his mind about telling you. I myself have debated whether I should give you the letter. You seem to have attained an enviable state of contentment, Lucius. Why should I give you news that may only disturb your tranquility? But I give it to you, nonetheless."

Epictetus handed him a small scroll. Lucius unrolled it and peered at Epaphroditus's familiar handwriting.

There are two things I have never told you.

The first of these is about the one you call Teacher. When I approached the two of you that day, just before the trial, I made a pretense of not knowing him. This was at his request. Forgive me for deceiving you. The Teacher's ideas are honest and simple, but the dangers of this world require him to be secretive sometimes, even devious. Perhaps you have realized that many of his exploits, which some attribute to magic, are realized through his remarkable ability to control the perceptions of others. I suspect he does this by using the power of suggestion, though how this works I do not know; I do know that it works more readily and more deeply with some people than with others. I seem to be immune to it, but our so-called Dominus is highly susceptible—as are you, my friend. The Teacher's disappearance that day was effected partly by the use of a device which was secreted on your person by me, without your knowledge, which you handed to the Teacher just before he used it. If you think back, you may recall other occasions when you thought you saw or heard something miraculous, when in fact your senses perceived an illusion planted in your mind by the Teacher. Who is to say this ability of his is not a gift from the Divine Singularity, which he has used not for malicious purposes but wisely, for the benefit of us all?

I hope this knowledge does nothing to damage your respect for the man or for his precepts. Yet, as I begin to think that I have not much longer to live, I feel compelled to confess to you what I know.

The second thing I want to tell you is of a more intimate nature. It is about the woman whom you loved in secret for so many years.

Not long before her tragic end, she asked me to visit her during her incarceration. She knew I was your friend, and she wanted to entrust a secret to me.

She was the mother of your child.

You may recall a period of several months when she was away from Roma. Her sisters in Alba knew of her condition and helped to conceal it. That was where she delivered the child. It was a boy. The unwanted baby was "exposed," as they call this ancient and all-too-common custom—taken to a desolate spot and abandoned to die, unless the gods or some passing mortal should take pity on it.

She kept this a secret from you. For that she felt guilty. Also, she was profoundly struck by the idea that she should die in the same way she condemned her own child to die—abandoned and left to starve. I think this was why she faced her fate so calmly. She believed her end was a punishment from Vesta, and that our so-called Dominus was merely a tool of the goddess.

She left it to me to decide whether or not to tell you this after she was gone. I could not bear to do so, nor did I see any reason to. Until now. For her story so disturbed my own peace of mind that I undertook to discover, if I could, the fate of her child—your son. Our so-called Dominus often holds court at his retreat outside Alba, where I am obliged to follow. I have used my position to obtain information from the local people and from the sisters who concealed the birth.

In recent days, I have found reasons to suspect that the exposed child was rescued—"harvested" (as they say) by a professional scavenger of exposed children and raised as a slave. (I am told such slaves are commonly called "foster children" and that this lucrative practice is widespread.) I have sought to find this boy—a task made possible, perhaps, by a characteristic which distinguished him as a baby: the second and third toes of his right foot are joined to the outermost knuckle. As yet I have not succeeded, but I am hopeful that your son may yet live and that I can locate him—though whether such a discovery would bring you joy or sadness, I do not know.

In the event that this letter should reach you after my death, I attach some of the information which I have thus far uncovered.

If anything should

The letter ended with an unfinished sentence.

Lucius put down the scroll. The revelation about Apollonius did not disturb him; he knew that the Teacher was a master of illusion, and he felt privileged to have served him in any capacity, with or without his own full knowledge. But the news about Cornelia and the child struck him like a thunderbolt. In retrospect, the reason for her withdrawal to Alba seemed painfully obvious. Why had he not guessed that she was pregnant? Why had she not told him?

He understood, at last, why she had mouthed "Forgive me" as she descended to her tomb. She was talking about the child.

The love he had felt for Cornelia, which he had so assiduously sought to bury along with everything else from the dead past, suddenly welled up inside him. The knowledge that he had a son changed his perception of the world in an instant.

No matter how long it took or how difficult the task, Lucius was determined to find the child.

A.D. 100

"When Vespasian saw that the treasury was empty, he filled it up again by looting Jerusalem," said Trajan. "For us, the obvious solution is the conquest of Dacia. The loot of Sarmizegetusa would be enormous. Imagine what I could build with all that gold!"

The emperor was holding a private conference in one of the more modest reception rooms in the House of the People. He sat alone on the dais. Plotina and Hadrian were seated in their own chairs nearby, one to each side of him. With his marriage to Trajan's grandniece Sabina, Hadrian was now an in-law of the emperor as well as his cousin, and Trajan frequently included him in his deliberations. Plotina's participation in all important discussions was taken for granted.

"The gold mines of Dacia and the hoard of King Decebalus are legendary," said Hadrian. He spoke slowly and carefully, not out of caution but because he was making a concerted effort to get rid of his provincial accent, which a year ago had been even more pronounced than Trajan's. More than once he had overheard a veteran courtier making fun of the emperor's Spanish accent. Trajan seemed to have no interest in changing his speech, but Hadrian was determined to speak Latin like a born Roman, and was taking lessons to learn to do so.

They were discussing the treasury and the means by which it could be replenished. Taxes were unpopular. Conquest was the preferred means, and had been throughout Roma's long history, as Plotina pointed out.

"The great generals of the Republic destroyed Carthage and took Spain and Greece. The Divine Julius conquered Gaul; the gold and slaves he captured made him the richest man in history and helped make him the sole ruler of the empire. The Divine Augustus took Egypt, the oldest and richest kingdom in the world. Vespasian sacked Jerusalem and brought back enough gold and slaves to build his amphitheater. When one looks at the map"—she gestured to a painting on the wall—"what remains to be taken of any value, except Dacia?"

"Or Parthia," said Trajan, stroking his chin and gazing at the vast empire that dominated the far-eastern portion of the map.

"There are dangers, of course," said Hadrian. "Even the Divine Augustus was thwarted when he tried to make slaves of the Germans. And no Roman has yet succeeded in taking Parthia; the empire is simply too big and too powerful. Dacia seems ripe for the picking, but that, too, presents a risk. Domitian did his best to get the better of King Decebalus and repeatedly failed."

"That's because Domitian was a military genius only in his imagination," said Plotina.

Hadrian nodded. "Certainly, Caesar is a far better military man than Domitian, but is he not also a better diplomat? Rather than attack King Decebalus head-on, perhaps the best strategy would be to win over the king's neighbors and allies, using statecraft to isolate the Dacians before directly confronting them."

"The less blood shed by Romans, the better," Plotina agreed. "Never forget what becomes of Roman soldiers when they're captured by the Dacians. They're handed over to the Dacian women, and the tortures inflicted on those poor men are the stuff of nightmares. If the way of conquest can be made easier by diplomacy, all the better."

"Might we not also send agents to tamper with the Dacians' religious ceremonies?" suggested Hadrian.

"How would that be of use?" asked Trajan.

"The Dacians' most important religious ceremony is an event held every five years, at which a youth is sacrificed to their god, Zalmoxis."

"I've never heard of him," said Plotina.

"Nor have most people outside Dacia," said Hadrian. "Zalmoxis was once a man, a Dacian who became a slave and then a disciple of the Greek philosopher Pythagoras. After Pythagoras freed him, Zalmoxis returned to Dacia and became a healer and religious teacher in his own right. He died but was resurrected, and preached to the Dacians about the immortality of the soul before he finally left this world for the next."

"Don't the Christians also worship a man who became a god?" said Trajan. "Or is it a god who became a man?"

"There are similarities in the two religions," acknowledged Hadrian, "but the worship of Zalmoxis is much older. The most important ceremony is held once every five years in a cave in the holy mountain of Kogaionon, where Zalmoxis spent three years in seclusion. A chosen youth is cast onto the points of three lances. His mission is to die, and then to deliver the requests of the Dacians to Zalmoxis in the other world. But sometimes the youth fails to die. If that happens, the messenger is deemed unworthy and another is chosen, but the omen is very bad."

"When does the next such ceremony take place?" asked Trajan.

"According to our spies, the next five-year ceremony will take place in just a few months. This has caused me to wonder, Caesar, if Roman agents inside Dacia might somehow sabotage the ceremony, and by doing so spread doubt and dissension among the Dacians."

Trajan laughed heartily and slapped his knee. "Little Greek! Only you could sift through all that foreign gibberish and find a way to use it to our advantage. Perhaps that endless education of yours will turn out to be more useful than I thought. I love this idea! By all means, yes, instruct our agents in Dacia to make a shambles of the upcoming ceremony."

"And if they should be uncovered?" asked Plotina.

"We'll disavow any knowledge. Decebalus will assume the agents originated from enemies within his own court."

"While the Dacian women have their way with the poor agents," said Plotina.

"Such men know the risks they take in return for the generous rewards I give them," said Trajan. "Ah, but this discourse on Zalmoxis reminded me of the Christians." He waved to a secretary, who brought him a scroll. "I've been asked by a provincial governor for official instructions on what to do about the Christians. Their refusal to pay allegiance to the imperial cult—indeed, to worship any of the gods—makes them a menace to society."

"But their numbers are quite small, are they not?" said Plotina.

"One of my ministers estimates they account for five percent of the population," said Trajan.

"Respectfully, Caesar, I think that estimate is much too high, even in the Eastern cities where their numbers are concentrated," said Hadrian. "The aggravation they cause is out of all proportion to their actual numbers. Most people see their flagrant atheism as a clear threat to the security of the Roman state, which has always depended on the favor of the gods. When a pious, law-abiding citizen—in Antioch, say—discovers that a Christian is living next door, that citizen is likely to demand that a magistrate do something about it."

"And if the magistrate acts?"

"The Christians are arrested, incarcerated, and given a choice: recognize the emperor and the gods by the simple act of burning incense on an altar, or be executed."

"And some of these fools actually choose to be executed?"

"These people are fanatics, Caesar."

"What if the magistrate does not act?"

"People take the law into their own hands. Christians have been burned out of their homes and driven off, even stoned to death by angry neighbors. As you can imagine, that sort of thing causes a huge headache for the authorities in charge of keeping the peace."

Trajan rubbed his nose thoughtfully. "But such incidents are rare, are they not? In my experience, whether one is in Antium or Antioch, most people try to get along with their neighbors and mind their own business, even if the neighbors are Christians."

"And what of the legions?" said Hadrian.

"Surely a Christian soldier is a contradiction in terms," said Plotina. "I thought these people were opposed to killing."

"Nonetheless, there are reports of Christians being found among Caesar's soldiers, where they greatly upset morale. A legionary who refuses to sacrifice to the gods before battle poses a clear danger to his comrades. No pious soldier of Roma wants to serve beside such people in combat."

Trajan shook his head. "It seems to me that an official policy of aggressively seeking out and punishing this tiny cult would be a waste of resources, more trouble than it's worth, likely to make people anxious and upset for no good reason. I certainly don't want to reward these death-worshipping fanatics with the attention they crave. And I am determined not to follow the example of Domitian, who was ready to believe that anyone was a Christian if an informer told him so. Such an accusation became an easy way to blackmail or get rid of an enemy, which is one reason our estimate of the number of Christians may be inflated—there are more people accused of being Christian than there are Christians!"

Trajan waved to the secretary, who brought a stylus and wax tablet, and began to dictate. "Notes for my response to a query from a provincial governor in regard to the Christians: These people are not to be sought out. If brought before you and found guilty, they must be punished. But even to the last minute, if such a person should repent and consent to worship the gods, he should be pardoned. Anonymous accusations must play no role in any prosecution; such practices are a discarded relic of a previous time. The official policy regarding the Christians, in a nutshell, may be summed up thusly: 'Ask not, tell not.' "

He turned to Hadrian. "There, what do you think of that?"

"Caesar is like a father who wishes to keep peace between his children, even the worst of them."

Trajan was amused. "Speak freely, Little Greek! What do you really think?"

"I think that Caesar is perhaps tolerant to a fault. But that is the opinion of a man much younger and less experienced than Caesar."

"Don't rub it in!" Trajan laughed. "Erudite, pious, *and* clever is our Little Greek."

"And don't forget handsome," said Plotina with a smile.

Hadrian nodded to acknowledge the compliment, but touched his fingers to one acne-scarred cheek.

"What else is on the agenda?" said Trajan. The secretary handed him another document. "Ah, the new census I commissioned. Can you believe that Roma has a million inhabitants? So many people!"

"And so much misery," said Plotina. "I took a walk yesterday through the Subura. The squalor was shocking; so many children, dressed in rags and running wild."

"The growing number of the destitute is not just a problem in Roma," said Hadrian, "but in every city of the empire."

"Domitian did nothing about the problem, of course," said Trajan, "but Nerva instituted a system of financial relief for the children of the poor, and also for orphans. I intend to continue that relief. Perhaps we can even expand the system, if we can fill the treasury."

"One hears there are more abandoned infants now than ever before," said Plotina, "newborns left to die, not on remote hillsides but just outside the city walls. The situation is so common that people traveling along the roads think nothing of seeing the corpse of an infant lying in the gutter. Where do these unfortunate children come from, in such great numbers?"

"I was just reading a discourse by Dio of Prusa on that very topic," said Hadrian. "He speculates that slave women, impregnated by a master or by another slave, often abort children, or else hide their pregnancies and then abandon the infant."

"But abandoning one's child to die—how could even a slave do such a thing?" said Plotina. After many years of marriage, she herself remained childless.

"Dio says that such a slave woman gets rid of her baby so as to escape the added slavery of having to raise a child that will simply become another slave for her master's use."

"What a vexing situation," said Plotina. "So many problems, so much suffering."

"And so very little we can do about it," said Trajan.

"All the more reason, husband, that we must do whatever we can."

Trajan smiled ruefully. "Speaking of Dio of Prusa, cousin, I almost regret introducing myself to the man. He's taken the liberty of sending me a lengthy piece with the title 'Oration on Kingship.' He seems to expect me to read the thing and send him a reply. I don't think he realizes that a man engaged in actually running the world hardly has time to read a long-winded compilation of helpful suggestions, however well intentioned."

"And are his suggestions helpful?" said Plotina.

"Honestly, I tried to skim the thing, but it's so full of high-flown phrases and obscure literary allusions that I couldn't make any sense of it. Perhaps, cousin, you could read Dio's oration and prepare a brief summary for me? Then I can send the fellow a suitable reply."

"I've already read it," said Hadrian.

Trajan raised an eyebrow. "He sent you a copy?"

"I think he sent copies to just about everyone he could think of. He's distributed the oration far and wide."

"The nerve of the man!"

"Dio wishes to have an influence on the world. To do that, he must influence the emperor. To influence the emperor, he uses the tool he knows best: words."

"Words can be very powerful," said Trajan.

"Indeed they can. Which is why it is better for Caesar to have these philosophers as friends rather than enemies. In point of fact, much of his advice is quite sound. I'll read his oration again and prepare a summary which Caesar can read at his leisure."

"Leisure!" Trajan laughed. "I have precious little of that. Well, we've talked enough of the great problems of the world. Let's see if we can actually get something done this morning. What sort of petitions are on the agenda?" He gestured to the secretary, who brought him a list of the citizens who were awaiting an audience, along with a description of their requests.

"What's this one?" Trajan peered more closely at the list. "Lucius Pinarius: the name sounds vaguely familiar. Have I ever met this fellow?"

"I don't think so," said Hadrian. "I looked at the list earlier, and I also noticed the name. The Pinarii are an ancient patrician family, cousins of the Divine Julius and the Divine Augustus, but this bearer of the name is a man of no particular importance—not even a senator—though he does appear to possess considerable wealth."

Trajan grunted. "According to these notes, his request is linked to an issue we were just discussing. This Lucius Pinarius desires to redeem a foster child from slavery; he claims the child is his offspring and he wants to have the boy legally recognized as such, so that the boy's name and citizenship are restored. That's not the same as manumission, is it? Legally, it would be saying that the boy was born a citizen and so was never a slave, despite the fact that he was raised as one."

"There are plenty of precedents for such cases," noted Hadrian, "but legal technicalities invariably arise that must be decided on a case-by-case basis. For example, should the foster child's current master be paid for the child's upbringing, or should the master relinquish the child to its lawful parent without payment?"

Trajan nodded thoughtfully. "How old is the boy?"

The secretary consulted his notes. "Fifteen, Caesar."

Trajan raised an eyebrow. "Ah! Well, let's have a look. Show them in."

Dressed in his best toga, Lucius Pinarius entered the room and stood before the emperor. His demeanor was humble but confident, and he glanced about the room in a way that suggested he was not unfamiliar with the surroundings. The wide-eyed boy who accompanied him, on the other hand, was obviously dazzled by the magnificence of the room.

Trajan and Hadrian exchanged brief but knowing glances. Both had an appreciative eye for male beauty, and the boy was extremely good-looking. With his dark blond hair and flashing green eyes, he did not much resemble his reputed father.

Trajan took the secretary's notes on the case and read them, then passed the notes to Hadrian. He looked at Lucius Pinarius.

"It would appear, citizen, that your claim of paternity for this boy is flimsy at best. You won't reveal the identity of the mother, for one thing. Why not?"

"My relationship with the boy's mother was irregular, Caesar."

"In other words, a cause for scandal."

"Had it not been kept secret, it would have caused a scandal, yes," said Lucius. "That is why I wish her identity to remain a secret, even though she is no longer alive. But I swear by the gods that she was a freeborn woman, and thus so was our child."

"You're certain the boy was your offspring, and not that of another man?"

"I am, Caesar."

Hadrian looked up from the notes. "If this account is correct, the boy was abandoned shortly after birth in the vicinity of Alba. He was harvested by a scavenger and sold as a slave, then passed through several hands before he was acquired by his current master. You've clearly documented all the steps you took to track him down, yet how can you be certain this individual is in fact the boy you seek?"

"By an unusual physical characteristic."

Hadrian glanced again at the notes. "Ah, yes, I see: his webbed toes." He looked at the boy and smiled. "His face is perfect, yet the gods have given him a hidden flaw. It's like a poem by Theocritus."

Trajan laughed and shook his head. "Little Greek! Was there ever a pretty boy who did not suggest to you a poem by someone or other? But what of the boy's current owner? Show him in."

The man who entered was dressed not in a toga but in a brightly colored tunic. That he was not a Roman citizen became evident when he spoke with a cosmopolitan Greek accent. "My name is Acacius, Caesar. I live in Neapolis. This boy is my property."

Trajan looked at the man's feet. "Your sandals are covered with dust."

"Marble dust, Caesar. I'm a sculptor. I acquired this boy because his previous owner noticed that he had a skill for shaping things with his hands, and offered to sell him to me. I've had him for five years. His talent is considerable. No, more than considerable: he has a gift from the gods. Thanks to the education I've given him, he's become a very skilled artisan, and I think he might eventually become a true artist, maybe even a great one. The slave represents a substantial investment of my time and money, Caesar, and if he's as gifted as I think, I stand to make a great deal of money from his skills in the future. I don't want to give him up."

Trajan rubbed his chin. "I see. You may all withdraw from the room while Caesar deliberates."

"But, Caesar," said Lucius, "I feel I've hardly had a chance to plead my case—"

"The facts are all in the notes, are they not? You may withdraw."

After the litigants were gone, Trajan ordered a slave to bring wine. "To settle this matter, I think we will need the inspiration of Bacchus," he said, then threw back his head and emptied his cup. "Well, cousin, what do you think? Is Lucius Pinarius a devoted father who's performed a labor worthy of Hercules in tracking down his long-lost son? Or he is simply a lusty old goat trying to get his hands on another man's slave?"

"My thoughts exactly," said Hadrian.

"Oh, the two of you!" said Plotina. "Must you always view the world through the lens of your own proclivities? Not *every* fifty-year-old man wants to sleep with pretty boys."

Trajan sipped from his second cup of wine, and smirked. "Plotina, dear, the man has never even been married. Do you seriously think he has no interest in boys?" He suddenly laughed out loud, so long and hard that he had to wipe a tear from his eye. "I'm remembering something one of my servants once said. This was back when my father was governor of Syria and I was serving under him as a tribune. I was retiring to my quarters one evening after a particularly stressful day, and the man asked me if he could bring me anything. I said, 'Well, I wouldn't mind if you could bring me a couple of fifteen-year-old Syrian boys.' And the servant replied, with a completely straight face, 'Certainly, Master; but if I can't find two fifteen-year-olds, shall I bring you one thirty-year-old?' What a wit that fellow had!"

Even Plotina laughed. She had long ago accepted her husband's proclivities and tended to be amused by them. She was glad that he had a sense of humor and could laugh at himself. Young Hadrian, on the other hand, took such matters very seriously. He was wont to declaim about the philosophical and mystical properties of desire, while Trajan simply wanted to have a good time.

"So," said Trajan, "what do we know about this Lucius Pinarius?"

Hadrian was reading the notes. "According to this, the fellow once fought a lion before Domitian. Can you imagine that? There's no note about what happened to the lion, but Pinarius obviously survived."

"A lot of people got on the wrong side of Domitian," said Plotina. "Even senators ended up in the arena as a punishment. That it happened to Pinarius is no mark against him. That he survived may indicate the favor of the gods."

"His father was closely tied to Nero," noted Hadrian. "The elder Pinarius performed auguries in furtherance of some of Nero's more disreputable schemes."

"Nero had many sycophants, some more willing and culpable than others," said Plotina. "A son shouldn't be held accountable for his father's mistakes."

"But look at this!" said Hadrian. "This should have been at the beginning of the notes, not at the end. The fellow has character references from Dio of Prusa and the philosopher Epictetus. Both have written glowing testimonials to his virtue and honesty."

"*That's* where I met him!" said Trajan, slapping his knee. "On the day we entered Roma, and you sent me to say hello to those two in the Forum. Lucius Pinarius was with them. Ah, well, if Dio and Epictetus speak well of him, I think that settles the matter, don't you, Plotina?"

Trajan called for the litigants to return.

"Lucius Pinarius, Acacius of Neapolis, this is my decision: this boy will be recognized as Pinarius's son. Though the boy was raised as a slave, he shall be considered as born free; he is not a freedman, but under the law was born and has always been a free person and the son of citizens. However, in consideration of the uncertainties involved in this case, no fault whatsoever shall accrue to you, Acacius, and in recognition of your lost investment, Lucius Pinarius will pay to you a sum adequate to purchase a similarly educated slave to replace the boy."

The sculptor protested. "Caesar, the boy is irreplaceable. I shall never find another boy as talented."

"If you think talent is too rare, complain to the gods, not to me," said Trajan.

"But, Caesar—"

"My judgment is final. Be gone!"

The unhappy sculptor withdrew. Lucius and the boy stood before the emperor.

Trajan leaned forward and smiled. "What are you called, boy?"

"My various masters have called me various names," said the boy, daring to look the emperor in the eye. "My master Acacius called me Pygmalion."

"Did he? And do you know the tale of Pygmalion?"

"He was a Greek sculptor who made a statue so beautiful he fell in love with it. Venus brought the statue to life, and Pygmalion married her."

"A Greek tale with a rare happy ending," noted Hadrian.

"And what will you call the boy, Lucius Pinarius?" asked Trajan. "Will you give him your own first name?"

"No. If I may, Caesar, in your honor and with your permission, I will give him the name Marcus."

"My own first name," said Trajan, smiling broadly. "Caesar is pleased."

Lucius turned to the boy. "Then from this moment forward, my son, you shall be Marcus Pinarius." Saying the name aloud for the first time, Lucius was overwhelmed by the reality of the moment. At fifteen, his son had not only been found and restored to him but was of age to put on the toga of manhood. On a sudden impulse, Lucius did something he had never dared to hope would be possible. With the emperor himself as witness, he took off the necklace he was wearing and placed it over his son's head. As countless generations of Pinarii had done before him, Lucius passed the fascinum to his heir. Father and son embraced.

Trajan caught only a brief glimpse of the golden amulet. Puzzled, he crooked a finger to summon Hadrian and whispered in his ear, "Is that a cross? And is a cross not a Christian symbol?"

Hadrian frowned. "Our intelligence said nothing to indicate Pinarius might be a Christian. If he were, would that have influenced Caesar's verdict?"

Trajan held out his cup to be refilled. He allowed his gaze to linger on the cupbearer, who happened to be attractive, though not as beautiful as young Marcus Pinarius.

"Does Caesar wish to retract his judgment and question Pinarius about his religious beliefs?" asked Hadrian.

"Certainly not," said Trajan, sipping his wine. "You know the official policy: ask not, tell not!"

PART IV
MARCUS
The Sculptor

A.D. 113

Marcus Pinarius woke with a shiver and a start. The first dim light of morning seeped through the shutters. In the distance, a cock crowed.

A hand touched his face. He drew back with a jerk, then saw his father standing over him.

"You were dreaming, my son," said Lucius Pinarius.

"Was I?"

"I heard you whimpering, even from my room. Was it the same dream?"

Marcus blinked. "Yes. I think so. It's already faded away. . . ."

For years, even before his father had found him, Marcus had been haunted by a recurring dream. In the dream he was shivering and frightened and naked, and the place in which he cowered was dank and dark and cold. A giant hand reached for him and grabbed him, and he gave a cry—and at that point in the dream he always woke up. He never saw the giant who caught hold of him. He never knew what happened next.

What did it mean? Did the dream recall a genuine memory, or was it a fantasy from his imagination? The dream always exerted such a powerful spell that after waking, it took Marcus a moment to remember who and what he was: not a child any longer, and not a helpless slave, but a man of twenty-eight, living with his father in their house on the Palatine Hill.

"Are you really my father?" he whispered.

Lucius sighed. "I am. By the shade of the blessed Apollonius of Tyana, I swear it. Never doubt it, my son."

"But who was my mother?" whispered Marcus.

After much deliberation, and despite the boy's desperate desire to know his origin, Lucius had made up his mind never to reveal to him the secret of his birth. The truth was simply too dangerous, and not only because Lucius himself had committed a capital crime each time he made love to Cornelia. How could it possibly benefit young Marcus to know that his mother had been a Vestal, that she had broken her sacred vow of chastity, that she had been buried alive, and that his own conception had been the result of a sacrilegious crime? Surely such knowledge could only plague him with more nightmares. Lucius would tell his son only that his mother had been a woman of patrician rank with whom Lucius had carried on an illicit and impossible liaison, whose family would never forgive her lapse, and who had died years ago. "I loved her deeply, and still miss her every day," he would add, for this was the truth. At the age of sixty-six, Lucius was determined to go to his grave without revealing to anyone the fact that Cornelia Cossa was the mother of his child.

"I, too, woke from a familiar dream," he said, ignoring his son's question.

"You were visited again by Apollonius?" said Marcus.

"Yes."

"He visits you often in your dreams."

"More often now than when he was alive!" said Lucius with a laugh. "I only wish he had returned to Roma before he died, so that you could have been blessed with the chance to meet him."

"I have been blessed by having a father who knew him," said Marcus. He flashed a weak smile. The dreadful spell cast by the nightmare was fading.

"Of course, there are those who question whether Apollonius actually died, at least in the usual sense," said Lucius, "since no corpse was ever discovered."

"Tell me the story," said Marcus, closing his eyes. His father had told him the tale many times before, but Marcus was always glad to hear it. It would help him to forget his bad dream.

"This occurred a few years ago on the island of Crete, where the Teacher had acquired a great following. He arrived late one night at the temple of the Minoan goddess Dictynna, which stands on a rocky promontory overlooking the sea. The wealthy people of Crete deposit their treasures in the temple for safekeeping. At night the doors are locked and fierce dogs stand guard. But when the Teacher approached, the dogs wagged their tales and licked his hands, and the doors of the temple sprang open. When the priests found him sleeping inside the next morning, they accused him of drugging the dogs and using magic to open the doors. They put him in chains and confined him in an iron cage suspended from a precipice overhanging the sea, with crashing waves below. But late that night, unfettered and free, again the Teacher approached the entrance to the temple, and this time there was a great crowd gathered in anticipation of his appearance. Again the dogs grew tame and fawned on him, and again the locked doors sprang open. He stepped inside. The doors shut after him, and from within there came the sound of women singing. 'Hurry, hurry, upward, upward!' they sang. 'Fly away from this place and ascend to the heavens!' When the doors opened, no singers were to be seen—and neither was the Teacher. Apollonius has never again been seen on this earth, except in the dreams of those who knew him."

"Do you think he'll ever visit me in my dreams, father?"

"I don't know, my son."

"What did he say to you this time?"

"He talked to me about the immortality of the soul. He said, 'Here is the proof, presented to you from beyond the grave, which I couldn't offer to you when I was a living man. The fact that I endure, and visit you in your dreams, shows you I have survived beyond my mortal life. Your soul is no less immortal than mine—but it is a fallacy to speak of 'your' soul and 'my' soul, for the soul is no one's possession; it emanates from and returns to the Divine Singularity, and the body it inhabits is mere gross matter, which decays and vanishes. When the body dies, the soul rejoices; like a swift horse freed from its traces, it leaps upward and mingles with the air, loathing the spell of harsh and painful servitude it has endured.'"

"You should write all this down, father."

Lucius shook his head. "I'm not sure that I should. Because in the next breath, the Teacher told me that all he had just said was of no real value to a living man. 'But of what use can this knowledge be to you while you live?' he said. 'The truth will be known to you soon enough, and you shall have no need for words to explain it or to convince you; you shall experience it for yourself. As long as you live, and move among other living beings, these things will be mysteries to you, like shadows cast on a wall by a light you cannot see.' "

Lucius looked down at his son, who gazed back at him with trusting green eyes—the eyes of his mother. Marcus sometimes still looked like a boy to him, though the world by every measure considered him a man.

"Come," Lucius said. "Wash your face and dress yourself. Hilarion will have woken the kitchen slaves by now, and our breakfast will be waiting. You have a busy day ahead of you."

Later that morning, holding a hammer in one hand and a chisel in the other, Marcus stepped back and read aloud the inscription on the massive marble pedestal to which he had been putting some finishing touches: " 'The Senate and People of Roma Dedicate this Monument to the Emperor Caesar Nerva Trajan Augustus Germanicus Dacicus, Son of the Divine Nerva, Pontifex Maximus, in His Seventeenth Year in the Office of Tribune, Six Times Acclaimed as Imperator, Six Times Consul, Father of His Country.' "

He stepped farther back from the immense pedestal and gazed up. The towering column was surrounded by scaffolding, but in his mind's eye Marcus could see the structure as it would appear when it was completed and the scaffolds were removed. Never before had there existed a monument like this one, and Marcus was immensely proud to have had a hand in creating it.

The column rose 100 feet—if one included the pedestal and the statue that would top the column, the total height would reach 125 feet—and was made of eighteen colossal marble drums stacked one atop another. Within the hollow column was a spiral staircase of 185 steps, lit by narrow slits in the drums. Wrapped around the column in an ascending spiral was a series of relief sculptures depicting Trajan's conquest of Dacia. These sculptures were the reason for the scaffolds that surrounded the column; the hundreds of images that circled the drums were still being finished and painted.

The height of the column corresponded to the height of the hillside that had been excavated to make room for it; the volume of earth that had been removed by human labor—mostly Dacian slave labor—was staggering. Where before a spur of the Quirinal Hill had blocked the way between the city's center and the Field of Mars, there was now a new forum bearing Trajan's name, the centerpiece of which was the enormous column that pierced the sky above Marcus's head.

He felt a hand on his shoulder. Standing beside him was the man who had designed not just the column but the entire forum complex. People called Apollodorus of Damascus a second Vitruvius, comparing him to the great architect and engineer who had served Julius Caesar. Trajan had met Apollodorus during his service in Syria, had realized his genius, and had kept him busy ever since.

In the Dacian campaigns, Apollodorus had served the emperor by designing siege engines and other weapons. To facilitate troop movements, he had constructed a stupendous bridge across the Danube River, the longest arch bridge ever built. To allow a vast army to move quickly and safely through the Iron Gates of the Danubian gorges, he had built a wooden roadway cantilevered from the sheer rock face; the legions had literally walked on top of the river and penetrated to the heart of the enemy's territory. Roman bravery, the favor of the gods, and the leadership of the emperor had won the day, but it was the brilliance of Apollodorus that had allowed the legions to move with the speed and force of a lightning bolt.

Early in the Dacian war, Apollodorus had asked Trajan to give him an assistant. The emperor recalled the strikingly handsome youth who had stood before him one day in the House of the People, and the comment made by the boy's onetime master: "His talent is considerable . . . he has a gift from the gods." It had been the great good fortune of Marcus Pinarius to be summoned by the emperor to serve under Apollodorus of Damascus. Throughout the Dacian war, Marcus was at the man's side day and night, assisting him, watching him work, learning from him, earning his trust and respect. Now, back in Roma, Apollodorus continued to work for the emperor, and Marcus continued to work under Apollodorus.

Marcus's aptitude for engineering was considerable, but his special gift had always been for sculpture. Anything he could visualize in his imagination he could render in stone with a sureness and ease that astounded even Apollodorus. While Apollodorus could take credit for the concept and the overall design of the great column, Marcus had sculpted many parts of the spiral relief, as well as the monumental sculpture at the base, a pile of weapons that symbolized the enemy's defeat. With vivid images of warfare, many witnessed by Marcus firsthand, the spiral relief recounted the struggle of the Dacians, ending in their slaughter and enslavement by the Roman legions. Over and over in the sequence of images, the figure of the emperor appeared, often sacrificing animals to the gods or taking part in a furious battle.

Apollodorus joined Marcus in gazing up at the column. He was a tall man with big arms who kept fit by taking part in the actual construction of his projects, not merely overseeing the work. Like many of Trajan's legionaries, his hair was shoulder length and he wore a beard, claiming that he had no time for barbers. At middle age, his hair was still thick and dark, with a bit of silver beginning to show at his temples and on his chin.

He gave Marcus's shoulder a friendly squeeze. His grip was painfully strong. "What do you feel when you look up at it?"

"Pride," Marcus said. It was true: Marcus took great pride in his artistry. And pride was what Romans were meant to feel when they gazed at the column—pride in their soldiers, pride in their emperor, pride in the conquest of another people. But pride was not all Marcus felt when he looked at the images that wrapped the column. Many of those images had been summoned from his own memories. Though he had not taken part in the fighting, Marcus had seen the aftermath of many battles, stepping over corpses, severed limbs, pools of blood, and scattered entrails. He had seen long trains of exhausted, naked Dacian prisoners, chained neck-to-neck with their hands tied, being driven to their new lives of slavery. He had seen the sack of villages and the rape of women and boys by Roman soldiers enjoying the privileges of victors after the terror and exhilaration of battle.

His father had taught Marcus the precepts of Apollonius of Tyana; it was hard to reconcile the ideas of a man who refused to kill an animal with the horrors Marcus had witnessed in the war, and the fact that the world glorified such horrors. Marcus had experienced life as a slave; it was hard for him to take pride in the enslavement of free men, even though their enslavement meant the enrichment of the Roman state and of Roman citizens like himself.

The war against Dacia had been necessary to secure Roma's frontiers, and had been sanctioned by the gods, whose favor was made manifest by auguries and other portents. To please Jupiter, the Romans desecrated every temple of the god Zalmoxis, pulling down his altars, smashing his images, and obliterating all inscriptions that referred to him. The Dacians' holiest shrine, the cave in Mount Kogaionon where Zalmoxis had lived as a mortal, had been ruined, its interior looted and the entrance filled with rubble. Zalmoxis must have been a very weak god, for he had been powerless to save his followers. Except in a few remote corners of Dacia, his worship was now extinct.

The Dacians were an ignorant, impious, and dangerous people, a threat to the Danube frontier and, with their vast hoard of wealth, a menace to Roma itself; so the legionaries were told as their commanders exhorted them to fight. But sometimes it seemed to Marcus that the Dacians were simply a proud people desperately fighting to save themselves, their religion, their language, and their native land. Just as the atrocities he had witnessed in the war sometimes caused him distress, so Marcus's work on the column that commemorated the war sometimes afflicted him with doubts. However dazzlingly executed the images on the column, were they not a celebration of brute strength and human suffering?

"Let's take a closer look, shall we?" said Apollodorus, who seemed never to be bothered by such thoughts. He and Marcus mounted the scaffolding. They had examined the images many times before, yet each time, Marcus always saw a bit more work to be done. The most vexing problem at this late stage was the placement of the miniature swords. In numerous places, tiny holes had been drilled so that tiny metal swords could be fitted into the hands of the figures on the relief; it had been Marcus's idea to use this novel effect, which gave the sculpture even greater depth, especially when seen at a distance. Unfortunately, the artisans responsible for the tedious task of fitting these embellishments had been quite careless and had missed a great many places on the first pass. Every time Marcus inspected the relief he found another area that had been overlooked. With 155 individual scenes, each blending into the next, and more than 2,500 individual figures, perhaps it was not surprising that the workmanship was not always consistent. Still, Apollodorus demanded perfection, and Marcus was determined to meet his expectations.

As the two men ascended the scaffolds, Marcus was swept into the encyclopedic history of the war recounted by the images. Taking thirteen legions—more than one hundred thousand men—into the field, Trajan's campaign had resulted not just in victory but in a cultural annihilation. The fortresses of the Dacians had been demolished along with their temples and cities. Facing defeat, King Decebalus made a last, desperate attempt to hide his vast treasure: he diverted a river, buried trunks of gold and silver in the soft riverbed, then returned the river to its course. But an informant revealed the secret to the Romans, and the treasure was recovered. Hundreds of tons of gold and silver had been seized, carted out of Dacia under heavy guard, and brought to Roma. There would be more treasure to come, for the mines of the Dacians had been discovered, and Dacian slaves had been put to work digging new veins.

His armies defeated, his people enslaved, his cities and towns in flames, his treasure stolen, King Decebalus at last killed himself. He was discovered sitting upright on a stone bench outside the sealed cave at Mount Kogaionon, wearing his robes of state and surrounded by a great many of his nobles, who had all taken poison. The body of Decebalus was stripped and decapitated. The robes were burned. The naked, headless body was thrown down the rocky mountainside to be consumed by vultures. The head was taken to Roma by the same speedy messengers who brought news of the war's successful conclusion. As the people of Roma thronged the Forum to celebrate, the head of Decebalus was displayed on the Capitoline Hill as proof of the Dacians' defeat, then thrown down the Gemonian Stairs. Someone kicked the head into the crowd, where it was batted about like a ball until it was dropped on the paving stones. The crowd swarmed around it, competing with one another to stamp the last remains of King Decebalus into the ground.

When Trajan returned to Roma, he celebrated with an unprecedented 123 days of games at the Flavian Amphitheater and at other sites across the city. Ten thousand gladiators fought. Eleven thousand animals were slaughtered. The scale of these spectacles had never been seen before; nor had the scale of his lavish building program, the results of which were to be seen in all directions from the uppermost tier of the scaffolding around the column. Apollodorus and Marcus gazed down at the largest basilica ever built, a vast hall revetted with marble and flooded with light. An adjoining courtyard, the largest open space in the city center, was dominated by an enormous statue of Trajan on horseback. Farther away, against the cliff face of the excavated Quirinal Hill, a sprawling, multistory shopping arcade was being built. There was also a gymnasium for sporting competitions and a new bathing complex even grander than the one Titus had built. On either side of the column, directly below them, were the two wings of Trajan's library. The wing for Latin literature was almost finished, and the extravagantly decorated reading room, lined with busts of famous authors, would soon open to the public; the Greek wing was still under construction. Apollodorus, who had served as chief architect and designer of these new constructions, called them "the fruits of Dacia."

As grand as they were, none of these buildings approached the height of the column. From the topmost scaffold, Apollodorus and Marcus stepped onto the top of the column. Their view of the city in all directions was virtually unimpeded; only the Temple of Jupiter atop the Capitoline loomed higher. Turning slowly, Marcus saw his father's house and the sprawling House of the People on the Palatine, the Flavian Amphitheater and the towering statue of Sol at the far end of the Forum, the cluttered tenements of the Subura, the Hill of Gardens, and the vast expanse of the Field of Mars with the bend of the Tiber beyond.

The only man-made object that reached to their level was an enormous crane situated just beyond the Greek wing of the library. Apollodorus pointed to it with a satisfied nod.

"I reworked the last of the calculations last night. Everything is ready. We'll lift the statue into place today."

Marcus gazed down at the workmen who surrounded the statue of Trajan that was to be placed atop the column. The men were securing the statue with padded chains and ropes connected to the crane. "How soon?"

"As soon as I can get all the workmen in place. Here, we'll go down using the stairway inside the column. You can observe as I give my final instructions. Come along, Pygmalion."

Long ago, from the emperor himself, Apollodorus had learned that Pygmalion had once been Marcus's name. To Marcus, the name was a reminder of his years as a slave, but when Apollodorus first used it as a pet name for him, he had been too intimidated to object. Apollodorus clearly intended no malice; he seemed to think that the name was a compliment, an acknowledgment of Marcus's skill as a sculptor.

As they descended, Marcus counted each of the 185 steps. He always did this. All the artisans and workmen practiced similar rituals—always tying an odd number of knots, or using an even number of nails, or stepping onto a scaffold with their right foot first.

They walked to the crane and stood before the gilded bronze statue of Trajan. Apollodorus had executed the basic design, but Marcus had sculpted most of the finer details, including Trajan's face and hands. This had meant spending long stretches of time with the emperor, who listened to reports and dictated correspondence while Marcus observed him and sculpted his likeness, first making preliminary models and then working on the full-scale statue. Marcus vividly remembered his first meeting with Trajan thirteen years ago, when his father had petitioned the emperor to recognize Marcus's status as a freeborn citizen. Trajan had seemed larger than life to Marcus then, and he still did.

Far more accessible was the emperor's protégé, Hadrian, who had often been present when Marcus was sculpting Trajan's likeness; perhaps Marcus found the man more approachable because he was closer to Marcus's own age. Hadrian had distinguished himself in the Dacian wars, commanding the First Legion Minerva, but he also had an avid interest in all things artistic and had strong opinions about everything from the poetry of Pindar ("incomparably beautiful") to Trajan's collection of silver Dacian drinking cups ("unspeakably hideous; they should be melted down"). He was known even to dabble in architecture, though none of his fanciful drawings had ever resulted in an actual building.

Hadrian joined them as Apollodorus and Marcus were making a final inspection to see that the statue was securely fitted for lifting.

"Is the operation on schedule?" asked Hadrian.

"We'll begin at any moment," said Apollodorus. "Will the emperor be present?"

"He intended to be here, but affairs of state preclude his presence," said Hadrian. He cracked a smile and lowered his voice. "Actually, I suspect he's a bit unnerved by the whole thing. I don't think he fancies the idea of seeing himself being hoisted a hundred feet in the air and dangling from a chain."

"Perhaps it's better that he's not here," said Apollodorus. "His presence might make the men nervous."

Hadrian slowly circled the statue, then nodded. "What a clever idea you came up with, Marcus Pinarius, to slightly exaggerate and elongate the emperor's features, so as to make them appear more natural when viewed by spectators on the ground. What's the word for that?"

"It's a trick of perspective called foreshortening," said Marcus. "I'm grateful that you supported my idea."

"Let's hope it works. Caesar was certainly skeptical when he saw the result. Horrified, actually. 'No man's nose is that long, not even mine!' he said. It does look a bit of a caricature when seen this close. But at a distance of a hundred feet and from a low angle, I suspect that nose will actually flatter him."

The workmen assigned to stand atop the column and guide the placement of the statue were in place; they called and waved to Apollodorus to signal their readiness. The workmen who would operate the various hoists and pulleys of the crane were also at their stations, as were the slaves who would supply the labor to pull the ropes, turn the winches, and steady the counterweights. The statue was ready to be lifted. Apollodorus closed his eyes and muttered a prayer. Marcus touched the fascinum at his breast.

Apollodorus gave the signal for the operation to begin. With a great groaning noise, the various parts of the crane began to move. The statue cleared the ground and began to ascend.

The statue rose to half the height of the column, and then higher still, until it dangled above the column. Apollodorus peered at all the various mechanisms in play, and suddenly seemed nervous. "Marcus, run up to the top of the column," he said. "See that everything is done correctly."

Marcus ran to the column, stepped inside, and bounded up the steps. He was so intent on reaching the top that he forgot to count them.

The workmen atop the column stood in a circle, ready to guide the statue into the spot intended for it, the outline of which had been drawn with chalk. Each of the men wore a rope around his waist that was secured to an iron pin driven into the marble, to catch them should they fall. Marcus was not wearing a rope.

The statue seemed to float on the air nearby, twisting slightly so that the gilding reflected sparkles of sunlight. Then it began slowly to move toward them, until it appeared just above their heads. The men reached up and touched the base of the statue, which then began very slowly to descend. Their foreman shouted instructions, making sure the orientation of the statue remained true as it was lowered into place. Marcus stayed out of the way, crouching to keep his balance.

The statue was still two feet above the top of the column when Marcus heard a sharp noise. Somewhere, a chain had snapped.

He looked at the statue, which swayed a bit. He looked at the crane, which also seemed to sway very slightly. Then the crane began to tilt to one side.

"Numa's balls!" cried the foreman. "The statue's coming down, right now! Keep it steady!"

The workmen grabbed hold of the statue, but they were powerless to guide it any longer as it swung one way and then the other. With a tremendous cracking noise, part of the crane collapsed. As he strove to keep his balance and stay clear of the statue, Marcus saw in glimpses that a section of the crane was falling and men on the ground were scrambling to get out of the way. He experienced a moment of vertigo in which it seemed that the huge statue was stationary while everything else—earth, sky, and the column under his feet—was spinning off-kilter.

The statue bumped one of the workmen. The movement was relatively small, but the weight of the statue lent tremendous force to the slight contact. The workman went tumbling backward, paddling his arms in the air. He stepped off the column and onto the topmost scaffold, but couldn't regain his balance and kept staggering backward. Marcus waited for the man's safety rope to stop his fall, but the knot at his waist had been poorly tied. The man slipped free from the rope and went flying off the scaffold, somersaulting backward. His scream pierced the air as he plummeted to the ground. There was a sickening sound of impact, then a moment of silence, then a tremendous crash as the broken section of the crane fell onto the Greek wing of the library.

Marcus experienced a moment of sheer panic. He imagined the statue swinging ever more wildly out of control, knocking off more and more of the workmen, until it actually struck the column, dislodging the top drum, throwing the whole column out of balance and causing it to topple over.

But that was not what happened.

The statue twisted one way, then the other, then suddenly dropped and landed with a jarring thud atop the column. None of the workmen were harmed, and when they took a closer look, they were amazed to see that the statue had landed precisely within the chalk outline. Despite the broken crane, the outcome could not have been more perfect.

For Marcus, the earth and the sky gradually stopped spinning and all was still. He realized that he was clutching the fascinum with his right hand. His knuckles were bone white. As he slowly unclenched his fist, he stepped onto the scaffolding and took stock of the damage below.

The crane was ruined beyond repair. One end of the Greek wing of the library was destroyed, but that part of the building was unfinished and the repairs would be relatively minor. The body of the man who had fallen lay twisted on the paving stones below, surrounded by a pool of blood. As Marcus watched, Apollodorus and Hadrian approached the lifeless body. Apollodorus gazed down at the corpse for a moment, then up at Marcus. His face was ashen.

Marcus, too stunned to speak, extended his arm and turned his thumb upward to signal that all was well atop the column. Apollodorus looked as if he might faint with relief.

Hadrian took a step back to avoid the spreading pool of blood, then stared up at Marcus, or rather, beyond him, at the towering statue of Trajan. "The nose!" he shouted.

What was Hadrian talking about? Marcus craned his neck to peer up at the statue. The gilding reflected the sunlight so brightly that he was blinded. He looked down at Hadrian and made a quizzical gesture.

Hadrian smiled broadly. He cupped his hands to his mouth and shouted. "The nose . . . looks . . . perfect!"

※

A month later, Lucius Pinarius hosted a small dinner party in honor of his son.

The Column would soon be officially dedicated, and in the various celebrations the emperor and his chief architect would be the focus of all attention. Before that happened, Lucius wanted to acknowledge his son's accomplishments and tremendous hard work. The dinner party was to be a major event for the Pinarius household, which seldom saw guests outside the small circle of Lucius's friends, most of whom were advanced in years and fellow followers of Apollonius of Tyana—not a group much given to traditional feasting, since they ate no meat and drank no wine.

No meat had been cooked or served in Lucius's house for many years, and he could not bring himself to include any sort of flesh, fowl, or fish on the menu; his cook assured him that no one would even notice the omission among the highly spiced delicacies and sumptuous sweets that would be offered. But for a dinner party that included a member of the imperial household—Hadrian had accepted an invitation—there would have to be wine. Lucius never drank wine, but Marcus occasionally did, and Lucius had no objection to serving it to his guests. If they should be disappointed by the absence of meat, he was determined that they would have no cause to be disappointed with the wine; he had stocked a variety of what a reputable merchant assured him were the very finest vintages, both Greek and Italian.

For such an occasion, his son informed him, there must be a scurra among the guests; no memorable social occasion could take place among the elite of the city without a scurra to amuse them. Apparently there existed an entire class of such persons in the city, men who literally made their way by their wit. A scurra cadged dinner invitations to the homes of the wealthy and in return shared gossip, told jokes, injected double entendres into the conversation, flattered the host, and gently mocked the guests.

"And where on earth will I find such a person?" Lucius had asked his son, quite certain there were no scurras among the staid acolytes of the Teacher.

"Apollodorus says he'll bring someone, a fellow named Favonius," said Marcus. Apollodorus had also invited the director of the imperial archives, a man in his forties named Gaius Suetonius, who had learned that the elder Pinarius had known Nero and his long-vanished circle and was eager to meet him.

After many days of preparation, the appointed hour arrived. The guests appeared in quick succession and were shown to their dining couches. The house was filled with the steady hum of conversation and laughter.

The scurra showed his worth early on. Favonius had frizzled red hair, plump cheeks, and a peculiar nose that skewed to one side; from his protruding belly, it appeared that he loved food and seldom missed a meal. When it became evident that no meat would be served, Favonius pretended to pout. "I see we're to be served a gladiators' diet tonight: no meat, just barley and beans! Ah, well, thank the gods that gladiators are allowed to drink wine." Both Lucius and Marcus were taken aback by the man's rudeness, but everyone else laughed, and not another word was said all night about the lack of meat or fish; the scurra's blatant complaint forestalled any further grumbling. Instead, the guests vied with one another to praise the cook's skill and ingenuity.

Hadrian and Suetonius engaged Lucius in conversation. The archivist was curious to learn anything about Nero, while Hadrian wanted to know every detail of his host's friendship with Apollonius of Tyana, Epictetus, and Dio of Prusa.

Marcus noticed that Apollodorus stayed largely out of the conversation. It seemed to him that there was some tension between the architect and Hadrian, who had always been on friendly terms.

Hadrian excused himself to go to the latrina. As soon as he was out of sight, the scurra grunted. "I do believe that fellow has lost his provincial accent entirely."

"I was just thinking the same thing," said Lucius. "When he first came to Roma, I seem to recall that his accent was quite pronounced."

"You recall correctly," said Favonius. "People still talk about the occasion, early in Trajan's reign, when Hadrian read one of the emperor's speeches aloud to the Senate, and the senators laughed out loud. Hadrian blushed so brightly you couldn't even see his acne scars."

"Hadrian's worked very hard to get rid of his accent, and I think he's succeeded," said Suetonius, whose own diction was elegant to the point of pedantry.

Apollodorus, who was from Damascus and whose Latin had its own provincial accent, shook his head. "He now sounds so much like a city-born Roman that Trajan has stopped calling him the Little Greek. He calls him the Little Roman."

Favonius tittered. "Oh, dear, I am going to have to steal that one from you."

"It's not a joke," insisted Apollodorus, "it's the truth!"

When Hadrian returned, the entire company fell silent. Hadrian took the opportunity to steer the conversation back to Dio of Prusa, whose latest writings had been much concerned with the subject of marriage. Happily restored to his native city, Dio also seemed to be quite happily married, and expressed his contentment by extolling the virtues of marital union above all other forms of love.

The topic cheered no one. Lucius Pinarius had known love, but never marriage. Apollodorus's wife had been very ill lately, and thoughts of her only made him gloomy. Hadrian had been married for several years to Trajan's grandniece Sabina, but their marriage was childless and thought by many to be in name only. As for Marcus, his irregular origins, a subject never openly discussed by those who knew him but apparently known to all, had made it difficult for him to find a match suited to his family's ancient name and patrician status; not yet married, and with no immediate prospects, he had given up thoughts of creating a family and devoted himself entirely to his work.

The scurra, seeing the gloominess caused by the subject, managed to crack a few crude jokes about marriage, but these seemed forced and stale. It was Suetonius who rescued the conversation. As a sidelight to his work as an archivist, he was a dedicated antiquarian and amateur historian, and kept a notebook dedicated especially to anecdotes about imperial marriages. He amused them at length with stories about the duel of wits between Livia and Augustus, Caligula's so-called marriages to his sisters, Claudius's misery with Messalina and his agony with Agrippina, and Nero's marriage to the beautiful but ill-fated Poppaea, followed by his betrothal to her double, the equally ill-fated Sporus.

"You must have known Sporus," said Suetonius, looking at their host.

Lucius made no answer for a long moment. "Yes, I did," he finally said.

"Was the eunuch as beautiful as they say?" asked Hadrian.

"Yes, she was," said Lucius, lowering his eyes. The others waited for him to elaborate, but instead he said, "Shall we retire to the garden? Carry your cups with you. I shall be serving a special wine from Samothrace with a jasmine flavor that emerges only under moonlight—so the merchant assured me."

As they stepped into the garden, Hadrian came to a sudden halt. He stared at the statue of Melancomas. Marcus had noticed that visitors were often a bit startled by the image of the naked boxer, probably because it stood at ground level and was so extraordinarily realistic that a casual observer might mistake it for a living man. But Hadrian's reaction went beyond mere surprise: his face was lit with wonder and delight. He reached out to touch the smooth marble of the statue's face. A moment later, he stepped back and touched his own cheek, running his fingertips over the rough, mottled blemishes.

"Melancomas," said Lucius.

"Yes, I've seen other images of him—but none that could match this one," said Hadrian, unable to take his eyes from the statue. "They say Melancomas was beloved by the Divine Titus. Lucky Titus! If only, someday, I could meet a youth as beautiful as this . . ."

Marcus smiled. "If only, someday, I could create a statue as beautiful as this."

Favonius stepped between them and tilted an eyebrow at each in turn. "May each of you be granted his desire—and be happy with it!"

Apollodorus joined them. He was a bit drunker than the rest. For Apollodorus, the evening was a rare break from months of unceasing labor, and he had imbibed a considerable quantity of the fine vintages on offer. Seeing that they were all gazing at the statue, he nodded. "Ah, the Melancomas. Superb! Without a doubt, the most beautiful and most valuable thing in the house." He looked from Marcus to Hadrian. "Look at the two of you—spellbound! But for rather different reasons, I suspect. Which of you is truly Pygmalion, and which is the Little Greek? It seems to me that Marcus here is more the pure connoisseur, the Greekling who loves art for its own sake, and you, Hadrian, are the lover who longs to see a statue brought to life! Perhaps we should call *you* Pygmalion!"

Favonius laughed, but Marcus was not amused. Being called Pygmalion in private was one thing, but hearing his old slave name used in front of others rankled him. Nor was Hadrian amused: he looked quietly furious, and the acne scars across his cheeks turned bright red. Again, Marcus was puzzled by the tension between the two men.

Favonius, who missed nothing, saw the look on Marcus's face and drew him aside. As they strolled to the far end of the garden, the scurra spoke in a low voice. "Are you not aware of the tiff between those two?"

Marcus wrinkled his brow. The scurra's eyes lit up. There was nothing that gave Favonius greater pleasure than the chance to deliver fresh gossip. "Everyone's talking about it! Where have you been the last couple of days?"

"Helping my father plan this party," said Marcus.

"Ah! Then you haven't heard about the meeting Caesar had with Apollodorus, about the reconstruction of the Greek wing of the library?"

"I know about that. It was two days ago."

"But you weren't there?"

"I won't be involved until the time comes to decorate the interior."

"I see." The scurra nodded knowingly. "Well, it so happens that Hadrian *did* attend that meeting."

"As he often does."

"But this time he put forward some plans of his own."

"What sort of plans?"

"Apollodorus was explaining to Caesar how long it will take to finish the repairs to the Greek wing, when Hadrian interrupted and proposed that the wing should have a dome on it—the man is crazy for domes—and produced some very elaborate drawings and plans which he insisted they both look at."

"But such an idea isn't possible. The Latin and Greek wings are intended to be symmetrical, and the Latin wing has no dome."

"That's exactly what Apollodorus said. Whereupon Hadrian said, 'That's why I propose to remodel the Latin wing and give it a dome as well.' Apparently he has some idea that a dome is absolutely necessary for such a building, something about letting in light from the ceiling. He produced another drawing to show how the library would look if *both* wings had a dome, with the Column rising up between them, and apparently Trajan rather liked the notion."

Marcus raised his eyebrows, thinking of all the time and effort such a scheme would entail. "How did Apollodorus react?"

"Apparently, he was absolutely scathing. You know he's not afraid to be outspoken when it comes to such things. Even as Hadrian was expounding on the beauty of his domes, Apollodorus pointed at the drawings and turned up his nose. 'What are these supposed to look like,' he said, 'two swollen testes flanking the upright Column?' Well, once that image is in your mind, you can't picture it any other way, can you? 'These bulbous monstrosities not only spoil the overall symmetry of the whole forum,' he says, 'but they'll collapse even before they're completed.' To which Hadrian made some crack about that unfortunate business with the broken crane, whereupon Apollodorus looked him straight in the eyes and said, 'It's one thing to draw your fantasy, young man, another to actually build it. Be off, now, and draw your giant gourds elsewhere. Caesar and I have a lot to talk about, and you understand nothing of these matters.'"

"Trajan let him speak that way to his own cousin?"

"The emperor gives Apollodorus a very long leash, as you know, at least in matters to do with art and architecture. He trusts his judgment implicitly, whereas Hadrian, when all is said and done, is still the Little Greek, an overeducated dabbler who would do better to concentrate on his military career and leave art to the hirelings who create it for the pleasure of their betters. Hadrian was crushed. He gathered up his precious drawings and stalked off, practically in tears. Oh dear, but now we've come full circle, and there they are, still staring at that statue and not saying a word to each other."

Marcus tried to think of a new topic for discussion. "What word, Hadrian, about this expedition being mounted by the emperor against Parthia?"

The question seemed to draw Hadrian out of a trance. He smiled. "I'm to go with him. It seems I'll finally see the cities of the East—perhaps even Ctesiphon."

He alluded to the capital of Parthia. Not content with the conquest of Dacia, Trajan had been seized by an even grander conceit—to fulfill the repeatedly thwarted Roman ambition that went back to the days of Julius Caesar, to follow in the footsteps of Alexander the Great and expand Roma's empire eastward into the realms of ancient Persia.

Lucius Pinarius, who had joined his guests in the garden, cleared his throat. "Of course, there's no real strategic purpose for inciting such a war, except that the Parthians present the only empire in the world to rival that of Roma."

"I should think there's every reason to conquer them," said Favonius. "Or rather, the only reason there ever is for a war—wealth to plunder. The Dacians were the last neighbor left on the edges of the empire who actually possessed anything worth taking. Beyond our provinces on the northern coast of Africa lies a trackless desert; beyond Egypt lies a land of savages and impassable jungles; the northern part of the island of Britannia is a frigid wasteland; and the realms beyond Germania and Dacia seem to be completely uncivilized, inhabited by such foul barbarians that they're not even worth taking as slaves. There is India, of course, and beyond that the kingdom of Serica, the land of silk, which surely must be wealthy, but the world beyond the Indus River is so remote that hardly any Roman has ever traveled there, except for a few intrepid merchants. Within our reach, only Parthia and its satellite kingdoms remain to be conquered—and the wealth of its empire must be staggering."

"As will be the challenge of taking it," said Hadrian. "Even the Flavians at their most ambitious never dreamed of such a thing. But Caesar is ready for the challenge."

"You won't be going, will you, Marcus?" said Lucius, with a slight quaver in his voice.

"No, father. The emperor has decided that Apollodorus and I should remain here in Roma."

Apollodorus nodded. "I'm compiling a handbook of designs for siege engines and such for the emperor to take with him, and training some of my best engineers for the expedition. But there's still a great deal of work to be done on Caesar's grand building projects here in the city, and whom could he possibly leave in charge but myself? Naturally, he looks to someone with experience, someone who knows how to get things done in strict accordance with his own high standards." His boasting seemed to Marcus a deliberate attempt to needle Hadrian. After another swallow of wine, Apollodorus spoke to Hadrian directly. "But while Pygmalion and I stay here in the city to finish the projects, I'm sure you'll manage to kill a Parthian or two, Little Greek! And like every conqueror, you'll find it's easier to demolish buildings and strip their ornaments than to put one up in the first place."

Hadrian blushed furiously. Apollodorus laughed and held out his cup for more wine. Did he not realize how deeply he had offended Hadrian? Did he not care?

Lucius stepped forward. "Caesar shows great trust to keep you here in Roma, Apollodorus. And you must have great trust in Marcus, to keep him here with you."

"No one else has the skill to finish the interior decorations of the Greek wing of the library, for one thing," said Apollodorus, looking askance at Hadrian.

"I'm gratified to hear you say that," said Lucius, "because, as our evening together draws to a close, I wish to remind you of the reason for this occasion: to honor my son for all he's accomplished in recent months. I ask you to drink a toast. Raise your cups, please. To Marcus Pinarius—the best son a man could ever hope for."

"To Marcus Pinarius!" said the rest, except for Apollodorus, who shouted, sounding quite drunk, "To Pygmalion!"

As soon as the toast was finished, Hilarion entered and spoke in Lucius's ear. Lucius hurried to Apollodorus. "Your daughter is in the vestibule," he said quietly. "Hilarion invited her to the garden, but she wouldn't come. Apparently she's quite upset. Your wife has taken a turn for the worse."

Apollodorus, looking suddenly sober, drew a deep breath and left them without a word.

The guests began to amble out of the garden, until no one was left except Marcus and Hadrian, who stood gazing at the statue of Melancomas and rubbing his chin. Marcus interpreted the gesture to mean that Hadrian was brooding or lost in thought, then realized that the man was once again touching the acne scars that disfigured his otherwise handsome face.

While the guests said their farewells to his father, Marcus proceeded to the vestibule, where Apollodorus was having a hushed conversation with his daughter. Marcus had met Apollodora when he first began working for her father. She had been a mere child then. He had not seen her since.

As Hilarion opened the door for Apollodorus and his daughter to make their exit, Apollodora looked back at Marcus for a moment. He was startled to see what a beauty she had grown into, with her lustrous dark hair, shimmering skin, and enormous eyes.

Later, when he went to bed, Marcus fell asleep thinking about her.

Lucius Pinarius claimed that wine disturbed sleep, and that this was yet another reason to avoid it; perhaps it was the wine that caused Marcus's strange dreams that night.

His pleasant thoughts about Apollodorus's daughter vanished as he fell asleep. He was back in Dacia. A village was in flames. As if he were a bird, he followed a boy with unkempt hair and ragged clothes who ran through the narrow streets. Laughing and making obscene noises, Roman soldiers pursued him. The boy tripped over a dead body, threaded his way through jumbled ruins, leaped over raging flames. Suddenly he reached a dead end. He was trapped. He screamed, but there were plenty of other people screaming in the village; he was just one more.

Suddenly, Marcus became the boy. The soldiers converged on him. He was tiny, and they were huge, looming above him in darkness so that he could not see their faces. A giant hand reached for him. . . .

Marcus had experienced this dream before, or dreams much like it. Always, this was the point at which he would awaken, shivering and covered with sweat. But this time he seemed to fall even deeper into the dream. The leering soldiers vanished, as did the ruins of the village. All was suffused with a golden light. Hovering before him was a beautiful, naked youth. He reminded Marcus of the statue of Melancomas, but this being was so radiantly beautiful that he seemed more than human. Was he a god? The youth regarded him with an expression of such tenderness and compassion that Marcus was suddenly close to tears.

The youth reached toward him. He whispered, "Do not fear. I will save you."

Then Marcus woke.

His room was lit by the first faint glow of dawn. He reached for the coverlet he had thrown off during his nightmare and pulled it to his chin. The warmth comforted him, but it was the lingering impression of the dream that filled him with an exquisite sense of well-being. He had never experienced such a feeling before, a certainty that somewhere in the universe there existed a power that was perfect and loving, that would shield him from all evil in the world.

Who was the divine youth of his dream? There had been nothing to identify him as one of the familiar gods of Olympus. Was he Apollonius of Tyana, who often visited Marcus's father in dreams? Marcus didn't think so; surely Apollonius would have shown himself as Marcus had always heard him described, an old man with a white beard. Was he a manifestation of the Divine Singularity, of which Marcus's father spoke? Perhaps. But it seemed to Marcus that the youth in his dream was a completely new being, never before seen by anyone in this world. He had shown himself to Marcus and to Marcus alone.

As the afterglow of the dream began to fade, Marcus tried to remember the face of the youth—he even tried to draw him, reaching for the stylus and wax tablet he kept at his bedside, but he found it impossible to recapture the features. The face Marcus drew was only a rough approximation that gave no hint of his unearthly perfection.

Perhaps the youth was nothing more than a creation of Marcus's imagination. And yet, the dream had seemed more real than waking life. Marcus was convinced that this being came from a place outside himself, a world that was unimaginably vast and beautiful and full of wonder.

A.D. 118

Trajan was dead.

Four years of campaigning in the East had yielded a series of conquests, including the capture of Ctesiphon and the subjugation of much of the Parthian empire. Armenia was made a Roman province, expanding Roma's empire to the shores of the Hyrcanian Sea, as were Mesopotamia and Assyria, which included the fabled city of Babylon and the Tigris and Euphrates rivers, giving Roma direct access to the Persian Gulf and control of all imports from India and Serica, including silk. Trajan sent a letter to the Senate in which he declared that his mission was accomplished; he regretted only that he was too old to follow the example of Alexander and march all the way to India. In fact, throughout the campaigns, he often displayed the vigor of a man half his age, marching on foot and fording swift rivers alongside his soldiers, who worshipped him like a god.

Then, even as scattered rebellions broke out in the newly conquered territories, Trajan fell ill. His condition became so grave that Plotina, who was with him, persuaded him to set sail for Roma. He did not get far. Off the coast of Cilicia, he suffered a paralyzing stroke, then was afflicted with a dropsy that caused parts of his body to swell to enormous size. Further travel was impossible, and the imperial fleet made harbor at the small port city of Selinus. Trajan died there at the age of sixty-four, ending a twenty-year reign that had added unprecedented wealth and territory to the empire.

Hadrian, serving as governor of Syria, was declared emperor.

He had arrived in Roma some days ago, but as yet he had been seen by only a handful of people. This was to be the day of his public debut as emperor, with a triumphal procession to celebrate the stupendous conquests in the East. The triumph would not be for Hadrian but in posthumous honor of the Divine Trajan.

In preparation for the triumph, Marcus and Apollodorus had been very busy. The entire route of the procession had to be decorated with pennants and wreaths, as did various temples and altars all over the city. Viewing stands had to be erected near the Column, where the procession would reach its climax. Stage sets had to be designed for the plays that would be produced in the days ahead. Decorations had to be made for a great many banquets, large and small. Apollodorus had been summoned for a private audience the first day Hadrian arrived and had been in daily contact with him ever since. Marcus, working under Apollodorus, had not yet seen the new emperor.

The hour was early. The city had not yet begun to stir, but Apollodorus and Marcus and their workers had already been up for hours, laboring by torchlight to ready the triumphal route. The procession was only a few hours away.

They stood near the Column, surveying the brightly colored streamers that had been affixed to the viewing stands. In the utterly still air the streamers hung as limp as shrouds, but with the slightest breeze they would snap to life, their undulations adding excitement and color to the acclamations of the crowd.

Marcus threw back his head, opened his mouth wide, and yawned.

"Did you get any sleep at all last night?" said Apollodorus.

"Last night? It's not dawn yet. This is still yesterday."

Apollodorus laughed. "You're babbling, Pygmalion. Did you go to bed early, as I told you to?"

"Yes, but . . ." Marcus was about to say, *My wife went to bed with me, which meant I got no sleep at all,* but since his wife was Apollodorus's daughter, he restrained himself. Apollodorus nevertheless read his thought—the two had worked together for so long that each usually knew what the other was thinking—and smiled indulgently. The relationship between Apollodora and Marcus had grown gradually, with a long courtship that had given both of their fathers a chance to get used to the idea. Apollodorus was aware of Marcus's irregular origins, but marriage into such an ancient patrician family was a great honor for the daughter of a Damascene Greek; for Lucius Pinarius, the match had seemed far below his son's station, but Marcus clearly loved the girl, and when Lucius asked himself, "What would Apollonius of Tyana do?"—always his test for making a difficult decision—he enthusiastically approved the union.

The marriage was a happy one. So far, there had been no children— but not for lack of trying, as Marcus made clear with another yawn and a dreamy smile.

"I never thought I'd see this day," declared Apollodorus, gazing at the cleaners who were sweeping the empty square soon to be thronged with people.

"The day we'd celebrate a triumph over the Parthians?" said Marcus.

"No, the day Hadrian would ride through the streets of Roma as Caesar. He still seems a boy to me. I suppose I thought Trajan would live forever."

"So did Trajan, apparently," said Marcus. "Even toward the end, when he was paralyzed and puffed up like an Arabian adder, they say he refused to make a will. Some say he wanted to die without naming a successor, in imitation of Alexander the Great. How *did* Hadrian become emperor?"

"It was all Plotina's doing," said Apollodorus. "Not that Hadrian wasn't the obvious choice. But it was Plotina who assured his legitimacy. She told everyone that her husband had adopted Hadrian with his very last breath, and she rallied her loyal courtiers to support Hadrian at every turn. Some say Plotina must be in love with Hadrian, and the two were carrying on an affair behind Trajan's back."

"Is that likely?"

Apollodorus laughed. "Knowing Hadrian, what do you think? I suspect Plotina's affection for him is more of the maternal variety, don't you? Oh, I'm sure she's infatuated with him, and has been for a very long time, in the way an older woman may be smitten by a younger man. But that doesn't mean their relationship is carnal."

"I suppose Hadrian will be heading off to war as soon as this triumph is over," said Marcus.

"Why do you say that?"

"I've heard that a great many of the newly conquered cities are in revolt. Insurgencies threaten to undo all those lightning-quick conquests made by Trajan. Hadrian will have to go back and reconquer everything to keep it from being lost."

"Or maybe not," said Apollodorus. "I was talking to him yesterday—you understand this is absolutely confidential, son-in-law?" When he was serious, Apollodorus tended to address Marcus as son-in-law, rather than as Pygmalion. "Hadrian says the new provinces in the East are untenable. He says Trajan overreached. Not only are the conquered territories in revolt, but the Jews are making trouble again—they've staged bloody riots in Alexandria and Cyrene and there's open warfare on the island of Cyprus. Tens of thousands have died. According to Hadrian, suppressing the Jews is far more important than holding on to Ctesiphon. So, instead of pouring soldiers and treasure into a perpetual war to hold the new Eastern provinces, he wants to cede the more troublesome areas to potentates beholden to Roma, creating a string of client states along a more defensible Eastern frontier."

"It sounds like he must have given the situation a great deal of thought, even before he became emperor."

"I suspect he did. You know Hadrian, never at a loss for an opinion, whatever the subject."

Marcus frowned. "So here we are, about to celebrate a triumph for the very conquests Hadrian is about to give up."

Apollodorus laughed. "Ironic, isn't it? But you and I have done our job.

We've decorated the city just as splendidly as if Hadrian intended to hold those provinces for a thousand years."

The first rays of the sun struck the top of the Column. The statue of Trajan seemed to burst into golden flames.

"Time to go home and change into our best togas," said Apollodorus.

Marcus nodded and yawned. He closed his eyes.

"Don't you dare fall asleep when you get home, Pygmalion, or you'll miss the triumph. And don't do the other thing, either—unless you and Apollodora intend to make a baby this time!" Apollodorus laughed heartily and slapped Marcus on the back, startling him into wakefulness even as he was about to fall asleep on his feet. "Will your father be coming?"

Marcus felt a twinge of anxiety at the mention of his father and was abruptly wide awake. "No, he won't be able to come. He hasn't been well lately."

In fact, Lucius Pinarius, who was now seventy, had been bedridden for a month, troubled by light-headedness and a weakness in his legs. Hilarion, who had also grown quite frail in recent years, was always at his old master's side, often reading aloud to him the letters Lucius had received from Apollonius of Tyana, who continued to visit Lucius regularly in his dreams. By his bedside, as a reminder that death was nothing to fear, Lucius kept the iron manacle that had been cast off by Apollonius. Just as Apollonius had been able to cast off his shackles, so Lucius anticipated the moment when his soul would cast off its earthly frame to rise up and merge with the Divine Singularity.

A few hours later, under a cloudless sky and a bright sun, Marcus awaited the arrival of the triumphal procession. Apollodorus, greeted by an acquaintance, had drawn a little distance away, taking Apollodora with him, so that Marcus stood unaccompanied in the crowd.

Long before the parade arrived at the Column, he heard the thunderous reactions of the multitude along the route that wound through the city. The sound of cheering grew nearer, until at last the vanguard of trumpeters came into sight.

They were followed by the magistrates and senators in their red-bordered togas, some chatting casually, as if unimpressed by all the pomp, while others carried themselves with all the dignity of their offices. Then came the white bulls on their way to be sacrificed at the Temple of Jupiter atop the Capitoline, followed by countless carts and wagons loaded high with the spoils of war, paintings and models of captured cities including Ctesiphon, Babylon, and Susa, and a great many captives in rags and chains, including some of the petty monarchs who had been deposed by Trajan.

At last, preceded by lictors brandishing fasces wreathed with laurel, the triumphal chariot arrived. Trajan had been famed for making his first entrance as emperor into the city on foot; on this day his effigy rode alongside Hadrian in the chariot. The effigy was made of wax, modeled and colored to look astonishingly lifelike. There was no need to make it larger than life, for Trajan in the flesh had towered above other men.

"Inevitably, the question arises: which of those two in the chariot is stiffer?" said a voice in Marcus's ear. He turned to see Favonius.

With the scurra was Suetonius. The director of the imperial archives raised an eyebrow. "I think our new emperor looks unusually relaxed and animated," he quipped. "Look there, how Hadrian smiles and salutes the crowd—no, wait, I'm looking at the effigy of Trajan!"

"I don't think Hadrian likes to be stared at," said Marcus, who had to admit that the new emperor looked distinctly uncomfortable standing next to the smiling waxen image of his predecessor.

"They say Vespasian found his triumph so tedious that he was bored to tears," said Suetonius. "There's a letter of his in the archives where he writes, 'What an old fool I was to demand such a grueling honor!'"

"Who can tell what our new emperor is thinking, with that beard concealing his face?" said Favonius. "The beard has everyone talking. Suetonius, have we ever before had an emperor with a beard?"

Suetonius considered. "One sees images of Nero wearing a partial beard, with his cheeks and chin clean-shaven. But a full beard? No. Hadrian is the first."

"Do you suppose he wants to remind us that he fancies himself a philosopher?" said Favonius. "Or is he affecting the unkempt look of the common soldiers who never shave while on campaign, as can be seen by all those images of bearded Romans killing Dacians on the Column over there?"

"His facial hair looks impeccably groomed to me," said Marcus. "Not every man can grow such a fine beard. I think the emperor looks quite handsome this way." It seemed to him that Hadrian's motivation was obvious: a beard was a way to cover the acne scars about which he was so self-conscious. As Trajan's protégé, Hadrian felt obliged to maintain the clean-shaven look favored by countless generations of the Roman elite. But now he was emperor and would do as he pleased—even grow a beard.

"This time next year," said Favonius, "I predict a majority of senators and practically every courtier in the House of the People will have a beard. Even the old eunuchs left over from the days of Titus will be sporting beards, if they have to paste them on!"

"Indeed, the only men without beards will be the young ones who want to attract Caesar's attention," said Suetonius.

The chariot drew alongside the base of the Column and came to a halt. Hadrian stepped from the car, bearing a funerary urn.

"So he's actually going to do it!" said Favonius. "Hadrian is going to deposit the old man's ashes in the base of his Column."

"That's the plan," said Marcus, who had been responsible for preparing the small vault that would receive the urn.

"It required an act of the Senate to make such a thing legal," noted Suetonius. "Until now, the remains of all the emperors have been interred in sarcophagi outside the old city walls. But Hadrian was determined that Trajan's Column should also serve as Trajan's tomb."

Favonius gazed up at the Column. "In his final resting place, Trajan shall remain upright and erect for all time. I envy the old fellow!"

Joined by Plotina, Hadrian deposited the urn in the chamber. Then Hadrian delivered a eulogy reciting Trajan's accomplishments, not only as a builder and a military man but as a friend of the people and the Senate of Roma. Trajan had kept his vow to kill no senators during his reign—a vow that Hadrian repeated—and one of his proudest achievements was his expansion of Nerva's welfare system for orphans and the children of the poor, which Hadrian promised to continue.

"But of course," said Hadrian, "on this day, we celebrate his triumphs in the field, and in particular the conquests for which the Senate saw fit to vote him the title Parthicus. We celebrate his victories over many foes, and his capture of many cities: Nisibis and Batnae, Adenystrae and Babylon, Artaxata and Edessa. . . ."

Hadrian continued in this singsong vein. His rhetorical style was surprisingly dull. Perhaps he was tired, or nervous, for he frequently reached up to tug at his beard, and every so often Marcus heard a hint of his old Spanish accent.

Favonius sighed. "He's merely reciting a catalog and leaving out the juicy details; that's like serving bones with no meat! Do you know the story of Trajan's encounter with King Abgarus of Osroene?"

Marcus shrugged. He was about to tell the scurra to hush, when Suetonius leaned in. "I've heard one version, but I should love to hear yours, Favonius."

The scurra's eyes lit up. "Well, I'm not sure where Osroene is, but it sounds terribly exotic—"

"It was one of those little kingdoms in the ancient land of Mesopotamia," said Suetonius. "The capital was Edessa, which is not far from the upper reaches of the Euphrates."

"Geography was never my strong point," admitted Favonius. "Anyway, King Abgarus was frightened to death of both the Romans and the Parthians, like a chicken caught between a fox and a wolf, and whenever one or the other tried to approach him for talks, he scuttled off in a panic. So, for the longest time, while Trajan was in the vicinity and trying to meet with him, Abgarus ignored every summons and stayed out of sight, hoping the Romans would simply go away. But when someone told him about Trajan's love of boys, Abgarus heaved a sigh of relief—for the most beautiful boy in all the East, by general consensus, happened to be his own son, Prince Arbandes. Trajan had finally given up on meeting the king and was moving on, leaving behind one of his generals with instructions to sack Edessa, when Abgarus and his royal entourage sped after Trajan and caught up with him at the border. That night, beside the road, Abgarus put up a huge tent and threw a sumptuous banquet for Trajan—and whom did he seat on the pillow next to Caesar but young Prince Arbandes. Trajan was utterly smitten; rumor has it he wrote a coded letter to Hadrian in which he proclaimed, 'I have met the most beautiful boy ever born!' To cap the evening, Abgarus had his son perform some barbaric dance for Trajan's amusement. What happened after the banquet we can only imagine, but apparently Arbandes's dancing-boy diplomacy was effective, because Trajan spared the city of Edessa and let Abgarus keep his throne as a Roman puppet."

Suetonius frowned. "But wasn't that Abgarus we saw earlier in chains, trudging along with the other monarchs deposed by Trajan?"

"Ah, yes, the king's fortunes later took a turn for the worse. After Trajan conquered Babylonia and was sailing down the Euphrates to have a look at the Persian Gulf, word arrived that a revolt had broken out in Osroene. King Abgarus blamed Parthian instigators and Jewish insurgents, but when Trajan's general Lusius Quietus and his bareheaded Berber cavalry arrived to put down the revolt, Edessa was sacked and Abgarus was deposed. Thus we saw Abgarus paraded before us in chains today."

"What happened to Prince Arbandes?" said Marcus.

"That's a good question," said Favonius. "He wasn't among the prisoners—a pretty puppy would have stood out among those mangy old dogs! Given Trajan's laudable practice of educating his boys after he was done with them, I'm betting Arbandes was given a tutor and sent off to some academy in Greece. Or perhaps he'll perform his savage dance for Hadrian at tonight's banquet!"

The scurra was being facetious. The fate of Arbandes was of no interest to him; the boy's history merely provided material for a salacious tale. Marcus, remembering all the suffering he had seen in Dacia, felt a stirring of pity for the dancing prince who had done everything he could to save his father's kingdom.

Hadrian had arrived at the end of the eulogy and was reciting all the late emperor's titles, including Dacicus, conqueror of Dacia, Germanicus, conqueror of Germania, and of course Parthicus. "But of all the titles bestowed on him by the grateful people and Senate of Roma, the one of which he was most proud was the one which had never been bestowed before: Optimus, best of all emperors."

Sensing that the speech was at an end, the crowd reacted with loud cheering. It was impossible to tell whether the cries of "Hail, Caesar!" were for Trajan or for Hadrian. It was Suetonius who stepped forward and acclaimed the new emperor by name: "Hail, Hadrian! Long may he reign!"

This cry was taken up by others. Hadrian, who looked as uncomfortable as ever receiving their accolades, but who had witnessed Suetonius's initiative, cast a grateful nod in the archivist's direction.

During a lull in the cheering, Favonius, who by the glint in his eye thought he had come up with something clever, stepped forward and shouted, "Hail, Hadrian! May he be luckier than Augustus! May he be better than Trajan!"

Suetonius pursed his lips at such a bold proclamation. "Luckier than the Luckiest? Better than the Best? Hear, hear!" He loudly repeated the phrase, and so did many others.

"May he be luckier than Augustus!" people shouted. "May he be better than Trajan!"

Marcus gazed at the new emperor, who appeared to be genuinely touched by the outpouring of goodwill. But even amid the jubilation, Marcus saw Hadrian touch his face. To others, the emperor might appear to be stroking his beard, as thoughtful philosophers do, but Marcus knew the man was thinking of the scars hidden beneath.

When Marcus and Apollodora arrived home that evening, Hilarion met them at the door with tears in his eyes. Marcus rushed to his father's room.

Lucius Pinarius had grown so thin in recent months that his body seemed hardly to press on the bed at all. His arms were folded across his chest. His eyes were closed. There was a smile on his face.

"It happened while he was asleep," said Hilarion. "I came to look in on him. I knew, the moment I stepped into the room. I held a mirror before his nostrils and saw there was no breath."

Marcus touched the fascinum at his breast. He gazed around the room, wondering if his father's spirit lingered or if it had already flitted off to join Apollonius and merge with the Divine Singularity. He looked at his father's face and began to weep.

He would never hear his father's voice again. He would never know the name of his mother.

A.D. 120

On a brisk autumn day, Marcus and Apollodorus found themselves engaged in one of the most challenging enterprises they had ever faced. They were moving the Colossus.

Originally, the towering statue of Nero stood in the courtyard of the Golden House. It was left in place when the courtyard was demolished by Vespasian, who remodeled the features so that the sun god Sol no longer resembled Nero. For decades the statue stood with its back to the Flavian Amphitheater, dominating the southern end of the ancient Forum and gazing over the rooftops of temples and offices of state toward the Capitoline Hill.

Hadrian had decided to build a vast new temple on the site. To make room for it, the Colossus would have to be moved. The project was especially important to the emperor because he was designing the new temple himself. Apollodorus had not even been allowed to see the plans.

"Your task is merely to relocate the Colossus," Hadrian told Apollodorus one sunny day as they surveyed the site. "I want the statue to be placed much closer to the amphitheater. Here, I'll show you the spot."

When Apollodorus saw the location, he expressed reservations. "The area around the amphitheater is already congested on game days. Putting the Colossus here will make the problem worse. And there's a question of proportion: having the statue so close to the amphitheater throws both structures out of scale. The viewer who sees them from a distance will find the contrast quite displeasing. Rather than clutter up this area—"

"On the contrary," Hadrian had snapped, "this open area is exactly the right spot to accommodate the statue. In fact, I see room for *two* such statues."

"Two, Caesar?"

"I intend to construct a new statue as a companion to the Colossus, equally as tall."

"But where will you put such a thing?"

"Right over there, in a spot equidistant between the amphitheater, the Colossus of Sol, and my new Temple of Venus and Roma. I think it must be a statue of Luna, so the two statues together will pay homage to the sun and moon. Does that not please your sense of balance?"

Apollodorus frowned. "In a religious sense, perhaps. But aesthetically—"

"I want you to design this new statue, Apollodorus. The style should match that of the Sol, of course, but I'll be interested to see what innovations you come up with. I realize that such a project is as much an engineering challenge as an artistic one. We mustn't have the goddess losing an arm or tumbling into rubble when there's an earthquake, as happened to the Colossus of Rhodes. The statue Nero built has stood the test of time, so as you move it, I suggest you take the opportunity to study the way it was cast and assembled, and learn whatever secrets you can about its construction."

The prospect of such a commission—the creation of a statue equal in size to the Colossus—silenced all Apollodorus's objections. Until that point, he had considered his work on Trajan's Column the crowning achievement of his career, but the Luna Colossus would eclipse all his other accomplishments. This was Apollodorus's opportunity to create a work of art that would endure for eternity.

In the meantime, the challenge was to move the Colossus of Sol.

The distance to be traversed was not great, only a few hundred feet, and the ground was flat and paved the entire way. The area had been cleared of spectators. First, the Colossus was hoisted by three cranes, just high enough for a conveyance on rollers to be placed underneath. The upright statue was gently lowered onto the conveyance. The ropes were left attached and were pulled taut by teams of men on all sides, to keep the statue steady as it was moved.

A team of twenty-four elephants was harnessed to the conveyance. At Apollodorus's signal, the elephant trainer drove the team forward. The rollers creaked under the strain. The taut ropes sang as if plucked. The elephants brandished their tusks and trumpeted.

Marcus watched the procedure with a tremor of anxiety. The near-disaster that had occurred when the statue of Trajan was set atop his Column was still vivid in his memory. This project was, if anything, even more ambitious, and the possibility of disaster, given the proximity of the amphitheater, was even greater. Despite careful planning and scrupulous attention to detail, unknown factors were in play, chief among them the uneven distribution of weight within the Colossus and the volatile temperament of elephants.

"*Merely* to relocate the Colossus!" said a voice behind him. It was Apollodorus, who stood with his arms crossed, gazing up intently at the statue as it lumbered forward.

"What's that?" said Marcus.

"The emperor's instructions to me: 'your task is *merely* to relocate the Colossus.' Ha! Compared to this, designing a new temple would be child's play. He's probably up there right now, sketching gourds to plop down on top of his temple."

Marcus glanced at the Palatine Hill. On a balcony high up in the House of the People, Hadrian and some of his courtiers stood watching their progress.

"I overheard a joke told by one of the workmen today," said Apollodorus, never taking his eyes off the statue.

"How did it go?" said Marcus.

"The fellow said, 'What will they call it if the Colossus goes tumbling into the Flavian Amphitheater?'"

Marcus shuddered at the thought. "What will they call it?"

"Nero's revenge!"

Marcus gave a dry laugh. He nervously fingered the fascinum and whispered a prayer—not to the ancient god the talisman represented, but to the radiant youth who had first appeared to him on the night of the dinner party in his honor, and since then had frequently visited him in dreams. Always the youth brought Marcus a sense of well-being and tranquility, yet never did he reveal his name. He only said what he always said: "Do not fear. I will save you."

The Colossus moved forward steadily. Marcus tried to imagine the astounding sight presented to Hadrian and to everyone else watching from a distance, to whom it must appear that a giant was striding slowly through the city. At last the statue reached the spot from which it was to be hoisted into its new location. Again it was lifted skyward, and then slowly, carefully, with utmost precision it was lowered onto its new base.

A cheer went up from the workers. The operation had been carried out without a hitch. Marcus sighed with relief. He turned to his father-in-law, who was grinning blithely, as if there had never been any possibility of error.

"No revenge for Nero today!" said Marcus.

⁂

Later that night, Marcus and his father-in-law, with Apollodora, quietly celebrated the day's good fortune with a dinner at Marcus's house. It was still a bit difficult for Marcus to think of the house as his, rather than as the house of his father. Marcus had been the sole heir to his father's estate and was one of the few Pinarii left in Roma. The ancient patrician family had dwindled to a handful of scattered cousins, a fact that lent a special urgency to Marcus's desire for a son to carry his name.

Apollodorus seemed to read his thoughts. "Any news from the two of you?" he said, looking at Marcus and then at his daughter.

Apollodora averted her eyes and blushed as she always did when questioned on the matter.

Apollodorus shrugged. "The world needs fresh blood as the older generation passes away. Do you know who just died? Your father's old friend Dio of Prusa."

"When did you hear this?" said Marcus.

"Earlier today, after we moved the Colossus. Suetonius happened to pass by and he gave me the news."

"Truly, that does mark the passing of a generation," said Marcus quietly. His father and almost all his father's closest friends were gone. Even Hilarion was gone. He had died of a sudden illness the preceding winter, surviving his old master by little more than a year.

"One generation passes and another takes its place," said Apollodorus. "It's a new age, with Hadrian at the helm. All sorts of changes are afoot. Imagine an emperor who fancies himself an architect!" He shook his head and emptied his wine cup.

"To be sure, there are those who speak ill of the emperor," said Marcus.

"Who? Only a handful of malcontents," said Apollodorus. Since Hadrian had instructed him to proceed with preliminary sketches of the Luna Colossus, Apollodorus would not hear a word against him.

"I'm thinking of the senators who were put to death at the outset of his reign, in contravention of his vow," said Marcus. Among the alleged conspirators had been Lusius Quietus, the despoiler of Edessa. "Perhaps they were indeed plotting to kill the emperor and deserved their sentences, but still—"

"The emperor never broke his vow," said Apollodorus, "at least, not technically. What he actually said was that he would punish no senators without the express consent of the Senate, and in fact a majority of the Senate voted in favor of the executions."

"Still, the appearance—"

"Really, Pygmalion, any hard feelings that resulted from that unfortunate turn of events were more than made up for by the goodwill Caesar garnered when he lit that bonfire of promissory notes in the courtyard of Trajan's Forum. Wholesale debt relief to those who owed money to the state—what an idea!"

"Some said the treasury would go bankrupt and the economy would come to a standstill," noted Marcus.

"Instead, that bonfire had the opposite effect. Confidence was restored and everyone began to spend again. The new tax revenues have more than made up for the debts that were forgiven. The emperor showed his own willingness to contribute to the public coffers when he melted down the famous Shield of Minerva, that glorified silver serving dish created by Vitellius. All the subsequent emperors had been afraid to touch the thing, even Trajan—they took it seriously as a sacred offering to the goddess. But when Hadrian was reviewing the imperial holdings, he took one look at the shield, declared it inconceivable that any goddess would care to have such a hideous thing consecrated to her, and ordered the shield to be melted down. They say he was able to mint enough coinage to pay an entire legion! Oh, he's a clever fellow, our Hadrian."

For the rest of the evening Apollodorus continued to dominate the conversation, fulsomely praising the emperor—Marcus almost preferred the old days when his father-in-law had aimed an occasional barb at Hadrian—and then praising his own accomplishments, his enthusiasm fueled by his continuous consumption of wine. Marcus was indulgent. If any man deserved to boast a bit and drink to his heart's content, it was Apollodorus, who had achieved something truly remarkable that day with the successful relocation of the Colossus.

At length, though Marcus and Apollodora offered him a bed for the night, Apollodorus departed for his house. He said he wanted to work on the sketches for the Luna statue in his private study. Marcus suspected he would fall into a drunken sleep before he picked up a stylus.

The house seemed very quiet after Apollodorus had left. Marcus took a stroll under starlight in the garden and paused to gaze at the statue of Melancomas. He was a lucky man to own such a thing. The emperor himself occasionally dropped by, just to sit alone in the garden and admire it. The statue almost, but not quite, captured the image of the divine being who visited Marcus in his dreams.

Occasionally Marcus considered sculpting his dream-god. So far, the demands of his work had prevented him from doing so—or so he told himself. In truth, Marcus was afraid to make the attempt, fearful that he would fall short of capturing the perfection of the divine youth. Perhaps one day he would be ready.

Apollodora joined him in the garden. She put her hand in his. "Husband, I have something to tell you."

He looked in her eyes and let out a gasp. "But why didn't you tell me earlier?"

"I wanted you to know before anyone else, including my father. I decided to wait until he left. We'll tell him tomorrow."

"A child? Our child! You're sure?"

"I'm sure."

He gazed at Apollodora's face under the starlight. He hoped the child would have her lustrous black hair and dark eyes. He touched the fascinum and whispered a prayer of thanksgiving to the youth who came to him in dreams.

A.D. 121

Marcus strolled through the ancient Forum, past the Temple of Castor and the House of the Vestals, happily whistling a marching tune he had learned in the Dacian campaigns.

It was a beautiful morning in late Aprilis, made all the more beautiful by the fact that his son had been born, healthy and whole, the preceding day. The infant appeared to take more after his father than his mother, having golden hair and bright blue eyes that the midwife predicted would change to green over time. Marcus named the boy Lucius. His only regret was that his father had not lived to see the grandson named for him.

Life was good. Marcus was happily occupied with his work, which at the moment meant collaborating with Apollodorus on designs for the Luna statue. He had never seen Apollodorus so excited by a project. Marcus was headed for the site now, to check some measurements. As he approached the Flavian Amphitheater and saw the Colossus looming beside it, he could see the Luna statue in his mind's eye, and the vision gave him a thrill of delight.

His route took him past the site where the Colossus had previously stood, where work was now in progress on the foundations of the Temple of Venus and Roma. What the finished temple would look like remained a secret. So far, Hadrian had insisted on overseeing all aspects of the project, excluding Apollodorus completely and forbidding the builders to show the plans to anyone not directly involved in the project. The emperor was determined to prove that he could conceive and create a masterpiece entirely on his own, with no help from anyone. Apollodorus was curious, of course, but had resisted any urge to pry into the matter; his energies were focused entirely on the Luna commission. Judging by the scale of the foundations, the temple was going to be enormous. Such a huge construction, commanding the prime location once occupied by the vestibule of the Golden House, would make the temple a landmark, whatever its appearance.

Marcus arrived at the site for the Luna statue, pulled out a ball of twine, a compass, a wax tablet, and a stylus, and took the measurements he needed. For a while he simply stood on the spot, basking in the knowledge that one day Apollodorus's crowning achievement would rise up for all the world to wonder at, and that he would be able to show it to little Lucius and say, "I had a hand in building that."

He walked past the Flavian Amphitheater and on to the great bath complex that had been built by Apollodorus for Trajan. Like all Trajan's projects, the baths had been constructed on a vast scale and decorated with exquisite taste. Paintings and sculptures adorned the public areas, and the pools were surrounded by colorful mosaics. Along with the bathing facilities and the courtyards for gymnastic exercises, there were a great many rooms where one could have one's hair cut or one's nails groomed, enjoy a cup of wine or a light meal, read a scroll from the library, or simply sit and talk with friends. There were also a great many dimly lit nooks and crannies where patrons could enjoy moments of intimacy, sometimes with prostitutes and sometimes with each other. Virtually every aspect of life was carried on at the baths. The scurra Favonius had once told Marcus that an ideal existence would be one in which a man was born, lived, procreated, and died at the baths, never leaving.

Marcus stripped and checked his clothing and shoes in the changing room. The floor, heated by piped hot water, was delightfully warm. The walls were heated as well. Carrying a drying cloth over his shoulder, he headed for the nearest hot plunge. The room was dim and steamy. Before his eyes could adjust, a familiar voice called his name. His father-in-law had arrived ahead of him.

"How is my new grandson this morning?" asked Apollodorus as Marcus stepped into the pool beside him. The water was so hot that he had to lower himself into it very gradually.

"As loud as he was yesterday," said Marcus, smiling broadly. "The midwife says he has a very powerful set of lungs."

"Good, good!" said Apollodorus.

"Congratulations on the birth of your son, Marcus Pinarius."

Marcus looked around, surprised to hear the voice of the emperor, whom he had not seen amid the rising vapors. Hadrian was nearby, immersed to his chest and leaning back against the side of the pool. A handsome young slave sat cross-legged behind him, using a set of tongs to curl the emperor's steam-dampened hair. Also in the room were a number of other retainers, whom Marcus took to be secretaries and bodyguards.

"Thank you, Caesar."

"Please accept my congratulations as well, Marcus Pinarius," said the man next to Hadrian, who turned out to be Suetonius, formerly of the imperial archives but now elevated to the post of private secretary to the emperor.

"Thank you, Suetonius."

"And I congratulate you, as well." The speaker was obscured behind a veil of mist—only a blur of frizzled red hair was visible—but Marcus recognized the voice. Thanks to his friendship with Suetonius, and his own dogged efforts to ingratiate himself, Favonius had managed to attract the favor of the emperor. "I offer congratulations not merely on the birth of your son, but also on that splendid beard you've grown. Your handsome face is like a painting framed with gold."

"Beards *are* the fashion," said Marcus, self-consciously touching the wiry blond hair that covered his jaw; he was still not used to it. "Father-in-law, when you sent me that message this morning asking me to meet you here, you didn't mention that Caesar would be present."

"What difference would that have made?" said Favonius. "Would you have worn something else?" He laughed at his own joke.

"Actually, our meeting here was purely by chance," said Hadrian. "But since Apollodorus happens to be here, and I happen to be here, I think perhaps the gods have brought us together. I take this as a sign that the time has finally arrived for me to show you something, Apollodorus."

"Whatever Caesar has to show me, I will be honored to view," said Apollodorus. Marcus looked at the scurra, expecting him to exploit the opportunity for a lewd comment, but Favonius held his tongue. Hadrian had a notoriously slippery sense of humor, especially when it came to himself or anything to do with his appearance. In that regard he was quite unlike Trajan, who had seemed incapable of being offended.

This was not the first time Marcus had encountered Hadrian at the baths. It was Hadrian's practice to see and be seen at the public baths, moving among the people as if he were simply another citizen enjoying the amenities of city life. Apollodorus thought Hadrian did this to demonstrate the common touch, something that came less easily to the "Little Greek" than it had to Trajan. Behind Hadrian's back, Favonius had once suggested to Marcus that the emperor frequented the public baths because he enjoyed looking at naked youths.

Hadrian, his forehead beaded with sweat, suggested that the party move to the cool plunge. As they all stepped from the pool and made their way to the next room, Marcus noticed that Favonius used his drying cloth to conceal as much of his plump, pink body as he could, while Hadrian remained naked and allowed the boy who had been curling his hair to carry his drying cloth. The man certainly had no need to be embarrassed about his physique. At the age of forty-five, Hadrian's broad shoulders, burly chest, and full beard, touched here and there with silver, suggested to Marcus the image of Jupiter as portrayed by the great sculptors of the past.

As they entered the room that had the cool plunge, Hadrian noticed a gray-bearded man leaning against the protruding corner of a wall and rubbing his back against it.

"What on earth are you doing, citizen?" said Hadrian.

The man hardly looked at him; clearly, he did not recognize the emperor. "What does it look like I'm doing? I'm massaging my back against this wall. I've got a terrible knot in my shoulder blade that won't go away. Old war wound. This is the only thing that seems to help."

"By Hercules, man, you look like a superannuated Ganymede performing an erotic dance! Get a slave to do that for you."

"A slave? Ha! The only slave I own is an old woman who does my cooking, and her hands are too crippled to give anyone a decent massage."

Hadrian pursed his lips. "A war wound, you say. You're a veteran, then?"

"I certainly am. First Legion Minerva, Dacian campaign. Got this wound fifteen years ago."

"In the back?"

"Not because I was running! Cursed Dacians ambushed us in the woods and attacked us from the rear. I took an arrow in the back and kept fighting until the last Dacian was dead. Sometimes it feels like that arrow is still in there." He rubbed his back furiously against the corner.

"First Legion Minerva, you say. Yet you don't recognize your old commander?"

The man stopped his movements. He took a closer look at Hadrian. His jaw dropped. "Caesar! Is that you? I had no idea! Sure, I recognize you now. You didn't have the beard back then."

"Let me see your wound."

The man turned around. There was a dark scar on the inside of one shoulder blade. Hadrian reached out and pressed his thumbs against the spot. "Here?" he said.

"Oh! That's the very spot!" The man let out a groan.

Hadrian stepped back and called to one of his secretaries. "Some of the slaves who work here at the baths must be skilled at massage. Purchase a couple for this fellow."

The veteran turned around and gaped. "Well, I never! You are truly a soldier's friend, Caesar, to do such a thing for an old veteran of the Minerva. May all the gods bless you! But how am I to pay for these slaves' upkeep? Slaves have to be fed, and I can barely afford to feed myself."

Hadrian turned to the secretary. "Along with the slaves, give this fellow a monthly stipend for their upkeep."

"How much, Caesar?"

"How should I know? Ask Suetonius for a figure. He knows that sort of thing."

Hadrian walked on. The veteran gazed after him in awe. "Bless you, Caesar!" he cried.

After a brief soak in the cool plunge, Hadrian sent slaves to fetch everyone's clothing. He put on a purple toga trimmed with gold, and those in his retinue wore togas, rather than the simple tunics that Marcus and Apollodorus found suitable for a visit to the baths. It was curious, Marcus thought, that the emperor didn't mind being seen naked by half of Roma, but, when dressed, he wished for himself and those in his train to be seen only in formal attire.

After everyone was dressed, Hadrian led them to a suite of private rooms reserved for the emperor's exclusive use. Marcus had seen these rooms when they were being built but had never been admitted into them since they were finished. The columns and walls were of the rarest marbles. The floors were decorated with extraordinarily detailed mosaics. The furniture was all of Greek design. The pillows and draperies were of silk. The paintings and statuary had been selected by Hadrian himself. There was no denying that the emperor had exquisite taste.

Hadrian called for delicacies and wine to be served. The conversation turned to the trip that Hadrian would soon be taking to visit the troops and talk with provincial magistrates along the Rhine and in Gaul and Britannia. Apollodorus ate little, Marcus noted, and drank his wine straight, without water. When Hadrian invited his guests to follow him into an adjoining room, Apollodorus called for a slave to refill his cup and carried it with him.

The room was dominated by a large table upon which architectural plans had been unrolled, the corners held down by marble weights in the shape of eagles' heads. There was also an architectural model of a temple, made not of painted wood but with actual marble columns and steps, a gilded tile roof, and bronze doors. Every aspect of the model, even to the painted friezes in the pediments and the finely carved capitals of the columns, was rendered with uncanny detail.

Hadrian stepped back and studied his guests, gratified to see the looks of astonishment on their faces. "As you will have realized, these are the plans for the Temple of Venus and Roma. The architect Decrianus made this model for me—amazing, is it not?—but the plans were entirely my own. Because progress has been so swift, and because there's no telling how long I may be away, I've decided to show these plans to you at last."

Apollodorus slowly circled the table, studying the plans and the model. He raised an eyebrow. "But where is the front of the temple, and where is the back? I think Decrianus must have misread your plans. Or perhaps Caesar can point out to me what I'm missing."

Hadrian smiled. "You see, Apollodorus, but you do not perceive. Decrianus was also taken aback when he saw what I had done, but soon enough he came to appreciate the novelty of it. Let me explain. This temple is situated at the very center of the city—which means it is at the center of the empire, and thus at the center of the world. I ask you, can a center have a front and a back? No. From the center of something, one faces outward, no matter what the direction."

"Perhaps this should have been a round temple, then," said Apollodorus.

Hadrian frowned. "That was my first conception, but the engineers were unable to guarantee that a dome of the span I envisioned could remain aloft. So this was my solution: a double temple, with a dividing wall running through the middle, which can be entered from either side. The side facing the Flavian Amphitheater is dedicated to Venus Felix, Bringer of Good Fortune. The side facing the ancient Forum is dedicated to Roma the Eternal. There will be no front or back, but rather two entrances of equal importance. Within their respective shrines, the statues of Venus and of Roma will sit back-to-back, with a wall between them, one gazing east, the other gazing west. Here, I'll show you. This is quite ingenious."

Hadrian took hold of the gilded roof of the model, which lifted completely off, exposing the interior, which was as finely finished and detailed as the exterior, with tiny porphyry columns, marble apses, and beautifully rendered statues of the goddesses.

Apollodorus gazed at the model without speaking.

Hadrian cleared his throat. "Of course, you will have grasped the rather clever wordplay at work here. Venus represents love—amor—and 'amor' spelled backwards is Roma. Thus, placing the two divinities of Venus and Roma back-to-back in a single temple creates a further symmetry with the back-to-back symmetry of their names. Within Roma's chamber there will be an altar where officials of the state will make sacrifices for the good fortune of the city. Within Venus's sanctuary, there will be an altar where newlywed couples can make sacrifices to the goddess. I've designed the altars myself, of course. . . ." His voice trailed off. He was waiting for Apollodorus to say something.

At last Apollodorus waved at the model and said, "I don't suppose the whole temple lifts up, to show what's underneath?"

"No," said Hadrian. "What would be the point of that?"

"To allow us to see the basement."

"There's a basement, but it's of no particular interest—"

"I presume there's also a tunnel, leading from that basement to the subterranean chambers beneath the Flavian Amphitheater?"

Hadrian shook his head. "I have no plans for such a tunnel—"

"That's too bad. The need for one is so obvious, I should think even Decrianus would have seen it. Probably he did, but was afraid to say anything."

"What are you talking about, Apollodorus?"

"The basement of this temple is going to be huge. That much space, in the heart of the city, shouldn't go to waste. It would have been the ideal place to store the various mechanisms for the amphitheater when they're not in use—the lifts and pumps and cranes and so forth. With an underground tunnel, those machines could have been moved from the basement of the temple to the amphitheater and back, out of sight. What a shame. What a wasted opportunity! If only I had been consulted—"

"Only *you* would look at a temple and see a closet!" said Hadrian. "This building isn't about creating storage space. It's about beauty, and worship, and—"

"Ah, yes, the temple itself." Apollodorus sighed. "I suppose we can be thankful that the engineers couldn't solve your dome problem, or else we'd have gotten a gigantic gourd plopped down in the very center of the empire. Instead, we have . . . this. Well, it has a normal ceiling and a normal roof; I can approve of that. Yes, the double-temple idea is clever—rather too clever, I think. The temple as palindrome! Personally, I think there's something unnatural about a building which has two fronts and no back—I can't say I find it pleasing. The whole conception is flawed, from the ground up—literally. The structure should have been built on higher ground to make it stand out more conspicuously at the head of the Sacred Way. If Trajan could excavate a hill to make space for his Forum, surely his successor could have built a hill on which to place his temple. That would have given you an even larger basement, and more storage space, by the way. Of course, you might yet be able to make the ceiling higher; it may not be too late to fix that problem, at least."

"Higher ceilings?" said Hadrian. His face was ashen.

"Obviously. Any beginning student of architecture could see that these statues are too large for the interiors."

"Too large?"

"What if the goddesses should wish to get up and leave? They'll hit their heads on the ceiling."

"But why would the goddesses—"

Apollodorus kept a straight face for a moment, then burst out laughing. No one joined him.

Despite the warmth that radiated from the heated floors and walls, it seemed to Marcus that the room was suddenly chilly. Hadrian's face was as red as if he had just stepped from the hottest pool in the building. Apollodorus seemed oblivious of the scene he had just caused. He gestured to one of the slaves and asked for more wine.

Without a word, Hadrian left the room. Suetonius and Favonius and the rest followed after him, but Apollodorus stayed where he was. He sipped his wine and gazed at the model, shaking his head.

"Father-in-law, what have you done?" said Marcus.

Apollodorus shrugged. "He asked me what I thought, and I told him. Better now than later. He may yet be able to salvage something from this folly."

"Father-in-law, do you imagine you're so important—do you think the emperor is so unfeeling—"

Apollodorus waved his hand dismissively. "If you have nothing intelligent to say, Pygmalion, go home and change my grandson's diapers."

Marcus hurried after the others. He hoped to find the emperor laughing and joking with his friends in the gallery, making light of Apollodorus's comments. But as Marcus caught up with the retinue, he saw that Hadrian's attention had been claimed by a most unseemly sight: two naked, middle-aged men, one on each side of the gallery, were furiously rubbing their backs against protruding corners, just as the impoverished veteran had done earlier.

Apparently, word of the emperor's kindness to the veteran had spread, and these two were hoping to elicit a similarly generous response. Hadrian angrily seized one of the men by the shoulders and pushed him toward the other, then called to his bodyguards.

"If these fellows need a backrub so badly, let them rub each other. Tie them together, back-to-back. Let them stay that way for the rest of the day, as an example to anyone who presumes to make a fool of Caesar."

Hadrian walked away at a fast clip. Marcus followed him for a while, then gradually slowed his pace and came to a stop, watching as the emperor and his retinue receded in the distance, listening to the echo of their footsteps down the long gallery.

A.D. 122

"Don't stack those stones here," said Marcus. "Can't you see there's more digging to be done? Stack them over there!"

The workmen charged with enlarging the basement of the Temple of Venus and Roma were probably the stupidest Marcus had ever dealt with, and he had dealt with some very stupid workers. These fellows did not have even the excuse of being slaves; they were all skilled stoneworkers. Hadrian had insisted that only artisans of a certain caliber be employed at each stage of the temple's construction, including the enlargement of the basement.

How had it fallen to Marcus to oversee the project? It was a matter of attrition, he thought. He had done nothing to rise in the emperor's favor;

rather, those of greater experience and standing had lost the emperor's favor, one by one, until Marcus had found himself called on to manage the work on the Temple of Venus and Roma while Hadrian was away from the city on his tour of the northern provinces. It was a great honor, but at this early stage there was nothing challenging about it and certainly nothing that called on his skills as an artist. Essentially, the temple was still just a hole in the ground, and at Hadrian's decree that hole was being made larger.

"I spend my days with idiots in a hole in the ground," Marcus muttered, shaking his head.

The slave who assisted him at the site each day—running errands, carrying messages, taking dictation—was a redheaded Macedonian named Amyntas. The youth scurried down the ladder and approached him.

"Master, your wife has come to visit you."

"Did she bring my son with her again?"

"Yes, Master."

Marcus sighed. How many times had he asked Apollodora not to visit him at the work site, and especially not to bring the baby? Even on the best of days, accidents happened—a cart stacked with stones might spill its load, or a carpenter with a sweaty hand might send a hammer flying through the air. But Apollodora was truly the daughter of her father; she would do as she pleased.

Marcus decided that the workmen could restack the stones without his supervision. He climbed up the ladder, secretly glad for a chance to get out of the hole and breathe some fresh air.

A little distance away, with the Flavian Amphitheater and the Colossus for a backdrop, Apollodora sat on a pile of neatly stacked bricks. Nearby, one of her slaves was holding little Lucius in her arms, cooing to him. Apollodora did not look happy.

"Has something happened?" asked Marcus.

"Two letters arrived for you," she said, producing the little scrolls. "Brought by separate messengers."

"Did you read them?" said Marcus, frowning.

"Of course not! That's why I'm here."

He understood. She wanted to know what was in the letters.

She handed him the first letter. The seal was familiar. Marcus himself had carved the carnelian stone in Apollodorus's ring; when pressed into the sealing wax, it left an image of Trajan's Column.

"This is from your father," he said. "You could have opened it, if you wished."

Apollodora shook her head. "I was too nervous. You read it, husband, and tell me what he says."

The letter had come from Damascus, where Apollodorus had been living for several months. Technically, Hadrian had not banished Apollodorus from Roma, but the imperial order that assigned him to an indefinite posting in his native city amounted to the same thing. Apollodorus had no desire to return to Damascus. Officially, Hadrian had claimed that he needed a builder with Apollodorus's experience to oversee repairs to the Roman garrison, but the posting was clearly a punishment.

In the letter, Apollodorus made no complaints and said nothing that might be construed as criticism of the emperor. Perhaps, Marcus thought, his father-in-law's exile had at last taught him to choose his words carefully. Marcus skipped over the formalities and found the gist of the letter, which he read aloud to Apollodora.

" 'You know that I am most eager to return to Roma, so that I can resume my work on the Luna statue and serve the emperor to my fullest capacity on any other projects that may please him. Toward that end, in my spare time—of which I sadly have too much here—I have composed a treatise on siege engines. This treatise I dedicated to the emperor. I sent him the first copy, with a note to express my hope that this small contribution to the science of war might meet with his approval. Though I sent this copy to him some months ago, I have not heard back from him. If you have any way to discover whether the emperor received this offering, and what he thought of it, I should be grateful if you could let me know, son-in-law. . . .' "

Marcus scanned the rest of the letter. Apollodorus described a sandstorm that had swept through the city, made some wry comments about Damascene cuisine ("goat, goat, and more goat"), and noted that unrest among the Jews throughout the region seemed to be on the rise again. Attached to the letter was a scrap of parchment upon which Apollodorus had drawn his latest version of the Luna statue.

"Poor father," said Apollodora. "He's so miserable."

"He doesn't say that."

"Because he's afraid to. That's the saddest thing of all."

Marcus had to agree. His father-in-law's vanity and bombast had sometimes been difficult to take, but Marcus cringed to see the once-proud man reduced to the status of a miscreant servant, desperate to return to the emperor's good graces.

"What's the other letter?" Marcus said.

Apollodora handed it to him. It bore the imperial seal in red wax, and the parchment was of the high quality that Hadrian always used when corresponding with Marcus, which he did quite often, using the new imperial postal service, which was far quicker and more reliable than the piecemeal system it replaced.

Marcus broke the seal and unrolled the scroll. The letter came from a far northern outpost in Britannia. He quickly scanned the letter for any mention of his father-in-law, but saw none.

As usual, Hadrian inquired about progress on the temple and offered highly detailed instructions on how the work was to be carried out. He described his tour of Gaul and Britannia, which had succeeded in making him known to the legions with whom he had previously had no contact. Hadrian relished his reputation as a soldier's soldier, able to endure hardship alongside his troops; like Trajan, he was not afraid to sleep on the ground, march for days, ford rivers, and climb mountains. He also included a few sketches he had made, studies for a massive wall that would cross the entire breadth of the island of Britannia at its narrowest point. To man this fortified wall he would need at least fifteen thousand auxiliaries from all over the empire.

"A wall across Britannia?" said Apollodora, looking at the drawings over his shoulder. Her dismissive tone made her sound uncannily like her father. "Trajan wouldn't have built a wall. He would have conquered whatever lay beyond."

"Only if the barbarians had something worth looting," said Marcus.

The wall was emblematic of the emperor's new frontier policy. Hadrian believed that there was no longer any incentive to push outward in conquest; nothing remained that was worth conquering except the western provinces of Parthia, which Trajan had briefly seized but could not control.

Under Hadrian, a consensus was forming that the empire had reached a natural limit; the wild, impoverished lands beyond its borders offered little to loot, and instead were full of potential looters. It was Hadrian's goal not to conquer these people but to keep them out. His task was to maintain peace and prosperity within the existing boundaries of the empire.

Almost as an afterthought, Hadrian mentioned that he had dismissed his private secretary, Suetonius, who would be returning from Britannia to private life in Roma. Marcus read aloud: " 'I realize that you have been on friendly terms with this person, so I wish to tell you this news myself. You will doubtless hear rumors regarding the reason for his dismissal. The fact is that this person developed an inappropriate professional relationship with the empress.' "

"What in Hades does that mean?" said Apollodora.

"Court politics," said Marcus. "Sabina has her courtiers and Hadrian has his, and when relations between the emperor and empress are strained, those courtiers sometimes find themselves in an awkward spot. Anyone too closely allied with Sabina runs the risk of being dismissed by Hadrian. I suspect that's what's happened to Suetonius."

"My father, and now Suetonius—and there have been quite a few others," said Apollodora. "Men whose lives have been ruined because they said a wrong word or gave the emperor a wrong look."

"I hardly think Suetonius's life is ruined," said Marcus. "He's coming back to Roma, isn't he? He'll finally have time to finish that history he's always dreamed of writing, about the first Caesars."

Apollodora gazed despondently at the letter. "No mention of my father, then, or the treatise he sent to Hadrian?"

"I'm afraid not."

"What will happen if you cross the emperor, husband?"

Marcus blew out his cheeks. "I shall try my best not to do so." He wanted to tell her there was no cause for fear, but in truth, there was a harsh and even petty side to Hadrian. Marcus told himself that the situation could be much worse. Except for the small number of executions that took place at the outset of his reign, Hadrian had kept his word to kill no senators, and his punishments were mild compared to those of some of his predecessors. When Marcus recalled the stories his father had told him about the reign of Domitian—who had forced Lucius Pinarius to face a lion in the arena, and whose favorite method of interrogation had been burning men's genitals—the reigns of Trajan and Hadrian seemed gentle by comparison.

Still, Marcus was acutely aware that he served at Hadrian's pleasure. In a state ruled absolutely by one man, no matter how enlightened that man might be, every other man was at his mercy. Marcus felt a sudden rush of anxiety, thinking how far he had risen in life and how much he had to lose. He calmed himself by touching the fascinum at his breast and thinking of the nameless god who visited him in dreams.

His distracted gaze fell on the Colossus beside the amphitheater, dazzling under the sunlight. He glanced again at the drawing of the Luna statue in Apollodorus's letter, and then at the nearby spot the statue was intended to occupy. Try as he might, he could not envision the Luna statue looming over him; he saw only empty sky. The masterpiece that was to be Apollodorus's crowning achievement, his monument for the ages—would it ever be built?

Apollodora began to weep. Tears ran down her cheeks. Little Lucius began to cry as well, filling the air with loud wailing.

Marcus looked on, feeling helpless to comfort either of them. He whispered a prayer. "God of the dream who protects me, give me a great work to do, and give me an emperor who will let me do it!"

A.D. 125

The city was abuzz with excitement at the emperor's long-awaited return to Roma. What had begun as a trip to the northern provinces had turned into a grand tour that spanned the empire, taking him from Britannia down to the Pillars of Hercules and Mauretania—where he put down a bloody revolt—then across the Mediterranean Sea to Asia Minor, and then to Greece, where Hadrian showered favors on the city of Athens, restoring it as a great seat of learning by endowing it with a new library as well as a forum and an arch and restoring the Temple of Olympian Zeus.

Now, at last, Hadrian was back in Roma, and on this day he was to visit the house of Marcus Pinarius.

The household was in a frenzy of last-minute preparations. Everything had to be made perfect. Marcus thought how very different this visit felt from the first time Hadrian had visited the house, some twelve years ago, when Marcus's father had hosted a dinner party to honor Marcus for his work on Trajan's Column. Hadrian had been an honored guest on that occasion, but today, one would have thought that a god was about to come calling. Apollodora was driving the slaves to tidy every corner, prune every bush in the garden, and polish every marble surface to a lustrous shine. Marcus knew what she was thinking: if only they could make the right impression on the emperor, perhaps he might yet relent in his banishment of her father, who continued to languish in Damascus.

"You *will* bring up the subject, won't you?" Apollodora asked him, for the tenth time that day.

"I'll try, wife. If the right moment arises—"

Amyntas came running. "Master, they're coming up the street! They'll be at the door any moment!"

"Calm yourself, Amyntas. Take a deep breath. When you answer the door—"

"I, Master? *I'm* to answer the door?"

Marcus smiled. Who else in the household was more suitable to greet the emperor than the handsomest of his young slaves? "Yes, Amyntas, you."

"But I'm so nervous, Master. Look how my hands tremble."

"The emperor will find your demeanor charming. Now go—I hear a knock at the door."

The retinue of some twenty people filed through the vestibule and the atrium, then into the formal reception room, where refreshments awaited them. Hadrian, resplendent in a purple toga, accepted Marcus's formal greeting, then drew him aside.

"Let's retire to your garden, Marcus Pinarius. Just the two of us."

Marcus walked beside the emperor. "You look well, Caesar," he said. It was true. Though close to fifty, with touches of gray in his hair and beard, Hadrian was as trim and muscular as ever, and his mood was buoyant. His years of travel had agreed with him.

"Ah, there it is!" he said as he stepped into the garden. Marcus remembered the awed expression on Hadrian's face when he first laid eyes on the statue of Melancomas. The emperor seemed less impressed now. He cocked his head and looked the statue up and down with an expression more wistful than astonished.

"Caesar must have seen many beautiful works of art during his travels," Marcus said.

"Oh, yes. Amazing things. Amazing experiences. My induction into the Mysteries of Eleusis was the most remarkable of those experiences, though I can say nothing specific about that, of course. My travels have opened my eyes. I received a very good education when I was young. My teachers did their best to enlighten me. But books and words can relate only so much. Actual experience is the key. Oh, before I forget, Epictetus asked me to give you his regards. I believe that he and your father were very close."

"Yes, Caesar. How is he?"

"As brilliant as ever, and still teaching at his school in Nicopolis. I hope that my wits will remain as quick when I'm in my seventies."

"I think Epictetus must be the very last of my father's circle who's still alive," said Marcus thoughtfully. Hadrian was in such high spirits that Marcus wondered if this might be a good time to bring up the matter of his father-in-law. He was clearing his throat to speak when Hadrian returned his attention to the statue of Melancomas.

"Do you recall, Pinarius, what we said about this statue, that evening many years ago? I said, 'If only, someday, I could meet a youth as beautiful as this.' To which you responded, 'If only, someday, I could create a statue as beautiful as this.'"

Marcus smiled, remembering. "Yes, and Favonius said, 'May each of you be granted his desire—and be happy with it!'"

"The scurra! I had forgotten he was here that night, but yes, you're right, I remember now. Well, Favonius was a wise man after all. You know, seeing it again after all this time, the Melancomas statue doesn't impress me as much as it once did. And you, Marcus, as an artist, with many more years of experience now: what do you think of it?"

Marcus tried to look at the familiar statue with fresh eyes. "Perhaps the shoulders are a bit too wide, and the hips too narrow; but of course the sculptor had a duty to record the actual proportions of the living model. The workmanship itself seems quite flawless to me."

"Does it? Here, there's someone I want you to meet."

Hadrian summoned a secretary who stood at the garden's edge and spoke in his ear. The man hurried to the reception room to fetch someone. Marcus noticed that Apollodora was peeking at them from behind a corner, looking anxious. As he wondered again if he should mention his father-in-law, Hadrian's young friend stepped into the garden and joined them.

Marcus was stunned. The youth who stood before him was the very incarnation of the god from his dreams.

Hadrian laughed. "That's a typical reaction of those meeting Antinous for the first time. But really, try not to gape, Pygmalion. That's what they used to call you, isn't it? Just as they used to call me the Little Greek?"

Marcus closed his mouth. The resemblance was too uncanny to be accidental. He touched the fascinum at his breast. "Forgive me, Caesar. It's only . . . that is, it's hard to explain . . ."

"Then don't try. Not with words, anyway." Hadrian shifted from speaking Latin to Greek. "Here, Antinous, what do you make of this statue?"

The youth likewise answered in Greek, with a Bithynian accent. "It's very beautiful. Who is it?"

"This is Melancomas, a famous wrestler."

"Is he still alive?"

Hadrian laughed. "Melancomas and the emperor Titus were lovers fifty years ago."

"So?" Antinous cocked his head. "He could be a handsome man in his seventies today."

Hadrian's smile faded. "No, Melancomas died young. But here, I want you to stand next to the statue. I want to see the two of you side by side. This is something I've been curious to see since I first met you. Take off your clothes, Antinous. There's no need to be modest before Pygmalion; he's an artist."

Antinous stood next to the Melancomas. He pulled off his chiton and dropped it to the ground, then undid his loincloth and let it fall.

Hadrian crossed his arms and nodded. "There, do you see, Pinarius? They're not really comparable, are they? As beautiful as we thought the Melancomas, it pales beside Antinous." He circled the youth and the statue, looking from one to the other. "Of course, cold marble can never compete with warm, living flesh, just as words in a book cannot match the actuality

of experience. But even if Melancomas were alive and breathing and standing next to Antinous, would there be any competition as to which was more
beautiful?"

Marcus was still too stunned to think clearly. "I don't know what to
say."

"Then say nothing. You're not a poet, after all, you're an artist. And
that's what I want from you—art. I want you to sculpt Antinous. Of course,
as I said, I know that marble or bronze can never fully capture the subtlety
and solidity of flesh, but you must do your best. What do you say, Pygmalion? Will you make me a statue of Antinous?"

"Of course I will, Caesar." Marcus, dazed, saw his wife peering at him
from her place of concealment. For the life of him, he could not remember
what she wanted.

⁂

To carry out the emperor's commission, Marcus set up a workshop at the
foot of the Aventine Hill, not far from the river. It was a lofty space with
excellent light and plenty of room. Soon the shelves were lined with scores
of clay models of the youth and all the various parts of his body. Occasionally Marcus heard the sounds of workers on the waterfront, but otherwise the space was very quiet.

Marcus had never enjoyed anything as much as he enjoyed working on
the statue. All his other work, even on the Temple of Venus and Roma,
was suspended.

Antinous was the ideal model. He was never late, had impeccable manners, and carried himself with a composure beyond his years. He was willing to quietly hold a pose for hours, content simply to exist and be still
inside his perfect body, letting whatever thoughts were behind his perfect
face remain a mystery.

From the brief conversations that occasionally took place between
them, Marcus learned that Hadrian had met the youth while traveling in
Bithynia. Marcus noted that Dio of Prusa had been a Bithynian, but Antinous had never heard of him. Philosophy did not interest him.

Nor was he much interested in religion or science, but when the subject of astrology came up, he told Marcus that the emperor himself was an

expert astrologer. "Caesar frequently casts his own horoscope," said Antinous. "He can't let anyone else do it, you see, because that would give them too much knowledge. That's why he won't allow any astrologers in the court and studies the heavens himself. How he can remember the meanings of all those configurations of the stars is beyond me, but of course he has a very scientific mind. He casts horoscopes for the people around him, too."

"Including you?"

Antinous frowned. "No, never for me. He seems to be superstitious about that. He says some things should remain a mystery."

What the boy really loved was hunting. One day, when the subject happened to come up—Marcus was talking about all the famous statues that had been made of the hunter Actaeon—Antinous became more animated than Marcus had ever seen him.

"I was very nearly killed by a lion once," he said.

"Really?"

"Caesar and I were hunting together, on horseback. We trapped a lion against a cliff face. Caesar wanted me to have the kill, so I threw my spear first. But I only wounded the beast. The lion was furious. It roared and crouched, and whipped its tail, and then it sprang at me. My heart stopped. I thought I was dead. But while the lion was in midair, Caesar's spear struck the beast and pierced its heart. It fell to the ground, dead. If Caesar hadn't killed the lion, it would surely have torn me to pieces. Caesar saved my life. I can never repay him for that."

"That's a remarkable story," said Marcus, seeing a glint in the youth's eyes that he was determined to capture. He seized a piece of charcoal and some parchment and began sketching furiously.

"I think someone is making a poem about it," Antinous said blandly, in his charming Bithynian accent, as if having one's activities recorded in verse were an everyday occurrence. There were probably a great many things Antinous took for granted, Marcus thought. What must it be like to go through life looking like that, attracting the admiration of every person you met?

After his initial awe, Marcus had come to realize that Antinous was not his dream-god. For one thing, despite Marcus's overwhelming first impression, he began to see that the youth was not exactly identical to the dream-god, or at least not all the time. There was something quicksilver about his appearance, as there was about every human face; it changed depending on his mood, the angle, the light. Sometimes Antinous did not resemble the dream-god at all, and Marcus could not imagine how he had ever thought he did; then, in the next instant, Antinous would turn his face just so, and he was the dream-god come to life. It was this elusive nature of the youth's appearance that Marcus was striving to capture, a challenge he found all-consuming. If Antinous was not a god, he was surely the vessel of a god, possessing some degree of divine power. Marcus would do his best to capture that divinity in marble.

Uncharacteristically, Hadrian had refrained from taking any part in the process, not even dropping by to look at Marcus's sketches or clay models. He declared his intention to wait until the statue was finished before he laid eyes on it. Marcus was touched by the emperor's trust, and the privacy of the process had allowed him to invest himself completely in his work.

Antinous had just left for the day when Marcus heard a knock on the door. A small vestibule separated the studio from the entrance, and it was here that he admitted an unexpected caller: Gaius Suetonius.

"Marcus Pinarius! I haven't seen you in ages," said Suetonius. "I pass by the site of the new temple occasionally, but I no longer see you there."

"My duties at the temple have been suspended for a while. I come here to the workshop every day."

"Hiding out, eh? I thought I'd never find this place, tucked away among the granaries and storehouses. Working on something for the emperor, are you?"

"Perhaps."

"Oh, come, Pinarius, everyone knows what you're up to. You're making a statue of that Bithynian boy."

Marcus frowned. "How did you know?"

"Favonius told me. I'm no longer privy to imperial comings and goings, but Favonius keeps me informed. He says everyone is talking about this statue of yours, just as everyone is talking about Hadrian and his new favorite."

"What do they say?"

"Some people claim to be scandalized by Hadrian's lack of propriety, elevating a foreign youth of no standing to a place of honor in his

household. Sabina's faction certainly isn't happy; Caesar has less time for
the empress than ever. But others are pleased to see the emperor so content. A happy Caesar is a benevolent Caesar. So, can I have a look at the
statue to see what all the fuss is about?"

Marcus shook his head. "No one is allowed to see the statue, I'm
afraid."

"No? Perhaps you could let me see a preliminary sketch? I've never
even seen this boy. I'm curious to know what he looks like."

"Not possible. Even Caesar hasn't seen my work yet, and no one can be
allowed to see it before Caesar."

Suetonius made a sour face. "Ah, well, one Bithynian youth looks like
another, I imagine. They're all available to a Roman with money, or so it
seemed when I was stationed there in the imperial service. You couldn't set
foot in the baths without those boys practically throwing themselves at you."

"I wouldn't know," said Marcus. "I've never been to Bithynia."

There was an awkward silence, broken by Suetonius. "I've been hard at
work, too."

"Have you?"

"Toiling away on my collection of imperial biographies. I've been writing about Domitian lately—that could put anyone in a bad mood. I was
wondering, did your father ever talk about those days? In particular, did
he ever mention a 'black room'? Apparently there was a chamber in the
imperial palace to which Domitian invited certain guests when he wanted
to frighten them half to death."

"No, I don't remember any stories about a black room."

"Ah, well, plenty of others have stories to tell. I have to say, some of the
tales I've collected about the emperors almost defy belief. They're quite
shocking, and all the more so because they're true. I rather hate to end my
collection with Domitian—such a grim fellow—but one can't yet write
this sort of biography about Trajan or Nerva, the emperor's father and
grandfather by adoption. One never knows what might cause offense.
Even the most flattering account might somehow provoke the emperor's
displeasure."

"Caesar is letting you write whatever you want about the previous dy-
nasties?"

"Amazing, isn't it? Everyone in a position of authority assures me that I may proceed as I wish. My biggest worry is what the emperor will say about my prose. Hadrian fancies himself a writer, you know. Architect, emperor, author, literary critic—is there nothing the man can't do? His own specialty is collecting odd bits of information and compiling catalogs of marvelous facts. His book will be forthcoming any day now. Of course he can't publish such a thing under his own name, so he's having his creature Phlegon put his name on the book. Trivial, time-wasting miscellany—just the sort of thing everyone's reading nowadays."

"Not a work of true merit, like your imperial biographies?"

"Exactly. Perhaps you'd like to read what I've written so far. I could profit from the reactions of a fellow like yourself, a man of learning and experience but with no literary pretensions or axes to grind. Shall I have a copy sent to you?"

"Yes, please do," said Marcus, just to get rid of the man. He was eager to return to the studio, where he could be alone to contemplate his progress on the statue of Antinous.

A few days later, while he was preparing to leave home for the workshop, an imperial messenger arrived with a request for Marcus to come to the House of the People.

"Do you know why I'm being summoned?" said Marcus.

"I'm afraid not," said the messenger.

Marcus was perturbed. His work on the statue had progressed to a stage that was particularly pleasurable to him—smoothing and polishing the stone and making very small adjustments. Now he would lose the best part of the day, when the light was brightest, and he would have to go through the bother of changing his simple tunic for a toga.

The summons also made him uneasy. If Hadrian was curious about progress on the statue, why did he not simply come to see it? Could it be that Suetonius's visit to the workshop had been observed and reported to the emperor? Surely Hadrian knew Marcus well enough by now to trust that he would never show the statue to anyone ahead of himself. While he dressed, Marcus decided that he was being unduly anxious. Probably there was some architectural detail about the temple that Hadrian wanted to discuss.

The chamber where Hadrian received him was tastefully appointed with Greek furnishings brought back from his travels; the room had the intimate atmosphere of a private home rather than of a regal reception hall. The slave who escorted Marcus showed him to a couch and brought him a cup of wine. A number of guests were already present, and more continued to arrive. Antinous was there, Marcus noticed; the empress Sabina was not. Some of the guests were senators and magistrates, but more were writers and philosophers. The mood was like that of a literary gathering. Almost all the men sported facial hair, though few could grow a beard as handsome as that of the emperor.

Eventually Hadrian rose and called forth the scholar Phlegon of Tralles, a small, nondescript man whom Hadrian introduced as the author of a new work titled *The Book of Marvels*. Phlegon stood before the company and read a number of excerpts, all of which he claimed had been verified by scrupulous research, having to do with wondrous things—sightings of live centaurs, appearances by ghosts, incidents of males giving birth, and stories about men and women who had changed their gender. He concluded with several accounts about the discovery of gigantic teeth and bones, the existence of which appeared to prove that huge creatures, now extinct, had once lived upon the earth.

" 'A tooth the size of a man's leg was uncovered by an earthquake in Sicily and shown to the emperor Tiberius,' " Phlegon read. " 'Tiberius called on a geometrician named Pulcher, who concluded that the creature who possessed such a tooth would have been as large as a ship—far larger than any creature known to exist today. Bones of gigantic size were found in a cave in Dalmatia, and equally enormous bones have been excavated in Rhodes, Athens, and Egypt. Some say these objects must be made of a stone which happens to look like bone, or are deliberate hoaxes, but I say we should not disbelieve this remarkable evidence. Rather, consider that in the beginning, when nature was in her prime, she reared everything near to the gods, but just as time is running down, so also living things have become smaller and smaller in stature.' "

Phlegon bowed. Marcus saw that Hadrian was beaming like a proud author. He remembered Suetonius's claim that the emperor was the true author of the work and joined the others in applauding.

After this bit of amusement, Hadrian moved on to a more serious matter.

"Our attention has been called to the recent death of a citizen, a case of murder, it would appear. A slave is suspected of killing his master."

There were mutterings of disdain from some of the guests, especially the senators.

Hadrian raised his hand. "As outrageous as such a crime may be, I bring up the matter because I see here an opportunity to reform certain laws handed down to us by our ancestors, specifically those harsh measures which demand the examination, by torture, of all the slaves in a household where such a crime occurs, and, if one of their number is found guilty, the execution of every slave. Marcus Pinarius—"

Marcus blinked and looked up, surprised at being called on.

"I asked you here today, Pinarius, because your grandfather once made an impassioned speech to the Senate on this very topic, in the reign of Nero. You are aware of that occasion, I presume?"

Marcus cleared his throat. "Yes, Caesar, my father told me something about it."

"I realize you never knew your grandfather, but you should be proud of what he said. Fortunately, his words were recorded and preserved in the Senate archives. I read them for the first time last night. Phlegon, would you be so kind as to read aloud the section I've marked?"

Phlegon took the scroll and stood before them again. " 'These slaves must be known not only to fellow slaves in other households, but to shop-keepers and artisans and all sorts of citizens who have dealings with them. Some are errand boys and messengers, some are seamstresses and hair-dressers, some are cooks and cleaners, some are bookkeepers and scribes, highly educated and valuable slaves deserving a degree of respect. Some are near the age of death. Some are newborn, just beginning life. Some are in the prime of life, at the peak of their usefulness and value. Some are preg-nant and about to bring forth new life. These victims of the law are not a faceless crowd but are human beings known to their neighbors, and so we cannot be surprised if there are murmurs throughout the city that the law is too harsh.' "

Hadrian nodded and took back the scroll. "I think those words are quite remarkable, considering the occasion and atmosphere in which they were delivered. Your grandfather spoke of those doomed slaves as if they were human beings, not mere property; as if their suffering mattered. At the time, your grandfather's sentiments were rebuked and ridiculed; but with the passing of the generations, and the general progress of mankind, I think we are able to see that your grandfather was not only brave and compassionate, but wise. As the Divine Trajan often told me, if the emperor can see a just way to reduce the suffering of those under his care, even the most wretched, he is obligated to do so. In the case at hand, I think we have an opportunity to do exactly that. Therefore, I am proclaiming a number of edicts involving the punishment of slaves.

"First, if a master is murdered in his house, no slaves shall be examined under torture except those who were near enough to have knowledge of the murder. This reform has been a long time coming."

There was a murmur of approval. A number of people nodded deferentially to Marcus, in honor of his farsighted grandfather.

"Further," said Hadrian, "a master may no longer kill a slave at will. Instead, the execution of a slave must be decided by a court. Further, no master may sell a slave, male or female, to a sexual procurer or a trainer of gladiators, unless the master can make a case that the slave is fit for nothing else. Further, I intend to abolish the existing houses of hard labor to which some masters consign their unwanted slaves for a fee, and where even some wretched freedmen end up, so desperate are they to work off their debts. I have visited those workhouses, which are places of unimaginable suffering, and I intend to shut them down."

The emperor's pronouncements were met with silence. Hadrian looked around the room. "Does anyone wish to comment on these ideas?"

A white-haired, clean-shaven senator stepped forward. "Caesar, today you have introduced us to a work called *The Book of Marvels*. But more marvelous than anything in that book are these radical ideas you put before us. I drew a breath when I heard about a tooth from a creature the size of a ship—but my jaw dropped to hear that a Roman citizen shall no longer have the power to discipline his slaves as he sees fit. I fear that Caesar's new laws are likely to be very unpopular, and not just with the rich, who own many slaves. Consider the common man, who owns only a handful of slaves. Unless his authority over those slaves is absolute—yes, even to the point of death—how can that man possibly feel safe inside his home at night? Our forefathers created these laws for a reason, and the Divine

Augustus restated them anew. I fear these pronouncements will stir considerable discontent, and such disorder that the magistrates will be unable to contain it."

Hadrian raised his hand for silence. "If disorder breaks out, then I will hold the magistrates responsible. It is their duty to contain such outbreaks, whatever the cause, and to see that laws are respected—all laws, including these. If the magistrates cannot do the job, then others who are more capable shall be appointed to take their place."

The senator bowed his head and stepped back. No one else dared to comment.

"If there's no other business this morning, then I'm ready for my lunch," said Hadrian.

As the various courses were served, the emperor called Marcus to his side.

"What do *you* think of my ideas, Pygmalion?"

"I'm not a statesman, Caesar."

"Perhaps not, but your grandfather was. Who knew? I had to check twice to be sure that the Pinarius who gave that speech before Nero and the Senate was indeed your grandfather. That took nerve. You can be proud of the blood in your veins, Pinarius."

"I am, Caesar. Thank you for inviting me here today, to hear the words of my grandfather."

"Yes, I thought you might enjoy that. How goes work on the statue?"

"It proceeds well, Caesar, and quickly. Very soon I'll be ready to unveil it for you."

"Very good!" Hadrian looked at Antinous, who was sitting next to Phlegon, scrolling through *The Book of Marvels*. "I can hardly wait to see it."

At last, Marcus was ready for the emperor's visit to the workshop.

Apollodora was with him, overseeing the slaves as they cleaned and tidied the place and decorated it especially for the occasion. Marcus had assured her that such preparations were unnecessary. "It's a workshop: it's supposed to be cluttered and covered in marble dust. The emperor knows that." But Apollodora had insisted that all must be perfect. If Hadrian was pleased—and of course he would be—this could at last be Marcus's opportunity to ask for a special favor: the return of his father-in-law from exile.

Apollodora had insisted on bringing along four-year-old Lucius as well, saying that the boy should be there to see his father's proud moment. No doubt she also thought that the sight of Lucius might move the emperor to be merciful to the boy's grandfather.

As the hour for the visit drew near, Marcus was increasingly fretful. Not only would Hadrian be judging his work, but Marcus would have to put the delicate matter of his father-in-law to the emperor, with his wife's happiness hanging on the outcome. Marcus stood before the statue a final time, studying the sensual curves of the naked body, the tilt of the head, the faraway look, and the elusive smile. Without a doubt, this was the finest and most beautiful thing Marcus had ever created. He reached for a sailcloth and threw it over the statue.

There was a sound from the vestibule. Amyntas came running. "Master—"

"Yes, I know, the emperor is here."

"He's left his retinue in the street. Only Antinous is with him."

"Well? Show them in!"

The emperor and Antinous entered. Marcus stood next to the draped statue. Apollodora stood nearby, with little Lucius beside her.

No one said a word. Hadrian smiled and gave a slight gesture with his hand, to indicate that Marcus should proceed.

Marcus pulled aside the sailcloth. The statue was unveiled.

Hadrian approached the statue. He slowly circled it, looking it up and down. His face was expressionless.

Antinous was smiling; he seemed pleased with his image. Of course, the statue offered no surprise to him, since he had seen it at every stage of its creation.

In his mind, Marcus rehearsed the little speech he had prepared: *Caesar, you recently saw fit to praise the plea my grandfather made, asking for clemency to be shown to even the lowliest of men. I also have a plea to make, which only Caesar can grant. I ask that you show mercy and forgiveness to—*

"A mistake," said Hadrian. He had concluded his full circuit of the statue and stood in front of it, staring at it. There was no expression on his face.

Marcus blinked. The utterance was so abrupt that he was not sure he had heard it correctly. "A mistake, Caesar? If some tiny flaw remains, an area where I failed to smooth the marble sufficiently . . ." said Marcus, though he knew every inch of the statue was perfect.

"No. The entire idea was a mistake." Hadrian's tone was frigid. He averted his eyes from both Marcus and the statue. "The fault is mine, Marcus Pinarius, not yours. I should never have expected that you, or anyone else, could do the thing I desired. I understand that now."

"Caesar, if the pose of the statue is not to your liking, or if the tilt of the head—"

"Nothing about the statue is to my liking. By Hercules, look at Antinous! And then look at this . . . this travesty."

Trembling, Apollodora stepped forward. "Caesar, it's a true likeness."

"What would you know? You might as well be blind. And so might you, Marcus. You possess a certain skill, yes. This is the image you intended to shape, I'm sure. But you have no eyes to see. This . . . *thing* . . . is not Antinous, not even a vague approximation. Am I the only one who can see him?"

Hadrian turned his back on the statue, as if disgusted by it.

Apollodora looked desperately at Marcus. "Husband, do it!" she whispered.

"Now is not the time," he said through clenched teeth.

But Apollodora had staked so much on this meeting that she could not let the chance go by. She rushed to Hadrian, even as he was departing, and dropped to her knees. "Caesar, we have a favor to ask. My father, in Damascus—he longs to return to Roma. If you could forgive him—we beg you!"

Hadrian shuddered. He waved his hand dismissively, turned away from her, and walked on.

Following him, Antinous looked over his shoulder and cast a parting glance at the statue. To Marcus, the face of the youth and the face of the statue were mirror images, perfectly alike in every way.

At the doorway to the vestibule, Hadrian stopped and collected himself. He kept his eyes averted. His voice was strained but calm. "You will return to work on the temple, Marcus Pinarius. There is still much you can accomplish there. But you will destroy this abomination, and everything to do with it. Do you understand? As soon as I'm gone, you will destroy every model and burn every drawing. You will break this statue into pieces. You will grind the pieces to dust. No one must ever see it."

A.D. 129

Work continued on the Temple of Venus and Roma—with the huge columns at last in place, the true massiveness of the structure was becoming evident—but on this day Marcus was at work at a different site, out on the Field of Mars, where Hadrian had decided to rebuild a neglected ruin called the Pantheon.

The original structure, a temple dedicated to the great gods, had been erected by Agrippa in the reign of Augustus. Damage caused by fire in the reign of Titus had been repaired by Domitian. Another fire, caused by lightning, virtually destroyed the temple while work was under way on Trajan's Column and Forum, and with those enormous projects claiming all available resources, the rebuilding of the Pantheon was neglected. For almost twenty years the Pantheon remained in ruins, a cordoned-off area in the bustling heart of the Field of Mars. Passing the familiar eyesore one day, Hadrian suddenly saw it afresh. The limitations of the site were such that any rebuilt temple would have to be nearly square in shape. It was hard to imagine an aesthetically pleasing temple no deeper than it was wide— essentially a cube. But what if the rebuilt temple was circular—or indeed, as Hadrian perceived in a flash of inspiration, spherical? Here at last, the emperor realized, was the project to which he could give full expression to his fascination for domes—the "giant gourds" that Apollodorus had derided. The rebuilt Pantheon would be unique, a sphere within a square, surmounted by a dome of almost inconceivable size. The challenge of constructing such a dome had defeated engineers in the past, but Hadrian insisted that it could be done, and had charged Marcus with doing so.

The emperor's expression of confidence in him had surprised Marcus, who had been badly shaken by Hadrian's rejection of the statue. But not once had Hadrian ever reminded Marcus of his displeasure on that occasion, and Marcus was determined to show the emperor that his trust was well placed. Fired by Hadrian's enthusiasm, Marcus and a team of engineers had conceived new ideas for making such a vast dome feasible—making the concrete thinner near the top, using coffers to lessen the mass, and using an oculus, an eyelike opening at the top, to admit light and further reduce the weight. Marcus was determined that his efforts should not disappoint the emperor. He often wished that Apollodorus were with him to offer advice and help oversee such a hazardous but thrilling enterprise.

The actual construction of the dome was still a long way off. On this day, Marcus was inspecting recent work on the thick, load-bearing walls when he heard a familiar cry and looked up to see his son's blond curls glinting in the sunlight.

At the age of eight, Lucius was now old enough to visit his father's work sites, as long as he was always supervised. Marcus was surprised to see that Lucius was accompanied not by one of the slaves who usually chaperoned him but by Amyntas, who had rapidly risen in the ranks of the household and was usually occupied with more important duties.

Marcus greeted the boy by lifting him in the air—not as easy a task as it once had been—then saw the reason why Amyntas had come. In the slave's hand was a scroll, and even at a distance Marcus could spot the imperial seal pressed into the wax.

Hadrian was again off traveling. He frequently corresponded with Marcus, but those letters were usually bundled with other imperial documents and delivered by couriers to the palace, where Marcus sent a slave to fetch them. A letter that had come not to the palace but directly to Marcus's house was unusual.

While Amyntas took Lucius to look at the walls, Marcus broke the seal and unrolled the scroll. Previous letters had come from Sicily, Carthage, the interior African city of Lambaesis, Athens, Ephesus, and Antioch. The heading of this letter showed that it had been posted from the desert trading city of Palmyra. Recalling its close proximity to Damascus, Marcus felt a twinge of hope. Apollodorus in his latest letter had expressed his intention to do his best to gain an audience with Hadrian, should the emperor's travels bring him anywhere near Damascus.

The letter was written not in Hadrian's usual first person, full of learned asides and literary allusions, but in a very stiff and formal third person. From the first words, Marcus knew the letter contained bad news:

> Caesar wishes to inform Marcus Pinarius personally of an unfortunate event, so that he will hear of it first from Caesar and not from some other source. Caesar will state the fact plainly: the father-in-law of Marcus Pinarius, Apollodorus of Damascus, has been executed for plotting against the life of the emperor. Because of irrefutable evidence supplied to Caesar, Caesar had no other recourse. This action was carried out swiftly and with respect to the person's status as a citizen.

Marcus knew what that meant: Apollodorus had been beheaded and not killed in some more disgraceful way, like crucifixion.

> Marcus Pinarius need fear no recrimination against himself. Although Caesar is aware of the natural bond of affection between Marcus Pinarius and his father-in-law, Caesar is of the belief that Marcus Pinarius played no part whatsoever in the plot, is certain of Marcus Pinarius's loyalty to the emperor, and desires Marcus Pinarius to continue his valuable work on the Temple of Venus and Roma and on the Pantheon. It is the wish of Caesar that this unfortunate event shall have no effect on the amity between himself and Marcus Pinarius. We shall not speak of it again.

Stunned, Marcus put down the letter. Could it be true that Apollodorus had conspired against the emperor? Had the bitterness of so many years of exile driven him to involve himself in some desperate plot? Hadrian's journeys exposed him not just to those who sought favors from the emperor but to those in each region who craved revenge, and in the vicinity of Damascus, where so many had been subjected to so much suffering under Roman rule, there must be many such persons. Had Apollodorus conspired with other malcontents and been discovered by Hadrian's agents? Or had he been the victim of rumors and lies? Hadrian spoke of "irrefutable evidence," but that phrase was invariably used when a declared enemy of the state was put to death.

Marcus would probably never know the truth. The emperor was above being questioned. Apollodorus was beyond giving answers.

Marcus saw something from the corner of his eye. It took him a moment to realize that it was a man in a toga. Only when the man spoke did he recognize Gaius Suetonius.

"Pinarius! I haven't seen you in a Titan's age. Only yesterday, I was revising a passage about Marcus Agrippa, and I thought to myself: I must drop by to see what you're up to here at Agrippa's ruined temple. Those walls look awfully thick—must be quite a heavy roof you're planning to put on top! You know, I never heard a word from you when I sent you my work in progress, all those years ago. Oh, that's alright, not everyone's a literary critic, and thank the gods for that. But now—good news! I've finally finished the work, and I have an army of scribes busy making copies. Shall I send you one? It's not a bad read, if I say so myself. I promise you won't be bored. Indeed, you may think I've written a book of marvels, like our friend Phlegon, it's so full of outrageous anecdotes. Amazing, what some of those emperors got up to! Even I was surprised at the details I discovered, and I spent years combing through the imperial archives. There's one story about Caligula—truly, it defies belief. . . ."

Marcus didn't hear. He was wondering how he was going to tell Apollodora the news.

He was suddenly distracted by a glint of sunlight on his son's blond curls. Lucius had wandered into an area where loose bricks had been piled in high stacks.

"Amyntas!" Marcus shouted. "Amyntas, look after Lucius! He doesn't belong over there. It's too dangerous."

Suetonius smiled. "Boys! Always getting into trouble, eh? A pity our emperor hasn't got one; that might keep *him* out of trouble. Oh, but I forget; Caesar *does* have a boy to look after. Takes him everywhere—so my correspondents along his travel route tell me. I hear he's headed for Jerusalem next—or what they used to call Jerusalem. Hadrian plans to rebuild the city Vespasian destroyed and give it a rather pretty new name: Aelia Capitolina, named for his ancestors, the Aelii. I suspect he'll put a statue of himself next to Jupiter and see if he can't convince those stubborn Jews to burn a bit of incense on the altar. Then he's to press on to Alexandria for his first look at Egypt. He and Antinous will play Caesar and Cleopatra, languidly cruising up the Nile past hippopotami and crocodiles. Do you suppose the Egyptians will put some sort of animal head on Hadrian's statue and declare him a god?"

The man chattered on and on. Marcus did not hear a word.

A.D. 132

Hadrian was back in Roma.

After years of travel, the emperor's return to the capital was to be marked with celebrations and banquets. But his very first excursion, bright and early on the morning after his first night back in the imperial palace, was an unannounced visit to the site of the Temple of Venus and Roma, to see what progress had been made in his absence. When the emperor was informed that Marcus Pinarius was not present, being occupied that morning at his workshop, Hadrian and his retinue headed directly to the Aventine Hill.

Marcus and his assistants were busy piecing together some sections of the gigantic bronze statue of Venus that was to be installed in the temple. When Amyntas came running in to announce that the emperor was in the vestibule, Marcus told everyone to cease working and stay exactly where they were. He put down his tools and dusted off his tunic. Amyntas, checking Marcus's appearance, flicked some bits of metal from his beard.

Impeccably dressed as always, the emperor made a cursory examination of the statue, then suggested that the workmen might be allowed a rest, so that he and Marcus could speak in private.

"I've just come from the temple," said Hadrian. "I'm pleased with the progress. You've done well, Pinarius."

"Thank you, Caesar. I'm but one of the many artisans and engineers who are privileged each day to carry out the emperor's grand vision."

"You needn't be so modest, Pinarius. I've spent a lifetime dealing with architects and artists all over the world. You may be the most talented of all."

Now that Apollodorus is dead, Marcus thought. Then he thought of the other death that had occurred in the course of Hadrian's journeys. During the trip up the Nile, Antinous had drowned.

It seemed to Marcus that the emperor had aged considerably since he had last seen him. There was more silver in his hair and his beard was now almost entirely gray. His face was more wrinkled. He spoke more slowly and with a quaver in his voice. His eyes were dull. Some essential spark had gone out of him.

Hadrian strolled around the studio, touching the various implements. "You spent so many hours with him here, in this room—alone with him, looking at him, observing him. More than anyone else on earth, except myself, you must remember what he looked like."

"Caesar speaks of Antinous," said Marcus quietly. "When I learned of his death, I wept." It was true. Marcus had grieved, not so much for the youth himself, whose personality had remained a mystery to him, but for the loss of so much beauty. In his mind, there was still some mysterious link between the Bithynian youth and the god who visited him in dreams. The death of Antinous had struck him as more than the death of a single mortal; his passing was emblematic of the death of all things.

"Do you know the circumstances of his death?" said Hadrian in a whisper.

"I know only what everyone knows, that Antinous drowned in the Nile."

"Egypt cast a spell over us—the heat, the buzzing insects, the oozing mud, the endlessly flowing river, the temples filled with strange symbols and animal-headed gods, the gigantic monuments from some unimaginably distant past. As we journeyed farther and farther up the Nile, we were gripped by some nameless, ancient dread.

"As I had explored the Mysteries of Eleusis, so I was initiated in the secret rites of the Egyptians. When the priests looked into my future, they saw something terrible. They declared that my life was over, that I would die in a matter of days, unless . . . unless another life was sacrificed in my place.

"I didn't want to believe them. But when I cast my horoscope, adjusting the reading for the greater influence of the southern stars, I saw they were right. I was in great danger. Death was very near."

Marcus drew a breath. "So Antinous . . ."

"He sacrificed himself in my place. I never asked him to do it. I was restless that night. I heard him leave the cabin. I heard the soft sound of a splash. I was half asleep and thought I was dreaming. . . ."

Marcus remembered the story Antinous had once told him, in this very room, about the time Hadrian and the boy hunted a lion. *If Caesar hadn't killed the lion, it would surely have torn me to pieces. Caesar saved my life. I can never repay him for that.*

The boy had been able to repay him, after all.

"What Antinous did was not the act of a mere mortal," said Hadrian. "I always sensed there was something divine in him. I think you sensed that, too, Pinarius. But I never truly understood the nature of his divinity until he left this world. In his honor I built a city on the Nile, where I consecrated a temple and appointed priests to worship him. In Ephesus and Athens, on the way back to Roma, I built more temples in honor of the god Antinous."

Marcus had heard about the emperor's activities on behalf of the new god. The grandiosity of Hadrian's grief was the talk of Roma; some dared to ridicule it, but others were in awe of it. Marcus had heard it compared to the madness of Alexander the Great after the death of Alexander's lover, Hephaestion, but it was hard for Marcus to look at the aging, paunchy Hadrian and see any resemblance to the dashing, doomed figure of Alexander.

"There will be no temple to Antinous here in Roma," said Hadrian. "Just as worship of the emperor is not required of citizens within Italy, so I will not ask the people of Roma to worship the youth who was my consort. But I plan to build a tomb for Antinous near the town of Tibur, east of the city. I also plan to build a residence there, a place where I can retreat from the world." Hadrian closed his eyes for a long moment, then opened them. "Naturally, Pinarius, I want you to be part of those projects."

"Of course, Caesar. I'll do whatever I can."

Hadrian stepped closer. He gazed steadily into Marcus's eyes. "What I really want, dear Pygmalion, is for you to sculpt Antinous."

Marcus stared back at him. Had grief erased the emperor's memory?

Hadrian smiled wanly. "I understand your hesitation, Pinarius. Let me explain. Temples have been erected. Temples must have statues, so artists in Egypt and Greece have sculpted images of the Divine Antinous. At best, these statues have been—what word can I use?—acceptable. But none has captured the divine essence of Antinous. I'm convinced that only you— because you alone sculpted him in life—can possibly do that. I want you to make a statue of Antinous. We'll collaborate on this project, you and I, working from memory."

Marcus felt many things at once—doubt, dread, and a twinge of anger, but also a thrill of excitement such as he had not experienced in a long time.

Hadrian looked at him with a plaintive expression. "I don't suppose . . . when I told you to destroy the statue . . ."

"I did as I was ordered, Caesar. I burned my sketches. I destroyed the models. I broke the arms and legs from the statue, smashed the torso, pulverized the hands and feet—"

Hadrian winced and shut his eyes.

"But . . ." Marcus hesitated for a long moment, then decided to tell the truth. "I kept the head."

Hadrian's eyes grew wide.

"It was the most beautiful thing I ever made, or ever could hope to make," said Marcus. "I couldn't bear to destroy it."

"Where is it?"

Marcus walked to a cluttered corner of the workshop. Hadrian followed him. Marcus cleared away a pile of implements and tattered scrolls to reveal a small cabinet covered with dust. The iron latch was rusty. Marcus had not opened the cabinet in years. It would have been too painful to look at the object it contained.

He managed to open the latch. He reached into the cabinet. He stood and held aloft the head of Antinous.

Hadrian gasped. He took the head from Marcus and held it in his hands. He touched his lips to the marble. His eyes filled with tears.

In the days and months that followed, the emperor spent every spare moment with Marcus in the workshop, surrounded first by drawings and small clay figurines, then by life-size models. Together they strove to recreate, to Hadrian's satisfaction, the true image of Antinous. Marcus drew and molded, and Hadrian gave his critiques, circling the life-size models, touching them and closing his eyes as if to summon up tactile memories, telling Marcus to make the chest larger, or the nose slightly longer, or the curvature of the calves more pronounced.

Having sculpted Antinous from life, Marcus trusted his memories of the youth's appearance; sometimes Hadrian's suggestions struck him as dubious, but Marcus did as he was told. Hadrian was pleased, and sometimes so shaken by the verisimilitude of the image that he wept. Strangely, to Marcus, their collaborative creation seemed to resemble more closely the god of his dreams than his recollection of the living Antinous.

At last came the day of the unveiling.

The statue would present no surprises to Hadrian, since he had overseen its creation from conception. Nonetheless, Marcus wished to make a formal unveiling, more for the benefit of his son than for the emperor. But young Lucius was late. Hadrian arrived ahead of the boy, but he did not seem to mind waiting. He strolled about the workshop, fiddling with various objects and taking deep breaths.

"Caesar has much on his mind today," observed Marcus. The two of them had grown increasingly comfortable in each other's presence. Hadrian now regularly unburdened himself to Marcus.

"The Jewish revolt," said Hadrian. It was the problem that most preoccupied him these days. "It's like the hydra: cut off one head and two more take its place. People continue to die by the tens of thousands. As long as a significant number of Jews persist in their belief that this firebrand Simon Bar Kochba is their long-awaited Messiah, there seems to be no way to suppress the revolt, short of complete extermination, of the sort that Trajan practiced in Dacia. But that's not possible in the case of the Jews; they're scattered all over the empire. The only long-term solution is to somehow assimilate these people, whether they wish to be assimilated or not. Toward that end, I've enacted a ban on their practice of amputating their foreskins. For reasons which defy comprehension, they attach some religious significance to this barbaric procedure. It's yet another way by which they deliberately set themselves apart. For their own good and to put an end to these insurrections, they must put aside their primitive religion and embrace the true gods, like the rest of the world."

"I understand you've renamed the province," said Marcus.

"The region that was Judaea is now to be called Syria Palestina, just as

Jerusalem is now Aelia Capitolina. These things make a difference—names and symbols and such."

"And Caesar's problems with the Christians?" said Marcus. This was another concern occasionally mentioned by the emperor.

Hadrian scoffed. "My travails with the Christians are as nothing compared to the trouble stirred up by the Jews. Some of my advisers lump the two groups together, but such thinking is ignorant and out of date; a great many Christians are not and never were Jews. Like the Jews, their atheism sets them apart from their neighbors, but unlike the Jews, they seem to be quite meek; meekness is actually a part of their teachings. As long as their numbers remain small and they keep their heads down, I think Trajan's policy of 'ask not, tell not' is best."

"What does that mean, exactly?" said Marcus, to whom this dictum had never quite made sense.

"It means that Roman magistrates take action against the Christians only when there is a formal complaint against them. No complaint, no action."

"That would seem to put a great deal of power in the hands of their neighbors," noted Marcus.

"If the Christians persist in their perversity, then they must live or die at the discretion of the decent, law-abiding majority." Hadrian put down the clay model he was examining and raised an eyebrow. "Wasn't one of your relatives a Christian?"

"I hardly think so," said Marcus with a laugh. His denial was genuine. Marcus had never been told about his Christian great-uncle.

"Oh, no, I'm quite sure about this," said Hadrian, who had reviewed every aspect of the imperial dossier on Marcus when he was deciding the fate of Apollodorus. "As a matter of fact, isn't that talisman you wear some sort of Christian amulet? I've always presumed it was handed down from the Christian in your family, and worn by you for sentimental rather than religious reasons, since you yourself clearly are not a Christian."

"A Christian symbol? My fascinum? Certainly not!" Marcus touched the fascinum. "This heirloom was given to me by father in the presence of yourself and the Divine Trajan. The fascinum long predates the first appearance of the Christians."

"Calm yourself, Pygmalion! Perhaps I'm mistaken about your amulet.

Nonetheless, I can assure you that the brother of your grandfather was indeed a Christian. I can't recall his name at the moment, but I know for a fact that he was executed by Nero after the Great Fire. It must have been quite a scandal at the time. That's probably why you never heard about it. Families have a way of falling silent about the scandals in their past; the children are the last to find out, if they ever do. If you don't believe me, ask your friend Suetonius the next time you see him. In his research, he's certain to have come across the Pinarius who was a Christian."

"With respect, Caesar, Suetonius is not my friend," said Marcus, flustered and taken aback by these revelations.

"No? Didn't Suetonius send you a personally inscribed copy of his imperial biographies?" Was there anything Hadrian didn't know, thanks to the vast network of imperial spies?

Marcus cleared his throat. "Yes, Suetonius sent me a copy—but I didn't ask for it, and I swear I've never read it."

"No? You should. It's not bad. Rather smutty, but I suppose the salacious details are what keep most readers scrolling forward. Ah, but I think your son has finally arrived."

They turned at a sound from the vestibule. Amyntas entered first, looking a bit shamefaced from fear that Marcus would blame him for the delay. Before he could speak, Apollodora swept into the room, wearing her best stola. She had never forgiven Hadrian for the death of her father, but in his presence she had been careful never to show a trace of bitterness. She was followed by Lucius, who at eleven was very big for his age, almost as tall as his father. Lucius's green eyes and fair hair had come from Marcus, but his build seemed to have come from his grandfather Apollodorus.

Glad to leave behind the emperor's unsettling revelations about a Christian relative, Marcus proceeded with the unveiling. He strode to the statue and pulled away the sailcloth.

Hadrian seemed to see the statue as if for the first time. He gazed at it for a long time, then reached out to touch it. Marcus saw on his face the same expression of awe he had displayed when he first saw the Melancomas statue, long ago.

"You captured him, Pinarius," Hadrian whispered. "You've done the impossible. Now you must do it again."

"Again, Caesar?"

"We must make more images. Each slightly different, so as to capture different aspects of his divinity, but all as true to life as this one. They can serve as models to the others who will make images of him all across the empire. Are you up for it, Pinarius?"

"Nothing would please me more, Caesar," said Marcus, with a quaver in his voice. The prospect of dedicating his time and talent to the creation of more such images—which to Marcus were as much an expression of devotion to his dream-god as to Hadrian's beloved—filled him with happiness.

"I'm glad your son is here today," said Hadrian. "To show my gratitude, I want to offer a very special opportunity to young Lucius. Recently, casting horoscopes, I discovered a curious fact: your son was born on the very same day as one of my protégés, Marcus Verus. Since the boys are exactly the same age—almost to the minute—I propose that we introduce your Lucius to young Verissimus—"

"Verissimus, Caesar?"

"I call Verus that sometimes. He so loves Truth that I can't resist punning on his name. Well, if Lucius and Verus are compatible, the two can be educated together."

Marcus looked at Lucius, who seemed a bit overwhelmed at this idea. "I fear my son might be at a disadvantage, Caesar. I've tried to provide good tutors for him, but his education thus far could hardly have rivaled that of your protégé."

Hadrian smiled. "Don't worry, I'm not expecting Lucius to provide competition in the fields of scholarship. Verus has a prodigious intellect; sometimes the breadth of his knowledge surprises even me. But Verus also loves every kind of sport. He could use a companion his own age for boxing, wrestling, ball games, riding, hunting, and so forth. What do you say?"

It occurred to Marcus that his son might be more than a match for young Verus in any sort of athletic competition; Lucius was uncommonly big and strong for his age. Marcus looked to Apollodora, whose eyes were wide with excitement. Despite her bitterness against the emperor, she could see what a tremendous opportunity was being offered to their son. At the age of eleven, Lucius Pinarius would be admitted into the innermost circle of the imperial court.

❧

Lucius was too young to wear a toga, but he did own a very finely made tunic that Marcus deemed suitable for his meeting with Verus. Apollodora fretted that the boy's recent spurts of growth had rendered the long sleeves a bit too short, but Marcus told her not to worry. "They're not as fussy about such things at the House of the People as you might think," he said.

"The House of the People?" Apollodora laughed. "No one but you calls it that anymore, husband."

"No?"

"I'm pretty sure all that pandering to the common folk ended when Plotina died."

"I stand corrected. Well, then, Lucius, are you ready for our visit to the House of Hadrian?"

A courtier met them at the entrance to the imperial palace at the appointed hour and escorted them to a lush garden with splashing fountains. It was here, for the time being, that the statue of Antinous had been installed. On a stone bench beside the statue sat Hadrian with the boy Marcus Verus, who was his distant cousin and a great-great-grandnephew of Trajan. The curly-headed Verus had a prominent nose and a small mouth. He had been brought up in the most rarefied atmosphere imaginable, surrounded by philosophers and scholars of great renown, and he carried himself with a composure beyond his years.

Hadrian introduced Verus to Marcus and his son. When Lucius expressed his honor at such a meeting, as his father had coached him to do, Verus shook his head. "The honor is mine, to meet a fellow my own age whose grandfather was a friend of the great Apollonius of Tyana." He turned to Marcus. "Did your father have many tales to tell about Apollonius?"

"As a matter of fact, no day passed without his recitation of a story about Apollonius. My father called him Teacher, and was greatly devoted to him, in life and in death."

Verus looked genuinely excited. "You must share those stories with me! They should be written down."

"Alas, my hand was meant for a chisel, not a stylus," said Marcus.

"But you must dictate those stories to a slave. The people who actually knew Apollonius are almost all dead now—"

"Adorable, isn't he?" said Hadrian, who reached out to muss the boy's hair. Verus responded with a very boyish roll of his eyes. "I'm thinking someone should sculpt him at this age. Perhaps you could find time to do it, Marcus, though I hate to interrupt your work on the next statue of Antinous."

"It would be my pleasure, Caesar." Marcus looked at the boy and envisioned at once the expression he would try to capture in stone—a mixture of innocence and wisdom, sophistication and guilelessness.

"I understand that your father was also a close friend of the late . . ." The boy hesitated and looked to Hadrian for guidance.

"Verissimus realizes that you cannot yet have heard the news, which arrived just this morning by imperial courier," said Hadrian. "Epictetus is dead."

Marcus drew a breath and lowered his eyes. "Truly, he was the very last of my father's circle."

Verus took Marcus's hand. "Perhaps we can find comfort in the words of Epictetus himself: 'We are disturbed not by events, but by the views which we take of them.' Is that not true, even of the death of loved ones?"

Marcus smiled ruefully. "I'm not the philosopher my father was. I'm not even sure what those words mean."

"If you are pained by an occurrence outside yourself, it is not that occurrence which disturbs you, but your own judgment about it. And it is in your power to wipe out that judgment *now*." Verus spoke with extraordinary conviction for one so young.

"Well spoken, Verissimus!" said Hadrian. He turned to Marcus. "The genealogists tell me the boy is descended from wise King Numa, and I think they must be right."

Marcus nodded. How was his awkward, taciturn son ever to keep up with the likes of young Verus?

"I propose that these two boys should spend some time with me at Tibur," said Hadrian. "What would you say to a bit of riding and hunting, Lucius?"

"Apollonius of Tyana was opposed to the killing of animals," said Lucius gravely.

Hadrian laughed. "Excellent! You and Verissimus have a ready-made subject for debate: can a lover of philosophy also enjoy the hunt? You shall come, too, Pygmalion. I've selected a site for the tomb of Antinous, and there are a number of other sites I want to show you—for the baths, the library, the great pool . . ."

"It will be an honor, Caesar." Marcus raised his eyes to the statue of Antinous, the god who had brought him so much good fortune.

A.D. 136

On the sixth day before the Nones of Maius, Marcus Pinarius and his son, Lucius, stood among the crowd of courtiers who filled the porticoes surrounding the ancient Auguratorium on the Palatine Hill. Before the altar, the emperor himself performed the augury to mark the passage to manhood of Marcus Verus, who stood in the middle of the gravel-strewn courtyard, wearing his first toga.

At fifteen, however mature his intellect, Verus still had no beard, and his delicate features were closer to those of a boy than a man. Hadrian's beard and hair had more gray than ever, and his face had an unhealthy pallor; it seemed to Marcus that the emperor looked considerably older than sixty. It was rumored that Hadrian was suffering a serious illness. He had begun construction on his own mausoleum.

Marcus was involved in the building of the new mausoleum. "All the other imperial tombs are already full," Hadrian had told him, "and I have no intention of spending eternity crammed next to Trajan inside the Column." The structure was to be a vast circular building not unlike the mausoleum of Augustus in design, but much larger, located on the banks of the Tiber across from the Field of Mars. It seemed to Marcus that Hadrian could not be content unless he had some vast building project under way. Now that the Temple of Venus and Roma was at last completed, along with the Pantheon with its magnificent dome and the sprawling imperial villa at Tibur, what was left to build except his mausoleum?

At the dedication ceremonies for all those grand projects, Marcus had been among a select group of architects and artists who had received the emperor's highest accolades, but those honors could not compare to the one that was to be bestowed on the Pinarii this day. No sooner had Hadrian taken the auspices for Marcus Verus, declaring them to be highly favorable, than he called out the name of Lucius Pinarius and asked him to step forward.

Lucius looked down at his father—at fifteen, he was already slightly taller than Marcus—with an expression of sudden terror. The boy's combination of athleticism and shyness had made him an ideal companion for Verus; their differences complemented each other. But this was no time to be timid. Marcus cast a look at the boy that he hoped was at once stern and supportive, then gave him a tiny shove to start him on his way.

Lucius stepped forward, hesitantly at first, but then with greater confidence. Instead of standing in place, Verus stepped forward to greet his friend. Hadrian made no objection to this lapse of decorum; he had grown quite fond of Lucius in recent months, and it had been his idea to make the donning of the manly toga a dual ceremony including both young men.

However awkward he might feel wearing it, Lucius looked splendid in his toga, Marcus thought. To him, the boy disproved the popular notion that humanity was in decline, dwindling in intellect and physical prowess with each generation. It seemed to Marcus that his son combined all that was best from the bloodlines of his parents, and Marcus could see no reason why Lucius should not surpass his ancestors in every way. Before the most important people in Roma, the emperor himself took the auspices, declared them favorable, and announced that Lucius Pinarius, son of Marcus Pinarius, had attained all the privileges and duties of a citizen of the greatest city on earth.

Among those who converged on the young men to congratulate them was the man whom Hadrian had recently adopted and named as his successor. Lucius Ceionius was in his middle thirties, too old to attract the sexual attentions of the emperor but nonetheless a wildly handsome man with a statuesque physique. As Hadrian had once remarked to Marcus

Pinarius, "In the whole empire, there is no handsomer man than Lucius Ceionius."

"Surely that's not the reason you picked him to be your successor," Marcus had responded, in jest.

"Don't be so certain of that," Hadrian said. "If beauty is a sign of divine favor, then Ceionius has it in abundance. Sometimes, when I look at him, I think I've adopted a god, not a son."

It struck Marcus that Ceionius, on this day, did not look particularly well; he had the same unhealthy pallor as Hadrian, and while Marcus looked on, the man suffered a fit of coughing so violent that he had to leave the courtyard. Hadrian watched him depart with a worried look. Someone leaned toward Marcus and spoke in his ear:

> *O handsome youth, the blissful vision of a day,*
> *No sooner glimpsed than snatched away.*

"Favonius!" said Marcus. "Leave it to you to twist the words of Virgil into an ill omen."

"Virgil? I had no idea," said the scurra. "I was quoting the emperor, actually. I overheard him utter those lines earlier today, when poor Ceionius first appeared."

"Is he seriously ill?"

"Caesar seems to think so. I'm told he cast a horoscope for Ceionius and the results were most alarming. Poor Hadrian! Just when he had the future all neatly planned out, with the empire cordoned off, and his temples finished, and his mausoleum under way, and the next emperor selected— poof! Fate deals an unforeseen reversal. Congratulations, by the way, on your son's ascent to manhood, and in such esteemed company. The future of the Pinarii looks very bright."

"Thank you." Marcus was irritated by the man's flippancy but managed a gracious nod.

"Almost as bright, if I may say so, as that curious bauble at your breast. How the gold catches the sunlight!"

Marcus reached up to touch the fascinum, which on this day he was wearing outside his toga, for all to see, since this was the last occasion on which he would ever wear it.

"You'll excuse me now," he said. "I need to go to my son."

Hadrian was already conducting the two young men to a private chamber just off the Auguratorium. For the ceremony that was to follow, Marcus had requested that no witnesses be present except the emperor and young Verus.

The small, quiet room was sparsely decorated. Dominating one wall was a bust of Antinous set in a niche. This, too, had been Marcus's request, that the only image present should be that of the Divine Youth.

While the emperor and Verus stood to one side, Marcus approached his son. Now that the public ceremony was over, Lucius looked quite relaxed. He smiled as Marcus lifted the chain over his neck and held the fascinum aloft.

"My son, you've seen this amulet many times, hanging from my neck. Before me, my father wore it, and before him, his father. The fascinum has been in our family for many generations, even before the founding of the city. It has protected us, guided us, given us strength in times of trouble. You are a man now, with all the uncertainties of life ahead of you. On this day, I wish to pass the fascinum to you, so that you may never face those uncertainties alone. As it has guided me, so let it now guide you. And just as it was given to me in the presence of the emperor—the Divine Trajan—so I wish to give it to you, here before Caesar."

Marcus placed the chain over his son's head. It was strange to see the gold talisman glimmering upon another breast, and for a moment Marcus felt a pang of regret. Had his father felt the same regret when he gave up the fascinum? If so, he had never spoken of it, and neither would Marcus.

For an hour or so, before the banquet was to begin, the young men were left to themselves.

"I don't know about you," said Verus, "but I'm taking off this toga and changing into something less cumbersome."

"You shall just have to put it on again for the banquet," said Lucius. "Besides, I have nothing to change into."

"You can wear one of my tunics, though it may be a bit short for you.

No matter, we're men now, and allowed to show our legs. Let's go to my rooms."

A statue of Minerva met them as they entered Verus's apartments. Around a corner, a bust of Socrates had pride of place upon a pedestal. On the ceilings and walls there were no paintings of warfare or scenes of seduction, or of maidens dancing or gladiators fighting; indeed, there were no paintings at all. The walls had been colored a placid sky blue, a color that was conducive to study and philosophical discussion, according to Verus.

As they discarded their togas and put on tunics, Verus's attention was drawn to the fascinum at his friend's breast. He asked to touch it.

"Can it really be as old as your father says?"

"So the Divine Claudius believed."

Verus nodded gravely. "Few men were more knowledgeable about the distant past than the Divine Claudius. How remarkable, that this object must have been in existence in the days of King Numa, and even before, in the age when demigods like Hercules walked the earth. What a wondrous thing, that you have this link to your ancestors. One of them must have worn it when Hannibal and his elephants crossed the Alps, and another when the Divine Julius was slain by assassins. Where will you keep it when you're not wearing it?"

"You've seen the shrine in the vestibule of our house. Among the niches that display the wax masks of the ancestors, there's one niche where we keep a small capsa that contains all the letters my grandfather received from Apollonius of Tyana, and the manacle that Apollonius cast off, and a small bust of Antinous made by my father. That's where the fascinum is kept."

Verus nodded. He had asked and been allowed to read the letters from Apollonius, but had been rather disappointed by them. A great teacher Apollonius must have been; a great writer he was not. The letters were nothing more than brief messages of encouragement, enthusiastic but without any philosophical content, and frequently ungrammatical. The manacle had impressed Verus even less; it looked like any rusty piece of iron, and he secretly wondered if it was genuine. As for Antinous, Verus did not share Hadrian's fascination for beautiful young males, and, though he was too circumspect to say so, he had little enthusiasm for the cult of the Divine Youth.

But the fascinum was another matter. To Verus it seemed a truly wondrous object, a repository of all the mysteries of the past, all the more intriguing because time had worn away its features yet was powerless to diminish its golden luster.

Lucius had shown him the fascinum. It seemed to Verus that he should show his friend something equally marvelous. "Follow me," he said.

They made their way to a part of the imperial palace that Lucius had never seen before. It soon became evident that they had entered a forbidden area; in a whisper, Verus told him to be silent, and whenever anyone passed, Verus pulled him out of sight.

They came to a locked door. To Lucius's amazement, Verus produced a small metal device and proceeded to pick the lock.

They proceeded down a long hallway and came to another locked door, which Verus picked with equal ease.

Once inside, Verus quietly closed the door behind them. They were in a stone vault. Narrow slits set high in the walls admitted bright beams of sunlight. Even before his eyes adjusted to the dimness that swallowed most of the room, Lucius saw that it was lined to the height of his waist with wooden cabinets, and atop the cabinets were objects that shone with bright points of colored light.

"This is the jewel room," Verus whispered.

Surrounding them was a vast collection of gemstones. Most were stored inside the cabinets, but some of the more spectacular examples were displayed on stands or hung on the wall or simply lay atop the cabinets, left there by Hadrian or Sabina or whatever courtier was allowed to handle such precious objects. Some were cut into cameos. Some were faceted and set as jewels into necklaces or bracelets of silver and gold. Some were in their natural state. There were rubies and sapphires, emeralds and lapis lazuli, amethyst and jasper, carnelian and agate, tiger's-eye and amber.

"Hadrian didn't acquire all these in his travels, did he?" whispered Lucius.

"Oh, no. These have been collected by generations of emperors. Nero ended up in such dire straits that he sold off most of the gems he inherited, but Vespasian and his successors managed to recover many of them. Do you see that carnelian necklace? Queen Cleopatra was wearing it the day she died. Augustus was furious that she killed herself, and took it off her with his own hands, as a trophy."

"I never imagined such a collection existed." Lucius was astounded by the treasure. He had seen the emperor's sprawling villa go up at Tibur. He had stood beside his father at the dedications of the Temple of Venus and Roma and of the Pantheon, the largest and grandest buildings ever constructed. That the wealth of Hadrian was immense he had always known, but now, gazing at the splendors that surrounded him, he realized that the emperor's fortune surpassed all reckoning.

"Very few people have ever seen this room," said Verus. "Even fewer have seen this." He opened a cabinet and pulled out a stone that he held between two fingers, thrusting it into the nearest beam of sunlight.

To Lucius, it seemed that the stone must have come from a world of dreams. It was octahedral and as large as a walnut. The stone was transparent yet captured the light and cast it back again in a dazzling array of colors. Lucius had never seen anything like it.

"It's called a diamond," said Verus. "This is by far the largest and most perfect specimen ever found. It's not only beautiful but indestructible. Fire will not burn it. No blade can cut it."

"Where did it come from?"

"We think Domitian acquired it. He had such a penchant for secrecy that no one knows its history, but it must have come from India, which is the source of all true diamonds. Nerva presented it to Trajan as a sign of his favor. Trajan presented it to Hadrian as a reward for leading the First Legion Minerva. It's the rarest jewel in all the collection, which means in all the world."

"It's amazing," said Lucius.

"I myself have little interest in gemstones," said Verus, "or in any of the other trappings of wealth. Material objects possess no intrinsic value, only that which men assign to them. And yet, when I gaze upon a thing as beautiful and perfect as this, I think it must in some way be a manifestation of that which Apollonius called the Divine Singularity."

"I could stare at it for hours," said Lucius. "Thank you for showing it to me."

Verus smiled. "And yet, the most precious thing in this room is not this diamond, but that object you wear upon your breast."

"Do you really think so?" Lucius looked down at the fascinum, which seemed to him a fragile, crudely fashioned thing compared to the adamantine perfection of the diamond. He could scarcely believe that Verus was serious, but it was not like his friend to joke about such a thing.

"I truly think so. I speak not just as Marcus Verus, your friend, but as Verissimus, who loves Truth above all else."

A.D. 138

The month of Junius had been uncommonly hot. The month of Julius promised to be even hotter. Wearing his toga and wiping sweat from his brow, Marcus Pinarius made his way to the imperial palace in answer to the emperor's summons.

He was sweating because the day was hot, he told himself; a man in his fifties should be carried in a sedan on such a day rather than travel on foot. But in fact, Marcus was also quite nervous. He had not seen the emperor for months, and these days, a summons to the palace was a cause not for celebration but for grave misgivings. Hadrian was now sixty-two. His health was rapidly declining, and his illness had brought out a dangerous, even murderous side of his personality. The vow he had made more than twenty years ago to kill no senators had fallen by the wayside. An atmosphere of gloom and fear had settled over everyone who had dealings with the emperor.

Marcus was conducted not to a reception hall but to the emperor's private quarters. The courtier left him in a room with a balcony perched above a garden. The bright sunlight from the balcony at first blinded Marcus to the contents of the room; only gradually did he perceive the sumptuous furnishings, the elegant statues, the paintings on the walls—and the fact that he was not alone. A figure in silhouette was seated on a couch with his back to the sunlight. For a moment, Marcus mistook the man for Hadrian—his hair and beard were much the same—but the man's posture was that of a younger man. Marcus gasped, thinking for just an instant that he was seeing Ceionius, who had died on the Kalends of Januarius. It was rumored that the man's lemur still lingered in the palace, held back by the anguish of Hadrian's mourning.

But this man was older than Ceionius had been, and younger than Hadrian—perhaps in his forties—and he appeared to be in the best of health, despite the strained look on his face. "You must be Marcus Pinarius," he said quietly. "I'm Titus Aurelius Antoninus. I don't think we've met, but I believe you're acquainted with my nephew, young Marcus Verus. Or rather, my son, as I suppose I should call him now."

So this was the man whom Hadrian, bitterly disappointed at the death of Ceionius and pressed by the imminence of his own death, had named to be his successor. Determined to control the succession even after his own death, Hadrian had required Antoninus to adopt as heirs the son of the late Ceionius and also young Marcus Verus. Verus had taken his new father's name and so was now Marcus Aurelius, third in the line of succession.

The forced adoptions had not been Hadrian's only gambit in his bid to control the future. He seemed determined to move or remove numerous people around him, like tokens on a game board. In his depressed, bed-ridden state, obsessed with protecting the succession, he had resorted to executing or forcing suicide on a number of men he considered too ambitious. The latest and most scandalous of these deaths had been the forced suicide of his ninety-year-old brother-in-law, Servianus, whom Hadrian suspected of seeking to advance his grandson. The death of the empress Sabina had also sparked a scandal: some of her relatives dared to whisper that Hadrian had poisoned her.

"I was told that Caesar asked for me," said Marcus.

Antoninus nodded. "It was the first thing he requested when he woke this morning."

"I pray that I may find Caesar in better health than when I last saw him," said Marcus.

"I presume that's your tactful way of inquiring about his condition. You'll see for yourself soon enough. Try not to be shocked at his appearance. His entire body is swollen with fluid. His face is so bloated you may hardly recognize him. They say something similar happened to Trajan, near the end."

"May I inquire about Caesar's state of mind?"

Antoninus gave him a piercing look. "You've known him a very long time, so I won't lie to you. In recent days, he's tried several times to take his own life. First he ordered a slave to stab him. When the slave refused, he tried to stab himself, but he was too weak. Then he sought poison from a doctor. 'Caesar asks me to be his murderer,' said the poor man, and Hadrian quoted Sophocles to him: 'I ask you to be my healer, the only physician who can cure my suffering'—the words of Hercules from *The Women of Trachis,* dying in agony and begging his son to set him afire. The doctor refused to give him poison, whereupon Caesar ordered that the man should be executed, along with everyone else who had thwarted his suicide attempts."

Marcus wiped fresh beads of sweat from his brow. "And was the doctor executed?"

"Of course not. I simply removed the offending persons from Caesar's presence and replaced them with others. They all have strict orders to keep close watch on Caesar and prevent any further suicide attempts. Meanwhile, since his physicians have failed to cure him, Caesar has called upon a series of wonder-workers and magicians. Mostly charlatans, I have no doubt, but just lately Caesar seems a little better. He insists that he's well enough to travel. He intends to depart for Baiae tomorrow. He says the sea air will improve his health. Before he goes, he wants to see you."

Antoninus escorted him to the door of the bedchamber. He opened it but stayed where he was, indicating that Marcus should enter alone.

Curtains had been pulled to block the sunlight. By the glow of several lamps, Marcus saw the grotesquely swollen figure of the emperor on the bed. A statue of Antinous, not quite life-size, stood on a pedestal at the foot of the bed, looking down on the emperor.

As Antoninus had warned him, the edema made Hadrian almost unrecognizable—his cheeks and chin and even his forehead were massively swollen, while his eyes and mouth looked small and pinched. But when he spoke, his voice was the same, except that a hint of his old Spanish accent kept breaking through.

"Pygmalion! Is that you?"

"It is. Caesar wished to see me?"

"Yes. Come closer. You're looking well, Pinarius. No, don't bother to return the compliment. I shudder to think what I must look like. You'll notice that Antoninus has thoughtfully removed all the mirrors from this room." Hadrian managed a weak laugh.

Marcus was surprised to find him in such good spirits. Was this the bitter man who had been ordering executions right and left?

"I called you here, Pinarius, because I wanted to thank you for all you've done for me over the years, and especially for your service to the worship of Antinous. The Divine Youth has no follower more devoted than you. The images you've created will outlast us all. The flesh is all we know in this life, but the flesh grows old and withers and rots, as I know only too well. Only perfection is immortal, and we were blessed by the god to witness perfection, and to touch it, you and I."

Speaking wearied him. Hadrian paused to rest for a while, then went on. "Have a look at the object on the table over there, by the window. Open the curtains, if you need more light."

On the table, Marcus saw a model of the new mausoleum. When he parted the curtains, he saw that the window framed a distant view of the building itself on the far side of the Tiber. Construction was well under way, but whatever decoration the emperor had in mind for the top of the huge circular building had remained a mystery—until now. The top of the model was fitted with a statue of Hadrian riding a chariot pulled by four horses. Marcus gaped. Judging by the scale of the model, the quadriga sculpture would be one of the largest statues ever made. Though not as tall, the sheer mass of the thing would rival the Colossus of Sol.

"What do you think, Pygmalion?"

"May I ask who made this model, Caesar?"

"I made it myself, with these swollen fingers of mine. Yes, it's a crude thing, but I never called myself a sculptor. The details I'll leave to a true artist—to you, Pinarius. So? What do you think?"

"Are the proportions of the statue to the mausoleum correctly rendered?"

"Closely enough."

Marcus frowned. "The mausoleum rises to almost sixty feet. This statue is very nearly as tall as the structure upon which it stands. Is Caesar aware of just how large the full-scale piece would be?"

"I am."

"But how is such a huge monument to be built? How is it to be transported and assembled atop the mausoleum? The enormous amount of bronze required—"

"I leave those petty details to you, Pygmalion!" Hadrian snapped. His face turned dark red and his eyes were reduced to two baleful points of light. For a moment Marcus imagined that the man's head might actually burst, like a grape squeezed between two fingers.

Then Hadrian laughed. "Listen to me! Did you hear that accent? Thicker than Trajan's! When I think of all those hours I spent with my elocution teachers, reading Cicero aloud until I was hoarse. Numa's balls, I haven't sounded so much like a Spaniard since I was a boy. That was so long ago. . . ." He closed his eyes and drifted off.

Marcus stared at him for a long time. What would Apollonius of Tyana have made of Hadrian? Certainly he was infinitely better than Domitian, and more knowledgeable of philosophy than Trajan, but if philosophy reconciled a man to life and prepared him to face death, then in Hadrian all the lessons of philosophy came to naught. As death approached, he was more tied to the material world than ever, craving a monument larger than anyone else's and determined to decide who would rule after him even to the second generation. Life obsessed him; death to him was unacceptable—his own death no less than the death of his beloved Antinous, whom Hadrian had sought to keep alive by populating the whole world with his image.

Perhaps no emperor could truly be a philosopher, since his duty was to care so deeply about the material world and the mortals in it, but Hadrian had come as close as anyone. Perhaps Hadrian, with all his flaws, was as good a ruler as the world could ever hope to see. Would Antoninus do a better job? Would young Marcus Aurelius, if he ever came to power?

Reflexively, Marcus reached to touch the fascinum, but it was not at his breast. The fascinum belonged to Lucius now. To the Divine Youth who looked over him, he whispered aloud, "I am a fortunate man, to have lived in such an age, and under such an emperor."

"What's that?" Hadrian muttered. He opened his eyes. "Are you still here, Pygmalion?"

"I am, Caesar."

"I almost forgot to tell you. I've made you a senator."

"I, Caesar?"

"Why not?"

"There are some in the Senate who'll say that a mere sculptor has no place among them."

"Who cares what those useless creatures think? I say you're a senator, and so you are. You've served me as well as any general or magistrate—better than most. And never forget that your grandfather was elevated to the Senate by the Divine Claudius, and that his father was a senator, and that your great-great-grandfather was one of the three heirs of Julius Caesar. So from now on, you are Senator Pinarius—except when I make a slip and call you Senator Pygmalion."

Marcus smiled. "Thank you, Caesar."

"I've also named you to the priesthood of Antinous."

"I, a priest?"

"Religious service is in your blood: you come from a long line of augurs. In essence you're already a priest of Antinous, so you might as well enjoy the title, and the stipend, along with the duties."

"What duties?"

"You will make more images of Antinous so as to propagate his worship."

"I'll do my best, Caesar."

Hadrian closed his eyes. His breathing slowed. Marcus thought he slept, but then he began to speak, very softly. He was reciting a poem. Perhaps he had composed it himself; Marcus had never heard it before.

> *Sweet soul that inhabits this clay,*
> *Soon you will flit away.*
> *Where will you go? To what place*
> *dark and cold and stripped of grace,*
> *never again to laugh and play?*

Hadrian sighed and fell asleep. Marcus quietly left the room.

The next day, the emperor and his retinue left for Baiae. Ten days later, word reached Roma that Hadrian was dead.

Antoninus, who had been running the state in Caesar's absence, departed at once for Baiae to look after the remains and bring them back to Roma. It fell to young Marcus Aurelius to oversee preparations for the funeral rites, including the gladiator games in honor of the dead.

Upon his return to Roma, Antoninus was recognized as emperor by unanimous declaration of the Senate. "May he be even luckier than Augustus!" they shouted. "May he be even better than Trajan!"

Hadrian's final months left a bitter taste in the mouths of many senators. There was a movement to annul many of his final acts—including the naming of several of his favorites to places in the Senate and other high positions. Antoninus said these annulments would dishonor the memory of his adoptive father and refused to allow them. He insisted that the Senate should deify Hadrian, despite widespread reluctance. Thus, Marcus Pinarius retained his status as a senator and a priest of Antinous, and the late emperor became the Divine Hadrian.

A.D. 141

The construction and decoration of the mausoleum of Hadrian was at last complete. On this day the late emperor's remains were to be officially interred.

To reach the mausoleum, a new bridge had been built across the Tiber. The bridge offered an impressive view of the huge structure, and it was here that the emperor Antoninus and a host of dignitaries assembled for the ceremony. Along with Hadrian, the remains of the empress Sabina and of Hadrian's onetime heir, Ceionius, would also be interred.

For Marcus Pinarius, dressed in his senatorial toga, the occasion marked the pinnacle of his long career; it also provided a rare moment to simply stop and catch his breath. Marcus had never been so busy in his life, not even during the hectic years of the Dacian campaigns, when he was Apollodorus's assistant. He regularly attended meetings of the Senate in Roma. He made frequent trips to the villa at Tibur to oversee the worship of Antinous, and he made new images of the Divine Youth whenever the inspiration struck him. But most of his efforts in the last few years had been consumed by the design and construction of the massive statue atop Hadrian's mausoleum. The images of Antinous were unquestionably the most beautiful of all the works Marcus had made, the closest he would ever come to creating perfection, but the quadriga statue with Hadrian was by far the grandest.

Constructing a work on such an immense scale had been one challenge; creating a sculpture of sufficient grandeur to properly honor Hadrian was another. As he stood on the new bridge, listening with only one ear to the endless speeches and invocations, Marcus gazed up at the gigantic sculptural group and felt tremendous satisfaction. Apollodorus would have said that the statue was much too big, its bulk reducing the mausoleum beneath to a mere pedestal, making the whole structure appear top-heavy. But Marcus had resisted the temptation to revise Hadrian's model and had stayed true to the emperor's wishes, though he had employed various tricks of perspective to give the figures a more pleasing proportion when seen from the ground. Over the last few days Marcus had ventured all over the Seven Hills and out on the roads that radiated from the city, seeing what the sculpture looked like from various viewpoints and distances. For sheer prominence, Hadrian in his quadriga rivaled the Temple of Jupiter atop the Capitoline, the Colossus of Sol, and even the Flavian Amphitheater. Indeed, Marcus had chanced upon one vantage point, north of the city, from which nothing of Roma could be seen except the quadriga; the illusion of seeing a titanic figure riding a gigantic chariot across a landscape devoid of humanity had been complete. As an artist, Marcus had known no moment of greater satisfaction, not even when gazing upon his images of the Divine Youth.

Next to Marcus stood Apollodora. Her features were those of an aging Eastern beauty, but she displayed the inscrutable expression of a true Roman matron. Marcus had no idea what she was feeling. It had been a long time since she had expressed resentment or grief about her father's death.

Next to her was Lucius, who had continued to grow until he was a head taller than his father. Lucius was wearing the fascinum, though the amulet was hidden under the folds of his toga. He saw his son exchange glances with young Verus—or Aurelius, as everyone now called him.

The emperor himself had recently acquired a new cognomen. He was Antoninus Pius now, so named by the Senate, ostensibly in recognition of his filial piety in discharging his duties to his adoptive father, including his insistence that the Senate vote divine honors to Hadrian; but many people thought the granting of the cognomen Pius was to thank Antoninus for saving the lives of a number of senators whom Hadrian would otherwise have put to death in the last days of his reign. "I'd rather save the life of one innocent citizen than take the lives of a thousand enemies," Antoninus had remarked. He had none of Hadrian's restlessness or brooding nature; he was known for a placid temperament and a gentle sense of humor. Under his benevolent rule, the bitterness that had marked the end of Hadrian's reign had almost faded from memory.

At last the speeches and rituals were done. Antoninus Pius carried the urn containing the ashes of Hadrian across the bridge and entered the mausoleum. In the vestibule, a niche housed a statue of Hadrian. To the right, a passageway lined with marble sloped gently upward as it followed a spiral course. The ramp made a full circle, ending in a chamber just above the entrance, and from this room another passage led to a circular chamber at the very center of the building. Niches had been carved in the wall to make room for the urns containing the ashes of Hadrian, Sabina, and Ceionius. The chamber was large enough to provide a resting place for many emperors to come. Thus, the mausoleum was both a monument to the past and an expression of faith in the future. Men died, but the empire of Roma would go on and on. Here was a place to house the remains of generations not yet born.

Marcus watched as Antoninus placed the urn in its niche. He felt the sense of sadness and release that comes with the ending of an era. Hadrian, the inveterate traveler, had reached the end of his final journey.

A banquet followed. Exhausted from standing all day, Marcus excused himself early. Apollodora left with him, but Lucius stayed behind, saying that he wanted to keep Aurelius company.

"How fortunate we are that those two have become such close friends," Marcus said to Apollodora as the litter carried them home. "For that happy outcome, as for so much else, we have the Divine Hadrian to thank."

Apollodora made no reply. She only nodded and closed her eyes, as if she was too tired to speak. When they arrived home, she went directly to bed.

Despite his weariness, Marcus felt restless. It was often so on days when he was called upon to take part in ceremonies and rituals; such events filled him with a nervous excitement that made it hard to sleep. He paced his garden for a while, then went to his library. Amyntas, knowing his master's habits and anticipating his needs, had left a lamp burning for him.

Marcus surveyed the scrolls in their pigeonholes, identified by dangling tags, and on a whim pulled out a volume from the late Suetonius's imperial biographies. Suetonius had recently come up in conversation with young Marcus Aurelius, who had expressed astonishment that Marcus had never read the man's work. "Are you telling me that you possess one of the very first copies, given to you by Suetonius himself, and you've never read it? Unbelievable! Really, you must read them."

Marcus located the other volumes and piled them on the table, then began to skim through the text. From the sternly moralistic Augustus, power had passed to the dour Tiberius, who had ended in utter debauchery and left the world at the mercy of the monstrous Caligula, whose bloody death had led to the reign of the hapless Claudius, cuckolded by one wife, Messalina, and probably murdered by another, Agrippina, who had put her son Nero on the throne and been rewarded with death. After Nero had come four emperors in quick succession: Galba, Otho, Vitellius, and then Vespasian, the bland but competent general who had left the empire to his sons, first the popular Titus, then the suspicious and cruel Domitian. There Suetonius's account ended, but Marcus needed no historian to tell him about the reigns of Nerva, Trajan, and Hadrian.

Marcus could see why the biographies were so popular. The stories told by Suetonius were brutal, funny, and shocking. The people he described were, for the most part, appalling. Had Caligula really given his horse Incitatus a stall of marble, a manger of ivory, purple blankets, and a collar of precious stones, all in preparation for making him a consul? Had Nero really tried to kill his mother by putting her on a collapsing boat? Had Domitian invited guests to a black room where he treated them like men already dead, and then released them, making a joke of their despair?

What amazing and terrible times Marcus's father and grandfather and great-grandfather had lived through—and how very little Marcus knew about their lives!

As the first faint light of dawn began to emanate from the garden, Marcus realized that he had been reading all night. He went to bed, thinking that an hour of sleep would be better than none, and dreamed of mad emperors.

※

When he woke, despite having slept so briefly, Marcus felt strangely energetic. After a leisurely breakfast with his wife and son, he invited Lucius to take a walk with him.

"Put on your toga," he said. "And wear the fascinum."

"Is this a special occasion, father?"

"Any walk across the city of Roma is a special occasion."

A litter carried them across the Field of Mars and deposited them at the new bridge that crossed the Tiber. Marcus wanted to gaze at the mausoleum without the distractions of a crowded ceremony. He had done so on many previous occasions, but that had been before Hadrian's remains were placed inside. The building seemed different to him now, more complete. Hadrian had desired a monument for the ages. Marcus had no doubt that the emperor's sepulcher would still be standing a thousand years hence.

Father and son walked to the Pantheon. They stepped inside to admire the statues of the gods and the extraordinary sense of light and space created by the lofty dome and the oculus that pierced it. Here, too, was a monument that would surely stand for all time, a worthy tribute to the gods and goddesses it celebrated.

Their stroll took them to the Flavian Amphitheater, the greatest gathering place ever created, where all Roma came to see and be seen and to witness spectacles of life and death. Nearby stood the Colossus of Sol, once a statue of Nero, which was the closest Nero had come to being deified. Marcus remembered the ambition of Apollodorus to construct an equally colossal statue of Luna; that dream had died forever along with his father-in-law. Apollodorus was hardly ever talked about in their household, due to the circumstances of his death. It occurred to Marcus that Lucius knew very little about either of his grandfathers. Marcus decided that he must make a point of telling his son all he knew about their ancestors, even the mysterious great-uncle who had been a Christian.

From the amphitheater it was only a short walk to the Temple of Venus and Roma. For years Marcus had labored to realize Hadrian's novel conception of a two-fronted temple; the result was surely one of the most splendid buildings on earth. In the sanctuary of Roma, priests were performing a rite in honor of the city. In the sanctuary of Venus, a newly wedded couple burned incense at the altar, praying to the goddess to bless their union.

"Look how happy they are," said Marcus. "You're of an age to marry now, son. Should I expect that someday soon—"

"Perhaps, father." The young man actually blushed. Thanks to his friendship with young Aurelius, chances were good that Lucius might join the house of Pinarius in marriage with one of the most prominent families in the city. Perhaps, once again, the Pinarii might serve as consuls and Vestals, as they had in the days of the kings and the first centuries of the Republic.

The steps of the temple took them down to the Sacred Way. They walked through the ancient Forum—found as bricks but left clad in marble by Augustus—and on to the much grander Forum of Trajan, where they ascended the spiral stairway to the top of Trajan's Column. This was Marcus's favorite view of the city. He remembered the day the statue of Trajan had been lowered into place, when disaster had very nearly struck. How young he had been then!

On the way back to their house on the Palatine, Marcus on a whim decided to drop by the Senate House, though there was no meeting that day. With Lucius beside him, he burned a bit of incense at the Altar of Victory and said a prayer. "Goddess, grant victory to Roma and defeat to her enemies. Watch over the empire which you delivered to Augustus. Protect Roma from all those who would cause her harm, whether from without or from within."

Why had he asked Lucius to take this walk with him? Reading Suetonius had given him the idea. The details were all a jumble in his head, but Marcus had been left with a vague impression that the world had progressed since the days of Augustus. In the rush of daily life, one tended to forget what a special place Roma was. One tended to forget, too, how strange was the past, and how much better, in every way, was the world of the present moment. Thinking of the outlandish tales of Suetonius, remembering the stories his father had told him, and reflecting on his own memories of a life that had begun in slavery but delivered him into the company of emperors and the care of the Divine Youth, it seemed to Marcus that the world had passed through a series of terrible trials to arrive at something resembling a perfect state, or as perfect as mortals could make it. He had done his part to create the stable, contented, truly civilized world that would be inherited by his son's generation. Time would pass, and the world of Hadrian would surely give way to the world of Marcus Aurelius—and then what?

Standing before the Altar of Victory with his son beside him, Senator Marcus Pinarius felt a rush of optimism. What did the future hold? Even the gods had no way of knowing.

AUTHOR'S NOTE

Empire is a novel about life in the city of Rome from the reign of Augustus, the first emperor, to the height of the empire under Hadrian; it spans the years A.D. 14 to 141. In a previous novel, *Roma,* I followed the same family line from the origin of the city to the rise of Augustus and the end of the Roman Republic.

In some ways, the time span portrayed in *Empire* is one of the most accessible periods of history. The major historians, including Suetonius, Tacitus, and Plutarch, are widely available to readers around the world in the original Latin or Greek or in numerous translations, and even the most minor written sources (inscriptions, fragments of poems, etc.) can be tracked down by a determined reader. The archaeological evidence is very rich: the entire city of Pompeii was preserved when Vesuvius buried it in A.D. 79, some of the major buildings of the era are still standing (such as the Pantheon), and excavations in the city of Rome continue to yield fresh finds, like the chamber believed to be the Lupercale of Augustus, the discovery of which was announced in January 2007. More evidence comes from numismatics, and worldwide trade in Roman coins on the Internet has made large, sharp images of even the most obscure coins widely accessible. With all these sources to draw on, the period is much favored by modern historians, who produce more books every year about the Roman Empire than any person could ever hope to read.

And yet, for the novelist, the period poses a special problem: the emperors. Or rather, emperor-centricism.

When I wrote *Roma,* I faced a very different challenge. The sources of information for the first thousand years of the city are far more limited, yet the narrative offered by those sources is almost unimaginably rich: legends of demigods and heroes, stories of social upheaval and violent class struggle, history as a pageant of powerful families, factions, and personalities all striving to fulfill their particular destinies. The challenge was somehow to find room for this teeming cast of characters in a single novel.

With the end of the Republic and the rise of autocratic rule, the storyline changes. Class conflict and individual heroes (and villains) recede. It's all about the emperors: their personalities, their families, their sexual habits, their often flamboyant lives and their sometimes bloody deaths. The story of Rome becomes a sequence of biographies of the men who ruled the empire. Everything and everyone else is secondary to the autocrat.

That's alright, if you want the emperors to be the focus of your fiction, as in Robert Graves's *I, Claudius* or Marguerite Yourcenar's *Memoirs of Hadrian.* But autocracies, where all power is concentrated in very few hands, where even the boldest generals serve at the whim of their master and even the best poets bend their talents to flatter the autocrat, do not produce the kind of larger-than-life heroes who populated *Roma,* like Coriolanus or Scipio Africanus. Instead, stripped of any hope of being able to affect the course of human events—or even their own lives—people seek diversion in spectacle and empowerment through magic, or they turn inward, pursuing mental or spiritual enlightenment rather than military glory or political action. Such a milieu makes for a very different sort of story than the one told in *Roma.* Heroes and villains give way to survivors and seekers.

It's popular these days to compare Rome to the United States, but life in the Roman Empire was probably more like life in the repressive Soviet Union. The Soviet empire never found its Trajan or Hadrian, but it's not hard to picture Stalin as Domitian.

Readers of *Empire* who wish to read the original sources can begin with Suetonius, who wrote biographies of the first twelve Caesars, from Julius to Domitian. Plutarch wrote biographies of Otho and Galba. Tacitus in his *Annals* and *Histories* wrote about the period from Tiberius to the Year of Four Emperors. We have no ancient biography of Nerva or Trajan, but the thread is picked up in a work called the *Historia Augusta,* which tells us about Hadrian and his successors. Given the biases and methods of these ancient authors, there is reason to doubt the veracity of all these works. Making sense of their mixture of the true and not-true keeps modern historians busy.

Dio Cassius is another important source, though the books of his *Roman History* that cover the period after Claudius survive only in fragments and in abridged form. Josephus's *The Jewish War* describes the bitter conflict between Rome and Jerusalem. Pliny's *Natural History* is full of historical details, hopefully more accurate than his scientific observations. The letters written by his nephew, Pliny the Younger, give us a vivid portrait of his times, including the eruption of Vesuvius, the paranoid reign of Domitian, and Trajan's "ask not, tell not" policy regarding the troublesome Christians. Our major source for the life of Apollonius of Tyana is a fanciful account by Philostratus, who lived a hundred years later; purportedly a biography, it might better be called a novel.

Poets and playwrights also provide many historical details and images of daily life. Under Augustus, we have Virgil, Horace, and Ovid; under Nero, Petronius, Seneca, and Lucan; under later emperors, Quintilian, Martial, and Juvenal.

The joke about two fifteen-year-olds versus one thirty-year-old comes from the oldest known joke book, a Greek text called the *Philogelos* (*The Laughter-Lover*). I first heard it from Mary Beard when she delivered the annual Sather Lecture series at the University of California at Berkeley in 2008. The joke as originally recorded does not mention Trajan, but it suits him. (A later emperor, Julian, made his own joke about Trajan in his satire *The Caesars;* when Trajan visits the Olympians, "Zeus had better look out, if he wants to keep Ganymede for himself!")

The sophist Dio of Prusa, who appears in the novel, is better known as Dio Chrysostom ("Golden-Mouthed," an epithet applied to him by later generations). It is Dio, in his Discourse 21, who tells us that Sporus had something to do with the death of Nero, who otherwise might have continued to reign. This is J. W. Cohoon's translation, with italics added: "It was solely on account of this wantonness of his, however, that he [Nero] lost his life—I mean the way he treated the eunuch [Sporus]. For the latter in anger disclosed the Emperor's designs to his retinue; and so they revolted from him and compelled him to make away with himself as best he could. Indeed *the truth about this has not come out even yet;* for so far as the rest of his subjects were concerned, there was nothing to prevent his continuing to be Emperor for all time, seeing that even now everybody wishes he were still alive."

Where poems are quoted in the novel, the translations are my own. Tacitus (*Annals,* 15.70) tells us that Lucan spoke his own verse as his dying words; historians conjecture he quoted *Pharsalia,* 4:516–17. The poem by Statius casting Earinus as the cupbearer of Domitian is *Silvae,* 3.4. Earinus's song is from Lucretius's *De Rerum Natura* (*On the Nature of Things*); a previous version appeared in my novel *Arms of Nemesis.* Martial's poem celebrating the arrival of Trajan in Rome is *Epigrams,* 10.6. The lines by Virgil used to describe Ceionius are from the *Aeneid,* 6:869–70. The poem by Hadrian is known to us from his biography in the *Historia Augusta.*

Almost all the sources cited above can be found, in English translation and in searchable formats, on the Internet; one merely has to open a search engine and start looking. My own research led me almost daily to Bill Thayer's site LacusCurtius, a remarkable fountainhead of information that includes the texts of Suetonius, Tacitus, Plutarch, the *Historia Augusta,* Dio Cassius, Dio Chrysostom, Samuel Ball Platner's *A Topographical Dictionary of Ancient Rome,* William Smith's *A Dictionary of Greek and Roman Antiquities,* and much more, beautifully presented and intelligently annotated. The home page is here: http://penelope.uchicago.edu/Thayer/E/Roman/home.html.

Another site of special interest is Jona Lendering's Livius (www.livius.org). His illustrated text of Philostratus's *Life of Apollonius* has become an old, dear friend. (I plan to post more links of interest to the readers of *Empire* at my own Web site, www.stevensaylor.com.)

In uncertain times, longtime relationships matter more than ever. Keith Kahla has been my editor since 1994, Alan Nevins my agent since 1995, and Rick Solomon my partner since 1976. Thank you all. And special thanks to my friend Gaylan DuBose, author of *Farrago Latina,* who kindly read and commented on the galleys. I also wish to thank five readers—Lyle O. Martin, Liz Bowes, Bob Conrad, Alan Beber, and Patty Elder—for their special contributions to this book.

Another old, dear friend—though we never met—is the late Michael Grant. When I was a boy growing up in Goldthwaite, Texas, Grant's were the first serious books about the ancient world I encountered. As my interest grew, I discovered more of his works; wherever my curiosity led, it seemed there was a book by Michael Grant on the subject—from biographies of Cleopatra, Julius Caesar, Nero, and Jesus to books about the Etruscans, gladiators, Roman coinage, and the ancient historians themselves. It was Grant's translation and notes for Cicero's *Murder Trials* (specifically the oration for Sextus Roscius) that inspired me to write my first novel, *Roman Blood. Catilina's Riddle, The Venus Throw,* and *A Murder on the Appian Way* (upon which Grant kindly commented) were inspired by his translations of Cicero in *Selected Political Speeches.* Deep into my research for *Empire,* I found myself without a compass in the brambles of the Roman thought-world, where astrology, Stoicism, the ancient gods, and the new cults all become tangled together; it was Grant who showed me a path with two brilliant books, *The World of Rome* and *The Climax of Rome.* With gratitude for all that Michael Grant has given me, and continues to give me, I dedicate this book to his memory.

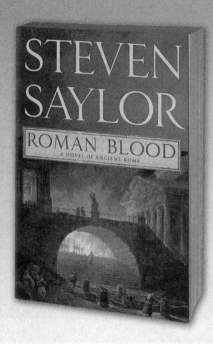

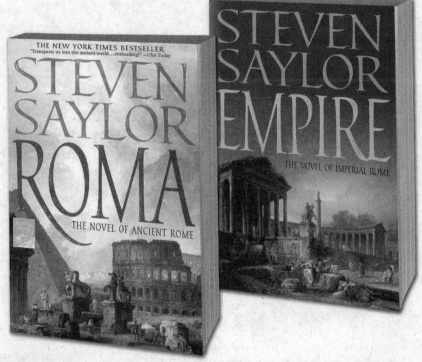